THE GREAT NOVEL
BY THE AUTHOR OF
THE TIN DRUM
AND **THE FLOUNDER**

DOG YEARS

GÜNTER GRASS

"Grass is a born storyteller"
—Life

Günter Grass was born in Danzig, Germany, in 1927. Sculptor, draftsman, novelist, playwright and poet, he has traveled widely in the United States and Europe. He is presently living in Berlin with his Swiss wife and their children.

His first novel, *The Tin Drum*, published in 1963, has been translated into every major European language. *Cat and Mouse* has the same milieu as *The Tin Drum*—Danzig and its petty bourgeoisie. *Dog Years* is his third novel.

Mr. Grass has been internationally acclaimed as one of the most imaginative and powerful contemporary novelists. *Time* has called him "Probably the most inventive talent to be heard from anywhere since the war."

> *"DOG YEARS is huge in scope and fantastic in content, a veritable 'comédie humaine' with overtones of Boccaccio, Rabelais, and Dante. . . ."*
> —SATURDAY REVIEW

> *"DOG YEARS is a savage invective against the German brand of human stupidity. Grass, the high-school dropout, has cut deeper than the professors of history who have tried to explain what happened."*
> —THE NEW YORK TIMES

"Nobody can read this book through to the end without being bruised by its power, pummeled into acknowledging that Grass is one of the most impressive talents of the present decade. More powerfully here even than in THE TIN DRUM he has given us the phantasmagoric history of the Germans during the last thirty years."

—THE ATLANTIC

"If I were assembling an orchestra of authors, I might put Henry James at violin, D. H. Lawrence at trumpet, Tolstoi at French horn, Scott Fitzgerald at saxophone, Saul Bellow at oboe, Norman Mailer at cymbals, J. D. Salinger at flute, and Günter Grass—Günter Grass would be my conductor. . . . In DOG YEARS there is a clear gain in power, however tumultuous."

—RICHARD KLUGER
HARPER'S

**Fawcett Crest Books
by Gunter Grass:**

DOG YEARS

THE FLOUNDER

GÜNTER GRASS

Dog Years

Translated by
RALPH MANHEIM

FAWCETT CREST • NEW YORK

A Fawcett Crest Book

Published by Ballantine Books

Copyright © 1963 by Hermann Luchterhand Verlag GmbH, Neuwied am Rhein, Berlin.

English translation © 1965 by Harcourt, Brace Jovanovich and Martin Secker & Warburg Limited.

Originally published in Germany under the title *Hundejahre*.

ISBN 0-449-20350-6

This edition published by arrangement with Harcourt, Brace Jovanovich

Printed in Canada

First Fawcett Crest Edition: January 1969
First Ballantine Books Edition: February 1983

Walter Henn *in memoriam*

BOOK ONE | **Morning Shifts**

FIRST MORNING SHIFT

You tell. No, you. Or you. Should the actor begin? Or the scarecrows, all at cross purposes? Or should we wait until the eight planets have collected in the sign of Aquarius? You begin, please. After all it was your dog. But before my dog, your dog and the dog descended from the dog. One of us has to begin: You or he or you or I . . . Many many sunsets ago, long before we existed, the Vistula flowed day in day out without reflecting us, and emptied forever and ever.

The present writer bears the name of Brauxel at the moment and runs a mine which produces neither potash, iron, nor coal, yet employs, from one shift to the next, a hundred and thirty-four workers and office help in galleries and drifts, in stalls and crosscuts, in the payroll office and packing house.

In former days the Vistula flowed dangerously, without regulation. And so a thousand day laborers were taken on, and in the year 1895 they dug the so-called cut, running northward from Einlage between Schiewenhorst and Nickelswalde, the two villages on the delta bar. By giving the Vistula a new estuary, straight as a die, this diminished the danger of floods.

The present writer usually writes Brauksel in the form of Castrop-Rauxel and occasionally of Häksel. When he's in the mood, Brauxel writes his name as Weichsel, the river which the Romans called the Vistula. There is no contradiction between playfulness and pedantry; the one brings on the other.

The Vistula dikes ran from horizon to horizon; under the supervision of the Dike Commission in Marienwerder, it was their business to withstand the spring floods, not to mention the St. Dominic's Day floods. And woe betide if there were mice in the dikes.

11

The present writer, who runs a mine and writes his name in various ways, has mapped out the course of the Vistula before and after regulation on an empty desk top: tobacco crumbs and powdery ashes indicate the river and its three mouths; burnt matches are the dikes that hold it on its course.

Many many sunsets ago; here comes the Dike Commissioner on his way from the district of Kulm, where the dike burst in '55 near Kokotzko, not far from the Mennonite cemetery—weeks later the coffins were still hanging in the trees—but he, on foot, on horseback, or in a boat, in his morning coat and never without his bottle of arrack in his wide pocket, he, Wilhelm Ehrenthal, who in classical yet humorous verses had written that "Epistle on the Contemplation of Dikes," a copy of which, soon after publication, was sent with an amiable dedication to all dike keepers, village mayors, and Mennonite preachers, he, here named never to be named again, inspects the dike tops, the enrockment and the groins, and drives off the pigs, because according to the Rural Police Regulations of November 1848, Clause 8, all animals, furred and feathered, are forbidden to graze and burrow on the dike.

The sun goes down on the left. Brauxel breaks a match into pieces: the second mouth of the Vistula came into being without the help of diggers on February 2, 1840, when in consequence of an ice jam the river broke through the delta bar below Plehnendorf, swept away two villages, and made it possible to establish two new fishing villages, East Neufähr and West Neufähr. Yet rich as the two Neufährs may be in tales, gossip, and startling events, we are concerned chiefly with the villages to the east and west of the first, though most recent, mouth: Schiewenhorst and Nickelswalde were, or are, the last villages with ferry service to the right and left of the Vistula cut; for five hundred yards downstream the sea still mingles its 1.8 percent saline solution with the often ash-gray, usually mud-yellow excretion of the far-flung republic of Poland.

Brauxel mutters conjuring words: "The Vistula is a broad stream, growing constantly broader in memory, navigable in spite of its many sandbanks . . ."—moves a piece of eraser in guise of a ferry back and forth across his desk top, which has been transformed into a graphic Vistula delta, and, now that the morning shift has been lowered, now that the sparrow-strident day has begun, puts the nine-year-old Walter Matern

—accent on the last syllable—down on top of the Nickelswalde dike across from the setting sun; he is grinding his
teeth.

What happens when the nine-year-old son of a miller
stands on a dike, watching the river, exposed to the setting
sun, grinding his teeth against the wind? He has inherited
that from his grandmother, who sat riveted to her chair
for nine years, able to move only her eyeballs.

All sorts of things rush by in the river and Walter Matern
sees them. Flood from Montau to Käsemark. Here, just
before the mouth, the sea helps. They say there were mice
in the dike. Whenever a dike bursts, there's talk of mice in
the dike. The Mennonites say that Catholics from the Polish
country put mice in the dike during the night. Others claim
to have seen the dike keeper on his white horse. But the insurance company refuses to believe either in burrowing mice
or in the dike keeper from Güttland. When the mice made
the dike burst, the white horse, so the legend has it, leapt
into the rising waters with the dike keeper, but it didn't
help much: for the Vistula took all the dike keepers. And
the Vistula took the Catholic mice from the Polish country.
And it took the rough Mennonites with hooks and eyes but
without pockets, took the more refined Mennonites with buttons, buttonholes, and diabolical pockets, it also took Güttland's three Protestants and the teacher, the Socialist. It
took Güttland's lowing cattle and Güttland's carved cradles,
it took all Güttland: Güttland's beds and Güttland's cupboards, Güttland's clocks and Güttland's canaries, it took
Güttland's preacher—he was a rough man with hooks and
eyes; it also took the preacher's daughter, and she is said
to have been beautiful.

All that and more rushed by. What does a river like the
Vistula carry away with it? Everything that goes to pieces:
wood, glass, pencils, pacts between Brauxel and Brauchsel,
chairs, bones, and sunsets too. What had long been forgotten
rose to memory, floating on its back or stomach, with the
help of the Vistula: Pomeranian princes. Adalbert came.
Adalbert comes on foot and dies by the ax. But Duke
Swantopolk allowed himself to be baptized. What will become
of Mestwin's daughters? Is one of them running away barefoot? Who will carry her off? The giant Miligedo with his
lead club? Or one of the ancient gods? The fiery-red
Perkunos? The pale Pikollos, who is always looking up from

below? The boy Potrimpos laughs and chews at his ear of wheat. Sacred oaks are felled. Grinding teeth— And Duke Kynstute's young daughter, who entered a convent: twelve headless knights and twelve headless nuns are dancing in the mill: the mill turns slow, the mill turns faster, it grinds the little souls to plaster; the mill turns slow, the mill speeds up, she has drunk with twelve knights from the selfsame cup; the mill turns slow, the mill speeds up, twelve knights twelve nuns in the cellar sup; the mill turns slow, the mill turns faster, they're feasting Candlemas with farting and laughter: the mill turns slow, the mill turns faster . . . but when the mill was burning inside and out and coaches for headless knights and headless nuns drove up, when much later— sunsets—St. Bruno passed through the fire and Bobrowski the robber with his crony Materna, with whom it all began, set fires in houses that had been previously notched—sunsets, sunsets—Napoleon before and after: then the city was ingeniously besieged, for several times they tried out Congreve rockets, with varying success: but in the city and on the walls, on Wolf, Bear, and Bay Horse Bastions, on Renegade, Maidenhole, and Rabbit Bastions, the French under Rapp coughed, the Poles under their prince Radziwil spat, the corps of the one-armed Capitaine de Chambure hawked. But on the fifth of August came the St. Dominic's Flood, climbed Bay Horse, Rabbit, and Renegade Bastions without a ladder, wet the powder, made the Congreve rockets fizzle out, and carried a good deal of fish, mostly pike, into the streets and kitchens: everyone was miraculously replenished, although the granaries along Hopfengasse had long since burned down—sunsets. Amazing how many things are becoming to the Vistula, how many things color a river like the Vistula: sunsets, blood, mud, and ashes. Actually the wind ought to have them. Orders are not always carried out; rivers that set out for heaven empty into the Vistula.

SECOND MORNING SHIFT

Here, on Brauxel's desk top and over the Schiewenhorst dike, she rolls, day after day. And on Nickelswalde dike stands Walter Matern with grinding teeth; for the sun is setting.

Swept bare, the dikes taper away in the distance. Only the sails of the windmills, blunt steeples, and poplars—Napoleon had those planted for his artillery—stick to the tops of the dikes. He alone is standing. Except maybe for the dog. But he's gone off, now here now there. Behind him, vanishing in the shadow and below the surface of the river, lies the Island, smelling of butter, curds, dairies, a wholesome, nauseatingly milky smell. Nine years old, legs apart, with red and blue March knees, stands Walter Matern, spreads his ten fingers, narrows his eyes to slits, lets the scars of his close-cropped head—bearing witness to falls, fights, and barbed wire—swell, take on profile, grinds his teeth from left to right—he has that from his grandmother—and looks for a stone.

There aren't any stones on the dike. But he looks. He finds dry sticks. But you can't throw a dry stick against the wind. And he wants to got to wants to throw something. He could whistle for Senta, here one second gone the next, but he does no such thing, all he does is grind—that blunts the wind—and feels like throwing something. He could catch Amsel's eye at the foot of the dike with a hey and a ho, but his mouth is full of grinding and not of hey and ho—nevertheless he wants to got to wants to, but there's no stone in his pockets either; usually he has a couple in one pocket or the other.

In these parts stones are called *zellacken*. The Protestants say *zellacken*, the few Catholics *zellacken*. The rough Mennonites say *zellacken*, the refined ones *zellacken*. Even Amsel, who likes to be different, says *zellack* when he means a stone; and Senta goes for a stone when someone says: Senta, go get a *zellack*. Kriwe says *zellacken*, Kornelius Kabrun, Beister, Folchert, August Sponagel, and Frau von Ankum, the major's wife, all say *zellacken;* and Pastor Daniel Kliewer from Pasewark says to his congregation, rough and refined alike: "Then little David picked up a *zellack* and flung it at the giant Goliath . . ." For a *zellack* is a handy little stone, the size of a pigeon's egg.

But Walter Matern couldn't find one in either pocket. In the right pocket there was nothing but crumbs and sunflower seeds, in the left pocket, in among pieces of string and the crackling remains of grasshoppers—while up above it grinds, while the sun has gone, while the Vistula flows, taking with it something from Güttland, something from

Mantau, Amsel hunched over and the whole time clouds, while Senta upwind, the gulls downwind, the dikes bare to the horizon, while the sun is gone gone gone—he finds his pocketknife. Sunsets last longer in eastern than in western regions; any child knows that. There flows the Vistula from sky to opposite sky. The steam ferry puts out from the Schiewenhorst dock and bucks the current, slant-wise and bumptious, carrying two narrow-gauge freight cars to Nickelswalde, where it will put them down on the Stutthof spur. The chunk of leather known as Kriwe has just turned his cowhide face to leeward and is pattering eyelashless along the opposite dike top: a few moving sails and poplars to count. A fixed stare, no bending over, but a hand in his pocket. And the eye slides down from the embankment: a curious round something, down below, that bends over, looks as if it wants to swipe something from the Vistula. That's Amsel, looking for old rags. What for? Any child knows that.

But Leather Kriwe doesn't know what Walter Matern, who has been looking for a *zellack* in his pocket, has found in his pocket. While Kriwe pulls his face out of the wind, the pocketknife grows warmer in Walter Matern's hand. Amsel had given it to him. It has three blades, a corkscrew, a saw, and a leather punch. Amsel plump, pink, and comical when crying. Amsel pokes about in the muck on the ledge, for though falling fast the Vistula is up to the dike top because there's a flood between Montau and Käsemark, and has things in it that used to be in Palschau.

Gone. Down yonder behind the dike, leaving behind a spreading red glow. In his pocket Walter Matern—as only Brauxel can know—clenches the knife in his fist. Amsel is a little younger than Walter Matern. Senta, far away looking for mice, is just about as black as the sky, upward from the Schiewenhorst dike, is red. A drifting cat is caught in the driftwood. Gulls multiply in flight: torn tissue paper crackles, is smoothed, is spread out wide; and the glass pinhead eyes see everything that drifts, hangs, runs, stands, or is just there, such as Amsel's two thousand freckles; also that he is wearing a helmet like those worn at Verdun. And the helmet slips forward, is pushed back over the neck, and slips again, while Amsel fishes fence laths and beanpoles, and also heavy, sodden rags out of the mud: the cat comes loose, spins downward, falls to the gulls. The mice in the dike begin to stir again. And the ferry is still coming closer. A dead yellow dog comes drifting and turns over. Senta is facing into the wind. Slantwise and bumptious the ferry transports its two freight cars. Down drifts a calf—dead. The wind falters but does not turn. The gulls stop still in mid-air, hesitating. Now Walter Matern—while the ferry, the wind and the calf and the sun behind the dike and the mice in the dike and the motionless gulls—has pulled his fist out of his pocket with the knife in it. While the Vistula flows, he holds it out in front of his sweater and makes his knuckles chalky white against the deepening red glow.

THIRD MORNING SHIFT

Every child between Hildesheim and Sarstedt knows what is mined in Brauksel's mine, situated between Hildesheim and Sarstedt.

Every child knows why the Hundred and Twentieth Infantry Regiment had to abandon in Bohnsack the steel helmet Amsel is wearing, as well as other steel helmets, a stock of fatigue uniforms, and several field kitchens, when it pulled out by train in '20.

The cat is back again. Every child knows that it's not the same cat, but the mice don't know and the gulls don't know. The cat is wet wet wet. Now something drifts by that is neither a dog nor a sheep. It's a clothes cupboard. The cupboard does not collide with the ferry. And as Amsel pulls a beanpole out of the mud and Walter Matern's fist begins to quiver around the knife, a cat finds freedom: it drifts out toward the open sea that reaches as far as the sky. The gulls grow fewer, the mice in the dike scamper, the Vistula flows, the fist around the knife quivers, the wind's name is Northwest, the dikes taper away, the open sea resists the river with everything it's got, still and for evermore the sun goes down, still and for evermore the ferry and two freight cars move closer: the ferry does not capsize, the dikes do not burst, the mice are not afraid, the sun has no intention of turning back, the Vistula has no intention of turning back, the ferry has no intention of turning back, the cat has no, the gulls have no, nor the clouds nor the infantry regiment, Senta has no intention of going back to the wolves, but merrily merrily . . . And Walter Matern has no intention of letting the pocketknife given him by Amsel short fat round return to his pocket; on the contrary, his fist around the knife manages to turn a shade chalkier. And up above teeth grind from left to right. While it flows approaches sinks drifts whirls rises and falls, the fist relaxes around the knife, so that all the expelled blood rushes back into the now loosely closed hand: Walter Matern thrusts the fist holding the now thoroughly warmed object behind him, stands on one leg, foot, ball of foot, on five toes in a high shoe, lifts his weight sockless in the shoe, lets his entire weight slip into the hand behind him, takes no aim, almost stops grinding; and in that flowing drifting setting lost moment—for even Brauchsel cannot save it, because he has forgotten, forgotten something—while Amsel looks up from the mud at the foot of the dike, with his left hand and a portion of his two thousand freckles pushes his steel helmet back, revealing another portion of his two thousand freckles, Walter Matern's hand is way out in front, empty and light, and discloses only the pressure marks of a pocketknife that had three blades, a corkscrew, a saw, and a leather punch; in the handle of which sea sand, powdered tree bark, a bit of jam, pine needles, and a vestige of mole's blood had become incrusted; whose barter value would have been a new bicycle bell; which no one had stolen, which Amsel had bought in his mother's shop with money he himself had earned, and then given his friend Walter Matern; which last summer had pinned a butterfly to Folchert's barn door, which under the dock of Kriwe's ferry had in one day speared four rats, had almost speared a rabbit in the dunes, and two weeks ago had pegged a mole before Senta could catch it. The inner surface of the hand still shows pressure marks made by the selfsame knife, with which Walter Matern and Eduard Amsel, when they were eight years old and intent on blood brotherhood, had scored their arms, because Kornelius Kabrun, who had been in German Southwest Africa and knew about Hottentots, had told them how it was done.

FOURTH MORNING SHIFT

Meanwhile—for while Brauxel lays bare the past of a pocket-knife and the same knife, turned missile, follows a trajectory determined by propulsive force, gravitation, and wind resistance, there is still time enough, from morning shift to morning shift, to write off a working day and meanwhile to say—meanwhile, then, Amsel with the back of his hand had pushed back his steel helmet. With one glance he swept the dike embankment, with the same glance took in the thrower, then sent his glance in pursuit of the thrown object; and the pocketknife, Brauxel maintains, has meanwhile reached the ultimate point allotted to every upward-striving object, while the Vistula flows, the cat drifts, the gull screams, the ferry approaches, while the bitch Senta is black, and the sun never ceases to set.

Meanwhile—for when a missile has reached that infinitesimal point after which descent begins, it hesitates for a moment, and pretends to stand still—while then the pocketknife stands still at its zenith, Amsel tears his gaze away from the object that has reached this infinitesimal point and once more—the object is already falling quickly fitfully, because now more exposed to the head wind, riverward—has his eye on his friend Matern who is still teetering on the ball of his foot and his toes sockless in high shoe, holding his right hand high and far from his body, while his left arm steers and tries to keep him in balance.

Meanwhile—for while Walter Matern teeters on one leg, concerned with his balance, while Vistula and cat, mice and ferry, dog and sun, while the pocketknife falls riverward, the morning shift has been lowered into Brauchsel's mine, the night shift has been raised and has ridden away on bicycles, the changehouse attendant has locked the change-house, the sparrows in every gutter have begun the day . . . At this point Amsel succeeded, with a brief glance and a directly ensuing cry, in throwing Walter Matern off his precarious balance. The boy on the top of the Nickelswalde dike did not fall, but he began to stagger and stumble so furiously that he lost sight of his pocketknife before it touched the flowing Vistula and became invisible.

"Hey, Grinder!" Amsel cries. "Is that all you can do? Grind your teeth and throw things?"

Walter Matern, here addressed as Grinder, is again standing stiff-kneed with parted legs, rubbing the palm of his left hand, which still bears the glowing negative imprint of a pocketknife.

"You saw me. I had to throw. What's the use of asking questions?"

"But you didn't throw no *zellack*."

"How could I when there ain't no *zellacks* up here?"

"So what do you throw when you ain't got no *zellack*?"

"Well, if I'd had a *zellack* I'd of thrown the *zellack*."

"If you'd sent Senta, she'd of brought you a *zellack*."

"If I'd sent Senta. Anybody can say that. You try and send a dog anyplace when she's chasing mice."

"So what did you throw if you didn't have no *zellack*?"

"Why do you keep asking questions? I threw some dingbat. You saw me."

"You threw my knife."

"It was my knife. Don't be an Indian giver. If I'd had a *zellack*, I wouldn't of thrown the knife, I'd of thrown the *zellack*."

"Whyn't you tell me? Couldn't you tell me you couldn't find a *zellack*, I'd have tossed you one, there's plenty of them down here."

"What's the good talking so much when it's gone?"

"Maybe I'll get a new knife for Ascension."

"I don't want no new knife."

"If I gave you one, you'd take it."

"You want to bet I wouldn't?"

"You want to bet you would?"

"Is it a bet?"

"It's a bet."

They shake hands on it: tin soldiers against magnifying glass. Amsel reaches his hand with its many freckles up the dike, Walter Matern reaches his hand with the pressure marks left by the pocketknife down the dike and with the handshake pulls Amsel up on the dike top.

Amsel is still friendly. "You're exactly like your grandma in the mill. All she does is grind the coupla teeth she's still got the whole time. Except she don't throw things. Only hits people with her spoon."

Amsel on the dike is a little shorter than Walter Matern. As he speaks, his thumb points over his shoulder to the spot where behind the dike lies the village of Nickelswalde and the Materns' postmill. Up the side of the dike Amsel pulls a bundle of roof laths, beanpoles, and wrung-out rags. He keeps having to push up the front rim of his steel helmet with the back of his hand. The ferry has tied up at the Nickelswalde dock. The two freight cars can be heard. Senta grows larger, smaller, larger, approaches black. More small farm animals drift by. Broad-shouldered flows the Vistula. Walter Matern wraps his right hand in the lower frayed edge of his sweater. Senta stands on four legs between the two of them. Her tongue hangs out to leftward and twitches. She keeps looking at Walter Matern, because his teeth. He has that from his grandmother who was riveted to her chair for nine years and only her eyeballs.

Now they have taken off: one taller, one smaller on the dike top against the ferry landing. The dog black. Half a pace ahead: Amsel. Half a pace behind: Walter Matern. He is dragging Amsel's rags. Behind the bundle, as the three grow smaller on the dike, the grass gradually straightens up again.

FIFTH MORNING SHIFT

And so Brauksel, as planned, sits bent over his paper and, while the other chroniclers bend likewise and punctually over the past and begin recording, has let the Vistula flow. It still amuses him to recall every detail: Many many years ago, when the child had been born but was not yet able to grind his teeth because like all babies he had been born toothless, Grandma Matern was sitting riveted to her chair in the overhang room, unable as she had been for the last nine years to move anything except her eyeballs, capable only of bubbling and drooling.

The overhang room jutted out over the kitchen, it had one window looking out on the kitchen, from which the maids could be observed at work, and another window in back, facing the Matern windmill, which sat there on its jack, with its tailpole pivoting on its post and was accordingly a genuine postmill; as it had been for a hundred years. The Materns had built it in 1815, shortly after the city and fortress of Danzig had been taken by the victorious Russian and Prussian armies; for August Matern, the grandfather of our grandmother sitting there riveted to her chair, had managed, during the long-drawn-out and listlessly conducted siege, to carry on a lucrative trade with both sides; on the one hand, he began in the spring to supply scaling ladders in exchange for good convention talers; on the other hand, he arranged, in return for Laubtalers and even more substantial Brabant currency, to smuggle little notes in to General Count d'Heudelet, calling his attention to the odd conduct of the Russians who were having quantities of ladders made, though it was only spring and the apples were in no shape to be picked.

When at length the governor, Count Rapp, signed the capitulation of the fortress, August Matern in out-of-the-way Nickelswalde counted the Danish specie and two-thirds pieces, the quickly rising rubles, the Hamburg mark pieces, the Laubtalers and convention talers, the little bags of Dutch gulden and the newly issued Danzig paper money; he found himself nicely off and abandoned himself to the joys of reconstruction: he had the old mill, where the fugitive Queen Louise is said to have spent the night after the defeat of Prussia, the historical mill whose sails had been damaged first on the occasion of the Danish attack from the sea, then of the night skirmish resulting from a sortie on the part of Capitaine de Chambure and his volunteer corps, torn down except for the jack which was still in good condition, and on the old jack built the new mill which was still sitting there with its pole on its jack when Grandmother Matern was reduced to sitting riveted and motionless in her chair. At this point Brauxel wishes, before it is too late, to concede that with his money, some hard, some easy-earned, August Matern not only built the new postmill, but also endowed the little chapel in Steegen, which numbered a few Catholics, with a Madonna, who, though not wanting in gold leaf, neither attracted any pilgrimages worth mentioning nor performed any miracles.

The Catholicism of the Matern family, as one might expect of a family of millers, was dependent on the wind, and since there was always a profitable breeze on the Island, the Matern mill ran year in year out, deterring them from the excessive churchgoing that would have antagonized the Mennonites. Only baptisms and funerals, marriages and the more important holidays sent part of the family to Steegen; and once a year on Corpus Christi, when the Catholics of Steegen put on a procession through the countryside, the mill, with its jack and all its dowels, with its mill post, its oak lever, and its meal bin, but most of all with its sails, came in for its share of blessing and holy water; a luxury which the Materns could never have afforded in such rough-Mennonite villages as Junkeracker and Pasewark. The Mennonites of Nickelswalde, who all raised wheat on rich Island soil and were dependent on the Catholic mill, proved to be the more refined type of Mennonites, in other words, they had buttons, buttonholes, and normal pockets that it was possible to put something into. Only Simon Beister, fisherman and small holder, was a genuine hook-and-eye Mennonite, rough and pocketless; over his boatshed hung a painted wooden sign with the ornate inscription:

> Wear hooks and eyes,
> Dear Jesus will save you.
> Wear buttons and pockets,
> The Devil will have you.

But Simon Beister was and remained the only inhabitant of Nickelswalde to have his wheat milled in Pasewark and not in the Catholic mill. Even so, it was not necessarily he who in '13, shortly before the outbreak of the Great War, incited a degenerate farmhand to haul kindling of all sorts to the Matern postmill and set it on fire. The flames were already creeping under jack and pole when Perkun, the young shepherd dog belonging to Pawel the miller's man, whom everyone called Paulchen, began, black and with tail straight back, to describe narrowing circles around hummock, jack, and mill, and brought miller's man and miller running out of the house with his staccato barks.

Pawel or Paul had brought the animal with him from Lithuania and on request exhibited a kind of pedigree, which made it clear to whom it may concern that Perkun's grandmother on her father's side had been a Lithuanian, Russian, or Polish she-wolf.

And Perkun sired Senta; and Senta whelped Harras; and Harras sired Prinz; and Prinz made history . . . But for the present Grandma Matern is still sitting riveted to her chair, able to move only her eyeballs. She is obliged to look on inactive as her daughter-in-law carries on in the house, her son in the mill, and her daughter Lorchen with the miller's man. But the war took the miller's man and Lorchen went out of her mind: after that, in the house, in the kitchen garden, on the dikes, in the nettles behind Folchert's barn, on the near side and far side of the dunes, barefoot on the beach and in among the blueberry bushes in the nearby woods, she goes looking for her Paulchen, and never will she know whether it was the Prussians or the Russians who sent him crawling underground. The gentle old maid's only companion is the dog Perkun, whose master had been her master.

SIXTH MORNING SHIFT

Long long ago—Brauxel counts on his fingers—when the world was in the third year of the war, when Paulchen had been left behind in Masuria, Lorchen was roaming about with the dog, but miller Matern was permitted to go on toting bags of flour, because he was hard of hearing on both sides, Grandma Matern sat one sunny day, while a child was being baptized—the pocketknife-throwing youngster of earlier morning shifts was receiving the name Walter— riveted to her chair, rolling her eyeballs, bubbling and drooling but unable to compose one word.

She sat in the overhang room and was assailed by mad shadows. She flared up, faded in the half-darkness, sat bright, sat somber. Pieces of furniture as well, the headpiece of the tall carved cupboard, the embossed cover of the chest, and the red, for nine years unused, velvet of the *prie-dieu* flared up, faded, disclosed silhouettes, resumed their massive gloom: glittering dust, dustless shadow over grandmother and her furniture. Her bonnet and the glass-blue drinking cup on the cupboard. Her frayed sleeves of her bedjacket. The floor scrubbed lusterless, over which the turtle, roughly the size of a man's hand, given to her by Paul the miller's man, moved from corner to corner, glittered and survived the miller's man by nibbling little scallops out of the edges of lettuce leaves. And all the lettuce leaves scattered about the room with their turtle-scallops were struck bright bright bright; for outside, behind the house, the Matern postmill, in a wind blowing thirty-nine feet a second, was grinding wheat into flour, blotting out the sun with its four sails four times in three-and-a-half seconds.

Concurrently with these demonic dazzling-dark goings-on in Grandma's room, the child was being driven to Steegen by way of Pasewark and Junkeracker to be baptized, the sunflowers by the fence separating the Matern kitchen garden from the road grew larger and larger, worshiped one another and were glorified without interruption by the very same sun which was blotted out four times in three-and-a-half seconds by the sails of the windmill; for the mill had not thrust itself between sun and sunflowers, but only, and this in the forenoon, between the riveted grandmother and a sun which shone not always but often on the Island.

How many years had Grandma been sitting motionless? Nine years in the overhang room.

How long behind asters, ice flowers, sweet peas, or convolvulus?

Nine years bright dark bright to one side of the windmill. Who had riveted her so solidly to her chair?

Her daughter-in-law Ernestine, née Stange.

How could such a thing come to pass?

This Protestant woman from Junkeracker had first expelled Tilde Matern, who was not yet a grandmother, but more on the strapping loud-mouthed side, from the kitchen; then she had appropriated the living room and taken to washing windows on Corpus Christi. When Stine drove her mother-in-law out of the barn, they came to blows for the first time. The two of them went at each other with feed pans in among the chickens, who lost quite a few feathers on the occasion.

This, Brauxel counts back, must have happened in 1905; for when two years later Stine Matern, née Stange, still failed to clamor for green apples and sour pickles and continued inexorably to come around in accordance with the calendar, Tilde Matern spoke to her daughter-in-law, who stood facing her with folded arms in the overhang room, in the following terms: "It's just like I always thought, Protestant women got the Devil's mouse in their hole. It

nibbles everything away so nothing can come out. All it
does is stink!"

These words unleashed a war of religion, fought with
wooden cooking spoons and ultimately reducing the Catholic
party to the chair: for the oaken armchair, which stood before the window between the stove and *prie-dieu,* received
a Tilde Matern felled by a stroke. For nine years now she
had been sitting in this chair except when Lorchen and the
maids, for reasons of cleanliness, lifted her out just long
enough to minister to her needs.

When the nine years were past and it had developed that
the wombs of Protestant women do not harbor a diabolical
mouse that nibbles everything away and won't let anything
germinate, when, on the contrary, something came full term,
was born as a son, and had his umbilical cord cut, Grandmother sat, was still sitting, while the christening was proceeding in Steegen under favorable weather conditions, still
and forever riveted, in the overhang room. Below the room,
in the kitchen, a goose lay in the oven, sizzling in its own
fat. This the goose did in the third year of the Great War,
when geese had become so rare that the goose was looked
upon as a species close to extinction. Lorchen Matern with
her birthmark, her flat bosom, her curly hair, Lorchen, who
had never got a husband—because Paulchen had crawled
into the earth, leaving nothing but his black dog behind—
Lorchen, who was supposed to be looking after the goose in
the oven, was not in the kitchen, didn't baste the goose at
all, neglected to turn it, to say the proper charms over it,
but stood in a row with the sunflowers behind the fence—
which the new miller's man had freshly whitewashed that
spring—and spoke first in a friendly, then in an anxious
tone, two sentences angrily, then lovingly, to someone who
was not standing behind the fence, who was not passing by
in greased yet squeaky shoes, who wore no baggy trousers,
and who was nevertheless addressed as Paul or Paulchen
and expected to return to her, Lorchen Matern with the
watery eyes, something he had taken from her. But Paul did
not give it back, although the time of day was favorable—
plenty of silence, or at any rate buzzing—and the wind
blowing at a velocity of twenty-six feet a second had boots
big enough to kick the mill on its jack in such a way that
it turned a mite faster than the wind and was able in one

uninterrupted session to transform Miehlke's—for it was his milling day—wheat into Miehlke's flour.

For even though a miller's son was being baptized in Steegen's wooden chapel, Matern's mill did not stand still. If a milling wind was blowing, there had to be milling. A windmill knows only days with and days without milling wind. Lorchen Matern knew only days when Paulchen passed by and days when nothing passed by and no one stopped at the fence. Because the mill was milling, Paulchen came by and stopped. Perkun barked. Far behind Napoleon's poplars, behind Folchert's, Miehlke's, Kabrun's, Beister's, Mombert's, and Kriwe's farmhouses, behind the flat-roofed school, and Lührmann's taproom and milk pool, the cows lowed by turns. And Lorchen said lovingly "Paulchen," several times "Paulchen," and while the goose in the oven, unbasted, unspoken-to, and never turned, grew steadily crisper and more dominical, she said: "Aw, give it back. Aw, don't be like that. Aw, don't act like that. Aw, give it back, 'cause I need it. Aw, give it, and don't be, not giving it to me . . ."

No one gave anything back. The dog Perkun turned his head on his neck and whimpering softly looked after the departing Paulchen. Under the cows, milk accumulated. The windmill sat with pole on jack and milled. Sunflowers recited sunflower prayers to each other. The air buzzed. And the goose in the oven began to burn, first slowly, then so fast and pungently that Grandmother Matern in her overhang room above the kitchen set her eyeballs spinning faster than the sails of the windmill were able to. While in Steegen the baptismal chapel was forsaken, while in the overhang room the turtle, hand-size, moved from one scrubbed plank to the next, she, because of the burnt goose fumes rising to the overhang room, began bright dark bright to drivel and drool and wheeze. First she blew hairs, such as all grandmothers have in their noses, out through nostrils, but when bitter fumes quivered bright through the whole room, making the turtle pause bewildered and the lettuce leaves shrivel, what issued from her nostrils was no longer hairs but steam. Nine years of grandmotherly indignation were discharged: the grandmotherly locomotive started up. Vesuvius and Etna. The Devil's favorite element, fire, made the unleashed grandmother quiver, contribute dragonlike to the chiaroscuro, and attempt, amid changing light after nine years, a dry grinding of the teeth; and she succeeded: from left to right, set on

edge by the acrid smell, her last remaining stumps rubbed
against each other; and in the end a cracking and splintering
mingled with the dragon's fuming, the expulsion of steam,
the spewing of fire, the grinding of teeth: the oaken chair,
fashioned in pre-Napoleonic times, the chair which had sustained the grandmother for nine years except for brief interruptions in behalf of cleanliness, gave up and disintegrated
just as the turtle leapt high from the floor and landed on
its back. At the same time several stove tiles sprung netlike
cracks. Down below the goose burst open, letting the stuffing
gush out. The chair disintegrated into powdery wood meal,
rose up in a cloud which proliferated, a sumptuously il-
lumined monument to transience, and settled on Grandmother Matern, who had not, as might be supposed, taken
her cue from the chair and turned to grandmotherly dust.
What lay on shriveled salad leaves, on the turtle turned
turtle, on furniture and floor, was merely the dust of pulverized oakwood; she, the terrible one, did not lie, but stood
crackling and electric, struck bright, struck dark by the
play of the windmill sails, upright amid dust and decay,
ground her teeth from left to right, and grinding took the
first step: stepped from bright to dark, stepped over the turtle,
who was getting ready to give up the ghost, whose belly was a
beautiful sulphur-yellow, after nine years of sitting still took
purposive steps, did not slip on lettuce leaves, kicked open
the door of the overhang room, descended, a paragon of
grandmotherhood, the kitchen stairs in felt shoes, and standing now on stone flags and sawdust took something from a
shelf with both hands, and attempted, with grandmotherly
cooking stratagems, to save the acridly burning baptismal
goose. And she did manage to save a little by scratching
away the charred part, dousing the flames, and turning the
goose over. But everyone who had ears in Nickelswalde
could hear Grandmother Matern, still engaged in her rescue
operations, screaming with terrifying distinctness out of a
well-rested throat: "You hussy! Lorchen, you hussy! I'll cook
your, you hussy. Damn hussy! Hussy, you hussy!"

Wielding a hardwood spoon, she was already out of the
burnt-smelling kitchen and in the middle of the buzzing
garden, with the mill behind her. To the left she stepped in
the strawberries, to the right in the cauliflowers, for the
first time in years she was back again among the broad beans,
but an instant later behind and between the sunflowers,

raising her right arm high and bringing it down, supported in every movement by the regular turning of the windmill sails, on poor Lorchen, also on the sunflowers, but not on Perkun, who leapt away black between the bean trellises.

In spite of the blows and though quite without Paulchen, poor Lorchen whimpered in his direction: "Oh help me please, Paulchen, oh do help me, Paulchen . . ." but all that came her way was wooden blows and the song of the unleashed grandmother: "You hussy! You hussy you! You damn hussy!"

SEVENTH MORNING SHIFT

Brauxel wonders whether he may not have put too much diabolical display into his account of Grandmother Matern's resurrection. Wouldn't it have been miracle enough if the good woman had simply and somewhat stiffly stood up and gone down to the kitchen to rescue the goose? Was it necessary to have her puff steam and spit fire? Did stove tiles have to crack and lettuce leaves shrivel? Did he need the moribund turtle and the pulverized armchair?

If nevertheless Brauksel, today a sober-minded man at home in a free-market economy, replies in the affirmative and insists on fire and steam, he will have to give his reasons. There was and remains only one reason for his elaborate staging of the grandmotherly resurrection scene: the Materns, especially the teeth-grinding branch of the family, descended from the medieval robber Materna, by way of Grandma, who was a genuine Matern—she had married her cousin—down to the baptizand Walter Matern, had an innate feeling for grandiose, nay operatic scenes; and the truth of the matter is that in May 1917, Grandmother Matern did not just go down quietly to rescue the goose as a matter of course, but began by setting off the above-described fireworks.

It must furthermore be said that while Grandmother Matern was trying to save the goose and immediately thereafter belaboring poor Lorchen with a cooking spoon, the three two-horse carriages bearing the hungry christening party were rolling past Junkeracker and Pasewark on their way from Steegen. And much as Brauxel may be tempted to record the ensuing christening dinner—because the goose didn't yield enough, preserved giblets and pickled pork were brought up from the cellar—he must nevertheless let the christening party sit down to dinner without witnesses. No one will ever learn how the Romeikes and the Kabruns, how Miehlke and the widow Stange stuffed themselves full of burnt goose, preserved giblets, pickled pork, and squash in vinegar in the midst of the third war year. Brauxel is especially sorry to miss the unleashed and newly nimble Grandmother Matern's great scene; it is the widow Amsel, and she alone, whom he is permitted at this point to excerpt from the village idyl, for she is the mother of our plumpish Eduard Amsel, who in the course of the first to fourth morning shifts fished beanpoles, roofing laths, and heavy waterlogged rags from the rising Vistula and is now, like Walter Matern, about to be baptized.

EIGHTH MORNING SHIFT

Many many years ago—for Brauksel tells nothing more gladly than fairy tales—there dwelt in Schiewenhorst, a fishing village to the left of the mouth of the Vistula, a merchant by the name of Albrecht Amsel. He sold kerosene, sailcloth, canisters for fresh water, rope, nets, fish traps, eel baskets, fishing tackle of all kinds, tar, paint, sandpaper, yarn, oilcloth, pitch, and tallow, but also carried tools, from axes to pocketknives, and had small carpenter's benches, grindstones, inner tubes for bicycles, carbide lamps, pulleys, winches, and vises in stock. Ship's biscuit was piled up beside cork jackets; a life preserver all ready to have a boat's name written on it embraced a large jar full of cough drops; a schnapps known as "Brotchen" was poured from a stout green bottle encased in basketry; he sold yard goods and remnants, but also new and used clothing, flatirons, secondhand sewing machines, and mothballs. And in spite of the mothballs, in spite of pitch and kerosene, shellac and carbide, Albrecht Amsel's store, a spacious wooden structure resting on a concrete foundation and painted dark green every seven years, smelled first and foremost of cologne and next, before the question of mothballs could even come up, of smoked fish; for side by side with all this retail trade, Albrecht Amsel was known as a wholesale purchaser of fresh-water fish as well as deep-sea fish: chests of the lightest pinewood, golden yellow and packed full of smoked flounder, smoked eel, sprats both loose and bundled, lampreys, codfish roe, and strongly or subtly smoked Vistula salmon, with the inscription: A. Amsel—Fresh Fish—Smoked Fish—Schiewenhorst—Great Island—burned into their front panels, were broken open with medium-sized chisels in the Danzig Market, a brick edifice situated between Lawendelgasse and Junkergasse, between the Dominican church and the Altstädtischer Graben. The top came open with a crisp crackling; nails were drawn squeaking from the sides. And from Neo-Gothic ogival windows market light fell on freshly smoked fish.

In addition, this farsighted merchant, deeply concerned with the future of the fish-smoking industry on the Vistula delta and the harbor-mouth bar, employed a stone-mason specializing in chimney construction, who was kept busy from Plehnendorf to Einlage, that is, in all the villages bordering the Dead Vistula, which villages with their smoke-house chimneys had the appearance of fantastic ruins: here he would fix a chimney that was drawing badly, elsewhere he would have to build one of those enormous smokehouse chimneys that towered over lilac bushes and squat fisher-men's huts; all this in the name of Albrecht Amsel, who not without reason was said to be wealthy. The rich Amsel, people said—or: "Amsel the Jew." Of course Amsel was not a Jew. Though he was also no Mennonite, he called him-self a good Protestant, possessed a permanent pew, which he occupied every Sunday, in the Fishermen's Church in Bohnsack, and married Lottchen Tiede, a reddish-blonde peasant girl inclined to stoutness from Gross-Zünder; which should be taken to mean: how could Albrecht Amsel be a Jew, when Tiede, the wealthy peasant, who never went from Goss-Zünder to Käsemark otherwise than in a coach-and-four and patent-leather shoes, who was a frequent caller at the District President's, who had put his sons in the Cavalry, or to be more precise, in the rather expensive Langfuhr Hussars, gave him his daughter Lottchen for his wife.

Later a good many people are said to have said that old

man Tiede had given the Jew Amsel his Lottchen only because he, like many peasants, merchants, fishermen, millers—including Miller Matern from Nickelswalde—was deep
in debt, dangerously so for the survival of his coach-and-four,
to Albrecht Amsel. In the intention of proving something it
was also said that speaking before the Provincial Market
Regulation Commission, Albrecht Amsel had expressed
strong opposition to the undue encouragement of hog
raising.

For the present Brauksel, who is a know-it-all, prefers to
have done with conjectures: for regardless of whether it
was love or debentures that brought Lottchen Tiede into his
house, and regardless of whether he sat in the Fishermen's
Church in Bohnsack on Sundays as a baptized Jew or a
baptized Christian, Albrecht Amsel, the dynamic merchant
of the Lower Vistula, who, it might be added, was also the
broad-shouldered cofounder of the Bohnsack Athletic Club
reg. 1905, a mighty-voiced baritone in the church choir, rose
to be a multiply-decorated reserve lieutenant by the banks
of the Somme and Marne, and fell in 1917, not far from
the fortress of Verdun, just two months before the birth of
his son Eduard.

NINTH MORNING SHIFT

Butted by the Ram, Walter Matern first saw the light of
day in April. The Fishes of March drew Eduard Amsel, restless and gifted, from the maternal cavern. In May, when the
goose burned and Grandmother Matern rose again, the
miller's son was baptized. The proceedings were Catholic.
As early as the end of April the son of the late merchant
Albrecht Amsel was already sprinkled in good Protestant
style in the Fishermen's Church in Bohnsack, half, as was
their customary, with Vistula water and half with water
taken from the Baltic.

Whatever the other chroniclers, who have been vying with
Brauksel for nine morning shifts, may record that is at
variance with Brauksel's opinion, they will have to take my
word for it in matters concerning the baptizand from
Schiewenhorst: among all the characters intended to breathe

life into this anniversary volume—Brauchsel's mine has been producing neither coal, nor iron ores, nor potash for almost ten years—Eduard Amsel, or Eddi Amsel, Haseloff, Goldmouth, and so on, is the most restless hero, except for Brauxel.

From the very start it was his vocation to invent scarecrows. Yet he had nothing against birds; on the other hand, birds, regardless of plumage and characteristics of flight, had plenty against him and his scarecrow-inventing mind. Immediately after the christening ceremony—the bells hadn't even stopped ringing—they knew him for what he was. Eduard Amsel, however, lay plump and rosy on a tight baptismal cushion, and if birds meant anything to him he didn't show it. His godmother was named Gertrud Karweise, later she took to knitting him woolen socks, year in year out, punctually for Christmas. In her robust arms the newly baptized child was presented to the large christening party, which had been invited to an interminable christening dinner. The widow Amsel, née Tiede, who had stayed home, was supervising the setting of the table, issuing last-minute instructions in the kitchen, and tasting sauces. But all the Tiedes from Gross-Zünder, except for the four sons who were living dangerously in the Cavalry—the second youngest was later killed—trudged along in their Sunday best behind the baptismal cushion. Along the Dead Vistula marched: Christian Glomme the Schiewenhorst fisherman and his wife Martha Glomme, née Liedke; Herbert Kienast and his wife Johanna, née Probst; Carl Jakob Ayke, whose son Daniel Ayke had met his death on Dogger Bank in the service of the Imperial Navy; the fisherman's widow Brigitte Kabus, whose boat was operated by her brother Jakob Nilenz; between Ernst Wilhelm Tiede's daughters-in-law, who tripped along city fashion in pink, pea-green, and violet-blue, strode, brushed gleaming black, the aged Pastor Blech—a descendant of the famous Deacon A. F. Blech, who, while Pastor of St. Mary's, had written a chronicle of the City of Danzig from 1807 to 1814, the years of the French occupation. Friedrich Bollhagen, owner of a large smoking establishment, walked behind the retired Captain Bronsard, who had found wartime occupation as a volunteer sluice operator in Plehnendorf. August Sponagel, inn-keeper at Wesslinken, walked beside Frau Major von Ankum, who towered over him by a head. In view of the fact that Dirk Heinrich von

Ankum, landowner in Klein-Zünder, had gone out of
existence early in 1915, Sponagel held the Frau Major's
rigidly-rectangularly offered arm. The rear guard, behind
Herr and Frau Busenitz, who had a coal business in
Bohnsack, consisted of Erich Lau, the disabled Schiewenhorst village mayor, and his superlatively pregnant Marga-
rete who, as daughter of the Nickelswalde village mayor
Momber, had not married below her station. Being on duty,
Dike Inspector Haberland had been obliged to take his
leave outside the church door. Quite likely the procession
also included a bevy of children, all too blond and all too
dressed up.

Over sandy paths which only sparsely covered the strag-
gling roots of the scrub pines, they made their way along the
right bank of the river to the waiting landaus, to old man
Tiede's four-in-hand, which he had managed to hold on to
in spite of the war and the shortage of horses. Shoes full of
sand. Captain Bronsard laughed loud and breathless, then
coughed at length. Conversation waited until after dinner.
The woods along the shore had a Prussian smell. Almost
motionless the river, a dead arm of the Vistula, which acquired a certain amount of current only farther down when
the Mottlau flowed into it. The sun shone cautiously on
holiday finery. Tiede's daughters-in-law shivered pink pea-
green violet-blue and would have been glad to have the
widows' shawls. Quite likely so much widow's black, the
gigantic Frau Major, and the disabled veteran's monumental limp contributed to the coming of an event which
had been in the making from the start: scarcely had the
company left the Bohnsack Fishermen's Church when the
ordinarily undisplaceable gulls clouded up from the square.
Not pigeons, for fishermen's churches harbor gulls and not
pigeons. Now in a steep slant bitterns, sea swallows, and
teals rise from the rushes and duckweed. Up go the crested
terns. Crows rise from the scrub pines. Starlings and blackbirds abandon the cemetery and the gardens of whitewashe l
fishermen's houses. From lilac and hawthorn come wag-
tails and titmice, robins, finches, and thrushes, every bird
in the song; clouds of sparrows from eaves and telegraph
wires; swallows from barns and crannies in masonry; whatever called itself bird shot up, exploded, flashed like an
arrow as soon as the baptismal cushion hove into sight, and
was carried across the river by the sea wind, to form a black-

torn cloud, in which birds that normally avoid one another mingled promiscuously, all spurred by the same dread: gulls and crows; a pair of hawks amid dappled songbirds; magpies with magpies!

And five hundred birds, not counting sparrows, fled in mass between the sun and the christening party. And five hundred birds cast their ominous shadow upon christening party, baptismal cushion, and baptized child.

And five hundred birds—who wants to count sparrows?—induced the christening party, from Lau, the disabled village mayor, to the Tiedes, to cluster together and first in silence, then muttering and exchanging stiff glances, to press from back to front and hurry their pace. August Sponagel stumbles over pine roots. Between Bronsard and Pastor Blech, who makes only the barest stab at raising his arms in pastoral appeasement, the gigantic Frau Major storms forward, gathering her skirts as in a rainstorm, and carries all in her wake: the Glommes and Kienast with wife, Ayke and the Kabus, Bollhagen and the Busenitzes; even the disabled Lau and his superlatively pregnant wife, who however did not suffer from shock and was delivered of a normal girl child, keep pace, panting heavily—only the godmother, bearing child and topsy-turvy cushion in her strong arms, drops back and is last to reach the waiting landaus and the Tiedes' four-in-hand amid the first poplars on the road to Schiewenhorst.

Did the baptizand cry? Not a whimper, but he didn't sleep either. Did the cloud of five hundred birds and uncounted sparrows disperse immediately after the hasty and not at all festive departure of the carriages? For a long while the cloud over the lazy river found no rest: for a time it hovered over Bohnsack, for a time it hung long and narrow over the woods and dunes, then broad and fluid over the opposite shore, dropping an old crow into a marshy meadow, where it stood out gray and stiff. Only when landaus and four-in-hand drove into Schiewenhorst did the cloud disperse into its various species, which found their way back to the square outside the church, to cemetery, gardens, barns, rushes, lilac bushes, and pines; but until evening, when the christening party, having eaten and drunk its fill, sat weighing down the long table with elbows, anguish darkened numerous bird hearts of varying sizes; for as Eduard lay on

his baptismal cushion, his scarecrow-inventing spirit had
made itself known to all the birds. From that moment on
they knew all about him.

TENTH MORNING SHIFT

Who can tell whether Albrecht Amsel, merchant and reserve
lieutenant, wasn't a Jew after all? The people of Schiewenhorst, Einlage, and Neufähr would hardly have called him
a rich Jew for no reason at all. And what about the name?
Isn't it typical? You say he's of Dutch descent, because in
the early Middle Ages Dutch settlers drained the Vistula
delta, having brought with them linguistic peculiarities,
windmills, and their names?

Now that Brauksel has insisted in the course of past
morning shifts that A. Amsel is not a Jew and declared in so
many words: "Of course Amsel was not a Jew," he can now,
with equal justification—for all origins are what we choose
to make of them—try to convince you that of course Albrecht Amsel was a Jew. He came of a family of tailors long
resident in Preussisch-Stargard and had been obliged—because his father's house was full of children—to leave Preussisch-Stargard at the age of sixteen for Schneidemühl,
Frankfurt on the Oder, and Berlin. Fourteen years later he
had come—metamorphosed, Protestant, and wealthy—to the
Vistula estuary by way of Schneidemühl, Neustadt, and
Dirschau. The cut which had made Schiewenhorst a village
on the river was not yet a year old when Albrecht Amsel
purchased his property on favorable terms.

And so he went into business. What else should he have
gone into? And so he sang in the church choir. Why
shouldn't he, a baritone, have sung in the church choir? And
so he helped to found an athletic club, and among all the
inhabitants of the village it was he who most staunchly believed that he Albrecht Amsel was not a Jew, that the name
of Amsel came from Holland: lots of people go by the name
of Specht (woodpecker), a famous African explorer was even
called Nachtigal (nightingale), only Adler (eagle) is a typically Jewish name, and certainly not Amsel (blackbird). The
tailor's son had devoted fourteen years to forgetting his ori-

gins and only as a sideline, though with equal success, to amassing a good-Protestant fortune.

And then in 1903 a precocious young man by the name of Otto Weininger wrote a book. This extraordinary book was named *Sex and Character*; published in Vienna and Leipzig, it labored for six hundred pages to demonstrate that women have no soul. Because the topic proved timely in those years of feminist agitation, and particularly because the thirteenth chapter, entitled "The Jewish Character," showed that the Jews, being a feminine race, also have no soul, the extraordinary book ran into an incredible number of editions and found its way into households where otherwise only the Bible was read. And so Weininger's brain child was also taken into the house of Albrecht Amsel.

Perhaps the merchant would not have opened the thick book if he had known that a certain Herr Pfennig was engaged in denouncing Otto Weininger as a plagiarist. In 1906 there appeared a vicious pamphlet attacking the late Weininger—the young man had meanwhile taken his own life—in the crudest terms. Much as he deplored the tone of the vicious pamphlet, even S. Freud, who had called the deceased Weininger an extremely gifted young man, could not overlook the well-documented fact that Weininger's central idea —bisexuality—was not original with him, but had first occurred to a certain Herr Fliess. And so Albrecht Amsel opened the book all unsuspecting and read in Weininger who in a footnote had introduced himself as a Jew: The Jew has no soul. The Jew does not sing. The Jew does not engage in sports. The Jew must surmount the Jewishness within him . . . And Albrecht Amsel surmounted by singing in the church choir, by not only founding the Bohnsack Athletic Club reg. 1905, but also by coming out for the squad in appropriate attire, by doing his part on the horse and horizontal bar, by high jumping, broad jumping, participating in relay races, and finally, despite opposition—here again a founder and pioneer—by introducing schlagball, a relatively new sport, in the territory to the right and left of all three mouths of the Vistula.

Like the villagers of the Island, Brauksel, who is recording these matters to the best of his ability, would know nothing of the town of Preussisch-Stargard and Eduard Amsel's tailor grandfather, if Lottchen Amsel, née Tiede, had kept silence. Many years after the fatal day in Verdun she opened her mouth.

Young Amsel, of whom we shall be speaking, though with interruptions, from now on, had hastened from the city to his mother's deathbed and she, who was succumbing to diabetes, had whispered feverishly in his ear: "Ah, son. Forgive your poor mother. Amsel, you never knew him but he was your very own father, was one of the circumcised as they say. I only hope they don't catch you now the laws are so strict."

At the time of the strict laws—which, however, were not yet in force in the Danzig Free State—Eduard Amsel inherited the business, the property, and the house with everything in it, including a shelf of books: *The Kings of Prussia, Prussia's Great Men, Frederick the Great, Count Schlieffen, The Battle of Leuthen, Frederick and Katte, Frederick the Great and La Barbarina*, and Otto Weininger's extraordinary book which Amsel henceforth kept about him, whereas the other books were gradually lost. In his own way he read in it, he even read the marginal notes which his singing, athletic father had jotted down. He saved the book down through hard times, and it is thanks to him that the book is now lying on Brauxel's desk, where it can be consulted today and at all times: Weininger has grafted quite a few ideas onto the present writer. The scarecrow is created in man's image.

ELEVENTH MORNING SHIFT

Brauschel's hair is growing. As he writes or manages the mine, it grows. As he dines, walks, slumbers, breathes, or holds his breath, as the morning shift is lowered, the night shift raised, and sparrows inaugurate the day, it grows. In fact, while with cold fingers the barber shortens Brauksel's hair at his request because the year is drawing to a close, it grows back under his scissors. One day Brauksel, like Weininger, will be dead, but his hair, toenails, and fingernails will survive him for a time—just as this handbook on the construction of effective scarecrows will be read long after the writer has gone out of existence.

Yesterday mention was made of strict laws. But at the present point in our story, which is just beginning, the laws are still mild, they do not punish Amsel's origin in any way; Lottchen Amsel, née Tiede, knows nothing about the horrors of diabetes; "naturally" Albrecht Amsel was not a Jew; Eduard Amsel is also a good Protestant and has his mother's quickly growing reddish-blond hair; plump, already in possession of all his freckles, he spends his time amid drying fishnets and his favorite way of viewing the world is: filtered through fishnets; small wonder that the world soon takes on for him a net-like pattern, obstructed by beanpoles.

Scarecrows! Here it is contended that at first little Eduard Amsel—he was five and a half when he built his first scarecrow deserving of the name—had no intention of building anything of the sort. But people from the village and salesmen on their way around the Island with fire insurance and seed samples, peasants on their way home from the notary's, in short, all those who watched him as he set up his fluttering figures on the dike near the Schiewenhorst dock, thought along those lines. And Kriwe said to Herbert Kienast: "Look what Amsel's kid has been making: honest-to-goodness scarecrows." As on the day of his christening, Eduard Amsel still had nothing against birds; but all those creatures to left and right of the Vistula that let themselves be carried bird-like by the wind had something against his products, namely scarecrows. He built one every day, and they were never alike. What the day before it had taken him three hours to make from striped pants, a jacketlike rag with bold checks, a brimless hat, and, with the help of an incomplete and ramshackle ladder, an armful of freshly cut willow switches, he tore down the following morning, to construct from the same materials an oddity of a very different race and faith, but which like its predecessor commanded birds to keep their distance.

Though all these transitory edifices revealed industry and imagination on the part of the architect, it was Eduard Amsel's keen sense of reality in all its innumerable forms, the curious eye surmounting his plump cheek, which provided his products with closely observed detail, which made them functional and crow-repellent. They differed not only in form but also in effect from the local scarecrows that stood wavering in the fields and gardens round about; whereas the run-of-the-mill article registered small success with the feathered folk, a *succès d'estime* at best, his creatures, though built for no purpose and with no enemy in view, had the power to instill panic in birds.

They seemed to be alive, and if you looked at them long enough, even in process of construction or when they were being torn down and nothing remained but the torso, they were alive in every way: they sprinted along the dike, running figures beckoned, threatened, attacked, thrashed, waved from shore to shore, let themselves be carried by the wind, engaged in conversation with the sun, blessed the river and its fish, counted the poplars, overtook the clouds, broke off the tips of steeples, tried to ascend to heaven, to board or pursue the ferry, to take flight, they were never anonymous, but signified Johann Lickfett the fisherman, Pastor Blech, time and time again Kriwe the ferryman, who stood with his mouth open and his head to one side, Captain Bronsard, Inspector Haberland, or whomever else those lowlands had to offer. Thus, although the rawboned Frau Major von Ankum had her small homestead in Klein-Zünder and seldom posed at the ferry landing, she made herself at home on the Schiewenhorst dike in the form of a giantess terrifying to birds and children alike, and remained there for three days.

A little later, when school began for Eduard Amsel, it was Herr Olschewski, the young schoolmaster in Nickelswalde—for Schiewenhorst did not maintain a school—who was obliged to stand still when his freckliest pupil planted him, insubstantial as a scarecrow, on the great dune to the right of the river mouth. Amid the wind-bowed pines on the crest of the dune Amsel planted the schoolmaster's double and before his canvas-shod feet laid out the griddle-flat Island from the Vistula to the Nogat, the plain as far as the towers of Danzig, the hills and woods beyond the city, the river from mouth to horizon, and the open sea reaching out toward an intimation of Hela Peninsula, including the ships anchored in the roadstead.

TWELFTH MORNING SHIFT

The year is running out. It is ending in an odd kind of way, because what with the Berlin crisis, New Year's Eve is to be celebrated not with noisy fireworks but only with the luminous kind. And still another reason for not celebrating New Year's Eve with the usual noise makers here in Lower Saxony is that Hinrich Kopf, a faithful likeness of a chief of state, has just been carried to his grave. As a precaution Brauxel, after consulting the shop committee, has put up a notice in the surface installations, in the administration building, in the gangways, and on the fill level, so worded: The workers and staff of Brauxel and Co.—Exporters and Importers—are requested to celebrate New Year's Eve quietly, in a manner befitting the troubled times. In addition the present writer, who could not resist the temptation to quote himself, has had his little motto—"The scarecrow is created in man's image"—printed on deckle-edged cards and sent to customers and business friends as a New Year's greeting.

The first school year brought Eduard Amsel a variety of surprises. Displayed each day ludicrously round and freckle-faced to the eyes of two villages, he became a whipping boy. Whatever games the children happened to be playing, he had to join in, or rather, he was joined in. Of course young Amsel cried when the gang dragged him into the nettles behind Folchert's barn or tied him to a post with rotten ropes that stank of tar and painfully if not imaginatively tortured him; but through the tears which, as everyone knows, confer a blurred but uncommonly precise vision, his greenish-gray, fat-encased little eyes never ceased to observe, to appraise, and to analyze typical movements. Two or three days after one of these beatings—and it was quite possible that in between blows, along with other insults and nicknames the word "Sheeny" would be uttered accidentally on purpose—the very same torture scene would be reproduced in the form of a single many-armed scarecrow between dunes or directly on the beach, licked by the sea.

Walter Matern put an end to these beatings and to the ensuing replicas of beatings. One day, perhaps because he had discovered on the beach a tattered but furiously flailing scarecrow, which far from looking unlike him looked like nine of him, he who for quite some time had taken an active part in beatings, who had even accidentally on purpose introduced the word "Sheeny," dropped his fists in mid-action, allowed both fists to reflect as it were for the time it would have taken to deal out five punches, and then went on punching: but from that time on it was no longer young Amsel who had to submit quietly when Walter Matern's fists declared their independence; instead, Matern attacked Amsel's tormentors, and this with so much dedication and rhythmic grinding of his teeth that he was still boxing at the soft summer air behind Folchert's barn long after all but the blinking Amsel had vanished.

As we all know from breathtaking movies, friendships concluded during or after beatings are often and breathtakingly put to the test. In the course of this book—and this in itself will make it kind of long—it will be necessary to subject the Matern-Amsel friendship to many more trials. From the very start Walter Matern's fists—luckily for the new friendship—were kept busy, because the local yokels, progeny of fishermen and peasants, were unable to digest this pact of friendship that had been so suddenly concluded; no sooner was school out than, succumbing to old habit, they dragged the struggling Amsel off behind Folchert's barn. For slowly flowed the Vistula, slowly the dikes tapered off, the seasons changed, slowly clouds drifted, slowly the ferry labored, slowly the denizens of the lowlands changed over from oil lamps to electric light, and only slowly did the children in the villages to the right and left of the Vistula get it through their heads that anyone who wanted to pick a bone with young Amsel would have Walter Matern to reckon with. The mystery of friendship began gradually to work wonders. A unique scene, representative of the many colorful situations that youthful friendship could involve in a rural district amid the unchanging embodiments of country life—peasant, farmhand, pastor, schoolmaster, postmaster, peddler, cheesemaker, dairy co-operative inspector, apprentice forester, and village idiot—perpetuated itself for many years without being photographed: somewhere in the dunes, with his back to the woods and their aisles, Amsel is at work. Garments of various cut are spread out in such a way that the artist can find what he needs at a glance. No one style is predominant. Driftwood and small sand heaps weigh down the cotton twill of the defunct Prussian Army and the checkered, stiff-dry yield of the latest flood, inhibiting their tendency to flutter away: nightgowns, morning coats, pants without seats, kitchen rags, jerkins, shriveled dress uniforms, curtains with peepholes, camisoles, pinafores, coachmen's coats, trusses, chest bandages, chewed-up carpets, the bowels of neckties, pennants from a shooting match, and a dowry of table linen stink and attract flies. A many-segmented caterpillar of felt and velours hats, caps, helmets, bonnets, nightcaps, garrison caps, low-crowned caps, and straw hats squirms, tries to bite its tail, clearly exhibits each one of its segments, lies there embroidered with flies, and waits to be used. The sun impels all the fence laths implanted in the sand, not to mention the fragments of ladders, the beanpoles, the smooth canes and knotted canes, and the common sticks washed ashore by sea and river, to cast moving shadows of varying lengths, which carry time along with them in their passage. Further: a mountain of string, wire, halfrotted rope, crumbling leather articles, matted veils, entangled woolens, and bundles of straw blackened with mildew, dislodged from the disintegrating roofs of barns. Potbellied bottles, bottomless milking pails, chamber pots, and soup tureens form a pile by themselves. And amid all this accumulated stock, astonishingly nimble: Eduard Amsel. Sweating, stepping on beach thistles with his bare feet but taking no notice, he groans, grunts, giggles some, plants a beanpole, tosses a roofing lath against it slantwise, throws some wire after it—he doesn't tie things together, just tosses, and they stay in place miraculously—makes a reddish-brown silverthreaded curtain climb three-and-a-half times around beanpole and roofing lath, allows matted bundles of straw to turn into a head around a mustard pot, selects a visor cap, exchanges the student cap for a Quaker's hat, mixes up the caterpillar of hats and the bright-colored sand flies as well, favors a nightcap for a time, but finally appoints a coffee cozy stiffened by the last flood to function as a summit. At the last moment he realizes that the whole lacks a vest and more specifically a vest that is shiny in back, chooses from among the mildewed tatterdemalion tatters, and, half over his shoulder and without really looking, tosses a vest on his creature under the coffee cozy. Already he is planting a tired little ladder to the left, crossing two man-size logs to

the right, twisting a triple-width section of garden fence into
a screwlike arabesque. He aims briefly, throws stiff army
twill and hits, joins with creaking belts, and with the help
of the tangled woolens gives this figure, the outrider of his
group, a certain military authority. An instant later, laden
with rags, hung with leather, entwined in rope, seven times
hatted, and surrounded by jubilant flies, he is in front, to
one side, to southeast and to starboard of his derelict junk-
pile, which is little by little metamorphosed into a crow-
repellent group; for from the dunes, the lyme grass, the
pine woods rise common and—ornithologically speaking—
rare birds. Cause and effect: they coagulate into a cloud
high above Eduard Amsel's place of work. They write their
terror in a birdscript that grows steadily steeper, narrower,
and more jumbled. The root sound of this text is *crah*,
which with the help of the wood pigeons puts forth the
branch *mah-roo-croo*. The text ends when it does end with
pee, but it also has its inner ferment comprising a great deal
of *uebü*, a great deal of *ek*, the *ra-atch* of the teals, and the
ox-like roar of the bitterns. Inspired by Amsel's creations,
every conceivable kind of terror found expression. But who
made his rounds over the rippling crests of the dunes, ensur-
ing the peace necessary to his friend's bird-repellent labors?

Those fists belong to Walter Matern. Seven years old, he
gazes gray-eyed over the sea as though it belonged to him.
Senta, his young she-dog, barks at the short-winded Baltic
waves. Perkun is gone, carried away by one of many canine
diseases. Senta of Perkun's line will whelp Harras. Harras of
Perkun's line will sire Prinz. Prinz of the Perkun-Senta-Har-
ras line—and at the very beginning the bark of a Lithuanian
she-wolf—will make history . . . but for the present Senta is
barking at the helpless Baltic. And he stands barefoot in the
sand. By sheer force of will and a slight vibration from his
knees to the soles of his feet, he is able to dig deeper and
deeper into the dune. Soon the sand will reach his rolled-up
corduroy trousers stiffened with sea water: but now Walter
Matern leaps out of the sand, flinging sand into the wind,
and is gone from the dune. Senta forsakes the short-winded
waves, both of them must have flaired something, they hurl
themselves, he brown and green in corduroy and wool, she
black and elongated, over the crest of the next dune into the
beach grass, and—after the sluggish sea has slapped the
beach six times—reappear, having gradually grown bored,

in an entirely different place. It seems to have been nothing. Air dumplings. Wind soup. Not even a rabbit.

But up above, where from Putzig Bay clouds of roughly equal size against blue drape drift in the direction of the Haff, the birds persist in giving Amsel's near-finished scarecrows the shrill and raucous recognition that any fully finished scarecrow would be proud of.

THIRTEENTH MORNING SHIFT

Fortunately the year ended peacefully at the mine. From the headframe the apprentices, under the supervision of Wernicke the head foreman, launched a few fine-looking rockets, which formed the company emblem, the well-known bird motif. Unfortunately the clouds hung so low that a good deal of the magic was lost.

This making of figures; this game played in the dunes, on top of the dike, or in a clearing rich in blueberries amid the scrub pine, took on new meaning late one afternoon when Kriwe the ferryman—the ferry had stopped for the day—took the Schiewenhorst village mayor with red-and-white-checked daughter to the edge of the woods where Eduard Amsel, guarded as usual by his friend Walter Matern and the dog Senta, had lined up six or seven of his most recent creations against the steeply rising wooded dunes, but not in military formation.

The sun let itself down behind Schiewenhorst. The friends cast long-drawn-out shadows. If Amsel's shadow was nevertheless more rotund, it was because the drooping sun bore witness to the little rascal's extraordinary fatness; he would grow still fatter in time to come.

Neither of them stirred a muscle when the lopsided Leather Kriwe and Lau, the disabled peasant, approached with a daughter in tow and two or three shadows. Senta adopted an attitude of wait and see, and uttered a short growl. The two boys gazed blankly—they had had lots of practice—from the top of the dune over the row of scarecrows, over the sloping meadow where moles had their dwellings, toward the Matern windmill. There it stood with pole on jack, raised windward by a little round hummock, but not running.

And who stood at the foot of the hummock with a sack bent over his right shoulder? The man beneath the sack was Matern, the white miller. He, too, like the sails of the mill, like the two boys on the crest of the dune, like Senta, stood motionless, though for different reasons.

Slowly Kriwe stretched out his left arm and a gnarled, leather-brown finger. Hedwig Lau, wearing her Sunday best on a weekday, dug a black and buckled patent-leather shoe into the sand. Kriwe's index finger pointed to Amsel's exhibition. "There you are, friend. See what I mean." And his finger pointed with slow thoroughness from scarecrow to scarecrow. Lau's approximately octagonal head followed the leathery finger, remaining two scarecrows behind—there were seven scarecrows—to the very end of the show.

"Them's fine scarecrows, friend; you won't have no more birds to worry about."

Because the patent-leather shoe was digging, its movement was transmitted to the hem of the little girl's dress and to her hair ribbons of like material. Lau scratched himself under his cap and once again, now slowly and solemnly, passed the seven scarecrows in review, this time in reverse order. Amsel and Walter Matern sat on the crest of the dune, dangling their legs unevenly, and kept their eyes on the motionless sails of the windmill. The elastic of Amsel's knee socks cut into his plump calves below the knee, leaving a bulge of doll-like pink flesh. The white miller remained frozen at the foot of the hummock, his right shoulder digging into the hundredweight sack. The miller was in plain sight, but far away. "If you want me to, I can ask the kid what one of them scarecrows costs if it costs anything." No one will ever nod more slowly than Erich Lau, the peasant and village mayor, nodded. For his little daughter every day was Sunday. Head cocked to one side, Senta followed every movement but usually got there first, for she was so young she couldn't help getting ahead of unhurried intimations. When Amsel was baptized and the birds gave the first sign, Hedwig Lau had still been swimming in amniotic fluid. Sea sand is bad for patent-leather shoes. Kriwe in wooden shoes made a half turn toward the crest of the dune and from the corner of his mouth spat brown juice that formed a ball in the sand: "Listen, kid, we'd like to know what one of them scarecrows would cost for the garden if it costs something."

The distant white miller with the bent sack did not drop the sack, Hedwig Lau did not remove her buckled patent-leather shoe from the sand, but Senta gave a short, dust-scattering leap as Eduard Amsel let himself drop from the crest of the dune. Twice he rolled. A moment later, propelled by the two rolls, he stood between the two men in woolen jackets, not far from Hedwig Lau's digging patent-leather shoe.

Step by step, the white miller began to climb the hummock. The patent-leather shoe stopped digging and a giggle dry as bread crumbs began to stir the red-and-white-checked dress and the red-and-white-checked hair ribbons. A deal was in the making. Amsel pointed an inverted thumb at the patent-leather shoes. A stubborn shaking of Lau's head made the shoes into a commodity that was not for sale, leastways not for the present. In response to the offer of barter, hard currency was jingled. While Amsel and Kriwe, but only infrequently Erich Lau the village mayor, figured and in so doing pressed fingers down and let them rise again, Walter Matern was still sitting on the crest of the dune. To judge by the sound his teeth were making, he harbored objections to the negotiations, which he later described as "haggling."

Kriwe and Eduard Amsel arrived at an agreement more quickly than Lau could nod. The daughter was digging again with her shoe. The price of a scarecrow was set at fifty pfennigs. The miller was gone. The mill was milling. Senta was heeling. For three scarecrows Amsel was asking one gulden. In addition and not without reason, for he was planning to expand his business, three rags per scarecrow and as a special premium Hedwig Lau's buckled patent-leather shoes as soon as they could be qualified as worn out.

Oh sober solemn day when a first deal is closed! Next morning the village mayor had the three scarecrows ferried across the river to Schiewenhorst and planted in his wheat behind the railroad. Since Lau, like many peasants on the Island, grew either the Epp or the Kujave variety, both beardless and consequently an easy prey for birds, the scarecrows had ample opportunity to prove their worth. With their coffee cozies, straw-bundle helmets, and crossed straps, they may well have passed for the last three grenadiers of the First Guards Regiment at the battle of Torgau, which, as Schlieffen tells us, was murderous. Already Amsel had given form to his penchant for Prussian precision; in any event the three soldiers were effective; a deathly stillness prevailed amid the ripening summer wheat, over the previously bird-winged and vociferously pillaged field.

Word got around. Soon peasants came from both shores, from Junkeracker and Pasewark, from Einlage and Schnakenburg, from deep in the interior of the Island: frgm Jungfer, Scharpau, and Ladekopp. Kriwe acted as go-between; but for the present Amsel did not raise his prices and, after remonstrances on the part of Walter Matern, took to accepting only every second and later every third offer. To himself and all his customers he said that he didn't want to botch his work and could turn out only one scarecrow a day, or two at the very most. He declined assistance. Only Walter Matern was permitted to help, to bring raw materials from both banks of the river and to continue guarding the artist and his work with two fists and a black dog.

Brauxel might also relate how Amsel soon had the wherewithal to rent Folchert's decrepit but still lockable barn for a small fee. In this wooden shelter, which had a reputation for spookiness because someone for some reason had hanged himself from one of its rafters, under a roof which would accordingly have inspired any artist, Amsel stored the materials that would subsequently come to life as scarecrows. In rainy weather the barn became his workshop. It was a regular shop, for Amsel let his capital work for him and had purchased in his mother's store, hence at cost price, hammers, two handsaws, drills, pliers, chisels, and the pocketknife equipped with three blades, a leather punch, a corkscrew, and a saw. This last article he gave to Walter Matern. And two years later when he couldn't find a stone on the Nickelswalde dike, Walter Matern had thrown it, in place of a stone, into the rising Vistula. We have heard about that.

FOURTEENTH MORNING SHIFT

Those characters ought to take Amsel's diary as an example and learn to keep their books properly. How many times has Brauchsel described the working method of both coauthors? Two trips at the expense of the firm brought us together and, at a time when those eminent citizens were leading a pampered existence, gave them an opportunity to take notes and to draw up a work plan as well as a few diagrams. Instead, they keep checking back: When does the manuscript have to be delivered? Should a manuscript page have thirty or thirty-four lines? Are you really satisfied with the letter form, or wouldn't something more modern be preferable, along the lines of the new French school, for instance? Is it sufficient for me to describe the Striessbach as a brook between Hochstriess and Langstriess? Or should historical references, such as the boundary dispute between the city of Danzig and the Cistercian monastery in Oliva, be brought in? And what about the letter of ratification written in 1235 by Duke Swantopolk, grandson of Subislaw I, who had founded the monastery? In it the Striessbach is mentioned in connection with Saspe Lake, *"Lacum Saspi usque in rivulum Strieza . . ."* Or the ratifying document issued by Mestwin II in 1283, in which the Striessbach, which constituted the border, is spelled as follows: *"Praefatum rivulum Striesz usque in Vislam . . ."*? Or the letter of 1291 confirming the monasteries of Oliva and Sarnowitz in all their possessions? Here Striessbach is written "Stricze" in one place, while elsewhere we read: *". . . praefatum fluuium Strycze cum utroque littore a lacu Colpin unde scaturit descendendo in Wislam . . ."*

The other coauthor is no more backward about checking back and seasons all his letters with requests for an advance: *". . . perhaps be permitted to point out that according to our verbal agreement each coauthor, on starting work on his manuscript, was to receive . . ."* That's the actor. All right, let him have his advance. But let Amsel's diary, a photostat if not the original, be his Bible.

The log must have inspired him. A log has to be kept on all ships, even a ferry. Kriwe: a cracked, lean chunk of leather with March-gray, lashless, and slightly crossed eyes, which nevertheless permitted him to guide the steam ferry diagonally, or it might be more apt to say crosswise, against the current from landing to landing. Vehicles, fisherwomen with flounder baskets, the pastor, school-children, travelers in transit, salesmen with sample cases, the coaches and freight cars of the Island narrow-gauge railway, cattle for slaughter or breeding, weddings and funerals with coffins and wreaths were squinted across the river by ferryman Kriwe, who entered all happenings in his log. So snugly and unjoltingly did Kriwe put in to his berth that a pfening could not have been inserted between the sheet metal sheathing on the bow of his ferryboat and the piles of the landing. Moreover he had long served the friends Walter Matern and Eduard Amsel as the most reliable of business agents, asking no commission for the deals he transacted and barely accepting tobacco. When the ferry wasn't operating, he took the two of them to places known only to Kriwe. He urged Amsel to study the terror-inspiring qualities of a willow tree, for the artistic theories of Kriwe and Amsel, which were later recorded in the diary, amounted to this: "Models should be taken primarily from nature." Years later, under the name of Haseloff, Amsel, in the same diary, amplified this dictum as follows: "Everything that can be stuffed should be classified as nature: dolls, for instance."

But the hollow willow tree to which Kriwe led the friends shook itself and had not yet been stuffed. Flat in the background, the mill milled. Slowly the last narrow-gauge train rounded the bend, ringing faster than it ran. Butter melted away. Milk turned sour. Four bare feet, two oiled boots. First grass and nettles, then clover. Over two fences, through three open stiles, then another fence to climb. On both sides of the brook the willows took a step forward, a step back, turned, had hips, navels; and one willow—for even among willows there is the one willow—was hollow hollow hollow, until three days later Amsel filled it in: squats there plump and friendly on both heels, studies the inside of a willow, because Kriwe said . . . and out of the willow in which he is sitting with his curiosity, he attentively examines the willows to the right and left of the brook; as a model Amsel especially prizes a three-headed one that has one foot on dry land but is cooling the other in the brook because the giant Miligedo, the one with the lead club, stepped on its willow foot long long ago. And the willow tree holds still, though to all appearances it would like to run away, especially as the ground fog—for it is very early, a century before school time—is creeping across the meadows from the river and eating away the trunks of the willows by the brook: soon only the three-headed head of the posing willow will be floating on the fog, carrying on a dialogue.

Amsel leaves his niche, but he doesn't feel like going home to his mother, who is mulling over her account books in her sleep, rechecking all her figures. He wants to witness the milk-drinking hour that Kriwe had been telling about. Walter Matern has the same idea. Senta isn't with them, because Kriwe had said: "Don't take the hound, boy; she's likely to whine and get scared when it starts."

So no dog. Between them a hole with four legs and a tail. Barefoot they creep over gray meadows, looking back over the eddying steam. They're on the point of whistling: Here, Senta! Heel! Heel! But they remain soundless, because Kriwe said . . . Ahead of them monuments: cows in the swirling soup. Not far from the cows, exactly between Beister's flax and the willows to either side of the brook, they lie in the dew and wait. From the dikes and the scrub pines graduated tones of gray. Above the steam and the poplars of the highway leading to Pasewark, Steegen, and Stutthof the cross pattern of the sails of the Matern wind-mill. Flat fretwork. No miller grinds wheat into flour so early in the morning. So far no cocks, but soon. Shadowy and suddenly close the nine scrub pines on the great dune, uniformly bent from northwest to southeast in obedience to the prevailing wind. Toads—or is it oxen?—toads or oxen are roaring. The frogs, slimmer, are praying. Gnats all in the same register. Something, but not a lapwing, calls: an invitation? or is it only announcing its presence? Still no cock. Islands in the steam, the cows breathe. Amsel's heart scurries across a tin roof. Walter Matern's heart kicks a door in. A cow moos warmly. Cozy warm belly-mooing from the other cows. What a noise in the fog; hearts on tin against doors, what is calling whom, nine cows, toads oxen gnats . . . And suddenly—for no sign has been given—silence. Frogs gone, toads oxen gnats gone, nothing calls hears answers anyone, cows lie down and Amsel and friend, almost without heartbeat, press their ears into the dew, into the clover: they are coming! From the brook a shuffling. A sobbing as of dishcloths, but regular, without crescendo, ploof ploof, pshish—ploof ploof pshish. Ghosts of the hanged? Headless nuns? Gypsies goblins elves? Who's there? Balderle Ashmodai Beng? Sir Peege Peegood? Bobrowski the incendiary and his crony Materna with whom it all began?

Kynstute's daughter, whose name was Tulla?—Then they
glisten: covered with bottom muck, eleven fifteen seventeen
brown river eels have come to bathe in the dew, this is
their hour, they slide slither whip through the clover and
flow in the direction of. The clover remains bowed in their
slimy track. The throats of the toads oxen gnats are still be-
numbed. Nothing calls and nothing answers. Warm lie the
cows on black-and-white flanks. Udders advertise themselves:
pale yellow matutinal full to bursting: nine cows, thirty-six
teats, eighteen eels. They arrive and suck themselves fast.
Brownish-black extensions to pink-spotted teats. Sucking
lapping glugging thirst. At first the eels quiver. Pleasure who
giving whom? Then one after another cows let their heavy-
heavy heads droop in the clover. Milk flows. Eels swell. The
toads are roaring again. The gnats start up. The slim frogs.
Still no cock, but Walter Matern has a swollen voice. He'd
like to go over and grab. It would be easy, child's play.
But Amsel's against it, he has something else in mind and is
already planning it out. The eels flow back to the brook.
The cows sigh. The first cock. The mill turns slowly. The
train rings as it rounds the bend. Amsel decides to build a
new scarecrow.

And it took form: a pig's bladder was to be had for
nothing because the Lickfetts had just slaughtered. It provided the taut udder. The smoked skin of real eels was
stuffed with straw and coiled wire, sewed up and attached
to the pig's bladder—upside down, so that the eels twined
and twisted like thick hair and stood on their heads on the
udder. The Gorgon's head was raised over Karweise's wheat
on two forked sticks.

And in his diary Amsel sketched the new scarecrow
just as Karweise would buy it—later the tattered hide of a
dead cow was thrown over the forked sticks like an overcoat. In the sketch it is overcoatless and more striking, a
finished product with its own ragged hide.

FIFTEENTH MORNING SHIFT

Our friend the actor is creating difficulties. Whereas
Brauxel and the young man write day after day—the one

about Amsel's diary, the other about and to his cousin—he has come down with a light case of January flu. Has to suspend operations, isn't getting proper care, has always been kind of delicate at this time of year, begs leave once again to remind me of the promised advance. It's been sent, my friend. Quarantine yourself, my friend; your manuscript will benefit by it. Oh sober joy of conscientious effort: There is a diary in which Amsel in beautiful newly learned Sütterlin script noted his expenses in connection with the fashioning of scarecrows for field and garden. The pig's bladder was free. Kriwe procured the worthless cowhide for two sticks of chewing tobacco.

On credit balance, what lovely round words: There is a diary in which Amsel, with figures plump and figures angular, entered his receipts from the sale of various scarecrows for garden and field—eels on udder netted him a whole gulden.

Eduard Amsel kept this diary for about two years, drew lines vertical and horizontal, painted Sütterlin pointed, Sütterlin rich in loops, put down blueprints and color studies for various scarecrows, immortalized almost every scarecrow he had sold, and gave himself and his products marks in red ink. Later, as a high school student, he wrapped the several times folded little notebook in cracked black oilcloth, and years later, when he had to hurry from the city to the Vistula to bury his mother, found it in a chest used for a bench. The diary lay among the books left by his father, side by side with those about the battles and heroes of Prussia and underneath Otto Weininger's thick volume, and had a dozen or more empty pages which Amsel later, under the names of Haseloff and Goldmouth, filled in with sententious utterances at irregular intervals separated by years of silence.

Today Brauxel, whose books are kept by an office manager and seven clerks, owns the touching little notebook wrapped in scraps of oilcloth. Not that he uses the fragile original as a prop to his memory! It is stowed away in his safe along with contracts, securities, patents, and essential business secrets, while a photostatic copy of the diary lies between his well-filled ash tray and his cup of lukewarm morning coffee and serves him as work material.

The first page of the notebook is wholly taken up by the

sentence, more painted than written: "Scarecrows made and sold by Eduard Heinrich Amsel."

Underneath, undated and painted in smaller letters, a kind of motto: "Began at Easter because I shouldn't forget anything. Kriwe said so the other day."

Brauksel holds that there isn't much point in reproducing here the broad Island idiom written by Eduard Amsel as an eight-year-old schoolboy; in the present narrative it will be possible at most to record in direct discourse the charms of this language, which will soon die out with the refugees' associations and once dead may prove to be of interest to science in very much the same way as Latin. Only when Amsel, his friend Walter, Kriwe, or Grandma Matern open their mouths in the Island dialect, will Brauchsel's pen follow suit. But since in his opinion the value of the diary is to be sought, not in the schoolboy's adventurous spelling but in his early and resolute efforts in behalf of scarecrow development, Eduard's village schoolboy idiom will be reproduced only in a stylized form, halfway between the Island brogue and the literary language. For example: "Today after milking recieved anuther gulden for scarcro what stands on one legg and holds the uther croocked Wilhelm Ledwormer tuk it. Throo in a Ulan's helmet and a peece of lining what uset to be a gote."

Brauksel will make a more serious attempt to describe the sketch that accompanies this entry: The scarecrow "what stands on one legg and holds the uther croocked" is not a preliminary study but was sketched after completion with all sorts of crayons, brown cinnabar lavender pea-green Prussian-blue, which, however, never reveal their tonality in pure strokes but are laid on in superimposed strata bearing witness to the transience of worn-out clothing. The actual construction sketch, tossed off in a few black lines and still fresh today, is startling when compared to this crayon drawing: the position "what stands on one legg . . ." is suggested by a slightly inclined ladder lacking two rungs; the position "and holds the uther croocked" must be that pole which tries to posture by inclining dancerlike at an angle of forty-five degrees to the middle of the ladder, while the ladder leans slightly to the left. Especially the construction sketch, but the ex post facto crayon drawing as well, suggested a dancer tightly clad in the late reflected splendor of a uniform worn by the musketeers of the Prince of Anhalt-Dessau Infantry Regiment at the battle of Liegnitz.

To come right out with it: Amsel's diary teems with uniformed scarecrows: here a grenadier of the Third Guards Battalion is storming Leuthen cemetery; the Poor Man of Toggenburg appears in the Itzenplitz Infantry Regiment; a Belling hussar capitulates at Maxen; blue and white Natzmer uhlans and Schorlem dragoons battle on foot; blue with red lining, a fusilier of the Baron de La Motte-Fouqué's regiment lives on; in short, just about everybody who for seven years and even earlier had frequented the battlefields of Bohemia and Saxony, Silesia and Pomerania, had escaped at Mollwitz, lost his tobacco pouch at Katholisch-Hennersdorf, sworn allegiance to Fritz in Pirna, deserted to the enemy at Kolin, and achieved sudden fame at Rossbach, came to life under Amsel's hands, though what it was their duty to disperse was no longer a motley Imperial Army, but the birds of the Vistula delta. Whereas Sevdlitz was under orders to chase Hildburghausen—". . . *voilà au moins mon martyre est fini . . .*"—to the Main via Weimar, Erfurt, and Saalfeld, the peasants Lickfett, Mommsen, Beister, Folchert, and Karweise were quite satisfied if the scarecrows itemized in Amsel's diary chased the birds of the Vistula delta from beardless Epp wheat to chestnut trees, willows, alders, and scrub pines.

SIXTEENTH MORNING SHIFT

He acknowledges by phone. The call, it goes without saying, is collect and goes on for a good seven minutes: the money has come, he's beginning to feel better, the crisis is past, his flu is clearing up, tomorrow or at latest the day after he'll be back at his typewriter; yes, unfortunately he has to write directly on the machine, for he is unable to read his own handwriting; but excellent ideas had come to him during his spell of flu . . . As though ideas fostered by fever ever looked like ideas when your temperature was back to normal. My actor friend doesn't think so much of double-entry bookkeeping, even though Brauxel, after years of reckoning up scrupulous accounts, has helped him to achieve a scrupulous credit balance.

It may be that Amsel learned the habit of bookkeeping not only from Kriwe's log but also from his mother, who sat up into the wee hours moaning over her books while her gifted son learned by looking on: conceivably he helped her to order, to file, and to check her accounts.

Despite the economic difficulties of the postwar years, Lottchen Amsel née Tiede managed to keep the firm of A. Amsel afloat and even to reorganize and expand the business—a risk her late husband would never have taken in times of crisis. She began to deal in cutters, some fresh from the Klawitter shipyard, others secondhand, which she had overhauled in Strohdeich, and in outboard motors. She sold the cutters or—as was more profitable—rented them to young fishermen who had just set up housekeeping.

Although Eduard's filial piety never permitted him to fashion even a remote likeness of his mother as a scarecrow, he had no inhibitions whatever, from the age of seven on, about copying her business practices: if she rented out fishing cutters, he rented out extra-stable scarecrows, made expressly for rental. Several pages of the diary show how often and to whom scarecrows were rented. In a steep column Brauxel has added up roughly what they netted him with their scaring: a tidy little sum. Here we shall be able to mention only one rental scarecrow which, though the fees it commanded were nothing out of the ordinary, played an illuminating part in the plot of our story and consequently in the history of scarecrows.

After the above-mentioned study of willows by the brook, after Amsel had built and sold a scarecrow featuring the milk-drinking eels motif, he devised a model revealing on the one hand the proportions of a three headed willow tree and on the other hand commemorating the spoon-swinging and teeth-grinding Grandmother Matern; it too left its trace in Amsel's diary; but beside the preliminary sketch stood a brief sentence which distinguished this product from all its fellows: "Have to smash it up today, cause Kriwe says it just makes trouble."

Max Folchert, who had it in for the Matern family, had rented the scarecrow, half willow half grandmother, from Amsel and set it up beside the fence of his garden, which bordered the Stutthof highway and faced the Matern vegetable garden. It soon became evident that this rented scarecrow not only drove away birds, but also made horses shy and run off in a shower of sparks. Cows on the way to the barn dispersed as soon as the spoon-swinging willow cast its shadow. The bewildered farm animals were joined by poor Lorchen of the curly hair, who had her daily cross to bear with the real spoon-swinging grandmother. Now she was so terrified and beset by an additional grandmother, who to make matters worse had three heads and was disguised as a willow, that she would wander, frantically wind-blown and disheveled, through fields and scrub pines, over dunes and dikes, though house and garden, and might almost have tangled with the moving sails of the Matern windmill if Lorchen's brother, miller Matern, hadn't grabbed her by the apron. On Kriwe's advice and against the will of old man Folchert, who afterward promptly demanded the refund of part of the rental fee, Walter Matern and Eduard Amsel destroyed the scarecrow during the night. Thus it was brought home to an artist for the first time that, when his works embodied a close enough study of nature, they had power not only over the birds of heaven, but over horses and cows as well and were also capable of disorganizing the tranquil rural gait of Lorchen, a human being. To this insight Amsel sacrificed one of his most successful scarecrows. Moreover, he never again took a willow tree for a model though he occasionally, in times of ground fog, found a niche in a hollow willow or deemed the thirsty eels on their way from the brook to the recumbent cows worthy of his attention. He avoided mating human and tree, and with self-imposed discipline limited his choice of models to the Island peasants, who, stolid and unoffending as they might be, were effective enough as scarecrows. He made the country folk, disguised as the King of Prussia's grenadiers, fusiliers, corporals, standard bearers, and officers, hover over vegetable gardens, wheat, and rye. He quietly perfected his rental system and, though he never suffered the consequences, became guilty of bribery by persuading a conductor on the Island railway, with the help of carefully wrapped gifts, to transport Amsel's rental scarecrows—or Prussian history put to profitable use—free of charge in the freight car of the narrow-gauge line.

SEVENTEENTH MORNING SHIFT

The actor is protesting. His waning flu, so he says, has not prevented him from carefully studying Brauxel's work schedule, which has been sent to both coauthors. It doesn't suit him that a monument should be erected to miller Matern in the course of this morning shift. Such a monument, he feels, is his affair. Brauksel, who fears for the cohesion of his literary consortium, has abandoned the sweeping portrait he was planning, but must insist on mirroring that aspect of the miller which had already cast its reflected splendor on Amsel's diary.

Though the eight-year-old was especially given to combing the battlefields of Prussia for ownerless uniforms, there was nonetheless a model, the above-mentioned miller Matern, who was portrayed directly, without Prussian trappings, but with his flour sack over his shoulder.

The result was a lopsided scarecrow, because the miller was an extremely lopsided man. Because he carried his sacks of grain and flour over his right shoulder, this shoulder was a hand's breadth broader, so that all who looked upon miller Matern full face had to fight down a strong temptation to seize the miller's head in both hands and straighten it out. Since neither his work smock nor his Sunday clothes were made to order, every one of his jackets, smocks, or overcoats looked twisted, formed wrinkles around the neck, was too short in the right sleeve, and had permanently burst seams. He was always screwing up his right eye. On the same side of his face, even when there was no hundred-weight sack bent over his right shoulder, something tugged the corner of his mouth upward. His nose went along with the movement. Finally—and this is why the present portrait is being drawn—his right ear, for many years subjected to the lateral pressure of thousands of hundredweight, lay creased and flattened against his head, while contrastingly his left ear protruded mightily in pursuit of its natural bent. Seen in front view, the miller had only one ear; but the ear that was missing or discernible only in relief was the more significant of the two.

Though not in a class with poor Lorchen, the miller was not exactly made for this world. The gossip of several villages had it that Grandma Matern had corrected him too freely with her cooking spoon in his childhood. The worst of the Matern family's oddities were traced back to Materna, the medieval robber and incendiary, who had ended up in the Stockturm with his companion in crime. The Mennonites, both rough and refined, exchanged winks, and Simon Beister, the rough, pocketless Mennonite, maintained that Catholicism had done the Materns no good, that there was certainly some Catholic deviltry in the way the brat, who was always prowling around with the tubby Amsel kid from over yonder, gnashed his teeth; and just take a look at their dog, eternal damnation could be no blacker. Yet miller Matern was of rather a gentle disposition and—like poor Lorchen—he had few if any enemies in the villages round about, though there were many who made fun of him.

The miller's ear—and when mention is made of the miller's ear, it is always the right flattened one, pressed down by flour sacks, that is meant—the miller's ear, then, is worth mentioning for two reasons: first, because in a scarecrow, the blueprint of which found its way into his diary, Amsel daringly omitted it, and secondly, because this miller's ear, though deaf to all ordinary sounds, such as coughing talking preaching, the singing of hymns, the tinkling of cowbells the forging of horseshoes, the barking of dogs, the singing of birds, the chirping of crickets, was endowed with the most sensitive understanding for everything down to the slightest whispers, murmurs, and hush-hush revelations that transpired inside a sack of grain or flour. Whether beardless wheat or the bearded variety that was seldom grown on the Island; whether threshed from tough or brittle ears; whether intended for brewing, for baking, for the making of semolina, noodles, or starch, whether vitreous, semivitreous, or mealy, the miller's otherwise deaf ear had the faculty of distinguishing exactly what percentage of vetch seed and mildewed or even sprouting grain it contained. It could also identify a sample, sight unseen, as pale-yellow Frankenstein, varicolored Kujave, reddish Probstein, red flower wheat, which grown in loamy soil yields a good brewer's mash, English club wheat, or as either of two varieties that were grown experimentally on the Island, Urtoba, a hard Siberian winter variety, and Schliephacke's white wheat, No. 5.

The miller's otherwise deaf ear was even more clairaudient when it came to flour. While as an earwitness he was able to tell how many wheat beetles, including pupas and doodle-bugs, how many ichneumon flies and flour beetles resided in it, he was able with his ear to the sack to indicate the exact number of mealworms—*Tenebrio molitor*—present in a hundredweight of wheat flour. Moreover—and this is in-deed astonishing—he knew, thanks to his flat ear, either instantly or after some minutes of clairaudient listening, how many dead mealworms the living mealworms in a sack had to deplore, because as he slyly revealed with puckered right eye, right corner of his mouth upward and nose acceding to the movement, the sound made by living worms indi-cated the number of their dead.

The Babylonians, Herodotus tells us, grew wheat with grains the size of peas; but who can lend credence to Herodotus?

Anton Matern the miller made detailed statements about grain and flour; was miller Matern believed?

In Lührmann's taproom, between Folchert's farm and Lührmann's dairy, he was put to the test. The taproom was an ideal testing ground and past tests had left visible traces. From the bar, first of all, there protruded an inch length of nail, allegedly belonging to a two-inch nail, which as a test Erich Block, master brewer in Tiegenhof, had driven into the plank with a single blow of his bare fist; secondly, the whitewashed ceiling of the taproom offered evidence of a different kind: ten or a dozen foot or rather shoe prints, suggesting that someone of succubine origin had been strolling about on the ceiling with his head down. Actually they bear witness to a perfectly human display of strength. When a certain fire insurance salesman expressed doubts about Karweise's muscular prowess, Karweise tossed him up at the ceiling head down and the soles of his shoes heavenward. This he did several times, always catching him in mid-air, careful that the man should incur no harm but live to corroborate the material evidence of an Island test of strength, namely, the prints of his salesman's shoes on a taproom ceiling.

When Anton Matern was put to the test, the atmosphere wasn't athletic—Matern seemed frail—but more on the spooky and mysterious side. It is Sunday. Door and windows closed. The summer is shut out. Four strips of flypaper, vociferous and variously pitched, are the only reminders of the season. In the bar the inch length of nail, shoe prints on gray, once whitewashed ceiling. The usual photographs of shooting matches and the usual prizes awarded at shooting matches. On the shelf only a few green glass bottles, contents distilled from grain. Competing smells are tobacco, shoe polish, and whey, but alcoholic breath, which had got off to a good start on Saturday, wins by a hair's breadth. They talk chew bet. Karweise, Momber, and young Folchert put up a keg of Neuteich bock beer. Silent over a little glass of goldwater—which only city people drink in these parts—miller Matern puts up an identical keg. From behind the bar Lührmann passes the twenty-pound sack and stands in readiness with the flour sieve for the control test. First a moment's contemplation as the sack rests on the hands of the utterly lopsided miller, then he beds the cushion against his flat ear. At once, because no one is chewing, talking broad brogue, or hardly even breathing alcohol fumes any longer, the flypaper becomes more audible: what is the song of dying swans in the theater beside the death song of iridescent flies in the lowlands!

Lührmann has slipped a slate with pencil attached under the miller's free hand. It lists, for inventory is to be taken: 1. mealworms; 2. pupas; 3. beetles. The miller is still listening. The flies drone. Whey and shoe polish predominate, because hardly anyone dares to expel any alcohol fumes. And now the awkward hand, for the miller's right hand is lightly supporting the sack, creeps across the bar to the slate: after mealworms the pencil grates a stiff 17. Twenty-two pupas it squeaks. These the sponge obliterates and as the wet spot dries, it becomes increasingly clear that there are only nineteen pupas. Eight living beetles are alleged to reside in the sack. And as an extra feature, for the rules of the bet do not demand it, the miller announces on strident slate: "Five dead beetles in the sack." Immediately thereafter alcohol fumes recapture the lead over shoe polish and whey. Someone has turned down the swan song of the flies. The spotlight is on Lührmann with his flour sieve.

To make a long story short, the predicted debit of parchment-hard worms, of soft pupae, horny only at the tip, and of grown beetles, otherwise known as flour beetles, was perfectly accurate. Only one dead beetle of the five dead flour beetles announced was missing; perhaps or undoubtedly its desiccated fragments had passed through the flour sieve.

And so miller Anton Matern received his keg of Neuteich bock beer and gave all those present, especially Karweise, Momber, and young Folchert who had staked the beer, a prophecy as a consolation and premium to take home with them. While setting the keg on his shoulder where the interrogated sack of flour had lain only a moment before, the miller with the flat ear told them, quite incidentally, as though relaying gossip he had just heard, how several mealworms—he couldn't say exactly how many, because they had all been talking at once—had been discussing the prospects for the next harvest—he had heard them distinctly with his flat ear while the twenty pounds had been lying beside it. Well, in the opinion of the mealworms, it would be advisable to mow the Epp variety a week before Seven Brothers and the Kujave wheat as well as Schliephacke's No. 5 two days after Seven Brothers.

Years before Amsel fashioned a scarecrow after the clairaudient miller, the miller had become part of a familiar formula of greeting: "Good morning to you, friend. I wonder what Matern's little mealworm is telling him today."

Skeptical or not, many of the peasants questioned the miller, meaning that he should question a well-filled sack capable of providing information as to when winter wheat or summer wheat should be sowed and knowing pretty well when the wheat should be mowed and when the sheaves should be brought in. And even before he was constructed as a scarecrow and put down in Amsel's diary as a preliminary sketch, the miller issued other predictions, more on the gloomy than on the bright side, which have always been borne out, even to this day when the actor in Düsseldorf has ideas about making the miller into a monument.

For he saw not only the threat of poisonous ergot in the grain, hailstorms warranting insurance benefits, and multitudes of field mice in the near future, but predicted to the day when prices would take a dive on the Berlin or Budapest grain exchange, bank crashes in the early thirties, Hindenburg's death, and the devaluation of the Danzig gulden in May 1935. And the mealworms also gave him advance notice of the day when the guns would begin to speak.

It goes without saying that thanks to his flat ear, he also knew more about the dog Senta, mother of Harras, than the dog, who stood black beside the white miller, revealed to the naked eye.

But after the war when the miller with his "A" refugee certificate was living between Krefeld and Düren, he was still able, with the help of a twenty-pound sack that had lived through the flight from the east and the turmoil of war, to prophesy how in the future . . . But as the authors' consortium has decided, not Brauxel but our friend the actor will be privileged to tell about that.

EIGHTEENTH MORNING SHIFT

Crows in the snow—what a subject! The snow puts caps on the rusty scoops and windlasses of potash-mining days. Brauxel is going to have that snow burnt, for who can bear such a sight: crows in the snow, which, if you keep looking, turn into nuns in the snow: the snow must go. Before the night shift pile into the changehouse, let them put in an hour of paid overtime; or else Brauxel will have the new models, which have already been tested—Perkunos, Pikollos, Potrimpos—brought up from the twenty-five-hundred-foot floor and put to work on the snow, then those crows and nuns will see what becomes of them and the snow won't have to be burnt. Unsprinkled, it will lie outside Brauxel's window and lend itself to description: And the Vistula flows, and the mill mills, and the narrow-gauge railway runs, and the butter melts, and the milk thickens—put a little sugar on top—and the spoon stands upright, and the ferry comes over, and the sun is gone, and the sun returns, and the sea sand passes, and the sea licks sand . . . Barefoot run the children and find blueberries and look for amber and step on thistles and dig up mice and climb barefoot into hollow willows . . . But he who looks for amber, steps on the thistle, jumps into the willow, and digs up the mouse will find in the dike a dead and mummified maiden: Tulla Tulla, that's Duke Swantopolk's little daughter Tulla, who was always shoveling about for mice in the sand, bit into things with two incisor teeth, and never wore shoes or stockings:

Barefoot run the children, and the willows shake themselves, and the Vistula flows for evermore, and the sun now gone now back again, and the ferry comes or goes or lies groaning in its berth, while the milk thickens until the spoon stands upright, and slowly runs the narrow-gauge train, ringing fast on the bend. And the mill creaks with the wind at a rate of twenty-five feet a second. And the miller hears what the mealworm says. And teeth grind when Walter Matern grinds his teeth from left to right. Same with his grandmother: all around the garden she chases poor Lorchen. Black and big with young, Senta crashes through a trellis of broad beans. For terrible she approaches, raising an angular arm: and in the hand on the arm the wooden spoon casts its shadow on curly-headed Lorchen and grows bigger and bigger, fatter and fatter, more and more . . . Also Eduard Amsel, who is always watching and forgets nothing because his diary stores it all up, has raised his prices some; now he is asking one gulden twenty for a single scarecrow.

This is because. Ever since Herr Olschewski in the low-ceilinged schoolhouse began to speak of all the gods there used to be, who still exist and who existed once upon a time, Amsel has devoted himself to mythology.

It began when a schnapps distiller's shepherd dog took the train with his master from Stutthof to Nickelswalde. The animal's name was Pluto, he had a flawless pedigree, and he came to cover Senta, which took effect. Amsel in the low-ceilinged room wished to know what Pluto was and meant. From that day on Herr Olschewski, a young teacher with ideas about the school system and glad to be inspired by questioning pupils, occupied hours which the schedule assigned to local geography and folklore with long-drawn-out stories revolving first around Wotan, Baldur, Hera, Fafnir, and later around Zeus, Juno, Pluto, Apollo, Mercury, and the Egyptian Isis. He waxed especially eloquent when making old Prussian gods—Perkunos, Pikollos, and Potrimpos—lodge in the branches of creaking oak trees.

Naturally Amsel not only listened but, as the sketches in his diary show, he also transmuted, and most ingeniously: he brought the fiery red Perkunos to life with decrepit red ticking obtained from houses where people had died. A split oak log became Perkunos' head; to right and left Amsel wedged superannuated horseshoes into it, and in the cracks he stuck the tail feathers of slaughtered roosters. Glowing, all fire god, the scarecrow was only briefly exhibited on the dike, then it was sold for one gulden twenty and moved to the interior of the Island, to Ladekopp.

The pale Pikollos, who was said to have looked up from below and for that reason had handled the affairs of the dead in pagan times, was not, as one might imagine, fashioned from the bedsheets of the deceased, young or old, for to costume the god of death in shrouds would have been much too unimaginative, but—Amsel procured his accessories in a house from which some peasants had just moved—was adorned in a fusty-yellow and crumbling bridal dress smelling of lavender, musk, and mouse droppings. This attire draped over his manly form made Pikollos imposing and terrible; when the mortuary-nuptial scarecrow was sold for use on a large farm in Schusterkrug, the god brought in two whole gulden.

And bright and gay as Amsel made him, Potrimpos, the forever laughing youth with the ear of wheat between his teeth, brought in only a single gulden, although Potrimpos protects summer and winter seed against corn cockle, charlock, and wild mustard, against couchgrass, vetches, spurry, and ergot. For over a week the youthful scarecrow, a hazelnut bush shirted in silver paper and skirted in cats' skins, stood exposed on the dike, tinkling invitingly with saffron-colored eggshells. Only then was he purchased by a peasant from Fischer-Babke. His wife, who was pregnant and for that reason more inclined than most to mythology, thought the fruit-promising scarecrow cute and giggly-comical: some weeks later she was delivered of twins.

But Senta too had come in for a portion of the boy Potrimpos' blessing: exactly sixty-four days later, under the jack of the Matern windmill, she whelped six blind but, in keeping with their pedigree, black puppies. All six were registered and gradually sold; among them a male, Harras, who will be spoken of frequently in the next book; for a Herr Liebenau bought Harras as a watchdog for his carpenter shop. In answer to an ad that miller Matern had put in the *Neueste Nachrichten,* the carpenter had taken the train to Nickelswalde and closed the deal.

In the obscure beginnings there is said to have been, there was, in Lithuania a she-wolf, whose grandson, the black dog Perkun, sired the bitch Senta; and Pluto covered Senta; and Senta whelped six puppies, among them the male Harras;

and Harras sired Prinz; and Prinz will make history in books that Brauxel does not have to write.

But Amsel never designed a scarecrow in the image of a dog, not even of Senta, who ambled about between him and Walter Matern. All the scarecrows in his diary, except for the one with the milk-drinking eels and the other—half grandmother, half three-headed willow—are likenesses of men or gods.

The lore that Herr Olschewski dispensed to dozing pupils through the summery droning of flies was reflected, out of school hours, in a series of bird-repellent creations modeled, when not on gods, on the grand masters of the order of Teutonic Knights from Hermann Balke via Konrad von Wallenrod down to von Jungingen: there was a considerable clanking of rusty corrugated iron, and black crosses were cut out of white waxed paper with spiked barrel staves. Various members of the Jagello family, the great Kasimir, the notorious robber Bobrowski, Beneke, Martin Bardewiek, and the unfortunate Lesczynski were obliged to pose in the company of Kniprode, Letzkau, and von Plauen. Amsel couldn't get enough of the history of Brandenburg-Prussia; he pottered through the centuries from Albrecht Achilles to Zieten and from the lees of eastern European history harvested scarecrows to disperse the birds of the heavens.

Soon after the carpenter, Harry Liebenau's father, bought the dog Harras from miller Anton Matern, but at a time when the world had not yet registered the presence either of Harry Liebenau or of his cousin Tulla, the *Neueste Nachrichten* offered all those who could read an article dealing lengthily and poetically with the Island. The region and its people were knowledgeably described. The author did not forget the anomalies of the storks' nests or the special features of the farmhouses, those old porch posts, for example. And in the middle section of this article, which Brauksel has had photostated in the East German newspaper archives, one could, and still can, read approximately the following knowledgeable lines: "Though in other respects everything runs its accustomed course on Great Island and the technology that is changing our whole world has not yet made its triumphant entry, an astonishing transformation is becoming discernible in what is, if you will, a secondary domain: The scarecrows in the far-billowing wheatfields of these magnificent plains—which only a few years ago were commonplace and merely useful or at most a trifle ludicrous and sad, but in any event closely resembled the scarecrows of other provinces and regions—now reveal, in the vicinity of Einlage, Jungfer, and Ladekopp, but also as far upstream as Käsemark and Montau and occasionally even in the region to the south of Neuteich, a new and richly variegated aspect: elements of fantasy mingle with immemorial folk ways; delightful figures, but gruesome ones as well, may be seen standing in surging fields and in gardens blessed with abundance; might it not even now be time to call the attention of the local folklore museums or of the provincial Museum to these treasure of naïve, yet formally mature folk art? For we have the impression that in the very midst of a civilization that is leveling everything in its path, the Nordic heritage is here flowering afresh and anew: the spirit of the Vikings and Christian simplicity in an East-German symbiosis. Especially a group of three figures in a far-billowing wheatfield between Scharpau and Bärwalde, which with its striking simplicity suggests the Crucifixion group on the mount of Calvary, the Lord and the two thieves, is marked by a simple piety which goes straight to the heart of the traveler wending his way amid these blessed far-billowing fields—and he does not know why."

Now let no one suppose that Amsel fashioned this group with its childlike piety—only one thief was sketched in the diary—with a view to divine reward: according to the diary, it brought in two gulden twenty.

What became of all the money that the peasants of the Great Island district spontaneously or after brief bargaining counted out into Amsel's palm? Walter Matern kept this mounting wealth in a small leather pouch. He guarded it with a dark frown and not without grinding of the teeth. Slung around his wrist he carried the pouch full of Free State silver currency between the poplars on the highway and through the windy clearings in the scrub pine forest; with it he had himself ferried across the river; he swung it, struck it against garden fences or slapped it challengingly against his own knee, and opened it ceremoniously when a peasant became a customer.

Amsel did not take payment. While Amsel made a show of indifference, Walter Matern had to state the price, seal the bargain with a handshake after the manner of cattle dealers, and pocket or pouch the coins. In addition Walter Matern was responsible for the transportation of sold or rented scarecrows. Amsel made him his flunky. Now and then he rebelled and tried to regain his freedom, but never for very long. The incident with the pocketknife was a feeble attempt of this kind; for Amsel, rolling through the world plump on short legs, was always ahead of him. When the two ran along the dike, the miller's son, after the manner of body servants, remained half a step behind the untiring builder of scarecrows. The servant also carried his master's materials: beanpoles and wet rags and whatever the Vistula had washed ashore.

NINETEENTH MORNING SHIFT

"Flunky, flunky!" blasphemed the children when Walter Matern flunkied for his friend Eduard Amsel. Many who blaspheme God are punished; but who is going to bring down the law on all the rancid little stinkpots who daily blaspheme the Devil? Like God and the Devil the two of them—Brauksel is now referring to the miller's son and little fatso from over yonder—were so smitten with each other that the blaspheming of the village youth was if anything incense to them. Moreover, the two of them, like Devil and God, had scored each other with the same knife.

Thus at one—for the occasional flunkying was an act of love—the two friends often sat in the overhang room, whose illumination was determined by the sun and the sails of the Matern windmill. They sat side by side on footstools at Grandmother Matern's feet. Outside it was late afternoon. The wood worms were silent. The shadows of the mill were falling somewhere else. The poultry yard was turned down very low, because the window was closed. Only on the flypaper a fly was dying of too much sweetness and couldn't stop. Far below the fly, grumpily, as though no ear were good enough for her yarns, Grandma was telling stories, always the same ones. With her bony grandmother's hands, which indicated all the dimensions that occurred in her tales, she dealt out stories about floods, stories about bewitched cows, the usual stories about eels, the one-eyed blacksmith, the three-legged horse, or how Duke Kynstute's young daughter went out to dig for mice, and the story about the enormous dolphin that a storm had washed ashore in the exact same year as Napoleon marched into Russia.

But decoyed by Amsel with adroit questions, she always ended up—though the detours could be very long—in the dark passageways and dungeons of the endless tale, endless because it has not been concluded to this day, about the twelve headless nuns and the twelve knights with their heads and helmets under their arms, who in four coaches—two drawn by white, two drawn by black horses—drove through Tiegenhof over resounding cobbles, stopped outside a deserted inn, and twelve and twelve went in: Music broke loose. Woodwinds brasses plucked strings. Tongues fluttered and voices twanged expertly. Sinful songs with sinful refrains from male throats—the heads and helmets under the sharply bent arms of the knights—alternated with the watery litanies of pious women. Then it was the turn of the headless nuns. From heads held out in hands a part song poured forth, obscene words to an obscene tune, and there was dancing and stamping and squealing and reeling. And in between, a humble shuffling procession cast headless shadows twelve and twelve through the windows of the inn and out on the paving stones, until once again leching and retching, roaring and stamping loosened the mortar and the dowels of the house. Finally toward morning, just before cockcrow, the four coaches with black horses and white horses drove up without coachmen. And twelve clanking knights, giving off clouds of rust, veils billowing on top, left the inn at Tiegenhof with maggot-pale nuns' faces. And twelve nuns, wearing knights' helmets with closed visors over their habits, left the inn. Into the four coaches, white horses black horses, they mounted six and six and six and six, but not mixed—they had already exchanged heads—and rode through the cowed village, and again the cobblestones resounded. To this day, said Grandma Matern, before spinning the story out some more, directing the coaches to other places and making them draw up outside chapels and castles—they say that to this day pious hymns and blasphemous prayers can be heard farting from the fireplace of that weird inn, where nobody is willing to live.

Thereupon the two friends would gladly have gone to Tiegenhof. But though they started out a number of times, they never got any farther than Steegen or at the farthest Ladekopp. Only in the following winter, which for a builder of scarecrows was naturally bound to be the quiet, truly creative season, did Eduard Amsel find occasion to take the measurements of those headless people: and that was how he came to build his first mechanical scarecrows, an undertaking that used up an appreciable part of the fortune in Matern's leather pouch.

TWENTIETH MORNING SHIFT

This thaw is drilling a hole in Brauxel's head. The water is dripping on the zinc ledge outside his window. Since there are windowless rooms available in the administration building, Brauksel could easily avoid this therapy; but Brauchsel stays put and welcomes the hole in his head: celluloid, celluloid—if you've got to be a doll, you may as well be a doll with little holes in your dry celluloid forehead. For Brauxel once lived through a thaw and underwent a transformation beneath the water dripping from a dwindling snow man; but before that, many many thaws ago, the Vistula flowed under a thick sheet of ice traversed by horse-drawn sleighs. The young people of the nearby fishing villages tried their hand at sailing on curved skates known as *Schlaiffen*. Two by two—a bedsheet nailed to roofing laths would fill with wind and send them whipping over the ice. Every mouth steamed. Snow was in the way and had to be shoveled. Behind the dunes, barren and fertile land was topped with the same snow. Snow on both dikes. The snow on the beach blended into the snow on the ice sheet that covered the rimless sea and its fish. Under a crooked snow cap, for the snow was falling from the east, the Matern windmill stood splay-footed on its round white hummock amid white fields distinguishable only by their unyielding fences, and milled. Napoleon's poplars sugar-coated. A Sunday painter had covered the scrub pines with white sizing fresh from the tube. When the snow turned gray, the mill was stopped for the day and turned out of the wind. Miller and miller's man went home. The lopsided miller stepped in the miller's man's footsteps. Senta the black dog, nervous since her puppies had been sold, was following trails of her own and biting into the snow. Across from the mill, on a fence that they had previously kicked clear of snow with the heels of their boots, sat Walter Matern and Eduard Amsel mufflered and mittened.

For a while they were silent straight ahead. Then they conversed in obscure technical terms. They talked about mills with runners and chasers, Dutch "smock" mills, without jack or tailpole but with three sets of runners and an extra set of burrs. They talked about vanes and sails and stabilizers which adjust themselves to the wind velocity. There were worm drives and rollers and oak levers and rods. There were relationships between drum and brake. Only children sing unwittingly: The mill turns slow, the mill turns faster. Amsel and Walter Matern did not sing, but knew why and when a mill: The mill turns slow and the mill turns faster when the brake puts slight or heavy pressure on the wheel shaft. Even when snow was falling, the mill turned evenly amid the fitful snow squalls, provided the wind kept up a good twenty-five feet a second. Nothing looks quite like a mill turning in a snowfall; not even a fire engine called upon to extinguish a burning water tower in the rain.

But when the mill was stopped for the day and the sails stood silhouetted in the falling snow, it turned out—but only because Amsel screwed up his eyes—that the mill was not yet slated for a rest. Silently the snow, now gray now white now black, drove across from the great dune. The poplars on the highway floated. In Lührmann's taproom light was burning egg-yellow. No train ringing on the bend. The wind grew biting. Bushes whimpered. Amsel glowed. His friend dozed. Amsel saw something. His friend saw nothing. Amsel's little fingers rubbed each other in his mittens, slipped out, looked for the right patent-leather shoe in the left-hand pocket of his jacket and found it: He was cooking with gas. Not a single snowflake kept its identity on Amsel's skin. His lips pursed and into his screwed-up eyes passed more than can be said in one breath: One after the other they drive up. Without coachmen. And the mill motionless. Four sleighs, two with white horses—blending; two with black horses—contrasting—and they help each other out: twelve and twelve, all headless. And a headless knight leads a headless nun into the mill. Altogether twelve headless knights lead twelve nuns without heads into the mill—but knights and nuns alike are carrying their heads under their arms or out in front of them. But on the trampled path things are getting complicated, for despite the likeness of veil and veil, armor and armor, they are still chewing on quarrels dating from the day when they broke up camp in Ragnit. The first nun isn't speaking to the fourth knight. But both are glad to chat with the knight Fitzwater, who knows Lithuania like the holes in his coat of mail. In May the ninth nun should have been delivered of a child, but wasn't, because the eighth knight—Engelhard Rabe his name—had cut off the heads and veils not only of the ninth but also of the sixth nun, who had overindulged in cherries summer after summer, with the sword of the tenth knight, the fat one, who was sitting on a beam and gnawing the meat from the bones of a chicken behind closed visor. And all because the embroidery on the banner of St. George wasn't finished and the River Szeszupe was conveniently frozen over. While the remaining nuns embroidered all the faster—the last red field was almost full—the third waxen nun, who was always following the eleventh knight in the shadows, came bringing the basin to put under the blood. Thereupon the seventh, second, fourth, and fifth nuns laughed, tossed their embroidery behind them, and held out their heads and veils to the eighth knight, the black Engelhard Rabe. He, nothing loath, turned first to the tenth knight, who was relieving himself still squatting on the beam with his chicken behind his visor, and cut off his head, chicken, and helmet with visor, then passed him his sword: and the fat, headless, but nevertheless chewing tenth knight helped the eighth, black knight, helped the second nun, the third waxen nun who had always remained in the shadow, and likewise the fourth and fifth nuns to dispose of their heads and veils and Engelhard Rabe's head. Laughing, they passed the basin from one to the other. Only a few nuns were embroidering on the banner of St. George, although the Szeszupe was conveniently frozen, although the English under Lancaster were already in the camp, although reports on the state of the roads had come in, although Prince Witold preferred to stand aside and Wallenrod was already summoning the company to table. But now the basin was full and running over. The tenth nun, the fat one—for just as there was a fat knight, there was also a fat nun—had to come waddling; and she was privileged to bring the basin three more times, the last time when the Szeszupe was already free of ice and Ursula, the eighth nun, whom everyone called Tulla affectionately and for short, had to kneel, showing the down on her neck.

She had taken her vow only the preceding March and had already broken it twelve times. But she didn't know with whom or in what order, because the visors had all been closed; and now the English under Henry Derby; freshly arrived in the camp, but already in a dreadful hurry. There was also a Percy among them, but it was Thomas Percy, not Henry. For him Tulla had cunningly embroidered an individual banner, although Wallenrod had forbidden individual banners. Jacob Doutremer and Pege Peegott were planning to follow Percy. In the end Wallenrod bearded Lancaster. He put Thomas Percy's pocket-sized banner to flight, bade Hattenstein bear the just-finished banner of St. George across the ice-free river, and ordered the eighth nun, known as Tulla, to kneel down while the bridge was being built, in the course of which operation four horses and a squire were drowned. She sang more beautifully than the eleventh and twelfth nuns had sung before her. She was able to twang, to chirp, and at the same time to make her bright-red tongue flutter in the dark-red cavern of her mouth. Lancaster wept behind his visor, for he would rather have stayed home, but he had had a falling out with his family, though he later became king notwithstanding. Suddenly and because no one wanted to cross the Szeszupe any more and all were whimpering to go home, the youngest of the knights jumped out of a tree in which he had been sleeping and took springy little steps toward the down on the neck. He had come all the way from Mörs in the lower Rhineland in the hope of converting the Barts. But the Barts had all been converted, and Bartenstein had already been founded. There was nothing left but Lithuania, but first the down on Tulla's neck. He smote it above the last vertebra, then tossed his sword in the air and caught it with his own neck. Such was the dexterity of the sixth and youngest knight. The fourth knight, who never spoke to the first nun, tried to imitate him, but had no luck and at the first attempt severed the head of the tenth nun, the fat one, and at the second attempt the sleek stern head of the stern first nun. Thereupon the third knight, who never changed his coat of mail and enjoyed a reputation for wisdom, had to bring the basin, because there wasn't a single nun left.

Followed by the bannerless English, by Hattenstein with banner and men-at-arms, the remaining knights with heads took a short trip into trackless Lithuania. Duke Kynstute gurgled in the bogs. Beneath giant ferns his daughter bleated. Croaking on all sides. Horses floundered. In the end Potrimpos was still unburied; Perkunos still had no inclination to burn; and unblinded Pikollos continued to look up from below. Ah! They should have made a movie. Plenty of extras and nature galore. Twelve hundred pair of greaves, crossbows, breastplates, rotting boots, chewed-up harnesses, seventy bolts of stiff linen, twelve inkwells, twenty thousand torches, tallow lamps, currycombs, balls of twine, sticks of licorice wood—the chewing gum of the fourteenth century —sooty armorers, packs of hounds, Teutonic Knights playing drafts, harpists jugglers muteleers, gallons of barley beer, bundles of pennants, arrows, lances, and smokejacks for Simon Bache, Erik Cruse, Clause Schone, Richard Westrall, Spannerle, Tylman, and Robert Wendell in the bridge-building scene, in the bridge-crossing scene, in ambush, in the pouring rain: sheaves of lightning, splintered oak trees, horses shy, owls blink, foxes track, arrows whir: the Teutonic Knights are getting nervous; and in the alder thicket the blind seeress cries out: "Wela! Wela!" Back back . . . but not until the following July were they again to see that little river which to this day the poet Bobrowski darkly sings. Clear flowed the Szeszupe, tinkling over the pebbles along the shore. Old friends in the crowd: there sat the twelve headless nuns, with their left hands holding their heads and veils and with the right hands pouring the water of the Szeszupe on overheated faces. In the background the headless knights stood sullen, refusing to cool themselves off. Thereupon the remaining knights decided to make common cause with those who were already headless. Near Ragnit they lifted off each other's heads and helmets in unison, harnessed their horses to four crude wagons, and set off with white horses and black horses through territories converted and unconverted. They exalted Potrimpos, dropped Christ, once again blinded Pikollos, but to no avail, and took up the Cross again. They stopped at inns, chapels, and mills and lived it up down through the centuries, terrifying Poles, Hussites, and Swedes. They were at Zorndorf when Seydlitz crossed Saverne Hollow with his squadrons, and when the Corsican had to hurry home, they found four ownerless coaches in his wake. For these they exchanged their crusaders' wagons, and so it was in carriages with comfortable springs that they witnessed the second battle of Tannenberg, which was not fought at Tannenberg any more than the first. In the van of Budenny's ferocious cavalry, they had barely time to turn back when, aided by the Virgin Mary, Pilsudski carried the day in a loop of the Vistula. In the years when Amsel was building and selling scarecrows, they had shuttled restlessly back and forth between Tapiau and Neuteich. Twelve and twelve, they were planning to go right on being restless until redemption should come their way and each one of them, or perhaps one should say each neck, should be enabled to carry his, her, or its own individual head.

Most recently they had been seen in Scharpau and Fischer-Babke. The first nun had taken to wearing the fourth knight's face now and then, but she still wouldn't speak to him. There they came riding through the fields between the dunes and the Stutthof highway; they stopped—only Amsel saw them—outside the Matern mill and alit. It happens to be the second of February, Feast of the Purification of the Virgin Mary, and they are going to celebrate it. They help each other out of the carriages, up the hummock, and into the windmill. A moment later flour loft and sack loft are full of buzzing, quick chatter, sharp screams, witch-sabbath oaths, and prayers said backwards. A chirping is heard and the sound of whistling on iron, while snow falls from the direction of the dune, possibly from the sky. Amsel glows and rubs the patent-leather shoe deep in his pocket, but his friend, aloof and turned inward, is dozing. Time out, for inside they are wallowing in flour, riding the mill post, wedging their fingers between drum and brake, and because it is Candlemas, turning the mill into the wind: slowly it turns, fitfully at first; then twelve heads strike up the sweet sequence: *Stabat mater dolorosa*—O Perkollos, seven of twelve are still so cold, seven frozen sevenfold—*juxta crucem lacrimosa*—O Perkunos, all twelve aflame; when I'm burned to ashes, eleven remain—*Dum pendebat filius*—O Potrimpos, all whitened with flour, we'll mourn Christ's blood in this white hour . . . Then at last, while the millstones jumble the head and helmet of the eighth, black knight with the fat friendly head of the tenth nun, the Matern postmill begins to turn faster and faster, although there is no wind at all. And the youngest, the knight from the lower Rhine, tosses his singing head with wide-open visor to the eighth nun. She affects ignorance, withholds recognition, calls herself Ursula and not Tulla, is quite sufficient to herself, and is riding the cotter that stops the wheel shaft. It begins to quake: The mill turns slow, the mill turns faster; the heads in the hopper howl off-key; staccato gasps on the wooden cotter; crows in the flour, the rafters groan and the bolts wrench loose; upstairs and down, headless forms; from sack loft to flour loft a transubstantiation is under way: amid lecherous grunts and crystalline prayer the old Matern postmill becomes young again and turns—only Amsel with his patent-leather shoe sees it—into a knight with pole on jack, flailing about him and smiting the snowfall; becomes—as only Amsel with his shoe understands—a nun in ample habit, bloated with beans and ecstasy, circling her arms: windmill knight windmill nun: poverty poverty poverty. But fermented mare's milk is guzzled. Corn cockle juice is distilled. Incisor teeth gnaw at fox bones, while the headless bodies go on starving: Poverty. Sweet simpering. And then nevertheless pulling over, pushing under, heads laid aside; and from the crosswise recumbents rise the pure sounds of ascetic discipline, renunciation limpid as water, the Song of Songs pleasing to God: windmill knight brandishes windmill scourge; windmill scourge strikes windmill nun—Amen—or not yet amen; for while silent and without passion snow falls from the sky, while Amsel with narrowed eyes sits on the fence, feels Hedwig Lau's right patent-leather shoe in the left-hand pocket of his jacket and is already hatching his little plan, the little flame that slumbers in every windmill has awakened.

And after heads had promiscuously found their way to bodies, they left the mill, which was now turning sluggishly, scarcely turning at all. And while they entered four carriages and glided away toward the dunes, it began to burn from the inside outward. Then Amsel slipped off the fence, pulling his friend along with him. "Fire, fire!" they shouted in the direction of the village: but the mill was beyond saving.

TWENTY-FIRST MORNING SHIFT

Finally the drawings have come. Brauksel had them glassed and hung at once. Medium formats: "Concentration of nuns between Cologne cathedral and railroad station. Eucharistic congress in Munich. Nuns and crows and crows and nuns."

Then the large items: DIN A 1, India ink, partly inked in: A Novice Takes the Veil; Large Abbess; Squatting Abbess— excellent. The artist is asking 500 marks. A fair price, absolutely fair. We'll put it right into the construction office. We'll use quiet electric motors: windmill nun brandishes windmill scourge . . .

For while the police were still investigating the scene of the fire, because arson was suspected, Eduard Amsel built his first, and in the ensuing spring when all snow had lost its meaning and it turned out that the Mennonite Simon Beister had set the Catholic postmill on fire on religious grounds, his second, mechanical scarecrow. He put a lot of money into it, the money from the little leather pouch. From sketches in his diary he fashioned a windmill knight and a windmill nun, made both of them, properly costumed in sails, sit on the jack and obey the wind; but though they soon found purchasers, neither windmill knight nor windmill nun did justice to the vision that snowy Candlemas night had given Eduard Amsel: the artist was dissatisfied; and it also seems unlikely that the firm of Brauxel & Co. will be able to complete its experimental series of mobiles and put them into mass production before mid-October.

TWENTY-SECOND MORNING SHIFT

After the mill had burned down, the ferry, followed by the Island narrow-gauge railway, brought the pocket and buttonless, in other words rough Mennonite Simon Beister, fisherman and small holder who had made a fire on religious grounds, to the city and then to the municipal prison of Schiessstange, situated in Neugarten at the foot of the Hagelsberg, which became Simon Beister's place of residence for the next few years.

Senta of Perkun's line, Senta who had whelped six puppies and whose blackness had always contrasted so strikingly with the white miller, showed signs of canine nervousness once the puppies were sold, and after the mill burned down went so destructively haywire—tearing a sheep limp from limb like a wolf and attacking an agent from the fire insurance company—that miller Matern was obliged to send his son Walter

to see Erich Lau, mayor of Schiewenhorst, for Hedwig
Lau's father owned a rifle.

The fire in the mill also brought the friends a certain
amount of change. Destiny, or rather the village teacher,
widow Amsel, and miller Matern, not to mention Dr.
Battke the high school principal, transformed the ten-year-
old Walter Matern and the ten-year-old Eduard Amsel into
two high school students, who succeeded in being assigned
to the same bench. While the new Matern windmill was still
being built—the project of a Dutch mill of masonry with a
rotating cap had to be abandoned for fear of marring the
historical profile of the mill where Queen Louise had passed
the night—Easter came around, accompanied by a moderate
rise in the river, the first signs of a plague of mice, and a
sudden bursting of pussy willows. Soon afterward Walter
Matern and Eduard Amsel donned the green velvet caps of
Sankt Johann High School. Their heads were the same size.
They wore the same size shoes, but Amsel was much stouter,
much much stouter. In addition Amsel had only one whorl
in his hair. Walter Matern had two, which is said to be-
token an early death.

The distance from the mouth of the Vistula to Sankt Johann High School made the friends into commuting schoolboys. Commuting schoolboys are rich in experience and
great liars. Commuting schoolboys can sleep sitting up. Commuting schoolboys are students who do their homework in
the train and so acquire a trembling script. Even in later
years when there is no more homework to be done, their
handwriting becomes hardly less cramped, at best it stops
trembling. That is why the actor has to write his story directly on the machine; as a former commuting schoolboy, he
still writes a cramped, illegible hand, jolted by imaginary
joints in the rails.

The narrow-gauge train left from the Island station, which
the city people call "Niederstadt Station." By way of Knüp-
pelkrug and Gottswalde, it made its way to Schusterkrug,
where it was ferried across the Dead Vistula, and Schiewenhorst, whence the steam ferry carried it across the so-called
cut to Nickelswalde. Amsel got out in Schiewenhorst and
Walter Matern in Nickelswalde. As soon as the locomotive
had pulled each of the four cars separately up the dike, the
train continued on to Pasewark, Junkeracker, Steegan, and
Stutthof, which was the terminus of the narrow-gauge line.

All the commuting scholars took the first car, right behind the locomotive. Peter Illing and Arnold Mathrey were from Einlage. Gregor Knessin and Joachim Bertulek got on in Schusterkrug. In Schiewenhorst Hedwig Lau's mother brought her to the station on schooldays. Often the child had tonsilitis and didn't come. Was it not unseemly that the narrow-chested narrow-gauge locomotive should chug away regardless of Hedwig Lau's absence? Like Walter Matern and Eduard Amsel, the village mayor's daughter went into sixth after Easter. Later on, beginning in fourth, her health improved, her tonsils stopped acting up; and now that there was no further reason to fear for her days, she became such a bore that Brauxel will soon find it unnecessary to go on mentioning her in these papers. But at the time Amsel still had a glance or two to spare for a quiet to sluggish, pretty little girl, or perhaps she was pretty only by coastwise standards. She sat across from him with hair that was somewhat too blond, eyes that were somewhat too blue, an unreasonably fresh complexion, and an open English book.

Hedwig Lau wears braids. Even as the train pulls in to the city, she smells of butter and whey. Amsel screws up his eyes and lets the coastwise blondness of her braids shimmer. Outside, the first frame saws come into view after Klein-Plehnendorf, and the timber port begins: swallows are replaced by gulls, the telegraph poles go on. Amsel opens his diary. Hedwig Lau's braids hang down, swaying gently just above the open English book. Amsel draws a sketch in his diary: lovely, lovely. From the loose braids which he rejects on formal grounds, he develops two spirals to cover the flaming redness of her ears. He doesn't say: Fix it this way, braids are dumb, you gotta wear spirals. Of course not, but while Kneipab passes outside, he thrusts his diary without a word over her open English book, and Hedwig Lau looks. Then with her eyelashes she nods in assent, almost obedience, although Amsel doesn't look like a boy whom schoolgirls would tend to obey.

TWENTY-THIRD MORNING SHIFT

Brauxel has an unblunting distaste for unused razor blades. A handy-man who formerly, in the days of the Burbach Pot-

ash Co. Inc., worked in the mine and opened up rich salt
deposits, breaks in Brauksel's razor blades and delivers them
to him after using them once. Thus Brauksel has no need to
overcome a revulsion which, though not directed against razor
blades, was equally innate and equally strong in Eduard Amsel. He had a thing about new, new-smelling clothes. The
smell of fresh underwear compelled him to fight down incipient nausea. As long as he attended the village school, natural
limits were imposed on his allergy, for the apparel in which
the small fry of Schiewenhorst as well as Nickelswalde
weighed down the school benches was baggy, worn, and
much mended. Sankt Johann High School had higher vesti-
mentary standards. His mother obliged him to put on new
and new-smelling clothes: the green velvet cap has already
been mentioned, in addition there were polo shirts, sand-gray
knee breeches of expensive material, a blue blazer with mother-of-pearl buttons, and—possibly at Amsel's request—patent-
leather shoes with buckles; for Amsel had no objection to
buckles or patent leather, he had no objection to mother-
of-pearl buttons or blazer, it was only the prospect of all these
new things actually touching his skin, the skin, it should not
be forgotten, of a scarecrow builder, that gave him the creeps,
especially as Amsel reacted to fresh underwear and unworn
clothes with an itching rash; just as Brauxel, if he shaves
with a fresh blade, must fear the onset of the dread barber's
itch.

Fortunately Walter Matern was in a position to help his
friend. His school clothes were made of turned cloth, his high
shoes had already been twice to the shoemaker's, Walter
Matern's thrifty mother had bought his high school cap
secondhand. And so for a good two weeks the trip in the narrow-gauge railway began with the same ceremony: in one of
the freight cars, amid unsuspecting cattle on their way to the
slaughterhouse, the friends changed clothes. The shoes and
cap presented no problem, but though Walter Matern was
hardly emaciated, his jacket, knee breeches, and shirt were
too tight for his friend. Yet uncomfortable as they were, they
were a blessed relief, because they had been worn and
turned, because they smelled old and not new. Needless to say,
Amsel's new clothes hung down limp and loose on his friend's
frame, and patent leather and buckles, mother-of-pearl buttons, and the ridiculous blazer looked odd on him. Amsel,
with his scarecrow builder's feet in rough, deeply furrowed

clodhoppers, was nevertheless delighted at the sight of his patent-leather shoes on Walter Matern's feet. Walter Matern had to break then in until Amsel pronounced them worn and found them just as cracked as the cracked patent-leather shoe that lay in his school satchel and meant something.

To anticipate, this exchange of clothing was for years a component, though not the cement, of the friendship between Walter Matern and Eduard Amsel. Even handkerchiefs, which his mother had slipped lovingly into his pocket, fresh and folded hem to hem, had to be initiated by his friend, and the same went for socks and stockings. And the exchange didn't stop at clothing; Amsel betrayed similar feelings about new pencils and pens: Walter Matern had to sharpen his pencils, take the shape off his new erasers, break in his Sütterlin pens—he would assuredly, like Brauksel's handyman, have had to initiate Amsel's new razor blades if reddish down had already ripened on Amsel's freckleface.

TWENTY-FOURTH MORNING SHIFT

Who, having relieved himself after breakfast, is standing here contemplating his excrement? A thoughtful, anxious man in search of the past. Why keep ogling a smooth and weightless death's-head? Theatrical ambiance, Hamletlike maunderings, histrionic gestures! Brauxel, the present writer, raises his eyes and pulls the chain; while contemplating, he has remembered a situation that gave the two friends, Amsel rather matter-of-factly, Walter Matern histrionically, an opportunity to meditate and to conjure up a theatrical ambiance.

The layout of the high school on Fleischergasse, was a fantastic jumble—the building had formerly been a Franciscan monastery. This prehistory made it an ideal establishment for the two friends, for the former monastery contained any number of passageways and hiding places known neither to the teachers nor to the caretaker.

Brauksel, who is running a mine that produces neither potash nor iron nor coal but is nevertheless functioning down to the twenty-five-hundred-foot floor, would also have taken pleasure in that subterranean confusion, for under all the classrooms, under the gymnasium and the urinals, under the auditorium, even under the board room there were low narrow corridors which, if you followed them, led to dungeons and shafts, but also in circles and astray. When school began after Easter, Amsel was first to enter the ground-floor classroom. Short-legged and wearing Walter Matern's shoes, he took little steps over oiled flooring and sniffed a little with pink nostrils—musty cellar air, theatrical ambiance—stopped still, interlocked his plump little fingers, took a bounce or two on the tips of his toes, and after bouncing and sniffing here and there, drew a cross on one of the floorboards with the tip of his right-hand shoe. When there was no whistle of understanding in response to his mark, he looked behind him with a rotation of his well-padded neck: there stood Walter Matern in Amsel's patent-leather shoes, presenting an obstinately uncommunicative face, but then he caught on from the bridge of his nose up and finally whistled understandingly through his teeth. Because there was a hollow spooky sound under the floorboards, they both felt immediately at home in this classroom assigned to the sixth, even though there was no Vistula flowing broad-shouldered between dikes outside the windows.

But after a week of high school, the two of them, who, as it happened, had rivers in their blood, found access to a little river, to take the place, however inadequately, of the Vistula. A lid had to be lifted in the locker room of the gymnasium, which in Franciscan days had been a library. The cracks around the small rectangle were caulked with the sweepings of many years, but for Amsel's eye that was no camouflage. Walter Matern lifted the lid: musty cellar air, theatrical ambiance! They had found the entrance to a dry musty passageway, which was distinguished from the other passageways beneath other classrooms by the fact that it led to the municipal sewage system and by way of the sewers to the Radaune. The little river with the mysterious name had its source in the Radaune Lakes in the district of Berent, flowed, rich in fish and prawns, past Petershagen, and entered the city to one side of the New Market. Sometimes visible, sometimes underground, it twined its way through the Old City, often bridged over and made picturesque by swans and weeping willows, and emptied into the Mottlau between Karpfenseigen and Barbank, shortly before the confluence of the Mottlau and the Dead Vistula.

As soon as the locker room emptied of witnesses, Amsel and his friend were able to lift the rectangle out of the floorboards—and so they did—, crawl through a low passageway—they crawled—, climb down—making use of the climbing irons inserted in the masonry at regular intervals—into a shaft that couldn't have been far from the urinal—Walter Matern went down first—, easily open a rusty iron door at the bottom of the shaft—Walter Matern opened it—, and pass through a dry, foul-smelling sewer alive with rats— each in the other's shoes they passed through it. To be precise, the sewer led under the Wiebenwall, under the Karrenwall, where stood the Provincial Insurance Company building, under the city park, and under the railroad tracks between Petershagen and the Main Station, and then into the Radaune. Across from Sankt Salvator cemetery, which was situated between Grenadiergasse and the Mennonite church at the foot of the Bischofsberg, the sewer fanned out and emptied. To one side of the opening more climbing irons led up a steeply sloping masonry wall to an ornate wrought-iron railing. Behind them lay a view known to Brauxel from numerous engravings: out of the fresh, spring-green park rises brick-red the panorama of the city: from Oliva Gate to Leege Gate, from St. Catherine's to St. Peter's on the Poggenpfuhl, the divergent height and girth of numerous towers bear witness to the fact that they are not of the same age.

Two or three times the friends took this excursion through the sewer. The second time they emerged over the Radaune, they were seen by some old folks who were passing the time of day in the park, but not reported. The possibilities seemed exhausted—for the Radaune is not the Vistula—when under the gymnasium, but before the shaft leading to the municipal sewers, they came across a second bifurcation, crudely stopped up with bricks. Amsel's flashlight discovered it. They crawled through the new passageway. It sloped downward. The man-high sewer to which it led was not part of the municipal sewage system, but led crumbling dripping medieval under the hundred-percent Gothic Church of the Trinity. Sankt Trinitatis was next to the museum, not a hundred paces from the high school. One Saturday, when after four hours of school the two friends were free to leave, two hours before train time, they made the above-mentioned discovery which is recorded here not only because medieval passageways are fun to describe, but also because the discovery

proved to be of interest to Eduard Amsel and gave Walter
Matern an opportunity for play-acting and teeth grinding.
Moreover Brauxel, who operates a mine, is able to express
himself with particular virtuosity below ground.

So the Grinder—Amsel invented the name, fellow students
have taken it up—so the Grinder goes first. In his left hand he
holds an army flashlight, while in his right he holds a
stick intended to frighten away or, as the case may be, de-
stroy rats. There aren't many rats. The masonry is rough
crumbly dry to the touch. The air cool but not glacial, more
on the drafty side, though it is not clear where the draft is
blowing from. Their steps do not echo as in the municipal
sewers. Like the passageway leading to it, this man-high corridor slopes steeply downward. Walter Matern is wearing his
own shoes, for Amsel's patent-leather shoes had suffered
enough as they were crawling through the low passageways.
So that's where the draft and ventilation were coming from:
from that hole! They might almost have missed it if Amsel
hadn't. It was on the left. Through the gap, seven bricks
high, five bricks wide, Amsel pushes the Grinder. Amsel himself has a harder time of it. Holding his flashlight between his
teeth, the Grinder tugs Amsel through the hole, helping to
transform Amsel's almost new school clothes into the customary school rags. Both stand there for a moment panting. They
are on the spacious floor of a round shaft. Their eyes are
drawn upward, for a watery light is trickling down from
above: the pierced, artfully forged grating on top of the
shaft is inserted in the stone floor of the Church of the Trinity: they will investigate that another time. Four eyes follow the diminishing light back down the shaft, and at the
bottom—the flashlight points it out to them—what lies in
front of the tips of four shoes but a skeleton!

It lies doubled up, incomplete, with interchanged or tele-
scoped details. The right shoulder blade has stove in four
ribs. The sternum is driven into the right ribs. The left collarbone is missing. The spinal column is bent above the first
lumbar vertebra. The arrangement of the arms and legs is ex-
ceedingly informal: a fallen man.

The Grinder stands rigid and allows himself to be relieved of
the flashlight. Amsel begins to throw light on the skeleton.
Without any intention on Amsel's part, effects of light and
shadow are produced. With the tip of one patent-leather
shoe—soon Brauxel will have no need to speak of patent

leather—he draws a circle through the dry, only superficially crusted dust, circumscribing all the fallen members, moves back, lets the cone of electric light follow the line, screws up his eyes as he always does when he sees something likely to serve as a model, tilts his head, waggles his tongue, covers one eye, turns around, looks behind him over his shoulder, conjures up a pocket mirror from somewhere, juggles with light, skeleton, and mirror image, directs the flashlight behind him under a sharply bent arm, tips the mirror slightly, stands briefly on tiptoes in order to lengthen the radius, then squats by way of comparison, stands again facing his model without mirror, corrects the line here and there, exaggerates the fallen man's pose with sketching shoe, still with his shoe erases and draws new lines to undo the exaggeration, harmonizes, sharpens, softens, strives for dynamic balance ecstasy, concentrates all his powers on sketching the skeleton, preserving the sketch in his memory, and perpetuating it at home in his diary. Small wonder that after all his preliminary studies are concluded, Amsel is taken with the desire to pick up the skull from between the skeleton's incomplete collarbones, and quietly put it into his school satchel with his books and notebooks and Hedwig Lau's crumbling shoe. He wants to carry the skull to the Vistula and put it on one of his scarecrows that are still in the framework stage, or if possible on the scarecrow that he has just sketched in the dust. His hand with its five pudgy, ludicrously spread fingers is already hovering over the vestiges of collarbone; it is about to reach into the eye sockets, the safest way to lift a skull, when the Grinder, who has long stood rigid, giving little sign of his presence, begins to grind several of his teeth. In his usual way: from left to right. But the acoustics of the shaft magnify and multiply the sound so forebodingly that Amsel stops in the middle of his skulduggery, looks behind him over his rounded back, and turns the flashlight on his friend.

The Grinder says nothing. His grinding is plain enough. It means: Amsel should not spread his little fingers. Amsel shouldn't take anything away. The skull is not to be removed. Don't disturb it. Don't touch it. Place of skulls. Golgotha. Barrow. Gnashing of teeth.

But Amsel, who is always at a loss for meaningful props and accessories, who is always short on what he needs most, is again preparing to dispatch his hand skullward and again—

for it isn't every day that you find a skull—outspread fingers
can be discerned amid the shimmering dust of the flashlight
beam. At this point the stick which thus far had struck
nothing but rats descends on him, once maybe twice. And
the acoustics of the shaft amplify a word uttered between
blow and blow: "Sheeny!" Walter Matern calls his friend
"Sheeny!" and strikes. Amsel falls sideways beside the skeleton. Dust rises and takes its time about settling. Amsel picks
himself up. Who can cry such fat, convulsively rolling tears?
But even as the tears roll from both his eyes and turn to
beads of dust on the floor of the shaft, Amsel manages to say
with a grin somewhere between good-natured and mocking:
"Walter is a very silly boy." Imitating the teacher's voice, he
several times repeats this sentence from his first-year English
book; for always, even when tears are flowing, he has to
imitate somebody, himself if need be: *"Walter is a very silly
boy."* And then in the idiom of the Island: "This here is my
head. Didn't I find it? I just wanna try it out. Then I'll bring it
back."

But the Grinder is in no mood to be spoken to. The sight
of the haphazardly disposed bones makes his face shrink
toward the inside corners of his eyebrows. He folds his arms,
leans on his stick, freezes in contemplation. Whenever he sees
anything dead: a drowned cat, rats he has slain with his own
hand, gulls slit open with a throw of his knife, when he sees
a bloated fish rolled in the sand by the lapping of the waves,
or when he sees a skeleton which Amsel wants to deprive of
its skull, his teeth start in from left to right. His bullish young
face twists into a grimace. His gaze, ordinarily dull to stupid,
becomes piercing, darkens, gives an intimation of directionless
hatred: theatrical ambiance in the passages, dungeons, and
shafts beneath the Gothic Church of the Trinity. Twice the
Grinder pounds his own forehead with his fist, bends down,
reaches out, raises the skull to himself and his thoughts, and
contemplates it while Eduard Amsel squats down to one side.

Who is squatting there, obliged to relieve himself? Who is
standing there, holding a stranger's skull far out in front of
him? Who looks behind him with curiosity, examining his
excrement? Who stares at a smooth skull, trying to recognize
himself? Who has no worms, but did once from salad? Who
holds the light skull and sees worms that will one day be his?
Who, who? Two human beings, pensive and troubled. Each
has his reasons. They are friends. Walter Matern puts the

skull back down where he found it. Amsel is scratching again in the dirt with his shoe, looking and looking. Walter Matern declaims high-sounding words into the void: "Let's be going now. This is the kingdom of the dead. Maybe that's Jan Bobrowski or Materna that our family comes from." Amsel has no ear for words of conjecture. He is unable to believe that Bobrowski the great robber, or Materna, robber, incendiary, and ancestor, ever gave flesh to this skeleton. He picks up something metallic, scratches at it, spits on it, rubs it off, and exhibits a metal button, which he confidently identifies as the button of one of Napoleon's dragoons. He dates the button from the second siege and puts it in his pocket. The Grinder does not protest, he has scarcely been listening, he is still with the robber Bobrowski or his ancestor Materna. The cooling feces drive the friends through the hole in the wall. Walter Matern goes first. Amsel squeezes through the hole backwards, his flashlight turned upon the death's- head.

TWENTY-FIFTH MORNING SHIFT

Change of shifts at Brauxel & Co.: The friends had to hurry on the way back. The train in Niederstadt station never waited more than ten minutes.

Change of shifts at Brauxel & Co.: Today we are celebrating the two-hundred-fiftieth birthday of Frederick the Great; it might be a good idea for Brauxel to fill one of the stalls with relics from Frederick's times: a kingdom of Prussia below ground!

Change of shifts at Brauxel & Co.: In the locker room of the gymnasium in the Sankt Johann High School Walter Matern fitted the rectangular lid back into the floorboards. They beat the dust from each other's clothes.

Change of shifts at Brauxel & Co.: What will the great conjunction of February 4-5 bring us? In the sign of Aquarius Uranus will enter into opposition, but not exactly, while Neptune completes the square. Two critical aspects, more than critical!—Shall we, will Brauxel, come through the Great Conjunction unscathed? Will it be possible to carry this book, dealing with Walter Matern, the dog Senta, the Vistula, Eduard Amsel, and his scarecrows, to a conclusion? Despite the critical aspects Brauxel, the present writer, wishes to avoid an apocalyptic tone and record the following events with equanimity, even though there is every reason to expect an auto-da-fé of the lesser apocalypse.

Change of shifts at Brauxel & Co.: After Walter Matern and Eduard Amsel had beaten the medieval dust from one another, they started out: down Katergasse, up the Lastadie. They follow Ankerschmiedgasse. Behind the Postal Savings Bank lies the new boathouse of the school oarsmen's association: boats are being put up on chocks. They wait for the open Cow's Bridge to close and crossing it spit several times into the Mottlau. Cries of gulls. Horse-drawn vehicles over wooden planks. Beer barrels are rolled. A drunken longshoreman is supporting himself on a sober longshoreman, he has designs on a salt herring, skin, bones, and . . . "You want to bet? You want to bet?" Across the Speicherinsel: Erich Karkutsch, flour, seed, dried peas, and beans; Fischer & Nickel—conveyor belts, asbestos goods; across the railroad tracks, shreds of cabbage, flocks of kapok. They stop outside the establishment of Eugen Flakowski, saddlers' and upholsterers' supplies: bales of seaweed, hemp, jute, horsehair, reels of awning string, porcelain rings and tassels, notions, notions! Through the puddles of horse piss in Münchengasse, across the New Mottlau. Up Mattenbuden. Then climb into the trailer of the Heubude streetcar, but only ride as far as Langgart Gate, and arrive at the station on time for the narrow-gauge train, which smells of butter and whey, which rings fast as it slowly rounds the bend, and which goes to the Island. Eduard Amsel is still holding Napoleon's dragoon's button hot in his pocket.

The friends—and they remain inseparable blood brothers in spite of the death's-head and the word "Sheeny"—spoke no more of the skeleton under the Church of the Trinity. Only once, on Milchkannengasse, between Deutschendorff's sporting goods store and a branch of the Valtinat dairy chain, outside a window displaying stuffed squirrels, martens, and owls, displaying mountain cocks and a stuffed eagle with outspread wings and a lamb in its claws, outside a window with shelves in the form of a grandstand that stopped just before the plate-glass pane, in the presence of rat traps, fox traps, packages of insect powder, little bags of moth flakes, in the presence of gnat bane, roaches' nemesis, and rough-on-rats, in the presence of exterminator's equipment, bird food, dog biscuit, empty fish bowls, tins full of dehydrated flies and waterbugs, in the presence of frogs, salamanders, and snakes in jars and alcohol, of incredible butterflies under glass, of beetles with antlers, hairy spiders, and the usual sea horses, in the presence of the human skeleton—to the right beside the shelf—in the presence of the chimpanzee's skeleton—to the left beside the grandstand—, and the skeleton of a running cat at the feet of the smaller chimpanzee, in the presence of the uppermost shelf of the grandstand, upon which stood instructively the skulls of man, woman, aged person, child, premature infant, and abortions, outside this world-embracing shop window—inside the store you could buy puppies or have kittens drowned by an officially licensed hand—, outside glass polished twice weekly, Walter Matern abruptly suggested to his friend that with the rest of the money in the leather pouch they might buy one or another of these skulls and use it in the construction of a scarecrow. Amsel made a negative gesture and said tersely, not with the terseness of one who is offended but with a lofty kind of terseness, that though the topic of death's-heads was not exactly dead or superseded, it was not urgent enough to justify a purchase with their last remaining funds; if they were going to buy anything, they could buy goose, duck, and chicken feathers of inferior quality cheap and by the pound from the peasants and poultry farmers of the Island; he, Amsel, was planning something paradoxical: he was going to create a scarecrow in the form of a giant bird—the shop window on Milchkannengasse full of stuffed zoological items had inspired him, especially the eagle above the lamb.

Sacred ludicrous moment of inspiration: angel taps on forehead. Muses with frayed rosebud mouths. Planets in Aquarius. A brick falls. The egg has two yolks. The ash tray is running over. Dripping from the roof: celluloid. Short circuit. Hatboxes. What turns the corner: a patent-leather shoe. What enters without knocking: La Barbarina, the Snow Queen, snow men. What lends itself to being stuffed: God, eels, and birds. What is extracted from mines: coal, iron, potash, scarecrows, the past.

This scarecrow comes into being soon thereafter. It is Amsel's last for many a year. For under the no doubt ironically intended title "The Great Cuckoo Bird"—suggested, as a note informs us, not by Amsel but by Kriwe the ferryman—this creation, handed down both in a preliminary sketch and in a color study, is the last recorded in the diary which is today still relatively safe in Brauxel's safe.

Rags—as the diary tells us in its own words—have first to be coated with pitch or tar. Rags coated with tar or pitch have to be studded on the outside with large and small feathers and on the inside as well if enough of them are available. But in an unnatural, not a natural, way.

And indeed, when the completed Great Cuckoo Bird, tarred, feathered, and superman-high, was set out on the dike to the amazement of all who approached, its feathers stood unnaturally on end. It looked altogether spooky. The most hardened fisherwomen fled, convinced that looking at the monster could induce goiter, swivel eye, or miscarriage. The men stood their ground stiff and stolid, but let their pipes grow cold. Johann Lickfett said: "Friend, I wouldn't want that thing for a present."

It was hard to find a purchaser. And yet for all the tar and feathers the price was not high. In the forenoon it stood alone on the Nickelswalde dike, silhouetted against the sky. Only when the commuting schoolchildren returned from the city did a few come strolling out as though by chance, but stopped at a safe distance, appraised it, expressed opinions, and were disinclined to buy. Not a gull in the cloudless sky. The mice in the dike looked for other lodgings. The Vistula was unable to make a loop or it would have. Everywhere cockchafers, not in Nickelswalde. When with a laugh that was much too loud Herr Olschewski, the schoolteacher who was by nature rather high-strung, expressed interest, more for the fun of it than to protect his sixty square feet of front garden —the Great Cuckoo Bird had to be unloaded far below the price originally set. It was moved in Olschewski's rack wagon.

For two weeks the monster stood in the front garden, casting its shadow upon the teacher's flat-roofed, whitewashed cottage. No bird dared to let out a peep. The sea wind ruffled tarry feathers. Cats grew hysterical and shunned the village. Schoolchildren made detours, dreamt wet at night, and woke up screaming, with white fingertips. In Schiewenhorst Hedwig Lau came down with a bad case of tonsillitis, complicated by sudden nosebleeds. While old man Folchert was chopping wood, a chip flew into his eye, which for a long time refused to heal. When Grandma Matern passed out in the middle of the poultry yard, there were many who blamed the Great Cuckoo Bird; however, both hens and rooster had been carrying straw around in their beaks for the last month: which has always been a presage of death. Everyone in the miller's house, beginning with poor Lorchen, had heard the woodworm, the deathwatch. Grandma Matern took note of all these omens and sent for the sacraments. Once they had been administered, she lay down and died in the midst of straw-toting chickens. In her coffin she looked surprisingly peaceful. Gloved in white, she was holding a lavender-scented lace handkerchief between her crookedly folded hands. It smelled just right. Unfortunately they forgot to take out her hairpins before the coffin was closed and relegated to Catholically consecrated earth. This omission was no doubt responsible for the shooting headaches that assailed Frau Matern née Stange immediately after the funeral and from then on left her no peace.

When the body was laid out in the overhang room, when the villagers all stiff and starched stood crowded together in the kitchen and on the stairs leading to the overhang room, while they muttered their "Now she's gone!," their "Now she don't need to scold no more," and their "Now her troubles are over, now she's earned eternal rest" over the body, Kriwe the ferryman asked leave to touch the dead woman's right index finger to one of his few teeth, which had been aching and suppurating for several days. Standing between window and armchair, the miller, an unfamiliar figure in black without sack or mealworm, struck by no changing light, for the new mill was not yet running, nodded slowly: gently Grandmother Matern's right glove was removed, and Kriwe conveyed his bad tooth to the tip of her crooked index finger: sacred ludicrous moment of miraculous healing: angel taps, lays on hands, strokes against the grain, and crosses fingers. Toad's blood, crow's eyes, mare's milk. In each of the Twelve Nights thrice over left shoulder, seven times eastward. Hairpins. Pubic hair. Neck fuzz. Exhume, scatter to the winds, drink of the corpse's bath water, pour it across the threshold alone at night before cockcrow on St. Matthew's Day. Poison made from cockles. Fat of a newborn babe. Sweat of the dead. Sheets of the dead. Fingers of the dead: for the truth of the matter is that the suppuration at the base of Kriwe's tooth was said to have subsided after contact with the deceased Grandmother Matern's crooked index finger and, in strict accordance with the superstitious belief that a dead

person's finger cures toothache, the pain was also said to have
eased and gone away.

When the coffin had been carried out of the house and was
swaying first past Folchert's farm, then past the teacher's
cottage, one of the pallbearers stumbled, because the Great
Cuckoo Bird was still standing hideous and gruesome in the
teacher's garden. Stumbling means something. Stumbling is an
omen. The pallbearer's stumbling was the last straw: the
peasants and fishermen of several villages submitted a petition to Herr Olschewski and threatened to send an even more
strongly worded one to the school board.

The following Monday, when Amsel and Walter Matern
came home from school, Herr Olschewski was waiting for
them at the Schiewenhorst ferry landing. He was standing
beneath a straw hat. He was standing in knickers, a sports
jacket with large checks, and canvas shoes. While the train
was being run onto the ferry, the schoolteacher, seconded by
Kriwe the ferryman, remonstrated with the two boys. This just
couldn't go on, he declared, a number of parents had com-
plained and were planning to write the school board, they had
already got wind of it in Tiegenhof, people *were* superstitious, of course that had something to do with it, even the
unfortunate death of Grandmother Matern—a fine woman!
—was being attributed—all this in our enlightened twentieth
century, but no one, especially here in the villages of the
Vistula delta, could swim against the stream, realities were
realities: beautiful as the scarecrow was, it was more than
village people, especially here on the Island, could stomach.

Literally, Herr Olschewski spoke as follows to Eduard
Amsel, his former pupil: "My boy, you're going to high
school now, you've taken quite a step out into the wide world.
From now on, the village will be too small for you. Let us
hope that your zeal, your artistic nature, that gift of God as
they say, will find new fields to conquer out there in the
world. But here let well enough alone. You know I'm saying
this for your own good."

The following day was marked by mildly apocalyptic do-
ings: Amsel broke up shop in Folchert's barn. In other words,
Matern opened the padlock and an amazing number of volunteer helpers carried the milliner's—as Amsel was called in the
villages—building materials into the open: four scarecrows
in process of construction, bundles of roofing laths and flower
stakes. Kapok was shredded. Mattresses vomited seaweed.

Horsehair exploded from sofa cushions. The helmet, the beautiful full-bottomed wig from Krampitz, the shako, the poke bonnets, the plumed hats, the butterfly bonnets, the felt-straw-velours hats, the sombrero and the Wellington hat donated by the Tiedes of Gross-Zünder, everything that can shelter a human crown passed from head to head, from the twilight of the barn to honey-yellow sunshine: "Milliner milliner!" Amsel's chest, which would have driven a hundred order-loving barracks orderlies out of their minds, poured forth ruffles, sequins, rhinestone beads, braid, clouds of lace, upholstery cord, and carnation-scented silk pompons. Everybody got into the act, pitched in to help the milliner, put things on, took them off, and threw them on the pile: jumpers and jackets, breeches and the frog-green litewka. A traveling agent for a dairy concern had given Amsel the zouave's jacket and a plum-blue vest. Hey, the corset, the corset! Two wrapped themselves in the Blücher overcoat. Brides dancing furiously in bridal dresses fragrant with lavender. Sack races in leggings. Pea-green screamed the shift. Muff equals ball. Young mice in the cape. Jagged holes. Shirts without collars. Roman collars and mustache holders, cloth violets, wax tulips, paper roses, shooting match medals, dogtags and pansies, beauty spots, tinsel. "Milliner milliner!" Whom the shoe fitted and whom it did not fit slipped or struggled into galoshes, top boots, knee boots, laced boots, strode in pointed shoes through tobacco-brown curtains, leapt shoeless but in gaiters through the curtains of a countess, princess, or even queen. Prussian, West Prussian, and Free City wares fell on the pile: What a shindig in the nettles behind Folchert's barn: "Milliner milliner!" And uppermost on the pyre, whence moths were still escaping, stood, supported by beanpoles, the public scandal, the bugaboo, Baal tarred and feathered, the Great Cuckoo Bird.

The sun shines down almost vertically. Kindled by Kriwe's hand with Kriwe's lighter, the fire spreads rapidly. All take a few steps backward, but stay on, eager to witness the great holocaust. While Walter Matern, as he always did at official functions, makes big noises, trying to drown out the crackling by sheer grinding of the teeth, Eduard Amsel, known as "the milliner" and occasionally—the merry bonfire is another such occasion—called "Sheeny," stands negligently on freckled legs, rubs his upholstered palms strenuously together, screws up his eyes and sees something. No green-yellow smoke, no stewing leather goods, no glittering flight of sparks and moths compels him to transform round eyes into oblique slits: no, it is the bird, spouting innumerable tongues of flame, the bird going up in smoke that falls to the ground and creeps over the nettles, which makes him a present of brisk ideas and suchlike flimflam. For as the burning beast, creature of rags, tar, and feathers, sizzling and showering sparks and very much alive, makes a last stab at flying, then collapses into dust, Amsel has resolved in his heart and diary that later, one day when he is big, he will revive the idea of the Great Cuckoo Bird: he will build a giant bird which will burn, spark, and blaze everlastingly, yet never be consumed, but continue in all eternity, forever and ever, by its very nature, apocalypse and ornament in one, to burn, spark, and blaze.

TWENTY-SIXTH MORNING SHIFT

A few days before the fourth of February, before the critical constellation of the heavenly luminaries calls this world into question, Brauxel decides to add an item to his stock or pandemonium: the burning *perpetuum mobile* in the form of a bird, inspired by Amsel—he will have it built. The world is not so rich in ideas that he should abjectly forgo one of the finest inspirations even if the world were coming to an end within the next few morning shifts; especially as Eduard Amsel, after the auto-da-fé behind Folchert's barn, offered an example of stoical fortitude by helping to put out the fire that flying sparks had kindled in Folchert's barn.

A few weeks after the public burning of Amsel's stock and his latest crow-scaring model, after a fire which, as we shall see, kindled all sorts of kindling in Amsel's little head and produced a fire that was never again to be quenched, the widow Lottchen Amsel, née Tiede, and Herr Anton Matern, miller in Nickelswalde, received blue letters, from which it could be gathered that Dr. Battke, principal of Sankt Johann High School, wished to see them in his office on a certain day and hour.

Widow Amsel and miller Matern took one and the same train to the city—they sat facing one another, each in a seat by the window. At Langgart Gate they took the streetcar a* far as Milchkannen Bridge. Because they were early, they were able to attend to a few business matters. She had to call on Hahn & Löchel, then on Haubold & Lanser; he had to drop in on the construction firm of Prochnow on Adebargasse in connection with the new mill. They met in Long Market, stopped at Springer's for a drink, and then—although they might have walked—took a taxi and reached Fleischergasse ahead of time.

To speak in round numbers, they had to wait for ten minutes in Dr. Rasmus Battke's waiting room, before the principal, in light gray shoes and the sports clothes they implied, appeared, imposing and without glasses, in the waiting room. With a small hand on a short arm, he motioned them into his office, and when the country folk hesitated to sit down in the club chairs, he cried out airily: "No formalities, please. I am sincerely delighted to meet the parents of two such promising students."

Two walls of books, one wall of windows. His pipe tobacco smelled English. Schopenhauer glowered between bookshelves, because Schopenhauer . . . Water glass, water pitcher, pipe cleaners on heavy red desk with green felt cover. Four embarrassed hands on upholstered leather arms. Miller Matern showed the principal his protruding ear, not the one that hearkened to mealworms. Widow Amsel nodded after every subordinate clause uttered by the fluent principal. The subjects of his discourse were: First, the economic situation in the countryside, hence the impending regulation of the market necessitated by the Polish customs laws, and the problems of the cheese producers on Great Island. Secondly, Great Island in general, and in particular the wind-swept far-billowing wheatfields; the advantages of the Epp variety and of the winter-resistant Siberian variety; the campaign against corn cockle—"but what a fertile blessed region, yes indeed . . ." Thirdly, Dr. Rasmus Battke had the following to say: Two such gifted students, though of course their gifts lay in very different directions—everything came so easily to little Eduard—two students bound by so productive a friendship—how touching it was to see little Matern defending his friend against the teasing, quite devoid of malice you may rest assured, of his fellow students—in short, two students so deserving of benevolent encouragement as Eduard Amsel, but in no less degree Walter Matern, were to say the least deterred by the long trip in the dreadful, though of course highly entertaining narrow-gauge railroad, from devoting their maximum energies to their work; he, the principal of the establishment, an old hand, as you may well imagine, at problems connected with schooling, who had learned a thing or two from his years of experience with commuting students, wished accordingly to suggest that even before the summer holidays broke upon the land, next Monday in fact, both boys should transfer to a different school. The Conradinum in Langfuhr, whose principal, an old friend, had already been consulted and supported his views wholeheartedly, had an in-student plan, or in plain German, a dormitory where a considerable number of students were provided with board and lodging—for a reasonable fee—thanks to the ample endowment from which the Conradinum benefited; in a word, they would both be well taken care of, it was an arrangement which he as principal of the Sankt Johann High School could only recommend.

And so on the following Monday Eduard Amsel and Walter Matern exchanged the green velvet caps of Sankt Johann for the red caps of the Conradinum. With the help of the narrow-gauge railway they and their suitcases left the Vistula estuary, Great Island, the dikes from horizon to horizon, Napoleon's poplars, the fish-smoking establishments, Kriwe's ferry, the new postmill, the eels between willows and cows, father and mother, poor Lorchen, the Mennonites rough and refined, Folchert, Kabrun, Lickfett, Lührmann, Karweise, schoolmaster Olschewski, and Grandmother Matern's ghost, which was haunting the house because they had forgotten to pour the water in which the corpse had been washed over the threshold in cross form.

TWENTY-SEVENTH MORNING SHIFT

The sons of rich peasants, the sons of landowners, the sons of West Prussian, slightly indebted country gentry, the sons of Kashubian brickworks owners, the son of the Neuteich druggist, the son of the pastor in Hohenstein, the son of the district president in Stüblau, Heini Kadlubek from Otroschken, little Probst from Schönwarling, the Dyck brothers from Ladekopp, Bobbe Ehlers from Quatschin, Rudi Kiesau from

Straschin, Waldemar Burau from Prangschin, and Dirk Heinrich von Pelz-Stilowski from Kladau on the Kladau—in short, the sons of rich man, poor man, beggar man, chief, not to mention the pastor, became, not all at once, but most of them shortly after Easter, boarders at the dormitory attached to the Conradinum. For many years the Conradinum had managed to keep afloat as a private institution thanks to an endowment, but by the time Walter Matern and Eduard Amsel became Conradinians, the city was making considerable contributions to its budget. Accordingly the Conradinum was looked upon as part of the municipal school system. Only the in-student facilities were not municipal, but still the private prerogative of the Conradinum and subject to an extra charge.

The sleeping quarters for students of sixth, fifth, and fourth, also called the small sleeping quarters, were situated on the ground floor, with their windows looking out on the school garden, that is to say, on gooseberries. There was always one bedwetter. The place smelled of him and seaweed mattresses. The two friends slept bed to bed under an oleograph showing the Crane Gate, the observatory, and the Long Bridge in winter with ice floes. The two friends never or seldom wet their beds. An attempt to initiate the newcomers, that is, to blacken Amsel's backside with shoe polish, was averted by Walter Matern before anybody could say Jack Robinson. In recreation period the two of them stood aloof under the same chestnut tree. At most little Probst and Heini Kadlubek, the son of a coal dealer, were privileged to listen while Walter Matern maintained a long dark staring silence and Eduard Amsel developed his secret language, giving new names to the new surroundings.

"I tnod ekil eht sdrib ereh."

I don't like the birds here.

"Sworraps ni eht ytic tnera sworraps ni eht yrtnuoc."

Sparrows in the city aren't sparrows in the country. "Draude Lesma sklat sdrawkcab."

With fluent ease he stood long and short sentences word for word on their heads and was even able to speak the new backward language with the broad accent of the Island: Dootendeetz (death's-head) became Zteednetood. With the help of a tongue molded to the Low German language, he smoothed out an awkward *c*, an unpronounceable *ps*, the difficult *sch*, and a tongue-twisting *nr*, and rendered "Lieb-

ärchen" (my friend) by the simplified "Nahkräbeil." Walter
Matern caught his meaning and gave brief, equally reversed,
and usually correct answers: "Good idea—doog aedi." And
impatient of shillyshallying: "Sey ro on?" Little Probst was
flabbergasted. But Heini Kadlubek, known as "Kebuldak,"
proved to be not at all backward at learning to talk backward.

Many inventions on a level with Amsel's linguistic arts
have been made in the playgrounds of this world; subsequently forgotten, they have ultimately been unearthed and
perfected by childish old people in city parks, which were
conceived as extensions of school playgrounds. When God
was a schoolboy, it occurred to him in the heavenly playground, along with young Satan, his school friend, who was
as bright as a button, to create the world. On the fourth of
February of this year, as Brauxel has read in a number of
newspaper articles, this world is expected to end; another
decision arrived at in playgrounds.

Playgrounds, it might also be noted, have something in
common with poultry yards: the strutting of the officiating
rooster resembles the strutting of the teacher in charge.
Roosters also stride about with their hands behind their
backs, turn unexpectedly, and cast menacing looks about
them.

Dr. Oswald Brunies, who is supervising at the moment—
the authors' consortium is planning to build him a monument—does his best to oblige the inventor of the poultry-
yard simile: every nine paces he scratches with the tip of his
left shoe in the gravel of the school yard; moreover, he crooks
his professorial leg—a habit not without significance. Dr.
Brunies is looking for something: not for gold, not for a
heart or for happiness God fame; he is looking for unusual
pebbles. The playground is asparkle with pebbles.

Small wonder if singly, or sometimes two at a time, students come up to him and call his attention, in earnest or
animated by the usual schoolboy whimsy, to perfectly ordinary pebbles they have just picked up. But Dr. Oswald
Brunies takes each one, even the most contemptible run of
the millstream, between the thumb and forefinger of his left
hand, holds it away from, then up to light, takes a magnifying glass secured by an elastic band from the breast pocket
of his peat-brown and partly threadbare jacket, moves the
glass on stretching elastic slowly and expertly into place be-

tween pebble and eye, then, elegantly and with full confidence in the elastic, lets the glass spring back into his breast pocket. An instant later he has the pebble in the cup of his left hand, lets it roll about in a small radius at first, then circle more boldly as far as the rim of the cup, and finally rejects it by tapping his left hand with his free right hand. "Pretty but superfluous!" says Dr. Brunies and digs the same hand into a bag which, always and as often as we shall speak of Oswald Brunies here, juts brown and rumpled from his side pocket. By ornamental detours, such as those made by priests in the course of Mass, he guides a cough drop from the bag to his mouth: celebrates, licks, sucks, diminishes, swirls juice between tobacco-stained teeth, shifts lump from cheek to cheek, while the intermission dwindles, while dread of intermission's end mounts in the muddled interiors of many children, while sparrows in chestnut trees yearn for the end of recreation, while he struts, scratches in the gravel of the playground, and causes the cough drop to become smaller and more vitreous.

Short intermission, long intermission. Intermission games, whisperings, sandwiches, and distress: anxiety, says Brauxel: in a moment the bell . . .

Empty playgrounds that belong to the sparrows. A thousand times seen and filmed, as the wind blows a sandwich paper through a deserted, melancholy, Prussian, humanistic, gravel-strewn playground.

The playground of the Conradinum consisted of a small rectangular playground, shaded irregularly by chestnut trees, and to the left of it with no fence intervening, an elongated Big Playground framed by young linden trees propped on poles and standing at regular intervals. The Neo-Gothic gymnasium, the Neo-Gothic urinal, and the Neo-Gothic old-brick-red, ivy-covered school building with its bell-less belfry bounded the Small Playground on three sides and sheltered it from the winds, which sent funnels of dust over the Big Playground from its southeast corner; for here nothing stood up to the wind but the low-lying school garden with its close-meshed wire fence and the two-storied, likewise Neo-Gothic dormitory. Until later, when a modern athletic field with cinder track and turf was laid out beneath the southern gable of the gymnasium, the Big Playground had to serve as an athletic field during gym classes. Also worth mentioning is a tarred wooden shed, some fifty feet in length, which stood between the young lindens and the school garden. Bicycles could be stored in it, front wheel upward. A little game: as soon as the upended front wheels were set in motion with strokes of the flat hand, the gravel that had stuck to the tires after the short ride through the Big Playground flew off and rained down on the gooseberry bushes in the school garden behind the wire network fence.

Anyone who has ever been obliged to play handball, football, völkerball, or faustball, let alone schlagball, in a field strewn with gravel will always, whenever he steps on gravel in later life, be forced to remember all the scraped knees, all those bruises which take forever to heal, which develop crusty scabs, and which transform all gravel-strewn playgrounds into blood-soaked playgrounds. Few things in the world make so lasting an impression as gravel.

But to him, the cock-of-the-playground, Dr. Oswald Brunies, the strutting, candy-sucking teacher—a monument will be erected to him—to him with magnifying glass on elastic, with sticky bag in sticky coat pocket, to him who collected big stones and little stones, rare pebbles, preferably mica gneiss—muscovy biotite—quartz, feldspar, and hornblende, who picked up pebbles, examined them, rejected or kept them, to him the Big Playground of the Conradinum was not an abrasive stumblingblock but a lasting invitation to scratch about with the tip of his shoe after nine rooster steps. For Oswald Brunies, who taught just about everything —geography, history, German, Latin, and when necessary religion—was not one of your universally dreaded gym teachers with shaggy black chest, bristling black legs, a policeman's whistle, and the key to the equipment room. Never did Brunies make a boy tremble under the horizontal bar, suffer on the parallel bars, or weep on hot climbing ropes. Never did he ask Amsel to do a front vault, not to mention a side vault over the long horse that is always too long. Never did he drive Amsel's fleshy knees across mordant gravel.

A man in his fifties with a cigar-singed mustache. The tip of every hair in his mustache sweet from ever-renewed cough drops. On his round head a gray felt hat, to which, often for a whole morning, clung burrs tossed on by his charges. From both ears swirling clumps of hair. A face seamed with wrinkles produced by laughing, giggling, grinning. Romantic poetry nestled in his tousled eyebrows. Schubert songs revolved around never-resting nostrils. Only in the corners of his mouth and on the bridge of his nose, a few blackheads: Heine's pungent *Winter's Tale* and Raabe's abrasive novel *Stopfkuchen*. Well liked and not taken seriously. A bachelor with a Bismarck hat and class director of the sixth, including Walter Matern and Eduard Amsel, the friends from the Vistula delta. By now the two of them smell only mildly of cow barn, curdled milk, and smoked fish; gone too is the smell of fire that clung to their hair and clothing after the public burning behind Folchert's barn.

TWENTY-EIGHTH MORNING SHIFT

After a punctual change of shifts, and business worries— the Brussels agricultural agreements are going to create marketing difficulties for the firm of Brauxel & Co.—back to the gravel in the playground. School life promised to be gay for the two friends. Scarcely had they been moved from Sankt Johann to the Conradinum, scarcely had they grown accustomed to the musty dormitory with its smell of nasty little boys—who doesn't know a few stories about dormitories?—scarcely had the gravel in the Big Playground impressed itself upon them, when word went around that in a few days the sixth would be going to Saskoschin for two weeks. They would be supervised by Dr. Brunies and by Dr. Mallenbrand the gym teacher.

Saskoschin! What a tender word!

The country school annex was situated in Saskoschin Forest. The nearest village was called Meisterswalde. Thither the class and two teachers were conveyed by bus via Schüddelkau, Straschin-Prengschin, and Gross-Salau. A village built around a market. The sandy market place big enough for a cattle fair, consequently surrounded by wooden stakes with worn iron rings. Shining puddles, ruffled by every gust of wind: there had been a violent shower shortly before the bus arrived. No cow dung or horse droppings, but several bevies of sparrows, which kept regrouping and raised their hubbub to the third power when Amsel alit from the bus. The market place was bordered by low peasant houses with small windows, some roofed with thatch. There was one new, unfinished two-story structure, Hirsch's emporium.

Brand-new plows, harrows, tedders were asking to be bought. Wagon shafts rose skyward. Directly across the way a brick-red factory, deserted, with boarded-up windows. Not until the end of October would the sugar-beet harvest bring life, stench, and profit. The inevitable branch of the Danzig Savings Bank, two churches, the milk pool, a spot of color: the mailbox. And outside the barbershop a second spot of color: the honey-yellow brass disk hung slantwise, sending out light signals as the clouds shifted. A cold treeless village.

Like the entire region to the south of the city, Meisterswalde was part of the Danzig Heights district. Compared to the marshland of the Vistula estuary, the soil was wretched. Beets, potatoes, Polish beardless oats, vitreous stunted rye. At every step the foot struck a stone. Peasants crossing their fields would bend down between steps, pick up one out of a nation of many, and hurl it in a blind rage: it would fall on someone else's field. Such gestures even on Sunday: holding umbrellas in their left hands, peasants in black caps with shiny patent-leather visors walk through the beet fields, bend down, pick things up, throw them in every direction. The stones fall: petrified sparrows, and no one, not even Eduard Amsel, could devise any kind of scarestone.

That was Meisterswalde: black humped backs, umbrella tips menacing the heavens, stones picked up and stones thrown, and an explanation for so many stones: It seems that the Devil, when refused what the peasants had solemnly sworn to give him, had punished them for their breach of faith by driving around the countryside all one night, vomiting up the damned souls that had accumulated in his stomach and scattering them over the fields and meadows. And the souls of the damned turned out to be stones, which there was no way to get rid of, let the peasants pick up and throw till they were old and bent.

The class was obliged to hike in loose formation for two miles, with Dr. Brunies at the head and Dr. Mallenbrand bringing up the rear, first over hilly country where the road was bordered on both sides by stunted, half-grown rye standing amid stone souls, then through the edge of Saskoschin Forest, until whitewashed walls behind beech trees announced the country annex.

Thin, thin! Brauxel, the present writer, suffers from inability to describe unpeopled landscapes. He knows how to begin; but once he has brushed in a rolling hill, rich green, and behind it innumerable graduated hills à la Stifter, ending in the distant gray-blue of the horizon, and gone on to scatter the stones inevitable in the region around Meisterswalde, as the Devil did in his time, through his still unformed foreground; once he has put in the bushes that consolidate the foreground—the moment he says: juniper, hazelnut, broom glossy-green, underbrush, bushes, spherical conical bushy up hill and down dale: withered bushes, thornbushes, bushes in the wind, whispering bushes—for in this region the wind is always blowing—he always itches to blow life into Stifter's wilderness. Brauksel says: And behind the third bush counting from the left, just a little above the one and one-half acres of feed beets, no, not the hazelnut bush —Oh, these wretched bushes!—there there there, below that lovely moss-covered stone, well anyway behind the third bush on the left, in the midst of this unpeopled landscape, a man is hidden.

Not a sower. Not the plowman so often seen in oil paintings. A man in his middle forties. Pale brown black impudent, hidden behind the bush. Hook-nosed rabbit-eared toothless. This *more,* this man, has an *angustri,* a ring, on his little finger and in the course of future morning shifts, while the schoolboys are playing schlagball and Brunies is sucking his cough drop, he will take on importance, because he has a little bundle with him. What is in the bundle? Who is the man?

He is Bidandengero the Gypsy, and the bundle whimpers.

TWENTY-NINTH MORNING SHIFT

Schlagball was the school sport in those days. In the gravel-strewn Big Playground at the Conradinum a fly had once been hit so high that while the ball was piercing the heavens and leathernly falling, a part of the team responsible for this feat had been able to run in fan formation to both goal posts, unmolested, and run back and collect points—an achievement compared to which twenty-five knee swings or skinning the cat seventeen times in a row were everyday occurrences. At the Saskoschin country annex schlagball was played morning and afternoon. A very moderate amount of class work was done before and after. Walter Matern, his friend Eduard Amsel, and Dr. Mallenbrand looked upon this game with three different sets of eyes.

For Mallenbrand the game of schlagball was a way of life, a philosophy. Walter Matern was a master of the high fly. He hit them and caught them openhanded, and when he caught one, he threw the ball directly from the catching position to a teammate: which brought in points.

Eduard Amsel, on the other hand, waddled about the schlagball field as though waddling through Purgatory. Stout and short-legged, he was perfect for blocking out and bouncing the ball off of. He was the team's weak spot. He was tracked and hunted down. Hedging him round, four players would execute a dance in which a leather ball figured prominently. Delectable feints would be practiced over his dead body until he rolled whimpering in the grass, smarting under the taut leather before it even reached him.

The ball spared Amsel only when his friend hit a fly; and the truth of the matter is that Walter Matern hit flies only to let Amsel make his way over the field in peace, under the protection of the soaring ball. But the flies didn't always remain in the air long enough: after a few days of philosophy played according to the rules, several black-and-blue moons blossomed on Amsel's freckled flesh—blooms that were long in fading.

A change of shift even then: after Amsel had enjoyed a gentle childhood to the right and left of the Vistula, Amsel's torments began far from the Vistula. They will go on for some time. For Dr. Mallenbrand passed as an expert and had written a book, or a chapter in a book, about German field games. In it he discussed the game of schlagball with succinct thoroughness. In the preface he expressed the opinion that the national character of schlagball was brought out most strikingly by a comparison with the international game of soccer. Then he went on to formulate the rules, point for point. A single blast of the whistle means: The ball is dead. A goal that counts is registered by the referee with two blasts of the whistle. A player is not allowed to run with the ball. There were many different kinds of ball: high-flying, known as flies, long balls, flat, corner, short balls, popflies, rollers, grounders, dribblers, goal balls, and triple-run balls. The ball was propelled by vertical blows, long blows, thrusts, or swings, by flat blows with underarm swing and by the two-hand blow, in which the ball must first be thrown to shoulder height. In catching a high-flying ball, a so-called fly—so spake Mallenbrand—the catcher's eye, his catching hand, and the falling ball must form a straight line. Moreover, and this was his title to fame, the field was lengthened from fifty to fifty-five yards at his suggestion. This feature which—as Amsel could testify—made the game more arduous was adopted by nearly every high school in eastern and northern Germany. He was the declared enemy of soccer and many regarded him as a strict Catholic. From his neck and alongside his hairy chest hung his metal referee's whistle. One blast meant: The ball is dead. Two blasts meant: Score obtained by hitting Eduard Amsel with the ball. Often enough he blew for flies that Walter Matern had struck for his friend: Out of bounds!

But his next fly is a good one. And the one after that. The following fly goes wrong: the hitter is out of position, the ball leaves the field and comes down with a whish and a tearing of foliage into the woods bordering the playground. In response to Mallenbrand's whistle—The ball is dead!— Walter Matern races to the fence, he's over and looks around in the moss and bushes at the edge of the forest: a hazelnut bush tosses him the ball.

He catches it and looks up: from a tangle of leaves grow the head and torso of a man. On his ear, the left one, a brass ring jiggles, because he is laughing soundlessly. Dark pale brown. Hasn't a tooth in his mouth. Bidandengero, that means the toothless. Under his arm he has a whimpering bundle. Holding the ball in both hands, Walter Matern moves backward out of the woods. He doesn't tell anyone, not even Amsel, about the soundless laughter behind the bush. The very next morning, or at any rate no later than the afternoon, Walter Matern intentionally hit an oblique fly that came down in the woods. Even before Mallenbrand could blow, he raced across ball field and fence. No bush and no underbrush threw him the ball. He found one ball under the ferns after a long search; as for the next one, the ants must have hauled it away.

THIRTIETH MORNING SHIFT

Diligent pencil strokes and sparrows: shading and open areas; breeding and explosions.

Diligent bees, diligent ants, diligent leghorns: diligent Saxons and diligent washerwomen.

Morning shifts, love letters, Materniads: Brauxel and his co-authors have taken an example from someone who worked diligently all his life—on lacquered tin.

And the eight planets? Sun Moon Mars Mercury Jupiter Venus Saturn Uranus, to which, such is the awesome rumor spread by the astrological calendars, the secret moon Lilith might be added. Can it be that they have orbited diligently for twenty thousand years solely in order to bring off that evil conjunction day after tomorrow in the sign of Aquarius?

Not every attempted fly was successful. Consequently the hitting of flies, as well as the hitting of oblique, intentionally off-center flies, had to be practiced diligently.

The meadow was bounded on the north side by a long wooden shed, the so-called rest porch. Forty-five wooden cots, forty-five shaggy, sour-smelling blankets neatly folded on the foot ends of the cots stood in readiness each day for the noonday rest period of the sixths. And after the noonday rest period Walter Matern practiced hitting flies to the east of the porch.

The country annex, the rest porch, the schlagball field, and the chickenwire fence running from end to end were surrounded on all sides by the dense, silent, or rustling Saskoschin Forest, a mixed woodland containing wild boar, badgers, adders, and a boundary line that cut across it. For the forest began in Poland, started out with pines and low-lying bushes on Tuchler Heath, acquired an admixture of birches and beeches on the mounds and ridges of Koshnavia, and continued northward into the milder coastal climate: the boulder glaze nurtured a mixed forest, which became purely deciduous as it approached the sea.

Sometimes forest Gypsies slipped back and forth across the border. They were regarded as harmless and lived on rabbits and hedgehogs, and by tinkering. They provided the school annex with wild mushrooms. The forester also needed their help when wasps and hornets nested in hollow tree trunks near the forest roads and made the horses of the timber wagons shy. They called themselves Gakkos, addressed one another as *More*, and were generally called *Mängische*, but sometimes *Ziganken*.

And once a Gakko tossed a high school student a schlagball after an unsuccessful fly had landed in the forest. *More* laughed soundlessly.

The student began to practice hitting out-of-bounds flies whereas previously he had only practiced regular flies.

The student succeeded in hitting two out-of-bounds flies that fell in the woods, but no Gypsy tossed him a ball.

Where did Walter Matern practice hitting good and no-good flies? At the east end of the rest porch there was a swimming pool, roughly twenty-five feet square, in which no one could swim, for it was out of order, clogged, and leaky. At the best rain water lay evaporating in the square of cracked concrete. Although no schoolboys were able to swim in the pool, it always had visitors: cool and active little frogs no bigger than a cough drop hopped about diligently as though practicing the art of hopping—less frequently, big heavily breathing toads—but always frogs, a congress of frogs, a playground of frogs, a ballet of frogs, a ball field of frogs; frogs you could blow up with blades of straw; frogs you could put down somebody's collar; frogs to stamp on; frogs to put in people's shoes; frogs that could be mixed with the always slightly burned pea soup; frogs in beds, frogs in inkwells, frogs in envelopes; frogs to practice flies with.

Every day Walter Matern practiced in the dry swimming pool. He picked slippery frogs out of the inexhaustible supply. If he hit thirty, thirty gray-blue frogs lost their cool young lives. As a rule, only twenty-seven brownish-black frogs were sacrificed to Walter Matern's dedicated devotions. It was not his purpose to send the green-gray frogs high in the air, higher than the trees of the rustling or silent forest. Nor did he practice hitting a common frog with just any portion of his bat. He had no wish to perfect himself in the hitting of long-distance balls, grounders, or treacherous bunts —besides, Heini Kadlubek was a past master at long-distance balls. What Walter Matern wanted was to hit the variously tinted frogs with that part of the bat which, when the bat was correctly raised alongside the body, gave promise of an exemplary, strictly vertical fly that would waver only slightly in the wind. If instead of the variously tinted frogs the dull-brown leather schlagball, shiny only at the seams, had offered resistance to the thick end of the bat, Walter Matern would have succeeded in half a midday hour in turning out twelve extra-special and fifteen to sixteen passable flies. In fairness it must be added that despite all this diligent fly swatting the frogs in the waterless swimming pool grew no fewer: merrily they hopped unequal heights and unequal distances while Walter Matern stood among them dealing death to frogs. They failed to understand, or else—like sparrows in this respect—they were so conscious of their numbers that there was never any possibility of a frog panic in the swimming pool.

In wet weather there were also newts, fire salamanders, and plain lizards in the death-shadowed pool. But these agile little creatures had no need to fear the bat; for the sixths developed a game, the rules of which only cost newts and salamanders their tails.

Courage was tested. The point was to take the twitching, wildly wriggling tail ends that newts and salamanders shed when you grab them with your hand—you can also knock them off with the flip of a hard finger—and swallow these living fragments in their mobile state. If possible, several tails should be swallowed successively as they leap from the concrete. The one who does it is a hero. Moreover, the three to five animated tails must go down unflushed by water and unpushed by crusts of bread. But even if the hero harbors three to five indefatigable tails, newt, salamander, or lizard, in his innards, he is also forbidden to make the slightest grimace. Amsel can do it. Harried and tormented on the schlagball field, Amsel understands and avails himself of the opportunity offered by the swallowing of salamander tails: not only does he successively incorporate seven vivacious tails into his round short-legged body, but he is also able, in return for a promise to set him free from the impending afternoon schlagball game and have him assigned to potato peeling in the kitchen, to withstand a counterordeal. One minute after his sevenfold swallowing and without putting his finger down his throat, he manages, thanks to sheer will power and even more to his abject terror of the leather schlagball, to yield up the seven tails: and lo and behold, they are still twitching, though with rather

less abandon because inhibited by the mucus that has come
up with them, on the concrete floor of the swimming pool,
amid hopping frogs that have grown no fewer although
Walter Matern, shortly before Amsel's feat of salamander
swallowing and the ensuing counter-ordeal, was practicing
flies.

The sixths are impressed. Over and over again they count
the seven resurrected tails, slap Amsel on his round freckly
back, and promise that if Mallenbrand has no objection they
will dispense with his services as the afternoon schlagball
victim. And in case Mallenbrand should take exception to
Amsel's k.p., they will only pretend to victimize him with
the schlagball.

Numerous frogs overhear this bargain. The seven swallowed and vomited salamander tails fall gradually asleep.
Walter Matern stands by the chickenwire fence, leaning on
his schlagball bat and staring into the bushes of the towering, enveloping Saskoschin Forest. Is he looking for something?

THIRTY-FIRST MORNING SHIFT

What is in store for us? Tomorrow, on account of the many
stars that are forming a clustering ferment above us, Brauksel is going to ride down with the morning shift and spend
the day in the archives on the twenty-five-hundred-foot level
—the powdermen used to keep their explosives there—concluding his record and endeavoring to the last to write with
equanimity.

The first vacation week in the Saskoschin country annex
passes amid schlagball games, well-regulated hikes, and moderate scholastic activities. On the one hand, steady consumption of frogs and, the weather permitting, an occasional
swallowing of salamander tails; on the other, singing while
gathered around the campfire in the evening—cold backs,
overheated faces. Someone gashes his knee. Two have sore
throats. First little Probst has a sty, then Jochen Witulski
has a sty. A fountain pen is stolen, or Horst Behlau has lost
it: tedious investigations. Bobbe Ehlers, a first-class goal
player, has to go back to Quatschin ahead of time, because

his mother is seriously ill. While one of the Syck brothers who had been a bedwetter back in the dormitory is able to report a dry bed in the Saskoschin country annex, his brother, hitherto dry, begins to wet his country annex bed regularly and his cot on the porch as well. Half-waking afternoon nap on the porch. Unplayed on, the schlagball field gleams in the sunlight. Amsel's slumbers raise beads on his smooth forehead. Back and forth, Walter Matern's eyes prod the distant chickenwire fence and the woods behind it. Nothing. With a little patience you can see hills growing out of the schlagball field: moles go on burrowing even in the midday rest period. At twelve there were peas with smoked pork—as usual slightly burnt. For supper supposedly sautéed mushrooms, followed by blueberry soup and farina pudding, actually there will be something else. And after supper postcards are written home.

No campfire. A few play Monopoly, others morris or checkers. In the dining hall the dry laborious sound of table tennis tries to make itself heard above the roar of the night-dark forest. In his room Dr. Brunies, while a cough drop grows smaller, classifies the yield of a collector's day: the region is rich in biotite and muscovite: they rub together gneissly. A silvery glimmer when gneisses grind; no silvery glimmer when Walter Matern's teeth grind.

At the edge of the night-dark schlagball field he sits on the concrete rim of the swimming pool rich in frogs and poor in water. Beside him Amsel: "Sti krad ni eht sdoow."

Walter Matern stares at the great black wall—near and coming nearer—of Saskoschin Forest.

Amsel rubs places where the schlagball has hit him that afternoon. Behind what bush? Is he laughing soundlessly? And is the little bundle? Is Bidandengero?

No mica gneiss; Walter Matern grinds from left to right. Heavily breathing toads answer. The forest with its birds groans. No Vistula opening out into sea.

THIRTY-SECOND MORNING SHIFT

Brauxel is writing below ground: Hoo, how dark it is in the German forest! Barbale, the ghost that is neither man nor woman, is afoot. Light-handed goblins sprinkle one another. Hoo, how dark it is in the Polish forest! Gakkos are crossing, tinkers. Ashmodai! Ashmodai! Or Beng Dirach Beelzebub, whom the peasants call Old Clootie. Servant girls' fingers that were once too curious, now spook candles, sleeping lights: so many sleeping lights, so many sleepers. Balderle steps on moss: Efta times efta is forty-nine.—Hoo! But it's darkest in the German-Polish forest. Beng is crouching there, Balderle flies upward, sleeping lights flit, ants crawl, trees copulate, Gypsies track through the woods: Leopold's bibi and Bibi the aunt and Estersweh's bibi and Hite's bibi, Gashpari's bibi, all all all strike fulminantes, make light until she shows herself: the immaculate Mashari showing the carpenter's baby where the milk pours from her goose-white crock. Green and resinous it flows and gathers the snakes, forty-nine of them, efta times efta.

Through the ferns the border runs on one leg. This side and that side: white, red-rimmed mushrooms battle black, white, and red ants. Estersweh, Estersweh! Who is looking for his little sister? Acorns fall in the moss. Ketterle calls because something glitters: gneiss lies beside granite and rubs. Glittering spray. Slate grinds. But who can hear it?

Romno, the man behind the bush. Bidandengero, toothless but keen of hearing: Acorns roll, slate slips, high shoe strikes the ground, hush little bundle, high shoe is coming, mushrooms ooze, the snake slithers away into the next century, blueberries burst, ferns tremble—for fear of whom? Light squeezes through the keyhole, steps downstairs into the mixed forest, Ketterle is the magpie—Por, its feather, flies. High shoes creak unpaid. Tittering comes the scrag, the schoolie, the brain buster, the teacher—Brunies, Brunies! Oswald Brunies!—tittering because as they rub, glitter sprays: gneissy slaty grainy scaly knotty: double spar, feldspar, and quartz. Rare, extremely rare, he says, and thrusts his high shoe forward, pulls out his magnifying glass on elastic band, and titters under his Bismarck hat.

He also picks up a beauty, beauty, a piece of reddish mica granite, turns it under the mixed forest into the sun that's on its way downstairs, until all the tiny mirrors say peep. This one he doesn't reject, he holds it out into the light, joins it in prayer, and does not turn around. He walks along, mumbling to himself. He lifts his mica granite into the next light and the next one and the next to next one, to let the thousand mirrors say peep again, one after another and only a few simultaneously. With his high shoe he steps close to the bush. Behind it sits Bidandengero, toothless and very still. And the bundle hushes too. No longer is Romno the magpie. Ketterle calls no more. Por, its feather, flies no more. Because nearby the scrag, the schoolie, the brain buster, the teacher Oswald Brunies.

Deep in the woods, he laughs under his hat, for in the deepest part of the German-Polish Saskoschin Forest he has found a piece of extremely rare flesh-colored mica granite. But because the thousand mirrors refuse to suspend their polyphonic peeping, Dr. Oswald Brunies begins to have a bitter dry taste in his mouth. Brushwood and pine cones have to be gathered. With three big stones that glitter only moderately he has to build a stove. Fulminantes from Swedish boxes have to strike a flame, deep in the woods; so that immediately afterward Ketterle calls again: Por—the magpie loses a feather.

The schoolmaster has a pan in his bag. It is oily, black, covered with tiny mica mirrors, because in his musette he keeps not only the pan, but also pieces of mica gneiss and mica granite and even his rare specimens of double spar. But in addition to pan and mica rock, the teacher's musette yields up several little brown and blue paper bags of varying sizes. As well as a bottle without a label and a tin can with a screw top. The little flame crackles dry. Resin boils. Mica mirrors leap in the hot pan. The pan sizzles when he pours something into it from the bottle. The fire crackles between three stones. Six heaping teaspoonfuls from the tin can. Moderate quantities shaken from the large blue and the pointed brown bag. He takes a spoon-handleful from the small blue, a pinch from the small brown bag. Then he stirs counterclockwise and with his left hand shakes powder from a tiny sprinkler can. Stirs clockwise while again the magpie, while far away beyond the border Estersweh is still being looked for, although there is no wind to carry.

He bends down on schoolmaster's knees and blows until it flares to a blaze. He has to keep stirring until the mash slowly boils down, becomes stickier and more sluggish. Back and forth over the steaming bubbling pan he moves a schoolmaster's nose with long hairs protruding from both nostrils: drops hang from his singed mustache, candy, and grow vitreous as he stirs the mash. From all directions come ants.

Undecided, the smoke creeps over the moss, tangles with the ferns. Under a shifting oblique light the great mound of mica stones—who can have made it?—cries aloud in polyphonic confusion: peep peep peep! The mash over the flame begins to burn, but the recipe says it has to burn. Brown has to rise from the bottom. Wax paper is spread out and greased. Two hands lift the pan: a thick weary dough flows brown bubbly lavalike over the greased paper, immediately takes on a glassy skin, wrinkles from the sudden coolness, and darkens. Quickly, before it grows cold, a knife in the schoolmaster's hand divides the flat cake into candy-sized squares; for what Dr. Oswald Brunies has brewed in the dark German-Polish woods under the trees of Saskoschin Forest, between Estersweh and Ketterle's cry, is cough drops.

Because he is lusting for sweets. Because his supply of sweetness was exhausted. Because his musette is always full of little bags and tins. Because in the bags, tins, and bottle, malt and sugar, ginger, anise, and salt of hartshorn, honey and beer, pepper and mutton suet are always in readiness. Because with tiny sprinkler can—that is his secret—he dusts the hardening mash with crushed cloves: now the forest is fragrant and the fragrance of mushrooms, blueberries, moss, decades-old shrubbery, ferns, and resin abandons the competition. Ants run wild. The snakes in the moss are candied. Ketterle's cry changes. Por, its feather, sticks. How is Estersweh to be looked for? The sweet way or the sour way? And who weeps behind the bush and snuffles behind the bush because he has been sitting in the acrid smoke? Had the little bundle been given poppy to be so still while the schoolmaster, hearing nothing, pried the cooled remnants of lava out of the pan with shrill spoon handle?

Dr. Oswald Brunies picks up what splinters have not fallen into the moss or jumped in among the mica stones and guides them beneath his oversweet mustache: sucks, draws juice, lets them melt away. With sticky fingers, kept busy crushing ants between them, he sits beside the fire, which has collapsed and is smoking only feebly, and breaks the hard, glassy-brown cake on the greased paper into some fifty previously scored squares. Along with fragments and candied ants he stuffs the sweet concoction into a large blue sack which before his candymaking had been full of sugar. Everything—the pan, the rumpled bags, the bag with the newly acquired supply of candy, the tin can, the empty bottle, and the tiny sprinkler can—finds its way back to the mica gneiss in the musette bag. Now he is standing, holding the brown-crusted spoon in his schoolmaster's mouth. Now he is striding over the moss in high shoes under Bismarck hat. He leaves nothing behind him except for tiny splinters and the greased paper. And now the schoolboys come loudly through the blueberries between the tree trunks. Little Probst is crying because of an encounter with wasps. Six have stung him. Four boys have to carry him. Dr. Oswald Brunies greets his colleague Dr. Mallenbrand.

When the class moved on, was no longer there, when nothing remained of it but calls, laughter, screams, and the voices of the scrags, schoolies, brain busters, in short, teachers, the magpie called three times. Por: its feather flew again. Then Bidandengero left his bush. And the other Gakkos as well: Gashpari, Hite, and Leopold disengaged themselves from the bushes, glided from the trees. Near the greased paper that had contained candy lava, they met. Black with ants, the paper moved in the direction of Poland. The Gakkos followed the ants: Hite, Gashpari, Leopold, and Bidandengero whished silently over moss and through ferns in a southerly direction. Bidandangero was the last to grow smaller amid the tree trunks. Along with him went a thin whimpering as though his little bundle, a toothless snuggle-bunny, a hungry mite, as though Estersweh were crying.

But the border was near, permitting a quick passage back and forth. Two days after the candymaking deep in the woods, Walter Matern, standing solidly planted in the striking zone, struck, quite contrary to his habit and only because Heini Kadlubek had said he could only hit flies but not long-distance balls, a long-distance ball that passed over both goals, over the whole field, and over the swimming pool rich in frogs and destitute of water. Walter Matern sent the schlagball into the woods. Before Mallenbrand came to count the balls, he had to go after it, hell bent for leather, over the chickenwire fence and into the mixed woods.

But he did not find the ball and kept looking where there was none. He lifted every fan of ferns. Outside a half-ruined foxhole, which he knew to be uninhabited, he went down on his knees. He poked about with a branch in the trickling hole. He was about to lie down on his belly and reach a long arm into the foxhole when the magpie screamed, the feather flew, the leather struck him: what bush had thrown it?

The bush was the man. The little bundle kept still. The brass ring in the man's ear jiggled, because the man was laughing soundlessly. His tongue fluttered bright red in his toothless mouth. A frayed string cut into his coat over his left shoulder. In front three hedgehogs dangled on the string, bleeding from pointed snouts. When the man turned slightly, a small bag hung down behind him, forming a counterweight to the hedgehogs. The man had braided the black oiled hair over his temples into short, stiffly protruding pigtails. Zieten's hussars had done the same.

"Are you a hussar?"

"Part hussar, part tinker."

"What's your name, anyway?"

"Bi-dan-den-gero. Have no tooth left."

"And the hedgehogs?"

"To cook in clay."

"And the bundle up front?"

"Estersweh, little Estersweh."

"And the bundle in back? And what are you looking for here? And how do you catch the hedgehogs? And where do you live? And have you really got such a funny name? And suppose the forester catches you? And is it true that the Gypsies? And the ring on your little finger? And the bundle up front?"

Por—that was the magpie calling from deep within the mixed forest. Bidandengero was in a hurry. He had, so he said, to go to the factory without windows. The schoolmaster was there. He was waiting for wild honey for his candy. He also wanted to bring the schoolmaster sparklers, and another little present too.

Walter Matern stood with the ball and didn't know what to do, in what direction. Finally he decided to climb back across the fence to the schlagball field—for the game was proceeding—when Amsel came rolling out of the bushes, asked no questions, had heard everything, and knew of only one direction: Bidandengero . . . He pulled his friend after him. They followed the man with the dead hedgehogs, and when they lost him, they found bright hedgehog blood from three hedgehog snouts on the ferns. They read the trace. And when the hedgehogs on Bidandengero's string were dry and silent, the magpie screamed in their stead: Por—Ketterle's feather—flew ahead. The forest grew denser, more crowded. Branches struck Amsel's face. Walter Matern stepped on the

white and red mushroom, fell in the moss, and bit into the
cushion. Trees made faces. A fox froze. Faces through spider-
webs. Fingers full of resin. Bark tasted sour. The woods
thinned out. Downstairs went the sun as far as the teacher's
mound of stones. Afternoon concert: gneisses, some augite,
hornblende, slate, mica, Mozart, twittering eunuchs from the
Kyrie to the chorale *Dona nobis:* polyphonic peeping—but
no sign of a teacher under a Bismarck hat.

Only the cold fireplace. Gone was the greased paper. And
only when the beeches came together again behind the clearing and screened off the sun, did they overtake the paper:
it was black with ants and on its way. Like Bidandengero
with his hedgehogs, the ants wished to make off across the
border with their prey. They marched in single file, just as
Walter Matern and his friend trotted along in single file,
following the magpie's lure: here here here. Through knee-
high ferns. Through neatly ordered beech trees. Through
green church light. Swallowed up again, far away, here again:
Bidandengero. But no longer alone. Ketterle had called the
Gakkos. Gashpari and Hite, Leopold and Hite's bibi, Aunt
Bibi and Leopold's bibi, all the Gypsies, tinkers, and forest
hussars had gathered under beech trees in the hushed ferns
around Bidandengero. Gashpari's bibi was pulling Bartmann,
the goat.

And when the forest thinned out again, eight or nine
Gakkos left the woods with Bartmann the goat. Until they
reached the trees on the other side, they were hidden by the
tall grass of the trough-shaped treeless meadow spreading
southward: and in the open meadow stands the factory,
shimmering.

An elongated one-story building, gutted. Untrimmed brick,
empty window holes blackened with soot. From the ground
to mid-height the chimney yawns, a brick maw with teeth
missing. All the same it stands upright, probably just topping
the beeches huddled close at the far end of the clearing. But
it isn't the chimney of a brickworks, although there are
plenty of those in the region. Formerly it evacuated the
smoke of a distillery, and now that the factory is dead and
the chimney cold, it houses a jutting stork's nest. But the
nest too is dead. Blackish rotting straw covers the cracked
chimney and shimmers emptily.

They approach the factory in fan formation. No more
magpie calling. Gakkos swimming in the tall grass. Butter-

flies staggering over the meadow. Amsel and Walter Matern reach the edge of the woods, lie flat, peer out over the trembling spikes, and see all the Gakkos climbing simultaneously but through different window holes into the dead factory. Gashpari's bibi has tied Bartmann to a hook in the wall.

A white long-haired goat. The factory is not alone in shimmering; the blackish straw on the cracked chimney and the meadow shimmer too, and Bartmann is dissolved in light. It's dangerous to watch staggering butterflies. They have a plan but it has no meaning.

Amsel isn't sure whether or not this is Polish territory. Walter Matern thinks he has recognized Bidandengero's head in a window hole: oily braids hussar style, brass in ear, gone again.

Amsel thinks he has seen the Bismarck hat first in one, then briefly in the next window hole.

Neither of them sees the border. Only bantering white butterflies. And above the variously pitched bumbling of the bumblebees a rising and falling garble. Not a distinct howling, cursing, or screaming. More like a crescendo of blubbering and squeaking. Bartmann the goat bleats two three volleys heavenward.

Then from the fourth window hole on the left leaps the first Gakko: Hite with Hite's bibi in tow. She unties Bartmann. Then another, and then two more in dappled Gypsy tatters: Gashpari and Leopold, his bibi, in numerous skirts. None through the open door, all the Gypsies through window holes, head-first, last of all Bidandengero.

For all Gypsies have sworn by the Virgin Mashari: never through doors, only through windows.

Fanwise as they have come, the Gakkos swim through the quaking grass to the woods that swallow them up. Once again the white goat. Ketterle does not call. Por, her feather, does not fly. Silence, until the clearing begins to buzz again: bantering butterflies. Bumblebees like double deckers, dragonflies pray, sumptuous flies, wasps, and such-like vagabonds.

And who shut the picture book? Who dripped lemon on homemade June clouds? Who let the milk clabber? How did Amsel's skin and Walter Matern's skin get that porous look, as though bombarded with sleet?

The little bundle. The snugglebunny. The toothless mite. From the dead factory Estersweh screamed over the living meadow. Not the dark window holes but the black gate spat the Bismarck hat into the open air. The scrag, schoolie, brain buster, teacher, Oswald Brunies, stood under the sun with the screaming bundle and didn't know how to hold it. "Bidandengero," he called, "Bidandengero!" But the woods didn't answer. Neither Amsel nor Walter Matern, who were picked up by the outcry and tugged step by step through the hissing grass to the factory, neither Dr. Brunies with the strident little bundle nor the picture-book meadow showed surprise when again something miraculous happened: from the south, from Poland, storks came flying over the meadow with measured wingbeat. Two of them described ceremonious loops and dropped, first one, then the other, into the blackened and disheveled nest on the cracked chimney.

Instantly they began to clatter. All eyes, the schoolmaster's under the Bismarck hat and the schoolboys' eyes as well, climbed up the chimney. The snugglebunny broke off its cries. Adebar Adebar the Stork. Oswald Brunies found a piece of mica gneiss, or was it double spar, in his pocket. Let the baby have it to play with. Adebar Adebar the Stork. Walter Matern wanted to give the little bundle the leather schlagball which had come with them so far, with which the whole thing had started. Adebar Adebar the Stork. But the six-months-old baby girl already has something to finger and play with: Angustri, Bidandengero's silver ring.

Quite possibly Jenny Brunies is wearing it to this day.

LAST MORNING SHIFT

It seems to have been nothing. No world has come discernibly to an end. Brauxel can write above ground again. Still, the date, February 4, has had something to show for itself: all three manuscripts have been punctually delivered, Brauchsel is able to set young Harry Liebenau's love letters down on his package of morning shifts; and on "morning shifts" and "love letters" he will pile the actor's confessions. Should a postscript seem desirable, Brauksel will write it, because he is in charge both of the mine and of the author's consortium, it is he who pays out the advances, sets the delivery dates, and will read the proof.

What happened when young Harry Liebenau came to us

and applied for the job of authoring the second book? Brauxel examined him. To date he had written and published lyric poetry. His radio plays have all been on the air. He was able to show flattering and encouraging reviews. His style was termed gripping, refreshing, and uneven. Brauchsel began by questioning him about Danzig: "What, young man, were the names of the streets connecting Hopfengasse with the New Mottlau?"

Harry Liebenau rattled them off: "Kiebitzgasse, Stützengasse, Mausegasse, Brandgasse, Adebargasse, Münchengasse, Judengasse, Milchkannengasse, Schleifengasse, Turmgasse, and Leitergasse."

"How, young man," Brauksel inquired, "will you kindly explain, did Portechaisengasse gets its delightful name?"

Harry Liebenau explained rather pedantically that it had taken its name from the litters, the taxis of the day, which had stood there in the eighteenth century and in which patricians and their ladies could be carried through muck and pestilence without fear for their costly attire.

In response to Brauxel's question as to who in the year 1936 had introduced the modern Italian rubber truncheon in the Danzig police force, Harry Liebenau spoke up like a recruit: "That was done by Police President Friboess!" But I was not yet satisfied: "Who, my young friend—I doubt if you remember—was the last chairman of the Center Party in Danzig? What was the honorable man's name?" Harry Liebenau had boned up very thoroughly, even Brauxel learned a thing or two: "Richard Stachnik, D.D., clergyman and schoolteacher, became chairman of the Center Party and member of the provincial diet in 1933. In 1937, after dissolution of the Center Party, he was imprisoned for six months: in 1944 he was deported to Stutthof concentration camp, but soon released. All his life Dr. Stachnik was active in behalf of the canonization of the Blessed Dorothea of Montau, who in the year 1392 had caused herself to be immured beside the cathedral of Marienwerder."

I still had a raft of tricky questions on hand. I asked him the course of the Striessbach, the names of all the chocolate factories in Langfuhr, the altitude of the Erbsberg in Jäschkental Forest, and obtained satisfactory answers. When in answer to the question: What well-known actors began their careers at the Danzig Stadttheater?—Harry Liebenau replied without hesitation Renate Müller, who died young, and Hans

Söhnker, the movie star, I, in my easy chair, gave him to understand that the examination was over and that he had passed.

And so, after three work sessions, we agreed to link up Brauxel's "morning shifts" and Harry Liebenau's "love letters" with a transitional passage. Here it is:

Tulla Pokriefke was born on June 11, 1927.

When Tulla was born, the weather was variable, mostly cloudy, with a possibility of showers. Light gyratory winds fluttered the chestnut trees in Kleinhammer Park.

When Tulla was born, Dr. Luther, the former chancellor, coming from Königsberg and on his way to Berlin, landed at the Danzig-Langfuhr airfield. In Königsberg he had spoken at a meeting of former German colonials; in Langfuhr he took a snack at the airport restaurant.

When Tulla was born, the Danzig police band, conducted by chief bandmaster Ernst Stieberitz, gave a concert in the gardens of the Zoppot casino.

When Tulla was born, Lindbergh, the transatlantic flier, boarded the cruiser *Memphis*.

When Tulla was born, the police, as their records for the eleventh of the month inform us, arrested seventeen persons.

When Tulla was born, the Danzig delegation to the forty-fifth session of the League of Nations council arrived in Geneva.

When Tulla was born, the Berlin stock exchange reported foreign buying of rayon and electrical industry stocks. Prices were generally firmer: Essen Anthracite: four and one-half points; Ilse and Stolberger Zinc: three points. Certain special securities also advanced. Glanzstoff opened at four points, Bemberg at two points above previous quotations.

When Tulla was born, the Odeon Cinema was showing *His Biggest Bluff* with Harry Piel in his dual and most brilliant role.

When Tulla was born, the NSDAP, Gau Danzig, called a monster mass meeting in the Sankt Josephshaus on Töpfergasse from five to eight. Party Comrade Heinz Haake of Cologne was to speak on the topic of "German workers of brawn and brain, unite!" On the day following Tulla's birth the meeting was to be repeated in the Red Room of the Zoppot casino under the motto: "Nation in distress: who will save it?" The poster was signed by a Herr Hohenfeld, member of the provincial diet, who called upon his fellow citizens to "Come in droves!"

When Tulla was born, the rediscount rate of the Bank of Danzig was unchanged at five and one-half per cent. At the grain exchange rye debentures brought nine gulden sixty a hundredweight: money.

When Tulla was born, the book *Being and Time* had not yet appeared, but had been written and announced.

When Tulla was born, Dr. Citron still had his practice in Langfuhr; later he was obliged to take refuge in Sweden.

When Tulla was born, the chimes in the City Hall tower played "Glory alone to God on high" when even hours were to be struck and "Heavenly Host of Angels" for the odd hours. The chimes of St. Catherine's played "Lord Jesus Christ, hear our prayer" every half hour.

When Tulla was born, the Swedish steamer *Oddewold* put in to Danzig empty, coming from Oxelösund.

When Tulla was born, the Danish steamer *Sophie* left for Grimsby with a cargo of timber.

When Tulla was born, a child's rep dress cost two gulden fifty at Sternfeld's department store. Girls' "princess" slips two gulden sixty-five. A pail and shovel cost eighty-five gulden pfennigs. Watering cans one gulden twenty-five. And tin drums lacquered, with accessories, were on sale for one gulden and seventy-five pfennigs.

When Tulla was born, it was Saturday.

When Tulla was born, the sun rose at three eleven.

When Tulla was born, the sun set at eight eighteen.

When Tulla was born, her cousin Harry Liebenau was one month and four days old.

When Tulla was born, Dr. Oswald Brunies adopted a foundling, aged six months, who was cutting her milk teeth.

When Tulla was born, Harras, her uncle's watchdog, was one year and two months old.

BOOK TWO | **Love Letters**

Dear Cousin Tulla:

I am advised to put you and your Christian name at the beginning, to address you, because you were, are, and will be matter everywhere, informally, as though this were the beginning of a letter. Yet I am telling my story to myself, only and incurably to myself; or can it be that I am telling you that I am telling it to myself? Your family, the Pokriefkes and the Damses, came from Koshnavia.

Dear Cousin:

since every one of my words to you is lost, since all my words, even if I speak obstinately to myself, have only you in mind, let us at last make peace on paper and cement a frail foundation for my livelihood and pastime: I speak to you. You don't listen. And the salutation—as though I were writing you one or a hundred letters—will be my formal crutch, which even now I would like to throw away, which I shall often and with fury in my arm throw into the Striessbach, into the sea, into Aktien Pond: but the dog, black on four legs, will bring it back as he has been trained to do.

Dear Tulla:

like all the Pokriefkes, my mother, a Pokriefke by birth and sister to your father August Pokriefke, hailed from Koshnavia. On the seventh of May, when Jenny Brunies was about six months old, I was normally and properly born. Seventeen years later somebody picked me up with two fingers and put me into a life-size tank as an ammunition loader. In the middle of Silesia, a region which is not as familiar to me as Koshnavia south of Konitz, the tank went into position and backed up, for purposes of camouflage, into a wooden shed which some Silesian glass blowers had filled with their products. Whereas hitherto I had never stopped searching for a word that would rhyme with you, Tulla, that tank backing into position and those screaming glasses showed your Cousin Harry the way to a rhymeless language: from then on I wrote simple sentences, and now that a certain Herr Brauxel has advised me to write a novel, I am writing a normal rhymeless novel.

Dear Cousin Tulla:

about Lake Constance and the girls around there I don't

know a thing; but about you and Koshnavia I know everything. The geographical co-ordinates of Koshnavia are north
latitude fifty-three twenty, east longitude thirty-five. You
weighed four pounds and ten ounces at birth. Koshnavia
proper consists of seven villages: Frankenhagen, Petztin,
Deutsch-Cekzin, Granau, Lichtnau, Schlangenthin, and Osterwick. Your two elder brothers Siegesmund and Alexander
were born in Koshnavia; Tulla and her brother Konrad were
registered in Langfuhr. The name of Pokriefke is to be found
even earlier than 1772 in the parish register of Osterwick.
The Damses, your mother's family, are mentioned years after
the partitions of Poland, first in Frankenhagen, then in
Schlangenthin; probably immigrants from Prussian Pomerania, for I am inclined to doubt that "Dams" is derived from
the archbishopric of Damerau, especially in view of the fact
that Damerau, along with Obkass and Gross Zirkwitz, was
donated to the Archbishop of Gnesen as early as 1275.
Damerau was then called Louisseva Dambrova, occasionally
Dubrawa; it is not properly a part of Koshnavia: the Damses
are outsiders.

Dear Cousin:
    you first saw the light of day in Elsenstrasse. We lived in
the same apartment house. It belonged to my father, master
carpenter Liebenau. Diagonally across the street, in the so-
called Aktienhaus, lived my future teacher, Dr. Oswald
Brunies. He had adopted a baby girl, whom he called Jenny,
although in our region no one had ever borne the name of
Jenny. The black shepherd dog in our yard was called Harras.
You were baptized Ursula, but called Tulla from the start,
a nickname probably derived from Thula the Koshnavian
water nymph, who lived in Osterwick Lake and was written
in various ways: Duller, Tolle, Tullatsch, Thula or Dul, Tul,
Thul. When the Pokriefkes were still living in Osterwick,
they were tenants on Mosbrauch Hill near the lake, on the
Konitz highway. From the middle of the fourteenth century
to the time of Tulla's birth in 1927, Osterwick was written
as follows: Ostirwig, Ostirwich, Osterwigh, Osterwig, Oster-
wyk. Ostrowit, Ostrowite, Osterwieck, Ostrowitte, Ostrôw.
The Koshnavians said: Oustewitsch. The Polish root of the
village name Osterwick, the word *ostrów*, means an island
in a river or lake; for originally, in the fourteenth century
that is, the village of Osterwick was situated on the island in
Osterwick Lake. Alders and birches surrounded this body of

water, which was rich in carp. In addition to carp and crucians, roaches, and the compulsory pike, the lake contained a red-blazed calf that could talk on St. John's Day, a legendary leather bridge, two sacks full of yellow gold from the days of the Hussite incursions, and a capricious water nymph: Thula Duller Tul.

Dear Tulla:

my father the carpenter liked to say and often did: "The Pokriefkes will never get anywhere around here. They should have stayed where they came from, with their cabbages."

The allusions to Koshnavian cabbage were for the benefit of my mother, a Pokriefke by birth; for it was she who had lured her brother with his wife and two children from sandy Koshnavia to the city suburb. At her behest carpenter Liebenau had taken on the cottager and farmhand August Pokriefke as an assistant in his shop. My mother had persuaded my father to rent the two-and-a-half-room apartment that had become vacant on the floor above us to the family of four—Erna Pokriefke was already pregnant with Tulla—at a low price.

For all these benefits your mother gave my father little thanks. On the contrary. Whenever there was a family scene, she blamed him and his carpenter shop for the deafness of her deaf-mute son Konrad. She maintained that our buzz saw, which roared from morning to closing time and only rarely fell silent, which made all the dogs in the neighborhood including our Harras howl themselves hoarse in accompaniment, had withered and deafened Konrad's tiny ears while he was still in the womb.

The carpenter listened to Erna Pokriefke with serenity, for she fulminated in the Koshnavian manner. Who could understand it? Who could pronounce it? The inhabitants of Koshnavia said *"Tchatchhoff"* for *Kirchhof* (churchyard). *Bäsch* was *Berg* (mountain)—*Wäsch* was *Weg* (way, path). The *"Preistewäs"* was the meadow (*Wiese*), some two acres in size, belonging to the priest in Osterwick.

You'll have to admit, Tulla,

that your father was a rotten helper. The machinist couldn't even use him on the buzz saw. The drive belt would keep slipping off, and he ruined the most expensive blades on nail-studded sheathing which he converted into kindling for his own use. There was only one job that he performed punctually and to the satisfaction of all: the gluepot on the cast-iron stove upstairs from the machine room was always hot and in readiness for five journeymen carpenters at five carpenter's benches. The glue ejected bubbles, blubbered sulkily, managed to turn honey-yellow or muddy-cloudy, succeeded in thickening to pea soup and forming elephant hide. In part cold and crusty, in part sluggishly flowing, the glue climbed over the rim of the pot, formed noses upon noses, leaving not so much as a speck of enamel uncovered and making it impossible to recognize the gluepot as an erstwhile cookpot. The boiling glue was stirred with a section of roofing lath. But the wood also put on skin over skin, swelled bumpy leathery crinkly, weighed heavier and heavier in August Pokriefke's hand and, when the five journeymen called the horny monster an elephant's trunk, had to be exchanged for a fresh section of always the same, positively endless roofing lath.

Bone glue, carpenter's glue! The brown, grooved cakes of glue were piled on a crooked shelf amid a finger-thick layer of dust. From the third to the seventeenth year of my life I faithfully carried a chunk of carpenter's glue in my pants pocket; to me glue was that sacred; I called your father a glue god; for not only had the glue god thoroughly gluey fingers which crackled brittlely whenever he moved, but in addition he invariably gave off a smell that followed him wherever he went. Your two-and-a-half-room apartment, your mother, your brothers smelled of it. But most generously he garnished his daughter with his aroma. He patted her with gluey fingers. He sprayed the child with particles of glue whenever he conjured up finger bunnies for her benefit. In short, the glue god metamorphosed Tulla into a glue maiden; for wherever Tulla went stood ran, wherever she had stood, wherever she had gone, whatever space she had traversed at a run, whatever Tulla took hold of, threw away, touched briefly or at length, whatever she wrapped clothed hid herself in, whatever she played with: shavings nails hinges, every place and object that Tulla had encountered retained a faint to infernal and in no wise to be quenched smell of bone glue. Your Cousin Harry stuck to you too: for quite a few years we clung together and smelled in unison.

Dear Tulla:

when we were four years old, they said you had a calcium

deficiency. The same contention was made concerning the marly soil of Koshnavia. The marl dating from the diluvian times, when the ground moraines formed, contains, as we know, calcium carbonate. But the weather-beaten, rain-washed layers of marl in the Koshnavian fields were poor in calcium. No fertilizer helped and no state subsidies. No amount of processions—the Koshnavians were Catholic to a man—could inject calcium into the fields; but Dr. Hollatz gave you calcium tablets: and soon, at the age of five, your calcium deficiency was overcome. None of your milk teeth wobbled. Your incisors protruded slightly: they were soon to become a source of dread to Jenny Brunies, the foundling from across the street.

Tulla and I never believed

that Gypsies and storks had anything to do with the finding of Jenny. A typical Papa Brunies story: with him nothing happened naturally, everywhere he sniffed out hidden forces, he always managed to dwell in an eerie eccentric light. Whether feeding his mania for mica gneiss with ever new and often magnificent specimens—there were similar cranks in cranky Germany with whom he corresponded—or, on the street, in the playground, or in his classroom, carrying on like an Old Celtic druid, a Prussian oak-tree god, or Zoroaster—he was generally thought to be a Freemason—he invariably displayed the qualities that we all of us love in our eccentrics. But it was Jenny, his association with the doll-like infant, that first made Dr. Brunies into an eccentric who acquired a standing not only within the precinct of the high school but also in Elsenstrasse and the streets intersecting or running parallel to it in the big little suburb of Langfuhr.

Jenny was a fat child. Even when Eddi Amsel was roaming around Jenny and Brunies, she seemed no slimmer. Amsel and his friend Walter Matern—they were both Dr. Brunies' students—were said to have witnessed the miraculous finding of Jenny. In any case Amsel and Matern made up half of the group which elicited smiles in our Elsenstrasse and in all Langfuhr.

For Tulla I am going to paint an early picture:

I want to show you an elderly gentleman with a bulbous nose, innumerable wrinkles, and a broad-brimmed soft hat on ice-gray matted hair. He is striding along in a green loden cape. To the left and right of him two schoolboys are trying to keep up with him. Eddi Amsel is what is commonly known as a fatty. His clothes are full to bursting. His knees are marked with little dimples. Wherever his flesh is visible, a crop of freckles burgeons. The general impression is one of boneless waddling. Not so his friend: rawboned and masterful, he stands beside Brunies, looking as though the teacher, Eddi Amsel, and plump little Jenny were under his protection. At the age of five and a half the little girl is still lying in a large baby carriage, because she has walking difficulties. Brunies is pushing. Sometimes Eddi Amsel pushes, rarely the Grinder. And at the foot end lies a half-open crumpled brown paper bag. Half the kids in the neighborhood are following the baby carriage; they are out for candy, which they call "blubblubs."

But only when we reached the Aktienhaus, across the street from where we lived, did Dr. Brunies bring the high-wheeled carriage to a halt and distribute a handful from the brown bag to Tulla, myself, and the other children, on which occasion he never forgot to help himself as well, even if he hadn't quite finished the vitreous remnant in his mumbling elderly mouth. Sometimes Eddi Amsel sucked a candy to keep him company. I never saw Walter Matern accept a candy. But Jenny's fingers were as tenaciously sticky with rectangular cough drops as Tulla's fingers with the bone glue which she rolled into marbles and played with.

Dear Cousin,

just as I am trying to gain clarity about you and your carpenter's glue, so I am determined to get things straight about the Koshnavians, or Koschneiders as they are also called. It would be absurd to accept an allegedly historical but thus far undocumented explanation of the term "Koshnavian." This so-called explanation is that during the Polish uprisings the Koshnavians had been stirred to acts of violence against the Germans, so that the collective noun "Koschneider" derives from the collective noun *"Kopfschneider"* (head cutter). Though I had good reason to adopt this exegesis—you, the scrawny Koshnavian maiden, had every aptitude for the head cutter's trade—I shall nevertheless content myself with the unimaginative but reasonable explanation that in the year 1484 a starosty official in Tuchel, Kosznewski by name, signed a document officially defining the rights and obligations of all the villages in the region, and that these villages later came to be known as Kosznew or Koshnavian villages after him. A vestige of uncertainty remains. The names of towns and districts may lend themselves to pedantry of this kind, but Kosznewski, the methodical starosty official, is no help in deciphering Tulla, more a something than a girl.

Tulla,
tautly encased in white skin, could hang head downward from the carpet-beating rack—for half an hour—all the while singing through her nose. Bones bruised black and blue, muscles uncushioned and unimpeded by fat made Tulla into a perpetually running, jumping, climbing, in a word, flying something. Since Tulla had her mother's deep-set, small-cut, narrow-placed eyes, her nostrils were the biggest thing in her face. When Tulla grew angry—and several times a day she became hard, rigid, and angry—she rolled her eyes so far back that her optical slits revealed nothing but white shot through with blood vessels. Her angry revulsed eyes looked like blinded eyes, the eyes of beggars and mountebanks who pass themselves off as blind beggars. When she went rigid and began to tremble, we used to say: "Tulla's bashed in her windows again."

From the first I was always running after my cousin, or more precisely, I was always two steps behind you and your smell of glue, trying to follow you. Your brothers Siegesmund and Alexander were already of school age and went their own ways. Only Konrad the deaf-mute curlyhead went with us. You and he; I, tolerated. We sat in the woodshed under the tar roof. The planks smelled and I was turned into a deaf-mute; for you and he could talk with your hands. The pushing down or crossing of certain fingers meant something and aroused my suspicions. You and he told each other stories that made you giggle and him shake silently. You and he hatched plans, of which I was mostly the victim. If you loved anyone at all, it was he, the little curlyhead; meanwhile the two of you persuaded me to put my hand under your dress. It was under the tar roof in the woodshed. Acrid was the smell of the wood. Salty was the taste of my hand. I couldn't get away, I was stuck; your bone glue. Outside sang the buzz saw, droned the power plane, howled the finishing machine. Outside whimpered Harras, our watchdog.

Listen Tulla,

that was him: a long-drawn-out black shepherd with erect
ears and a long tail. Not a long-haired Belgian Groenendael,
but a short-haired German shepherd. Shortly before we
were born, my father the carpenter had bought him as a
puppy, in Nickelswalde, a village on the Vistula delta. The
owner, who also owned Queen Louise's mill in Nickelswalde,
asked thirty gulden. Harras had a powerful muzzle with dry,
tight lips. Dark eyes set a little obliquely followed our steps.
Neck firm, free from dewlap or throatiness. Barrel length
two inches in excess of shoulder height: I measured it. Harras
could bear scrutiny from all sides: legs always straight and
parallel. Toes well closed. Pads thick and hard. Long, slightly sloping croup. Shoulders buttocks knuckles: powerful,
well muscled. And every single hair straight, close to the body,
harsh and black. Undercoat likewise black. No wolf colors,
dark on a gray or yellow ground. No, all over him, even
inside the erect slightly forward-tilted ears, on his deep
crinkled chest, along his moderately coated hocks, his hair
glistened black, umbrella-black, priest-black, widow-black,
SS-black, black-board-black, Falange-black, blackbird-black,
Othello-black, dysentery-black, violet-black, tomato-black,
lemon-black, flour-black, milk-black, snow-black.

Harras searched, found, pointed, retrieved, and did trail
work with his nose to the ground. In a herding contest on
the Bürgerwiesen he proved a failure. He was a stud dog
with his name in the studbook. Unsatisfactory on the leash:
he pulled. Good at barking at intruders but only average at
following strange tracks. My father had had him trained by
the police in Hochstriess. They thrashed him till he stopped
eating his dirt: a nasty habit with puppies. The number
517 was stamped on his dog tag: sum of digits thirteen.

All over Langfuhr, in Schellmühl, in the Schichau housing
development, from Saspe to Brösen, up Jäschkentaler Weg,
down Heiligenbrunn, all around the Heinrich Ehlers Athletic
Field, behind the crematory, outside Sternfeld's department
store, along the shores of Aktien Pond, in the trenches of the
municipal police, on certain trees of Uphagen Park, on certain lindens of the Hindenburgallee, on the bases of advertising pillars, on the flagpoles of the demonstration-hungry athletic field, on the still unblacked-out lampposts of the suburb
of Langfuhr, Harras left his scent marks: he remained true
to them for many dog years.

Up to the withers Harras measured twenty-five inches. Five-year-old Tulla measured three foot six. Her cousin Harry was an inch and a half taller. His father, the imposingly built carpenter, stood six foot two in the morning and an inch less at closing time. As for August and Erna Pokriefke, as well as Johanna Liebenau, née Pokriefke, none of them was more than five foot five: the Koshnavians are a short race.

Dear Cousin Tulla,

what would I care about Koshnavia if you, the Pokriefkes, were not from there? But as it is, I know that from 1237 to 1308 the villages of Koshnavia belonged to the dukes of Pomerelia. After they died out, the Koshnavians paid taxes to the Teutonic Knights until 1466. Until 1772 the kingdom of Poland absorbed them. In the course of the European auction Koshnavia fell to the Prussians. They kept order until 1920. As of February 1920 the villages of Koshnavia became villages of the Polish Republic, until the autumn of 1933 when they were incorporated into the Greater German Reich as part of the Province of West Prussia-Danzig: Violence. Bent safety pins. Pennants in the wind. Billeting: Swedes Hussites Waffen-SS. Andifyoudon't. Rootandbranch. Asoffourfortyfivethismorning. Circles described with compasses on military maps. Schlangenthin taken in counter-attack. Anti-tank spearheads on the road to Damerau. Our troops resist heavy pressure northwest of Osterwick. Diversionary attacks of the twelfth division of airborne infantry thrown back south of Konitz. In line with the decision to straighten the front, the so-called territory of Koshnavia is evacuated. Last-ditch fighters take up positions south of Danzig. Panic-makers, bogeymen, terrible jokesters are shaking the paper-weight again, the fist . . .

Oh Tulla,

how can I tell you about Koshnavia, about Harras and his scent marks, about bone glue, cough drops, and the baby carriage, when I have this compulsion to stare at my fist!— Yet roll it must. Once upon a time there rolled a baby carriage. Many many years ago there rolled a baby carriage on four high wheels. On four old-fashioned high wheels it rolled, enameled black and hooded with cracking oilcloth. Dull-gray spots where the chromium-plated spokes of the wheels, the springs, the handle to push it by, had peeled. From day to day the spots grew imperceptibly larger: Past: Once upon a time. When in the summer of '33: in the days in the days when I was a boy of five, when the Olympic Games were being held in Los Angeles, fists were already being moved swift, dry, down to earth; and yet, as though unaware of the draft that was blowing, millions of baby carriages on wheels high and low were being propelled into the sunlight, into the shade.

On four old-fashioned high wheels there rolled, in the summer of 1932, a black-enameled, slightly decrepit baby carriage which Eddi Amsel the high school student, who knew all the junkshops, had negotiated in Tagnetergasse. He, Dr. Oswald Brunies, and Walter Matern took turns at pushing the vehicle. The tarred, oiled, and yet dry boards on which the baby carriage was being pushed were the boards of the Brösen pier. The friendly seaside resort—where sea baths were taken as early as 1823—with its low-lying fishing village and dome-surmounted casino, its medium-high dunes and scrub pine forest, with its fishing boats, its hundred and fifty feet of pier, and its tripartite bathhouse, with the watch-tower of the German Lifesaving Society, was situated exactly halfway between Neufahrwasser and Glettkau on the shores of the Gulf of Danzig. The Brösen pier had two levels and branched off to the right into a short breakwater designed to resist the waves of the Baltic Sea. Sunday in Sunday out: the Brösen pier floated twelve flags on twelve flagpoles: at first only the flags of the Baltic cities—gradually more and more swastika flags.

Under flags and over boards rolls the baby carriage. Dressed much too black and shaded by his soft hat, Dr. Brunies is pushing now and will be relieved by Amsel the fat or Matern the bullish. In the carriage sits Jenny, who will soon be six years old and is not allowed to walk.

"Couldn't we let Jenny walk a little? Please, sir. Just for a try. We'll hold her on both sides."

Jenny Brunies mustn't. "Do we want the child to get lost? To be pushed about in the Sunday crowd?" People come and go, meet separate bow, or take no notice of each other. They wave, take each other's arms, point to the big break-water, to Adlerhorst, feed gulls with food brought from home, greet, remind, are vexed. And all so well dressed: large flower patterns for the special occasion. The sleeveless get-ups of the season. Tennis dress and sailing togs. Neckties in

the east wind. Insatiable cameras. Straw hats with new sweat-
bands. Toothpaste-white canvas shoes. High heels dread the
cracks between the boards. Pseudo captains aiming spy-
glasses. Or hands shading far-seeing eyes. So many sailor
suits. So many children running, playing, hiding, and scaring
each other. I see something you do not see. Eenymeeny-
minymo. Sour herring one two three. There's Herr Anglicker
from Neuer Markt with his twins. They're wearing sailor ties
and one as slowly as the other licking raspberry ice with pale
tongues. Herr Koschnick from Hertastrasse with his wife
and a visitor from Germany. Herr Sellke allows his sons, first
one, then the other, to look through his spyglass: smoke trail,
superstructure, the *Kaiser* is rising above the horizon. Herr
and Frau Behrendt have used up their sea gull biscuit. Frau
Grunau, who owns the laundry on Heeresanger, with her
three apprentice girls. Scheffler the baker from Kleinhammerweg with giggling wife. Heini Pilenz and Hotten Sonntag
without parents. And there's Herr Pokriefke with his gluey
fingers. Hanging on his arm, his shriveled little wife, who
can't stop moving her head this way and that with ratlike
swiftness. "Tulla!" she can't help crying. And "Come here,
Alexander." And "Siegesmund, keep an eye on Konrad!" For
on the pier the Koshnavians don't talk like Koshnavians,
although Herr Liebenau and his wife are not present. On Sunday morning he has to stay in his shop, drawing up a work
schedule, so the machinist will know on Monday what
goes into the buzz saw. She doesn't go out without her husband. But his son is there because Tulla is there. Though
younger than Jenny, both are allowed to walk. Allowed to
hop skip jump behind Dr. right up to where it ends in a
sharp wind-swept triangle. Allowed down the steps, right
left, to the lower story, where the fishermen Brunies and
his mildly embarrassed students. Allowed on the pier, squat
catching sticklebacks. Allowed to run sandal-swift along narrow runways and to dwell secretly in the framework of the
pier, beneath five hundred pairs of Sunday shoes, beneath
the gentle tapping of canes and umbrellas. It's cool shady
greenish down there. The water smells of salt and is transparent all the way down to the shells and bottles rolling
about on the bottom. On the piles supporting the pier and the
people on the pier beards of seaweed wave fitfully: back and
forth sticklebacks busy silvery commonplace. Cigarette butts
fall from the top deck, disintegrate brownish, attract fin-

ger-length fishes, repel them. Schools react spasmodically,
dart forward, hesitate, turn, regather a floor lower, and emigrate someplace where other seaweed waves. A cork bobs up
and down. A sandwich paper grows heavy, twists and turns.
Between tarred beams Tulla Pokriefke hikes up her Sunday
dress, it already has tar spots on it. Her cousin is expected to
hold his open hand underneath. But he doesn't feel like it and
looks away. Then she can't, doesn't have to any more and
jumps from crossed beams to the ramp and runs with clattering sandals, making pigtails fly and fishermen wake up, she's
already on the stairs to the pier, the stairs to the twelve
flags, stairs to the Sunday forenoon; and her cousin Harry
follows her glue smell, which uproariously drowns out the
smell of the seaweed, the smell of the tarred and yet rotting
beams, the smell of the wind-dry runways, the smell of the
sea air.

And you Tulla

said one Sunday morning: "Aw let her. I want to see how
she walks."

Wonder of wonders, Dr. Brunies nods and Jenny is allowed
to walk on the boards of the Brösen pier. Some laugh, many
smile, because Jenny is so fat and walks over the boards on
two pillars of fat encased in white, bulge-surmounted knee
socks and in buckled patent-leather shoes.

"Amsel!" says Brunies under his black felt hat. "When
you were little, say at the age of six, did you suffer from
your, well, to put it bluntly, your corpulence?"

"Not especially, sir. Matern always looked out for me. Only
I had trouble sitting down in school, because the seat was too
narrow."

Brunies offers candy. The empty baby carriage stands off
to one side. Matern guides Jenny awkwardly carefully. The
flags all strain in the same direction. Tulla wants to guide
Jenny. If only the baby carriage doesn't roll away. Brunies
sucks cough drops. Jenny doesn't want to go with Tulla, is
on the verge of tears, but Matern is there, and Eddi Amsel
quickly and accurately imitates a barnyard. Tulla turns on
her heels. At the pointed pier end a crowd is gathering: there's
going to be singing. Tulla's face turns triangular and so small
that fury gains the upper hand. They are singing on the end
of the pier. Tulla rolls her eyes back: bashed-in windows.
Up front Hitler cubs are standing in a semicircle. Scrawny

Koshnavian rage: Dul Dul, Tuller. The boys aren't all in uniform, but all join in the singing, and many listen and nod in approval: "Welovethestorms . . ." they all sing; the only nonsinger strains to hold a black triangular pennant with runic writing straight up in the air. Empty and forsaken stands the baby carriage. Now they sing: "Andtheearlymorn- ingthatisthetimeforus." Then something gay: "Amanwho- calledhimselfColumbus." A fifteen-year-old curlyhead, who is wearing his right arm in a sling, possibly because he has real- ly hurt it, invites the audience in a tone half of command, half of embarrassment, to join in singing the Columbus song, at least the refrain. Young girls who have taken their boy friends' arms and enterprising husbands, among them Herr Pokriefke, Herr Berendt, and Matzerath the gro- cer, join in the chorus. The northeast wind aligns the flags and smooths out the false notes in the merry song. Anyone who listens closely can hear, now below now above the singing, a child's tin drum. That must be the grocer's son. He isn't quite right in the head. "Gloriaviktoria" and "Wiedewie- dewittjuchheirassa" is the refrain of the well-nigh intermin- able song. Little by little it becomes imperative to join in: "Why isn't *he* singing?" Sidelong glances: Herr and Frau Ropinski are singing too. Even old Sawatzki is with us, and he's an out-and-out Socialist. So come on! Chin up! Aren't Herr Zureck and Postal Secretary Bronski singing, though they both work at the Polish Post Office? "Wiedewiede- wittbumbum." And what about Dr. Brunies? Couldn't he at least stop sucking that eternal cough drop and pretend? "Gloriaviktoria!" To one side and empty stands the baby carriage on four high wheels. It glitters black and de- crepit. "Wiedewiedewittjuchheirassa!" Papa Brunies wants to pick up Jenny in his arms and unburden her pillars of fat in patent-leather shoes. But his students—"Gloriaviktoria!"— especially Walter Matern, advise him against it. Eddi Am- sel joins in the singing: "Wiedewiedewittjuchheirassa!" Be- cause he is an obese child, he has a lovely velvety boy so- prano voice, which at certain points in the refrain, in the "juchheirassaaah" for instance, is a silvery bubbling. That's known as descant singing. A number of people look around, curious to know where the spring is gushing.

Now, because contrary to all expectation the Columbus song has a last verse, they are singing a harvest song: "I'veloaded- mywagonfull." Now, although such things are best sung in the evening: "Nolovelierlandatthishour." Eddi Amsel lets his fat-boy soprano stand on its head. Brunies sucks ostentatiously and turns on irony lights. Matern darkens under a cloudless sky. The baby carriage casts a solitary shadow . . .

Where is Tulla?

Her cousin has joined in six stanzas of the Columbus song. During the seventh stanza he has erased himself. Only sea air, no more glue smell; for August Pokriefke is standing with his wife and the deaf-mute Konrad on the west side of the triangle at the end of the pier, and the wind has shifted from northeast to east. The Pokriefkes have their backs turned to the sea. They are singing. Even Konrad is opening his mouth in the right places, pursing his lips soundlessly, and he doesn't miss an entrance when the canon Meisterjakobmeisterjakob is attempted with little luck.

Where is Tulla?

Her brothers Siegesmund and Alexander have beat it. Their cousin Harry sees them both on the breakwater. They are diving. Siegesmund is practicing flips and handstand dives. The brothers' clothes are lying, weighted down by shoes, on the windy spur of the pier. Tulla isn't with them. From the direction of the Glettkau pier—even the big Zoppot pier can be made out in the distance—the excursion steamer is approaching on schedule. It is white with a big black smoke trail, like the steamers in children's drawings. Those who wish to take the steamer from Brösen to Neufahrwasser are crowding onto the left side of the pier end. Where is Tulla? The Cubs are still singing, but no one is listening any more, because the steamer is getting bigger and bigger. Eddi Amsel has also withdrawn his high soprano. The tin drum has abandoned the song rhythm and succumbed to the pounding of the engine. It's the *Pike*. But the *Swan* looks exactly the same. Only the side-wheeler, the *Paul Beneke*, looks different. In the first place it has side wheels; in the second place it is bigger, much bigger; and in the third place its run is from Danzig-Langebrücke to Zoppot, Gdingen, and Hela and back—it doesn't come to Glettkau and Brösen at all. Where is Tulla? At first it looks as if the *Pike* had no intention of putting in to the Brösen pier, then she heaves to and is alongside quicker than anyone expected. She churns up foam and not only at bow and stern. She hesitates, marks time, and whips up the sea. Lines are cast: bollards grind. Tobacco-brown cushions on the starboard side muffle the shock. All the children and some of the women are scared because the *Pike* is going to toot in a minute. Children stop their ears, open their mouths, tremble in advance: there she toots with the dark voice that goes hoarse at the end, and is made fast. Ice-cream cones are being licked again, but a few children on board the steamer and on the pier are crying, still stopping their ears and staring at the smokestack, because they know that before casting off the *Pike* will toot again and let off white steam that smells of rotten eggs.

Where is Tulla?

A white steamer is lovely if it has no rust spots. The *Pike* hasn't a single one, though the Danzig Free State flag at the stern and the pennant of the "Vistula" shipyard are washed out and frayed. Some land—some go aboard. Tulla? Her cousin looks behind him: on the right side of the pier stands solely and eternally the baby carriage on four high wheels. It casts a crooked eleven-o'clock shadow, which merges seamlessly with the shadow of the pier railing. A thin unramified shadow approaches this tangle of shadows: Tulla coming up from below. She had been with the waving beards of seaweed, the spellbound fishermen, the exercising sticklebacks. Bony in short dress, she mounts the steps. Her knees kick against the crocheted hem. From the top of the stairs she heads directly for the carriage. The last passengers go aboard the *Pike*. A few children are still crying or have started up again. Tulla has hooked her arms behind her back. Although her skin is bluish-white in the winter, she turns quickly brown. A dry yellow-brown, the carpenter's glue has missed her vaccination marks: one two three four cherry-size islands on her left arm remain conspicuously ashen. Every steamer brings gulls with it—takes gulls away. The starboard side of the steamer exchanges words with the left side of the pier end: "And drop in again. And take the film to be developed, we can't wait. And give everybody our best regards, hear?" Tulla stands beside the empty baby carriage. The steamer toots high low and its voice cracks. Tulla doesn't stop her ears. Her cousin would like to stop his ears but doesn't. The deaf-mute Konrad, between Erna and August Pokriefke, watches the steamer's wake and holds both ears. The bag lies rumpled wrapping-paper-brown at the foot end. Tulla doesn't take a candy. On the breakwater two boys are fighting with one boy: two fall in the water, reappear: all three laugh. Dr. Brunies has picked up Jenny after all. Jenny doesn't know whether she should cry because the steamer has tooted. The teacher and his pupils advise her not to cry. Eddi Amsel has made four knots in his handkerchief and pulled the head covering thus produced over his flaming red hair. Because he looks comical to begin with, the knotted handkerchief makes him look no more comical. Walter Matern stares darkly at the white steamer as it detaches itself trembling from the pier. On board men, women, children, Hitler Cubs with their black pennant wave laugh shout. The gulls circle, fall, rise, and ogle out of heads screwed slantwise. Tulla Pokriefke gives the right hind wheel of the baby carriage a gentle kick: the carriage shadow is scarcely moved. Men, women, and children move slowly away from the left flank of the pier end. The *Pike* sends up a scrawl of black smoke, stamps, puts about, and, growing quickly smaller, takes a course for the Neufahrwasser harbor mouth. Through the calm sea she digs a foaming furrow which is quickly effaced. Not all the gulls follow her. Tulla acts; she throws back her head with its pigtails, lets it snap forward, and spits. Her cousin blushes to kingdom come. He looks around to see if anyone was looking when Tulla spat into the baby carriage. By the left-hand rail of the pier stands a three-year-old in a sailor suit. His sailor cap is encased in a silk ribbon with a gold-embroidered inscription: "HMS Seydlitz." The ends of the ribbon flutter in the northeast wind. At his side hangs a child's tin drum. From his fists grow battered wooden drumsticks. He doesn't drum, has blue eyes, and watches as Tulla spits a second time into the empty baby carriage. A multitude of summer shoes, canvas shoes, sandals, canes, and parasols approach from the end of the pier as Tulla takes aim a third time.

I don't know whether there was any other witness besides me and the grocer's son when my cousin spat three times in quick succession into Jenny's empty baby carriage and then shuffled off skinny angry slowly in the direction of the casino.

Dear Cousin,

I still can't stop putting you on the shimmering boards of the Brösen pier: One Sunday in the following year, but in the same month, to wit, the stormy month of August crawling with jellyfish, when once again men, women, and children with beach bags and rubber animals left the dusty suburb of Langfuhr and rode to Brösen, for the most part to station themselves on the free beach and in the bathing establishment, in lesser part to promenade on the pier, on a day when eight flags of Baltic cities and four swastika flags flapped sluggishly on twelve flagpoles, when out at sea a storm was piling up over Oxhöft, when the red jellyfish were stinging and the nonstinging bluish-white jellyfish were blossoming in the lukewarm sea—one Sunday, then, in August Jenny got lost.

Dr. Brunies had nodded assent. Walter Matern had picked Jenny up out of the baby carriage and Eddi Amsel had failed to take notice when Jenny wandered off in the dominically attired throng. The storm over Oxhöft put on an extra story. Walter Matern didn't find Jenny. Eddi Amsel didn't. I found her, because I was looking for my cousin Tulla: I was always looking for you and found mostly Jenny Brunies.

That time, as the storm built up from the west, I found both of them, and Tulla was holding our Harras, whom I had taken along with my father's permission, by the collar.

On one of the runways that ran lengthwise and crosswise under the pier, at the end of a blind runway, or alley if you will, I found them both. Concealed by beams and struts, huddled in a white dress in green changing light traversed by shadow—above her the scraping of light summer shoes, below her, licking lapping glugging sighing—Jenny Brunies, plump dismayed tearful. Tulla was scaring her. Tulla commanded our Harras to lick Jenny's face. And Harras obeyed Tulla.

"Say shit," said Tulla, and Jenny said it.

"Say: my father farts all the time," said Tulla, and Jenny admitted what Dr. Brunies sometimes did.

"Say: my brother is always swiping things," said Tulla.

But Jenny said: "I haven't got any brother, honest I haven't."

Thereupon Tulla fished under the runway with a long arm and brought up a wobbling nonstinging jellyfish. It took both her hands to hold the whitish glassy pudding, in whose soft center violet-blue veins and knots converged.

"You're going to eat it till there's nothing left," Tulla

commanded. "It hasn't any taste, go ahead." Jenny remained frozen and Tulla showed her how you eat jellyfish. She sucked in two soupspoonfuls, swished the gelatinous mass between her teeth, and from the gap between her two upper incisors spat a jet of gook that barely missed Jenny's face. High over the pier the storm front had begun to nibble at the sun.

"You saw me do it. Now do it yourself."

Jenny's face was getting ready to cry. Tulla theatened: "Should I tell the dog?" Before Tulla could sick our Harras on Jenny—I'm sure he wouldn't have hurt her—I whistled Harras to heel. He didn't obey right away, but he turned his head and collar toward me. I had him. But up above, though still at a distance, it was thundering. Tulla, right next to me, smacked the rest of the jellyfish against my shirt, pushed by, and was gone. Harras wanted to follow her. Twice I had to call: "Stay!" With my left hand I held the dog, with my right I took Jenny's hand and led her up to the storm-anticipating pier, where Dr. Brunies and his students were looking for Jenny amid the scurrying bathers, crying "Jenny!" and fearing the worst.

Even before the first gust of wind the caretakers brought in eight different and four identical flags. Papa Brunies held the baby carriage by the handle: the carriage trembled. The first drops broke loose overhead. Walter Matern lifted Jenny into the baby carriage: the trembling did not subside. Even when we had taken shelter and Dr. Brunies with trembling fingers had given me three cough drops, the baby carriage was still trembling. The storm, a traveling theater, passed quickly by with a great to-do.

My Cousin Tulla

had to scream at the top of her lungs on the same pier. By then we were able to write our names. Jenny was no longer being wheeled in a baby carriage, but like us went step by little step to the Pestalozzi School. Punctually vacation came with special fares for school-children, bathing weather, and ever new Brösen pier. On the twelve flagpoles of the pier there now blew, when it was windy, six Free State flags and six swastika flags, which were no longer the property of the resort management, but of the Brösen Party group. And before vacation was over, one morning shortly after eleven o'clock, Konrad Pokriefke drowned.

Your brother, the curlyhead. Who laughed soundlessly, joined in the singing, understood everything. Never again to talk with hands, elbows, forehead, lower eyelid, fingers crossed beside right ear, two fingers cheek to cheek: Tulla and Konrad. Now one small finger pressed down, because under the breakwater . . .

The winter was to blame. With ice, thaws, pack ice, and February storms it had severely battered the pier. The management, to be sure, had had the pier repaired more or less; painted white and equipped with new flagpoles, it had the right holiday sparkle, but some of the old piles, which pack ice and heavy breakers had broken off deep under the surface of the water, still protruded treacherously from the bottom, spelling disaster for Tulla's little brother.

Although bathing off the breakwater was forbidden that year, there were plenty of kids who, starting from the free beach, swam out to the breakwater and used it as a diving board. Siegesmund and Alexander Pokriefke hadn't taken their brother with them; he swam after them dog paddle, arms and legs flailing, and managed to swim, though not in any recognized style. All three together dove perhaps fifty times from the breakwater and came up fifty times. Then they dove together another seventeen times and came up together only sixteen times. No one would have noticed so quickly that Konrad had failed to come up if our Harras hadn't acted like he'd gone crazy. From the pier he had joined in their counting and now he ran up and down the breakwater, yelping uncertainly here and there, and finally stood still, keening at the high heavens.

The steamer *Swan* was just docking; but all the people crowded onto the right side of the pier. Only the ice-cream vendor, who never caught on to anything, continued to call out his flavors: "Vanilla, lemon, woodruff, strawberry, vanilla, lemon . . ."

Walter Matern slipped off only his shoes and dove head-first from the rail of the pier. He dove exactly across from the spot which our Harras indicated, first whimpering, then scratching with both forepaws. Eddi Amsel held his friend's shoes. He came up, but dove again. Fortunately Jenny didn't have to watch this: Dr. Brunies and she were sitting under the trees in the casino park. Only when Siegesmund Pokriefke and a man, who however was not a lifeguard, took turns in helping, was the deaf-mute Konrad, whose head had been wedged between two poles that had snapped close to the bottom, finally dislodged.

They had scarcely laid him on the runway when the life-saving team came with the oxygen apparatus. The steamer *Swan* whistled a second time and resumed its circuit of beach resorts. No one turned off the ice-cream vendor: "Vanilla, lemon, woodruff . . ." Konrad's face had turned blue. His hands and feet, like those of all the drowned, were yellow. The lobe of one ear had been torn between the piles: bright red blood dripped on the boards. His eyes refused to close. His curly hair had remained curly under water. Around him, who looked even tinier drowned than alive, a puddle grew. During the efforts to revive him—they applied the oxygen apparatus as the regulations prescribed—I held Tulla's mouth closed. When they removed the apparatus, she bit into my hand and screamed above the voice of the ice-cream vendor to high heaven, because she could no longer talk silently with Konrad for hours, with fingers, cheek to cheek, with the sign on the forehead and the sign for love: hidden in the woodshed, cool under the pier, secretly in the trenches, or quite openly and yet secretly on busy Elsenstrasse.

Dear Tulla,

your scream was to be long-lived: to this day it nests in my ear and holds that one heaven-high tone.

The following summer and the one after that nothing could move our Harras to go out on the breakwater. He remained with Tulla, who also avoided the pier. Their solidarity had a story behind it:

In the summer of the same year, but shortly before the deaf-mute Konrad drowned while bathing, Harras was summoned for mating purposes. The police were acquainted with the dog's pedigree and once or twice a year sent a letter signed by a Police Lieutenant Mirchau. My father never said no to these letters which were framed more or less as commands. As a master carpenter he wished in the first place to avoid trouble with the police; in the second place stud service, when performed by a male of Harras' parts, brought in a tidy little sum; in the third place my father took manifest pride in his shepherd: when the two of them set out for the profitable mating ceremony, an onlooker could easily have been led to believe that the police had called not upon Harras but upon my father to mate.

For the first time I was allowed to go along: unenlightened, but not ignorant. My father despite the heat wearing a suit, which he otherwise put on only when the carpenter's guild had a meeting. A respectable charcoal with belly-spanning vest. Under his velour hat he held a fifteen-pfennig cigar—he was in the habit of buying seconds. No sooner was Harras out of his kennel and muzzled into inoffensiveness—because we were going to the police—than he lit out and was up to his old trick, pulling on the leash: to judge by the ample remains of the cigar, we were in Hochstriess sooner than anyone would have thought possible.

Hochstriess was the name of the street that ran southward from the Main Street of Langfuhr. Past two-family houses where police officers lived with their families; on the right, the gloomy brick barracks built for Mackensen's Hussars, now inhabited by the police. At the Pelonker Weg entrance, which was little used and had no sentry box but only a barrier and a guardroom, my father, without removing his hat, produced Lieutenant Mirchau's letter. Although my father knew the way, a policeman escorted us across gravel-strewn barracks yards where policemen in light-gray twill were drilling or standing in a semicircle around a superior. All the recruits stood at ease with their hands behind their backs and gave the impression of listening to a lecture. The offshore wind sent dust cones whirling through the hole between the police garages and the police gymnasium. Along the endless stables of the mounted police, recruits were hurrying over the obstacle course, hurdling walls and ditches, bars and barbed-wire entanglements. All the barracks yards were framed by evenly spaced young lindens about the thickness of a child's arm, supported by props. At that point it became advisable to hold our Harras close. In a small square —to the left and right windowless storerooms, in the background a flat-roofed building—police dogs, perhaps nine of them, were obliged to heel, to point, to retrieve, to bark, to hurdle walls like the recruits, and finally, after complicated trail work with nose to the ground, attack a policeman who, disguised as a thief and protected by padding, was acting out a classical attempt at a getaway. Well-kept beasts, but none like Harras. All of them iron-gray, ash-gray with white markings, dull yellow with black saddle or dark-brindled on light-brown undercoat. The yard resounded with commands and with the commanded barking of the dogs.

In the orderly room of the police kennels we had to wait. Lieutenant Mirchau wore his very straight part on the left side. Lieutenant Mirchau exchanged such words with my father as a carpenter exchanges with a police lieutenant when they are seated in a room for a short while. Then Mirchau lowered his head. His part moved back and forth over his work—he was probably looking through reports. The room had two windows to the left and right of the door. The drilling police dogs would have been visible if the windows hadn't been painted opaque except for the upper third. On the whitewashed wall across from the window front hung two dozen photographs in narrow black frames. All were of the same format; in two pyramidal groups—six photographs at the bottom, then four, and at the top two—they flanked a picture of large upright format, which though broader was also framed in black. Each of the twenty-four of the pyramidally ordered photographs represented a shepherd heeling for a policeman. The large ceremoniously flanked picture presented the face of an elderly man in a spiked helmet, with tired eyes under heavy eyelids. Much too loudly I asked the man's name. Lieutenant Mirchau replied, without raising head or part, that this was a picture of the Reichspräsident, and that the signature at the bottom had been affixed by the old gentleman in person. There were also ink tracks crowded in under the photographs of dogs and policemen: probably the names of the dogs, references to their pedigrees, the names and ranks of the policemen, possibly, since these were obviously police dogs, allusions to actions performed in line of duty by the dogs and dog-leading policemen, for instance, the names of the burglars, smugglers, and murderers who had been apprehended with the help of the dog in question.

Behind the desk and Lieutenant Mirchau's back hung, again symmetrically echeloned, six framed and glassed paper rectangles, illegible from where I was sitting. To judge by the type and sizes of the lettering, they must have been certificates in Gothic print with gold embossing, seals, and raised stamps. Probably dogs, who had served with the police, who had been drilled in the Langfuhr-Hochstriess police kennels, had won first, second, or even third prize at interregional police dog meets. On the desk, to the right of the inclined part, slowly moving back and forth over the lieutenant's work, stood in tense posture a bronze, or perhaps only plaster shepherd about the height of a dachshund, who, as any dog fancier could see at a glance, was cow-hocked and let his croup, to the onset of the tail, slope much too steeply.

Despite all this emphasis on cynology, the orderly room of the Langfuhr-Hochstriess police kennels didn't smell of dogs, but rather of lime; for the room had been freshly whitewashed—and the six or seven potted dwarf lindens that adorned both window sills gave off a dry acrid smell: my father was obliged to sneeze loudly several times, which embarrassed me.

After a good half hour Harras was brought back. He didn't look any different. My father received twenty-five gulden of stud money and the bright-blue stud certificate, the text of which indicated the circumstances of the covering, such as the male's immediate readiness to mate, and the numbers of two entries in the studbook. To help me preserve it in my memory to this day, Lieutenant Mirchau spat into a white-enameled spittoon, which stood by the left hind leg of his desk, and said they would send word whether it had taken. If the desired result should materialize, he would see to it that the balance of the stud fee was sent as usual.

Harras had his muzzle on again, my father had put away the stud certificate and the five five-gulden pieces, we were already on our way to the door when Mirchau resurfaced from his reports: "You've got to keep that animal more in check. His habits on the leash are deplorable. His pedigree makes it quite clear that the animal came from Lithuania three generations back. Suddenly, from one day to the next, a mutation can set in. We've seen all sorts of things. Moreover, breeder Matern should have had the mating of the bitch Senta of Queen Louise's mill with the stud dog Pluto supervised and confirmed by the local dog club in Neuteich." He shot a finger at me: "And don't leave the dog with children too often. He shows signs of reverting to wildness. It's all the same to us, but you'll have trouble later on."

It wasn't you,
    but me the lieutenant's finger was aimed at. But it was you who demoralized Harras.

Tulla, skinny bony. Through the cracks in every fence. Under the stairs a tangle; a tangle down the banister.

Tulla's face, in which the overly large, usually crusted nostrils—she talked through her nose—outweighed everything, even the narrow-set eyes, in importance.

Tulla's scraped, scab-forming, healing, newly scraped knees.

Tulla's aroma of bone glue, her carpenter's glue dolls and her wigs of wood shavings, which one of the carpenters had to plane specially for her from long boards.

Tulla could do what she liked with Harras; and she did with Harras everything that entered her head. Our dog and her deaf-mute brother were for a long time her real retinue, whereas I, who wanted passionately to belong, was always just tagging around after the three of them, and yet obliged to do my breathing at a distance from Tulla's aroma of bone glue when I finally caught up with them by the Striessbach, on Aktien Pond, on the Fröbelwiese, in the coconut pile of the Amada margarine factory, or in the police trenches; for when my cousin had wheedled my father long enough—which Tulla was very good at doing—Harras was allowed to go along. Tulla led our Harras to Oliva Forest, to Saspe and across the sewage fields, through the lumber yards behind the New City or to the Brösen pier, until the deaf-mute Konrad drowned while swimming.

Tulla screamed for five hours,
then played deaf and dumb. For two days, until Konrad lay beneath the ground in the Consolidated Cemeteries beside Hindenburgallee, she lay stiff in bed, beside the bed, under the bed, tried to waste away completely, and on the fourth day after Konrad's death moved into the kennel by the front wall of the lumber and plywood shed, which was properly intended only for Harras.

But it turned out that both found room in the kennel. They lay side by side. Or Tulla lay alone in the kennel and Harras lay across the entrance. This never went on for long, then they were back again, lying flank to flank in the kennel. When it became necessary to bark and growl briefly at a delivery man, bringing door frames or blades for the buzz saw, Harras left the kennel; and when he was drawn to his dinner plate or drinking bowl, Harras left Tulla for a short while, only to push hurriedly and backwards—for in the cramped kennel he had difficulty in turning around—back into the warm hole. He let his superimposed paws, she her thin braids tied up in string, hang out over the threshold of the kennel. Either the sun shone on the tar paper of the kennel roof or they heard the rain on the tar-paper roof; or they didn't hear the rain, heard perhaps the lathe, the finishing machine, the booming planing machine, and the agitated, tranquillized, freshly and more furiously agitated buzz saw, which went its arduous ways even when the rain was beating down on the yard, forming always the same puddles.

They lay on shavings. On the first day my father came out, and Dreesen the machinist, who called my father by his first name and vice versa after work hours. August Pokriefke came out in wooden shoes. Erna Pokriefke came out in felt slippers. My mother didn't come out. They all said: "Now come on out of there and get up and stop that." But Tulla didn't come out, didn't get up, and didn't stop. Anyone attempting to set foot in the vicinity of the kennel quailed after the first step; for the kennel—and Harras had no need to take one paw off the other—emitted a growling that meant something. Born Koshnavians, long-time residents of Langfuhr, the tenants of the two-and-a-half-room apartments exchanged the opinion from floor to floor: "She'll come when she's had enough and when she sees she can't bring little Konrad back to life by going on that way."

But Tulla didn't see,

didn't come out, and didn't have enough on the evening of her first dog-kennel day. Two lay on wood shavings. They were renewed every day. August Pokriefke had been doing that for years; and Harras attached importance to the renewal of the shavings. Consequently, of all those who were concerned over Tulla, only old man Pokriefke was allowed to approach the kennel with a basket of crisp shavings. In addition he had a broom and shovel wedged under his arm. As soon as August Pokriefke came padding along thus laden, Harras left the kennel unasked, tugged a little, then harder at Tulla's dress, until he dragged herself out into the daylight and crouched down beside the kennel. As she crouched, her eyes, quite sightless, rolled back so that only the whites shimmered; with "bashed-in windows," she passed water. Not defiantly, indifferently would be more accurate, she waited until August Pokriefke had renewed the shavings and come out with the little speech that was bound to occur to him as a father: "Come on up now. You're still on vacation now, but pretty soon you'll have to go to school. D'you think you're the only one? D'you think we didn't love the boy? And don't act like you was nuts. They'll come and get you and put you in an institution where they swat you from morning to night. They'll think you're crazy. So come up now. It'll be dark soon. Mama's making potato pancakes. Come along now or they'll take you away."

Tulla's first dog-kennel day ended like this:

she stayed in the kennel. August Pokriefke took Harras off the chain. With different keys he locked the lumber shed, the plywood shed, the machine room, and the office where the varnishes and frames, the saw blades and the cakes of bone glue were kept, left the yard, also locked the door to the yard; and no sooner had he locked up than it grew darker and darker. It grew so dark that I, looking out between the curtains of our kitchen window, could no longer distinguish the tar paper of the dog kennel from the ordinarily lighter front wall of the lumber shed.

On the second dog-kennel day,

a Tuesday, Harras no longer had to tug when August Pokriefke wanted to renew the shavings. Tulla began to take food, that is, she ate with Harras out of his dish, after Harras had dragged a boneless chunk of dog meat into the kennel and whetted her appetite by nuzzling the meat with his cold nose.

Now this dog meat really wasn't bad. Usually it was stringy cow meat and was cooked in large quantities on our kitchen stove, always in the same rust-brown enamel pot. We had all of us, Tulla and her brothers and myself as well, eaten this meat in our bare hands, without bread to push it down. It tasted best when cold and hard. We cut it into cubes with our pocketknives. It was cooked twice a week and was compact, gray-brown, traversed by pale-blue little veins, sinews, and sweating strips of fat. It smelled sweetish soapy forbidden. Long after gulping down the marbled cubes of meat—often while playing we had both pockets full of them —our palates were still deadened and tallowy. We even spoke differently when we had eaten of those meat cubes: our speech became palatal metamorphosed four-legged: we barked at each other. We preferred this dish to many that were served at the family board. We called it dog meat. When it wasn't cow meat, it was never anything worse than horse meat or the mutton from a forced slaughtering. My mother threw coarse-grained salt—a handful—into the enamel pot, piled up the foot-long tatters of meat in the boiling salt water, let the water boil up again for a moment, put in marjoram, because marjoram is supposed to be good for a dog's sense of smell, turned the gas down, covered the pot, and didn't touch it for a whole hour; for that was the time required by cow-horse-sheep meat to turn into the dog meat which Harras and we ate and which, thanks to the marjoram cooked with it, provided us all, Harras and the rest of us, with sensitive olfactories. It was a Koshnavian recipe. Between Osterwick and Schlangenthin they said: Marjoram is good for your looks. Marjoram makes money go further. Against Devil and hell strew marjoram over the threshold. The squat long-haired Koshnavian sheep dogs were celebrated for their marjoram-favored keenness of smell.

Rarely, when there was no meat displayed on the low-price counter, the pot was filled with innards: knotted fatty beef hearts, pissy, because unsoaked, pig's kidneys, also small lamb kidneys which my mother had to detach from a finger-thick coat of fat lined with crackling parchment: the kidneys went into the dog pot, the suet was rendered in a cast-iron frying pan and used in the family cooking, because mutton suet wards off tuberculosis. Sometimes, too, a piece of dark spleen, halfway between purple and violet, went into the pot, or a chunk of sinewy beef liver. But because lung took longer to cook, required a larger cooking pot, and when you come right down to it doesn't yield much meat, it almost never went into the enamel pot, in actual fact only during the occasional summer meat shortages brought on by the cattle plague that sometimes came to Kashubia as well as Koshnavia. We never ate the boiled innards. Only Tulla, unbeknownst to the grownups, but before our eyes as we looked on with a tightening of the throat, took long avid gulps of the brownish-gray broth in which the coagulated excretion of the kidneys floated sleetlike and mingled with blackish marjoram to form islands.

On the fourth dog-kennel day

—on the advice of the neighbors and of the doctor who came in when there was an accident in the shop, Tulla was given her way—I brought her—no one was up yet, even the machinist, who was always first at work, hadn't arrived yet—a bowlful of heart, kidney, spleen, and liver broth. The broth in the bowl was cold, for Tulla preferred to drink her broth cold. A layer of fat, a mixture of beef tallow and mutton tallow, covered the bowl like an icecap. The cloudy liquid emerged only at the edges, and drops of it rolled over the layer of tallow. I tiptoed cautiously in my pajamas. I had taken the key to the yard from the big key rack without jangling the other keys. Very early and very late all staircases creak. On the flat roof of the woodshed the sparrows were starting up. In the kennel no sign of life. But varicolored flies on tar paper already touched by slanting sun. I ventured as far as the semicircular earthworks and foot-deep ditch which marked the range of the dog's chain. Inside the kennel: peace, darkness, and not a single varicolored fly. Then there awakened in the darkness: Tulla's hair mixed with shavings. Harras held his head on his paws. Lips pressed tight. Ears scarcely playing, but playing. Several times I called, but there was sleep in my throat and I didn't do very well, swallowed, and called louder: "Tulla!" I also stated my name: "It's Harry and I've brought you something." I tried to lure her with the broth in the bowl, attempted lip-smacking sounds, whistled softly and hissingly, as though trying to lure not Tulla but Harras to the edge of the semicircle.

When there was no life or sign of life but flies, a little oblique sun, and sparrow chatter, at the most dog ears—and once Harras yawned at length but kept his eyes shut—I set down the bowl at the edge of the semicircle, or more precisely, in the ditch dug by the dog's forepaws, left it, and without turning went back into the house. Behind my back: sparrows, varicolored flies, climbing sun, and the kennel.

The machinist was just pushing his bicycle through the passage. He asked, but I didn't answer. In our apartment the windows were still shuttered. My father's sleep was peaceful, confident in the alarm clock. I pushed a stool up to the kitchen window, grabbed a big chunk of dry bread and the pot of plum butter, pushed the curtains to left and right, dipped the bread into the plum butter, and was already gnawing and tugging when Tulla crawled out of the kennel. Even when Tulla had the threshold of the kennel behind her, she stayed on all fours, shook herself limply, shed wood shavings, crawled sluggish and wobbly toward the semicircle described by the dog's chain, reached ditch and earthworks right next to the door to plywood shed, hove to with a sharp twist of the hips, shook off more shavings— her light blue cotton dress was gradually developing blue and white checks—yawned in the direction of the yard— there in the shade, only his cap struck by the oblique rays

of the sun, stood the machinist beside his bicycle, rolling
himself a cigarette and looking toward the kennel; while I
with bread and plum butter looked down on Tulla, ignored
the kennel, and aimed only at her, her and her back. And
Tulla with sluggish sleepy movements crawled along the
semicircle, letting her head and matted hair hang down, and
stopped only, but still behind lowered head, when she
reached the glazed brown earthenware bowl, whose contents
were covered by an unbroken layer of tallow.

As long as I upstairs forgot to chew, as long as the machinist, whose cap was growing more and more into the sun,
used both hands to light his conical handmade cigarette—
three times his lighter failed to light—Tulla held her face
rigid against the sand, then turned slowly but again from
the hips, without raising her head with its hair and shavings.
When her face was over the bowl and would have been mirrored if the layer of tallow had been a round pocket mirror,
all movement was suspended. And I too, up above, was still
not chewing. Almost imperceptibly Tulla's weight was shifted from two supporting arms to her left supporting arm,
until seen from the kitchen window her left open palm disappeared under her body. And then, though I couldn't see
her free arm coming, she had her right hand on the basin,
while I dipped my chunk of bread in the plum butter.

The machinist smoked rhythmically and let his cigarette
cling to his lower lip as he blew out smoke till the still-
horizontal sun struck it. Strained with propping, Tulla's left
shoulder blade stretched the blue-and-white gingham of her
dress. Harras, head on paws, raised his eyelids one more
slowly than the other and looked toward Tulla: she extended the little finger of her right hand; he slowly and successively lowered his lids. Now, because the sun disclosed
the dog's ears, flies flared up and were extinguished in the
kennel.

While the sun climbed and a cock crowed nearby—there
were roosters in the neighborhood—Tulla stuck the extended
little finger of her right hand vertically into the middle of
the layer of tallow, and began cautiously but tenaciously to
bore a hole in the tallow. I put the bread aside. The machinist shifted to the other leg and let his face slip out of the
sunlight. That was something I wanted to see, how Tulla's
little finger would bore through the layer of tallow, penetrate
to the broth, and break open the layer several times more;

but I didn't see how Tulla's little finger reached into the broth, and the layer of tallow didn't break into floes, but was picked up from the basin, round and in one piece, by Tulla's little finger. High over shoulder, hair, and shavings she raises the disk the size of a beer mug mat into the early seven-o'clock sky, offers a glimpse of her screwed-up face, and then hurls the disk with a snap of her wrist into the yard, in the direction of the machinist: in the sand it broke forever, the shards rolled in the sand; and a few fragments of tallow, transformed into tallowy balls of sand, grew after the manner of snowballs and rolled down close to the smoking machinist and his bicycle with its new bell.

As I then looked back from the shattered disk of tallow to Tulla, she was kneeling bony and steep, but still cool, under the sun. She spreads the fingers of her left, overstrained hand five times sideways, folds them over three joints and then back over the same joints. Cupping the bowl in her right hand, which rests on the ground, she slowly guides her mouth and the edge of the bowl together. She laps, sips, wastes nothing. In one breath, without removing the bowl from her lips, Tulla drinks the fatless spleen-heart-kidney-liver broth with all its granular delicacies and surprises, with the tiny bits of cartilage at the bottom, with Koshnavian marjoram and coagulated urea. Tulla drinks to the dregs: her chin raises the bowl. The bowl raises the hand beneath the bowl into the beam of the oblique sun. A neck is exposed and grows steadily longer. A head with hair and shavings leans back and beds itself on shoulders. Two narrow-set eyes remain closed. Skinny, sinewy, and pale, Tulla's childlike neck labors until the bowl lies on top of her face and she is able to lift her hand from the bowl and move it away between the bottom of the bowl and the side-slipping sun. The overturned bowl conceals the screwed-up eyes, the crusty nostrils, the mouth that has had enough.

I think I was happy in my pajamas behind our kitchen window. Plum butter had set my teeth on edge. In my parents' bedroom the alarm clock put an end to my father's slumbers. Down below the machinist was obliged to light up again. Harras raised eyelids. Tulla let the bowl tip off her face. The bowl fell in the sand. It did not break. Tulla fell slowly onto both palms. A few shavings, which the lathe may have spat out, crumbled off her. She executed a ninety-degree turn from the hip, crawled slow sated sluggish first into the oblique sun, then carried sun along with her on her back to the kennel door, pivoted outside the hole, and pushed herself backwards, with hanging head and hair, charged with horizontal sun that made both hair and shavings shimmer, across the threshold into the kennel.

Then Harras closed his eyes again. Varicolored flies returned. My edgy teeth. Beyond his collar his black neck which no illumination could make lighter. My father's getting-up sounds. Sparrows strewn around the empty bowl. A patch of material: blue-and-white checks. Wisps of hair, shimmering light, shavings, paws, flies, ears, sleep, morning sun: tar paper grew soft and smelled.

Dreesen the machinist pushed his bicycle toward the half-glass door to the machine shop. Slowly and in step he shook his head from left to right and right to left. In the machine shop the buzz saw, the band saw, the lathe, the finishing machine, and the planing machine were still cold but hungry. My father coughed solemnly in the toilet. I slipped down off the kitchen stool.

Toward evening of the fifth dog-kennel day,
   a Friday, the carpenter tried to reason with Tulla. His fifteen-pfennig cigar formed a right angle to his well-cut face and made his paunch—he was standing in side view— look less protuberant. The imposing-looking man spoke sensibly. Kindness as bait. Then he spoke more forcefully, let the ash break prematurely from his teetering cigar, and took on a more protuberant paunch. Prospect of punishment held out. When he crossed the semicircle, whose radius was measured by the dog's chain, Harras, accompanied by wood shavings, stormed out of the kennel and hurled his blackness and both forepaws against the carpenter's chest. My father staggered back and went red and blue in the face, his cigar still clung to his lips, though the angle had lost its precision. He seized a roofing lath from one of the piles propped up on sawhorses, but did not strike out at Harras, who tense and unbarking was testing the strength of his chain. Arm and lath were lowered, and it was not until half an hour later that he thrashed the apprentice Hotten Scherwinski with his bare hands, because according to the machinest, Hotten Scherwinski had neglected to clean and oil the lathe, and moreover, the apprentice had allegedly

made off with some door mountings and a couple of pounds of one-inch nails.

Tulla's next dog-kennel day,
the sixth, was a Saturday. August Pokriefke in wooden shoes moved the sawhorses out of the way, cleaned up Harras' droppings, swept and raked the yard, grooving the sand with patterns that were not even ugly, but more on the strong, simple side. Desperately and over and over again, while the sand grew steadily darker and wetter, he raked in the vicinity of the dangerous semicircle. Tulla was not to be seen. She peed, when she had to pee—and Tulla had to make water regularly every hour—in shavings which August Pokriefke had to change in the evening. But on the evening of the sixth dog-kennel day he did not dare to renew the couch of shavings. As soon as he took venturesome steps with clumsy wooden shoes, with shovel and broom, with his basket of curly shavings from the lathe and finishing machine, and thrust himself and his evening chore across the clawed-up ditch of the semicircle, mumbling "good boy, good boy, be a good boy," the kennel emitted a growling which was not exactly malignant but more in the nature of a warning.

On Saturday the shavings in the kennel were not renewed; and August Pokriefke did not let the dog Harras off the chain. With watchdog fierce but chained the shop lay unguarded beneath a thin moon. But no burglars called.

Sunday,
Tulla's seventh dog-kennel day brought Erna Pokriefke into the picture. In the early afternoon she came out, drawing behind her on the left a chair, whose fourth leg cut a sharp track across the patterns of her yard-raking husband. On the right she carried the dog's dish full of knotty beef kidney and halved lamb's hearts: all the heart chambers lay wide open, revealing their tubes, ligaments, sinews, and smooth inner walls. Near the door of the plywood shed she put down the dish full of innards. A respectful step back from the center of the semicircle, directly across from the kennel door, she set up the chair, and finally sat huddled and askew in her black Sunday dress, with her rat's eyes and her bobbed hair that seemed more chewed than cut. She pulled her

knitting out of her front-buttoned taffeta and knitted in the direction of kennel, Harras, and daughter Tulla.

We, that is, the carpenter, my mother, August Pokriefke, as well as his sons Alexander and Siegesmund, spent the whole afternoon standing at the kitchen window, looking, bunched together or singly, out into the yard. At the windows of the other apartments on the court stood and sat neighbors and their children; or else a spinster, such as Fräulein Dobslaff, stood at the window of her ground-floor apartment, looking out into the yard.

I declined to be relieved and stood steadfast the whole time. No game of Monopoly and no Sunday crumb cake could lure me away. It was a balmy August day and on the following day school was to begin. At Erna Pokriefke's request we had had to close the lower double windows. The square upper windows, also double, were open a crack, admitting air, flies, and the crowing of the neighborhood cocks to our kitchen. Sounds came and went, including the trumpet notes emitted by a man who Sunday after Sunday practiced the trumpet in the attic of a house on Labesweg. But all the while a breathless whispering, babbling, chattering, burbling, and twanging: the penetrating nasal clamor of Koshnavian alders in the sandy wind, quantities of lace, a rosary, beads, crumpled paper smoothing out of its own accord, the mouse is cleaning house, straw grows to bundles: not only did Mother Pokriefke knit in the direction of the dog kennel, she whispered, murmured, muttered, smacked her lips, chirped, and whistled luringly in the same direction. I saw her lips in profile, her twitching, grinding, hammering chin, receding and darting forward, her seventeen fingers and four dancing needles, under which something light blue grew in her taffeta lap, something intended for Tulla, and later Tulla actually wore it.

The dog kennel with its inhabitants gave no sign. At the beginning of the knitting and while a lament refused to die down, Harras had come out of the kennel lazily and unseeing. After yawning with cracking jaws and after stretching exercises, he had found his way to his dish, on his way going into a convulsive crouch to expel his knotty sausage and also lifting a leg. He moved the dish over in front of the kennel, where jerkily, with dancing hocks, he bolted the beef kidney and the lamb's hearts with all their wide-open chambers, but covered the kennel door with his bulk, making it impossible to tell whether Tulla like himself was eating of the kidney and the hearts.

Toward evening Erna Pokriefke went back into the house with an almost finished light-blue knitted jacket. She said nothing. We were afraid to ask questions. The Monopoly game had to be put away. There was crumb cake left over. After supper my father pulled himself up to his full height, stared grimly at the oil painting of the Kurish elk, and said that this had been going on too long and something had to be done.

On Monday morning:

the carpenter made ready to go to the police; Erna Pokriefke, her legs firmly planted in our kitchen, reviled him in an amplified voice, calling him a no-good dumbhead; I alone, already harnessed with my school satchel, looking out the kitchen window. And then Tulla tottering, bony, followed by Harras with hanging head, left the kennel. At first she crawled on all fours, then stood up like a normal human and, without interference from Harras, crossed the semicircle with fragile steps. On two legs, grimy, gray, licked shiny in places by a long dog's tongue, she found the yard door.

Harras howled after her only once, but his howl cut through the screaming of the buzz saw.

While for Tulla and me,

for Jenny and all the other schoolchildren school began again, Harras resumed his dog's life, a varied routine which was not even interrupted by the arrival, exactly three weeks later, of the news that the stud dog Harras had once again earned twenty-five gulden for my father. Brief as it had been, his visit to the kennels of the Langfuhr-Hochstriess police barracks had produced the desired effect. After an appropriate lapse of time we were informed by a card specially printed for the correspondence of the police kennels that the shepherd dam Thekla of Schüddelkau, breeder: Albrecht Leeb, registration no. 4356, had whelped five puppies. And then, several months later, after the Sundays of Advent, after Christmas, after New Year's, after snow, thaw, more snow, long-lasting snow, after the beginning of spring and the distribution of Easter report cards—everybody was promoted—after a period in which nothing happened—unless I should mention the accident in the machine shop: the apprentice Hotten Scherwinski lost the middle finger and index finger of his left hand to the buzz saw—came the registered letter announcing, over the signature of Gauleiter Forster, that the shepherd puppy Prinz of the litter Falko, Kastor, Bodo, Mira, Prinz—out of Thekla of Schüddelkau, breeder A. Leeb, Danzig-Ohra, by Harras of Queen Louise's mill, breeder and owner Friedrich Liebenau, master carpenter in Danzig-Langfuhr, had been purchased from the police kennels in Langfuhr-Hochstriess and that it had been decided in the name of the Party and the German population of the German city of Danzig, to present the shepherd Prinz to the Führer and Chancellor through a delegation on the occasion of his forty-sixth birthday. The Führer and Chancellor, so the communication went on, had graciously accepted the gift of the Gau of Danzig and declared his intention of keeping the shepherd Prinz along with his other dogs.

Enclosed in the registered letter was a postcard-size photograph of the Führer, signed by his own hand. In the picture he wore the costume of an Upper Bavarian villager, except that the jacket was more fashionably cut. At his feet, with his tongue hanging out, a gray-clouded shepherd dog with light, probably yellow markings on his chest and over his stop. Mountains towered in the distance. The Führer was laughing in the direction of someone who was not in the picture.

Letter and picture of the Führer—both were immediately placed under glass and framed in our own shop—went on long excursions in the neighborhood. As a result, first my father, then August Pokriefke, and finally quite a few of the neighbors joined the Party, while Gustav Mielawske—for over fifteen years a journeyman in our shop and a quiet Social Democrat—gave notice and did not return to his bench until two months later, after a good deal of coaxing by the master carpenter.

Tulla received a new school satchel from my father. I was given a complete Hitler Cub uniform. Harras was presented with a new collar, but couldn't be given better care because he was well taken care of as it was.

Dear Tulla,

did our dog Harras' sudden career have consequences for us? To me Harras brought schoolboy fame. I had to step up to the blackboard and tell the class all about it. Of course

I was not allowed to speak about breeding and mating, about the stud certificate and the stud money, about Harras' prowess at stud as noted in the stud-book, or about the heat of the bitch Thekla. I was obliged and permitted to babble in baby talk about Papa Harras and Mama Thekla, about their babies Falko, Kastor, Bodo, Mira, and Prinz. Fräulein Spollenhauer wanted to know all about it: "Why did the Herr Gauleiter make our Führer a present of the little dog Prinz?"

"Because it was the Führer's birthday and he'd always wanted a little dog from our city."

"And why is the little dog Prinz so happy on the Obersalzberg that he isn't the least bit homesick for his mama?"

"Because our Führer loves dogs and is always kind to dogs."

"And why should we be glad that Prinz is with the Führer?"

"Because Harry Liebenau is a member of our class."

"Because Harras belongs to his father."

"Because Harras is the little dog Prinz's father."

"And because it is a great honor for our class and our school and our beautiful city."

Were you there, Tulla,

when Fräulein Spollenhauer with me and the whole class paid a visit to our carpenter shop? You were not there, you were in school.

The class stood in a semicircle around the semicircle that Harras had described around his domain. Once again I had to repeat my lecture, then Fräulein Spollenhauer asked my father to say a few words to the children. Assuming that the class had been apprised of the dog's political career, the carpenter obliged with a few sidelights on our Harras' pedigree. He spoke of a she-dog named Senta and of a male by the name of Pluto, both of them just as black as Harras or little Prinz for that matter. They had been Harras' parents. The she-dog Senta had belonged to a miller in Nickelswalde in the Vistula estuary—"Have you ever been in Nickelswalde, children? I went there years ago on the narrow-gauge railway, and the mill there is a place of historical importance, because Queen Louise of Prussia spent the night there when she was fleeing before the French." Under the jack of the mill, said the carpenter, he had found six whelps—"That's what they call dog babies"—and he had bought one baby dog from the miller. "That was our Harras, who has always been such a joy to us, especially lately."

Where were you, Tulla,

when I, under the machinist's supervision, was allowed to show our class through the machine shop? You were in school, unable to see or hear me naming all the machines to my classmates and Fräulein Spollenhauer: The lathe. The finishing machine. The band saw. The planing machine. The buzz saw.

Then Herr Dreesen explained the different kinds of wood to the children. He drew a distinction between cross-grained wood and long-grained, knocked on elm, pine, pear wood, oak, maple, beech, and soft linden wood, chatted about rare woods and the annual rings in trees.

Then we had to stand out in the yard and sing a song that Harras didn't want to listen to.

Where was Tulla

when Hauptbannführer Göpfert accompanied by Jungbannführer Wendt and several lesser leaders visited our shop? We were both in school and not present when the decision was made to name a newly formed squad of Cubs after our Harras.

And Tulla and Harry were absent

when after the Röhm putsch and the death of the old gentleman at Neudeck a get-together was arranged on the Obersalzberg behind bright rustic cotton curtains in a low-ceilinged imitation of a peasants' living room; but Frau Raubal, Rudolf Hess, Herr Hanfstaengl, Danzig SA leader Linsmayer, Rauschning, Forster, August Wilhelm of Prussia, called "Auwi" for short, Beanpole Brückner, and Reich Peasant Leader Darré listened to the Führer—and Prinz was there. Prinz out of our Harras, whom Senta had whelped, and Perkun sired Senta.

They ate apple tart that Frau Raubal had baked and spoke of branch and root, of Strasser, Schleicher, Röhm, root and branch. Then they discussed Spengler, Gobineau, and the Protocols of the Elders of Zion. Then Hermann Rauschning mistakenly called Prinz the shepherd pup a "magnificent black wolfhound." Later on all the historians unthinkingly followed him. Yet every cynologist will agree with me that the only real wolfhound is the Irish wolfhound, which differs significantly from the German shepherd. With his long fine-drawn head he is related to the degenerate greyhound. He measures thirty-two inches at the withers or seven inches more than our Harras. The Irish wolfhound has long hair. And small, soft ears which do not stand erect but topple. A decorative luxury dog, which the Führer would never have had in his kennels; whereby it is proved for all time that Rauschning was mistaken: no Irish wolfhound weaved nervously around the legs of the cake-eating company; Prinz, our Prinz, listened to conversations and worried about his master with canine fidelity. For the Führer feared for his life. Artful plots might well have been baked into every piece of cake. Fearfully he drank his soda water and often had to vomit for no reason.

But Tulla was present

when the newspapermen and photographers came. Not only did the *Vorposten* and the *Neueste Nachrichten* send their reporters. Gentlemen as well as ladies in sports clothes came from Elbing, Königsberg, Schneidemühl, Stettin, and even from the national capital. Only Brost, editor of the *Volksstimme,* soon to be suppressed, refused to interview our Harras. Instead, he commented on the hubbub in the newspapers under the title: "Gone to the Dogs." On the other hand, denominational newspapers and specialized journals sent reporters. The organ of the German Shepherd Dog Association sent a cynologist, whom my father was obliged to turn out of the house. For this dog expert began at once to carp at our Harras' pedigree. The names, he declared, were revolting and alien to the breed; there were no data about the bitch that had whelped Senta; the animal itself was not bad, but it would be his duty to inveigh against such methods of dog raising; precisely because this was a historical dog, a sense of responsibility was in order.

In a word, whether inveighingly or in terms of uncritical praise, Harras was described, printed, and photographed. The carpenter shop with machinist, journeymen, helpers, and apprentices also broke into print. Statements by my father, such as: "We are simple artisans with our noses to the grindstone, but all the same we are glad that our Harras . . ."— in brief, the unvarnished utterances of a carpenter were quoted verbatim, often as photograph captions.

My guess would be that eight solo pictures of Harras were printed in the papers. Three times, I'd say, he appeared with my father, once in a group picture with the entire personnel of the shop, never with me; but exactly twelve times Tulla found her way with our Harras into German-language and international newspapers: slender, on fragile pins, she held still beside our Harras.

Dear Cousin,

and yet you helped him when he moved in. You carried his music, pile after pile, and the porcelain ballerina. For though fourteen tenants went on living in our apartment house, Fräulein Dobslaff moved out of the apartment on the ground floor left, whose windows could be opened on the court. With her remnants of dress material and her numbered photograph albums, with furniture from which wood meal trickled, she went to live with her sister in Schönwarling; and Herr Felsner-Imbs the piano teacher, with his piano and his yellowish stacks of music, his goldfish and his hourglass, his countless photographs of once famous artists, and his porcelain figurine in a porcelain tutu, immobilized on pointed porcelain slipper in a perfect arabesque, moved into the empty apartment, without changing the faded wallpaper in the living room or the large flower pattern that covered the walls of the bedroom. To make matters worse, the erstwhile Dobslaffian rooms were dark by nature, because, not seven paces from the windows of both rooms, the gable end of the carpenter shop with its outside staircase reached up to the second floor of the apartment house and cast shadow. And between apartment house and carpenter shop there were two lilac bushes, which did their duty spring after spring. With my father's permission Fräulein Dobslaff had had a garden fence put up around the two bushes, which did not prevent Harras from depositing his scent marks in her garden. Still, it was not because of the dog droppings or the darkness of the apartment that Fräulein Dobslaff moved, but because she wished to die in Schönwarling, where she had come from.

Felsner-Imbs had to burn electric light surrounded by a greenish glass-bead lamp shade when pupils called in the morning or afternoon while the sunshine was putting on an orgy outside. To the left of the house entrance he had had an enamel sign put up: Felix Felsner-Imbs—concert pianist and licensed piano teacher. The wobbly old gentleman had not been living in our house for two weeks when the first pupils came, bringing with them the price of a lesson and Damm's *Piano Method,* and were obliged by lamplight to pound out scales and études with right hand, with left hand, with both hands, and once again, until the big hour-glass on the piano harbored not a single grain of sand in its upper compartment, so demonstrating in its medieval way that the piano lesson was over.

Felsner-Imbs didn't wear a velvet tam. But flowing blowing hair, snow-white and powdered to boot, hung down over his Schiller collar. Between little boy's lesson and little girl's lesson he brushed his artist's mane. And when on the treeless Neuer Markt a gust of wind had ruffled his mane, he reached for the little brush in the ample pocket of his jacket and, while publicly dressing his astonishing hair, quickly acquired an audience: housewives, schoolchildren, ourselves. As he brushed his hair, an expression of unadulterated pride moved into his eyes. Light blue and lashless, they looked out upon concert halls in which an imaginary public refused to stop applauding him, Felsner-Imbs the concert pianist. Beneath the glass-bead lamp shade a greenish glow fell on the part in his hair: seated on a solidly built piano stool, an Oberon, masterful interpreter of the piano pieces drawn from the opera of that name, metamorphosed boy pupils and girl pupils into water sprites.

The pupils who sat facing the open *Piano Method* at Herr Felsner-Imbs' piano must have been keen of hearing, for from the omnipresent all-day arias of the buzz saw and the lathe, from the modulations of the finishing machine and planing machine, and the ingenuous singsong of the band saw, only a remarkable ear could have hoped to pluck, neatly and note by note, the scales that had to be pounded out beneath the lashless gaze of Felsner-Imbs. Because this concert of machines buried even a fortissimo run of the pupil's hand fathoms deep, the green drawing room behind the lilac bushes resembled an aquarium, silent but full of movement. The piano teacher's goldfish in its bowl on the little lacquered stand was not needed to confirm this impression; it was an accessory too many.

Felsner-Imbs attached particular importance to a correct position of the hands. With a little luck wrong notes could be submerged by the replete yet all-devouring soprano of the buzz saw, but if in playing an étude a pupil let the balls of his hands sink down upon the black wood of the altogether black piano in the course of an ascending or descending scale, if the backs of his hands departed from the desired horizontal position, no amount of carpenter's din could make this obvious lapse in technique unseen. Moreover Felsner-Imbs had made it a feature of his teaching method to lay a pencil across any pupil's hand condemned to execute scales. The hand that failed the test by slumping on the wood in quest of repose sent the control pencil hurtling downward.

Jenny Brunies, the schoolteacher's adoptive daughter from across the street, also had to ride a control pencil on her pudgy right and left hands for the duration of many scales; for, a month after the piano teacher moved in, she became one of his pupils.

You and I

watched Jenny from the little lilac garden. We pressed our faces flat against the windowpanes of the seaweed-green aquarium and saw her sitting on the piano stool; plump and doll-like in brown corduroy. An enormous pinwheel bow performed the function of a brimstone butterfly—in reality the bow was white—on her smoothly falling, approximately medium-brown hair, which was cut to shoulder length. Whereas other pupils frequently enough received a quick painful smack on the back of their hand with the previously fallen pencil, Jenny, although her pencil too fell occasionally on the polar bear skin under the piano stool, never had to fear the punishing blow; at the worst she came in for a look of concern from Felsner-Imbs.

Possibly Jenny was extremely musical—with the buzz saw and the lathe behind us, we, Tulla and I, outside the windowpanes, seldom heard the faintest note; besides, we were not equipped by nature to distinguish winged, accomplished scales from painfully climbed scales—in any case the pudgy little creature from across the street was permitted to ply the keys with both hands sooner than other pupils; moreover, the pencil toppled more and more infrequently and in the end the writing instrument and sword of Damocles was set aside altogether. Through the screaming and squeaking of the daily sawing, planing, and falsetto singing of the carpenter's opera, one could, by trying very hard, more surmise than hear the

thin melodies of Damm's *Piano Method:* "Winter Adieu"—
"A Hunter from the Palatinate"—"I graze by the Neckar,
I graze by the Rhine" ...

Tulla and I,
    we remember that Jenny was favored. Whereas the les-
sons of the other pupils sometimes came to an abrupt end
in the middle of "With Bow and Arrow," because the last
grain of sand in the medieval hourglass had said amen to
the piano, no hourglass hour struck for either teacher or
pupil when Jenny's doll flesh submitted to instruction on the
piano stool. And when plump Eddi Amsel got into the habit
of escorting plump Jenny Brunies to her piano lesson—
Amsel was Dr. Brunies' favorite student and came and went
as he pleased across the street—it was perfectly possible
that the next pupil would have to wait his turn for an hourglass quarter of an hour on the lumpy sofa in the dusky
background of the music room; for Eddi Amsel, who seems
to have taken piano lessons at the Conradinum, liked to sit
beside the green-maned Felsner-Imbs, playing "Prussia's
Glory," the "Finnish Cavalry March," and "Old Comrades"
with four-handed gusto.
    Amsel also sang. Not only in the high school chorus did
his high soprano triumph; Amsel also sang in St. Mary's
choir in the venerable Church of St. Mary, whose nave once
every month resounded full and round with Bach cantatas
and Mozart Masses. Eddi Amsel's high soprano was discovered when the choir decided to do Mozart's early work,
the *Missa Brevis.* Every school chorus in town was scoured
for a boy soprano. The esteemed conductor of St. Mary's
choir surged up to Amsel and assailed him with his enthusiasm: "Truly, my son, you will sing the *Benedictus* more
sweetly than Antonio Cesarelli, the celebrated eunuch, who
lent his voice when the Mass was first performed. I can hear
you rise to such heights of jubilation in the *Dona nobis* that
everyone will think: Verily, St. Mary's is too small for that
voice."
    The story is that although Mr. Lester still represented the
League of Nations in the Danzig Free State and all racial
laws were constrained to halt at the borders of the diminutive state, Amsel expressed misgivings: "But, sir, they say
I'm a half-Jew."
    The conductor's answer: "Nonsense, you're a soprano, I

expect you to introduce the *Kyrie*!" This succinct reply proved to be long-lived and is said to have been cited with respect many years later in conservative resistance circles.

In any case the chosen boy soprano practiced the difficult passages of the *Missa Brevis* in Felsner-Imbs' green music room. The two of us, Tulla and I, once heard his voice when buzz saw and lathe both had to catch their breath at once: He mined silver. Little knives ground thin as angel's breath quartered the air. Nails melted. Sparrows were ashamed. Apartment houses grew pious, for a corpulent angel sang *Dona nobis* over and over again.

Dear Cousin Tulla,

the only reason for this long and scaly introduction is that Eddi Amsel took to frequenting our apartment house. At first he came only with Jenny, then he brought his bullish friend. Walter Matern might have been regarded as our relation, because his father's shepherd bitch Senta had whelped our Harras. Often my father, as soon as he saw the boy, asked him questions about how the miller was getting along and the economic situation on Great Island. As a rule Eddi Amsel, who was well versed in economics, answered prolixly and with facts which made the employment-promoting plan of the Party and Senate seem unrealistic. He recommended closer relations with the sterling bloc, for want of which he predicted an appreciable devaluation of the gulden. Eddi Amsel even cited figures: the devaluation would have to come to roughly 42 per cent; goods imported from Poland could expect to cost 70 per cent more; even now the devaluation could be predicted for the first days in May; he had all these facts and figures from Matern's father, the miller, who always knew everything in advance. Needless to say, the miller's predictions were confirmed on May 2, 1935.

Amsel and his friend were then in first, working moderately toward their final exams. Both wore real suits with long pants, drank Aktien beer at the Sports Palace or on Zinglers Höhe, and Walter Matern, who smoked Regatta and Artus cigarettes, was said to have seduced a girl in second from the Helene Lange School in Oliva Forest the previous year. No one would have thought of imputing such achievements to the copious Eddi Amsel. Fellow students and girls who were occasionally invited to hear the school choir regarded him as something which they daringly designated as a eunuch. Others expressed themselves more cautiously, saying that Eddi was still rather infantile, more in the neuter gender. As far as I know from hearsay, Walter Matern long put up with this calumny in silence, until one day in the presence of several schoolboys and some girls who were more or less members of the group, he made a speech of some length showing his friend in his true light. Amsel, he said approximately, was far in advance of all the boys present as far as girls etcetera were concerned. He called quite regularly on the whores in Tischlergasse across the street from Adler's Beer Hall. But he did not limit his calls to the usual five minutes, he was a respected guest, because the girls regarded him as an artist. With India ink, brush and pen, at first with pencil as well, he had done a whole pile of portraits and nudes, which were not in the least obscene and not half bad as art. For with a portfolio full of such drawings Eddi Amsel had gone unannounced to see Pfuhle, the celebrated teacher and painter of horses, who taught the architects drawing at the Engineering School, and submitted his drawings. And Pfuhle, who was known as a hard man to approach, had recognized his talent and promised to help him.

After this speech, which I can repeat only in substance, Amsel, or so I heard, was almost exempted from teasing. On several occasions classmates came to see him and wanted to be taken along to Tischlergasse, a request which he, amiably and with Matern's support, turned down. One day, however, when Eddi Amsel—as I was later told—asked his friend to accompany him to Tischlergasse, he met with a rebuff. He, said Walter Matern with precocious assurance, had no wish to disappoint the poor girls. The professional aspect of the thing repelled him. He'd never be able to get a hard on. That would only make him behave like a brute, which in the end would be embarrassing for both parties. It had to be admitted that love was indispensable, or at least passion.

Amsel had no doubt listened to his friend's firm utterances with a shake of the head and, taking his portfolio and an attractive box of assorted candies, gone by himself to call on the girls across the street from Adler's Beer Hall. And yet— if I am correctly informed—he succeeded one wretched day in December in persuading his friend to celebrate the second or third Sunday of Advent with him and the girls. It was only on the fourth Sunday that Matern screwed up the courage. It turned out, however, that the professional aspect of the thing repelled him so attractively that despite his prognosis he did get a hard on, which he was able to lodge securely and discharge at student's prices with a girl of few words by the name of Elisabeth. Yet, I was told, the kindness that had been shown him did not prevent him on the way home, up Altstädtischer Graben and down Pfefferstadt, from grinding his teeth malignantly and lapsing into dark meditations about venal womanhood.

Dear Cousin,

with exactly the same chocolate-brown and egg-yellow tiger-striped portfolio that had made his visits to the ill-famed Tischlergasse into legitimate artistic excursions, Eddi Amsel, accompanied by Walter Matern, came to our apartment house. In Felsner-Imbs' music room we both saw him breathing sketches of the porcelain ballerina onto paper. And one brightly decked day in May I saw him step up to my father, point to his tiger-striped portfolio, and open the portfolio forthwith in an attempt to let his drawings speak for him. But my father, without further ado, gave him permission to draw our watchdog Harras. Only he advised him to station himself and his equipment outside the semi-circle which demonstrated with ditch and wall the range of the dog's chain. "The dog is ferocious and I'm sure he doesn't think much of artists," said my father.

From the very first day our Harras heeded Eddie Amsel's slightest word. Amsel made Harras into a canine model. Amsel did not, for instance, say "Sit, Harras!" as Tulla said "Harras, sit!" when Harras was supposed to sit down. From the very first day Amsel ignored the name Harras and said to our dog when he wanted a change of pose: "Now, Pluto, would you kindly first stand on all four legs, then raise the right foreleg and bend it slightly, but make it relaxed, a little more relaxed. And now would you be so kind as to turn your noble shepherd's head half left, like that, that's good, now, Pluto, if you please, stay that way."

And Harras hearkened to the name of Pluto as if he had always been a hound of hell. The ungainly Amsel almost burst his gray-checked sports suit. His head was covered by a white linen visor cap, that gave him somewhat the look of an English reporter. But his clothes were not new: everything Eddi Amsel wore on his body made an impression of secondhandness and was indeed secondhand; for the story

was that, although he received a fabulous allowance, he purchased only worn clothes, either from the pawnshop or from
the junkshops on Tagnetergasse. His shoes must have belonged
previously to a postman. He sat with broad posterior on a
preposterous little camp chair, which proved however to be
inexplicably stable. While on his left bulging thigh he supported the stiff cardboard to which his drawing paper was
clamped and with his right hand, with remarkable ease,
guided an always rich-black brush, which covered the drawing paper from the upper left to the lower right-hand corner
with daintily skimming sketches, some unsuccessful, others
excellent and strikingly fresh, of the watchdog Harras or
the hellhound Pluto, our yard became each day a little
more—and Eddi Amsel spent about six afternoons drawing
in our yard—the scene of various tensions.

There stood Walter Matern in the background. Disreputably
dressed; a costumed proletarian in a problem play, who has
learned social indictments by heart, who in the third act will
become an agitator and ringleader, and who nevertheless
fell a victim to our buzz saw. Like our Harras, who time and
time again, under certain weather conditions, accompanied
the song of the buzz saw—never that of the lathe—with a
rising and falling howl out of a vertically held head, so the
gloomy young man from Nickelswalde reacted directly to the
buzz saw. He did not, to be sure, move his head into a
vertical position, he did not stammer anarchist manifestoes,
but in his old familiar way underscored the sound of work
with a dry grinding of the teeth.

This grinding had its effect on Harras: it drew his lips
above his scissors bite. He drooled at the lips. The holes on
either side of his nose dilated. The bridge of his nose puckered up to the stop. The noted shepherd ears, erect but pointing slightly forward, became uncertain, tilted. Harras drew
in his tail, rounded his back from withers to crown to cring-
ing hump, in short he cringed like a dog. And several times
Eddi Amsel produced a painful likeness of these shameful
positions with dashing rich-black brush, with scratching
spread-foot pen, with gushing and gifted bamboo quill. Our
buzz saw, Walter Matern's grinding teeth, and our Harras,
whom the buzz saw and the grinding teeth turned into a
mongrel, played into the artist's hand of Eddi Amsel; taken
together, the buzz saw, Matern, the dog, and Amsel formed
as productive a work team as Herr Brauxel's authors'

consortium: he, I, and yet another are writing simultaneously and are supposed to be finished when the applesauce with the stars begins on the fourth of February.

But my cousin Tulla,
who stood by, more furious from day to day, refused to stand aside any longer. Amsel's power over Pluto the hellhound became for her a loss of power over our Harras. Not that the dog stopped obeying her—just as before he sat when Tulla said "Harras, sit!"—but he carried out her commands, which she snapped out more and more sternly, in a manner so absent and mechanical that neither could Tulla conceal it from herself nor I from myself and Tulla that this Amsel was ruining our dog.

Tulla,
blind with rage, started out by throwing pebbles, and several times hit Amsel's round back and the blubbery back of his head. He, however, gave it to be understood by a graceful shrug of the shoulders and a lazy turn of the head that though aware of the blow, he did not acknowledge it.

Tulla,
with tiny white face, tipped over his bottle of India ink. A black puddle with a metallic sheen stood on the sand in our yard and took a long time to seep away. Amsel took a fresh bottle of India ink from his coat pocket and nonchalantly showed that he had a third bottle in reserve.

When Tulla,
storming up from behind, threw a handful of sawdust that settled in the drive belt casing of the buzz saw at an almost finished, still damp and freshly glistening picture, Eddi Amsel, only briefly astonished, gave a partly annoyed, partly good-natured laugh, sedately shook a sausagelike forefinger at Tulla, who watched the effect of her performance from a distance, and then began, more and more interested in the new technique, to work the sawdust clinging to the paper and to give the drawing what is nowadays known as structure. He developed the amusing but short-lived method of making capital of chance. Reaching into the drive belt casing of the buzz saw, he made a mixture in his handkerchief of sawdust, of the knotty shavings from the lathe, the

short curls of the power plane, the fine-grained droppings of the band saw, and with his own hand and no need of an assault from Tulla gave his brush drawings a pimply relief, the charm of which was further enhanced when a part of the superficially blackened wood particles fell off, revealing the white paper ground in mysterious islands. Once —probably dissatisfied with his overly conscious strewings and sawdust groundings—he asked Tulla to storm up from behind and to fling sawdust, shavings, or even sand as though at random. He expected a good deal from Tulla's collaboration; but Tulla declined and made "bashed-in windows."

My cousin Tulla was unable to get the better of Eddi Amsel, artist and dog tamer. It took August Pokriefke to trip him up. Several times, laden with sawhorses, he stood beside the artist, accompanied words of criticism or praise with crackling glue fingers, spoke in elaborate detail about a painter who had used to come to Koshnavia summer after summer and had painted Osterwick Lake, the church at Schlangenthin, made oil portraits of a few Koshnavian types, such as Joseph Butt from Annafeld, Musolf the tailor from Damerau, and the widow Wanda Jentak. He too had been painted while cutting peat and then been exhibited in Konitz as a peat cutter. Eddi Amsel expressed interest in his colleague but did not interrupt his deft sketching. August Pokriefke left Koshnavia and began to speak about our watchdog's political career. He explained in great detail how the Führer on the Obersalzberg had come by the shepherd Prinz. He told about the signed photograph that hung in our parlor over a pear-wood miniature and figured up how often his daughter Tulla had been snapshot and printed in the papers with or in between long articles about Harras. Amsel voiced gratification at Tulla's early triumphs and began to sketch a seated Harras or Pluto. August Pokriefke expressed the opinion that the Führer would set everything to rights, you could bank on that, he knew more than all the rest of them lumped together, and he could draw too. What was more, the Führer wasn't one of those people who always want to act big. "When the Führer rides in a car, he sits next to the driver and not in back like a bigshot." Amsel found words of praise for the Führer's homespun modesty and made the hellhound's ears stand exaggeratedly erect on his paper. August

Pokriefke asked whether Amsel was still in the Hitler Youth or already a Party member; for he, Amsel—that was his name, wasn't it?—must be in the movement somewhere.

At this point Amsel slowly let his hand and brush drop, glanced once again with tilted head at the drawing of the seated Harras or Pluto, then turned his full, shining, and freckle-strewn face toward the inquirer, and answered with alacrity that, he was sorry to say, he was a member of neither nor, that this was the first time he had heard of the man—what was his name again?—but that he would be glad to inquire who the gentleman was, where he came from, and what plans he had for the future.

Tulla

made Eddi Amsel pay for his ignorance the following afternoon. No sooner was he seated on his stable camp chair, no sooner was he holding cardboard and drawing paper on his bursting left thigh, no sooner had Harras as Pluto taken up his new pose, lying with outstretched forepaws and sharply alert neck, no sooner had Amsel's brush steeped itself in India ink, than the door to the yard spat out first August Pokriefke, the glue cook, then the glue stirrer's daughter.

He stands with Tulla in the doorway, whispers, casts side-long glances at the heavily laden camp chair, vaccinates his daughter with orders: and there she comes, first lazily and by sauntering detours, holding thin arms interlocked across the back of her dirndl dress, flings bare legs aimlessly, then describes quick, narrowing semicircles around the brush-guiding Eddi Amsel, is now to the left, now to the right of him: "Hey!" and then from the left: "Hey, you!" again from the left: "What are you doing around here anyway?" Spoken from the left: "I'm asking you what you're doing around here" and from the right: "You got no business here!" Spoken from the left: " 'Cause you're . . ." and from close up on the right: "Do you know what you are?" Then from the left into his ear: "Want me to tell you?" Now, threaded into the right ear: "You're a sheeny. A sheeny. That's right, a sheeny. Or if you're not a sheeny, what do you come around here for drawing pictures of our dog if you're not a sheeny?" Amsel's brush stops. Tulla at a distance but inexorably: "Sheeny." Eddi Amsel with rigid brush. Tulla: "Sheeny." The word flung into the yard, first only for Amsel, then loud enough to make Matern withdraw his ear from the buzz saw that is just starting up. He reaches out for the thing that's screaming sheeny. Matern fails to catch Tulla: "Sheeny!" The cardboard with the first still moist India ink entries has fallen, sketch down, into the sand. "Sheeny!" Upstairs, on the fourth, fifth, then the second floor, windows are thrust open: Housewives cool their faces. From Tulla's mouth: "Sheeny!" Above the sound of the buzz saw. Matern grabs but misses. Tulla's tongue. Swift legs. Amsel stands beside the camp chair. The word. Matern picks up cardboard and drawing. Tulla bounces up and down on planks laid over sawhorses: "Sheeny, sheeny!" Matern screws the top on the India ink bottle. Tulla bounces off the plank—"Sheeny!"—rolls in the sand: "Sheeny!" Now all windows occupied and carpenters at the windows on the second floor. The word, three times in succession the word. Amsel's face, overheated while he was sketching, cools off. A smile refuses to fade. Sweat, but now cold and clammy, runs over fat and freckles. Matern lays his hand on Amsel's shoulder. Freckles turn gray. The word. Always the same one word. Matern's hand is heavy. Now from the stairs leading to the second floor. Tulla giddily jumping about: "Sheenysheenysheeny!" On his right Matern leads Amsel by the arm. Eddi Amsel is trembling. To the left, Matern, already charged with the portfolio, picks up the camp chair. Released from constraint, Harras relinquishes his pose. He sniffs, understands. Already his chain is taut: The dog's voice. Tulla's voice. The buzz saw bites into a sixteen-foot plank. The finishing machine is still silent. Now it too. Now the lathe. Long twenty-seven steps to the yard door. Harras tries to move the lumber shed to which he is chained. Tulla, dancing wildly, over and over again the word. And by the yard door, where August Pokriefke with crackling fingers stands in wooden shoes, the smell of glue battles with the smell from the little garden outside the piano teacher's windows: the scent of lilacs strikes and wins. It's the month of May after all. The word stops coming but it's still in the air. August Pokriefke wants to spit out what he's been storing up in the hollow of his mouth for some minutes. But he doesn't spit, because Matern is looking at him with clamoring teeth.

Dear Cousin Tulla,

I skip: Eddi Amsel and Walter Matern were turned out of our yard. Nothing was done to you. Because Amsel had spoiled Harras, Harras was sent to the trainer's twice a week. You like me had to learn reading, writing, and 'rithmetic. Amsel and Matern had their oral and written examinations behind them. Harras was trained to bark at strangers and to refuse food from strange hands; but Amsel had already spoiled him too radically. You had trouble with writing, I with arithmetic. We both liked school. Amsel and his friend passed their examinations—the former with distinction, the latter with a certain amount of luck. Turning point. Life began or was supposed to begin: After the devaluation of the gulden the economic situation improved slightly. Orders came in. My father was able to rehire a journeyman whom he had discharged four weeks before devaluation. After their final exams Eddi Amsel and Walter Matern began to play faustball.

Dear Tulla,

faustball is a ball game played by two teams of five in two adjacent fields with a ball that is roughly the size of a football but somewhat lighter. Like schlagball it is a German game, even though Plautus in the third century B.C. mentions a *follis pugilatorius*. In corroboration of the strictly German character of the game—for Plautus was assuredly speaking of faustball-playing Germanic slaves—it is worth recalling that during the First World War fifty teams were engaged in playing faustball in the Vladivostok PW camp; in the PW camp at Oswestry—England—more than seventy teams participated in faustball tournaments which were lost or won without bloodshed.

The game does not involve too much running and can consequently be played by sexagenarians and even by excessively corpulent men and women: Amsel became a faustball player. Who would have thought it? That soft little fist, that fistling, good for concealing a private laugh, that fist that never pounded a table. At the most he could have weighed down letters with his fistling, prevented them from flying away. It was no fist at all, more like a meat ball, two little meat balls, two rosy pompons swinging from abbreviated arms. Not a worker's fist, not a proletarian's fist, not a Red Front salute, for the air was harder than his fist. Little fists for guessing: which one? The law of the fist pronounced him guilty; fist fights made him into a punching bag; and only in the game of faustball did Amsel's fistling triumph; for that reason it will be related here, in chronological order, how Eddi Amsel became a player of faustball, in other words, an athlete who with closed fists—to stick out the thumb was forbidden—punched the faustball from below, from above, from the side.

Tulla and I had been promoted;

a well-earned vacation took Amsel and his friend to the Vistula estuary. The fishermen looked on as Amsel brushed in fishing boats and nets. The ferryman looked over Eddi Amsel's shoulder as he sketched the steam ferry. He visited the Materns on the other side, exchanged oracles about the future with miller Matern and sketched the Matern postmill from all sides. Eddi Amsel also attempted a chat with the village schoolteacher; but the village schoolteacher was said to have snubbed his former pupil. I wonder why. Similarly a Schiewenhorst village beauty seems to have given Amsel a saucy rebuff when he wished to draw her picture on the beach with the wind in her hair and her dress on the beach in the wind. Nevertheless Amsel filled his portfolio and went back to the city with a full portfolio. He had, to be sure, promised his mother to study something serious—engineering—but for the present he frequented Professor Pfuhle, the painter of horses, and like Walter Matern, who was supposed to study economics but much preferred to declaim into the wind in the role of Franz or Karl Moor, couldn't make up his mind to embark on his studies.

Then a telegram came: his mother called him back to Schiewenhorst to her deathbed. The cause of her death seems to have been diabetes. From the dead face of his mother, Eddi Amsel first did a pen-and-ink drawing, then a red crayon drawing. During the funeral in Bohnsack he was said to have wept. Only a few people were at the grave. I wonder why. After the funeral Amsel began to liquidate the widow's household. He sold everything: the house, the business, the fishing boats, the outboard motors, the dragnets, the smokehouses, and the store with its pulleys, tool boxes, and variously smelling miscellaneous wares. In the end Eddi Amsel was looked upon as a wealthy young man. He deposited a part of his fortune in the Agricultural Bank of the City of Danzig, but managed to invest the greater part on profitable terms in Switzerland: for years it worked quietly and did not diminish.

Amsel took but a few tangible possessions with him from Schiewenhorst. Two photograph albums, hardly any letters, his father's war decorations—he had died a reserve lieutenant in the First World War—the family Bible, a school diary full of drawings from his days as a village schoolboy, some old books about Frederick the Great and his generals, and Otto Weininger's *Sex and Character* rode away with Eddie Amsel on the Island narrow-gauge railway.

This last standard work had meant a great deal to his father. Weininger attempted, in twelve long chapters, to prove that woman has no soul, and went on, in the thirteenth chapter entitled "Judaism," to develop his theory that the Jews were a feminine race and therefore soulless, that only if the Jew overcame the Jewishness within him could the world hope to be redeemed from the Jews. Amsel's father had underlined memorable sentences with a red pencil, with the frequent marginal comment: "Very true!" Reserve Lieutenant Albrecht Amsel had found the following very true on p. 408: "The Jews, like women, like to stick together, but they have no social intercourse with each other . . ." On p. 413 he had entered three exclamation marks: "Men who are middlemen always have Jewish blood . . ." On p. 434 he had several times underlined the tail end of a sentence and written "God help us!" in the margin: ". . . things that will forever be beyond the reach of the authentic Jew: spontaneous being, divine right, the oak tree, the trumpet, the Siegfried motif, self-creation, the words: 'I am.' "

Two passages endorsed by his father in red pencil took on meaning for the son as well. Because it was said in the standard work that the Jew does not sing and does not engage in sports, Albrecht Amsel, by way of disproving at least these theses, had founded an athletic club in Bohnsack and lent his baritone to the church choir. In regard to music, Eddi Amsel played the piano in a smooth and dashing manner, let his boy soprano, which even after graduation refused to come down from the upper story, jubilate in Mozart Masses and short arias, and in regard to sports threw himself body and soul into the game of faustball.

He who for years had been the victim of school schlagball slipped of his own free will into the chrome-green gym pants of the Young Prussia Athletic Club and moved his friend, who had hitherto played field hockey at the Danzig Hockey Club, to join with him the Young Prussians. With the permission of the head of his club and after pledging himself to support his hockey club at least twice a week in the Niederstadt field, Walter Matern signed up for handball and light athletics; for the leisurely game of faustball would not in itself have made sufficient demands on the young man's physique.

Tulla and I knew the Heinrich Ehlers Athletic Field

situated between the Municipal Hospitals and the Heiligen-brunn Home for the Blind. Good turf, but run-down wooden grandstand and locker room, through whose cracks the wind found its way. The large field and the two small subsidiary fields were used by players of handball, schlagball, and faust-ball. Sometimes football players and track men came too, until the sumptuous Albert Forster Stadium was built not far from the crematory and Heinrich Ehlers Field was thought fit only for school sports.

Because Walter Matern had won the shot-put and the three-thousand-meter run at the interschool track meet the preceding year, so earning the reputation of a promising athlete, he was able to gain admission for Eddi Amsel and make him into a Young Prussian. At first they wished to use him only as a handyman. The field manager handed him a broom: locker rooms must be kept spotlessly clean. He also had to keep the balls greased and sprinkle the foul lines of the handball field with lime. Only when Walter Matern pro-tested was Eddi Amsel assigned to a faustball team. Horst Plötz and Siegi Lewand were the guards. Willi Dobbeck played left forward. And Walter Matern served as line player in a team that soon came to be feared and was to become first in the league. For Eddi Amsel directed, he was the heart and switchboard of the team: a born play maker. What Horst Plötz and Siegi Lewand picked up in the rear and conveyed to the center of the field, he deftly, with supple forearm, dispatched to the line: there stood Walter Matern, the smasher and line player. He received the ball from the air and seldom hit it dead center, but put a twist on it. While Amsel knew how to receive treacherously dealt balls and turn them into neat passes, Matern was unstoppable, piling up points with balls that had been harmlessly roaming around: for when a ball lands without spin, it rebounds at exactly the same angle, it is predictable; but Matern's balls, hit on the lower third of the ball, took on backspin and bounced back the moment they landed. Amsel's specialty was the seemingly simple forearm shot, which however he handled with unusual precision. He picked up low balls. When the opposing team laid down smashes at his feet, he saved them from dopping dead with backhand shots. He recognized spin balls at once, tapped them up with the edge of his little finger, or slammed them with a swift forehand. Often he ironed out balls that his own guards had bungled and, Weininger's assertions to the contrary notwithstanding, was a smiled-at, but respectfully smiled-at non-Aryan faustball player, Young Prussian, and sportsman.

Tulla and I were witnesses

as Eddi Amsel succeeded in taking off a few pounds, a loss which, apart from us, was observed only by Jenny Brunies, the little dumpling who had meanwhile turned ten. She too noticed that Amsel's gelatinous chin was turning into a firm, full-rounded pediment. His chest too lost its tremulous teats and, as his thorax filled out, slipped back into low relief. Yet quite conceivably Eddi Amsel didn't lost a single pound, but only distributed his fat more evenly, his athletically developed muscles lending athletic structure to his previously structureless layer of fat. His torso, formerly a shapeless sack stuffed with down, took on the contours of a barrel. He began to look like a Chinese idol or the tutelary deity of all faustball players. No, Eddie Amsel didn't lose so much as half a pound while playing center; it seems more likely that he gained two and a half pounds; but he sublimated the gain after the manner of an athlete: to what speculations the relativity of a man's weight will lend itself!

In any event Amsel's juggling with his hundred and ninety-eight pounds, in which no one would have discerned his two hundred and three pounds, may have moved Dr. Brunies to prescribe physical exercise for his doll-like Jenny as well. Dr. Brunies and Felsner-Imbs the piano teacher decided to send Jenny to a ballet school three times a week. In the suburb of Oliva there was a street named Rosengasse, which began at the market and zigzagged its way into Oliva Forest. On it stood a modest early-nineteenth-century villa, to whose sand-yellow stucco clung, half concealed by red-blowing hawthorn, the enamel sign of the ballet school. Like Amsel's admission to the Young Prussia Athletic Club, Jenny's admission to the ballet school was obtained through pull: for many years Felix Felsner-Imbs had been the ballet school pianist. No one was so expert at accompanying bar exercises: Every *demi-plié,* from the first to the fifth position, hearkened to his adagio. He sprinkled the *port de bras.* His exemplary rhythm for *battement dégagé* and his sweat-raising rhythm for the *petits battements sur le cou-de-pied.* Besides, he had millions of stories. One had the impression that he had seen Marius Petipa and Preobrajenska, the tragic Nijinsky and the miraculous Massine, Fanny Elssler and la Barbarina all dance simultaneously and in person. No one doubted that this was an eyewitness to historical performances: thus he must have been present when, in the early-romantic days of the last century, la Taglioni, la Grisi, Fanny Cerito, and Lucile Grahn danced the famous *Grand Pas de Quatre* and were showered with roses. He had had difficulty in obtaining a seat on Olympus for the first performance of the ballet *Coppélia.* It went without saying that so accomplished a ballet pianist was able to render the scores of the entire repertory, from the melancholy *Giselle* to the evanescent *Sylphides,* on the piano; and on his recommendation Madame Lara began to make an Ulanova of Jenny.

It was not long before Eddi Amsel became a persevering onlooker. Sitting by the piano equipped with his sketching pad, extracting mana from soft lead, he followed the bar exercises with swift eyes and was soon able to transfer the various positions to paper more pleasingly than the boys and girls, some of them members of the child ballet at the Stadttheater, could perform them at the bar. Often Madame Lara took advantage of Amsel's skill and explained a regulation *plié* to her pupils with the help of his sketches.

Jenny on the dancing floor cut a half-miserable, half-endearingly ludicrous figure. Conscientiously the child learned all the combinations—how diligently she reversed her little feet in the *pas de bourrée,* how touchingly her roly-poly *petit changement de pieds* stood out against the *changements* of the practiced *rats de ballet,* how brightly, when Madame Lara practiced *Little Swans* with the children's class, shone Jenny's dust- and time-dispelling gaze, which the austere Madame called her "Swan Lake look"—and yet, for all the glamour that inevitably attaches to a ballerina, Jenny looked like a little pink pig trying to turn into a weightless *sylphide.*

Why did Amsel, over and over again, take Jenny's lamentable arabesque, Jenny's heart-rending *tour à la seconde* as an occasion for lightly tossed-off sketches? Because his pencil, without flattering the plumpness away, discerned the dancer's line behind all the fat, proving to Madame Lara that within the fat a diminutive star was preparing to rise in the heaven of ballet dancers; it would only be necessary to render the tallow and lard, to increase the heat under the pan until a crisp and slender Terpsichorean rind should be able to execute the famous thirty-two *fouettés en tournant* in the crackling flame.

Dear Tulla,

just as Eddi Amsel became Jenny's audience, so Jenny Brunies looked on from the lawn terraces in the late afternoon as Amsel helped his faustball team to victory. Even when Amsel was practicing, while he was making a light faustball hop on his broad forearm for the time it takes to say three rosaries, wonderment gaped from Jenny's open buttonhole mouth. The two of them with their total of three hundred and twenty pounds came to be a familiar sight throughout the suburb if not the city; everybody in the suburb of Langfuhr knew about Jenny and Eddi, just as they all knew about a tiny little fellow with a tin drum. Except that the dwarf, whom everybody called Oskar, was reputed to be an incorrigible lone wolf.

We all of us,

Tulla, I, and Tulla's brothers, met Amsel, roly-poly Jenny, and Walter Matern, the smasher, on the athletic field. Other nine-year-olds, Hänschen Matull, Horst Kanuth, Georg Ziehm, Helmut Lewandowski, Heini Pilenz, and the Rennwand brothers met there as well. We were in the same Cub squad, and over the protests of many athletic clubs our squad leader Heini Wasmuth had obtained permission for us to practice relay racing on the cinder track and to drill in uniform and street shoes on the turf of the athletic field. Once Walter Matern gave our squad leader a piece of his mind. They bellowed at each other. Heini Wasmuth showed official orders and a permit issued by the field management, but Matern, who openly threatened violence, managed to put through a new policy, making the cinder track and the turf of the athletic field out of bounds to persons in uniform and street shoes. From then on we drilled on the Johanneswiese and went to Heinrich Ehlers Field only privately and in gym shoes. There the sun fell obliquely because it was afternoon. Activity on all the fields. Variously pitched referees' whistles put the ball into or took it out of play in a wide variety of games. Goals were tossed, sides changed, flies struck, announcements roared. Balls were passed, opponents thrown off; fake-outs, block plays, encirclement; teams were outplayed, contestants played out, games lost and won. Painful cinders in gym shoes. Players dozed while waiting for the return game. The smell from the crematory indicated the direction of the wind. Bats were rubbed, balls greased, foul lines drawn, scores kept, and victors cheered. Lots of laughing, constant yelling, some crying, and frequent irritation over the field manager's cat. Everyone obeyed my cousin Tulla. Everyone was afraid of Walter Matern. Some covertly threw pebbles at Eddi Amsel. Many made a detour around our Harras. The last one out had to lock the locker room and leave the key with the caretaker; Tulla never did that, I did it sometimes.

And once—

Tulla and I were there—Jenny Brunies cried because somebody had burned a hole in her brand-new spring-green dress with a magnifying glass.

Years later—Tulla and I were absent—some high school boys, who were putting on a schlagball tournament, were said to have put the field manager's cat on the neck of a dozing fellow student.

Another time—Jenny, Amsel, and Matern were absent because Jenny was having her ballet lesson—Tulla swiped two schlagball balls for us, and a kid from the Athletic and Fencing Club was suspected.

And once after the faustball game—Walter Matern, Eddi Amsel, and Jenny Brunies were lying on the terrace wall to one side of the small ball field—something really happened and it was marvelous:

We park ourselves a few steps to one side. Tulla, Harras, and I can't take our eyes off the group. The whole time the setting sun is peeping into the athletic fields from Jäschkental Forest. The uncut grass on the edge of the cinder track casts long shadows. We aren't even giving a thought to the smoke that rises up vertically from the chimney of the crematory. Now and then Eddi Amsel's high laugh comes over to us.

Harras lets out a brief bark and I have to grab him by the collar. Tulla is pulling up grass with both hands. She isn't listening to me. Over yonder Walter Matern is miming some part in a play. They say he's studying to be an actor. Once Jenny waves to us in her white dress that probably has grass spots on it. I wave cautiously back until Tulla turns toward me with her nostrils and incisor teeth. Butterflies go about their business. Nature crawls aimlessly, bumblebees bumble . . . no, not bumblebees; what we first see, then hear on a late summer afternoon in the year 1936, as we sit in separate groups on Heinrich Ehlers Field, on an early summer evening when the last teams have been whistled off and the broad-jump pit is being raked, is the airship *Graf Zeppelin*. We've been expecting it. The newspapers had said it was coming. First Harras gets restless, then we too—Tulla first —hear the sound. It swells, although the zeppelin is supposed to come from the west, from all directions at once. And then suddenly there it is in mid-air, over Oliva Forest. Of course the sun just happens to be setting. Accordingly, the zeppelin isn't silvery but pink. Now that the sun is slipping behind the Karlsberg and the airship is heading toward the open sea, pink gives way to silver. All stand shading their eyes. Choral singing is wafted over to us from the vocational and home economics school. Polyphonically the girls sing at the zeppelin. On Zinglers Höhe a brass band attempts something along the same lines with the "Hohenfriedberger March." Matern looks hard in a different direction. He has something against the zeppelin. Eddi Amsel applauds with small hands on short arms. Jenny too is jubilant. "Zeppelin, zeppelin!" she cries and bounces like a ball. Even Tulla distends her nostrils, trying to suck up the zeppelin. All Harras' restlessness has gone into his tail. It's so silvery a magpie would want to steal it. While on Zinglers Höhe the "Badenweiler March" follows the "Hohenfriedberger March," while the vocational girls interminably sing "Sacred Fatherland," while the zeppelin out toward Hela grows smaller, yet more silvery, smoke—I'm positive—rises imperturbably and vertically from the chimney of the municipal crematory. Matern, who doesn't believe in the zeppelin, watches the Protestant smog.

My cousin Tulla,
   otherwise invariably guilty, or at least an accomplice, was

not to blame for the scandal at Heinrich Ehlers Field. Walter Matern did something. What he did was recounted in three versions: Either he distributed leaflets in the locker room; or he pasted leaflets on the grandstand benches shortly before the handball game between Schellmühl 98 and the Athletic and Fencing Club; or, while all the fields were busy with games or practice, he secretly stuck leaflets into the hanging pants and jackets of the junior and senior athletes in the locker room; and the manager caught him in the act. It doesn't matter much which version is accredited, for the leaflets, whether openly distributed, pasted, or secretly stuck in pockets, were all identically red.

But since the Danzig senate, first under Rauschning, then under Greiser, had dissolved the Communist Party in '34 and the Social Democratic Party in '36—the Center Party, under its chairman Dr. Stachnik, dissolved itself in October 1937—the propagandist activities of the student Walter Matern—he still wasn't studying but doing something connected with dramatics—could only be regarded as illegal.

Nevertheless, no one wanted to create a disturbance. After brief proceedings in the manager's house, amid loving cups, photographs of athletes, and framed certificates—Koschnik, the field manager, had made a name for himself as a track man in the early twenties—Walter Matern was expelled from the Young Prussians. Eddi Amsel, who, it appears, had been closely and critically examining the bronze statue of a javelin thrower during the proceedings, was also urgently advised, though no reasons were stated, to resign from the club. The two erstwhile Young Prussians were given handwritten documents commemorating the victory of Amsel's faustball team in the last tournament and hands were shaken in a spirit of sportsmanship. All the Young Prussians and the field manager as well took leave of Eddi Amsel and Walter Matern with guarded words of regret and a promise to make no report to the Athletic Association.

Walter Matern remained an esteemed member of the Hockey Club and even joined up for a course in gliding. Near Kahlberg on the Frische Nehrung he is said to have made a number of twelve-minute glider flights and to have photographed the lagoon from the air. But Eddi Amsel had had his fill of sports: he took another fling at the fine arts, and my cousin Tulla helped him.

Listen, Tulla:
sometimes, and it doesn't even have to be quiet in the street outside, I hear my hair growing. I don't hear my fingernails, I don't hear any toenails growing, only my hair. Because you once reached into my hair, because you left your hand for a second and eternity in my hair—we were sitting in the lumber shed amid your collection of extra-long shavings that were wavy like my hair—because afterward, but still in the lumber shed you said: "But that's the only thing that's any good about you." Because you recognized this one and only quality in me, my hair made itself independent, it doesn't really belong to me, it belongs to you. Our Harras belonged to you. The lumber shed belonged to you. All the gluepots and beautiful curly wood shavings belonged to you. It's you I'm writing to, even if I'm writing for Brauxel.

But no sooner had Tulla withdrawn her hand from my hair and said something about my hair than she was gone, over resinous planks, between tall sections of plywood. She was outside in the yard and I, with still electric hair, was too slow in following to prevent her assault on the piano teacher and ballet pianist.

Felsner-Imbs had entered the yard. Stooped, he strode stiffly to the machine shop and inquired of the machinist when the buzz saw and lathe were planning to take a fairly protracted intermission, because he, the ballet pianist and former concert pianist, wished to practice, very softly, something complicated, a so-called adagio. Once or twice a week Felsner-Imbs asked this favor of our machinist or of my father, and it was always granted, though not always immediately. No sooner had the machinist nodded and, pointing a thumb at the buzz saw, said that he just had to run through two more planks; no sooner had Felsner-Imbs, after elaborate bows that looked perilous so near the buzz saw, left the machine shop; scarcely had he covered half the distance to the yard door—I was just crawling out of the lumber shed—when my cousin Tulla let Harras, our watchdog, off the chain.

At first Harras didn't know quite what to do with his sudden freedom, for ordinarily he was put right on the leash when released from his chain; but then he, who a moment before had stood distrustful, with head cocked, bounded into the air with all four legs, landed, shot diagonally across the yard, turned just before the lilac bushes, hurdled a sawhorse with neck outstretched, and went leaping frolicsomely around the pianist who had frozen into a statue: playful barking, a harmless snap, dancing hindquarters; and only when Felsner-Imbs sought safety in flight and Tulla from in front of the kennel—she was still holding the snap of the chain—had sicked our Harras on the game with an inflammatory skiss-skiss-skiss, did Harras pursue the pianist and catch him by his flowing swallowtails; for Felsner-Imbs, who during piano lessons wore only a velvet artist's jacket, slipped, as soon as he had to practice a difficult concert piece or play to an imaginary or actually present audience, into the swallowtails of a concert performer.

The coat was done for and my father had to replace it. Otherwise the pianist had suffered no injury, for the machinist and the master carpenter had managed to pull Harras, who as a matter of fact was only playing, away from the festive cloth.

Tulla was supposed to be spanked. But Tulla had turned to unpunishable air. I got a licking instead, for I had failed to restrain Tulla, I had stood by inactive and as the boss's son I was responsible. My father smacked me with a piece of roofing lath until Felsner-Imbs, whom Dreesen the machinist had put back on his legs, interceded. While with a hairbrush, which in the inside pocket of his swallowtail coat had survived Harras' onslaught, he first brushed his artist's mane against the grain—a sight that made Harras growl—then curried it into his usual leonine hairdo, he remarked that actually not I, but Tulla or the dog was deserving of punishment. But where Tulla had been standing there was only a hole; and my father never laid a hand on our Harras.

Listen, Tulla:

half an hour later buzz saw, lathe, and finishing machine fell silent, as arranged, the band saw was soundless, Harras lay once more lazily on his chain, the deep booming of the planing machine ceased, and from Felsner-Imbs' music room delicate, elaborately slow sounds, now solemn, now sad, detached themselves. Fragilely they strutted across the yard, climbed the façade of the apartment house as far as the third story, then fell headlong, gathered together, and dispersed: Imbs was practicing his complicated piece, the so-called adagio, and the machinist, with a manipulation of the black switch box, had turned off all the machines for the time required to go through the piece three times.

Tulla, I presumed, was sitting deep within the lumber shed, under the tar-paper roof with her long-curled wood shavings. She could probably hear the melody, but she didn't run after it. I was lured by the pianist's concert piece. I climbed the fence around the lilac garden and pressed my face to the windowpanes: a cone of glass-green light in the music room. Inside the cone of electric light two conjuring hands and a snow-white but green-glowing head: Felsner-Imbs at conjured keyboard, with his music. The big hourglass silent and hard at work. The porcelain ballerina also thrusts her horizontal leg, frozen in its arabesque, into the cone of green light. Eddi Amsel and Jenny Brunies huddle mustily on the sofa in the background. Jenny is filling a lemon-yellow dress. Amsel isn't drawing. A sickly pallor coats the ordinarily healthy and apple-glowing faces of the listeners. Jenny has clasped her ten sausage fingers, which the submarine light has transformed into fleshy algae. Amsel builds his hands into a flat roof under his chin. Several times and with relish Felsner repeats a particularly sad passage—Hail and farewell: lapping of waves, army of clouds, birds in flight, love potion, idyl in the woods, early death—then once again, while far in the rear of the room, on the little lacquered stand, the goldfish quivers in its bowl, he plays the whole soft and gentle piece—weary unto death, transition, serene joy —and listens to the last chord with all ten fingers in green air until the half-hour intermission arranged for the lathe and finishing machine, the buzz saw and band saw all at once is at an end.

The congealed group in the Imbs music room began to move again: Jenny's fingers unlocked themselves; Amsel's finger roof collapsed; Felsner removed his fingers from the cone of green light and only then showed his guests his swallowtails, tattered on the sides and in back. The ill-fated garment passed back and forth and finally came to rest with Amsel.

And Amsel lifted it up, counted the remaining fabric-covered buttons, tested every rent with parted fingers, demonstrated what a shepherd's incited fangs can do, and after this instructive Introit, proceeded to the Mass: he ogled through jagged holes, peered through slits, widened burst seams with two malignant fingers, was wind under coattails, finally crawled in, became entirely one with the festive tatter, transubstantiated himself and the cloth, and treated the audience to a performance featuring a disabled swallowtail coat: Amsel looked terrifying; Amsel aroused pity; Amsel the hobbler; Amsel the dodderer; Amsel in the wind and rain, on sheet ice; the merchant on the flying carpet; roc, the fabled bird; the caliph turned stork; the crow, the owl, the woodpecker; the sparrow at its morning bath, behind the horse, with the dog; many sparrows meet, scold each other, take counsel, entertain, and thank the audience for applauding. Then came Amsel's swallowtail divertimenti: the unleashed grandmother; the ferryman has a toothache; the parson fights the wind; Leo Schugger at the cemetery gate; teachers in playgrounds. But let it not be supposed that all were fat, with the build of a lifeguard. Once inside the coat, he conjured up towering beanpoles and windmills, he was Balderle and Ashmodai, the cross by the wayside, and the evil number efta. A dancing, pathetically withered spook seized the porcelain ballerina, abducted her from the piano, courted her with bat's wings, ravished her heart-rendingly, made her vanish ruthlessly, as though forever, in Harras-black cloth that grew longer and longer, reappear safe and thank goodness sound, and return to her native piano. Pressed for encores, he wound up with a few more numbers; still in love with his masquerade, he transformed himself, confident of applause, into this and that, and was grateful to our Harras, for his scissors bite had, he thanked Tulla far away in the lumber shed for Tulla had sicked, and Harras had beset, and Felsner-Imbs' swallowtail coat had released catches deep within Eddi Amsel, unearthed wells, tossed pennies in, and fostered the growth of a whole crop of ideas, which, sowed during Amsel's childhood, gave promise of a barn-bursting harvest.

Hardly a moment after Eddi Amsel had unwrapped himself from black cloth viscera, disclosing the easygoing and old-familiar Amsel in the flowing green light of the music room, he neatly folded his equipment, took the half-frightened, half-amused Jenny by her plump little hand, and, carrying away the Imbsian swallowtails, left the pianist and his goldfish.

Tulla and I

naturally thought Amsel had carried away the hopelessly

tattered garment with the intention of taking it to the tailor's. But no tailor received work because our Harras had leapt. My allowance was cut in half because my father had to provide a brand-new coat. The carpenter might have exacted the rag in return, perhaps for use in the machine shop—where wiping rags were always needed—but my father paid, exacted nothing, and even apologized, as carpenters tend to apologize, with embarrassed condescension and a clearing of the throat, and Amsel remained the usufructuary of the garment which, though fragmentary, was susceptible of transformation. From then on he ceased to devote his talents exclusively to drawing and watercoloring; from then on, though he had no intention of scaring crows, Eddi Amsel built life-size scarecrows.

Here it is contended that Eddi Amsel had no special knowledge of birds. Neither was Tulla's cousin a cynologist nor could Eddi Amsel be termed an ornithologist because of his scarecrows. Just about anybody can distinguish sparrows from swallows, an owl from a woodpecker. Even Eddi Amsel did not believe starlings and magpies to be equally thieving; but as far as he was concerned, robin and bullfinch, titmouse and chaffinch were all indifferently songbirds. He was not up to question games such as "What kind of bird is that?" No one had ever seen him leafing through Brehm's *Life of the Birds*. When I once asked him: "Which is bigger, an eagle or a wren?" he dodged the question with a twinkle: "The Angel Gabriel naturally." But he had a keen eye for sparrows. What no bird expert can do, Amsel could: he was able to distinguish as individuals the members of a crowd bevy congress of sparrows, whom everybody believes to be equally colorless. He took a statistical view of all those who bathed in roof gutters, clamored behind horse-drawn vehicles, and descended on playgrounds after the last bell: in his opinion they were all individualists that had camouflaged themselves as a mass society. And to his eyes blackbirds were never, not even in snow-covered gardens, identically black and yellow-billed.

Nevertheless Eddie Amsel built no scarecrows to ward off the sparrows and magpies with which he was familiar; he built with no adversary in mind, on formal grounds. At the most he wished to convince a dangerously productive environment of his own productivity.

Tulla and I

knew where Eddi Amsel designed and built his scarecrows, though he didn't call them scarecrows but figures. He had rented a spacious villa on Steffensweg. Amsel's inheritance was considerable and the ground floor of the villa was said to be paneled in oak. Steffensweg was situated in the south-western part of the suburb of Langfuhr. Below Jäschkental Forest it branched off from Jäschkentaler Weg and proceeded in the direction of the Almshouse and Orphanage along the grounds of the Langfuhr fire department. One villa after another. A few consulates: the Latvian and the Argentine. French gardens behind wrought-iron fences, none of them wanting for ornament. Boxwoods, yew trees, and red-flowering hawthorn. Expensive English lawns that had to be sprinkled in the summer and in winter lay gratis beneath the snow. Weeping willows and silver firs flanked, overtowered, and shaded the villas. Espaliered fruit gave a good deal of trouble. Fountains required frequent repairs. Gardeners gave notice. The watch-and-ward society provided burglary insurance. Two consuls and the wife of a chocolate manufacturer put in a petition for a fire alarm, which was immediately granted, although the fire department was right behind the Orphanage and its training tower overlooked all the silver firs, promising the ivy on white house fronts and all the many cornices and porticoes that knew Schinkel from hearsay to dispatch two fire brigades, within twenty-seven seconds. At night but few windows were lit up, unless the owner of the Anglas chocolate factory happened to be giving a reception. Footfalls between lampposts could long be heard coming and going. In a word, a quiet genteel neighborhood, where in ten years only two murders and one attempted murder had become audible, that is to say, known.

Soon Walter Matern, who had previously lived in a furnished room in the Old City, on Karpfenseigen, moved into Amsel's villa, where he occupied two oak-paneled rooms. Sometimes an actress or two lived with him for a week at a time, for he still hadn't made up his mind to start studying economics. Instead he had found a place among the supers of the Stadttheater on Kohlenmarkt. As a member of a large crowd, as a soldier among soldiers, as one of six candle-bearing servants, as a drunkard among drunken mercenaries, as a grumbler among grumbling peasants, as a masked Vene-tian, as a mutinous soldier, and as one among six gentlemen who with six ladies had to provide a birthday party in the first act, a garden party in the second act, a funeral in the third act, and a merry reading of the will in the last act with numbers and with a chatting, joking, mourning, and joyfully animated background, Walter Matern, though not yet privileged to utter two consecutive sentences, was acquiring his first experience of the stage. At the same time, having decided to broaden the original foundation of his histrionic gift, his gruesome grinding of the teeth, he took two lessons a week in comedy with Gustav Nord, a comedian of city-wide reputation; for Matern was convinced that a talent for tragedy had come to him with his mother's milk and that if there were still rough edges, it was only in comedy.

While two oak-paneled rooms of Amsel's villa were constrained to hear Walter Matern in the role of Florian Geyer, the third and largest room, oak-paneled like the actor's, became the witness of Amsel's working methods. Scantily furnished. Crude meathooks in the solid oak ceiling. Chains on trolleys. Close under the paneling, they were hanging big as life. A similiar principle is observed in miners' change-houses: air and freedom on the floor; under the ceiling, congestion. Still, there was one piece of furniture, a writing desk, a genuine Renaissance desk. Lying open upon it: the standard work, a work of six hundred pages, a work without equal, a diabolical work, Weininger's work, the unappreciated over-estimated best-selling misunderstood too-well-understood stroke of genius, provided with marginal notes by Amsel's father and footnotes by Weininger: *Sex and Character*, Chapter 13, p. 405: ". . . and perhaps, provisionally speaking, the world-historical significance and enormous achievement of Jewry consists solely in this: in having continually brought the Aryan to consciousness of his self, in having reminded him of himself ["of himself" in bold-face type]. It is for this that the Aryan owes the Jew a debt of gratitude; thanks to him, he knows what to guard against: against Jewishness as a possibility in himself."

These and similar sentences, as well as sentences that said the exact opposite or were in themselves paradoxical, Amsel declaimed with a preacher's pathos to already-finished figures dangling from the oak ceiling and to the many wooden and wire frames that occupied the polished floor and peopled the oak-paneled room with an amorphous yet eagerly debating company: and in the course of an easy informal discussion

Eddi Amsel, their knowledgeable, sophistical, always original, objective, when necessary subjective, urbane, omnipresent, never offended Olympian host, explained the true
nature of women and Jews: "Must we say with Weininger that
women and Jews have no soul or does it suffice to say that
this applies only to women or only to Jews, and are the
Jews, from an anthropological point of view, for in an
empirical sense, the tenets of faith argue to the contrary?
The Chosen People, begging your pardon. But, and only for
the sake of argument, don't we often observe Jewish characteristics in rabid anti-Semites: Wagner, for example, although *Parsifal* will always be incomprehensible to an authentic Jew, and in the same way we can distinguish between Aryan socialism and typically Jewish socialism, for
Marx, as we all know, was. That is why women and Jews
are equally deficient in Kantian reason, and even Zionism
doesn't. The Jews, you see, prefer movable goods. The same
with the English. Exactly, exactly, what are we discussing:
the Jew lacks, he is fundamentally, no, not only a foreign
body in the state, but. But what can you expect when in the
Middle Ages and down to the nineteenth century and again
today: the Christians are to blame, begging your pardon.
Quite the contrary, my dear girl: see here, you know your
Bible, don't you, well then, what did Jacob do to his dying
father? He lied to Isaac ha-ha-ha, and he swindled Esau, if
you please, and Laban didn't come off any better. But such
things happen everywhere. Speaking in terms of percentages,
the Aryans take the lead in crime and not. Which proves if
it proves anything that the Jew has no knowledge either of
good or evil, that's why the Jews lack the very concept of
angel, not to mention the Devil. May I call your attention to
Belial and the Garden of Eden? Still, I think we can agree
that the highest ethical elevation and the profoundest moral
degradation are equally unknown to him: hence the few
crimes of violence, and the same goes for women, which
proves again that he lacks stature in every respect, or can
you offhand name a saint who. Very clever! That's why I say:
we're talking about species, not individuals. Even his prover-
bial feeling for the family serves only the one purpose of
multiplying, that's right, that's why they're such panders:
the Jewish pander in antithesis to the aristocrat. But doesn't
Weininger say distinctly that he neither nor, that he has no
desire whatever to play into the hands of the mob, neither

boycott nor expulsion, after all he was one. But he wasn't for Zionism either. And when he quotes Chamberlain. After all, he himself says that the parallel with women doesn't always. But he says both are without a soul. Yes, yes, but only in a platonic sense, so to speak. You forget. I forget nothing, my friend. He states cold facts. For instance: Take your time, with facts anything . . . A quotation from Lenin, eh? You see what I mean? Look here. Darwinism found most of its supporters, because the ape theory: so it's no accident if chemistry is still in the hands, like the Arabs in the past, a related race after all, hence the purely chemical tendency in medicine, whereas naturopathy, in the end it all boils down to the question of the organic and the inorganic as such: it was not without reason that Goethe identified the effort to make a homunculus not with Faust but with Wagner his famulus, because Wagner, it is safe to assume, represents the typically Jewish element, whereas Faust: because one thing is certain, they are without genius of any kind. What about Spinoza? You've taken the word out of my mouth. Because if he hadn't been Goethe's favorite author. Not to mention Heine. The same with the English who also haven't, because if I'm not mistaken Swift and Sterne were. And about Shakespeare we're still insufficiently informed. Able empiricists. Yes, I agree, practical politicians, psychologists, but never. Just the same there's—no, no, let me have my say, my dear, I'm referring to English humor, which the Jew will never, but at the very most clever mockery, exactly like women, but humor? Never! And I'll tell you why, because they believe in nothing, because they *are* nothing and for that very reason they can become anything they please, because with their inclination for abstraction, hence jurisprudence, and because to them nothing, absolutely nothing is inviolable or sacred, because they drag everything into the, because they refuse to respect either a Christian's Christianity or a Jew's baptism, because they are utterly without piety or any true enthusiasm, because they can neither search nor doubt, I'm speaking of authentic doubt, because they are irreligious, because they are neither sunlike nor demonic, because they are neither fearful nor brave, because they are unheroic and never anything but ironic, because like Heine, because they have no ground under their feet, because all they can do is undermine, yes, that they can do all right and never, because they don't even despair, because they are not creative, because they have no song, because they never identify themselves with any cause or idea, because they lack simplicity, shame, dignity, awe, because they never experience wonderment or shattering emotion, only the material side, because they are without honor or profound erotic impulse, because grace, love, humor, yes, that's right, humor I say, and grace and honor and song and faith, the oak tree, the Siegfried motif, the trumpet, and spontaneous being, I say, are forever beyond their grasp, yes, grasp, let me finish: grasp grasp!"

Thereupon Eddi Amsel detaches himself nimbly from the genuine Renaissance writing desk, but nevertheless, as the cocktail party amid the oak paneling turns to other topics, such as the Olympiad and its side effects, does not close Otto Weininger's standard work. He merely takes his distance and appraises the figures which, though possessed of only a framework existence, swagger and express opinions all the same. He reaches behind him into boxes, but not haphazardly, grasps, rejects, selects, and begins to dress up the motley company on the floor in very much the same way as he has done with the company hanging on chains and meathooks under the oak ceiling. Eddi Amsel covers them with old newspapers and vestiges of wallpaper obtained from renovated apartments. Discarded scraps of banners formerly belonging to the seaside resort fleet, rolls of toilet paper, empty tin cans, bicycle spokes, lamp shades, cast-off notions, and Christmas tree decorations set the style. With an ample pot of paste, with motheaten odds and ends picked up at auctions or simply picked up, he performs magic. But it has to be admitted that for all their aesthetic harmony, for all their refinement of detail and morbid elegance of line, these scarecrows or, as Amsel said, figures, were less impressive than the scarecrows which Eddi Amsel the village schoolboy seems to have built for many years in his native Schiewenhorst, exhibited on the Vistula dikes, and sold at a profit.

Amsel was the first to notice this loss of substance. Later, when Walter Matern left his own oak paneling and his pocket-sized paperbacks of dramatic works, he too, though remarking on Amsel's amazing talent, called attention to the undeniable absence of the old creative fury.

Amsel tried to show that his friend was mistaken; he placed one of his splendidly bedizened figures on the terrace outside the paneled room, shaded by the beech trees of Jäschkental Forest. The figure enjoyed a modicum of success, for the good old faithful sparrows shut their eyes to the artistic aspect and as usual allowed themselves to be scared a little; but no one could have said that a cloud of feathered beasts, thrown into panic by the sight, had risen screaming from the treetops and re-enacted a scene from Amsel's village childhood over the forest. His art was stagnant. Weininger's text remained paper. Perfection proved tedious. Sparrows were unmoved. Crows yawned. Wood pigeons refused to believe. Chaffinches, sparrows, crows, and wood pigeons took turns in sitting on Amsel's artistic figure—a paradoxical sight which Eddi Amsel bore with a smile. But we, in the bushes behind the fence, heard him sigh.

Neither Tulla nor I could help him;

nature helped: in October Walter Matern had a fist fight with the platoon leader of a platoon of Hitler Cubs, who were putting on so-called war games in the nearby forest. A squad of uniformed Cubs moved into Amsel's garden with the pennant around which the operation revolved. From the open window Walter Matern dove head-first into the wet foliage; and undoubtedly I too would have come in for a licking if I like my squad leader had tried to stand by Heini Wasmuth our group leader.

The following night we were ordered to throw stones at the villa from the woods: we heard several windowpanes crash. That would have been the end of the affair if Amsel, who had remained on the terrace while blows were falling in the garden, had contented himself with looking on: but he sketched his observations on cheap paper and built models the size of upright cigar boxes: wrestling groups, a muddled shapeless free-for-all of scrawny Cubs, short-panted, knee-socked, shoulder-strapped, brown-tattered, pennant-maddened, rune-bepatched, dagger belts askew, Führer-vaccinated and hoarse with triumph—the living image of our Cub squad fighting over the pennant in Amsel's garden. Amsel had found his way back to reality; from that day on he stopped wasting his talent on fashion plates, hothouse plants, studio art; avid with curiosity, he went out into the street.

He developed a mania for uniforms, especially black and brown ones, which were taking on a larger and larger part in the street scene. In a junkshop on Tagnetergasse he managed to scare up an old SA uniform dating back to the heroic period before the seizure of power. But one did not satisfy his needs. With considerable effort he abstained from putting an ad in the *Vorposten* under his own name: "Wanted: Old SA uniforms." In the stores specializing in uniforms the Party rig was obtainable only on presentation of a Party card. Because it was impossible for Eddi Amsel to join the Party or any of its organizations, Eddi Amsel set about, with coaxing, blasphemous, comical, and always adroit words, persuading his friend Walter Matern, who, though he had stopped distributing Communist leaflets, had a photograph of Rosa Luxemburg pinned to his oak paneling, to do what Amsel would have liked to do for the sake of the uniforms he needed, but couldn't.

Out of friendship—the two of them were said to have been blood brothers—half for the hell of it and half out of curiosity, but especially in order that Amsel might obtain those intensely brown uniforms for which he and the skeletons of future scarecrows were thirsting, Walter Matern, step by little step, gave in: he put aside his pocket-sized paperbacks and filled out an application in which he made no secret of the fact that he had been a member of the Red Falcons and later of the C.P.

Laughing, shaking his head, grinding, no longer outwardly but deep within, every tooth in his head, he joined a Langfuhr SA sturm, whose headquarters and meeting place was the Kleinhammerpark Beer Hall, a spacious establishment with a park by the same name, with dance hall, bowling alley, and home cooking, situated between the Aktien Brewery and the Langfuhr railroad station.

Students from the engineering school made up the bulk of this largely petit-bourgeois sturm. At demonstrations on the Maiwiese beside the Sports Palace the sturm performed guard duty. For years its main function was to start fights on Heeresanger, near the Polish student house, with members of the "Bratnia Pomoc" student organization, and to wreck the Polish clubhouse. At first Walter Matern had difficulties, because his Red past and even the leaflet incident were known. But since he was not the only former Communist in SA Sturm 84, Langfuhr-North, and since the former Communists began to exchange Red Front salutes as soon as they had a few drinks under their belts, he soon felt at home, especially as the group leader took him under his wing: before '33 Sturmführer Jochen Sawatzki had made speeches as a Red Front Fighter and had read strike proclamations to the shipyard workers in the Schichau housing development: Sawatzki was loyal to his past and said when making his brief and popular speeches in the Kleinhammerpark: "Take it from me, boys, if I know anything about the Führer, he'd get a bigger kick about one Communist that joins the SA than about ten Center Party big shots, that only join the Party because they're scared shitless and not because they realize the new day has dawned, yep, believe you me, she's dawned all right. And the only ones that haven't caught on is the big shots, because all they do is saw wood."

When early in November a delegation from the trusty sturm was sent to the Party congress in Munich and consequently put into new uniforms, Walter Matern succeeded in diverting the old rags that had weathered full many a beer-hall battle, to Steffensweg. Actually Matern, whom Sturm-führer Sawatzki had soon appointed squad leader, should have taken the whole kit and boodle including boots and harness to Tiegenhof, where they were just organizing a new SA sturm, which was short on funds. But Eddi Amsel gave his friend a check that had zeroes enough on it to put twenty men into new-smelling togs. Between Amsel's oak panels brown tatters piled up: beer spots, grease spots, blood spots, tar and sweat spots gave the rags additional value in his eyes. He began at once to take measurements. He sorted, counted, piled, took his distance, dreamed of marching columns, let them march by, salute, march by, salute, looked on with screwed-up eyes: beer-hall battles, movement, tumult, men against men, bones and table edges, eyes and thumbs, beer bottles and teeth, screams, crashing pianos, potted plants, chandeliers, and more than two hundred and fifty well-tempered knives; and yet, apart from the piled-up rags there was no one between the oak panels but Walter Matern. He was drinking a bottle of seltzer and didn't see what Eddi Amsel saw.

My cousin Tulla,
    of whom I am writing, to whom I am writing, although if Brauxel had his way, I should be writing of nothing but Eddi Amsel, Tulla arranged for our watchdog Harras to attack Felsner-Imbs, the piano teacher and ballet pianist, a second time. On the open street, on Kastanienweg, Tulla let the dog off the leash. Imbs and Jenny—she in a yellowish fluffy coat—were probably on their way from the ballet school,

for the laces of her ballet slippers were dangling pink and silky out of a gym bag that Jenny was carrying. Tulla let Harras loose, and the rain was slanting down from all sides because the wind kept shifting. Over rilled and bubbling puddles leapt Harras, whom Tulla had let loose. Felsner-Imbs was holding an umbrella over himself and Jenny. Harras made no detours and knew whom Tulla meant when she released him. This time it was the pianist's umbrella my father had to replace, for Imbs defended himself when the black beast, rain-smooth and distended, sprang at him and his pupil, withdrawing the umbrella from its rain-combating function and wielding it, transformed into a shield with a point in the middle, against the dog. Naturally the umbrella gave way. But the metal stays, radiating toward the star-shaped edge of the umbrella, remained. A few of them bent and broke through the cloth; but they confronted our Harras with a painful obstacle. Both his forepaws became entangled in the forbidding spokes; a couple of passers-by and a butcher, who dashed out of his shop in spotted apron, were able to hold him in check. The umbrella was done for. Harras panted. Tulla wouldn't let me run for it. The butcher and the pianist got wet. Harras was put on the leash. The pianist's inspired mane was reduced to matted strands: diluted hair powder dripped on dark cloth. Jenny, the roly-poly, lay in a gutter which gushed Novemberly, gurgled, and secreted gray bubbles.

The butcher didn't go back to his blood sausage; exactly as he had dashed out of his shop, as bald and hatless and porcine as a heel of bologna, he delivered me and Harras to the master carpenter. He described the incident in terms unfavorable to me, representing Tulla as a timid little girl who had run away in terror when I had been unable to hold the dog on the leash; when the truth of the matter is that Tulla had looked on to the end and beaten it only after I had taken the leash away from her.

The butcher took his leave with a shake of a large hairy hand. I got my licking, this time not with a rectangular roofing lath but with a flat woodworking hand. My father promised Dr. Brunies to pay for cleaning the fluffy yellowish coat: fortunately Jenny's gym bag with the pink silk ballet slippers hadn't been carried away in the gutter, for the gutter flowed into the Striessbach, and the Striessbach flowed into Aktien Pond, and the Striessbach flowed out the other end

of Aktien Pond and made its way through the whole of
Langfuhr, under Elsenstrasse, Hertastrasse, Luisenstrasse, past
Neuschottland, up Leegstriess, and emptied near Broschken-
weg, opposite Weichselmünde, into the Dead Vistula,
whence, mingled with Vistula water and Mottlau water, it
passed through the harbor channel between Neufahrwasser
and Westerplatte to merge with the Baltic Sea.

Tulla and I were present
    when in the first week of Advent, at 13 Marienstrasse, in
Langfuhr's largest and finest garden restaurant, the Kleinhammerpark, Manager August Koschinski, Tel. 41-09-40—
fresh waffles every Tuesday—one thing and another led to a
brawl that was quelled only an hour and a half later by the
police detachment which during Party meetings was always
on standby duty in the small Hunt Room: Sergeant Burau
put in a call for reinforcements: One one eight, whereupon
sixteen policemen drove up and restored order with beauty
doctors.

The meeting, held under the motto "Home to the Reich
—Down with the tyranny of Versailles!," was well attended.
Two hundred and fifty people had crowded into the Green
Room.

According to the agenda one speaker followed another at
the speaker's desk between the potted plants: first Sturmführer Jochen Sawatzki spoke tersely huskily vigorously.
Then Local Group Leader Sellke spoke of his impressions at
the Reich Party Congress in Nuremberg. The spades of the
Labor Service, thousands upon thousands, had particularly
impressed him, because sunshine had kissed the blades of
Labor Service spades: "I can only tell you, dear citizens of
Langfuhr, who have turned out in such gratifying numbers
that was unique, absolutely unique. It's something a man won't
forget as long as he lives, how they glittered, thousands upon
thousands of them. A shout went up as from thousands upon
thousands of throats: our hearts were full to overflowing, dear
citizens of Langfuhr, and many a hardened fighter had tears
in his eyes. But that's nothing to be ashamed of, not on such
an occasion. And I thought to myself, dear citizens of Langfuhr, when I go home, I'll tell all those who could not be
present what it's like when thousands upon thousands of Reich
Labor Service spades . . ." Then Kreisleiter Kampe spoke of
his impressions at the harvest thanksgiving festival in Bücke-

burg and of the projected new apartments in the projected Albert Forster Housing Development. Then SA Sturm-führer Sawatzki, supported by two hundred and fifty citizens of Langfuhr, shouted a triple *Siegheil* for the Führer and Chancellor. Both anthems, one too slow and one too fast, were sung too low by the men, too high by the women, and by the children off-key and out of time. This concluded the official part of the program and Local Group Leader Sellke informed the citizens of Langfuhr that the second part would now begin, a friendly informal get-together in the course of which useful and tasty products would be raffled off for the benefit of Winter Aid. The prizes had been donated by: Valtinat Dairy Products, Amada Margarine, Anglas Chocolates, Kanold Candies, Kiesau Wines, Haubold & Lanser Wholesalers, the Kühne Mustard Co., the Danzig Glass Works, and the Aktien Brewery of Langfuhr, which had donated beer, two cases to be raffled off and an extra keg "for SA Sturm 84, Langfuhr-North; for the boys of Langfuhr SA Sturm 84; for our storm troopers, of whom we are proud; a triple hip-hip-hurray for our storm troopers of Sturm 84 —hurray, hurray!"

And then came the tangle which could be disentangled only after a phone call to the police—one one eight—and with the help of beauty doctors. It should not be supposed that the peace was disturbed by Communists or Socialists. By that time they were all washed up. What set off the battle at the Kleinhammerpark was booze, the barrel fever that rises up from within to hit the eyeballs from behind. For, as is only natural after long speeches that have had to be made and listened to, liquid nourishment was drunk, guzzled, lushed, slushed, and sopped up; sitting or standing, one good thing led to another; some ran from table to table, growing damper all the while; many leaned on the bar, pouring it in with both hands; few stood upright and gargled headless, for a dense cloud of smoke cut the hall, which was low to begin with, off at shoulder height. Those whose euphoria had made the longest strides struck up a part song as they drank: Know-youtheforestallshottobits; Inacoolvalley; Ohheadboweddown-withbloodandwounds.

A family affair, everybody was there, all old friends: Alfons Bublitz with Lotte and Fränzchen Wollschläger: "You 'member the time in Höhne Park. Along the Radaune on the way to Ohra, who do we run into but Dulleck and his brother, and there he is, stewed to the gills."

And in a row at the bar stood beer-assed the SA men Bruno Dulleck, Willy Eggers, Paule Hoppe, Walter Matern, and Otto Warnke. "And one time at the Café Derra! You're nuts, man, that was in Zinglers Höhe, they beat Brill up. And then another time, only a coupla days ago. Where was that? By the dam in Straschin-Prangschin. I hear they chucked him into the basin. But he climbed out. Not like Wichmann in Klein-Katz, they gave it to him good, with gun butts: shoilem boil 'em! They say he's gone to Spain. That's what you think! They done him in and stuffed the pieces in a sack. I remember him from the Sharpshooters' Club, before they elected him to the Diet with Brost and Kruppke. They got away, slipped across the border near Goldkrug. Say, would you look at Dau. The guy's a walking bank. One time in Müggenwinkel he said . . ."

Gustav Dau came ambling over, arm in arm with Lothar Budzinski. Wherever he went, he stood a couple of rounds and then another round. Tulla and I sat at a table with the Pokriefkes. My father had left immediately after the speeches. There weren't many children left. Tulla looked at the toilet door: MEN. She drank nothing, said nothing, just looked. August Pokriefke was stewed. He was explaining the railroad connections in Koshnavia to a Herr Mikoteit. Tulla was trying to nail the toilet door closed by just looking: but it swung, moved by full and emptied bladders. The express line Berlin, Schneidemühl, Dirschau passed through Koshnavia. But the express didn't stop. Tulla looked at the door of the ladies' toilet: she saw Walter Matern, disappearing into the men's toilet. Mikoteit worked for the Polish railroad, but that didn't prevent August Pokriefke from listing every single local station on the Konitz-Laskowitz run. Every five sips of beer Erna Pokriefke said: "Now go on home to beddy-bye, children, it's time." But Tulla kept her grip on the fluttering toilet door: every exit and entrance was snapshot by her slit-eyes. Now August Pokriefke was rattling off the stations on the third Koshnavian run—Nakel-Konitz: Gersdorf, Obkass, Schlangenthin . . . Chances were being sold for the Winter Aid raffle. First prize: a dessert set for twelve, including wine glasses; all crystal, pure crystal! Tulla was allowed to draw three lots, because one time, last year, she had drawn an eleven-pound goose. From the all but full SA cap she drew, without removing her eyes from the toilet door: first, a bar of Anglas chocolate; and then, with small scratched hand, she draws the second lot: blank! But none the less the first prize, the crystal: the door to the men's toilet is slammed and wrenched open. Where pants are being unbuttoned or dropped, things are starting up. Quick on the draw, out come the knives. Stabbing each other and slicing each other's jackets, because Tulla is drawing the lot: China against Japan. Shoilem boil 'em.

And kick and clout and turn over and lay out flat and bellow: "Shut up your trap! You crazy loon! You lousy bastard! You stinking ape! Not so rough!" And all the drunks at the bar: Willy Eggers, Paule Hoppe, Alfons Bublitz, the younger Dulleck, and Otto Warnke pull out their clasp knives: "Shoilem boil 'em!" A brawny-armed chorus, stewed to the gills, take their pick of fruit plates, behead glasses, and oil the toilet door. Because Tulla has pulled a blank, they brawl around and tickle each other with knives hooks chivies. Chair and bone, here and now, nobody's yellow, gimme room, plunk on the head, artifacts crack, Willy stands, self-point totters, beer and blood, exaltation. For all ten are champs and have no need to catch their breath. Each looking for each. Who's crawling down there? Whose ink is running out? What are them plug-uglies hollering about? How are toilet doors lifted off their hinges? Who drew the lot? Blank. Uppercut. Tackle. Inside-out. Squirting brains. Telephone: one one eight. Police, shoilem boil 'em! Sneaky and underhanded. Never never. *Existenz*. Green Room. Chandelier crashes. Being and Time. Fuse blows. No lights. Darkness: for in the Black Room the black beauty doctors of the Black Maria look for pitch-black round heads, until brains, black under black chandelier, and the black women scream: "Light! Where's the light? Oh, my, the police! Shoilem boil 'em."

Only when Tulla in the darkness drew a third lot from the SA cap that had stayed with us between her knees, only when my cousin had drawn and unrolled the third lot—it won her a pail of dill pickles from the Kühne Mustard Co. —did the lights go on again. The four stand-by policemen under Sergeant Burau and the sixteen reinforcements under Police Lieutenant Sausin moved in: from the bar and the swinging door to the cloakroom: green, loved, and feared. All twenty-two cops had police whistles between their lips and warbled down on the crowd. They worked with the new night sticks, introduced from Italy by Police President Froboess, there termed *manganelli*, here beauty doctors. The new billies had the advantage over the old ones that they left no open wounds, but operated dryly, almost silently. After one blow with the new police truncheon, each victim turned two and a half times in patent consternation on his own axis and then, but still in corkscrew fashion, collapsed to the floor. Near the toilet door August Pokriefke also submitted to the authority of the article imported from Mussolini's Italy. Without open wounds he was laid up for a week. Not counting him, the final count was three seriously injured and seventeen slightly injured, including four cops. SA men Willy Eggers and Fränzchen Wollschläger, Gustav Dau, the mason, and Lothar Budzinski, the coal dealer, were taken to police headquarters but released the following morning. Herr Koschinski, manager of the Kleinhammerpark, reported one thousand two hundred gulden worth of damages to the insurance company: glass, chairs, the chandelier, the demolished toilet door, the mirror in the toilet, the potted plants around the speaker's stand, the first prize: crystal crystal!—and so on. A police investigation revealed that there had been a short circuit, that someone—I know who!—had unscrewed the fuses.

But nobody suspected that by drawing the blank lot my cousin Tulla had given the signal, had unleashed the beerhall battle.

Dear Tulla,

all that was within your power. You had the eye and the finger. But what is important for this story is not your beerhall battle—although you had a part in it, it was a commonplace affair, indistinguishable from other beer-hall battles—the significant item is that Eddi Amsel, owner of a villa on Steffensweg, was able to take delivery of a beer-sour bundle of battle-scarred and blood-encrusted uniforms: Walter Matern was the slightly injured donor.

This time the loot wasn't limited to SA uniforms. It included the togs of plain Party members. But everything was brown: not the brown of summer oxfords; not hazelnut-brown or witch-brown; no brown Africa; no grated tree bark, no furniture, brown with age; no medium-brown or sand-brown; neither young soft coal nor old peat, dug with a peat spade; no breakfast chocolate, no morning coffee enriched

with cream; tobacco, so many varieties, but none so brown
as; neither the roebuck brown that so deceives the eye nor
the suntan-lotion brown of a two weeks' vacation; no autumn
spat on the palette when this brown: shit brown, at best clay
brown, sodden, pasty, Party brown, SA brown, the brown of
all Brown Books, Brown Houses, Braunau brown, Eva Braun,
uniform brown, a far cry from khaki brown, the brown shat
on white plates by a thousand pimply asses, brown derived
from split peas and sausages; no, no, ye gentle witch-brown,
hazelnut-brown brunettes, you were not the godmothers
when this brown was boiled, born, and dyed, when this
dungheap brown—I'm still being polite about it—lay before
Eddi Amsel.

Amsel sorted out the brown, took the big scissors from
Solingen and made them twitter experimentally. Amsel began
to cut into the indescribable brown. A new implement stood
voluted beside the genuine Renaissance writing desk supporting Weininger's always open standard work: the tailor's horse,
the tailor's organ, the tailor's confessional: a Singer sewing
machine. How the kitten purred when from coarse burlap,
onion sacks, and other permeable material Eddi Amsel sewed
shirtlike undergarments. And the puffed-up Amsel behind the
slender little machine: were they not one? Might not the two
of them, born, baptized, vaccinated, educated as they were,
have borne witness to the same identical development? And
with big stitches and little stitches, he sewed scraps of the
horrible brown on the burlap shirts like beauty spots. But he
also fragmented the armband-red and the sunstroke-mad-
dened bellyache of the swastika. He stuffed with kapok and
sawdust. In illustrated magazines and yearbooks he looked
for and found faces, a coarse-grained photograph of Gerhard
Hauptmann or a glossy black-and-white print of a popular
actor of those years: Birgel or Jannings. He fastened Schmel-
ing and Pacelli, the bruiser and the ascetic, under the visors
of the brown caps. He turned the League of Nations High
Commissioner into an SA man Brand. Undaunted, he snipped
at reproductions of old engravings and played God with
Solingen scissors until Schiller's bold profile or the dandyface
of the young Goethe gave its features to one or another of
the movement's martyrs, Herbert Norkus or Horst Wessel.
Amsel dismembered, speculated, cross-bred, and gave the centuries a chance to kiss each other under SA caps.

From page 4 of his copy he cut the head of the full-length

photograph of the slender, boyish Otto Weininger, author of the standard work, who had committed suicide while still a young man, had the section enlarged to life size at Sönnker's, and then proceeded to work at length but always with unsatisfactory results, on "SA man Weininger."

Eddi Amsel's self-portrait was more successful. In addition to the Renaissance desk and the Singer sewing machine, his equipment included a tall, narrow mirror, reaching up to the ceiling paneling, of the kind to be found in tailor shops and ballet schools. Before this responsive glass he sat in a self-tailored Party uniform—among the SA uniforms he had found none capable of containing him—and hung his full-figure likeness on a naked skeleton which, in the middle, as a sort of solar plexus, lodged a winding mechanism. In the end the authentic Amsel sat Buddhalike tailor fashion, appraising the constructed and still more authentic Party Comrade Amsel. He stood blown up to capacity in burlap and Party brown. The shoulder strap circumscribed him like a tropic. Insignia of rank on his collar made him into a modest section chief. A pig's bladder, daringly simplified and daubed only with a few suggestive black strokes, supported, an excellent likeness, the section chief's cap. And then in the Party comrade's solar plexus the winding mechanism began to operate: the breeches came to attention. Starting at the belt buckle, the right rubber glove, full to bursting, moved jerkily, by remote control, to chest, then to shoulder level, presented first the straight-arm, then the bent-arm Party salute, returned sluggishly, just barely in time, for the mechanism was running down, to the belt buckle, gave a senile tremor or two and fell asleep. Eddi Amsel was in love with his new creation. At the narrow studio mirror he imitated the salute of his life-size facsimile: the Amsel quartet. Walter Matern, to whom Amsel displayed himself and the figure on the floor as well as the mirror images of himself and the figure, laughed, at first overloudly and then with embarrassment. Then he just stared in silence at Amsel, at the scarecrow, and at the mirror by turns. He stood in civilian clothes among four figures in uniform. The sight provoked the inborn grinding of his teeth. And grinding he gave it to be understood that he could take a joke but that too much was enough; Amsel should stop harping on one and the same theme; after all there were plenty of people in the SA and the Party as well who were seriously striving for an ideal, good guys and not just bastards.

Amsel replied that precisely this had been his artistic purpose, that he hadn't intended criticism of any kind, but merely wished, through his art, to create a hodgepodge of good guys and bastards, after the manner of life itself.

Thereupon he tinkered with a prefabricated frame until he had turned out a bullish-looking good guy: SA man Walter Matern. Tulla and I, who were peering from the night-black garden into the electrically lit up and oak-paneled studio, saw with round eyes how Walter Matern's uniformed likeness—blood spots still bore witness to the brawl at the Kleinhammerpark—bared the teeth of his photographed face with the help of a built-in mechanism and ground its mechanically moved teeth: yes, we only saw it—but anyone who saw Walter Matern's teeth heard them too.

Tulla and I saw

how Walter Matern, who with his SA sturm had to do guard duty at a monster mass meeting on the snow-covered Maiwiese, caught sight of the uniformed Eddi Amsel in the crowd. Löbsack spoke. Greiser and Forster spoke. Snow was falling in big flakes, and the crowd shouted *Heil* so long that snowflakes slipped into the open mouths of the *Heil*-shouters. Party Comrade Eddi Amsel also shouted *Heil* and snapped after particularly large snowflakes, until SA man Walter Matern fished him out of the crowd and pushed him off the slushy field into Hindenburgallee. There he gave him hell and we thought in another minute he was going to slug him.

Tulla and I saw

Eddi Amsel in uniform collecting money for the Winter Aid in the Langfuhr market. He jiggled his can, distributed his little jokes among the populace, and took in more coins than the genuine Party comrades; and we thought: if Matern should turn up now and see this, well . . .

Tulla and I

surprised Eddi Amsel and the grocer's son in a snow squall on Fröbelwiese. We were huddled under a trailer that was wintering on the Fröbelwiese. Amsel and the gnome were silhouetted like shadows against the snow flurries. No shad-

ows could have been more different than those shadows. The
gnome shadow held out his shadow drum into the snowfall.
The Amsel shadow bent down. Both shadows held their ears
to the drum as though listening to the sound of December
snow on white-lacquered tin. Because we had never seen
anything so silent, we too kept still, with frost-red ears: but
all we could hear was the snow, we couldn't hear the tin.

Tulla and I

kept an eye peeled for Eddi Amsel when between Christmas and New Year's Day our families went for a walk in
Oliva Forest; but he was somewhere else and not in
Freudental. There we drank coffee with milk and ate potato
pancakes under deer antlers. There wasn't much doing in the
outdoor zoo, because in cold weather the monkeys were
kept warm in the basement of the forestry house. We
shouldn't have taken Harras with us. But my father, the master carpenter, said: "The dog needs a run."

Freudental was a popular place for excursions. We took the
Number 2 streetcar to Friedensschluss and then walked
through the woods, between trees with red markings, until
the valley opened and the forestry house and the outdoor zoo
lay before us. As a carpenter, my father was unable to look
at any good-sized tree, whether beech or pine, without esti-
mating its utility in cubic feet. This put my mother, who
looked upon nature and hence trees more as the adornment
of the world, into a bad humor, which was dispelled only
by the potato pancakes and coffee. Herr Kamin, the conces-
sionaire of the forestry house and inn, took a seat between
August Pokriefke and my mother. Whenever guests appeared,
he told the story of how the zoo had come into being. And
so Tulla and I heard for the tenth time how a Herr Pikuritz
from Zoppot had donated the male bison. The zoo hadn't
started with the bison, though, but with a pair of red deer,
given by the director of the railroad car factory. Next came
the wild boar and the fallow deer. Somebody contributed a
monkey, somebody else two monkeys. Nikolai, head of the
forestry commission, had provided the foxes and the beavers.
A Canadian consul had furnished the raccoons. And the
wolves? Who gave the wolves? Wolves that later broke out of
the enclosure, tore a berry-picking child to pieces, and, once
shot, had their picture in the papers? Who gave the wolves?
Before Herr Kamin can tell us that the Breslau zoo had

donated the two wolves, we are outside with Harras. Past Jack, the bison bull. Around the frozen pond. Chestnuts and acorns for wild boar. Brief barking at the foxes. The wolves' den barred. Harras turned to stone. The wolves restless behind iron bars. Pace longer than Harras'. But the chest not so well developed, the stop not so clearly marked, eyes set at a slant, smaller, more protected. Head more thickset, trunk barrel-shaped, height to the withers: less than Harras, coat stiff, light gray with black clouds, on yellow undercoat. A hoarse whining Harras. The wolves pace restlessly. One day the guardian will forget to close . . . Snow falls in plaques from firs. For the time it takes to glance, the wolves stop still behind bars: six eyes, quivering flews. Three noses curl. Breath steams from fangs. Gray wolves—black shepherd. Black as a result of consistent breeding. Oversaturation of the pigment cells, from Perkun by way of Senta and Pluto to Harras of Queen Louise's mill, gives our dog his stiff, unclouded, unbrindled, unmarked black. My father whistles and August Pokriefke claps his hands. Tulla's family and my parents standing outside the forestry house in winter coats. Restless wolves stay behind. But for us and Harras the Sunday walk isn't over yet. In every mouth an aftertaste of potato pancakes.

My father led us all to Oliva. There we took the streetcar to Glettkau. The Baltic was frozen as far as the misty horizon. Sheathed in ice, the Glettkau pier glistened strangely. Consequently my father had to take his camera out of its leather case and we had to group ourselves around Harras against the fantastic sugar candy. It took my father a long while to get focused. Six times we were told to hold still, which Harras did with ease—he was used to having his picture taken from the days when the press photographers had courted him. Of the six pictures my father took, four turned out to be overexposed: the ice shed extra light.

From Glettkau we walked across the crunching sea to Brösen. Black dots as far as the ice-bound steamers in the roadstead. A good many people had had the same idea. No need for the gulls to go hungry. Two days later four schoolboys on their way to Hela across the ice got lost in the fog and, despite a search with private planes, were never seen again.

Shortly before the Brösen pier, which was also wildly ice-covered—we were meaning to turn off toward the fishing village and the streetcar stop, because the Pokriefkes, especially Tulla, had a horror of the Brösen pier, where years before the little deaf-mute Konrad—after my father with flat wood-working hand had indicated the new line of march, at approximately four in the afternoon, shortly before New Year's, 1937, on December 28, 1936, Harras, whom my father had been holding on the leash because there were so many other dogs about, broke loose, leash and all, took ten long flat leaps over the ice, disappeared in the screaming crowd and, by the time we caught up to him, had merged with a fluttering overcoat to form a black snow-spewing bundle.

Without a word from Tulla, Felsner-Imbs, the pianist and piano teacher, who with Dr. Brunies and ten-year-old Jenny had come out for a Sunday excursion like ourselves, was attacked a third time by our Harras. This time the damage was not confined to a swallowtail coat or umbrella that had to be replaced. My father had every reason to call the unfortunate episode an expensive joke. Felsner's right thigh had been badly mangled. He had to spend three weeks in Deaconesses' Hospital, over and above which he demanded exemplary damages.

Tulla,
it's snowing. Then and now it snowed and is snowing. Snow drifted, is drifting. Fell, is falling. Came down, is coming down. Swirled, is swirling. Flakes floated, are floating. Powdered, is powdering. Tons of snow on Jäschkental Forest, on the Grunewald; on Hindenburgallee, on Clay-Allee; on Langfuhr Market and on Berka Market in Smaragdendorf; on the Baltic and on the lakes of the Havel; on Oliva, on Spandau; on Danzig-Schidlitz, on Berlin-Lichterfelde; on Emmaus and Moabit; Neufahrwasser and Prenzlauer Berg; on Saspe and Brösen, on Babelsberg and Steinstücken; on the brick wall around the Westerplatte and the rapidly built wall between the two Berlins, snow is falling and lies on the ground, snow was falling and lay on the ground.

For Tulla and me,
who were waiting for snow with sleds, snow fell for two days and remained on the ground. Occasionally the snowfall was slanting, resolute, hard-working, then for a time the flakes were large and aimless—in this light, toothpaste-white with jagged edges; against the light, gray to black: a damp

sticky snow, on top of which more resolute slanting snow came powdering down from the east. Through the night the moderate cold remained gray and spongy, so that in the morning all the fences were freshly laden and overloaded branches snapped. Countless janitors, columns of unemployed, the Emergency Technical Aid, and every available municipal vehicle were needed before streets, car tracks, and sidewalks were again discernible. Mountain chains of snow, crusty and lumpy, lined both sides of Elsenstrasse, concealing Harras completely and my father up to his chest. Tulla's woolen cap was two fingers' breadths of blue when there was a slight dip in the ridge. Sand, ashes, and red rock salt were strewn. With long poles men pushed the snow off the fruit trees in the Reichskolonie kitchen gardens and behind Abbot's Mill. And as they shoveled, strewed, and relieved branches, new snow kept falling. Children were amazed. Old people thought back: When had so much snow fallen? Janitors grumbled and said to one another: Who's going to pay for all this? There won't be any sand, ashes, rock salt left. And if it doesn't stop snowing. And if the snow thaws—and thaw it will as sure as we're janitors—it'll all flow into the cellars and the children will get the flu, and so will the grownups, like in '17.

When it's snowing, you can look out of the window and try to count. That's what your cousin Harry is doing, though he's not really supposed to be counting, he's supposed to be writing you letters. When the snow is coming down in big flakes, you can run out in the snow and hold up your open mouth. I'd love to, but I can't, because Brauxel says I've got to write you. If you're a black shepherd, you can run out of your white-capped kennel and bite into the snow. If your name is Eddi Amsel and you've built scarecrows from childhood up, you can build birdhouses for the birds at times when the snow falls breathlessly, and perform acts of mercy with bird food. While white snow is falling on a brown SA cap, you can grind your teeth. If your name is Tulla and you're very light, you can run through and over the snow and leave no trace. As long as vacation lasts and the sky keeps coming down, you can sit in a warm study and sort out your mica gneiss, your double spar, your mica granite and mica slate, and at the same time be a schoolteacher and suck candy. If you're paid for working in a carpentry shop, you can try to earn extra money on days when suddenly a pile of snow is falling, by making snow pushers out of the wood in the car-

pentry shop. If you have to make water, you can piss into
the snow, engrave your name with a yellowish steaming
stroke; but it has to be a short name: I wrote Harry in the
snow in this manner; whereupon Tulla grew jealous and
destroyed my signature with her shoes. If you have long eyelashes, you can catch the falling snow with long eyelashes; but
they don't have to be long, thick eyelashes will do; Jenny
had that kind in her doll face; when she stood still and gaped
in amazement, she was soon looking out sea-blue from under
white, snow-covered roofs. If you stand motionless in the
falling snow, you can close your eyes and hear the snow
fall; I often did so and heard plenty. You can see the likeness of a shroud in the snow; but you don't have to. If
you're a roly-poly foundling who's been given a sled for
Christmas, you may want to go coasting; but nobody wants to
take the foundling along. You can cry in the middle of the
snowfall and nobody notices, except for Tulla with her big
nostrils who notices everything and says to Jenny: "Do you
want to go coasting with us?"

We all went coasting and took Jenny along, because the
snow was lying there for all children. The snow had blan-
keted memories from the days when the rain was pelting
down and Jenny lay in the gutter: several times over. Jenny's
joy at Tulla's offer was almost frightening. Her phiz was
radiant, while Tulla's face revealed nothing. Perhaps Tulla
had made the offer only because Jenny's sled was new and
modern. The Pokriefkes' intricate iron frame was gone with
Tulla's brothers; and Tulla didn't like to sit on my sled, because I always had to hold on to her and that impaired my
coasting technique. Our Harras wasn't allowed to come along,
because the dog behaved like a lunatic in the snow; and yet
he was no longer young: a ten-year-old dog corresponds to a
man of seventy.

We pulled our empty sleds through Langfuhr as far as the
Johanneswiese. Only Tulla let herself be pulled, sometimes
by me, sometimes by Jenny. Jenny liked to pull Tulla and
often offered to pull. But Tulla let herself be pulled only
when she felt like it and not when somebody offered. We
coasted on Zinglers Höhe, on Albrechtshöhe, or on the big
sled run on the Johannesberg, which was maintained by the
city. The sled run was regarded as dangerous and I, a rather
scary child, preferred to coast on the gently sloping Johanneswiese, at the foot of the sled run. Often when the city

slopes were too crowded, we went coasting in the part of the
forest that began to the right of Jäschkentaler Weg and
merged with Oliva Forest behind Hochstriess. The hill we
coasted on was called the Erbsberg. From its top a sled run
led directly to Eddi Amsel's garden on Steffensweg. We lay
on our bellies on our sleds, peering through snow-bearing
hazelnut bushes and through gorse that gave off a sharp smell
even in winter.

Amsel often worked in the open. He was wearing a traffic-
light-red sweater. Knitted tights, also red, disappeared into
rubber boots. A white muffler, crossed over the chest of his
sweater, was held together in back by a conspicuously large
safety pin. Red again and for the third time, a fuzzy cap
with a white pompon stretched over his head: we felt like
laughing, but we couldn't, because the snow would have
fallen off the hazelnut bushes. He was pottering with five
figures that looked like the orphans from the Almshouse and
Orphanage. Sometimes as we lurked behind snow-covered
gorse and black gorse pods, a few orphans with a lady super-
visor came into Amsel's garden. In blue-gray smocks under
blue-gray caps, with mouse-gray earmuffs and black woolen
mufflers, they posed parentless and shivering until Amsel
dismissed them with little bags of candy.

Tulla and I knew
that Amsel was filling an order at the time. The stage manager of the Stadttheater, to whom Walter Matern had introduced his friend, had examined a portfolio full of sketches
and designs submitted by Eddi Amsel, stage and costume de-
signer. Amsel's stage sets and figurines had appealed to the
stage manager, who had commissioned him to design the
scenery and costumes for a patriotic play. Since during the
last act—the scene was laid in the days of Napoleon: the city
was being besieged by Prussians and Russians—orphans had
to run back and forth between the advance lines and sing
before the duke of Württemberg, Amsel conceived the Amselian idea of putting not real orphans but mechanical orphans on the stage, because, so he maintained, nothing tugs
at the heartstrings so much as a quavering mechanical toy;
think of the touching music boxes of bygone times. And so
Amsel invited the Almshouse children to his garden and
dispensed charitable gifts in exchange. He had them pose and
sing chorales. "Lord on high, we praise Thee!" sang the

Protestant orphans. We, behind the bushes, suppressed our laughter and were all of us glad to have father and mother.

When Eddi Amsel was working in his studio, we couldn't make out what he was working on: the windows behind the terrace with the busily visited birdhouses reflected nothing but Jäschkental Forest. The other children thought he must be pottering with the same kind of thing as outside, comical orphans or cotton and toilet paper brides; only Tulla and I knew he was making SA men who could march and salute, because they had a mechanism in their tummies. Sometimes we thought we could hear the mechanism. We felt our own bellies, looking for the mechanism inside us: Tulla had one.

Tulla and I
didn't stick it out very long behind the bushes. In the first place it was getting too cold; in the second place it was too much of a struggle to keep from laughing; in the third place we wanted to coast.

While one sled run led down Philosophenweg and the second carried our sleds down to Amsel's garden, the third sled run deposited us near the Gutenberg monument. You never saw many children in that clearing, because all the children, except for Tulla, were afraid of Gutenberg. I didn't like to get too close to the Gutenberg monument either. No one knew how the monument had got into the forest; probably the monument builders had been unable to find a suitable place in town; or else they chose the forest, because Jäschkental Forest was a beech woods and Gutenberg, before casting metal type, had carved the letters he printed his books with out of beech wood. Tulla made us coast down to the Gutenberg monument from the Erbsberg, because she wanted to scare us.

For in the middle of the white clearing stood a soot-black cast-iron temple. Seven cast-iron columns supported the embossed cast-iron mushroom roof. Between the columns hung cold cast-iron chains held by cast-iron lion jaws. Blue granite steps, five of them, surrounded the temple, giving it elevation. And in the middle of the iron temple, amidst the seven columns, stood a cast-iron man: a curly iron beard flowed down over his cast-iron printer's apron. On the left he held a black iron book wedged against apron and beard. With the iron index finger of his iron right hand he pointed at the letters of the iron book. You could have read in the book if you had climbed the five granite steps and stood by the iron chain. But we never dared to take those few paces. Only Tulla, the feather-light exception, hopped, as we stood by with bated breath, up the steps to the chain, stood slim and tiny in front of the temple without touching the chain, sat between two iron columns on an iron garland, swung wildly, then more calmly, slipped off the still swinging chain, was in the temple, danced around the gloomy Gutenberg, and climbed up on his left cast-iron knee. It provided support, because he had set his left cast-iron foot with its cast-iron sandal sole on the upper edge of a cast-iron memorial tablet with the informative inscription: Here stands Johannes Gutenberg. To get an idea of how black the man reigned in the Harras-black temple, you have to remember that in front of, above, and behind the temple snow was falling, now in big, now in little flakes: the cast-iron mushroom roof of the temple was wearing a snowcap. While the snow fell, while the chain, set in motion by Tulla, came slowly to rest, while Tulla sat on the iron man's left thigh, Tulla's white index finger—she never wore gloves—spelled out the selfsame iron letters that Gutenberg was pointing at with his iron finger.

When Tulla came back—we had been standing motionless and were snowed in—she asked if we'd like to know what was written in the iron book. We didn't want to know and shook our heads violently, without a word. Tulla claimed the letters were changed from day to day, that every day you could read new but always terrible words in the iron book. This time they were especially terrible: "D'yuh wanna or don'tcha wanna?" We didn't. Then one of the Esch brothers wanted to know. Hänschen Matull and Rudi Ziegler wanted to know. Heini Pilenz and Georg Ziehm still didn't want to know and then they did want to know. Finally Jenny Brunies also wanted to know what was written in Johannes Gutenberg's iron book.

We were frozen to the spot and Tulla danced around us. Our sleds had thick pillows on them. Around the Gutenberg monument the forest cleared, letting the inexhaustible sky down on us. Tulla's bare finger pointed at Hänschen Matull: "You!" His lips became uncertain. "No, you!" Tulla's finger meant me. I'd surely have burst into tears if a moment later Tulla hadn't tapped little Esch and then reached into Jenny's fluffy duffel coat: "You you you! it says. You! You gotta go up or he's coming down and getcha."

The snow melted on our caps. "Kuddenpech said you. He said you. He wants Jenny, nobody else." Repetitions poured out of Tulla, more and more close-knit. As she described witch's circles in the snow around Jenny, the cast-iron Kuddenpech looked gloomily over our heads out of his cast-iron temple.

We began to confer. What, we asked, did Kuddenpech want of Jenny? Does he want to eat her or turn her into an iron chain? Does he want to stick her under his apron or press her flat in his iron book? Tulla knew what Kuddenpech wanted of Jenny. "She's gotta dance for Kuddenpech, 'cause she's always doing ballet with Imbs."

Jenny stood rigid, a doll-like ball in a teddy-bear fur, clutching the rope of her sled. The two snow roofs fell from her long, thick eyelashes: "NonoIdon'twanttoIdon't-wantto!" she whispered, probably meaning to scream. But because she had no mouth for screaming, she ran away with her sled: floundered, rolled over, picked herself up, rolled into the beech woods in the direction of Johanneswiese.

Tulla and I let Jenny run;
we knew she couldn't get away from Kuddenpech. If it was written in Kuddenpech's iron book: "It's Jenny's turn!" —then she'd just have to dance for Kuddenpech the way she was taught to at ballet school.

The next day, when we gathered our sleds on the hard-stamped snow of Elsenstrasse after lunch, Jenny didn't come out, although we whistled up at Dr. Brunies' windows, with fingers and without fingers. We didn't wait long: she was bound to come sooner or later.

Jenny Brunies came the day after. Without a word she fell into line, as usual filling her fluffy yellowish coat.

Tulla and I had no way of knowing
that Eddi Amsel stepped out into his garden at the same time. As usual he had on his knottily knitted traffic-light-red tights. Red again was his fluffy sweater. His matted white muffler was held together in back by a safety pin. He had had all his woolens knitted from unraveled wool: he never wore anything new. A lead-gray afternoon. It has stopped snowing; but there's a smell of snow that wants to fall. Amsel carries a figure over his shoulder into the garden. He puts it down man-high in the snow. Purse-lipped, he

whistles his way across the terrace and into the house, and comes back laden with another figure. He plants the second beside the first. With the march—"We are the guard . . ."— he whistles his way back into the studio and sweats round beads as he totes the third figure to join the two that are waiting in the garden. But he has to whistle the march all over again from the beginning: a path is gradually beaten through the knee-high snow until nine full-grown figures stand lined up in the garden, waiting for his orders. Burlap faced with dry brown. Chin strap under pig's bladder chin. Shined and polished and ready for duty: one-dish-devouring Spartans, nine against Thebes, at Leuthen, in Teutoburg Forest, the nine loyal stalwarts, the nine Swabians, nine brown swans, the last levy, the lost platoon, the rear guard, the advance guard, nine alliterated Burgundian noses: this is the sorrow of the Nibelungs in Eddi Etzel's snow-covered garden.

Tulla, I, and the others
had meanwhile left Jäschkentaler Weg behind us. Single file: sled track in sled track. Good crunchy snow. Imprints in the snow: many variously outlined rubber heels and hobnailed soles, with two, five, or no hobnails missing. Jenny stepped in Tulla's tracks; I in Jenny's tracks; Hänschen Matull in my tracks; obediently, little Esch and all who followed. Silently, without shouting or arguing, we trotted along behind Tulla. Only the little sleigh bells tinkled brightly. We were not, as might be supposed, going to cross the Johanneswiese to the top of the big sled run; shortly before the forester's house Tulla hove to: under the beeches we grew tiny. At first we met other children with sleds or on barrel staves. When there was no one left but us, the cast-iron monument had to be near. With short steps we entered Kuddenpech's realm.

While we crept stealthily, still stealthily,
Eddi Amsel was still whistling merrily merrily, still merrily. From one SA man he hurried to the next. Into the left pants pocket of nine storm troopers he reached: and then he released the mechanism inherent in all of them. They still sat fast on their central axes—metal pipes affixed to broad feet, rather like umbrella stands—and nevertheless, but without gaining ground, they fling eighteen twilightofthe-

godsy booted legs a hand's breadth above the snow. Nine creaky-boned marchers that have to be taught to march in time. This Amsel does to two of the marchers with the old faithful thrust into their left pockets: now they're in order, functioning, marching calmly firmly resolutely forward onward across toward upon and past, first in march step, then in goose step, as required in parades; all nine of them. And nine times the chin-strapped pig's bladders under SA visor caps snap almost simultaneously to the right: eyes right. They all look at him, for Eddi Amsel has pasted pig's bladder faces on all of them. Reproductions from paintings by Schnorr von Carolsfeld, who, as everyone should know, painted the sorrow of the Nibelungs, provide the features: the gloomy SA man Hagen of Tronje; the SA men, father and son, Hildebrand and Hadubrand; the luminous SA Sturmführer Siegfried of Xanten; the sensitive Obersturmführer Gunther; the ever-merry Volker Baumann; and three doughty heroes who had capitalized on the sorrows of the Nibelungs: the noble Hebbel of Wesselburen, Richard the Wagoner, and the painter who with subdued Nazarene palette had portrayed the sorrows of the Nibelungs. And as they, all nine of them, are still looking rigidly to the right, their arms, which only a moment before were swinging in march time, rise up jerkily and yet with a remarkable steadiness: slowly but conscientiously right arms climb to the regulation height for the German salute, while left arms bend stiffly until blackened rubber gloves stop near belt buckles. But who is being saluted? To whom are the eyes right addressed? What is the name of the Führer who is expected to look into all their pasted eyes? Who looks, returns the salute, and passes them in review?

In the manner of the Reich Chancellor, with arm bent at an angle, Eddi Amsel answers the salute of the parading storm troopers. For his own benefit and that of his nine mobile men, he whistles a march, this time the Badenweiler.

What Tulla didn't know:

while Eddi Amsel was still whistling, Gutenberg cast his terrible cast-iron gaze over the little group who, with sleds of various sizes, were crowding into his sphere of influence yet remaining at a respectful distance, and who finally excreted one little individual: doll-like fluffy condemned. Step by step, Jenny plodded in the direction of the cast iron.

New snow on old snow stuck to rubber soles: Jenny grew a good inch. Believe it or not, crows rose from the white beeches of Jäschkental Forest. Snowy burdens tumbled from branches. Subdued terror lifted Jenny's chubby hands. She grew another half inch because she was again, step by step, approaching the iron temple; while overhead the crows creaked unoiled, while nine black holes glided over the Erbsberg and fell into the beeches bordering the forest and Amsel's garden.

What Tulla couldn't know:

when the crows moved, Eddi Amsel and his nine parading storm troopers were not alone in Amsel's garden; five, six, or more figures with mechanisms built in not by Amsel but by Our Father who art in Heaven, are trampling down the snow. It's not Amsel's studio that has spat them out. They've come in from outside, over the fence: masked disguised shady. With their pulled-down civilian caps, with wide loden capes and black rags slit at eye level, they seem scarecrowy and invented, but it's not scarecrows, it's warm-blooded men who climb over the fence the moment the mechanism in Amsel's figures begins running down: nine saluting right cudgels fall with a jerk; rubber gloves slide away from belt buckles; goose step simplifies itself into marchstep funeral-march dragstep, halt; tinkling, the mechanism runs down; at this point Amsel unpurses his lips; the pig's snout has stopped whistling; cocking his fat head so that his fuzzy cap dangles, he is intrigued by his uninvited guests. While his nine invented creatures stand at attention as commanded, while gradually their over-heated mechanism cools off, the nine masked figures move according to plan: they form a semicircle, breathe warm breath through black masks into the January air, and approaching step by step, transform the semicircle around Eddi Amsel into a circle around Eddi Amsel. Soon he will be able to smell them.

Then Tulla called the crows back:

she called the cacophonous birds from across the Erbsberg into the beeches around the Gutenberg monument. The crows saw Jenny stiffen at the foot of the granite steps leading to Kuddenpech's iron temple and look back with her round face: Jenny saw Tulla, saw me, little Esch, Hänschen Matull, Rudi Ziegler, she saw the lot of them far in the distance. Did she count? Did the nine crows count: seven eight nine children in a cluster and one child alone? It wasn't cold. A smell of wet snow and cast iron. "Gwan dance around, dance around him!" Tulla yelled. The forest had an echo. We yelled too and echoed, to make her start dancing, to get the fool dancing over with. All the crows in the beeches, Kuddenpech under his iron mushroom roof, and we saw Jenny pull her right shoe, into which a knitted pants leg disappeared, out of the snow and with her right suggest something in the nature of a *battement développé: passer la jambe.* A plaque of snow fell from her shoe sole just before she sank the right shoe into the snow again and pulled out the left one. She repeated the awkward angle, stood on her right foot, lifted her left, ventured a cautious *rond de jambe en l'air,* went into fifth position, left her hands lying on the air in the *port de bras,* embarked on an *attitude croisée devant,* wobbled an *attitude éffacée,* and took her first fall when her *attitude croisée derriére* went wrong. When she emerged, her coat was no longer yellowish but dusted with white. Under a topsy-turvy woolen cap short leaps were now supposed to continue the dance in Kuddenpech's honor: from the fifth position into the *demi-plié: petit changement de pieds.* The ensuing figure was probably supposed to be the difficult *pas assemblé,* but Jenny took a second fall; and when, in an attempt to shine with a daring *pas de chat,* she took a third fall, tumbling when she should have been floating on air, when instead of weightlessly rejoicing the iron Kuddenpech's heart she flopped like a sack of potatoes into the snow, the crows rose up out of the beeches and squawked their heads off.

Tulla dismissed the crows:
on the north side of the Erbsberg they saw that the masked men had not only closed their circle around Eddi Amsel but had narrowed it. Nine loden capes trying to rub shoulders. Jerkily Amsel turns his glistening face from one to the next. He picks up his feet but makes no headway. His wool bunches up and has barbs. He conjures sweat from his smooth forehead. He gives a high-pitched laugh and wonders with nervous tongue between his lips: "What can I do for the gentlemen?" Pitiful ideas come to him: "Would you like me to make you some coffee? There may be some cake in the house. Or how about a little story? Do you know the one about the

milk-drinking eels; or the one about the miller and the talking mealworms; or the one about the twelve headless nuns and the twelve headless knights?" The nine black rags with eighteen eye slits seem to have taken a vow of silence. But when, possibly in order to put on water for coffee, he concentrates his spherical energies and tries to break through the circle of loden capes and pulled-down caps, he receives an answer: a bare, dry, unmasked fist: he falls back with his matted wool, pops quickly up again, begins to brush off the snow that is clinging to him. Then a second fist strikes and the crows rise up from the beeches.

Tulla had called them

because Jenny had had enough. After the second and third tumble she crawled over to us, a whimpering snowball. But Tulla wasn't through. While we stayed where we were, she darted swift and trackless over the snow: toward the snowball Jenny. And when Jenny tried to get up, Tulla pushed her back. No sooner did Jenny stand than she was lying down again. Who would have supposed that she was wearing a fluffy coat under the snow? We retreated toward the edge of the forest and from there saw Tulla at work. Above us the crows were enthusiastic. The Gutenberg monument was as black as Jenny was white. Tulla sent a bleating laugh with echo across the clearing and motioned us to come over. We stayed under the beeches while Jenny was being rolled in the snow. In utter silence she grew fatter and fatter. When Jenny had no legs left to get up with, the crows had done enough spying and projected themselves over the Erbsberg.

Tulla had an easy time of it with Jenny;

but Eddi Amsel, as the crows can bear witness, has to be answered with fists as long as he asks questions. All the fists that answer him are mute except for one. As this fist strikes him, it grinds its teeth behind a black rag. From Amsel's red-foaming mouth, a question blows bubbles: "Is it you? Si ti uoy?" But the grinding fist doesn't speak, it only punches. The other fists are taking a rest. Only the grinding one is working, bending over Amsel because Amsel refuses to get up any more. Several times, with downward thrust, it rams the red-gushing mouth. Possibly the mouth still wants to form the question: Isityou?—but all it can come up with is small, well-shaped pearly teeth: warm blood in cold snow, tin drums, Poles, cherries with whipped cream: blood in the snow. Now they're rolling him as Tulla rolled the girl Jenny.

But Tulla was finished with her snow man first.

With the flat of her hands she beat him firm all around, set him upright, gave him a nose modeled with a few swift strokes, looked around, found Jenny's woolen cap, stretched the cap over the snow man's pumpkin-round head, scratched in the snow with the tips of her shoes until she found leaves, hollow beechnuts, and dry branches, struck two branches left right into the snow man, gave the snow man beechnut eyes, and stepped back to survey her work from a distance.

Tulla might have drawn comparisons,

for behind the Erbsberg, in Amsel's garden, another snow man is standing. Tulla did not compare, but the crows compared. In the middle of the garden he reigns, while nine scarecrows, hung with brown-tattered burlap, stand dimly in the background. The snow man in Amsel's garden has no nose. No one has put beechnut eyes in his face. There's no woolen cap over his head. He cannot salute, wave, despair with fagot arms. But to make up for all that he has a red mouth that grows larger and larger.

The nine men in loden capes are in more of a hurry than Tulla. Over the fence they climb and vanish into the woods, while we, with Tulla, are still standing by our sleds at the edge of the woods, staring at the snow man in Jenny's woolen cap. Again the crows descend on the clearing, but instead of stopping in the beeches, they circle cacophonously unoiled over Gutenberg's iron temple, then over the snow man. Kuddenpech breathes on us coolly. The crows in the snow are black holes. The sky is darkening on both sides of the Erbsberg. We run away with our sleds. We're hot in our winter clothes.

Dear Cousin Tulla,

you hadn't thought of that: with evening came a thaw. A thaw is said to set in. All right: a thaw set in. The air became pliant. The beeches sweated. The branches gave up burdens of snow. Thudding sounds were heard in the woods. A warm breeze helped. Holes dripped into the snow. A hole dripped into my head, for I had stayed among the beeches. But even if I had gone home with the others and their sleds, a hole would have dripped into my head. No one, regardless of whether he stays or goes home, can get away from a thaw.

The snow men were still standing—the one in Kuddenpech's domain, the one in Amsel's garden—motionless. The gathering dusk excepted a dim whiteness. The crows were somewhere else, telling about what they had seen somewhere else. The snowcap slipped off the cast-iron mushroom roof of the Gutenberg monument. Not only were the beeches sweating, so was I. Johannes Gutenberg, normally a dull cast iron, exuded damply and glittered amid shimmering columns. Above the clearing and also where the forest ends and borders on the gardens of villas, over Langfuhr, the sky moved several stories higher. Hurrying clouds drove in slovenly ranks toward the sea. Through holes the night sky dotted stars. And finally a puffed-up thawtide moon came out and shone with intermissions. It showed me, now through a good-sized hole, now with half its disk, now nibbled, now behind a brittle veil, what had changed in the clearing, in Kuddenpech's domain, now that a thaw had set in.

Gutenberg glistened alive, but stayed in his temple. At first it looked as though the forest were going to take a step forward; but then in the broad light it stepped back; stepped forward on a solid front as soon as the moon was shut off; stepped back again, couldn't make up its mind, and with so much coming and going lost all the snow it had caught in its branches during the days of snow. Thus unburdened and with the help of the mild wind, it began to murmur. In league with the shivery moon, the agitated Jäschkental Forest and the cast-iron Johannes Gutenberg inspired me, Harry-in-the-Woods, with a sopping wet fear. I fled: Away from here! I stumbled up the Erbsberg. Two hundred and seventy-five feet above sea level.

I slid down the Erbsberg with moving snow, I wanted to get away away away, but landed outside Amsel's garden. I peered in through dripping hazelnut bushes and tart-smelling gorse under an absent moon. With thumb and forefinger, as soon as the moon permitted, I took the measure of the snow man in Amsel's garden: he was shrinking but still sizable.

Then I was seized with ambition to measure another snow man on the other side of the Erbsberg. Slipping time and again, I struggled up and in coasting down took care that no accompanying avalanche should carry me into the clearing,

into Kuddenpech's realm. A jump to one side saved me: I
hugged a sweating beech tree. I let water run down over burning fingers. Now to the right, now to the left of the trunk, I
peered into the clearing and, as soon as the moon took the
measure of the clearing, took measuring fingers to the snow
man outside Gutenberg's temple: Tulla's snow man was
shrinking no faster than the snow man to Amselward of the
Erbsberg; but he gave clearer indications: his fagot arms
were drooping. His nose was falling off. It seemed to
Harry-in-the-Woods that the beechnut eyes had come closer
together, giving him a crafty expression.

And once again, if I was to keep abreast of developments,
I had to climb the shifting Erbsberg and coast down, braking,
into the gorse: parched pods rustled. The scent of the gorse
tried to make me sleepy. But gorse pods woke me up and
compelled me, with thumb and forefinger, to keep faith with
shrinking snow men. After a few more of my ups and downs
both of them fell haltingly to their knees, which is meant to
mean that they grew thinner up above, swelled into a mealy
mass below the belt line, and stood on spreading feet.

And once, to Amselward, a snow man slanted to one side,
as though too short a right leg had made him slant. Once,
in Kuddenpech's realm, a snow man stuck out his belly and
disclosed in profile a rachitic incurving of the spine.

Another time—I was checking Amsel's garden—the snow
man's right leg had grown back; that deplorable slant had
straightened itself out.

And once—I had just come back from Amsel's garden and
was clinging, wet-hot and wool-sticky, to my dripping beech
tree—Gutenberg's iron temple, as the moonlight proved, was
empty: Horror! briefly the moon flared up: temple's empty.
And under the blacked-out moon: the temple an eerie
shadow, and Kuddenpech at large: sweating, glittering cast
iron with a curly iron beard. With open iron book, with
angular iron script he was looking for me among the beeches,
fixing to grab me with the book, to press me flat in the iron
book, he was after me, Harry-in-the-Woods. And that rustling sound: was it the woods, was it Gutenberg with his
rustling beard, whishing between beech trunks, whishing
through bushes? Had he opened his book—a hungry maw—
where Harry was standing? Now he's going to. What is
Harry looking for? Shouldn't he go home to supper? Punishment. *Poena*. Cast iron. And one more demonstration of how

terrifyingly deceptive the moonlight can be: when the clouds granted the deceiver a good-sized hole, the iron man was immutably in his house, emitting thawtide glitter.

How glad I was not to be pasted in Gutenberg's album. Exhausted, I slipped down along my dripping beech tree. I forced my tired, terror-popping eyes to be conscientious and go on watching the snow man. But they closed and opened, unfastened window shutters, at every gust of wind. Maybe they rattled. And in between I admonished myself, obsessed by the job I had taken upon myself: You mustn't sleep, Harry. You've got to go up the Erbsberg and down the Erbsberg. The summit is two hundred and seventy-five feet above sea level. You've got to go into the gorse, through the parched pods. You've got to register any alterations the snow man in Amsel's garden may have thought up. Arise, Harry. Ascend!

But I stuck to the dripping beech and would surely, if not for the loud crows, have missed the moment when the snow man in Gutenberg's realm fell apart. As they had done in the afternoon, so in the thickening night they announced the unusual by suddenly erupting and creaking unoiled. Quickly the snow of the snow man collapsed. The crows winged their way, as though for them only one direction existed, across the Erbsberg, Amselward: there too, no doubt, the snow was rapidly collapsing.

Who does not rub his eyes when he looks on at transmutations, but is unable to believe either his eyes or the snow miracle? Is it not strange that the bells always have to ring when snow men collapse: first the Church of the Sacred Heart, then Luther Church on Hermannshöfer Weg. Seven strokes. At home dinner was on the table. And my parents in among the heavy carved and polished furniture—sideboard, buffet, glass cabinet—looked at my empty carved chair: Harry, where are you? What are you doing? What are you looking at? You're going to make your eyes sore with all that rubbing.—There in the slushy, porous gray snow stood no Jenny Brunies, no frozen roly-poly, no ice dumpling, no pudding on legs, there stood a frail line, on which Jenny's yellowish fluffy coat hung loose, as though shrunk after improper washing. And the line had a tiny doll-like face, just as Jenny's face had been doll-like. But there stood a very different doll, thin, so thin you could easily have looked past her, and didn't budge.

Already the crows were returning loudly, plummeting down on the black forest. Assuredly they too had had to rub their eyes on the other side of the Erbsberg. There too wool had assuredly shrunk. A force drew me up the Erbsberg. Certainty seized me though I was reeling yet never slipped. Who had stretched a dry cable to pull me up? Who cabled me down without falling?

His arms folded over his chest, well balanced on supporting leg and unweighted leg, a young man stood in the dingy snow. Skin-tight the woolen sweater: pink; many washings ago it must have been traffic-light red. A white, coarsely knitted muffler, such as Eddi Amsel had owned, was thrown negligently over his left shoulder, not crossed and held together by a safety pin in back. Gentlemen in fashion magazines tend to wear their mufflers thus asymmetrically. Hamlet and Dorian Gray were posing jointly. Mimosa and carnations mingled their aromas. And the pain around the mouth cleverly enhanced the pose, gave it counterweight, and raised the price. And indeed the young man's first movement had to do with the painful mouth. Spasmodically, as though in obedience to an inadequately lubricated mechanism, the right hand climbed and fingered sunken lips; the left hand followed and poked around in the mouth: had the young man boiled-beef fibers between his teeth?

What was he doing when he stopped poking and bent straight-kneed from the hips? Was the young man with his very long fingers looking for something in the snow? Beechnuts? A key? A five-gulden piece? Was he looking for goods of another, intangible kind? The past in the snow? Happiness in the snow? Was he looking in the snow for the meaning of existence, hell's victory, death's sting. Was he looking for God in Eddi Amsel's thawing garden?

And then the young man with the painful mouth found something, found something else, found four times, seven times, found behind before beside him. And as soon as he had found, he held his find out into the moonlight with two long fingers: it glistened, it shimmered, white as sea foam.

Then I was drawn back up the Erbsberg. While he was looking, finding, and holding out into the moonlight, I coasted safely downhill, found my beech tree, and hoped to find the old familiar roly-poly Jenny in Gutenberg's clearing. But still it was the whippety line, hung with Jenny's shrunken coat, that cast a narrow shadow as soon as moonlight broke against it. But the line had meanwhile moved its arms sideways and turned out its feet, heel to heel. In other words, the line stood in the ballet dancer's first position and embarked forthwith, though without any visible exercise bar, on a difficult bar exercise: *grand plié—demie-pointe—équilibre, bras en couronne,* twice each in the first, second, and fifth positions. Next eight *dégagés* outstretched and eight *dégagés en l'air* with closed *plié.* Sixteen *battements dégagés* limbered the line up. In the *rond de jambes à la seconde,* ending in *équilibre en attitude fermée,* and in the *grand port de bras en avant, puis en arrière,* the line showed suppleness. Softer and softer grew the line. Marionettelike arm movements changed to fluid arm movements: already Jenny's coat slipped from shoulders no broader than a hand. Exercise under lateral floodlight: eight *grands battements en croix:* long legs, not quite enough instep, but a line as if Victor Gsovsky had dreamed the line and the line's line: *Finir en arabesque croisée!*

When again I was drawn up the Erbsberg, the hard-working line was reeling off *petits battements sur le cou-de-pied:* fine sweeping arm movements that sprinkled innumerable classical dots on the soft thawing air.

And the other side of the Erbsberg? With the moon looking on for a moment, I was ready to believe that the young man in Amsel's garden not only had Amsel's white muffler, but also Amsel's red hair. But it didn't stand up in flaming stubbles, it lay flat. Now he was standing to one side of a crumbling pile of snow. He had his back turned to the scarecrow group in burlap and brown rags, standing in the shadow of the woods: broad shoulders, narrow hips. Who had given him such ideal proportions? In the hollow of his right hand, held out to one side, lay something that was worth looking at. Supporting leg at a slant. Unweighted leg negligent. Bent neck line, part line, dotted line between eyes and the hollow of his hand: spellbound, ecstatic, photographed: Narcissus! I was already thinking of going up the mountain to watch the low *pliés* of the hard-working line, for nothing worth looking at was shown me in the hollow hand, when the young man acted: what he threw behind him glistened perhaps twenty or thirty-two times in the moonlight before raining down in the hazelnut bushes, in my gorse. I groped for it, especially as he had hit me with something that felt like pebbles. I found two teeth: small, well cared for,

with healthy roots; worth saving. Human teeth cast away
with a gesture. He didn't look behind him but strode springily
across the garden. He took the steps to the terrace in one
jump: gone with the moon. But a moment later a small
light bulb, possibly veiled in cloth, showed him bustling about
Amsel's villa. A glimmer of light in one window, then in the
next. Swift comings and goings. Something being carried,
something else: the young man was packing Amsel's suitcase
and was in a hurry.

I too in a hurry, climbing the Erbsberg for the last time.
O everlasting two hundred and seventy-five feet above sea
level. For to this day every third dream, I need only have
eaten something heavy for dinner, makes me climb the Erbsberg over and over again until I wake: painfully up, wildly
down, and then again, for ever and ever.

From my beech tree I saw the line dancing. No more bar
exercises, but a soundless adagio: solemnly arms are moved,
rest on the air. Steps secure on insecure ground. One leg is
enough, the other has been given away. Scales that tip slightly and go back to sleep, weightless. Turning, but not fast,
in slow motion, a pencil could follow. It's not the clearing
that's turning, but the line, turning two neat pirouettes. No
lifting, no balloon flights through the air; Gutenberg
should come out of his temple and play the partner. But he
as I: audience, while lightfoot the line measures the clearing. Speechless the crows. The beeches weep. *Pas de bourrée, pas de bourrée.* Changing feet. Allegro now, because
an allegro has to follow an adagio. Swift little feet. *Échappé
échappé.* And out of the *demi-plié* burgeon the *pas as-
semblés.* What Jenny couldn't quite manage: the merry
pas de chat; the line wouldn't want to stop on that, it
leaps, lingers in the air and manages, while persevering in
weightlessness, to bend its knees and touch toe to toe. Is it
Gutenberg who, after the bright allegro, whistles an adagio
as a finale? What a tender line. The line keeps listening. An
accommodating line. Line can grow longer or shorter. A
dash, drawn in one line. Line can do a curtsy. Applause.
That's the crows, the beeches, the thawtide wind.

And after the final curtain—the moon rang it down—the
line began with tiny little steps to look for something in the
dance-furrowed clearing. But it wasn't looking for lost teeth,
its mouth wasn't drawn with pain like the young man's to
Amselward of the Erbsberg, but rather with the ghost of a

frozen smile, which didn't expand or grow warmer when the line found what it was looking for: with Jenny's new sled the line moved across the clearing, no longer a dancer but a somewhat hesitant child, picked up Jenny's fallen fuzzy coat, threw it over its shoulders, and—Gutenberg raised no objection—vanished in the woods, in the direction of Jäschkentaler Weg.

Instantly, now that the clearing was deserted, terror was back again with cast iron and murmuring trees. Turning my back on the deserted clearing, I hurried through the beeches, and when the woods stopped and the street-lamp-studded Jäschkentaler Weg welcomed me, my hopping and hurrying did not abate. I didn't stop till I was on Hauptstrasse, outside Sternfeld's department store.

Across the square the clock outside the optician's indicated a few minutes after eight. The street was full of people. Moviegoers were hurrying into the movie house. A picture with Luis Trenker was being shown, I think. And then, probably after the picture had started, the young man came along, ambling and yet tense, with a suitcase. It couldn't have held much. Which of Amsel's spacious garments could the young man have taken with him? The streetcar came from Oliva, meaning to continue toward the main railroad station. He got into the trailer and stayed on the platform. When the car began to move, he lighted a cigarette. Sorrowfully sunken lips had to hold the cigarette. I'd never seen Eddi Amsel smoke.

And no sooner was he gone than primly, step by little step, the line came along with Jenny's sled. I followed it down Baumbachallee. We were going the same way. Behind the Church of the Sacred Heart I speeded up till I was beside the line, keeping step. I spoke more or less as follows: "Good evening, Jenny."

The line wasn't surprised: "Good evening, Harry."

I, to be saying something: "Have you been coasting?"

The line nodded: "You can pull my sled if you like."

"You're late getting home."

"I'm good and tired, too."

"Have you seen Tulla?"

"Tulla and the others left before seven."

The new Jenny had just as long eyelashes as the other: "I left a little before seven too. But I didn't see you." Jenny informed me politely: "I can see why you didn't see me. I was inside a snow man."

Elsenstrasse grew shorter and shorter: "What was it like in there?"

On the bridge over the Striessbach the new Jenny said: "It was awfully hot in there."

My solicitude, I think, was sincere: "I hope you didn't catch cold in there."

Outside the Aktienhaus, where Dr. Brunies lived with Jenny, the new Jenny said: "Before I go to bed, I'll take a hot lemonade as a precaution."

Many more questions occurred to me: "How did you get out of the snow man?"

The new Jenny said good-by in the entrance: "It began to thaw. But now I'm tired. Because I danced a little. For the first time I did two successful pirouettes. Cross my heart. Good night, Harry."

And then the door closed. I was hungry. I hoped there was something left in the kitchen. It seems, incidentally, that the young man took the train at ten o'clock. He and Amsel's suitcase rode away. It seems that they crossed both borders without any trouble.

Dear Tulla,

Jenny didn't catch cold inside the snow man but on the way home: the ballet in the clearing must have overheated her. She had to stay in bed for a week.

Dear Tulla,

you already know that a young man slipped out of the corpulent Amsel. With a light step, carrying Amsel's suitcase, he hurried through the station and took the train to Berlin. What you don't know yet: in his suitcase the light-footed young man has a passport, and it's forged. A certain "Hütchen," a piano maker by trade, manufactured the passport some weeks before the double miracle in the snow. The forger's hand thought of everything: for strange to say, the passport is graced with a photograph reproducing the tense, somewhat rigid features of the young man with the painful lips. Moreover, Herr Huth didn't issue this passport in the name of Eduard Amsel: he named the owner of the passport Hermann Haseloff, born in Riga on February 24, 1917.

Dear Tulla,

when Jenny was well again, I showed her the two teeth that the young man had flung into my gorse.

Jenny was delighted. "Oh," she said, "why, those are Herr Amsel's teeth. Will you give me one?" I kept the other tooth and still carry it on me; for Herr Brauxel, who could claim the tooth, leaves it in my purse.

Dear Tulla,

what did Herr Haseloff do when he arrived in Berlin-Stettin Station? He moved into a hotel room and went next day to a dental clinic where he had his sunken mouth filled with gold in exchange for good, erstwhile Amselian, now Haseloffian money. In the new passport Herr Huth had to note, after "Distinguishing Marks": "Artificial denture. Gold crowns." Henceforth when Herr Haseloff laughs, he will be seen laughing with thirty-two gold teeth; but Haseloff seldom laughs.

Dear Tulla,

those gold teeth became famous; they still are. Yesterday as I was sitting in Paul's Taproom with some associates, I made an experiment to prove that Haseloff's gold teeth are not a myth. This bar on Augsburger Strasse is frequented mostly by wrestlers, shippers, and unaccompanied ladies. The upholstered bench around our table—the one we always occupied—offered the possibility of arguing hard on a soft foundation. We talked about things people talk about in Berlin. The wall behind us was papered helter-skelter with the photographs of famous boxers, six-day bicycle racers, and track stars. Signatures and dedications offered reading matter; but we weren't reading, we were pondering, as we often do between eleven and twelve o'clock at night, where we could go when we had to leave. Then we joked about the impending fourth of February. The end of the world over beer and gin. I told them about Herr Brauxel, my eccentric employer; and that brought us to Haseloff and his gold teeth, which I called genuine whereas my colleagues refused to believe they were anything more than a myth.

So I called over to the bar: "Hannchen, have you seen Herr Haseloff lately?"

Over her rinsing of glasses Hannchen called back: "Naw. When Goldmouth's in town, he's been going someplace else lately, he's been going to Diener's."

Dear Tulla,

so it's true about the false teeth. Haseloff was and is known as Goldmouth; and the new Jenny, when she was allowed to get up after her bad cold, was given a pair of toe-dancing slippers covered with glittering silvery silk. Dr. Brunies wanted to see her standing on silver points. From then on she danced in Madame Lara's ballet room: Little Swans. The pianist Felsner-Imbs, whose dog bite was healing, poured out Chopin. And I, at Herr Brauxel's request, dismiss Goldmouth and listen to the scraping of silvery exercising ballet slippers: Jenny is holding the bar, embarking on a career.

Dear Tulla,

at that time we were all transferred to different schools: I was sent to the Conradinum; you and Jenny became pupils at the Helene Lange School, which soon had its name changed to the Gudrun School. My father, the master carpenter, had suggested sending you to high school: "The child is bright but unsteady. Why not give it a try?"

From sixth on Dr. Brunies signed our report cards. He taught us German and history. From the start I was conscientious but no grind and nevertheless first in my class: I allowed others to copy from me. Brunies was a lenient teacher. It was easy to divert him from strict insistence on his actual subject: someone only had to bring a piece of mica gneiss to class and ask him to talk about this kind of gneiss or all kinds of gneiss, about his collection of mica gneiss specimens, and instantly Brunies would drop the Cimbri and the Teutons to lecture about his science. But he didn't restrict himself to his hobby; he reeled off his whole litany of minerals: plutonite and pyroxenite; amorphous and crystalline rocks; it is from him that I have the words: multifaceted, tabular, and needle-shaped; the colors: leek-green, air-blue, pea-yellow, silver-white, clove-brown, smoke-gray, iron-black, and dawn-red are from his palette; he taught me tender words: rose quartz, moonstone, lapis lazuli; I adopted little words of reproach: "You tufahead, you hornblender, you nagelfluh!" But even now I couldn't distinguish agate from opal, malachite from labradorite, biotite from muscovite.

When we were unable to distract him with minerals from teaching according to the curriculum, his adoptive daughter Jenny had to fill the bill. The class speaker politely requested permission to speak and asked Dr. Brunies to tell us about Jenny's progress as a ballet dancer. The class, he said, would be pleased. Everyone was eager to know what had happened at the ballet school since the day before yesterday. And just as regularly as the key word "mica gneiss," the key word "Jenny" was able to lead Dr. Brunies astray: he broke off the migrations, let Ostrogoths and Visigoths rot by the Black Sea, and shifted to the new topic. He no longer sat motionless behind his desk: like a dancing bear he hopped about between bookcase and blackboard, seized the sponge and effaced the just outlined itineraries of the Goths. And over a still wet ground he made chalk squeak swiftly: not until a good minute later—he was still writing in the lower lefthand corner—did the wetness begin to dry at the upper right:

"First position, second position, third position, fourth position." That is what was written on the blackboard when Dr. Oswald Brunies began his theoretical instruction in ballet dancing with the words: "As is customary throughout the world, we shall begin with the basic positions and then turn our attention to the bar exercises." The schoolmaster invoked the authority of Arbeau, the first theoretician of the dance. According to Arbeau and Brunies there were five basic positions, all based on the principle of turned-out toes. During my first years in high school the word "turned-out" acquired more weight than the word "spelling." To this day a glance at a ballet dancer's feet tells me whether they are turned out enough; but spelling—with or without an *h*, for instance, or how many *r*'s in porridge—is still a puzzle to me.

We uncertain spellers, five or six ballet fans, sat in the gallery of the Stadttheater and looked on critically at the recital that the ballet master had ventured to stage with the help of Madame Lara. The program consisted of *Polovetsian Dances, Sleeping Beauty* with Petipa's ambitious choreography, and the *Valse Triste,* which Madame Lara had rehearsed.

My opinion: "La Petrich has plenty of sparkle in the *adagio,* but she's not turned out enough."

Little Pioch blasphemed: "Man, take a look at la Reinerl: those lopsided pirouettes, and her turnout is just plain embarrassing." Herbert Penzoldt shook his head. "If Irma Leuwelt can't develop a better instep, she won't hold on as first soloist very long, even if her turnout is terrific."

In addition to the word "instep" and the word "turnout," the word "sparkle" took on importance. So-and-so "may have plenty of technique, but there's no sparkle." Or a certain superannuated male dancer at the Stadttheater, who had to start in the wings when venturing a *grand jeté*, but then described a magnificent slow arc, received a magnanimous testimonial from the gallery: "With his sparkle, Brake can do what he likes; it's true that he only does three turns but they've got something."

A fourth word that was fashionable during my days in sixth was "balloon." In the *entrechat six de volée*, in the *grand jeté*, in every variety of leap, a dancer either had "balloon" or he didn't have balloon. Which meant either that in leaping he was able to hover weightlessly in air, or that he did not succeed in calling the laws of gravity into question. In fifth I coined the expression: "The new first soloist leaps so slowly a pencil could follow." That is what I still call leaps that are skillfully delayed: leaps that a pencil could follow. If only I could do that: follow leaps with a pencil.

Dear Cousin,

my class teacher, Dr. Brunies, did not content himself with teaching the ABC of ballet as a substitute for a ballad with seventeen stanzas and a regular joggle; he also taught us exactly what stands on tips when a ballet dancer succeeds in remaining faultlessly and effortlessly on her toes for the length of a single pirouette.

One day—I don't remember whether we were still on the Ostrogoths or whether the Vandals were already on their way to Rome—he brought Jenny's silver ballet slippers to class with him. At first he acted mysterious, huddled behind his desk, and hid his potato face with all its little creases behind the silvery pair. Then, without showing his hands, he set both slippers on their tips. His old-man's voice intoned a bit of the *Nutcracker Suite:* and between the inkwell and the tin box with his ten-o'clock sandwiches he made the slippers practice all the positions: *petits battements sur le coude-pied*.

When the show was over, he whispered, flanked by the silver slippers, that on the one hand the ballet slipper was a still-modern instrument of torture; while on the other hand, a ballet slipper must be regarded as the only kind of shoe in which a young girl can go to heaven in her lifetime.

Then he let Jenny's ballet slippers, accompanied by the class monitor, pass down the rows from desk to desk: Jenny's silver slippers meant something to us. Not that we kissed them. We barely caressed them, we gazed upon their frayed silver glitter, tapped their hard unsilvered tips, played absently with silver ribbons, and all of us attributed magical power to the slippers: out of the poor roly-poly they had been able to make something ethereal which, thanks to ballet slippers, was capable, day in day out, of going to heaven on foot. We dreamed sorrowfully of ballet slippers. Boys who suffered from exaggerated love for their mothers saw her enter their room at night dancing on her toes. Those who had fallen in love with a movie poster dreamt of seeing a film with a toe-dancing Lil Dagover. The Catholics among us waited at altars of Our Lady to see whether the Virgin might not deign to exchange the customary sandals for Jenny's ballet slippers.

I alone knew that it wasn't the ballet slippers that had metamorphosed Jenny. I had been a witness: with the help of plain snow Jenny Brunies had been miraculously alleviated, and so had Eddi Amsel—it all came out in the same wash.

Dear Cousin,

our families and all the neighbors were surprised at the obvious change in the child who was not yet eleven. But with an oddly smug wagging of the head as though they had all had a presentiment of Jenny's metamorphosis and prayed for it in common, they expressed their approval of what the snow had brought to pass. Punctually every afternoon at a quarter after four Jenny left the Aktienhaus across the street from us and walked primly, with a small head on a long neck, up Elsenstrasse. She propelled herself entirely with her legs and scarcely moved her body. Many neighbors pasted themselves to their streetside windowpanes every day at this hour. As soon as Jenny hove in sight, they said over geraniums and cactuses: "Now Jenny's going to balley."

When my mother missed Jenny's entrance by a minute for housewifely reasons or because she had been gossiping in the hallway, I heard her complaining: "Now I've gone and missed Brunies' Jenny. Well, tomorrow I'll set the alarm clock for a quarter after four, or maybe a little earlier."

The sight of Jenny had the power to move my mother: "What a string bean she's got to be, what a little broomstick." Yet Tulla was just as thin, but thin in a different way. Tulla's wiry figure frightened people. Jenny's figure made them pensive.

Dear Cousin,

our walk to school shaped itself into a strange procession. The girls of the Helene-Lange School and I went the same way as far as Neuschottland. At Max-Halbe-Platz I had to turn off to the right, whereas the girls took Bärenweg in the direction of Christ Church. Because Tulla waited in the half-darkness of our entranceway and made me wait until Jenny had left the Aktienhaus, Jenny had a head start: she walked fifteen, sometimes only ten paces ahead of us. All three of us took pains to maintain the interval. When one of Jenny's shoelaces came undone, Tulla had to retie a shoelace. Before I turned off to the right, I stopped behind the advertising pillar on Max-Halbe-Platz and followed the two of them with my eyes: Tulla was still behind Jenny. But one never had the picture of a dogged chase. On the contrary, it became clear that Tulla was running after Jenny without wishing to overtake the girl with the stiff, artificial gait. Sometimes when the morning sun was halfway up and Jenny cast her shadow, long and as wide as a telegraph pole, behind her, Tulla, prolonging Jenny's shadow with her shadow, stepped pace for pace on Jenny's shadow head.

Tulla made it her business to follow in Jenny's wake, and not only on the way to school. Also at a quarter after four, when the neighbors said: "Now Jenny's going to balley," she slipped out of the stair well and dogged her steps.

At first Tulla kept her distance only as far as the streetcar stop and turned back as soon as the car bound for Oliva clanged away. Then she began to spend money for the car, taking my pfennigs. Tulla never borrowed money, she took it. She reached into Mother Pokriefke's kitchen cupboard without asking. She rode in the same trailer as Jenny, but Tulla stood on the rear, Jenny on the front platform. Along the Oliva Castle Park Tulla followed in Jenny's trace at the usual distance, which was slightly diminished only in narrow Rosengasse. And beside the enamel sign "Lara Bock-

Fedorova, Ballet School," Tulla stood for a whole hour and no amount of stray cats could distract her attention. After the ballet lesson, she stood with locked-up face, letting the bevy of chattering ballet rats pass with their swinging gym bags. All the girls walked slightly pigeon-toed and carried overly small heads on stem-necks that seemed to need props. For the time it takes to draw a breath Rosengasse smelled, although it was May, of chalk and sour jerseys. Only when Jenny stepped through the garden gate beside the pianist Felsner-Imbs, did Tulla, once the two had a suitable head start, set herself in motion.

What a trio! Always in the lead the stooped Felsner-Imbs in spats and the child with the ash-blond pigtail down her neck; Tulla following at a distance. Once Felsner-Imbs looks around. Jenny doesn't look around. Tulla stands up to the pianist's gaze.

Once Imbs slows down and without stopping plucks a sprig of hawthorn. He puts it in Jenny's hair. Then Tulla likewise breaks off a sprig of hawthorn, but doesn't stick it in her hair, she throws it, after rectifying the interval with rapid steps, into a garden where no hawthorn grows.

Once Felsner-Imbs stops: Jenny stops. Tulla stops. While Jenny and Tulla stand still, the pianist turns about with frightening determination, takes ten paces toward Tulla, raises his right arm, shakes his artist's mane, and points an outstretched finger in the direction of the Castle Park: "Can't you stop molesting us? Haven't you any homework to do? Get along! Go away! We've seen enough of you!" Again and with desperate rashness he turns about, for Tulla neither answers nor obeys the index finger recommending the Castle Park. Imbs is at Jenny's right again. The procession doesn't start moving yet, for while he was sermoning Tulla the pianist's hair has got mussed and has to be brushed. Now it is billowing properly again. Felsner-Imbs takes steps. Jenny takes pigeon steps with feet turned out. Tulla keeps her distance. All three approach the streetcar stop across from the entrance to the Castle Park.

Dear Cousin,

the sight of you exerted a discipline. Passers-by carefully avoided entering the gap between Jenny and Tulla. In busy streets the effect of the two children was amazing.

By merely walking in dispersed Indian file they succeeded in creating a moving hole in the crowd.

Tulla never took our Harras with her when she was following Jenny. But I attached myself to them and, as in going to school, left the house with Tulla and walked up Elsenstrasse beside her: the Mozart pigtail ahead of us belonged to Jenny. In June the sun shines with particular beauty between old apartment houses. On the bridge across the Striessbach I detached myself from Tulla and with quick steps moved up to Jenny's left side. It was a cockchafer year. They hung excitedly in the air and scrambled wildly on sidewalks. Some had been stepped on, we stepped on others. The dry remnants of belated cockchafers were always sticking to the soles of our shoes. By Jenny's side—she took pains not to step on any bugs—I offered to carry her gym bag. She handed it to me: air-blue cloth in which the tips of the ballet slippers marked their contours. Behind Kleinhammerpark—clusters of cockchafers buzzed between chestnut trees —I slackened my pace until with Jenny's gym bag I was keeping step beside Tulla. After the railroad underpass, between the empty market booths of the weekly market, on wet pavement and in among the singing brooms of the street sweepers, Tulla asked me for Jenny's bag. Since Jenny never looked around, I allowed Tulla to carry Jenny's bag as far as Hauptstrasse. Outside the moviehouse Jenny was looking at pictures, in which a movie actress had broad cheekbones and was wearing a white doctor's smock. We looked at pictures in another case. Next week: A little actor smirked six times. Shortly before the streetcar stop I took the gym bag back and climbed with Jenny and Jenny's bag into the trailer of the Oliva car. In the course of the ride cockchafers crackled against the windowpanes of the front platform. After the "White Lamb" stop, I, still carrying the bag, left Jenny and visited Tulla on the rear platform but didn't give her the bag. I paid her fare, for at that time I had learned how to earn pocket money, selling firewood from my father's carpenter shop. After the Friedensschluss stop, when I was visiting with Jenny again, I would have paid for her too, but Jenny presented her monthly pass.

Dear Cousin,

before summer vacation was over, it became known that Herr Sterneck, the ballet master of the Stadttheather, had admitted Jenny to the children's ballet. I heard she was going to dance in the Christmas play, that rehearsals had already begun. The play this year, I learned, was called *The Snow Queen* and Jenny, as one could read in the *Vorposten* and the *Neueste Nachrichten* as well, would be playing the part of the Snow Queen, for the Snow Queen was not a speaking part but a dancing part.

In addition to taking the Number 2 to Oliva, Jenny now took the Number 5 to Kohlenmarkt three times a week; there stood the Stadttheater, as Herr Matzerath, who looked down on it from the Stockturm, described it in his book.

I had to cut a lot of firewood and sell it in secret to raise the carfare for Tulla and myself. My father had strictly forbidden this business, but the machinist stood by me. Once —I was late and made my heels clatter on the cobbles of Labesweg—I caught up with the two girls just before Max-Halbe-Platz. Someone had usurped my place: sturdy and diminutive, the grocer's son was marching along, now beside Tulla, now beside Jenny. Occasionally he did what no one else ever dared to do: he thrust himself into the empty gap. Whether he was beside Tulla, beside Jenny, or between them, his tin drum hung down over his belly. And he pounded the drum louder than necessary to provide two slender girls with march time. His mother, so they said, had died recently. Of fish poisoning. A beautiful woman.

Dear Cousin,
it wasn't until late summer that I heard you talk to Jenny. All spring and summer dialogue had been replaced by Jenny's gym bag, passing from hand to hand. Or by cockchafers, avoided by Jenny, stepped on by you. Or in a pinch Felsner-Imbs or I would toss back a word or carry one to and fro.

When Jenny left the Aktienhaus, Tulla was standing in her path and said, more past Jenny than to Jenny: "May I carry your bag with the silver shoes in it?" Without a word Jenny gave Tulla the bag but looked just as far past Tulla as Tulla had spoken past Jenny. Tulla carried the bag. Not that she walked beside Jenny as she carried it; she kept her distance as before, and when we took the Number 2 to Oliva, she stood on the rear platform with Jenny's bag. I was allowed to pay and was superfluous just the same. Not until we were outside the ballet school in Rosengasse did Tulla return the bag with the word "thanks" to Jenny.

So it continued into the fall. I never saw her carry Jenny's school satchel, only her bag. Every afternoon she stood ready in knee socks. Through me she found out when Jenny had rehearsal, when she had ballet school. She stood outside the Aktienhaus, no longer asked, held out her hand without a word, thrust her hand into the loop of the string, carried the bag after Jenny, and observed an unchanging distance.

Jenny possessed several gym bags: leek-green, dawn-red, air-blue, clove-brown, and pea-yellow. She changed colors without method. As Jenny was leaving the ballet school one October afternoon, Tulla, without looking past her, said to Jenny: "I'd like to look at the ballet slippers, to see if they're really silver." Felsner-Imbs was against, but Jenny nodded and pushed the pianist's hand aside with a gentle look. Tulla removed the slippers, which had been neatly packaged with the help of their silk ribbons, from the pea-yellow bag. She didn't open the package, she held it up to eye level on the palms of her hands, let her narrow-set eyes move along the slippers from the heels to the hard tips, tested the slippers for silver content and, though they were worn down and shabby-looking, found them silvery enough. Jenny held the bag open and Tulla let the ballet slippers vanish inside the yellow cloth.

At the end of November, three days before the first night, Jenny spoke to Tulla for the first time. In a gray loden coat she stepped out of the stage entrance of the Stadttheater, and Imbs was not escorting her. Right in front of Tulla she stopped; and while reaching into her leek-green gym bag, she said, without looking very far past Tulla: "Now I know what the iron man in Jäschkental Forest is called."

"His book said something different than what I said."

Jenny had to come out with her knowledge: "His name isn't Kuddenpech, it's Johannes Gutenberg."

"The book said that someday you're going to balley something terrific for thousands of people."

Jenny nodded: "That's very likely, but Johannes Gutenberg invented the printing press in the city of Mainz."

"Sure. That's what I was trying to tell you. He knows everything."

Jenny knows even more: "And he died in fourteen hundred and sixty-eight."

Tulla wanted to know: "Say, what's your weight?"

Jenny gave a precise answer: "Two days ago I weighed seventy-five pounds and two ounces. What's yours?"

Tulla lied: "Seventy-four pounds and eight ounces."

Jenny: "With your shoes on?"

Tulla: "In gym shoes."

Jenny: "Me without shoes, only in my jersey."

Tulla: "Then we're the same weight."

Jenny was delighted: "Very nearly. And I'm not afraid of Gutenberg any more. And here are two tickets for the first night, for Harry and you, if you'd like to come."

Tulla took the tickets. The car arrived. Jenny as usual gets on in front. Tulla gets on in front too. I too of course. At Max-Halbe-Platz Jenny gets out first, then Tulla, I last. Down Labesweg the two of them keep no interval, they walk side by side, looking like friends. I am allowed to carry the green gym bag behind them.

Dear Cousin,

you have to admit that as far as Jenny was concerned that first night was terrific. She turned two neat pirouettes and wasn't afraid to do the *grand pas de basque,* which makes even experienced ballet dancers tremble. She was marvelously turned out. Her "sparkle" made the stage too narrow. When she leapt, she leapt so slowly a pencil could follow, she had "balloon." And it was hardly noticeable that Jenny didn't have enough instep.

As the Snow Queen she wore a silver jersey, an icy silvery crown, and a veil that was supposed to symbolize the frost: everything Snow Queen Jenny touched froze fast instantly. With her came the winter. Icicle music announced her entrances. The *corps de ballet,* snow-flakes, and three funny-looking snow men obeyed her frost-chattering commands.

I don't remember the plot. But in all three acts there was a talking reindeer. He had to pull a sleigh full of mirrors, and in it, on snow cushions, sat the Snow Queen. The reindeer spoke in verse, ran faster than the wind, and rang silver bells off stage, announcing the Snow Queen's arrival.

This reindeer, as you could read in the program, was played by Walter Matern. It was his first part of any length. Shortly afterward, I heard, he obtained an engagement at the municipal theater in Schwerin. He did the reindeer very nicely and had a benevolent press next day. But the real discovery proclaimed in both papers was Jenny Brunies. One critic expressed the opinion that if Jenny had wanted to, the Snow Queen could have turned the orchestra and both balconies to ice for a thousand years.

My hands were hot from clapping. Tulla didn't clap when the performance was over. She had folded up the program very small and eaten it during the last act. Dr. Brunies, who was sitting between me and the other ballet fans in our class, sucked a whole bag of cough drops empty in the course of the three acts and the intermission after the second act.

After seventeen curtain calls Felsner-Imbs, Dr. Brunies, and I waited outside Jenny's dressing room. Tulla had already gone.

Dear Tulla,

the actor who played the reindeer and who could hit a schlagball into a fly and put a treacherous backspin on a faustball, that actor and athlete who played field hockey and was able to stay up for twelve minutes in a glider, that actor and glider pilot who always had a different lady on his arm—they all looked ailing and afflicted—that actor and lover, who had distributed red leaflets, who systematically read advertising prospectuses, mysteries, and introductions to metaphysics all in a jumble, whose father was a miller with the power of prophecy, whose medieval ancestors had gone by the name of Materna and been terrifying rebels, that well-built, moody, thick-set, tragic, short-haired, unmusical, poetry-loving, lonely, and healthy actor and SA man, that SA squad leader who after an action in January had been promoted platoon leader, that actor, athlete, lover, metaphysician, and platoon leader who on and without occasion could grind his teeth, that is, delve penetratingly and inescapably into last things, that grinder who would have liked to play Othello but had to play the reindeer when Jenny danced the Snow Queen, for one reason or another that SA man, grinder, and actor, even before leaving for the Schwerin Stadttheater where he had been engaged as *jeune premier*, took to drink.

Eddi Amsel, who went into the snow man and left it as Hermann Haseloff, did not become an alcoholic: he began to smoke.

Do you know why he called himself Haseloff and not Thrush, Finch, or Starling? For a whole year, while the two of you, Jenny and you, were keeping your distance, this question plagued me hermeneutically and even in my sleep. Before I suspected that Amsel now had another name, I paid perhaps a real, in any event an imagined visit to the empty villa on Steffensweg, which is conceivably still standing empty for Amsel on the strength of a long lease. Possibly Walter Matern, his faithful—one would think—subtenant, had just left the house—he probably had a show—when I made my way, let us suppose, from the garden across the terrace into Amsel's former studio. I pushed in approximately two windowpanes. In all likelihood I owned a flashlight. What I was looking for I could only find, and actually did find, in the Renaissance desk: important papers. Above me Amsel's scarecrow production of the previous year was still hanging. As I know myself, I wasn't afraid of weird shadows, or only tolerably afraid. The papers were slips of foolscap covered, in big letters, with chains of association and names, as though put there expressly for me. On one scrap of paper Amsel had tried to work himself up a name out of Steppenhuhn (moor hen): Stephun, Steppuh, Steputat, Stepius, Steppat, Stopoteit, Stappanowski, Stoppka, Steffen. When he dropped Steppenhuhn because it had brought him back so quickly and treacherously to the vicinity of the hastily abandoned Steffensweg, he tried the birds Sperling, Specht, and Sperber (sparrow, woodpecker, sparrow hawk) in combination: Sperla, Sperlinski, Sperluch, Spekun, Sperballa, Spercherling, Spechling. This unsuccessful series was followed by an original development on Sonntag, the Sabbath day: Sonntau, Sonntowski, Sonatowski, Sopalla, Sorau, Sosath, Sowert, Sorge. He abandoned it. He carried the series Rosin, Rossinna, Rosenoth no further. Probably he was looking for a counterpart to the *A* in Amsel when he began with Zoch, wrote Zocholl after Zuchel, squeezed Zuphat from Zuber, and lost interest with the attractive name of Zylinski; for outcries such as "New names and teeth are worth their weight in gold" or "A name is as good as teeth" told me, the at least conceivable spy, how hard a time he had finding a name that was different and yet right. Finally, between two half-developed series deriving from Krisun-Krisin and Krupat-Krupkat, I found a name all by itself and underlined. No series had spawned it. It had sprung from the air and landed on paper. It stood there meaningless and self-evident. Original and yet to be found in every telephone directory. More readily traceable to the circuitous rabbit than to the lunging hawk. The double *f* justified a Russian, or if need be Baltic, twitter. An artist's name. A secret agent's name. An alias. Names cling. Names are worn. Everybody has a name.

I left Eddi Amsel's oak-paneled studio with the name of Haseloff in my heart. I am willing to swear that no one had got wind of it before I came and pushed windowpanes in. All the scarecrows under the ceiling must have had moth balls in their pockets. Had Walter Matern played the housewife and insured Amsel's legacy against decay?

I ought to have taken some papers with me as proof for later.

Dear Tulla,

that actor who even in school and later consistently in his SA sturm was referred to as the "Grinder"—"Where's the Grinder? I want the Grinder to take three men and guard the Feldstrasse car stop, while we comb Mirchauerweg on the other side of the synagogue. I want the Grinder to give three loud grinds as soon as he leaves the town hall"—that enormously busy Grinder was to perfect the art of tooth-grinding very considerably when he took to boozing not off and on but regularly: he barely took time to pour the stuff into a glass; his breakfast began with juniper juice.

Thereupon he was thrown out of the SA. But they didn't bounce him out for drinking—they all tippled—they threw him out because he had stolen when drunk. At first Sturmführer Sawatzki covered him, for the two of them were close friends, they stood shoulder to shoulder at the bar, soaking themselves in the same liquid. It was only when SA Sturm 84 became restive that Sawatzki set up a court of honor. The seven men, all experienced platoon leaders, proved that Matern—only once—had dipped into the Section treasury. Witnesses reported that he had boasted about it when sozzled. The sum spoken of was fifty-three gulden. Matern had spent it buying rounds of gin. Sawatzki argued that the bilge people talked under the influence couldn't be accepted as proof. Matern protested vehemently: weren't they satisfied with him?—"Without me you'd never have caught Brill in Kahlbude."—What was more, he took full responsibility for whatever he had done—"Besides, you all helped me sop it up, every man jack of you. That's not stealing, it's boosting morale."

Then Jochen Sawatzki had to make one of his terse speeches. He is reported to have wept while settling Matern's hash. Intermittently he spoke of friendship: "But I won't put up with any rats in my sturm. None of us wants to throw his best buddy to the dogs. But stealing from your comrades is the worst kind. That's something no Lux or Ivory Soap can wash clean." The story was that he laid his hand on Walter Matern's shoulder and advised him in a voice choked with tears to disappear as quietly as possible. He could go to the Reich and join the SS: "You're through in my sturm, but not with me!"

After that they—nine men in civilian clothing—seem to have paid a visit to the Kleinhammerpark. Undisguised and without loden capes, they occupied the bar. They poured in beer and schnapps and ate blood sausage. They intoned: *"Ich hatt' einen Kameraden . . ."* Matern was said to have snarled obscene poems and croaked something about the essence of the ground. One of the nine was always in the toilet. But there was no Tulla sitting on a high stool, growing thinner and thinner like a tear-off calendar. No Tulla kept her eye on the toilet door: no beer-hall battle took place.

Dear Tulla,

Walter Matern didn't go to the Reich: the theatrical season continued; *The Snow Queen* was on the program until mid-February; and *The Snow Queen* needed a reindeer. Nor did Matern become a member of the SS, he became what he had forgotten but had been since baptism: a Catholic. In that, alcohol helped him. In May '38—they were doing Billinger's play, *The Giant*; Matern, who played the son of Donata Opferkuch, was fined a number of times for coming to rehearsals drunk—as the theatrical season was drawing to an end, he spent a good deal of his time knocking around the Holm, the waterfront suburb, and Strohdeich. To see him was to hear him. Not only did he perform his usual grinding act on docks and between warehouses, he also quoted with storm and bluster. Only lately, since I have been able to look things up in books, have I begun to unscramble the anthology of quotations that Matern had cooked up: he mixed liturgical texts, the phenomenology of a stocking-cap, and abstrusely secular lyrical poetry into a stew sea-

soned with the cheapest gin. The poetry especially—I sometimes chased after him—formed marbles that stuck in my
ears: expressionist poems. Lemurs were sitting on a raft.
There was talk of rubble and bacchanalias. How I, a boy
plagued by curiosity, puzzled my head over the word "gilly-
flowerwave." Matern writes finis. The longshoremen, good-
natured when they didn't have to unload plywood with the
wind in their beam, listened: ". . . it is late." The stevedores
nodded. "O soul, rotted through and through . . ." They
patted him on the shoulder and he thanked them: "What
brotherly joy round Cain and Abel, for whom God journeyed
through the clouds—causal-genetic, *haïssable*: the late I."

At that time I only dimly suspected who was meant by
Cain and Abel. I padded along behind him, as he reeled—
his mouth full of morgue, thrownness, and *Dies irae, dies illa*
—between the loading cranes in Strohdeich. And as he sat
there with the Klawitter shipyard behind him and the breath
of the Mottlau upon him, the Virgin Mary appeared to him.

He is sitting on a bollard and has already sent me home
several times. But I don't want any supper. To his bollard
and to the others that no one is sitting on, a medium-sized
Swedish freighter is made fast. It's a night beneath hasty
clouds, for the freighter is sleeping fitfully and the Mottlau
is pulling and pushing. All the hawsers by which the Swede
is clinging to the bollards are grinding. But he wants to
drown them out. He has already spat out the late I, all his
thrownness, and the Sequence for the Dead, now he starts
competing with the hawsers. In windbreaker and knickers
he sticks fast to his bollard, he grinds, before attacking the
bottle, goes on grinding the same song as soon as the bottle
neck is released, and keeps on blunting his teeth.

At the far end of Strohdeich he sits: by Polish Hook, at
the confluence of the Mottlau and the Dead Vistula. A good
place for tooth grinding. The ferry from Milchpeter had
brought him, me, and the longshoremen across. He had
started up with his teeth on the ferry, no, already on
Fuchswall and Jakobswall, after the gasworks, but it's only
on the bollard that he's started drinking and grinding himself
into a state: *"Tuba mirum spargens sonum . . ."* The low-
lying Swede helps. The Mottlau pushes, pulls, and mixes
with the sluggish waters of the Dead Vistula. The shipyards help, they're working the night shift: Klawitter behind
him; the shipyard on the other side of Milchpeter; farther

off the Schichau shipyard and the railroad car factory. The clouds devouring each other help him too. And I help, because he needs an audience.

That has always been my forte: to pad along behind, to be curious, to listen.

Now that the riveters fall silent and briefly, in all the shipyards at once, hold their breath, there's nothing left but Matern's teeth and the sullen Swede, until the wind blows around from Kielgraben: there, on Englischer Damm, cattle are being driven into the slaughterhouse. The Germania bread factory is quiet, though all three floors are lit up. Matern has finished his bottle. The Swede slips away. I wide awake in a freight-car shed. With its hangars, grain elevators, ramps, and cranes Strohdeich stretches out as far as Bay Horse Bastion, where the ferryboat with lights on is chugging across to the Brabank pier. His grinding has dwindled to leftovers and he has stopped listening to hawsers. What can he hear when he hears no riveters? Hoarse cattle and sensitive hogs? Does he hear angels? *Liber scriptus proferetur.* Is he reading masthead lights, port and starboard lights for line? Is he plotting nihilation or writing finis: last rose's dying, raft of lemurs, boulders of the east, barcaroles, Hades rises, morgue, Inca tablets, castle of the moon? This last of course is still at large, still sharp after a second shaving. Over the lead foundry and the pumping station it is licking at the municipal salt elevator, pissing sideways along silhouetted backdrop—Altstadt, Pfefferstadt, Jungstadt, that is to say, the churches of St. John, St. Catherine, St. Bartholomew, St. Mary; until with moon-inflated shift She appears. She must have come on the ferry from Brabank. From lamppost to lamppost She saunters up Strohdeich, disappears behind bird-necked cranes on the waterfront, hovers between shunting tracks, blossoms up again under a street lamp; and closer and closer he grinds her over to his bollard: "Hail, Mary!" But as she stands billowing before him, sheltering a little lamp under her shift, he doesn't get up but sticks fast and sulks: "Say, you. What should I do? Thou'rt weary and footsore from seeking me . . . So see here, Mary: do you know where he's taken himself? Hail, Mary, O.K., but now tell me, could I help it, it was that cynical streak I couldn't stomach: nothing was sacred to him. That's why. Actually we only wanted to teach him a little lesson: *Confutatis maledictis . . .* and now he's gone, he's left me his rags. I've mothproofed them, can you imagine, mothproofed, the whole damn lot! Come sit down, Mary. The thing with the money out of the cash drawer, O.K., I did it, but what about him, where is he? Has he run off to Sweden? Or to Switzerland where his dough is stashed away? Or to Paris?— that's where he belongs. Or Holland? Or overseas? Come on, sit down for God's sake. Bathed in tears, the day will dawn . . . Even as a kid—good Lord, was he fat!—he was always overdoing it: once he wanted a skull from under the Church of the Trinity. To him everything was funny, and always Weininger, that's why we. Where is he? I've got to. Tell me. Blessed art Thou among . . . But only if you. The Germania bread factory is working the night shift. See? Who's going to eat all that bread? Tell me. That's not riveters, it's. Sit down. Where?"

But the illuminated shift doesn't want to sit down. Standing, two hands' breadths above the pavement, She has prepared a little piece: *"Dona eis requiem:* things will be better soon. You will live in the true faith and be an actor in Schwerin. But before you depart for Schwerin, a dog will stand in your path. Fear not."

He on the bollard wants details: "A black dog?"

She with "balloon" in her shift: "A hound of hell."

He nailed to the bollard: "Does he belong to a carpenter?"

She enlightens him: "How can the dog belong to a carpenter when he is dedicated to hell and trained to serve Satan?"

He remembers: "Eddi called him Pluto, but only as a joke."

She with raised index finger: "He will stand in your path."

He tries to worm out of it: "Send him the distemper."

She counsels him: "Poison is obtainable in every drugstore."

He tries to blackmail her: "But first you've got to tell me where Eddi . . ."

Her last word: "Amen!"

I in the freight-car shed know more than both of them put together: he smokes cigarettes and has an entirely different name.

Dear Tulla,

on her way home the Virgin Mary probably took the ferry to Milchpeter beside the gasworks; and Walter Matern crossed with me at Brabank. One thing is certain, that he became even more Catholic than before: he even drank cheap vermouth, because schnapps and gin didn't do the trick any more. His teeth on edge from sugared sweet wine, he may have ground the Virgin to within speaking distance two or three times more: on the Holm, between the lumberyards on either side of Breitenbach Bridge or, as usual, at Strohdeich. It's doubtful whether they discussed anything new. He wanted to know where someone had taken himself to; she no doubt sicked him on the dog: "Formerly people used crow's eyes, but nowadays Grönke, the pharmacist, has a pharmacy on Neuer Markt that carries everything, corrosive, narcotic, and septic poisons. For instance: As_2O_3—a white vitreous powder extracted from ores, a simple arsenic salt, in a word, rat poison, but if you don't stint, it can do for a dog too."

So it happened that Walter Matern, after long absence, reappeared in our apartment house. Of course he didn't stagger straight into our yard and start caterwauling up at the eaves; he knocked at Felsner-Imbs' door and plumped himself down on the decrepit divan. The pianist brewed tea and kept his patience when Matern began to question him: "Where is he? Man, don't be like that. You know where he is. He can't just have evaporated. If anybody knows, it's you. So speak up!"

Behind windows left ajar I wasn't sure whether the pianist knew any more than I did. Matern threatened. From the divan he worked with his teeth and Imbs clutched a pile of music. Matern reeled in the electric-green music room. Once he reached into the goldfish bowl and threw a handful of water at the flowered wallpaper, unaware that he had thrown only water. But he hit the porcelain ballerina when he tried to smash the big hourglass with his shag pipe. The horizontal arabesque leg fell, after a clean break, on soft sheet music. Matern apologized and promised to pay for the damage, but Imbs mended the figure himself with a glue called "Omnistick." Walter Matern wanted to help but the pianist stood there stooped over and unapproachable. He poured more tea and gave Matern photographs to look at: in a stiff tutu stood Jenny doing an arabesque, like the porcelain ballerina except that her leg was all in one piece. Apparently Matern saw more than the picture, for he muttered things that didn't stand on their toes in silver slippers. The usual questions: "Where? He can't just have. Clears out without even leaving a message. Pushes off without. I've asked all over, even in Tischlergasse and in Schiewenhorst. Hedwig Lau has married in the meantime and broken off all relations with him, she says, broken off . . ."

Walter Matern pushed the music-room window wide open, slipped over the sill, and shoved me into the lilac bushes. By the time I had scrambled to my feet, he was approaching the ravaged semicircle indicating the reach of the chain that attached Harras to the lumber shed in the daytime.

Harras was still keen and black. Only above the eyes he had two little ice-gray islands. And the lips were no longer quite tight. The moment Walter Matern left the lilac garden, Harras was out of his kennel, straining his chain as far as the semicircle. Matern ventured to within two or three feet. Harras panted and Matern looked for a word. But the buzz saw interfered, or the lathe. And to our black shepherd Walter Matern, when he had found the word between buzz saw and lathe, when he had coughed it up and chewed it over, when it lay indigestible between his teeth, said "Nazi!"; to our Harras he said: "Nazi!"

Dear Tulla,

these visits went on for a week or more. Matern brought the word with him; and Harras stood straining forward, for to him was attached the lumber shed where we lodged: you and I and sometimes Jenny, who didn't take up much room. We knelt narrow-eyed behind peepholes. Outside, Matern went down on his knees and assumed the attitude of the dog. Human cranium versus dog's skull, with a child's head's worth of air in between. On one side growling: rising, falling, yet restrained; on the other side a grinding more of sea sand than of gravel, and then in rapid fire the word: "Nazi Nazi Nazi Nazi!"

Lucky that no one, except for us in the shed, heard the snapped word. Yet the windows on the court were chock-full. "The actor's here again," said the neighbors from window to window when Walter Matern came calling on our dog Harras. August Pokriefke ought to have turned him out of his yard, but the machinist said this was none of his business.

And so my father had to cross the yard. He kept one hand in his pocket, and I am sure he was holding a chisel warm. He stopped behind Matern and laid his free hand momentously on Matern's shoulder. In a loud voice, meant to be heard by all the occupied windows of the apartment house and by the journeymen in the second-floor windows of the shop, he said: "Leave the dog alone. Right away. And get out of here. You're drunk. You ought to be ashamed of yourself."

Matern, whom my father had raised to his feet with his carpenter's grip, couldn't resist the temptation to look him menacingly, ominously in the eye in the worst ham actor tradition. My father had very blue, firmly rounded eyes, which blunted Matern's stare. "It won't do you any good to make eyes. There's the door." But Matern chose the route through the lilac garden to Felsner-Imbs' music room.

And once, when Matern did not leave our yard through the pianist's apartment, he said to my father from the doorway of the yard: "Your dog has distemper, hadn't you noticed?"

My father with the chisel in his pocket: "Let me worry about that. And the dog hasn't got distemper, but you're stewed and you'd better not show your face around here any more."

The journeymen made menacing noises behind him and brandished drills and spirit levels. Nevertheless my father sent for the veterinary: Harras didn't have distemper. No mucous discharge from his eyes or nose, no drowsy look, no vomiting after feeding. Even so, brewer's yeast was spooned into him: "You never can tell."

Dear Tulla,

then the theatrical season of 1937 to 1938 was over, and Jenny told us: "Now he's in the theater in Schwerin." He didn't stay in Schwerin long but went, this too we heard from Jenny, to Düsseldorf on the Rhine. But because he had been fired without notice in Schwerin, he was unable to find work in any other theater, either in Düsseldorf or elsewhere. "Those things get around," said Jenny. As one might have expected, the next letter informed us that he was working on the radio, lending his voice to children's programs; the letter said he had become engaged but it wouldn't last long; that he still didn't know where Eddi Amsel was keeping himself, but he was sure he must be; that liquor was plaguing him less, he had gone back to sports: field hockey and even faustball, as in happier days; that he had a number of friends, all of them ex-Communists, who like him had their bellies full; but that Catholicism was a lot of shit, he'd got to know a few priests in Neuss and Maria Laach, they were revolting specimens; there'd probably be war soon; and Walter Matern wanted to know whether the beastly black dog was still alive —but Felsner-Imbs didn't answer.

Dear Tulla,
then Matern in person took the train and turned up in Langfuhr to see whether our Harras was still alive. As if it were the most natural thing in the world, as if months hadn't passed since his last visit, he was suddenly standing in our yard, dressed fit to kill: English cloth, red carnation in buttonhole, short-haired, and stewed to the gills. He had left all caution in the train or somewhere else, he no longer went down on his knees in front of Harras, no longer hissed and ground the word, but bellowed it into the yard. He didn't mean only our Harras; the neighbors in the windows, our journeymen, the machinist, and my father were all sick. The word. The neighbors all vanished into their two-and-a-half-room apartments. The journeymen fastened hinges. The machinist unleashed the buzz saw. My father manned the lathe. Nobody wanted to have heard that. August Pokriefke stirred carpenter's glue.

For to our Harras who alone remained available Walter Matern was saying: "You black Catholic hog!" Hymnally he spewed up his guts: "You Catholic Nazi hog! I'm going to grind you up into dogballs. Dominican! Christian dog! I'm twenty-two dog years old, and I still haven't done anything to earn immortality . . . just wait!"

Felsner-Imbs took the raving young man, who was breathless from roaring against lathe and buzz saw, by the sleeve and led him into the music room, where he served him tea.

In many apartments, on the second floor of our shop and in the machine shop, denunciations to the police were formulated; but no one turned him in.

Dear Tulla,
from May '39 to June 7, '39, Walter Matern was held for questioning in the cellar of police headquarters in Düsseldorf.

This was no theater gossip, passed on to us by Jenny; I sleuthed it out from the records.

For two weeks he was in the Marien Hospital in Düsseldorf, because they had cracked a few of his ribs in the cellar of police headquarters. For a long while he had to wear a bandage and wasn't allowed to laugh, which wasn't very hard on him. No teeth were knocked out.

I had no need to sleuth out these details, they were written black on white—though without mention of the police cellar —on a picture postcard, the picture side of which disclosed the Church of St. Lambert in Düsseldorf. The addressee was not the pianist Felsner-Imbs but Dr. Oswald Brunies.

Who had sent Walter Matern to the police cellar? The director of the Schwerin Stadttheater had not reported him. He had not been dismissed for political unreliability; it was because of continuous drunkenness that he was no longer allowed to act in Schwerin. This information didn't fall in my lap, it had to be painstakingly sleuthed out.

But why did Walter Matern remain in custody for only five weeks? Why only a few ribs and no teeth? He would not have been released from the police cellar if he had not volunteered for the Army: his Free City of Danzig passport saved him. In civilian clothes but with an induction order over still painful ribs he was sent to his home city. There he reported to the Langfuhr-Hochstriess police barracks. Until they were permitted to don uniforms, Walter Matern and several hundred civilians from the Reich had to spoon up one-dish meals for a good eight weeks: the war wasn't quite ripe.

Dear Tulla,

in August 1939—the two battleships had already anchored off the Westerplatte; in our carpentry shop finished parts for army barracks and double- and triple-decker beds were being hammered together—on the twenty-seventh of August our Harras breathed his last.

Somebody poisoned him; for Harras did not have distemper. Walter Matern, who had said: "The dog has distemper," gave him As_2O_3: rat poison.

Dear Tulla,

you and I could have testified against him.

It was a Saturday night: we're sitting in the lumber shed, in your hiding place. How did you arrange, what with the constant coming and going of logs, planks, and plywood, to have your nest spared?

Probably August Pokriefke knows his daughter's hiding place. When shipments of lumber come in, he alone sits in

the shed, directs the piling of the planks, and sees to it that
Tulla's hiding place is not buried. No one, not even he,
dares to touch the furnishings of her hide-out. No one puts
on her wood-shaving wigs, lies in her wood-shaving bed,
and covers himself with plaited shavings.

After supper we removed to the shed. Actually we wanted
to take Jenny with us, but Jenny was tired; and we understand: after an afternoon of ballet practice and rehearsal,
she has to go to bed early, for she has a rehearsal even on
Sunday: they are working up *The Bartered Bride*, with all
those Bohemian dances.

So the two of us are huddled in the dark, playing silence.
Tulla wins four times. Outside, August Pokriefke lets
Harras off his chain. For a long while he scratches at the
shed walls, whimpers softly, and wants to come in with us:
but we want to be alone. Tulla lights a candle and puts on
one of her wood-shaving wigs. Her hands around the flame
are parchment. She sits behind the candle tailor fashion and
moves her head with its dangling fringe of wood shavings
over the flame. Several times I say "Cut it out, Tulla!" so
she can continue her little tinder-dry game. Once a crisp
shaving crackles, but no lumber shed goes up sky-high in
flames, contributing an item to the local papers: Langfuhr
carpenter shop a total loss.

Now Tulla removes the wig with both hands and I have to
lie down in the wood-shaving bed. With the plaited blanket—
extra-long shavings that journeyman carpenter Wischnewski
planes from long planks—she covers me up. I am the patient
and have to feel sick. Actually I'm too old for this game. But
Tulla likes to be a doctor and sometimes I get fun out of
being sick. I speak in a hoarse voice: "Doctor, I feel sick."

"I don't believe you."

"Oh yes, Doctor, all over."

"All over where?"

"All over, Doctor, all over."

"Maybe it's the spleen this time."

"The spleen, the heart, and the kidneys."

Tulla with her hand under the wood-shaving blanket:
"Then you've got diabetes."

Now I have to say: "And I've got hose fever too."

She pinches my watering can. "Is that it? Is that where it
hurts?"

In accordance with the rules and because it really hurts, I

let out a scream. Now we play the game again, the other way around. Tulla crawls under the wood shavings and I, because she is sick, have to take her temperature with my little finger in her aperture. That too comes to an end. Twice we play stare and don't blink. Tulla wins again. Then, because we can't think of any other game, we play silence again. Once Tulla wins, and then I win, because in the middle of her silence Tulla explodes: out of her frozen face lit up from below, she hisses through ten bright-red paper fingers: "Somebody's crawling on the roof, d'you hear?"

She blows out the candle. I hear the crackling of the tar paper on the roof of the lumber shed. Somebody, possibly with rubber soles, is taking steps, pausing in between. Harras has started to growl. The rubber soles follow the tar paper to the end of the roof. We, Tulla in the lead, creep over the logs in the same direction. He's standing right over the dog kennel. Under him there's barely room for us between roof and piled logs. He's sitting down, with his legs dangling over the gutter. Harras keeps growling, always in the same low register. We peer through the ventilation slit between the roof and the edge of the shed. Tulla's little hand could slip through the slit if she liked and pinch him in either leg. Now he whispers: "Good boy, Harras, good boy." We can't see whoever is whispering "Good boy, Harras" and "Mum's the word," all we can see is his pants; but I bet the shadow he casts on the yard with the half-moon behind him is Walter Matern's shadow.

And what Matern throws into the yard is meat. I breathe in Tulla's ear: "It's poisoned for sure." But Tulla doesn't stir. Now Harras is nuzzling the chunk of meat while Matern on the roof encourages him: "Go on, eat. Eat, will you?" Harras tugs at the chunk of meat, tosses it up in the air. He doesn't feel like eating, he wants to play, although he's an old dog: thirteen dog years and a few months.

Then Tulla says, not even quietly, but with just about her usual voice: "Harras!" through the slit between the roof and the wall of the shed: "Take it, Harras, take it." And our Harras first tilts his head, then devours the meat, scrap by scrap.

Above us rubber soles squeak hastily over the tar paper: heading for adjoining yards. I bet it's him. Today I know it was he.

Dear Tulla,

we let ourselves into the house with your key. Harras was still busy with the meat and didn't come bounding after us, as he usually did. In the stair well I brushed the sawdust and shavings off my clothes and asked you urgently: "Why did you let Harras eat it, why?"

You were up the stairs before me: "Well, he wouldn't have done it for him, would he?"

I, ten steps behind you: "And suppose there was poison in it?"

You, a landing higher: "Well, then he'll kick off."

I over the rising banister: "But why?"

"Because!" Tulla laughed through her nose and was gone.

Dear Tulla,

next morning—I slept heartlessly without any particular dreams—my father woke me. He was really crying and he said: "Our good Harras is dead." And I was able to cry and dressed quickly. The vet came and wrote out a certificate: "The dog would certainly have lived another three years. Too bad."

My mother said it: "I wonder if it wasn't the actor, that used to be a Communist and that's always hollering in the yard." Of course she was crying too. Somebody suspected Felsner-Imbs.

Harras was buried in the police cemetery for dogs between Pelonken and Brennau, and his grave received regular visits. My father filed a complaint. He mentioned Walter Matern and the pianist. Imbs was questioned, but he had spent the evening playing chess with Dr. Brunies, looking at mica stones and drinking two bottles of Moselle. The proceedings against Walter Matern, who also had an alibi handy, bogged down: two days later the war began in Danzig, in Langfuhr, and in other localities as well. Walter Matern marched into Poland.

Not you, Tulla,

but I almost got to see the Führer. He announced his coming with crashing and pounding. On the first of September cannon were firing in just about every direction. Two of the carpenters took me up on the roof of our house. They had borrowed a spyglass from Semrau the optician: the war looked phony and disappointing. All I could ever see was shells being fired—Oliva Forest sent up little cottony clouds

—I never saw them landing. Only when the dive bombers began to do acrobatics over Neufahrwasser, showing the spyglass luxuriant smoke trails where the Westerplatte must have been, did I believe that they weren't playing. But as soon as I peered down from the roof into Elsenstrasse and on all ten fingers counted out housewives shopping and loafing kids and cats in the sunshine, I wasn't so sure: Maybe they're only playing and school will start again tomorrow.

But the noise was tremendous. The dive bombers, the twelve knock-kneed howlers, would certanly have made our Harras bark himself hoarse; but our Harras was dead. Not of distemper; someone poisoned our shepherd with poisoned meat. My father wept manly tears and let his cigar dangle cold in his face. Forlorn he stood at his drawing table with inactive carpenter's pencil, and the German troops marching into town couldn't comfort him. Even the news on the radio that Dirschau, Konitz, and Tuchel—all Koshnavia—were in German hands, brought him no consolation, although his wife and the Pokriefkes, all born Koshnavians, trumpeted the news across the yard: "Now they've occupied Petzin, and they've taken Schlangenthin, and Lichtnau and Granau. Did you hear that, Friedrich, they marched into Osterwick a few hours ago."

True consolation came to the carpenter only on September 3, in the form of a motorcyclist in uniform. The courier's letter announced that the Führer and Chancellor was sojourning in the liberated city of Danzig and wished to make the acquaintance of deserving citizens, one of these being Friedrich Liebenau, whose shepherd dog Harras had sired the Führer's shepherd dog Prinz. The shepherd dog Prinz was also sojourning in the city. Master carpenter Liebenau was requested to be at the Zoppot casino at such and such a time and report to SS Sturmbannführer So-and-so, the duty adjutant. It would not be necessary to bring the dog Harras, but a member of the family, preferably a child, would be admitted. Required: identification papers. Attire: uniform or well-pressed street clothes.

My father selected his Sunday suit. I, the requisite member of the family, hadn't been wearing anything but my Hitler Cub uniform for the last three days anyway, because something was always going on. My mother brushed my hair until my scalp tingled. Not a button was missing from father or son. When we left the house, the entrance was cramped with neighbors. Only Tulla was absent: she was collecting shell fragments in Neufahrwasser. But outside, every window was occupied with curiosity and admiration. Across the street in the Aktienhaus, a window was open in the Brunies apartment: wispy Jenny was waving to me excitedly; but Dr. Brunies didn't show himself. I long missed his potato face: when we were seated in the open official car behind the uniformed driver, when Elsenstrasse ended, when we had Marienstrasse, Kleinhammerpark, and Kastanienweg behind us, when we were speeding first down Haupstrasse, then down Zoppoter Chaussee in the direction of Zoppot, I still missed the face with the thousand wrinkles.

Not counting the bus, this was my first real ride in an automobile. During the ride my father leaned over and shouted in my ear: "This is a big moment in your life. Open your eyes wide, take it all in, so you can tell about it later on."

I opened my eyes so wide that the wind made them water; and even now as, quite in keeping with my father's, not to mention Herr Brauxel's wishes, I relate what I took in through wide-open eyes and stored up in my memory, my eyes grow strained and moist: at the time I feared that I might look upon the Führer through eyes blinded by tears, and today I have to make an effort to prevent the tears from blurring anything which was then angular, uniformed, beflagged, sunlit, world-shatteringly important, sweat-drenched, and real.

The Zoppot casino and Grand Hotel made us very small as we climbed out of the official car. The casino gardens were cordoned off; they—the population!—were standing outside and were already hoarse. There were two sentries on the broad driveway leading to the entrance. The driver had to stop three times and wave a pass. I have forgotten to speak of the flags in the streets. Even in our neighborhood, on Elsenstrasse, there were swastika flags of varying lengths. Poor or thrifty people, who couldn't or wouldn't afford a proper flag, had stuck little paper pennants in their flowerpots. One flagpole was empty, cast doubt upon all the occupied flagpoles, and belonged to Dr. Brunies. But in Zoppot, I believe, the whole population had put out flags; or at least so it seemed. From the round window in the gable of the Grand Hotel a flagpole grew at right angles to the façade. The swastika flag hung down over four stories, stopping above the main entrance. The flag looked very new and scarcely stirred, for that side of the hotel was sheltered from the wind. If I had had a monkey on my shoulder, the monkey could have climbed up the flag four stories high, until the flag had to give up.

In the lobby of the hotel, a giant in uniform under visor cap that was much too small and squashed down on one side, took us in charge. Across a carpet that made me weak in the knees he led us diagonally through the lobby. Bustle: figures came, went, relieved one another, announced one another, delivered, took reception: oodles of victories, numbers of prisoners with lots of zeroes. A stairway led down into the cellar. An iron door opened for us on the right: in the air-raid shelter of the Grand Hotel several deserving citizens were already waiting. We were searched for weapons. I was allowed, after a telephonic inquiry, to keep my Hitler Cub knife. My father had to deposit the pretty little penknife with which he cut off the tips of his cigars. All the deserving citizens, among them Herr Leeb of Ohra, to whom the meanwhile deceased Thekla of Schüddelkau had belonged—Thekla and Harras parented Prinz—well, then, my father, Herr Leeb, a few gentlemen with gold Party badges, four or five young whippersnappers in uniform but older than I, we all stood in silence, steeling ourselves. Several times the telephone rang. "Yes, sir. Yes, Sturmführer, I'll take care of it." Some ten minutes after my father had given up his penknife, it was returned to him. With an "All listen please!" the giant and duty adjutant began his explanation: "The Führer cannot receive anyone at the moment. Great tasks, decisive tasks require his attention. At such a time we can only stand back in silence, for on every front weapons are speaking for us all, and that means you and you and you."

Immediately and with a conspicuously practiced hand, he began to distribute postcard-size photographs of the Führer. The Führer's personal signature made them valuable. We already had one such signed postcard; but the second postcard, which we glassed and framed like the first, showed a more earnest Führer: he was wearing field gray and not any Upper Bavarian peasant jacket.

Half relieved, half disappointed, the deserving citizens were crowding through the door of the air-raid shelter, when my father addressed the duty adjutant. I admired his spunk; but he was known for that: in the Carpenters' Guild and in the Chamber of Commerce. He held out the ancient letter from the gauleiter's office, written in the days when Harras was still eager to mate, gave the adjutant a brief and factual account of the events leading up to and following the letter, reeled off Harras' pedigree—Perkun, Senta, Pluto, Harras, Prinz. The adjutant showed interest. My father concluded: "Since the shepherd dog Prinz is now in Zoppot, I request permission to see him." Permission was granted; and Herr Leeb, who had been standing diffidently to one side, was also given permission. In the lobby the duty adjutant motioned to another colossus in uniform and gave him instructions. The second giant had the face of a mountain climber and said to us: "Follow me." We followed. We crossed a room in which twelve typewriters were rattling and even more telephones were being used. A corridor showed no sign of ending. Doors opened. People streaming in our direction. Folders under arms. We stepped aside. Herr Leeb greeted everyone. In a vestibule six oval-backed chairs stood around a heavy oak table. The carpenter's eyes appraised the furniture. Veneers and inlays. Three walls crowded with heavily framed assortments of fruit, hunt still lifes, peasant scenes —and the fourth wall is glazed and sky-bright. We see the Grand Hotel winter garden: insane incredible forbidden dangerous plants: they must be fragrant, but we smell nothing through the glass.

And in the middle of the winter garden, drowsy perhaps from the emanations of the plants, sits a man in uniform, a little man compared to our giant. At his feet a full-grown shepherd is playing with a medium-sized flowerpot. The plant, something pale green and fibrous, is lying off to one side with its roots and compact soil. The shepherd rolls the flowerpot. We seem to hear the rolling. The giant beside us taps on the glass wall with his knuckles. Instantly the dog stands alert. The guard turns his head without moving his body, grins like an old friend, stands up, apparently meaning to come over to us, then sits down again. The outer glass front of the winter garden offers an expensive view: the terrace of the casino park, the big fountain—turned off— the pier, broad at the beginning, tapering down, fatter again at the end: many flags of the same kind, but no people except for the sentries. The Baltic can't make up its mind: now green, now gray, it tries in vain to glitter blue. But the dog is black. He stands on four legs, his head cocked. The spit and image of our Harras when he was young.

"Like our Harras," says my father.

I say: "The spittin' image of our Harras."

Herr Leeb remarks: "But he could have got his long croup from my Thekla."

My father and I: "Harras had that too: a long, gently sloping croup."

Herr Leeb admiringly: "How tight and dry the lips are—like my Thekla."

Father and son: "Our Harras was tight too. And the toes. And the way he holds his ears. The spittin' image."

Herr Leeb sees only his Thekla: "I guess—of course I can be mistaken—that the Führer's dog's tail is the same length as Thekla's was."

I put in for my father: "And I'm willing to bet the Führer's dog measures sixty-four centimeters to the withers, exactly like our Harras."

My father knocks on the pane. The Führer's dog barks briefly; Harras would have given tongue in exactly the same way.

My father inquires through the pane: "Excuse me. Could you tell us how many centimeters Prinz measures to the withers?" "Centimeters?" "Yes, to the withers."

The man in the winter garden has no objection to telling us the Führer's dog's height to the withers: six times he shows ten fingers, once his right hand shows only four fingers. My father gives Herr Leeb a good-natured tap on the shoulder: "He's a male after all. They come four or five centimeters taller."

All three of us agree about the coat of the dog in the winter garden: short-haired, every hair straight, every hair smooth, harsh, and black.

My father and I: "Like our Harras."

Herr Leeb undaunted: "Like my Thekla."

Our giant in uniform says: "Come off it, don't make such a much. Shepherds all look pretty much the same. The Führer has a whole kennel full of them in the mountains. This trip he took this one. Sometimes he takes different ones, it all depends."

My father wants to give him a lecture about our Harras and his ancestry, but the giant motions him to desist and angles his watch arm.

The Führer's dog is playing with the empty flowerpot again as I, in leaving, venture to tap on the pane: he doesn't

even raise his head. And the man in the winter garden
prefers to look at the Baltic.

Our withdrawal over soft carpets, past fruit still lifes, peasant scenes, hunt still lifes: pointers licking at dead rabbits
and wild boars, no shepherd dogs have been painted. My
father caresses furniture. The room full of typewriters and
telephones. A dense crowd in the lobby. My father takes me
by the hand. Actually he ought to take Herr Leeb's hand
too: he's always being jostled. Motorcyclists with dust-gray
coats and helmets stagger in among the correct uniforms.
Dispatch riders with victory dispatches in their bags. Has
Modlin fallen yet? The dispatch riders hand in their bags and
drop into wide armchairs. Officers give them a light and stop
to chat. Our giant pushes us through the entrance under the
four-story flag. I still have no monkey on my shoulder that
wants to climb up. We are escorted through all the road-
blocks, then dismissed. The population behind the fence
wants to know if we've seen the Führer. My father shakes
his head: "No, folks, not the Führer, but we've seen his dog,
and let me tell you, he's black, just like our Harras."

Dear Cousin Tulla,

no official car carried us back to Langfuhr. My father,
Herr Leeb, and I took the suburban railway. We got out
first. Herr Leeb stayed in the train and promised to come and
see us. I felt humiliated at our having to pass through Elsenstrasse on foot. All the same it had been a wonderful day,
and the essay I had, at Father's suggestion, to write the day
after our visit to Zoppot and submit to Dr. Brunies, was entitled: "My most wonderful day."

While returning my essay with his corrections, Dr. Brunies
looked down from his desk and said: "Very well observed,
excellently, in fact. There are, indeed, a number of hunt still
lifes, fruit still lifes, and hearty peasant scenes hanging in
the Grand Hotel, mostly Dutch masters of the seventeenth
century."

I was not allowed to read my essay aloud. Dr. Brunies
dwelt at some length on the hunt still lifes and peasant
scenes, spoke about genre painting and Adriaen Brouwer, his
favorite painter. Then he came back to the Grand Hotel and
casino—"The Red Room is especially fine and festive. And
in that Red Room Jenny is going to dance." He whispered
mysteriously: "As soon as the momentarily reigning warrior

caste leaves, as soon they have taken their clanking sabers and shouts of victory to other watering places, the director of the casino, in collaboration with the manager of the Stadttheater, is going to stage an unpretentious but distinguished ballet program."

"Can we come and see it?" asked forty pupils.

"It's to be a charity benefit. The proceeds are going to the Winter Aid." Brunies shared our dismay that Jenny would be dancing for a restricted audience: "She is going to make two appearances. She is actually going to do the famous *Pas de Quatre;* in a simplified version for children, to be sure, but even so."

I returned to my desk with my exercise book. "My most wonderful day" was far behind me.

Neither Tulla nor I

saw Jenny balley. But she must have been good, for someone from Berlin wished to engage her immediately. The performance took place shortly before Christmas. The audience consisted of the usual Party bigwigs, but also of scientists, artists, high Navy and Air Force officers, even diplomats. Brunies told us that immediately after the applause had died down at the end, a fashionably dressed gentleman had appeared, had kissed Jenny on both cheeks, and asked to take her away with him. To him, Brunies, he had shown his card and identified himself as the first ballet master of the German Ballet, the former Strength-through-Joy Ballet.

But Dr. Brunies had declined and had put the ballet master off until some later date: Jenny was still an immature child. She still needed a few more years in her familiar environment: school and home, the good old Stadttheater, Madame Lara.

I went up to Dr. Oswald Brunies in the playground. As usual he is sucking his cough drops, left and right, left and right.

"Dr. Brunies," I ask, "what was that ballet master's name?"

"He didn't tell me, my boy."

"But didn't you say he showed you some kind of a visiting card?"

Dr. Brunies claps his hands. "Right you are, a visiting card. But what on earth was on it? I've forgotten, my boy, forgotten."

Then I begin to guess: "Was he called Steppuhn, or Stepoteit, or Steppanowski?"

Brunies sucks merrily at his cough drop: "Far from it, my boy."

I try other birds: "Was he called Sperla or Sperlinski or Sperballa?"

Brunies titters: "Wrong, my boy, wrong."

I pause for breath: "Then his name was Sorius. Or it was Zuchel, Zocholl, Zylinski. Well, if it wasn't one of those and it wasn't Krisin or Krupkat, I've only got one name left."

Dr. Brunies hops from one leg to the other. His cough drop hops with him: "And what would that last name be?" I whisper in his ear and he stops hopping. I repeat the name softly, and under his matted eyebrows he makes frightened eyes. Then I mollify him, saying: "I asked the clerk at the Grand Hotel and he told me." The bell rings and the recreation period is up. Dr. Brunies wants to go on merrily sucking, but he fails to find the cough drop in his mouth. He fishes a fresh one from his jacket pocket and says, while giving me one too: "You're very curious, my boy, mighty curious."

Dear Cousin Tulla,

then we celebrated Jenny's thirteenth birthday. It was Dr. Brunies who had picked the foundling's birthday: we celebrated it on January 18th—King of Prussia proclaimed Emperor of Germany. It was winter outside, but Jenny had asked for a *bombe*. Dr. Brunies, who knew how to cook candy, had made the ice-cream mold at Koschnick's bakery according to a recipe of his own. That was Jenny's unvarying desire. If anyone said: "Would you like something to eat? What can I bring you? What would you like for Christmas, for your birthday, to celebrate your first night?" she always wanted ice cream, ice cream to lick, ice cream to eat.

We too liked to lick ice cream, but we had other desires. Tulla, for instance, who was a good six months younger than Jenny, was beginning to want a child. Both Jenny and Tulla, in the period after the Polish campaign, had the barest intimations of breasts. It was not until the following summer, during the French campaign and in the weeks after Dunkirk, that a change set in. They would feel each other in the lumber shed: it was as if they had been stung first by wasps, then by hornets. The swellings had come to stay;

they were carried about by Tulla with sophistication, by Jenny with wonderment.

Gradually I had to make up my mind. Actually I preferred to be with Tulla; but the minute we were alone in the lumber shed, Tulla wanted a child by me. So I attached myself to Jenny, who at most demanded a ten-pfennig ice-cream cone or a thirty-five-pfennig dish at Toskani's, an ice-cream parlor of repute. What gave her the greatest pleasure was to be taken to the icehouse between the Klein-hammerpark and Aktien Pond; it belonged to the Aktien Brewery, but was situated outside the brick wall spiked with broken glass, which encircled all three of the brewery buildings.

The icehouse was cubical, Aktien Pond was round. Willows stood with their feet in the water. Coming from Hochstriess, the Striessbach flowed into it, through it, and out of it, divided the suburb of Langfuhr into two halves, left Langfuhr at Leegstriess, and emptied, near Brosch-kescher Weg, into the Dead Vistula. The earliest record of the Striessbach, *"Fluuium Strycze,"* occurs in a document dated 1299, in which it is identified as a brook forming the boundary between the lands of Oliva monastery and those of the township. The Striessbach was neither wide nor deep, but it was rich in leeches. Aktien Pond was also alive with leeches, frogs, and tadpoles. As for the fish in Aktien Pond, we shall get around to them. Over the usually smooth water gnats sustained a single high note, dragonflies hovered transparent and precarious. When Tulla was with us, we had to collect leeches from the inlet in a tin can. A rotting, tumble-down swan house stood crookedly in the muck along the shore. Some years before, there had been swans in Aktien Pond for a single season, then they had died; only the swan house remained. Year in year out, regardless of changes in government, long editorials and indignant letters from readers kept up a stir over Aktien Pond, all demanding, in view of the gnats and the demise of the swans, that it be filled in. But then the Aktien Brewery made a contribution toward a municipal old people's home, and the pond wasn't filled in. During the war the pond was out of danger. It obtained a subtitle, it wasn't just plain Aktien Pond any more, but also the "Kleinhammerpark Fire-fighting Pond." The air-raid defense people had discovered it and entered it in their operations maps. But the swan house belonged neither to the brewery nor to the air-raid defense; the swan house, somewhat larger than our Harras' kennel, belonged to Tulla. In it she spent whole afternoons, and we handed the cans with the leeches in to her. She undid her clothing and applied them; on the belly and the legs. The leeches swelled up, turned blue-black like blood blisters, trembled slightly and ever more slightly, and as soon as they were full and easily detachable, Tulla, now green about the gills, tossed them into a second tin can.

We too had to apply leeches: I three, Jenny one, on the forearm and not on the legs, because she had to dance. With finely chopped nettles and water from Aktien Pond, Tulla cooked her leeches and ours over a small wood fire until they were done; then they burst, and despite the nettles cooked up with them, colored the soup a brownish black. We had to drink the muddy broth; for to Tulla the cooking of leeches was sacred. If we didn't want to drink, she said: "The sheeny and his friend were blood brothers too, the sheeny told me one time." We drank to the lees and all felt akin.

But one time Tulla almost spoiled the fun. When her cookery was done, she frightened Jenny: "If we drink now, we'll both get a baby and it'll be from him." But I didn't want to be a father. And Jenny said it was too soon for her, she wanted to dance first, in Berlin and all over.

And once when there was already a certain amount of friction between me and Tulla about the baby routine, Tulla forced Jenny in the swan house to put on nine leeches: "If you don't do it this minute, my oldest brother that's fighting in France will bleed to death this minute." Jenny applied all nine leeches all over her, went white, and then fainted. Tulla evaporated and I pulled off the leeches with both hands. They stuck because they weren't full yet. Some of them burst and I had to wash Jenny off. The water brought her to, but she was still livid. The first thing she wanted to know was whether Siegesmund Pokriefke, Tulla's brother in France, was safe now.

"Sure thing," I said, "for the present."

The self-sacrificing Jenny said: "Then we'll have to do it every few months."

I enlightened Jenny. "Now they have blood banks all over. I've read about it."

"Oh!" said Jenny and was a little disappointed. We sat down in the sun beside the swan house. The broad front of the icehouse building was reflected in the smooth surface of Aktien Pond.

Tulla,

I'm telling you what you already know: the icehouse was a box with a flat roof. From corner to corner they had covered it with tar paper. Its door was a tar-paper door. Windows it had none. A black die without white dots. We couldn't stop staring at it. It had nothing to do with Kuddenpech; but Kuddenpech might have put it there, although it wasn't made of cast iron but of tar paper, but Jenny wasn't afraid of Kuddenpech any more and always wanted to go inside the icehouse. If Tulla said: "Now I want a baby, right away," Jenny said: "I'd awfully like to see the icehouse on the inside, will you come with me?" I wanted neither nor; I still don't.

The icehouse smelled like the empty kennel in our yard. Only the dog kennel didn't have a flat roof and actually, in spite of the tar paper, it smelled entirely different: it still smelled of Harras. On the one hand my father didn't want to get another dog, but on the other hand he still didn't wish to chop the kennel into kindling but often, as the journeymen were working at their benches and the machines were biting into wood, stood in front of the kennel for five minutes, staring at it.

The icehouse was reflected in Aktien Pond and darkened the water. Nevertheless, there were fish in Aktien Pond. Old men, with chewing tobacco behind sunken lips, fished from the Kleinhammerpark shore and toward evening caught hand-size roaches. Either they tossed the roaches back or they gave them to us. For they weren't really fit to eat. They were putrid through and through and even when washed in clean water lost none of their living corruption. On two occasions corpses were fished out of Aktien Pond. By the outlet an iron grating collected driftwood. The corpses drifted into it: one was an old man, the other a housewife from Pelonken. Both times I got there too late to see the corpses. For as fervently as Jenny longed to penetrate into the icehouse and Tulla to be with child, I wanted to see an honest-to-goodness corpse; but when relatives died in Koshnavia—

my mother had aunts and cousins there—the coffin was always closed by the time we reached Osterwick. Tulla claimed there were little children on the bottom of Aktien Pond, weighted down with stones. In any event Aktien Pond was a convenient place for drowning kittens and puppies. Sometimes there were also elderly cats, floating aimless and bloated; in the end they got caught in the grating and were fished out with a hooked pole by the municipal park guard—his name was Ohnesorge like the Reich Postmaster General. But that is not why Aktien Pond stank, it stank because the waste from the brewery flowed into it. "Bathing prohibited," said a wooden sign. Not we, only the kids from Indian Village went swimming regardless, and always, even in winter, smelled of Aktien beer.

That was what everyone called the housing development which extended from behind the pond, all the way to the airfield. In the development lived longshoremen with large families, widowed grandmothers, and retired bricklayers. I incline to a political explanation of the name "Indian Village." Once upon a time, long before the war, many Socialists and Communists had lived there, and "Red Village" may well have become metamorphosed into "Indian Village." In any case, when Walter Matern was still an SA man, a worker at the Schichau Shipyard was murdered in Indian Village. "Murder in Indian Village," said the headline in the *Vorposten*. But the murderers—possibly nine masked men in loden capes—were never caught.

Neither Tulla's
stories about Aktien Pond nor mine—I'm full of them and have to hold myself back—can outdo certain stories revolving around the icehouse. One of them was that the murderers of the Schichau Shipyard worker had taken refuge in the icehouse and had been sitting ever since, eight or nine frozen murderers, in the iciest part of the icehouse. Many also presumed Eddi Amsel, who had disappeared without trace, to be in the icehouse, but not I. Mothers threatened children who didn't want to finish their soup with the black windowless cube. And it was rumored that because little Matzerath hadn't wanted to eat, his mother had punished him by shutting him up in the icehouse for several hours, and since then he hadn't grown so much as a fraction of an inch.

For there was something mysterious inside that icehouse. As long as the ice trucks were standing out in front and resonant ice blocks were being loaded on, the tar paper door stood open. When to prove our courage we leaped past the open door, the icehouse breathed on us, and we had to stand in the sun. Especially Tulla, who was unable to pass an open door, was afraid of the icehouse and hid when she saw the broad swaying men who wore black leather aprons and had purple faces. When the icemen pulled the blocks out of the icehouse with iron hooks, Jenny went up to the men and asked if she could touch a block of ice. Sometimes they let her. Then she held one hand on the block until a cubical man pulled her hand away: "That's enough now. You want to get stuck?"

Later there were Frenchmen among the ice haulers. They shouldered the blocks in exactly the same way as the native ice haulers, were exactly as cubical, and had the same purple faces. They were called "foreign workers," and we didn't know whether we were allowed to talk to them. But Jenny, who was learning French in school, accosted one of the Frenchmen: *"Bonjour, Monsieur."*

He, very courteous: *"Bonjour, Mademoiselle."*

Jenny curtsied: *"Pardon, Monsieur, vous permettez, Monsieur, que j'entre pour quelques minutes?"*

The Frenchman with a gracious gesture: *"Avec plaisir, Mademoiselle."*

Jenny curtsied again: *"Merci Monsieur,"* and let her hand disappear in the hand of the French ice hauler. The two of them, hand in hand, were swallowed up by the icehouse. The other ice haulers laughed and cracked jokes.

We didn't laugh but began to count slowly: twenty-four, twenty-five . . . If she isn't out by two hundred, we'll shout for help.

They came out at a hundred and ninety-two, still hand in hand. In the left she held a chunk of ice, curtsied once again to her ice hauler, and then withdrew into the sun with us. We were shivering. Jenny licked the ice with a pale tongue and offered Tulla the ice to lick. Tulla didn't feel like it. I licked: that's how cold iron tastes.

Dear Cousin Tulla,

after the incident with your leeches and Jenny's fainting, when we were on the outs over that, and because you kept wanting to have a child by me, when you had just about stopped coming to Aktien Pond with us and we, Jenny and I, didn't feel like crawling into the lumber shed with you, when the summer was over and school had begun, Jenny and I took to sitting either in the dill outside the garden fences of Indian Village or beside the swan house, and I helped Jenny by fastening my eyes to the icehouse, for Jenny had eyes only for the black, windowless cube. That is why the icehouse is clearer in my memory than the buildings of the Aktien Brewery behind the chestnut trees. Possibly the compound rose like a turreted castle behind the gloomy brick wall. Definitely, the high church windows of the machine house were framed in smooth Dutch brick. The chimney was squat but nevertheless, regardless of what direction you looked from, dominated the whole of Langfuhr. I could swear that the Aktien chimney wore a complicated helmet, a knight's helmet. Regulated by the wind, it gave off churning black smoke and had to be cleaned twice a year. New and dressed in bright brick-red, the administration building, when I screw up my eyes, looks at me over the glass-spiked wall. Regularly, I assume, trucks drawn by two horses left the yard of the brewery. Stout short-tailed Belgians. Behind leather aprons, under leather caps, with rigid purple faces: the driver and his helper. The whip in the holder. Order book and money pouch under the apron. Wads of tobacco for the day's work. Harness studded with metal buttons. The jolting and clanking of beer cases as front and hind wheels stumble over the iron threshold of the exit. Iron letters on the arch over the portal: D.A.B. Wet sounds: bottle-washing plant. At half past twelve the whistle blows. At one the whistle repeats itself. The xylophone notes of the bottle washers: the score has been lost, but the smell is still with me.

When the east wind turned the helmet on the brewery chimney and rolled black smoke over the chestnut trees, across Aktien Pond, the icehouse, and Indian Village in the direction of the airfield, a sour smell came down: surface-fermented yeast out of copper kettles: Bock Pils Malt Barley March-Beer Urquell. Not to mention the waste. Despite persistent claims that it drained somewhere else, the discharge from Aktien Brewery mixed with the pond, turned it sour and fetid. Accordingly, when we drank

Tulla's leech soup, we drank a bitter beer soup. Anyone who trampled a toad was *ipso facto* opening a bottle of bock beer. When one of the tobacco ruminants threw me a hand-size roach and I cleaned the roach beside the swan house, the liver, the milt, and the rest were overdone malt candy. And when I browned it over a crackling little fire, it rose for Jenny like yeast dough, bubbled, and tasted—I had stuffed it full of fresh dill—like last year's pickling fluid. Jenny ate little of the fish.

But when the wind came from the airfield and blew the vapors of the pond and the smoke from the brewery chimney against Kleinhammerpark and the Langfuhr railroad station, Jenny stood up, withdrew her gaze from the ice-filled tar-paper cube, and described numbered steps in the dill. Light to begin with, she weighed only half as much when she balleyed. With a little leap and a graceful curtsy she concluded her act, and I had to applaud as in the theater. Occasionally I gave her a nosegay of dill, having drawn the stems through a rubber beer-bottle washer. These never-fading, ever-red flowers floated by the hundreds on Aktien Pond, formed islands, and were collected: Between the Polish campaign and the taking of the island of Crete, I accumulated over two thousand beer-bottle washers, and felt rich as I counted them. Once I made Jenny a chain out of rubber washers. She wore it like a real necklace, and I was embarrassed for her: "You don't have to wear those things on the street, only by the pond or at home."

But to Jenny the necklace was not without value: "I'm fond of it, because you made it. It seems so personal, you know."

The necklace wasn't bad-looking. Actually I had strung it for Tulla. But Tulla would have thrown it away. When Jenny danced in the dill, the necklace actually looked very nice. After the dance she always said: "But now I'm tired," and looked past the icehouse: "I still have homework to do. And tomorrow we rehearse and the day after tomorrow too."

With the icehouse behind me I made a try: "Have you heard any more from the ballet master in Berlin?"

Jenny supplied information: "Not long ago Herr Haseloff wrote us a postcard from Paris. He says I have to exercise my instep."

I burrowed: "What does this Haseloff look like?"

Jenny's indulgent reproach: "But you've asked me that a dozen times. He's very slim and elegant. He's always smoking long cigarettes. He never laughs or at most with his eyes."

I systematically repeated myself: "But when he does laugh with his mouth for a change and when he speaks?"

Jenny came out with it: "It looks funny but also a little spooky, because when he talks, he has a mouth full of gold teeth."

I: "Real gold?"

Jenny: "I don't know."

I: "Ask him sometime."

Jenny: "I wouldn't like to do that. Maybe they're not real gold."

I: "After all your necklace is only made out of beer-bottle washers."

Jenny: "All right, then I'll write and ask him."

I: "Tonight?"

Jenny: "Tonight I'll be too tired."

I: "Then tomorrow."

Jenny: "But how should I put it?"

I dictated: "Just write: Herr Haseloff, there's something I've been wanting to ask you. Are your teeth real gold? Did you have different teeth before? And if so, what became of them?"

Jenny wrote the letter and Herr Haseloff answered by return mail that the gold was genuine, that he had formerly had white teeth, thirty-two of them; that he had thrown them behind him into the bushes and had bought himself new ones, gold ones; that they had been more expensive than thirty-two pair of ballet slippers.

I said to Jenny: "Now count how many bottle washers there are in your necklace."

Jenny counted and didn't understand: "What a coincidence, exactly thirty-two."

Dear Tulla,

it was inevitable that you should come around again with your scratched-up legs.

At the end of September—the dill went to seed and turned yellow, and the choppy waves of Aktien Pond made a soapy wreath of foam along the shore—at the end of September came Tulla.

Indian Village spat her out, and seven or eight boys. One

was smoking a pipe. He stood behind Tulla, using her for a windbreak, and handed her the boiler. Speechlessly she smoked. Slowly, by a calculated detour, they approached, stood looking in the air, looked past us, turned back and were gone: behind the fences and whitewashed cottages of Indian Village.

And once toward evening—we had the sun behind us, the helmet of the brewery chimney sat on the bleeding head of a bleeding knight—they appeared to one side of the icehouse and came goose-stepping through the nettles along the front tar-paper wall. In the dill they spread out, Tulla handed the pipe to the left and said to the gnats: "They've forgotten to close up. Wouldn't you like to go in, Jenny, and see what it's like?"

Jenny was so friendly and always polite: "Oh no, it's late and I'm rather tired. We have English tomorrow, you know, and I have to be rested for my dancing lesson."

Tulla had the pipe again: "O.K., if you don't want to. Then we'll go tell the caretaker to lock up."

But Jenny was already on her feet and I had to stand up: "You can't go, Jenny, it's out of the question. Anyway, you're tired, you just said so." Jenny wasn't tired any more and wanted to look in just for a second: "It's very interesting in there, please, Harry."

I stuck by her side and got into the nettles. Tulla in the lead, the others behind us. Tulla's thumb pointed at the tar-paper door: it was open just a crack and scarcely breathed. Then I had to say: "But I won't let you go alone." And Jenny, slender in the door jamb, said ever so politely: "That's awfully nice of you, Harry."

Who else but Tulla

pushed me through the doorway behind Jenny. And I had forgotten to disarm you and the boys outside with a crossyourheartandhopetodie. As the breath of the icehouse took us in tow—Jenny's little finger hooked itself into my little finger—as icy lungs drew us in, I knew: now Tulla, alone or with that young thug, is going to the caretaker and getting the key, or she's getting the caretaker with the key: and the gang are palavering in nine voices so the caretaker won't hear us while he's locking up.

For that reason or because Jenny had me by the finger, I didn't succeed in calling for help. She led me surefootedly through the black crackling windpipe. From all sides, from the top and bottom too, breath made us light until there was no ground under our feet. We passed over trestles and stairways that were marked with red position lights. And Jenny said in a perfectly normal voice: "Watch out, please, Harry: we'll be going downstairs now, twelve steps."

But hard as I tried to find ground from step to step, I sank, breathed in by a suction coming from below. And when Jenny said: "Now we're in the first basement, we've got to keep to the left, that's where the entrance to the second basement is supposed to be," I would gladly, though busy with a skin itch, have stayed in the first basement. That was the nettles from before; but what was beating down on my skin was the breath coming from all sides. And every direction creaked, no, crackled, no, crunched: piled blocks, complete sets of teeth rubbed against each other till the enamel splintered, and the breath of iron was yeasty stale stomach-sour furry clammy. The barest touch of tar paper. Yeast rose. Vinegar evaporated. Mushrooms sprouted. "Careful, a step," said Jenny. In whose malt-bitter maw? The second basement of what hell had left pickles uncovered to spoil? What devil had stoked the furnace to subzero?

I wanted to scream and whispered: "They'll lock us in if we don't . . ."

But Jenny was still her methodical self: "They always lock up at seven."

"Where are we?"

"Now we're in the second basement. Some of these blocks are many years old."

My hand wanted to know exactly: "How many years?" and reached out to the left, looked for resistance, found it, and stuck fast on prehistoric giant's teeth: "I'm stuck, Jenny! I'm stuck!"

Then Jenny rests her hand on my sticking hand: instantly I am able to remove my fingers from the giant tooth, but I keep hold of Jenny's arm, arm lovely from dancing, arm that can lie and sleep on air, the other one too. And both rubbed hot by breath in blocks. In the armpits: August. Jenny titters: "You mustn't tickle me, Harry."

But I just want "to hold tight, Jenny."

She lets me and is again "a little tired, Harry."

I don't think "there's a bench here, Jenny."

She is not of little faith: "Why shouldn't there be a bench here, Harry?" And because she says so, there is one, an iron bench. But because Jenny sits down, the iron bench turns, the longer she sits on it, into a cozy well-worn wooden bench. Now Jenny, precociously motherly, says to me in the second basement of the icehouse: "You mustn't shiver any more, Harry. You know, once I was hidden inside a snow man. And I learned a great deal in there. So if you can't stop shivering, you must hold me tight. And then if you're still cold, because you weren't ever in a snow man, you must kiss me, that helps, you know. I could give you my dress too, I don't need it, I'm positive. You mustn't be embarrassed. We're all alone. And I'm perfectly at home here. You can throw it around your neck like a muffler. Later on I'll sleep a little, because I have to go to Madame Lara's tomorrow, and the day after tomorrow I have to practice again. Besides, I really am a little tired, you know."

And so we sat through the night on the iron wooden bench. I held Jenny tight. Her dry lips were tasteless. I threw her cotton dress—if I only knew whether it had dots, stripes, or checks—I threw her short-sleeve summer dress over my shoulders and around my neck. Dressless but in her slip, she lay in my arms, which didn't tire, because Jenny was light even when she slept. I didn't sleep, for fear she'd slip away from me. For I'd never been inside a snow man, and without her dry lips, without her cotton dress, without her weightless weight in my arms, without Jenny, I'd have been lost. Surrounded by crackling, sighing, and crunching, in the breath of the ice blocks, breathed on breathed in: the ice would have held me in its clutches to this day.

But as it was, we lived to see the next day. The morning rumbled in the basement above us. That was the icemen in the leather aprons. Jenny in her dress wanted to know: "Did you sleep a little too?"

"Of course not. Somebody had to be on the lookout."

"Imagine, I dreamt my instep had improved and in the end I was able to do the thirty-two *fouettés*: and Herr Haseloff laughed."

"With his gold teeth?"

"Every single one of them, while I turned and turned."

Without difficulty, amid whispering and interpretation of dreams, we made our way to the first basement and then up some more steps. The red position lights showed the path between piled ice blocks to the exit, the rectangular light. But Jenny held me back. We mustn't let anybody see us, because "If they catch us," said Jenny, "they'll never let us in again."

When the glaring rectangle disclosed no more men in leather aprons, when the hefty Belgian horses pulled up and the ice truck rolled away on rubber tires, we dashed through the door before the next ice truck drove up. The sun slanted down from chestnut trees. We slipped along tar-paper walls. Everything smelled different from the day before. My legs were in the nettles again. On Kleinhammerweg, while Jenny was saying her irregular English verbs, I began to dread the carpenter's hand waiting for me at home.

You know,
that night we spent in the icehouse had several consequences: I got a licking; the police, notified by Dr. Brunies, asked questions; we had grown older and left Aktien Pond with its smells to the twelve-year-olds. I got rid of my collection of bottle washers the next time the junkman came around. Whether Jenny stopped wearing her bottle-washer necklace, I don't know: We elaborately went out of each other's way. Jenny blushed when we couldn't avoid each other on Elsenstrasse; and I went red in the face every time Tulla met me on the stairs or in our kitchen, when she came in for salt or to borrow a saucepan.

Is your memory any good?
There are at least five months, with Christmas in the middle, that I can't piece together. During this period, in the gap between the French campaign and the Balkan campaign, more and more of our workmen were drafted and later, when the war had started in the East, replaced by Ukrainian helpers and one French carpenter. Wischnewski fell in Greece; Arthur Kuleise, another of our carpenters, fell right in the beginning at Lemberg; and then my cousin, Tulla's brother Alexander Pokriefke, fell—that is, he didn't fall, he was drowned in a submarine: the battle of the Atlantic had started. Not only the Pokriefkes, but the master carpenter and his wife as well, each wore crape. I too wore crape and was very proud of it. Whenever anyone asked me why I was in mourning, I said: "A cousin of mine, who was very close to me, was on duty in the Caribbean Sea in a submarine

and he didn't come home." Actually I hardly knew Alexander Pokriefke, and the Caribbean Sea was hokum too.

Did something else happen?

My father received big orders. His shop was turning out nothing but doors and windows for Navy barracks in Putzig. Suddenly and for no apparent reason he began to drink, and once, of a Sunday morning, beat my mother because she was standing where he wanted to stand. But he never neglected his work and went on smoking his seconds, which he obtained on the black market in exchange for door frames.

What else happened?

They made your father a cell leader. August Pokriefke threw himself body and soul into his Party claptrap. He got a certificate of disability from a Party doctor—the usual knee injury—and decided to give indoctrination lectures in our machine shop. But my father wouldn't allow it. Old family quarrels were dug up. Something about two acres of pasture land left by my grandparents in Osterwick. My mother's dowry was itemized on fingers. My father argued to the contrary that he was paying for Tulla's schooling. August Pokriefke pounded the table: the Party would advance the money for Tulla's school, you bet they will! And he, August Pokriefke, would deliver his indoctrination lectures come hell and high water, after hours if necessary.

And where were you that summer?

Off in Brösen with the thirds. If anyone went looking for you, he found you on the hulk of a Polish mine sweeper, which lay on the bottom not far from the harbor mouth. The thirds dived down into the mine sweeper and brought stuff up. I was a poor swimmer and never dared to open my eyes under water. Consequently I went looking for you in other places and never on the barge. Besides, I had Jenny; and you always wanted the same old thing: a baby. Did they make you one on the mine sweeper?

You showed no sign of it. Or the kids in Indian Village? They left you no reminders. The two Ukrainians in our shop with their perpetually frightened potato faces? Neither of them took you into the shed, and nevertheless my father was always grilling them. And August Pokriefke knocked one of them, Kleba was his name, cold with a spirit level between

finishing machine and lathe, because he was always begging
for bread. Whereupon my father threw your father out of
the shop. Your father threatened to put in a report; but it
was my father, who enjoyed a certain standing with the
Chamber of Commerce and with the Party as well, who did the
reporting. A court of honor of sorts was held. August Pokriefke and master carpenter Liebenau were instructed to
make up; the Ukrainians were exchanged for two other
Ukrainians—there were plenty of them—and the first two, so
we heard, were sent to Stutthof.

Stutthof: on your account!

That little word took on more and more meaning. "Hey,
you! You got a yen for Stutthof?"—"If you don't keep that
trap of yours shut, you'll end up in Stutthof." A sinister word
had moved into apartment houses, went upstairs and downstairs, sat at kitchen tables, was supposed to be a joke, and
some actually laughed: "They're making soap in Stutthof now,
it makes you want to stop washing."

You and I were never in Stutthof.

Tulla didn't even know Nickelswalde; a Hitler Cub
camp took me to Steegen; but Herr Brauxel, who pays me
my advances and calls my letters to Tulla important, is familiar with the region between the Vistula and Frisches Haff.
In his day Stutthof was a rich village, larger than Schiewenhorst and Nickelswalde and smaller than Neuteich, the county
seat. Stutthof had 2698 inhabitants. They made money
when soon after the outbreak of the war a concentration
camp was built near the village and had to be enlarged again
and again. Railroad tracks were even laid in the camp. The
tracks connected with the Island narrow-gauge railway from
Danzig-Niederstadt. Everybody knew that, and those who
have forgotten may as well remember: Stutthof: Danzig-Lowlands County, Reich Province of Danzig-West Prussia, judicial
District of Danzig, known for its fine timber-frame church,
popular as a quiet seaside resort, an early German settlement.
In the fourteenth century the Teutonic Knights drained the
flats; in the sixteenth century hard-working Mennonites moved
in from Holland; in the seventeenth century the Swedes
several times pillaged the Island; in 1813 Napoleon's retreat
route ran straight across the flats; and between 1939 and

1945, in Stutthof Concentration Camp, Danzig-Lowlands County, people died, I don't know how many.

Not you but we,
   the thirds at the Conradinum, were taken out to Nickels-walde near Stutthof by our school. The Party had acquired the old Saskoschin country annex and turned it into a staff school. A piece of land between Queen Louise's mill in Nickelswalde and the scrub pine forest was purchased half from miller Matern, half from the village of Nickelswalde, and on it was erected a one-story building with a tall brick roof. As in Saskoschin we played schlagball in Nickelswalde. In every class there were crack players who could hit flies sky-high and whipping boys who were encircled with hard leather balls and made into mincemeat. In the morning the flag was raised; in the evening it was taken down. The food was bad; nevertheless we gained weight; the air on the Island was nourishing.

Often between games I watched miller Matern. He stood between mill and house. On the left a sack of flour pressed against his ear. He listened to the mealworms and saw the future.

Let us assume that I carried on a conversation with the lopsided miller. Maybe I said in a loud voice, for he was hard of hearing: "What's new, Herr Matern?"

He definitely answered: "In Russia the winter will set in too early."

Possibly I wanted to know more: "Will we get to Moscow?"

He oracularly: "Many of us will get as far as Siberia."

Then I may have changed the subject: "Do you know a man by the name of Haseloff, who lives mostly in Berlin?"

No doubt he listened at length to his flour sack: "I only hear about somebody who had a different name before. The birds were afraid of him."

I'd have had reason enough to be curious: "Has he gold in his mouth and does he never laugh?"

The miller's mealworms never spoke directly: "He smokes a lot of cigarettes, one after another, though he's always hoarse because he caught cold once."

I'm sure I concluded: "Then it's him."

The miller saw the future with precison: "It always will be."

Since there was no Tulla and no Jenny in Nickelswalde,

it cannot be my job to write about the adventures of the thirds in Nickelswalde; anyway the summer was drawing to an end.

The fall brought changes in the school system. The Gudrun School, formerly the Helene Lange School, was turned into an Air Force barracks. All the girls' classes moved to our Conradinum with its stench of boys. The school was operated in shifts: girls in the morning, boys in the afternoon, or vice versa. Some of our teachers, among them Dr. Brunies, also had to teach girls' classes. He taught Tulla's and Jenny's class history.

We no longer saw each other at all. Because we went to school in shifts, we had no difficulty in avoiding each other: Jenny no longer had to blush; I ceased to go red in the face; exceptions are memorable:

for once, around noon—I had left home early and was carrying my school satchel in my right hand—Jenny Brunies came toward me under the hazelnut bushes on Uphagenweg. She must have had five periods that morning and stayed on at the Conradinum for reasons unknown to me. In any case she was coming from school and also carrying her satchel in her right hand. Green hazelnuts and a few pale brownish ones were already lying on the ground, because a wind had been blowing the day before. Jenny in a dark blue woolen dress with white cuffs and a dark blue hat, but not a beret, something more like a tam, Jenny blushed and shifted her satchel from right to left when she was still five hazelnut bushes away from me.

The villas on either side of Uphagenweg seemed to be uninhabited. Everywhere silver firs and weeping willows, red maples and birches, dropping leaf after leaf. We were fourteen years old and walked toward each other. Jenny seemed thinner than I remembered her.

Her toes turned out from all the balleying. Why was she wearing blue when she could have said to herself: I'll turn red if he comes along.

Because I was early and because she flushed to the edge of her tam, because she had shifted her satchel, I stopped, also shifted my satchel, and held out my hand. She briefly let a dry anxious hand slip into mine. We stood amid unripe nuts. Some had been stepped on or were hollow. When a bird in a maple tree had finished, I began: "Hi there, Jenny, why so late? Have you tried the nuts? Want me to crack you a few? They haven't any taste, but after all they're the first. And what have you been doing with yourself? Your old man is still mighty chipper. Only the other day he had his pocket full of sparklers again: must have been ten pounds of them, or at least eight, not bad. And all that tramping around at his age, but what I wanted to ask you: how's the ballet going? How many pirouettes can you do? And how's the instep, improving? I wish I could get to the old Coffee Mill one of these days. How's the first soloist, the one you got from Vienna? I heard you're in *The Masked Ball*. Unfortunately I haven't been able to, because I. But they say you're good, I'm mighty glad. And have you been back to the icehouse? Don't be like that. It was only a joke. But I remember well because when I got home my father. Have you still got the necklace, the one made of bottle washers? And what about Berlin? Have you heard any more from those people?"

I chatted stammered repeated myself. I cracked hazelnuts with my heel, picked half-crushed kernels from splintered shells with nimble fingers, gave some took some; and Jenny amiably ate soapy nuts that dulled the teeth. My fingers were sticky. She stood stiffly, still kept all her blood in her head, and replied slowly monotonously compliantly. Her eyes had agoraphobia. They clung to the birches, weeping willows, silver firs: "Yes, thank you, my father is very well. Except he's been teaching too much. Sometimes I have to help him correct papers. And he smokes too much. Yes, I'm still with Madame Lara. She's really an excellent teacher and widely recognized. Soloists come to her from Dresden and even from Berlin for a little extra workout. You see, she's had the Russian style in her bones ever since she was a child. She learned all sorts of things from watching Preobrajensky and Trefilova. Even if she does seem dreadfully pedantic, always correcting and fussing over something, she never loses sight of the dance, and we learn something more than technique. There's really no need for you to see *The Masked Ball*. Our standards here aren't really the highest. Yes, Harry, of course I remember. But I've never gone back. I read somewhere that you can't or shouldn't repeat certain things, or they disappear entirely. But I wear your necklace sometimes. Yes, Herr Haseloff has written again. To Papa of course. He's really a funny man and writes about thousands of little things other people wouldn't notice. But Papa says he's a great success in Berlin. He's been doing all sorts of things, stage designs too. He's said to be a very strict teacher, but a good one. He goes on the road with Neroda, who really directs the ballet: Paris, Belgrade, Salonika. They don't only dance for soldiers. But Papa says I'm not ready for it yet."

Then there were no nuts left on the ground. And a few schoolboys had passed by. I knew one of them; he grinned. Jenny hurriedly let her right hand disappear in my right hand. I turned her hand over for a moment: five smooth light fingers; and on the ring finger she was wearing a tarnished, primitively wrought silver ring. I took it off without asking.

Jenny with empty ring finger: "That's Angustri, that's its name."

I rub the ring: "Angustri? How come?"

"That's Gypsy language and it means ring."

"Have you always had it?"

"But you mustn't tell anybody. It was on my pillow when I was found."

"And how do you know its name?"

Jenny's blush rises, falls: "That's what the man who left me there called the ring."

I: "A Gypsy?"

Jenny: "His name was Bidandengero."

I: "Then maybe you're one too."

Jenny: "Certainly not, Harry. They have black hair."

I clinch it: "But they can all dance!"

I told Tulla all about it:

she, I, and a lot of other people were crazy about the ring. We thought there was some hocus-pocus in the silver, and when the conversation revolved around Jenny, we called her not Jenny but Angustri. Undoubtedly those of my fellow pupils who had fallen in love with Jenny's ballet slippers from the start were now pining for Angustri. I alone remained calm-to-curious toward Jenny and Angustri. We had been through too much together. And from the very start I had been contaminated by Tulla. Even as a high school student, in relatively clean clothes, she still had her smell of bone glue; and I stuck fast with hardly a struggle.

When Tulla said: "Swipe the ring next time," I said no, and when I waylaid Jenny in Uphagenweg I only half meant to pull the silver off her finger. Twice in one week she blushed, because I crossed her path. Both times she had no Angustri on her, but was wearing the silly bottle-washer necklace.

But Tulla, who was in mourning for her brother Alexander, soon arranged nevertheless for Jenny to wear mourning. By the late fall of 1941—the special dispatches about victories in the East had stopped—the Conradinum boasted twenty-two fallen Conradinians. The marble tablet with the names, dates, and ranks hung in the main entrance between Schopenhauer and Copernicus. The fallen included one holder of the Knight's Cross. Two holders of the Knight's Cross were still alive and when they had leave regularly visited their old school. Sometimes they made terse or long-winded speeches in the auditorium. We sat spellbound and the teachers nodded approval. After the lectures questions were permitted. The students wanted to know how many Spitfires you had to shoot down, how many gross register tons you had to sink. For we were all determined to win the Knight's Cross later on. The teachers either asked practical questions—were replacements still coming in all right?—or they indulged in high-sounding periods about sticking it out and final victory. Dr. Brunies asked a holder of the Knight's Cross—I think it was the one from the Air Force—what his thoughts had been on first seeing a dead soldier, friend or foe. The fighter pilot's answer has slipped my mind.

Brunies asked the same question of Sergeant Walter Matern, who, because he wasn't a holder of the Knight's Cross, was only entitled to deliver a lecture from the teacher's desk in our classroom on the "Role of Ground Forces Anti-Aircraft in the East." I've also forgotten the answer of the sergeant with the Iron Cross first and second class. All I see is that field-gray, at once haggard and bullish, he clutches the desk top with both hands and stares over our heads at an oleograph on the rear wall of the classroom: the spinach-green Thoma landscape. Wherever he breathes, the air becomes rarefied. We want to know something about the Caucasus, but he talks unswervingly about the Nothing.

A few days after his lecture Walter was sent back to Russia, where he came by a wound which made him unfit for combat in the Ground Forces AA: with a slight limp he was assigned to the home front AA, first in Königsberg, then in Danzig. In the Brösen-Glettkau shore battery and the Kaiserhafen battery he trained Air Force auxiliaries.

He was liked and feared by all, and to me became a shining ideal; only Dr. Brunies, when Matern came for a visit and stood behind the desk, questioned his sergeant's existence by turning on irony lights and asking Matern, instead of delivering a lecture about the fighting at Orel, to read us a poem by Eichendorff, perhaps: "Dark gables, lofty windows . . ."

I can't recall that Dr. Brunies seriously taught us anything. A few subjects for compositions come to mind: "Preparations for marriage among the Zulus." Or: "The destinies of a tin can." Or: "When I was a cough drop, growing smaller and smaller in a little girl's mouth." Apparently his idea was to feed our imaginations, and since out of forty students two can reasonably be expected to have an imagination, thirty-eight thirds were permitted to doze while two—another and myself—unrolled the destinies of the tin can, thought up original marriage customs for the Zulus, and spied on a cough drop growing smaller in a little girl's mouth.

This topic kept me, my classmate, and Dr. Brunies busy for two weeks or more. Tuberous and leathery-crinkly, he sat huddled behind his worn desk top and, by way of inspiring us, gave an imitation of sucking, nibbling, and drawing juice. He made an imaginary cough drop move from one cheek to the other, almost swallowed it, diminished it with closed eyes, let the cough drop speak, narrate; in short, at a time when sweets were rare and rationed, Dr. Brunies' addiction to candy redoubled: if he had none in his pocket, he would invent some. And we wrote on the same topic.

Beginning roughly in the fall of '41, vitamin tablets were distributed to all our students. They were called Cebion tablets and kept in large brown-glass apothecary jars. In the conference room, where previously Meyers Konversations Lexikon had stood back beside back, there now stood a row of labeled jars—sixth to first. Each day they were carried by the class teachers into the classrooms for the vitamin-deficient schoolboys of the third war year.

Of course it did not escape our notice that Dr. Brunies was already sucking and that there was sweet enjoyment around his old man's mouth when he entered the class with the apothecary jar under his arm. The distribution of the Cebion tablets took up a good half of the period, for Brunies did not let the glass pass from seat to seat: in alphabetical order, in strict accordance with the class roster, he let the students step forward one by one, reached elaborately into the glass jar, acted as if he was fishing for something very special, and then, with triumph in every wrinkle, brought out one of the perhaps five hundred Cebion tablets, displayed it as the outcome of a difficult magician's act, and handed it to the student.

We all knew that Dr. Brunies' coat pockets were full of Cebion tablets. They had a sweet-sour taste: a little like lemon, a little like grape sugar, a little like a hospital. Since we liked to suck Cebion tablets, Brunies, who was wild about everything sweet, had good reason to fill his coat pockets. Every day, on his way from the conference room to our classroom, he would stop in the teachers' toilet with the brown apothecary jar and a moment later would be back in the corridor, sucking his way forward; his pocket flaps would be powdered with Cebion dust.

I would like to say that Brunies knew that we knew. Often he vanished behind the blackboard during the class, victualed up, and showed us his busy mouth: "I assume that you haven't seen anything; and if you have seen something, you've seen wrong."

Like other teachers Oswald Brunies had to sneeze often and sonorously; like his colleagues he pulled out a big handkerchief on such occasions; but unlike his colleagues he sent Cebion tablets, whole or broken, tumbling from his pockets along with his snot rag. Those that went rolling on the waxed floor we rescued. A cluster of bowed zealously collecting schoolboys handed Dr. Brunies half and quarter tablets. We said—the words became a stock phrase—: "Dr. Brunies, you've dropped some of your sparkling stones."

Brunies answered gravely: "If they are common mica gneiss, you may keep them; but if you have found one or several pieces of double spar, I should like you to return them."

We, and that was our tacit agreement, found only pieces of double spar which Brunies caused to disappear between brownish tooth stumps and tested by letting them travel from cheek to cheek until he had attained certainty: "Indeed, you have discovered several pieces of extremely rare double spar; how gratifying to have found them."

Later Dr. Brunies dropped the detours; he stopped going behind the blackboard and never again referred to lost pieces of double spar. On his way from the conference room to our classroom he gave up visiting the teachers' toilet with his apothecary jar, but avidly and openly helped himself to our

Cebion tablets during class. The trembling of his hands was pitiful. It overcame him in the middle of a sentence, between two stanzas of Eichendorff: he didn't pick out a solitary tablet; with three bony fingers he seized five tablets, tossed all five into his insatiable mouth, and smacked his lips so shamelessly that we had to look away.

No, Tulla,
we didn't report him. Several reports were turned in; but none came from our class. A few members of my class, it is true, and I was one of them, were later called into the conference room to testify; but we were extremely reserved, all we said was yes, Dr. Brunies had eaten candy during class, but not Cebion tablets, only ordinary cough drops. This, we said, was a habit he had always had, even when we were in sixth and fifth; and in those days no one had even heard of Cebion tablets.

Our testimony didn't help much; when Brunies was arrested, Cebion dust was found in the linings of his pockets.

At first it was rumored that Dr. Klohse, our principal, had reported him; some said it was Lingenberg, a mathematics teacher; then word got around that certain pupils in the Gudrun School, some of the girls in Brunies' history class, had turned him in. Before I had time to think: It must have been Tulla, Tulla Pokriefke's name came up.

You did it!
Why? Because. Two weeks later—Dr. Brunies had been obliged to hand our class over to Dr. Hoffmann; he was suspended from teaching but not yet under arrest; he was at home on Elsenstrasse with his sparkling stones—two weeks later we saw the old gentleman once again. Two of my classmates and I were called to the conference room. Two seconds and five girls from the Gudrun School were already waiting; among them: Tulla. We put on a strained grin, and the sun grazed all the brown apothecary jars on the shelf. We stood on a soft carpet and were not allowed to sit down. The classical authors on the walls exchanged disparaging looks. Over the green velvet on the long conference table sunlight wallowed in dust. The door was oiled: Dr. Brunies was led in by a man in civilian clothes, who however was not a teacher but a plain-clothes man. Dr. Klohse came in after them. Brunies gave us a friendly, absent-minded nod, rubbed his brown

bony hands, turned on irony lights as though eager to get down to business and tell us about the marriage preparations of the Zulus, the destinies of a tin can, or the cough drop in the mouth of a little girl. But it was the man in civilian clothes who did the speaking. He termed the meeting in the conference room a necessary confrontation. In a drawling voice he asked Dr. Brunies the familiar questions. They dealt with Cebion and the removal of Cebion tablets from jars. Regretfully and headshakingly, Brunies answered all questions in the negative. The seconds were questioned, then we. He was inculpated exculpated. Contradictory stammerings: "No, I didn't see anything, only hearsay. We always thought. We knew he was fond of candy, so we supposed. In my presence, no. But it's true that he . . ."

I don't believe it was I who finally said: "It's true that Dr. Brunies dipped into the Cebion tablets, three or at the very most four times. But we couldn't begrudge him his little pleasure. We knew he was fond of sweets, always had been."

During the questioning and answering I noticed how absurdly and helplessly Dr. Brunies was rummaging left right left through his coat pockets. In so doing he moistened his lips excitedly. The man in civilian clothes ignored this rummaging through pockets and licking of lips. First he spoke, beside the tall window, with Dr. Klohse, then he motioned Tulla over to the window: she was wearing a black pleated skirt. If Brunies had only had his pipe; but he had left it in his overcoat. The plain-clothes man whispered obscenely in Tulla's ear. The soles of my feet burned on the soft carpet. Dr. Brunies' restless hands and the perpetual motion of his tongue. Now Tulla is taking steps in her black pleated skirt. The goods rustles until she comes to a stop. With both hands she takes hold of a brown apothecary jar half full of Cebion tablets. She lifts it down from the shelf and no one stops her. Around the unoccupied green conference table she moves, step by step, in her pleated skirt, her eyes small and narrowed. All look after her and Brunies sees her coming. She stops an arm's length from Dr. Brunies, draws the jar to her bosom, holds it with her left hand, and with her right hand removes the glass cover. Brunies wipes his hands dry on his jacket. She puts the glass cover down to one side: the sunlight strikes it on the green felt of the conference table. Dr. Brunies' tongue has stopped moving but is still between his lips. Again she holds the jar with both hands, lifts it higher, stands on tiptoes in her pleated skirt. Tulla says: "Won't you have some, Dr. Brunies?"

Brunies offered no resistance. He did not hide his hands in his pockets. He did not avert his head and his mouth full of brown tooth stumps. No one heard: "What is the meaning of this nonsense?" Dr. Brunies grabbed, he hastily put his whole hand in. When his three fingers emerged from the jar, they raised six or seven Cebion tablets; two fell back into the jar; one dropped on the light-brown plush carpet and rolled under the conference table; what he had managed to keep between his fingers he stuffed into his mouth. But then he felt badly about the one Cebion tablet that had been lost under the table. He went down on his knees. In front of us, the principal, the man in civilian clothes, and Tulla, he went down on both knees, searched with groping hands beside and under the table; he would have found the tablet and raised it to his sweets-craving mouth, if they hadn't interfered: the principal and the man in civilian clothes. To right and left they picked him up by the arms and set him on his feet. A second opened the oiled door. "Good gracious, Herr Colleague!" said Dr. Klohse. "Really!" Tulla bent down to pick up the tablet under the conference table.

Later we were questioned once again. One after another, we entered the conference room. The business with the Cebion tablets hadn't proved sufficient. The seconds had written down some of Dr. Brunies' utterances. They sounded subversive and negative. All of a sudden everybody said: He was a Freemason. Though none of us knew what a Freemason was. I hung back, as my father had advised me to do. Maybe I shouldn't have said anything about Dr. Brunies' perpetually ungarnished flagpole, but after all he was our neighbor, and everyone saw that he never put out a flag when everybody was putting out flags. The man in civilian clothes knew all about it and nodded impatiently when I said: "Well, for instance on the Führer's birthday, when they all put out flags, Dr. Brunies never hangs out a flag, though he owns one."

Jenny's foster father was placed under arrest. I heard that they let him return home for a few days and then took him away for good. Felsner-Imbs the pianist, who came to the apartment in the Aktienhaus every day and looked after Jenny, said to my father: "Now they've taken the old gentleman to Stutthof. If only he lives through it!"

The Pokriefkes and the Liebenaus,

your family and mine, put off their mourning because your brother Alexander had been dead for a full year; Jenny had her clothes dyed. Once a week a social worker visited the house across the street; Jenny received her in black. At first we heard that Jenny was going to be sent to a welfare home; the Brunies apartment was being vacated. But black-clad Jenny found people to intercede for her. Felsner-Imbs wrote letters; the principal of the Gudrun School put in a petition; the manager of the Stadttheater appealed to the gauleiter's office; and Madame Lara Bock-Fedorova had connections. And so Jenny, though in black, kept on going to school, to ballet classes and rehearsals, wearing a soft black tam and a black coat that was too big for her, advancing step by step in black cotton stockings. But in the street her face showed no sign of tears. A trifle pale, but that may have been the effect of her black clothing, rigid from the waist up, her shoes turned outward as befits a ballet dancer, she carried her school satchel—which was brown, of artificial leather—to school and her leek-green, dawn-red, and air-blue gym bags, dyed black, to Oliva or to the theater, and returned punctually and pigeon-toed, more well behaved than rebellious, to Elsenstrasse.

Yet there were voices that interpreted Jenny's daily black as a rebellious color: in those days you were allowed to wear mourning only if you could produce a stamped and certified reason. You were allowed to mourn for fallen sons and deceased grandmothers; but the terse notification of the Danzig-Neugarten police that it had been necessary to place Dr. Oswald Brunies under arrest for unseemly conduct and crimes against the national welfare, was not a document acceptable to the rationing office; for there alone, in the clothing section, were purchase permits for mourning garments obtainable.

"What's the matter with her? He's still alive, isn't he? An old man like him, they wouldn't. She's certainly not helping him any, on the contrary. Somebody ought to tell her she's not doing any good, only making a spectacle of herself."

The neighbors and the social worker spoke to Felsner-Imbs. The pianist tried to persuade Jenny to stop wearing her mourning. He said it wasn't the externals that counted. If there was mourning in her heart, that was quite sufficient. His grief was hardly less, for he had lost a friend, his only friend.

But Jenny Brunies stuck to her external black and continued to wear it in accusation all over Langfuhr and on Elsenstrasse. Once at the car stop of the Number 2 to Oliva I
spoke to her. Of course she turned red, framed in black. If I
had to paint her portrait from memory, she would have
light-gray eyes, shadow-casting lashes, brown hair parted in
the middle, flowing smooth and lusterless in two tired curves
from her forehead down over her cheeks and ears, and
plaited into a stiff pigtail behind. I would paint her long
slender face ivory-pale, for her blush was an exception. A
face made for mourning: Giselle in the cemetery scene. Her
inconspicuous mouth spoke only when asked.

At the streetcar stop I said: "Must you wear mourning the
whole time, Jenny? Why, Papa Brunies may be home again
any minute."

"My feeling is that he's dead, even if they haven't notified
me."

I cast about for a subject, because the car wasn't coming:
"Are you always home alone in the evening?"

"Herr Imbs often comes to see me. We sort out the stones
and label them. He left lots of unsorted stones, you know."

I wanted to shove off, but the car didn't come: "I suppose
you never go to the movies, or do you?"

"When Papa was still alive, we sometimes went to the
Ufa-Palast on Sunday morning. He liked educational films
best."

I was more interested in the feature: "Wouldn't you like to
go to the movies with me sometime?"

Jenny's car approached, straw-yellow: "I'd be glad to if
you feel like it." People in winter coats got out: "It wouldn't
have to be a funny picture, we could go to a serious one,
couldn't we?"

Jenny got in: "They're playing *Liberated Hands* at the
Filmpalast. Young people of sixteen and over are admitted."

If Tulla had said:

"One in the orchestra," the cashier would certainly have
asked for Tulla's identification; but we didn't have to prove
we were sixteen, because Jenny was in mourning. We kept
our coats on, because the movie house was poorly heated. No
acquaintances in sight. We didn't have to talk, because they
kept playing potpourris. Simultaneously the curtain purred
up, a fanfare introduced the newsreel, and the lights went

out. Only then did I put my arm around Jenny's shoulder. It didn't stay there long, because for at least thirty seconds heavy artillery shelled Leningrad. As an English bomber was downed by our fighter planes, Jenny didn't want to see and buried her forehead in my overcoat. I let my arm wander again, but my eyes pursued the fighter planes, counted Rommel's tanks advancing in Cyrenaica, followed the foaming track of a torpedo, I saw the tanker rocking in the sights, quivered when the torpedo struck, and transferred the flickering and quivering of the disintegrating tanker to Jenny. When the newsreel camera visited the Führer's headquarters, I whispered: "Jenny, look, the Führer is coming on in a second, maybe he'll have the dog with him." We were both disappointed when only Keitel, Jodl, and somebody else were standing around him amid trees on gravel paths.

When the lights went on again, Jenny took her coat off, I didn't. The educational film was about deer which have to be fed in the winter, because otherwise they would starve. Without her coat Jenny was even thinner. The deer were not shy. The pine trees in the mountains were laden with snow. In the movie house everybody's clothes were black, not only Jenny's mourning sweater.

Actually I wanted to during the educational film, but I didn't until the feature had started. *Liberated Hands* wasn't a crime thriller with shooting and handcuffing. The hands belonged to a sculptress, who was nuts about the sculptor who was her teacher, and her real name was Brigitte Horney. Just about every time she did it on the screen, I did it to Jenny in the movie house. She closed her eyes; I could see her. On the screen hands were always kneading lumps of clay into naked figures and frolicking foals. Jenny's skin was cool and dry. She had her thighs pressed together and I was of the opinion she ought to relax. She complied at once but kept her eyes on the feature. Her hole was even smaller than Tulla's; that's what I'd what I'd wanted to know. When I inserted a second finger, Jenny turned her head away from the feature: "Please, Harry. You're hurting me." I stopped right away, but left my other arm with her. Horney's sultry, brittle voice filled the sparsely attended movie house. Shortly before the end I smelled my fingers: they smelled like the unripe hazelnuts on our way to school: bitter soapy insipid.

On the way home I became impersonal. Along Bahnhofstrasse I chattered away to the effect that the feature had been tops but the newsreels were always the same old stuff; the thing with the deer had been pretty boring; and tomorrow back to that stupid school; surely it would all come out all right with Papa Brunies: "What do they say about it in Berlin? Have you written Haseloff all about it?" Jenny also thought the feature had been good; Horney was really a great artist; she too hoped it would come out all right with Papa Brunies, though she felt in her bones that he; but Herr Haseloff had written twice since then; he was coming soon to take her away: "He says Langfuhr isn't the right place for me any more. Herr Imbs thinks so too. Will you write me sometimes when I'm in Berlin with the ballet?"

Jenny's information cheered me up. The prospect of soon having her and her mourning black far away from me inspired friendly words. I took her good-naturedly by the shoulder, made detours through dark side streets, stopped with her in February or March under blue blackout lamps, propelled her along to the next lamppost, pressed her against wrought-iron garden fences, and encouraged her to go to Berlin with Haseloff. Over and over again I promised to write not just now and then but regularly. In the end I commanded her to leave Langfuhr, for Jenny transferred the full responsibility to me: "If you don't want me to leave you, I'll stay with you; but if you think Herr Haseloff is right, I'll go."

I invoked someone who had been taken to Stutthof: "I'll bet that if Papa Brunies were here, he'd say exactly the same as me: Off to Berlin with you! It's the best thing that could happen to you."

On Elsenstrasse Jenny thanked me for the movies. I kissed her again quickly dryly. Her concluding words as usual: "But now I'm a little tired and besides I have English to do for tomorrow."

I was glad she didn't ask me up to Dr. Brunies' empty apartment. What could I have done with her amid crates full of assorted mica gneiss, amid uncleaned pipes, and with desires in my head that asked nothing of Jenny but a good deal of Tulla.

Dear Cousin,

then, shortly before Easter, snow fell. It soon melted away. At the same time you started carrying on with soldiers on furlough, but didn't contract a child. Then shortly after Easter there was an air-raid alarm; but no bombs fell around our way. And early in May Haseloff came and took Jenny away.

He drove up in a black Mercedes with a chauffeur and got out: slender smooth strange. A much too spacious overcoat with strikingly large checks hung loosely over his shoulders. He rubbed white-gloved hands, inspected the front of the Aktienhaus, appraised our house, every floor: I, half behind the curtains, stepped back into the room to the edge of the carpet. My mother had called me to the window: "Say, would you take a look at him!"

I knew him. I was first to see him when he was still new. He threw me a tooth into the hazelnut bush. He went off in the train soon after being reborn. He began to smoke and still smokes—with white gloves. I have his tooth in my change purse. He went away with a sunken mouth. He comes back with a mug full of gold: for he's laughing, he trots down Elsenstrasse a little way and back a little way, laughs, trots, and takes it all in. The houses on both sides, house numbers, odd and even, little strips of garden, pansies. Can't look enough, and breaks into open laughter, showing all the windows Haseloff's mouth full of gold. With thirty-two gold teeth he spits soundless laughter, as though in all this egg-shaped world there were no better reason for showing one's teeth than our Elsenstrasse. But then Felsner-Imbs comes out of our house, respectfully. And then the curtain falls on too much gold on a sunny day in May. Foreshortened as seen from my curtain, the two men greet each other with four hands, as though celebrating a reunion. The chauffeur is stretching his legs beside the Mercedes and takes no interest. But all the windows are loges. The eternally sprouting younger generation form a circle around the reunion. I and the sparrows on the eaves understand: he's back again, takes the pianist by the arm, breaks through the eternally sprouting circle, pushes the pianist into the Aktienhaus, respectfully holds the door open for him, and follows him without looking back.

Jenny had her two suitcases ready, for in less than half an hour she left the Aktienhaus with Felsner-Imbs and Haseloff. She left in mourning. She left with Angustri on her finger and without my bottle-washer necklace; it was in with her underwear in one of the two suitcases that Imbs and Haseloff handed to the chauffeur. The kids drew little men in the dust on the black Mercedes. Jenny stood undecided. The chauffeur took off his cap. Haseloff was about to push Jenny gently into the interior of the car. He had turned up his coat collar, he no longer showed Elsenstrasse his face, he was in a hurry. But Jenny didn't want to get into the car just yet, she pointed at our curtains, and before Imbs and Haseloff could hold her back, she had vanished into our house.

To my mother, who always did what I wanted, I, behind curtains, said: "Don't open if she rings. What on earth can she want?"

Four times the bell rang. Our bell wasn't the kind you press, it was the kind you turn. Our turnbell didn't just scream, it snarled four times, but my mother and I didn't stir from our place behind the curtains.

What our bell repeated four times will stay in my ears.

"Now they're gone," said my mother; but I looked at the miniature chests of walnut, pearwood, and oak in our dining room.

The diminishing engine sound of a receding car has also stayed with me and will probably stay forever.

Dear Cousin Tulla,

a week later a letter came from Berlin; Jenny had written it with her fountain pen. The letter made me as happy as if Tulla had written it with her own hand. But Tulla's hand was writing to a sailor. I ran about with Jenny's letter, telling everybody it was from my girl friend in Berlin, from Jenny Brunies or Jenny Angustri, as she now called herself, for Haseloff her ballet master and Madame Neroda, the managing director of the Strength-through-Joy Ballet, now the German Ballet, had advised her to take a stage name. Her ballet school had already started, and in addition they were rehearsing country dances to early German music which Madame Neroda, who was actually an Englishwoman, had unearthed. This Madame Neroda seemed to be an unusual woman. For instance: "When she goes out, to make calls or even to attend a formal reception, she wears an expensive fur coat but no dress under it, only her dancing tights. But she can afford to do such things. And she has a dog, a Scotty, with eyes exactly like hers. Some people think she's a spy. But I don't believe it and neither does my girl friend."

At intervals of a few days I wrote Jenny a string of love letters, very repetitious and full of overt desires. I had to write every letter twice, because the first version was always crawling with slips. Any number of times I wrote: "Believe me, Tulla," wrote: "Why, Tulla? This morning, Tulla. If you want to, Tulla. I want you, Tulla. I dreamed Tulla. Eating Tulla up, holding her tight, loving her, making Tulla a baby."

Jenny answered me promptly in a small tidy hand. Evenly but respecting the margins, she filled two sheets of blue writing paper—both sides—with replies to my propositions and descriptions of her new surroundings. To everything I wanted of Tulla Jenny said yes; except for having babies, it was rather too soon for that —I had myself to consider too; first we must get ahead in our work, she on the stage and I as a historian; that's what I wanted to be.

About Neroda she wrote that this extraordinary woman owned the world's largest collection of books on the dance, that she even had an original manuscript from the hand of the great Noverre. She spoke of Herr Haseloff as a rather weird but occasionally comical eccentric, who, once he was through with his strict but imaginatively conducted ballet exercises, cooked up strangely human machines in his cellar workshop. Jenny wrote: "Actually he doesn't think too much of the classical ballet, for often, when the exercises aren't going quite as he would wish, he cracks rather nasty jokes. 'Tomorrow,' he says, 'I'm going to fire you jumping jacks, the whole lot of you. They can put you to work in the munitions factories. If you can't turn a single pirouette as neatly as my little machines, you'll be better off turning out shells.' He claims that his figures in the cellar go into positions lovely enough to give you religion; he says his figures are always well turned out; that he's planning to put one of them up in front of the class, at the bar: 'It'll make you green with envy. Then you'll realize what classical ballet can be, you little holes and stoppers.' "

That's what Herr Haseloff called girl and boy dancers. In one of the next letters Jenny wrote me at Elsenstrasse I found a P.S. in which one such mechanical figure was described and summarily sketched. It stood at the bar, displaying a regulation *port de bras* for the benefit of the little holes and stoppers.

Jenny wrote: "You wouldn't believe it, but I've learned a lot from the mechanical figure, which, incidentally, is neither a hole nor a stopper. Especially, I've learned to carry my back properly, and the little dots in the *port de bras*—Madame Lara neglected that—have become quite clear to me. Whatever I do, whether I'm polishing my shoes or picking up a glass of milk, I always make dots in the air. And even when I yawn—because when the day is over we're all frankly tired—and cover my mouth with my hand, I always watch the dots. But now I must close. I'll love you and hold you tight as I fall asleep and tomorrow morning, too, when I wake up. And please don't read too much or you'll ruin your eyes.—As ever, Your Jenny."

Dear Tulla:
   with one of these Jenny letters I tried to strike a bridge: to you. We ran into each other in the stair well of our apartment house, and I made no attempt to dispel the usual blush: "Look, Jenny's written me again. You interested? It's pretty funny, the stuff she writes about love and all that. If you feel like a laugh, you ought to read the stuff she writes. Now she calls herself Angustri like the ring, and pretty soon she's going on tour with the troupe."
   I held out the letter as if it were something unimportant and mildly amusing. Tulla flipped the paper with one finger: "You really ought to get some sense into you and stop coming around all the time with the same old applesauce and ballet rubbish."
   Tulla wore her hair loose, mustard-brown, shoulder-length, and stringy. There were still faint signs of a permanent wave that the sailor from Putzig had treated her to. A strand of hair hung down over her left eye. With a mechanical movement—Haseloff's figure couldn't have done anything more mechanical—she pushed back the strand of hair with a contemptuous expulsion of breath, and with a shrug of her bony shoulders sent it back down over the same eye. But she wasn't wearing make-up yet. By the time the Hitler-Youth patrol caught her in the railroad station after midnight and then on a bench in Uphagenpark with an ensign from the Neuschottland Naval Training School, she wore make-up all over.
   She was kicked out of school. My father spoke of money thrown out the window. To the principal of the Gudrun School, who despite the report of the patrol service wanted to give Tulla another chance, Tulla was said to have said: "Never mind, ma'am, go ahead and throw me out. I've got the joint up to here anyway. What I want is to have a baby by somebody, just to get a little action around here."

Why did you want a baby? Because!—Tulla was thrown out but didn't get a baby. In the daytime she sat home listening to the radio, after supper she went out. Once she brought home six yards of the best Navy serge for herself and her mother. Once she came home with a fox fur from the Arctic front. Once her loot was a bolt of parachute silk. She and her mother wore underthings from all over Europe. When somebody came from the Labor Office and wanted to put her to work in the power plant, she had Dr. Hollatz make out a certificate of poor health: anemia and a shadow on her lung. Tulla obtained extra food tickets and a sick benefit, but not much.

When Felsner-Imbs moved to Berlin with hourglass, porcelain ballerina, goldfish, stacks of music, and faded photographs—Haseloff had engaged him as pianist for the ballet—Tulla gave him a letter to take with him: for Jenny. I have never been able to find out what Tulla wrote with her fountain pen, for all Jenny said in her next to next letter was that Felsner-Imbs had arrived safely, that she had received a very nice letter from Tulla, and that she sent Tulla her very best regards.

There I was on the outside again, and the two of them had something in common. When I ran into Tulla, I didn't turn red any more but chalky. Yes, I stuck to you, but I gradually learned to hate you and your glue; and hatred —a disease of the soul with which one can live to a ripe old age—made it easier for me to get along with Tulla: amiably and condescendingly, I gave her good advice. My hatred never made me violent, for in the first place I watched myself even in my sleep, in the second place I read too much, in the third place I was a conscientious student, almost a grind, with no time to vent my hatred, and in the fourth place I built myself an altar, on which stood Jenny turned out in her tutu, her arms opened for second position; or more accurately, I piled up Jenny's letters and resolved to become engaged to her.

My darling Tulla,
Jenny could be awfully prim and boring when you sat facing her or walked beside her, but she could be very entertaining with her witty saucy letters. Seen from without, her eyes were silly under melancholy lashes; appraised from within, they had the gift of seeing things dryly and sharply

etched, even things that stood on the tips of silver slippers and in stage lighting signified a dying swam.

Thus she described for my benefit a ballet class that Haseloff had given his little holes and stoppers. They were rehearsing a ballet that was going to be called *Scarecrows* or *The Scarecrows* or *The Gardener and the Scarecrows*.

And everything—at the bar and on the floor—went wrong. Felsner-Imbs sat with endlessly bowed back and repeated the bit of Chopin to no avail. In the rain outside the windows stood pine trees full of squirrels and the Prussian past. In the morning there had been an air-raid alarm and practice in the furnace room. Now the little holes in leotards were wilting on the long practice bar. Injected with cod-liver oil, the stoppers flapped their eyelashes until Haseloff with a tensing of his knees jumped up on the piano, an occurrence quite familiar to Felsner-Imbs and not at all harmful to the piano, for Haseloff was able, from a standing position, to make high, slow, and long leaps and land delicately on the brown piano lid without jolting the innards of the hard-tuned instrument. At this the holes and stoppers should have come to life, for they all knew perfectly well what Haseloff's rage-propelled leap to the piano meant and boded.

From aloft, not directly but into the big mirror that turned the front wall into a spy, Haseloff spoke warningly to the holes and stoppers: "Do you want my brush to show you how to dance? Haven't you any *joie de vivre*? Do you want rats to bite the swans from underneath? Must Haseloff take out his bag of pepper?"

Once again he built up his notorious bar exercise: "*Grand plié*—twice each in the first, second, and fifth position; eight slow *dégagés* and sixteen quick ones in the second position; eight *petits battements dégagés*, dabbed on the floor with the accent on the outside." But only the holes put the accent on the outside and dabbed in the dot; as for the stoppers, neither the threatened bag of pepper nor Chopin in league with Felsner-Imbs could give them *joie de vivre* or a tidy *plié*: batter on a spoon, mayonnaise, Turkish honey make threads: so stretched the boys, or stoppers— Wolf, Marcel, Schmitt, Serge, Gotti, Eberhard, and Bastian. They fluttered their eyelashes, sighed a little between *battements tendus* on half-toe, in the *rond de jambes à la seconde* they twisted their necks like swans just before feeding, and waited in resignation, seven sleep-warm stoppers, for

Haseloff's second leap, which, on the occasion of the *grand battement,* was not long in coming.

Haseloff's second leap also started from the standing position: from the piano lid it carried him, with straight knees and amazingly high instep, over the pianist's snow-white hair into the middle of the room, in front of the mirror. And concealing nothing from the mirror, he produced the announced bag, miraculously. The pointed bag, the cone-shaped bag, feared, familiar, the bag, powder-soft doesaworldofgood butinmoderation, he drew the two-ounce bag from his special breast pocket and ordered all the girls or holes to desist from the bar. He sent them into the corner beside the sizzling, glow-cheeked pot-belled stove. There they crowded together twittering, turned toward the wall, covering their eyes with pale fingers. And Felsner-Imbs also covered his leonine head with his silk scarf.

For while eyes were covered and a head modestly veiled, Haseloff commanded: *"Face à la barre!"* Seven boys or stoppers excitedly peeled black, pink, egg-yellow, and springgreen leotards from each other's boyish flesh. *"Préparation!"* cried Haseloff with a dry snap of the fingers: their faces to the wall, they lined up along the bar with their indefatigable eyelashes and with fourteen hands clutched the worn wood. Supported by blindly played Chopin, seven trunks bent forward with straight arms and knees, making one and the same soft-skinned boyish bottom jut sevenfold into the wellheated room.

Then Haseloff went into first position alongside the first bottom; in his left hand he held the little conical bag; in the right, as though conjured out of the air, he had a paint brush between his fingers. He dipped the badger-hair brush, expensive and durable, into the little bag and, sustained by Felsner-Imbs, began to whistle merrily the time-honored polonaise as he shifted nimbly, always sure of the mirror, from boy-bottom to stopper-bottom.

In so doing—and this is what all the fuss was about—he made the powder-charged badger brush emerge seven times from the bag and vanish seven times powder-charged in the young men's rear ends, the stopper-bottoms, abracadabra.

No foot powder this. Nor was sleeping powder injected. Nor reducing powder, nor anti-lion powder, nor baking powder, not insect powder, nor milk powder; neither cocoa nor powdered sugar, nor flour to bake buns with, nor face powder nor tooth powder; it was pepper, black, finely ground pepper, that Haseloff discharged seven times unflaggingly with his brush. Finally, only a hair's breadth from the mirror, he concluded his educational performance with a slow pirouette, stood, his mouth full of gold teeth, facing the room and trumpeted: *"Alors, mes enfants!* Stoppers first, then holes. *Première position: Grand plié, bras en couronne."*

And scarcely had Imbs, no longer blind, flung his Chopin-laden fingers at the keys, than quick as a flash and as though self-propelled, colored leotards rolled over seven peppered stopper-bottoms. An exercise got a wiggle on: swift feet, long legs, graceful arm movements. Eyelashes fell silent, lines awakened, beauty perspired; and Haseloff made his badger brush disappear—somewhere. Such was the long-lasting effect of the pepper that after a successful exercise the holes without pepper and the pepper-animated stoppers could be summoned to a rehearsal of the scarecrow ballet: Third Act, Destruction of the garden by the massed scarecrows, culminating in a *pas de deux.*

Because subsequently the big scene, danced to traditional Prussian military music, was so spicily successful—a precise chaos *sur pointes*—Haseloff called it a day with thirty-two gold teeth, waved his towel, bade Felsner-Imbs close the piano and bury Chopin and Prussia's marches in his brief case, and distributed compliments: "Bravo Wölfchen, bravo Schmittchen, bravo all holes and stoppers! A special bravo for Marcel and Jenny. Hang around, the two of you. We'll do the gardener's daughter and the Prince, first act, without music *en demie-pointe.* The rest of you, go right to bed and no gallivanting around. Tomorrow morning, the whole *corps de ballet,* abduction of the gardener's daughter and grand finale."

Dear Tulla,

in the Jenny letter whose contents I have tried to reproduce, as in all other Jenny letters, it was written how very much she loved me now and forever, even though Haseloff was making up to her—with restraint and ever so ironically. But I mustn't worry about that. Incidentally, she would be coming to Langfuhr, though only for two days: "The apartment after all has to be vacated. And so we've decided to move the furniture and the stone collection to a safe place. You can imagine all the red tape it took to get permission to move the things. But Haseloff knows how to handle people. But he thinks the furniture will be safer in Langfuhr, because Berlin is being bombed more and more. Just the same he wants to move the mica stones to Lower Saxony, where he knows some peasants and the manager of a mine."

Dear Tulla,

first a moving van drove up across the street. Fifteen families occupied the windows of our house. Then, soundlessly, the Mercedes pulled up behind the moving van, but left room for loading. The chauffeur stood promptly at the door with lifted cap: in a black fur coat, possibly mole, her face ensconced in the turned-up collar, Jenny stood on the sidewalk, and raised her eyes for a moment to our windows: a lady who isn't allowed to catch cold. In a black ulster with a brown fur collar, nutria, Haseloff took Jenny's arm. The switchman, the great impresario, half a head shorter than Jenny: Hermann Haseloff, his mouth full of gold teeth. But he didn't laugh, didn't look at our house. Elsenstrasse didn't exist.

My father said from behind his newspaper: "There's no reason why you shouldn't help with the moving as long as you're always writing each other."

I almost missed Jenny's hand in the wide sleeve of her fur coat. She introduced me. Haseloff had only an eighth of a glance available. "Hm," he said, and "Nice-looking stopper." Then he directed the moving men like a *corps de ballet*. I wasn't allowed to help or even to go up to the apartment. The loading of the furniture, heavy pieces, dark brown for the most part, all oak, was exciting, because under Haseloff's direction a bookcase as wide as a wall became weightless. When Jenny's room left the Aktienhaus—Biedermeier in light birch—the pieces hovered over the cubical men and had "balloon." Between the coat rack and the Flemish chest Haseloff half turned to me. Without leaving the movers to their own strength he invited Jenny and me to dinner at the Hotel Eden by the Main Station, where they were staying. Heavy open crates were piled on the sidewalk in among the last kitchen chairs. I accepted: "At half past seven." All at once, as though Haseloff had staged it, the sun broke through up above, awakening sparkle in open crates. The smell of the absent teacher revived too: cold pipe smoke joined in the moving; but some of the mica gneiss had to stay behind.

Eight or nine crates walled up the moving van, for two
there was no room. That gave me my entrance in Haseloff's
moving-man's ballet, for I offered to make room in our cellar for mica gneiss and mica granite, for biotite and muscovite.

My father, whom I asked for permission in the machine
room, surprised me by calmly consenting: "That's a good
idea, my son. There's plenty of room in the second cellar
next to the window frames. Put Dr. Bruines' crates in there.
If the old gentleman collected stones all his life, he must
have had his reasons."

Dear Tulla,

the crates were moved to our cellar and in the evening I
sat beside Jenny, across from Haseloff, in the dining room of
the Hotel Eden. Allegedly you had met Jenny in town that
afternoon, without Haseloff. Why? Because. We hardly spoke,
and Haseloff looked between Jenny and me. You had met, so
I heard, at the Café Weitzke on Wollwebergasse. What did
you have to talk about? All sorts of things! Jenny's little
finger had meanwhile hooked itself to my little finger under
the table. I'm sure Haseloff noticed. What had there been to
eat at the Cafté Weitzke? Bad cake and watery ice cream
for Jenny. At the Hotel Eden there was turtle soup, breaded
veal cutlet with canned asparagus, and for dessert, at Jenny's
request, frozen pudding. Maybe I rode after you as far as
Kohlenmarkt and saw you in the Café Weitzke: sitting, talking, laughing, saying nothing, crying. Why? Because. After
dinner I noticed a thousand and more ice-gray freckles on
Haseloff's tense or rigid face. Eddi Amsel, when he still
existed, had fewer but larger freckles in his fat face, brownish and genuine. You spent at least two hours chattering
away in the Café Weitzke. At half past nine I had to speak:
"I used to know somebody who looked like you, but he had a
different name."

Haseloff summoned the waiter: "A glass of hot lemonade,
please."

I had my lines ready: "First he was called Stephuhn, then
he was called Sperballa, then Sperlinski. Do you know him?"

Haseloff, who had a cold, received his hot lemonade:
"Thank you. Check please."

Behind me the waiter added up the bill: "For a few minutes the man I knew was even called Zocholl. Then he was

called Zylinski. And then he found a name that he still goes by. Would you like to know what it is, or would you, Jenny?"

Haseloff let two white tablets dissolve in a teaspoon and paid with bank notes hidden under the check: "Keep the change."

When I wanted to tell them the man's name, Haseloff swallowed the tablets and took a long drink from the lemonade glass. Then it was too late. And Jenny was tired. Only in the hotel lobby, after Jenny had been allowed to give me a kiss, Haseloff showed a few of his gold teeth and said in a hoarse voice: "You're talented. You know lots of names. I'll help you, today or the day after tomorrow, and now let me tell you one more name: Brauxel written with an x; or Brauksel written like Häksel; or Brauchsel, written like Weichsel. Remember that name and the three ways of spelling it."

Then they both, elegantly and with unnatural slowness, climbed the stairs. Jenny looked round and round and round; even when I wasn't in the hotel lobby any more with three times Brauxel in my head.

Dear Tulla,

he exists. I found him while I was looking for you. He tells me how to write when I write to you. He sends me money so I can write you without having to worry. He owns a mine between Hildesheim and Sarstedt. Or maybe he only manages it. Or holds the biggest block of shares. Or maybe the whole thing is sculduggery camouflage fifth column, even if his name is Brauxel Brauksel Brauchsel. Brauksel's mine produces no ore, no salt, no coal. Brauksel's mine produces something else. I am not allowed to name it. All I am allowed and ordered to say is Tulla, over and over again. And I have to keep the deadline, the fourth of February. And I have to heap up the pile of bones. And I have to start on the last story, for Brauchsel has sent me an urgent telegram: "Aquarius conjunction approaching stop heap up bone pile stop start miscarriage stop let dog loose and finish on time."

There was once a girl, her name was Tulla,

and she had the pure forehead of a child. But nothing is pure. Not even the snow is pure. No virgin is pure. Even a pig isn't pure. The Devil never entirely pure. No note rises pure. Every violin knows that. Every star chimes that. Every knife peels it: even a potato isn't pure: it has eyes, they have to be scooped out.

But what about salt? Salt is pure! Nothing, not even salt, is pure. It's only on boxes that it says: Salt is pure. After all, it keeps. What keeps with it? But it's washed. Nothing can be washed clean. But the elements: pure? They are sterile but not pure. The idea? Isn't it always pure? Even in the beginning not pure. Jesus Christ not pure. Marx Engels not pure. Ashes not pure. And the host not pure. No idea stays pure. Even the flowering of art isn't pure. And the sun has spots. All geniuses menstruate. On sorrow floats laughter. In the heart of roaring lurks silence. In angles lean compasses.— But the circle, the circle is pure!

No closing of the circle is pure. For if the circle is pure, then the snow is pure, the virgin is, the pigs are, Jesus Christ, Marx and Engels, white ashes, all sorrows, laughter, to the left roaring, to the right silence, ideas immaculate, wafers no longer bleeders and geniuses without efflux, all angles pure angles, piously compasses would describe circles: pure and human, dirty, salty, diabolical, Christian and Marxist, laughing and roaring, ruminant, silent, holy, round pure angular. And the bones, white mounds that were recently heaped up, would grow immaculately without crows: pyramids of glory. But the crows, which are not pure, were creaking unoiled, even yesterday: nothing is pure, no circle, no bone. And piles of bones, heaped up for the sake of purity, will melt cook boil in order that soap, pure and cheap; but even soap cannot wash pure.

There was once a girl, her name was Tulla,

and she let numerous pimples, big and little, bloom and fade on her childlike forehead. Her cousin Harry long combated pimples of his own. Tulla never tried tinctures and remedies. Neither ground almonds nor stinky sulphur nor cucumber milk nor zinc ointment found a place on her forehead. Untroubled, she strode through the world pimples first, for she still had the jutting forehead of a child, and dragged sergeants and ensigns into night-black parks: for she wanted to have a baby, but didn't.

After Tulla had vainly tried every rank and branch of service, Harry advised her to try uniformed high school students. He had lately been wearing attractive Air Force blue and living no longer in Elsenstrasse but, in tiptop bathing weather, in the barracks of the Brösen-Glettkau shore battery, a large battery strung out behind the dunes, equipped with twelve 88-millimeter guns and a whole raft of 40-millimeter AA-guns.

At the very start Harry was assigned as Number 6 to an 88-millimeter gun with outriggers. The Number 6 had to adjust the fuze setter with the aid of two cranks. This Harry did throughout his term as an Air Force auxiliary. A priviledged job, for the Number 6 alone of nine cannoneers was entitled to sit on a little stool attached to the gun; when the gun was rotated quickly, he traveled along free of charge and didn't bash his shins against the iron of the outriggers. During gunnery practice Harry sat with his back to the muzzle of the cannon and while with his cranks he made two mechanical pointers hurry after two electrical pointers, he pounded back and forth between Tulla and Jenny. This he did rather adroitly: the mechanical pointer chased the electrical pointer, Tulla chased Jenny, and as far as Harry Liebenau was concerned, the fuze setter was operated to the complete satisfaction of the tech sergeant in charge of training.

Once there was a tech sergeant,

who could grind his teeth loudly. Along with other decorations he wore the silver wound insignia. Accordingly he limped slightly but obviously between the shacks of the Brösen-Glettkau shore battery. He was looked upon as strict but fair, admired, and superficially imitated. When he went out to the dunes to hunt dune rabbits, he chose as his companion an Air Force auxiliary whom the others called Störtebeker. While hunting dune rabbits the tech sergeant either didn't say a single word or he uttered quotations, interspersed by ponderous pauses, from one and the same philosopher. Störtebeker repeated his quotations and created a philosophical schoolboy language that was soon prattled by many, with varying success.

Störtebeker prefixed most of his sentences with "I, as a pre-Socratic." Anyone who looked on as he mounted guard could see him drawing in the sand with a stick. With a superiorly guided stick he plotted the advent of the still unuttered essence of unconcealment, or to put it more bluntly, of Being. But if Harry said: "Being," Störtebeker corrected him impatiently: "There you go again. What you really mean is essents—things that are."

Even in everyday matters philosophical tongues made pre-Socratic leaps, appraising every commonplace incident or object with the tech sergeant's painstakingly acquired knowledge. Underdone potatoes in their jackets—the kitchen was poorly supplied and even more poorly run—were called "spuds forgetful of Being." If someone reminded someone of something that had been borrowed, promised, or asserted days before, the answer came prompt and absolute: "Who thinks about thoughts any more," or, analogically, about the borrowed, the promised, or the asserted? The daily facts of life in an AA battery, such as semi-serious disciplinary drill, tedious practice alerts, or greasy-messy rifle cleaning, were disposed of with an expression overheard from the tech sergeant: "After all, the essence of being-there is its existence."

The word "existence" and its collaterals met all requirements: "Would you exist me a cigarette? Who feels like existing a movie with me? Shut your trap or I'll exist you one."

To go on sick call was to plug for a sack existence. And anybody who had hooked a girl—as Strötebeker had hooked Harry's cousin Tulla—boasted after taps how often he had bucked the girl's existence.

And existence itself—Strötebeker tried to draw it in the sand with a stick: it looked different each time.

There was once an Air Force auxiliary

named Störtebeker, who was supposed to get Harry's cousin with child and probably did his best. On Sundays when the Brösen-Glettkau battery was open to visitors, Tulla came out in high-heeled shoes and took her nostrils and pimply forehead for a stroll amid 88-millimeter guns. Or she hobbled into the dunes between the tech sergeant and Air Force auxiliary Störtebeker, in the hope that they would both make her a baby; but tech sergeant and Air Force auxiliary preferred to indulge in other proofs of existence: they shot dune rabbits.

There was once a cousin,

his name was Harry Liebenau and all he was good for was looking on and saying what he'd heard other people say. There he lay flat with half-closed eyes in the sand amid wind-flattened beach grass and made himself still flatter when three figures appeared on the crest of the dune. The four-square staff sergeant, with the sun behind him, held a heavy protective arm around Tulla's shoulder. Tulla was carrying her high-heeled shoes in her right hand and with the left clutched the hind paws of a bleeding dune rabbit. To the right of Tulla—but without touching her—Störtebeker held carbine, barrel down. The three figures didn't notice Harry. For an eternity they stood motionlessly silhouetted, because the sun was still behind them, on the crest of the dune. Tulla reached up to the tech sergeant's chest. She carried his arm like a crossbeam. Störtebeker to one side and yet belonging, rigid and on the lookout for Being. A handsome and precise picture that grieved the flat-lying Harry, for he had less rapport than the bleeding rabbit with the three figures against the drooping sun.

There was once a picture,
    painful at sunset; Air Force auxiliary Harry Liebenau was never to see it again for suddenly one day he had to pack. Inscrutable decree transferred him, Störtebeker, thirty other Air Force auxiliaries, and the tech sergeant to another battery. No more dunes gently-wavy. No Baltic Sea, smoothly virginal. Beach flexibly musical. No longer did twelve eighty-eights jut somberly into the balmy bugle-call sky. Never again the reminders of home in the background: Brösen's wooden church, Brösen's black and white fishermen's cows, Brösen's fishnets hung on poles to be dried or photographed. Never again did the sun set for them behind rabbits sitting on their haunches and worshiping the departing sun with erect ears.

In the Kaiserhafen battery there were no such pious animals, only rats; and rats worship fixed stars.

The way to the battery led from Troyl, a harbor quarter between the Lower City and the Holm, for three quarters of an hour over sand roads through sparse woods in the direction of Weichselmünde. Left behind: the widely scattered repair shops of the German Railways, the lumber sheds behind the Wojahn shipyard; and here, projected into the area between the Troyl streetcar stop and the Kaiserhafen battery, the water rats held uncontested sway.

But the smell that hung over the battery and didn't budge a step even in a violent west wind, didn't come from rats.

The first night after Harry moved into the battery, his gym shoes were gnawed, both of them. The regulations prohibited getting out of bed with bare feet. Everywhere they sat and grew fatter; on what? They were reviled as the grounds of the ground; but to this name they did not answer. The battery was equipped with metal ratproof lockers. Many were slain, unsystematically. It didn't help much. Then the tech sergeant, who performed the functions of top sergeant in his battery and every morning reported to his Captain Hufnagel how many corporals and sergeants, how many Air Force auxiliaries and Ukrainian volunteers had fallen in, issued an order of the day whereby the water rats were appreciably diminished; but the smell that hung over the battery did not diminish: it didn't come from the grounds of the ground.

There was once an order of the day;
it promised premiums for slain rodents. The p.f.c.s and corporals, all matured in the service, received a cigarette for three rats. The Ukrainian volunteers were illicitly given a package of machorka if they could produce eighteen. The Air Force auxiliaries received a roll of raspberry drops for five rats. Some of the corporals gave us three cigarettes for two rolls of raspberry drops. We didn't smoke machorka. In accordance with the order of the day, the battery split up into hunt groups. Harry belonged to a group that staked out its territory in the washroom, which had only one door and no window. First the washroom door was left open and left-overs of food were deposited in the washtroughs. Then both drains were plugged up. Thereupon we waited behind the windows of the school shack until it began to grow dark. Soon we saw the long shadows pouring past the shack toward the washroom door with a single monotone whistle. No flute strains lured; the suction of an open door. And yet nothing was there but cold grits and kohlrabi stalks. Strewn across the threshold, beef bones ten times boiled and two handfuls of moldy oat flakes—contributed by the kitchen—were expected to lure rats. They would have come even without the oats.

When the washroom promised sufficient game, the school shack spat out five men in high rubber boots, armed with clubs, whose tips were armed with hooks. The washroom swallowed up the five. The last slammed the door. Obliged to remain outside: belated rats, forgetful of Being; the smell grounded on the battery; the moon in case it should nihilate; stars in so far as they were thrown; the radio, blaring from world-related noncoms' barracks; the ontic voices of ships. For inside rose up a music *sui generis*. No longer monotone, but leaping over octaves: grit-shrill kohlrabi-soft bony tinny plucked nasal inauthentic. And, as rehearsed, suddenly illumination came-to-be: five left-handed flashlights part the darkness. For the space of two sighs, silence. Now they rise up lead-gray in the light, slide on their bellies over tinsheathed washtroughs, smack halfpoundly on the tile flooring, crowd around the drains plugged with oakum, try to climb up the concrete pillar and get at the brown wood. Claw themselves fast, scurry away. Unwilling to leave the grits and stalks. Eager to save beef bones and not their own skins: smooth, waxed, waterproof, sound, lovely, precious, vulnerable, currycombed for thousands of years, upon which the hooks descend without regard: No, rat blood is not green but. Are stripped off with boots and nothing else. Are spitted, two with the same hook: Being-beside—Being-with. Are caught in mid-air: music! The same old song since the days of Noah. Rat stories, true and made up. World-relation attitude irruption: grain ships gnawed bare. Hollowed-out granaries. The Nothing acknowledged. Egypt's lean years. And when Paris was besieged. And when the rat sat in the tabernacle. And when thought forsook metaphysics. And when help was most needed. And when the rats left the ship. And when the rats came back. When they attacked even infants and old people riveted to their chairs. When they negated the newborn babe away from the young mother's breast. When they attacked the cats and nothing was left of the rat-terriers but bare teeth, which sparkle to this day, lined up in the museum. And when they carried the plague back and forth and pierced the pink flesh of the pigs. When they devoured the Bible and multiplied in accordance with its instructions. When they disemboweled the clocks and confuted time. When they were sanctified in Hamelin. And when someone invented the poison that struck their fancy. When rattail knotted with rattail to make the rope that plumbed the well. When they grew wise, as long as poems, and appeared on the stage. When they channelized transcendence and crowded into the light. When they nibbled away the rainbow. When they announced the beginning of the world and made leaks in hell. When rats went to heaven and sweetened St. Cecilia's organ. When rats squeaked in the ether and were resettled on stars, ratless stars. When rats existed self-grounded. When an order of the day became known, which offered rewards for rats, slain ones: coarse tobacco, hand-rolled cigarettes, sweet-and-sour raspberry drops. Rat stories rat stories: They collect in the corners. If it doesn't hit them, it hits concrete. They pile up. Stringtails. Curly noses. Fleeing forward. Vulnerable, they attack. Club must help club. Flashlights fall soft, roll hard, are rolled; but buried crosswise, they still glare through, and when dug up they point again to something bounding from a mound that lay still, already written off. For each club counts as it goes along: seventeen, eighteen, thirty-one. But the thirty-second runs, is gone, back again, two hooks too late, a club pounces too soon, whereupon it bites its way through and through and through and topples Harry over: the soles of his rubber boots slip on terror-wet tiles. He falls back soft and screams loud; from the other clubs constrained laughter. On blood-soaked furs, on prey, on quivering layers, on gluttonous generations, on never-ending rat history, on consumed grits, on stalks, Harry screams: "I've been bitten. Been bitten. Bitten . . ." But no rat had. Only fear when he fell, when he fell not hard but soft.

Then all grew still within the washroom walls. Anyone who had an ear available heard the world-related radio blaring from the noncoms' barracks. A few clubs kept aiming dispiritedly and struck what was quivering-to-an-end. Perhaps clubs couldn't cease-to-exist from one second to the next just because there was silence. The clubs still hold a vestige of life; it had to emerge and carry on a vestigial existence. But even when on top of the silence club-peace set in, the rat story wasn't over; for Harry Liebenau filled in this existential pause. Because he had fallen soft, he was obliged to throw up at length into an empty bowl that had contained grits. He couldn't empty his stomach on the rats. They had to be counted, lined up, and tied by their tails to a wire. There were four heavily tenanted lengths of wire, which the tech sergeant, aided by the company clerk who kept the tally, was able to count at morning roll call: A hundred and fifty-eight rats, rounded out on the friendly side, yielded thirty-two rolls of raspberry drops, half of which Harry's hunt group exchanged for cigarettes.

The strung-up rats—that same morning they had to be buried behind the latrine—smelled damp, earthy, with an

overtone of sourness, like an open potato cellar. The smell
over the battery had greater density: no rat exhaled it.

There was once a battery—
    it was near Kaiserhafen and for that reason was called the
Kaiserhafen battery. Conjointly with the Brösen-Glettkau
battery, the Heubude, Pelonken, Zigankenberg, Camp Narvik,
and Altschottland batteries, it guarded the air space over
Danzig and its harbor.

During Harry's term of service in the Kaiserhafen battery,
there were only two air-raid alerts; but rats were hunted every
day. When once a four-engine bomber was shot down over
Oliva Forest, the Pelonken and Altschottland batteries shared
the credit; the Kaiserhafen battery came off empty-handed,
but could point to increasing success in purging the battery
area of water rats.

Ah yes, this being-in-the-midst-of surpassed itself, attaining
the dimension of a world-project! And Harry's hunt group
was among the most successful. But all the groups, even the
volunteer auxiliaries who worked behind the latrine, were
outdone by Störtebeker, who joined no group.

He withdrew rats in broad daylight and always had an
audience. As a rule he lay on his belly in front of the kitchen
shack, right next to the drain cover. He grounded with long
arm in a drain which provided Störtebeker with overarching
withdrawal from the sewer that ran from Troyl to the drainage fields.

O manifold why! Why thus and not otherwise? Why water
rats and not other essents? Why anything at all rather than
nothing? These questions in themselves contained the first-
last primordial answer to all questioning: "The essence of the
rat is the transcendentally originating threefold dispersion of
the rat in the world-project or in the sewage system."

You couldn't help admiring Störtebeker, although a heavy
leather glove, such as welders wear, protected his right hand
that lurked open in the drain. To tell the truth, we all waited
to see rats, four or five of them, chew up his glove and
lacerate his bare hand. But Störtebeker lay serenely with
barely open eyes, sucking his raspberry drop—he didn't smoke
—and every two minutes with suddenly rising leather glove
smacked down a water rat with rat head on the corrugated edge of the drain cover. Between rat death and rat
death he whispered in his own tongue, which however had

been infected with obscurity by the tech sergeant's language, rat propositions and ontological rat truths, which, so we all believed, lured the prey within reach of his glove and made possible his overarching withdrawal. Imperturbably, while he harvested below and piled up above, his discourse ran its course: "The rat withdraws itself by unconcealing itself into the ratty. So the rat errates the ratty, illuminating it with errancy. For the ratty has come-to-be in the errancy where the rat errs and so fosters error. That is the essential area of all history."

Sometimes he called not-yet-withdrawn rats "latecomers." He referred to the piled-up rats as "foretimely" or as "essents." When, his work accomplished, Störtebeker surveyed his ordered prey, he spoke almost tenderly and with a mild didacticism: "The rat can endure without the ratty, but never can there be rattiness without the rat." In an hour he produced as many as twenty-five water rats and could have withdrawn more if he had wanted to. Störtebeker used the same wire as we did for stringing up water rats. This tail-knotted and enumerable demonstration, repeated every morning, he termed his being-there-relatedness. With it he earned quantities of raspberry drops. Sometimes he gave Harry's cousin a roll. Often, as though to appease the ratty, he tossed three separate drops ceremonially into the open drain outside the kitchen shack. Concepts gave rise to a controversy among schoolboys. We were never sure whether the sewer should be termed world-project or errancy.

But the smell that grounded on the battery came neither from world-project nor from errancy, as Störtebeker called his multirelational drain.

There was once a battery,

over which, from first gray to last gray, there flew busy, never-resting crows. Not gulls but crows. There were gulls over Kaiserhafen proper, over the lumber warehouses, but not over the battery. If gulls ever invaded the area, a furious cloud immediately darkened brief happening. Crows do not tolerate gulls.

But the smell that hung over the battery came neither from crows nor from gulls, which weren't there anyway. While p.f.c.s, corporals, Ukrainian volunteer auxiliaries, and Air Force auxiliaries slew rats for reward, the ranks from sergeant to Captain Hufnagel had a different distraction: shooting—though not for promised rewards, but only to fire and hit something—individuals crows out of the agglomeration of crows over the battery. Yet the crows remained and became no fewer.

But the smell which hung over the battery, which stood between barracks and gun positions, between the computer and the shrapnel trenches, and scarcely moved its supporting leg, the smell which, as Harry and everyone else knew, was projected neither by rats nor by crows, which arose from no drain and hence from no errancy, this smell was wafted, regardless of whether the wind was working from Putzig or Dirschau, from the harbor-mouth bar or from the open sea, by a whitish mound blocked off by barbed wire and situated to the south of the battery. This mound stood in front of, and half hid, a brick-red factory, which from squat chimney discharged self-involved smoke, which probably dropped its fallout on Troyl or the Lower City. Between mound and factory ended railroad tracks leading to the Island Station. The mound, neatly conical, rose just a little higher than a rusty shaking-conveyor similar to those used in coal yards and potash mines for piling waste. At the foot of the mound tip cars stood motionless on a movable track. The mound shimmered faintly when struck by the sun. It stood out, sharply silhouetted, when the sky hung low and touched it. If you disregarded the crows that inhabited it, the mound was clean; but it has been written at the beginning of this concluding tale, that nothing is pure. And thus, for all its whiteness, the mound to one side of the Kaiserhafen battery was not pure; it was a pile of bones, and its components, even after processing in the factory, were still overgrown with remnants; and the crows couldn't stop living there, restlessly black. So it came about that a smell, which hovered over the battery like the bell that didn't feel like going to Rome, injected into every mouth, Harry's too, a taste which, even after immoderate consumption of raspberry drops, lost none of its heavy sweetness.

No one talked about the pile of bones. But everybody saw smelled tasted it. Anyone who stepped out of a barracks whose doors opened southward had the cone-shaped mound in his field of vision. Anyone who like Harry, the Number 6, sat upraised beside a gun and who, in gunnery practice, was swung around with gun and fuze setter in accordance with instructions given by the computer, was time and time again, as though computer and bone-pile were engaged in conversation, confronted with a picture: a whitish mountain beside a smoke-spewing factory, an idle shaking-conveyor, motionless tip cars, and a moving blanket of crows. Nobody spoke of the picture. Anyone who dreamed teeming images of the mound remarked over his morning coffee that he had had a funny dream: about climbing stairs or about school. At the most, a phrase which had been used emptily until then took on, in the usual conversations, a vague weightiness that may have come from the unnamed mound. Words occur to Harry: placedness—instandingness—nihilation; for in the daytime workers never moved tip cars to diminish the placedness, although the factory was under steam. No freight cars rolled on tracks and came from the Island Station. In the daytime the shaking-conveyor gave instandingness nothing to chew on. But once during a night maneuver —for one hour the eighty-eight had to chase a target plane caught in four searchlights—Harry and everybody else heard work sounds for the first time. The factory was still blacked out, but lanterns red and white were waved on the railroad tracks. Freight cars bumped each other. A monotonous clanking started up; the shaking-conveyor. Rust against rust: the tip cars. Voices, commands, laughter: for an hour activity prevailed in the nihilation area, while the target plane flew over the city again from the sea side, slipped away from the searchlights, and, caught again, became a Platonic target: The Number 6 manned the fuze setter, trying with cranks to make two mechanical pointers coincide with two electrical pointers and unflinchingly nihilating the evasive essent.

The next day the placedness took on a quality of growth, for Harry and all those who had been disregarding the mound. The crows had received visitors. The smell remained unchanged. But no one inquired after its meaning, although Harry and everyone else had it on their tongues.

There was once a pile of bones—
so it was called, ever since Harry's cousin Tulla had spat out the words in the direction of the mound.

"That's a pile o' bones," she said, helping with her thumb. Harry and many others contradicted, but didn't state exactly what was piled up to the south of the battery.

"Bet you it's bones. And what's more, human bones. Everybody knows that." Tulla offered to bet with Störtebeker rather than her cousin. All three and others were sucking raspberry drops.

Though freshly uttered, Störtebeker's answer had been ready for weeks: "We must conceive of piledupedness in the openness of Being, the divulgation of care, and endurance to death as the consummate essence of existence."

Tulla demanded greater precision: "And I'm telling you they come straight from Stutthof, want to bet?"

Störtebeker refused to be pinned down geographically. He declined the bet and became impatient: "Will you stop chewing my ear off with your threadbare scientific concepts. The most we can say is that here Being has come into unconcealment."

But when Tulla kept harping on Stutthof and called unconcealment by its name, Störtebeker evaded the proffered bet with a grandiose gesture of blessing which took in the battery and the mound of bones: "There lies the essence-ground of all history."

Rats went on being slain after duty hours and even during policing-and-mending period. The ranks from sergeant up shot crows. The smell clung to the battery, no relief showed up. And Tulla said, not to Störtebeker, who was standing aside, drawing figures in the sand, but to the tech sergeant, who had twice exhausted the magazine of his carbine: "Want to bet that they're not honest-to-God human bones, a whole pile of them?"

It was Sunday, visitors' day. But only a few visitors, mostly parents, stood strange in civilian clothes beside their sons who had shot up too fast. Harry's parents hadn't come. November was dragging on, and rain hovered the whole time between low clouds and the earth with its barracks. Harry was standing with the group around Tulla and the tech sergeant, who was loading his carbine for the third time.

"Want to bet that . . ." said Tulla and held out a small white hand ready to shake on it. Nobody wanted to. The hand remained alone. Störtebeker's stick projected the world in the sand. On Tulla's forehead pimples crumbled. Harry's hand played with pieces of bone glue in pants pockets. And then the tech sergeant said: "I bet they're not . . ." and shook on it, without looking at Tulla.

Instantly, as though in possession of a complete plan, Tulla turned on her heels and took the broad strip of weeds between two gun positions as her path. Despite the damp cold

she had on only a sweater and a pleated skirt. She strode
along on bare spindly legs, arms locked behind back, hair
stringy, colorless, and far removed from her last permanent.
She grew smaller as she walked, but remained distinct in the
damp air.

At first Harry and everybody thought: Moving so unswervingly, she'll pass straight through the barbed-wire fence; but
just before the barbs, she dropped to the ground, lifted the
bottommost strand of the fence between battery area and factory area, rolled under without difficulty, stood again knee-
deep in withered-brown weeds, and strode again, but now
as though bucking resistance, toward the crow-in-habited
mound.

Harry and everybody looked after Tulla and forgot the
raspberry drops on their palates. Störtebeker's stick hesitated
in the sand. A grinding gathered strength: somebody had
grit between his teeth. And only when Tulla stood tiny in
front of the mound, when crows lazily rose up, when Tulla
stooped down—bending in the middle—only when Tulla
about-faced and came back, more quickly than everybody
and Harry had feared, the grinding between the tech sergeant's
teeth ebbed away; whereupon silence broke out, the silence
that scoops out the ears.

She didn't come back empty-handed. What she carried between two hands rolled under the wire of the barbed-wire
fence with her into the battery area. Between two 88-milli-
meter guns, which in line with the last order of the computer
pointed to northwest at exactly the same angle as the other
two guns, Tulla grew larger. A short school intermission
takes as long as Tulla's trip there and back. For five minutes
she shrank to toy size and then expanded: almost grown
up. Her forehead was still pimpleless, but what she carried in
front of her already meant something. Störtebeker started a
new world-project. Again the tech sergeant ground gravel,
coarse gravel this time, between his teeth. The silence was
hatchmarked with self-grounded sounds.

When Tulla stood in front of everybody and to one side
of her cousin with her gift, she said without special emphasis: "See? Do I win or don't I?"

The tech sergeant's flat hand struck the left side of her face
from the temple over the ear to the chin. Her ear didn't fall
off. Tulla's head grew hardly smaller. But she dropped the
skull, the one she had brought back, on the spot.

With two clammy yellow hands Tulla rubbed her struck cheek, but didn't run away. On her forehead crumbled exactly as many pimples as before. The skull was a human skull and didn't break when Tulla dropped it, but bounced twice in the weeds. The tech sergeant seemed to see more than the skull. A few looked away over barracks roofs. Harry was unable to pry his eyes away. A piece of the skull's lower jaw was missing. Mister and little Thrasher cracked jokes. Quite a few laughed gratefully in the right places. Störtebeker tried to make the oncoming manifest itself in the sand. His narrow-set eyes saw the essent which clings to itself in its fate, whereupon, suddenly and unexpectedly, world came-to-be; for the tech sergeant shouted with his carbine on safety: "You bastards! Get moving! To your barracks! Policing-and-mending time!"

All moved lethargically and made detours. Jokes congealed. Between the shacks Harry turned his head on shoulders that didn't want to join in the turning: the tech sergeant stood rigid and rectangular with dangling carbine, self-conscious as on the stage. Behind him held geometrically still: placedness, instandingness, nihilation, the essence-ground of history, the difference between Being and the essent—the ontological difference.

But the volunteer auxiliaries were batting the breeze as they peeled potatoes in the kitchen shack. The noncoms' radio was dishing out a request concert. The Sunday visitors took their leave in an undertone. Tulla was standing right next to her cousin, rubbing the struck side of her face. Her mouth, distorted by her massaging hand, muttered past Harry: "Is this the way to treat me when I'm pregnant?"

Naturally Harry had to say: "By whom?"

But she didn't care about that: "Want to bet I'm not?"

Harry didn't want to, because Tulla won all bets. Outside the washroom he pointed his thumb at the half-open door: "In that case, you'd better wash your hands right away, with soap."

Tulla obeyed.—Nothing is pure.

There was once a city—

in addition to the suburbs of Ohra, Schidlitz, Oliva, Emmaus, Praust, Sankt Albrecht, Schellmühl, and the seaport suburb of Neufahrwasser, it had a suburb named Langfuhr. Langfuhr was so big and so little that whatever happens or could happen in this world, also happened or could have happened in Langfuhr.

In this suburb, with its kitchen gardens, drill grounds, drainage fields, slightly sloping cemeteries, shipyards, athletic fields, and military compounds, in Langfuhr, which harbored roughly 72,000 registered inhabitants, which possessed three churches and a chapel, four high schools, a vocational and home-economics school, at all times too few elementary schools, but a brewery with Aktien Pond and icehouse, in Langfuhr, which derived prestige from the Baltic Chocolate Factory, the municipal airfield, the railroad station, the celebrated Engineering School, two movie houses of unequal size, a car barn, the always overcrowded Stadium, and a burned-out synagogue; in the well-known suburb of Langfuhr, whose authorities operated a municpal poorhouse-and-orphanage and a home for the blind, picturesquely situated near Heiligenbrunn, in Langfuhr, incorporated in 1854, a pleasant residential section on the fringe of Jäschkental Forest where the Gutenberg monument was located, in Langfuhr, whose streetcar lines went to Brösen, the seaside resort, Oliva, the episcopal seat, and the city of Danzig—in Danzig-Langfuhr, then, a suburb made famous by the Mackensen Hussars and the last Crown Prince, a suburb traversed from end to end by the Striessbach, there lived a girl by the name of Tulla Pokriefke, who was pregnant but didn't know by whom.

In the same suburb, actually in the same apartment house on Elsenstrasse, which like Hertastrasse and Luisenstrasse connects Labesweg with Marienstrasse, lived Tulla's cousin; his name was Harry Liebenau, he was serving as an Air Force auxiliary in the Kaiserhafen AA battery and was not one of those who might have impregnated Tulla. For Harry merely cogitated in his little head what others actually did. A sixteen-year-old who suffered from cold feet and always stood slightly to one side. A knowledgeable young man, who read a hodgepodge of books on history and philosophy and took care of his handsomely wavy medium-brown hair. A bundle of curiosity who mirrored everything with his gray, but not cold-gray eyes and had a fragile, porous feeling about his smooth but not sickly body. An always cautious Harry, who believed not in God but in the Nothing, yet did not want to have his sensitive tonsils removed. A melancholic, who liked honey cake, poppy-seed cake, and shredded coconut, and though not a good swimmer had volunteered for the Navy. A young man of inaction, who tried to murder his father by means of long poems in school copybooks and referred to his mother as the cook. A hypersensitive boy, who, standing and lying, broke out in sweat over his cousin and unswervingly though secretly thought of a black shepherd dog. A fetishist, who for reasons carried a pearl-white incisor tooth in his purse. A visionary, who lied a good deal, spoke softly, turned red when, believed this and that, and regarded the never-ending war as an extension of his schooling. A boy, a young man, a uniformed high school student, who venerated the Führer, Ulrich von Hutten, General Rommel, the historian Heinrich von Treitschke, for brief moments Napoleon, the panting movie actor Emil Jannings, for a while Savonarola, then again Luther, and of late the philospher Martin Heidegger. With the help of these models he succeeded in burying a real mound made of human bones under medieval allegories. The pile of bones, which in reality cried out to high heaven between Troyl and Kaiserhafen, was mentioned in his diary as a place of sacrifice, erected in order that purity might come-to-be in the luminous, which transluminates purity and so fosters light.

In addition to the diary Harry Liebenau kept up an often languishing and then for a time lively correspondence with a girl friend, who under the stage name of Jenny Angustri danced in the German Ballet in Berlin and who in the capital and on tours of the occupied regions appeared first as a member of the *corps de ballet*, later as a soloist.

When Air Force auxiliary Harry Liebenau had a pass, he went to the movies and took the pregnant Tulla Pokriefke. Before Tulla was pregnant, Harry had tried several times in vain to persuade her to attend the movies by his side. Now that she was telling all Langfuhr: "Somebody's knocked me up"—though there were still no visible signs—she was more indulgent and said to Harry: "It's O.K. with me if you'll pay."

They let several films flicker past them in Langfuhr's two movie houses. The Art Cinema ran first the newsreel, then the educational film, then the feature. Harry was in uniform; Tulla was sitting there in a much too spacious coat of Navy serge, which she had had tailored especially for her condition. While grapes were being harvested on rainy screen and peasant girls, festooned with grapes, wreathed with vineleaves, and forced into corsets, were smiling, Harry tried to clinch with his cousin. But Tulla disengaged herself with the mild reproach: "Cut that out, Harry. There's no sense in it now. You should have come around sooner."

In the movies Harry always had a supply of raspberry drops on him, which were paid out in his battery every time you had laid low a specific number of water rats. Accordingly, they were known as rat drops. In the darkness, while up front the newsreel started up with a din, Harry peeled paper and tin foil from a roll of raspberry drops, thrust his thumbnail between the first and the second drop, and offered Tulla the roll. Tulla lifted off the raspberry drop with two fingers, clung to the newsreel with both pupils, sucked audibly, and whispered while up front the muddy season was setting in in Center Sector: "Everything stinks in that battery of yours, even the raspberry drops, of that whatchacallit behind the fence. You ought to ask for a transfer."

But Harry had other desires, which were fulfilled in the movies: Gone: the muddy season. No more Christmas preparations on the Arctic front. Counted: the gutted T-34 tanks. Docked: the U-boat after a successful expedition. Taken off: our fighter planes to attack the terror bombers. Different music. Different cameraman: a quiet pebble-strewn afternoon, sunlight sprinkling through autumn leaves: the Führer's headquarters. "Hey, look. There he runs stands wags his tail. Between him and the aviator. Sure thing, that's him: our dog. Our dog's dog, I mean; it's him all over. Prinz, that's Prinz, that our Harras . . ."

For a good minute, while the Führer and Chancellor under low-pulled visor cap, behind anchored hands, chats with an Air Force officer—was it Rudel?—and walks back and forth among the trees at the Führer's headquarters, an obviously black shepherd is privileged to stand beside his boots, rub against the Führer's boots, let the side of his neck be patted—for once the Führer unlocks his anchored hands, only to recouple them as soon as the newsreel has captured the cordiality prevailing between master and dog.

Before Harry took the last streetcar to Troyl—he had to change at the Main Station for the Heubude train—he took Tulla home. They talked by turns: neither listened: she about the feature; he about the newsreel. In Tulla's picture a girl was raped while picking mushrooms and consequently—something Tulla refused to understand—jumped in the river; Harry tried, in Störtebeker's philosophical language, to keep the newsreel alive and at the same time define it: "The way I see it, dog-being—the very fact of it—implies that an essent dog is thrown into his there. His being-in-the-world is the dog-there, regardless of whether his there is a carpenter's yard or the Führer's headquarters or some realm removed from vulgar time. For future dog-being is not later than the dog-there of having-beenness, which in turn is not anterior to being-held-out-into the dog-now."

Nevertheless, Tulla said outside the Pokriefkes' door: "Beginning next week I'll be in my second month, and by Christmas you're sure to see something."

Harry dropped in at his parents' apartment for fifteen minutes, meaning to take some fresh underwear and edibles. His father, the carpenter, had swollen feet because he had been on them all day: from one building site to another. Consequently he was soaking his feet in the kitchen. Large and gnarled, they moved sadly in the basin. You couldn't tell from the carpenter's sighs whether it was the well-being bestowed by his footbath or tangled memories that made him sigh. Harry's mother was already holding the towel. She was kneeling and had taken off her reading glasses. Harry pulled a chair over from the table and sat down between father and mother: "Want me to tell you a terrific story?"

As his father took one foot out of the basin and his mother expertly received the foot in the Turkish towel, Harry began: "There was once a dog, his name was Perkun. Perkun sired the bitch Senta. And Senta whelped Harras. And the stud dog Harras sired Prinz. And do you know where I just saw our Prinz? In the newsreel. At the Führer's headquarters. Between the Führer and Rudel. Plain as day, out of doors. Might have been our Harras. You've got to go see it, Papa. You can leave before the feature if you've had enough. I'm definitely going again, maybe twice."

With one dry but still steaming foot, the carpenter nodded absently. He said of course he was glad to hear it and would go see the newsreel if he could find time. He was too tired to be pleased aloud though he tried hard, and later, with two dry feet, actually did put his pleasure into words: "You don't say, our Harras' Prinz. And the Führer patted him in the newsreel. And Rudel was there too. You don't say."

There was once a newsreel:
it showed the muddy season in Center Sector, Christmas

preparations on the Arctic front, the aftermath of a tank battle, laughing workers in a munitions plant, wild geese in Norway, Hitler Cubs collecting junk, sentries on the Atlantic Wall, and a visit to the Führer's headquarters. All this and more could be seen not only in the two movie houses of the suburb of Langfuhr, but in Salonika as well. For from there came a letter written to Harry Liebenau by Jenny Brunies, who under the stage name of Jenny Angustri was performing for German and Italian soldiers.

"Just imagine," Jenny wrote, "what a small world it is: last night—for once we weren't playing—I went to the movies with Herr Haseloff. And whom did I see in the newsreel? I couldn't have been mistaken. And Herr Haseloff also thought the black shepherd, who was there for at least a minute in the headquarters scene, could only be Prinz, your Harras' Prinz.

"The funny part of it is that Herr Haseloff can't possibly have seen your Harras except in the photographs I've shown him. But he has tremendous imagination, and not only in artistic matters. And he always wants to know about things down to the slightest details. That's probably why he has sent in a request to the propaganda unit here. He wants a copy of the newsreel for purposes of documentation. He'll probably get it, for Herr Haseloff has connections all over, and it's unusual for anyone to refuse him anything. Oh, Harry, then we'll be able to look at the newsreel together, any time we please, later, when the war is over. And someday when we have children, we'll be able to show them on the screen how things used to be.

"It's stupid here. I haven't seen a bit of Greece, just rain. Unfortunately we had to leave our good Felsner-Imbs in Berlin. The school goes on even when we're on tour.

"But just imagine—but of course you know all about it— Tulla is expecting a baby. She told me about it on an open postcard. I'm glad for her, though I sometimes think she's going to have a hard time of it, all alone without a husband to take care of her or any real profession . . ."

Jenny did not conclude her letter without pointing out how very much the unaccustomed climate fatigued her and how very much—even in far-off Salonika—she loved her Harry. In a postscript she asked Harry to look out for his cousin as much as possible. "In her condition, you know, she needs a prop, especially as her home isn't exactly what you would call well regulated. I'm going to send her a package with Greek honey in it. Besides, I've unraveled two practically new sweaters I was recently able to buy in Amsterdam. One light-blue, the other pale-pink. I'll be able to knit her at least four pairs of rompers and two little jackets. We have so much time between rehearsals and even during performances."

There was once a baby,

which, although rompers were already being knitted for him, was not to be born. Not that Tulla didn't want the baby. She still showed no sign, but she represented herself, with a sweetness verging on the maudlin, as an expectant mother. Nor was there any father growling with averted face: I don't want a child! for all the fathers that might have come into consideration were absorbed from morning till night in their own affairs. To mention only the tech sergeant from the Kaiserhafen battery and Air Force auxiliary Störtebeker: the tech sergeant shot crows with his carbine and ground his teeth whenever he made a bull's-eye: Störtebeker soundlessly drew in the sand what his tongue whispered: errancy, the ontological difference, the world-project in all its variations. How, with such existential occupations, could the two of them find time to think of a baby that suffused Tulla Pokriefke with sweetness though it did not yet round out her expressly tailored coat?

Only Harry, the receiver of letters, the writer of letters, said: "How are you feeling? Are you sick to your stomach before breakfast? What does Dr. Hollatz say? Don't strain yourself. You really ought to stop smoking. Should I get you some malt beer? Matzerath will give me dill pickles for food tickets. Don't worry. I'll take care of the child later on."

And sometimes, as though to replace the two plausible but persistently absent fathers in the expectant mother's eyes, he stared gloomily at two imaginary points, ground inexperienced teeth in the tech sergeant's manner, drew Störtebeker's symbols in the sand with a stick, and prattled with Störtebeker's philosophical tongue, which, with slight variations, might also have been the tech sergeant's tongue: "Listen to me, Tulla, I'll explain. The fact is that the average everydayness of child-being can be defined as thrown, projected being-in-the-child-world, which in its child-being-in-the-world and its child-being-with-others involves the very core of child-being capacity.—Understand? No? Let's try again . . ."

But it was not only his innate imitativeness that inspired Harry with such sayings; in the becoming uniform of an Air Force auxiliary he occasionally took up his stance in the middle of the Pokriefkes' kitchen and delivered self-assured lectures to Tulla's grumbling father, a dyspeptic Koshnavian from the region between Konitz and Tuchel. He made no profession of fatherhood, but took everything on himself. He even offered—"I know what I'm doing"—to become his pregnant cousin's future husband, yet was relieved when, instead of taking him up, August Pokriefke found troubles of his own to chew on: August Pokriefke had been drafted. Near Oxhöft—he had been declared fit only for home-front duty—he had to guard military installations, an occupation which enabled him, in the course of long weekend furloughs, to tell the whole family—the master carpenter and his wife were also obliged to lend their ears—interminable stories about partisans; for in the winter of '43 the Poles began to extend their field of operations: whereas previously they had made only Tuchler Heath insecure, now partisan activity was also reported in Koshnavia. Even in the wooded country inland from the Gulf of Danzig and extending to the foot of Hela Peninsula, they were making raids and imperiling August Pokriefke.

But Tulla, with flat hands on still-flat tummy, had other things to think about besides guerrillas stealthy and insidious, and guerrilla-fighter groups. Often she stood up in the middle of a night attack west of Heisternest and left the kitchen so noticeably that August Pokriefke was unable to bring in his two prisoners and save his motor pool from plunder.

When Tulla left the kitchen, she went to the lumber shed. What could her cousin do but follow her as in the years when he had been permitted to carry the school satchel on his back. Tulla's hiding place was still there among the timber. The logs were still piled in such a way as to leave an empty space just big enough for Tulla and Harry.

There sit an expectant sixteen-year-old mother and an Air Force auxiliary who has enlisted in the Army and is looking forward to his induction, in a children's hiding place: Harry had to lay a hand on Tulla and say: "I can feel something. Plain as day. There it is again." Tulla potters with tiny wood-shaving wigs, weaves wood-shaving dolls from soft linden shavings, and as ever disseminates her aroma of bone glue.

Unquestionably the baby, as soon as emerged, will distill his mother's unbanishable smell; but only months later, when sufficient milk teeth are present, and still later at the sandbox age, will it become apparent whether the child often and significantly grinds his teeth or whether he prefers to draw little men and world-projects in the sand.

Neither bone-glue aroma nor grinding tech sergeant nor sign-setting Störtebeker. The baby didn't feel like it; and on the occasion of an outing—Tulla obeyed Harry, who, putting on the airs of a father, said an expectant mother needed plenty of fresh air—under the open sky, the infant gave it to be understood that it had no desire to disseminate the aroma of bone glue after the manner of its mother, or to perpetuate the paternal habits of teeth-grinding or world-projecting.

Harry had a weekend pass: an existential pause. Because the air was so Decemberly, cousin and cousin decided to go out to Oliva Forest, and if it wasn't too much for Tulla, to walk as far as the Schwedenschanze. The streetcar, Line Number 2, was crowded, and Tulla was furious because nobody stood up for her. Several times she poked Harry, but the sometimes bashful Air Force auxiliary was disinclined to speak up and demand a seat for Tulla. In front of her, with rounded knees, sat a dozing infantry p.f.c. Tulla fumed at him: couldn't he see she was expecting? Instantly the p.f.c. transformed his rounded sitting knees into neatly pressed standing knees. Tulla sat down, and on all sides total strangers exchanged glances of complicity. Harry was ashamed not to have demanded a seat and ashamed a second time that Tulla had asked for a seat so loudly.

The car had already passed the big bend on Hohenfriedberger Weg and was jogging from stop to stop on a stretch that was straight as a die. They had agreed to get out at "White Lamb." Right after "Friedensschluss," Tulla stood up and directly behind Harry pushed her way through winter coats to the rear platform. Even before the trailer reached the traffic island at "White Lamb"—so called after an inn favored by excursionists—Tulla was standing on the bottommost running board, screwing up her eyes in the head wind.

"Don't be a fool," said Harry above her.

Tulla had always like to jump off streetcars.

"Wait till it stops," Harry had to say from above.

From way back, jumping on and off had been Tulla's favorite sport.

"Don't do it, Tulla, watch out, be careful!" But Harry didn't hold her back.

Beginning roughly in her eighth year, Tulla had jumped from moving streetcars. She had never fallen. Never, as stupid, foolhardy people do, had she risked jumping against the motion of the car; and now, on the trailer of the Number 2, which had been running between Main Station and the suburb of Oliva since the turn of the century, she did not jump from the front platform, but from the rear platform. Nimbly and light as a cat, she jumped with the motion of the car and landed with an easy flexing of the knees and gravel-scraping soles.

Tulla said to Harry, who had jumped off right behind her: "Watcha always nagging for? You think I'm dumb?"

They took a dirt road to one side of the White Lamb Inn. Turning off through the fields at right angles to the rectilinear streetcar line, it led toward the dark forest, huddled on hills. The sun was shining with spinsterish caution. Rifle practice somewhere near Saspe punctuated the afternoon with irregular dots. The White Lamb, haven of excursionists, was closed, shuttered, boarded. The owner, it seemed, had been jailed for economic subversion—buying canned fish on the black market. The furrows of the field and the frozen ruts of the road were filled with wind-blown snow. Ahead of them hooded crows were shifting from stone to stone. Small, under a sky too high and too blue, Tulla clutched her belly first over, then under, the material of her coat. For all the fresh December air, her face couldn't produce a healthy color: two nostrils dilated with fright in a shrinking, chalky phiz. Luckily Tulla was wearing ski pants.

"Something's gone wrong."

"What's wrong? I don't get it. You feel sick? You want to sit down? Or can you make it to the woods? What is it, anyway?"

Harry was frightfully excited, knew nothing, understood nothing, half suspected and didn't want to know. Tulla's nose crinkled, the bridge sprouted beads of sweat that didn't want to fall off. He dragged her to the nearest stone—the crows abandoned it—then to a farm roller, its shaft spitting the December air. Then at the edge of the woods, after crows had had to move another few times, Harry leaned his cousin against the trunk of a beech tree. Her breath flew white. Harry's breath too came in puffs of white steam. Distant rifle practice was still putting sharp pencil points on nearby paper. From crumbly furrows ending just before the woods, crows peered out with cocked heads. "It's good I got pants on, or I wouldn't have made it this far. It's all running off!"

Their breath at the edge of the woods rose up and blew away. Undecided. "Should I?" First Tulla let her Navy serge coat slip off. Harry folded it neatly. She herself undid her waistband, Harry did the rest with horrified curiosity: the finger-size two-months-old fetus lay there in her panties. Made manifest: there. Sponge in gelatin: there. In bloody and in colorless fluids: there. Through world onset: there. A small handful: unkept, beforelike, partly there. Dismal in sharp December air. Grounding as fostering steamed and cooled off quickly. Grounding as taking root, and Tulla's handkerchief as well. Unconcealed into what? By whom attuned? Space-taking never without world-disclosure. Therefore: panties off. Ski pants up, no child, but. What a vision of essence! Lay there warm, then cold: Withdrawal provides the commitment of the enduring project with a hole at the edge of Oliva Forest: "Don't stand there! Do something. Dig a hole. Not there, that's a better place." Ah, are we ourselves ever, is mine ever, now under the leaves, in the ground, not deeply frozen; for higher than reality is potentiality: here manifested: what primarily and ordinarily does not show itself, what is hidden but at the same time is an essential part of what does primarily and ordinarily show itself, namely, its meaning and ground, which is not frozen but loosened with heels of shoes from the Air Force supply room, in order that the baby may come into its there. There into its there. But only project there. Shorn of its essence: there. A mere neuter, a mere impersonal pronoun—and the impersonal pronoun not there in the same sense as the there in general. And happening-to-be-present confronts being-there with the facticity of its there and without disgust sets it down with bare fingers, unprotected by gloves: Ah, the ecstatic-horizontal structure! There only toward death, which means: tossed in layers, with a few leaves and hollow beechnuts on top, lest the crows, or if foxes should come, the forester, diviners, vultures, treasure seekers, witches, if there are any, gather fetuses, make tallow candles out of them or powder to strew the memorable spot. Later a fatso by the name of Amsel spent hours drawing the dog with pen and brush. He didn't call Harras by his right name, he called him Pluto; the carpenter's little niece didn't call Amsel by his right name, but reviled him as "Sheeny." Then Amsel was turned out of the yard. And once a disaster was barely averted. But an article of clothing belonging to a piano teacher, who lived in the right-hand rear apartment on the ground floor, was badly ripped and had to be paid for. And once, or several times, somebody came around reeling drunk and insulted Harras in political terms, louder than buzz saw and lathe could scream to high heaven. And one time somebody who was good at grinding his teeth tossed poisoned meat from the roof of the lumber shed and it landed right in front of the kennel. The meat was not left lying.

Memories. But let no one try to read the thoughts of a carpenter who hesitates in front of an empty kennel and stops in his tracks. Maybe he's thinking back. Maybe he's thinking about lumber prices. Maybe he isn't thinking about anything in particular, but losing himself, while smoking his fifteen-pfennig cigar, between memories and lumber prices. And this for half an hour until the machinist cautiously calls him back: time to cut panels for prefabricated Navy barracks. Empty and full of memories, the kennel doesn't run away.

No, the dog had never been sick, only black: coat and undercoat. Short-haired like the five other members of his litter, who were doing well in police work. The lips closed dry. Neck taut and without dewlap. Croup long and gently sloping. Ears always erect and slightly tilted. And once again now: every single Harras hair straight, smooth, harsh, and black.

. . . . ds a few stray hairs, now dull and brittle, ... times, after clos-

across thresholds ointments for everything and nothing. And so: fieldstone on it. Grounding in the ground. Placedness and abortion. Matter and work. Mother and child. Being and time. Tulla and Harry. Jumps off the streetcar into her there, without stumbling. Jumps shortly before Christmas, nimbly but too overarchingly: pushed in two moons ago, out through the same hole. Bankrupt! The nihilating Nothing. Lousy luck. Come-to-be in errancy. Spitting cunt. Not even transcendental but vulgar ontic unconcealed ungrinded unstörtebekert. Washed up. Error fostered. Empty egg. Wasn't a pre-Socratic. A bit of care. Bullshit. Was a latecomer. Vaporized, evaporated, cleared out. "You shut your trap. Stinking luck. Why did it have to happen to me? Beans. I was going to call him Konrad or after *him*. After who? After him. Come on, Tulla. Let's go. Yes, come on, let's go."

And cousin and cousin left after securing the site with one large and several small stones against crows, foresters, foxes, treasure seekers, and witches.

A little lighter, they left; and at first Harry was allowed to support Tulla's arm. Distant practice shots continued irregularly to punctuate the written-off afternoon. Their mouths were fuzzy. But Harry had a roll of raspberry drops in his breast pocket.

When they were standing at the "White Lamb" car stop and the car coming from Oliva grew yellow and larger, Tulla said out of gray face into his rosy face: "We'll wait till it starts to move. Then you jump in front and me on the rear platform."

There was once an abortion

named Konrad, and no one heard about him, not even Jenny Brunies, who, under the name of Jenny Angustri, was dancing in Salonika, Athens, Belgrade, and Budapest in pointed slippers for sound and convalescent soldiers and knitting little things from unraveled wool, pink and blue, intended for a girl friend's baby who was supposed to be named Konrad, the name by which they had called the girl friend's little brother before he drowned while swimming.

In every letter that came fluttering Harry Liebenau's way —four in January, in February only three—Jenny wrote something about slowly growing woolies: "In between I've been working hard. Rehearsals drag out dreadfully, because there's always something wrong with the lighting and the stage hands here act as if they didn't understand a word. Sometimes, when they take forever to shift scenes, one's tempted to think of sabotage. At any rate the routine here leaves me lots of time for knitting. One pair of rompers is done and I've finished the first jacket except for crocheting the scallops on the collar. You can't imagine how I enjoy doing it. Once when Herr Haseloff caught me in the dressing room with an almost finished pair of rompers, he had a terrible scare, and I've kept him on the hook by not telling him whom I was knitting for.

"He certainly thinks I'm expecting. In ballet practice, for instance, he sometimes stares at me for minutes on end, in the weirdest way. But otherwise he's nice and ever so considerate. For my birthday he gave me a pair of fur-lined gloves, though I never wear anything on my fingers, no matter how cold it is. And about other things, too, he's as kind as he could be: for instance, he often talks about Papa Brunies, in the most natural way, as if we were expecting him back any minute. When we both know perfectly well that it will never be."

Every week Jenny filled a letter with her babbling. And in the middle of February she announced, apart from the completion of the third pair of rompers and the second jacket, the death of Papa Brunies. Matter-of-factly and without making a new paragraph, Jenny wrote: "The official notice has finally come. He died in Stutthof camp on November 12, 1943. Stated cause of death: heart failure."

The signature, the unvarying "As ever, your faithful and somewhat tired Jenny," was followed by a postscript with a bit of special news for Harry: "Incidentally, the newsreel came, the one with the Führer's Headquarters and your Harras' pup in it. Herr Haseloff ran the scene off at least ten times, even in slow motion, so as to sketch the dog. Twice was as much as I could bear. Don't be cross with me, but the news of Papa's death—the announcement was so awfully official— has affected me quite a lot. Sometimes I feel like crying the whole time, but I can't."

There was once a dog,
 his name was Perkun, and he belonged to a Lithuanian miller's man who had found work on the Vistula delta. Perkun survived the miller's man and sired Senta. The bitch Senta, who belonged to a miller in Nickelswalde, whelped

Harras. The stud dog, who belonged to a carpenter in Danzi Langfuhr, covered the bitch Thekla, who belonged to a He Leeb, who died early in 1942, shortly after the bitch Thekl But the dog Prinz, sired by the shepherd male Harras ar whelped by the shepherd bitch Thekla, made history: he w given to the Führer and Chancellor for his birthday an because he was the Führer's favorite dog, shown in tl newsreels.

When dog breeder Leeb was buried, the carpenter attende his funeral. When Perkun died, a normal canine ailme was entered on the studbook. Senta had to be shot becaus she grew hysterical and did damage. According to an entr in the studbook, the bitch Thekla died of old age. But Ha ras, who had sired the Führer's favorite dog Prinz, wa poisoned on political grounds with poisoned meat, and burie in the dog cemetery. An empty kennel was left behind.

There was once a kennel
 which had been inhabited by a black shepherd by the name of Harras until he was poisoned. Since then the kennel had stood empty in the yard of the carpenter shop, for carpenter Liebenau had no desire to acquire a new dog; as far as he was concerned, Harras had been the one and only.

Often on his way to the machine shop, the imposing man could be seen to hesitate outside the kennel, long enough to draw a few puffs from his cigar or even longer. The wall of earth which Harras, on taut chain, had thrown up with his two forepaws had been leveled by the rain and the apprentices' wooden shoes. But the open kennel still gave off the smell of a dog who, in love with his own smell, had deposited his scent marks in the yard and all over Langfuhr. Especially under the piercing August sun or in t the kennel smelled across thresholds ointments for everything and nothing. And so: fieldstone on it. Grounding in the ground. Placedness and abortion. Matter and work. Mother and child. Being and time. Tulla and Harry. Jumps off the streetcar into her there, without stumbling. Jumps shortly before Christmas, nimbly but too overarchingly: pushed in two moons ago, out through the same hole. Bankrupt! The nihilating Nothing. Lousy luck. Come-to-be in errancy. Spitting cunt. Not even transcendental but vulgar ontic unconcealed ungrinded unstörtebekert. Washed up. Error fostered. Empty egg. Wasn't a pre-Socratic. A bit of care. Bullshit. Was a latecomer. Vaporized, evaporated, cleared out. "You shut your trap. Stinking luck. Why did it have to happen to me? Beans. I was going to call him Konrad or after *him*. After who? After him. Come on, Tulla. Let's go. Yes, come on, let's go."

And cousin and cousin left after securing the site with one large and several small stones against crows, foresters, foxes, treasure seekers, and witches.

A little lighter, they left; and at first Harry was allowed to support Tulla's arm. Distant practice shots continued irregularly to punctuate the written-off afternoon. Their mouths were fuzzy. But Harry had a roll of raspberry drops in his breast pocket.

When they were standing at the "White Lamb" car stop and the car coming from Oliva grew yellow and larger, Tulla said out of gray face into his rosy face: "We'll wait till it starts to move. Then you jump in front and me on the rear platform."

There was once an abortion

named Konrad, and no one heard about him, not even Jenny Brunies, who, under the name of Jenny Angustri, was dancing in Salonika, Athens, Belgrade, and Budapest in pointed slippers for sound and convalescent soldiers and knitting little things from unraveled wool, pink and blue, intended for a girl friend's baby who was supposed to be named Konrad, the name by which they had called the girl friend's little brother before he drowned while swimming.

In every letter that came fluttering Harry Liebenau's way —four in January, in February only three—Jenny wrote something about slowly growing woolies: "In between I've been working hard. Rehearsals drag out dreadfully, because there's always something wrong with the lighting and the stage hands here act as if they didn't understand a word. Sometimes, when they take forever to shift scenes, one's tempted to think of sabotage. At any rate the routine here leaves me lots of time for knitting. One pair of rompers is done and I've finished the first jacket except for crocheting the scallops on the collar. You can't imagine how I enjoy doing it. Once when Herr Haseloff caught me in the dressing room with an almost finished pair of rompers, he had a terrible scare, and I've kept him on the hook by not telling him whom I was knitting for.

"He certainly thinks I'm expecting. In ballet practice, for instance, he sometimes stares at me for minutes on end, in the weirdest way. But otherwise he's nice and ever so considerate. For my birthday he gave me a pair of fur-lined gloves, though I never wear anything on my fingers, no matter how cold it is. And about other things, too, he's as kind as he could be: for instance, he often talks about Papa Brunies, in the most natural way, as if we were expecting him back any minute. When we both know perfectly well that it will never be."

Every week Jenny filled a letter with her babbling. And in the middle of February she announced, apart from the completion of the third pair of rompers and the second jacket, the death of Papa Brunies. Matter-of-factly and without making a new paragraph, Jenny wrote: "The official notice has finally come. He died in Stutthof camp on November 12, 1943. Stated cause of death: heart failure."

The signature, the unvarying "As ever, your faithful and somewhat tired Jenny," was followed by a postscript with a bit of special news for Harry: "Incidentally, the newsreel came, the one with the Führer's Headquarters and your Harras' pup in it. Herr Haseloff ran the scene off at least ten times, even in slow motion, so as to sketch the dog. Twice was as much as I could bear. Don't be cross with me, but the news of Papa's death—the announcement was so awfully official— has affected me quite a lot. Sometimes I feel like crying the whole time, but I can't."

There was once a dog,
  his name was Perkun, and he belonged to a Lithuanian miller's man who had found work on the Vistula delta. Perkun survived the miller's man and sired Senta. The bitch Senta, who belonged to a miller in Nickelswalde, whelped

Harras. The stud dog, who belonged to a carpenter in Danzig-Langfuhr, covered the bitch Thekla, who belonged to a Herr Leeb, who died early in 1942, shortly after the bitch Thekla. But the dog Prinz, sired by the shepherd male Harras and whelped by the shepherd bitch Thekla, made history: he was given to the Führer and Chancellor for his birthday and, because he was the Führer's favorite dog, shown in the newsreels.

When dog breeder Leeb was buried, the carpenter attended his funeral. When Perkun died, a normal canine ailment was entered on the studbook. Senta had to be shot because she grew hysterical and did damage. According to an entry in the studbook, the bitch Thekla died of old age. But Harras, who had sired the Führer's favorite dog Prinz, was poisoned on political grounds with poisoned meat, and buried in the dog cemetery. An empty kennel was left behind.

There was once a kennel

which had been inhabited by a black shepherd by the name of Harras until he was poisoned. Since then the kennel had stood empty in the yard of the carpenter shop, for carpenter Liebenau had no desire to acquire a new dog; as far as he was concerned, Harras had been the one and only.

Often on his way to the machine shop, the imposing man could be seen to hesitate outside the kennel, long enough to draw a few puffs from his cigar or even longer. The wall of earth which Harras, on taut chain, had thrown up with his two forepaws had been leveled by the rain and the apprentices' wooden shoes. But the open kennel still gave off the smell of a dog who, in love with his own smell, had deposited his scent marks in the yard and all over Langfuhr. Especially under the piercing August sun or in the damp spring air, the kennel smelled pungently of Harras and attracted flies. Not a suitable ornament for an active carpenter shop. The tar paper of the kennel roof had begun to fray around roofing nails, which seemed to be coming loose. A sad sight, empty and full of memories: once when Harras still lay keen and chained, the carpenter's little niece had lived beside him in the kennel for a whole week. Later, photographers and newspapermen came, snapped the dog's picture and described him. Numerous papers termed the yard of the carpenter shop a historical site because of the celebrated kennel. Celebrities, even foreigners, came and tarried as much as five minutes on the memorable spot. Later a fatso by the name of Amsel spent hours drawing the dog with pen and brush. He didn't call Harras by his right name, he called him Pluto; the carpenter's little niece didn't call Amsel by his right name, but reviled him as "Sheeny." Then Amsel was turned out of the yard. And once a disaster was barely averted. But an article of clothing belonging to a piano teacher, who lived in the right-hand rear apartment on the ground floor, was badly ripped and had to be paid for. And once, or several times, somebody came around reeling drunk and insulted Harras in political terms, louder than buzz saw and lathe could scream to high heaven. And one time somebody who was good at grinding his teeth tossed poisoned meat from the roof of the lumber shed and it landed right in front of the kennel. The meat was not left lying.

Memories. But let no one try to read the thoughts of a carpenter who hesitates in front of an empty kennel and stops in his tracks. Maybe he's thinking back. Maybe he's thinking about lumber prices. Maybe he isn't thinking about anything in particular, but losing himself, while smoking his fifteen-pfennig cigar, between memories and lumber prices. And this for half an hour until the machinist cautiously calls him back: time to cut panels for prefabricated Navy barracks. Empty and full of memories, the kennel doesn't run away.

No, the dog had never been sick, only black: coat and undercoat. Short-haired like the five other members of his litter, who were doing well in police work. The lips closed dry. Neck taut and without dewlap. Croup long and gently sloping. Ears always erect and slightly tilted. And once again now: every single Harras hair straight, smooth, harsh, and black.

The carpenter finds a few stray hairs, now dull and brittle, between the floorboards of the kennel. Sometimes, after closing time, he bends down and pokes about in the moldy warm hole, paying no attention to the tenants hanging out the windows.

But when one day the carpenter lost his purse, containing aside from change a bundle of faded dog hairs; but when the carpenter went to see the Führer's favorite dog, whom Harras had sired, in the newsreel, but next week's newsreel unrolled before his eyes without the Führer's dog; but when news came that a fourth former journeyman of the Liebenau carpenter shop had met a soldier's death; when heavy oak buffets, walnut sideboards, extensible dining-room tables on richly carved legs could no longer be turned out at the carpenter's workbenches, and the only operation permitted was the nailing together of numbered pine boards: parts for Army barracks; when the year 1944 was in its fourth month; when people said: "Now they've done old Herr Brunies in too"; when Odessa was evacuated and Tarnopol was encircled and had to surrender; when the bell rang for the next-to-last round; when food tickets stopped keeping their promises; when carpenter Liebenau heard that his only son had volunteered for the Navy; when all this—the lost purse and the flickering newsreel, the fallen journeyman and the lousy barracks parts, Odessa evacuated and the lying food tickets, old Herr Brunies and his enlisted son—when all this added up to a round sum demanding to be written off, carpenter Friedrich Leibenau walked out of his office, picked up an ax that was new and still coated with grease, crossed the yard on April 20, 1944, at two in the afternoon, planted himself with parted legs in front of the empty kennel of the poisoned shepherd Harras, and with steady overhead strokes, lonely and speechless, smashed the edifice into kindling.

But because the fifty-fifth birthday of the selfsame Führer and Chancellor, to whom the young shepherd dog Prinz of Harras' line had been presented ten years before, was celebrated on April 20th, everybody at the apartment house windows and at the workbenches in the shop understood that more had been smashed than rotting wood and torn tar paper.

After this deed the carpenter had to stay in bed for a good two weeks. He had overtaxed himself.

There was once a carpenter,
who with practiced overhead strokes chopped into kindling a dog kennel that stood for a good many things.

There was once an assassin, who packed a bomb, experimentally, in his brief case.

There was once an Air Force auxiliary who was waiting impatiently to be inducted into the Navy; he wanted to submerge and to sink enemy ships.

There was once a ballet dancer who, in Budapest, Vienna, and Copenhagen, was knitting rompers and jackets for a baby that had long lain buried at the edge of Oliva Forest, weighted down with stones.

There was once an expectant mother who liked to jump off moving streetcars and in so doing, although she had jumped nimbly and not against the motion of the car, lost her two-months child. Thereupon the expectant mother, again a flat young girl, went to work: Tulla Pokriefke became—as one might have expected—a streetcar conductress.

There was once a police president whose son, generally known as Störtebeker, who intended to study philosophy later on, who might almost have become a father, and who, after projecting the world in sand, founded a teen-agers' gang, which later became famous under the name of the Dusters. He stopped drawing symbols in the sand; instead, he drew the rationing office, the Church of the Sacred Heart, the Post Office Administration Building: all angular buildings into which he later, and at night, led the self-grounded Dusters. The conductorette Tulla Pokriefke belonged halfway to the gang. Her cousin didn't belong at all. At the most he stood lookout when the gang met in the storage sheds of the Baltic Chocolate Factory. A permanent possession of the gang appears to have been a three-year-old child, their mascot, who was addressed as Jesus and survived the gang.

There was once a tech sergeant who trained Air Force auxiliaries as AA gunners and quasi-philosophers, who limped slightly, had a way of grinding his teeth, and might almost have become a father, but was tried, first by a special, then by a general court-martial, was broken of his rank and transferred to a punitive battalion, because, while in a state of drunkenness between the barracks of the Kaiserhafen battery, he had insulted the Führer and Chancellor in sentences marked by such locutions as: forgetful of Being, mound of bones, structure of care, Stutthof, Todtnau, and concentration camp. As they were taking him away—in broad daylight—he bawled mysteriously: "You ontic dog! Alemannic dog! You dog with stocking cap and buckled shoes! What did you do to little Husserl? What did you do to tubby Amsel? You pre-Socratic Nazi dog!" On account of this unrhymed hymn, he was compelled, in spite of his bad leg, to dig up mines on the steadily advancing Eastern front and later, when the invasion had begun, in the West; but the demoted tech sergeant was lucky and wasn't blown sky-high.

There was once a black shepherd, his name was Prinz. He was transferred, along with the Führer's headquarters, to Rastenburg in East Prussia. He was lucky, he didn't step on any mines; but the wild rabbit he was chasing jumped on a mine and could be retrieved only very partially.

Like "Camp Werewolf" northeast of Vinnitsa, the Führer's Headquarters in East Prussia bordered on mined woods. The Führer and his favorite dog lived a secluded life in Zone A of the "Wolf's Lair." To give Prinz exercise, the officer in charge of dogs, an SS captain, who had owned a well-known dog kennel before the war, took him for walks in Zones I and II; but the Führer had to stay in his constricted Zone A, because he was always busy with staff conferences.

Life was tedious at the Führer's headquarters. Always the same barracks, where the Führer Escort Battalion, the Army Chiefs of Staff, or guests come to comment on the situation, were lodged. Some distraction was provided by the goings-on at the gate of Zone II.

It was there that a rabbit ran between the sentries on the perimeter of the Zone, was shooed away amid hoots of laughter, and made a black shepherd forget the lessons learned in his school days at the police kennel: Prinz broke loose, bounded through the gate, past the still laughing sentries, crossed with dragging leash the road leading to the camp—rabbits pucker up their noses, which is something no dog can stand—resolved to follow a pucker-nosed rabbit which luckily had a good head start; for when the rabbit lit out into the mined woods and disintegrated on an exploding mine, the dog incurred little danger, although he had taken a bound or two into the mined area. Cautiously, step by step, the officer in charge of dogs led him back.

When the report was drawn up and had found its way through channels—first SS Major Fegelein appended comments, then it was submitted to the Führer—the officer in charge of dogs was broken to private and assigned to the very same punitive battalion as the demoted tech sergeant reduced to clearing mines.

The onetime officer in charge of dogs took an unlucky step east of Mogilev; but when the battalion was transferred to the West, the tech sergeant, with limping yet lucky leg, deserted to the Allies. He was moved from one PW camp to the next and finally found peace in an English camp for antifascist prisoners, for along with the usual guardhouse peccadilloes the reason for his demotion was noted in his paybook. Shortly after, at a time when the *Götterdämmerung* recording was all ready to be put on, he and some like-minded companions organized a camp theater. On an improvised stage he, a professional actor, played leading roles in plays by German classical authors; a slightly limping Nathan the Wise and a teeth-grinding Götz.

But the would-be assassin, who months before had concluded his experiments with bomb and brief case, couldn't get himself admitted to a camp for antifascist prisoners of war. His attempt at assassination was also a failure, because he wasn't a professional assassin, because in his inexperience he neglected to go the whole hog, because he decamped before his bomb had plainly said yes, and tried to save himself for great tasks after a successful assassination.

There he stands between General Warlimont and Navy Captain Assmann as the Führer's staff conference drags on, and can't figure out where to put his brief case. A liaison officer of the Field Economic Office concludes his talk on the fuel question. Materials in short supply, such as rubber, nickel, bauxite, manganese, and wolfram are listed. The ball-bearing shortage is general. Somebody from the Foreign Office—is it Ambassador Hewel?—speculates on the situation in Japan now that the Tojo cabinet has resigned. Still the brief case has found no satisfactory resting place. The new alignment of the Tenth Army after the evacuation of Ancona, the fighting strength of the Fourteenth Army after the fall of Livorno are discussed. General Schmundt asks for the floor, but He does all the talking. Where to put the brief case? A freshly arrived report creates animation in the group around the card table: the Americans have entered Saint-Lô! Hastily, before the Eastern front, the position around Bialystok for instance, can come up, action is taken: hapazardly the assassin puts the brief case with contents under the card table, on which lie the general staff maps with their complicated markings, around which Messrs. Jodl, Scherff, Schmundt, and Warlimont stand calmly or bob up and down on booted toes, around which the Führer's black shepherd rambles restlessly, because his master, likewise restless, wants to stand now here now there, rejecting this, demanding that with hard knuckle, talking constantly, about those defective 152-millimeter howitzers, then a moment later about the excellent 210-millimeter Skoda howitzer. "Had all-round firing capacity; with the trailer mount removed, just the thing for coastal fortifications, Saint-Lô, for instance." What a memory! Names, figures, distances pell-mell, and moving about the whole time, always with the dog at heel, all over the place except in the vicinity of the brief case at the feet of Generals Schmundt and Warlimont.

To sum it up, the assassin was a dud; but the bomb wasn't a dud, it went off punctually, cut off several officer's careers, but removed neither the Führer nor the Führer's favorite dog from the world. For Prinz, to whom as to all dogs the region under the table belonged, had sniffed at the abandoned brief case and possibly heard an uncanny ticking: in any event, his cursory sniffing commanded him to transact a piece of business that well-trained dogs transact only out of doors.

An attentive adjutant, standing by the shack door, saw what the dog wanted, opened the door a crack—wide enough for Prinz—and closed it without disturbing noise. But his solicitude brought him no reward; for when the bomb said Now!, when it said Time's up! Pickupthechips! Endoftheline!, when the bomb in the brief case of the assassin who had meanwhile run for it said Amen, the adjutant among others was hit by several splinters, but not a one touched the Führer or his favorite dog.

Air Force auxiliary Harry Liebenau—to get back to the suburb of Langfuhr from the great world of assassins, general staff maps, and the unscathed Führer figure—heard about the unsuccessful attempt on the Führer's life on the turned-up radio. The names of the assassin and his fellow conspirators were given. Thereupon Harry began to worry about the dog Prinz, descended from the dog Harras; for no special communiqué, not a line in the papers, not so much as a whispered word revealed whether the dog was among the victims or whether Providence had spared him as well as his master.

It wasn't until the next newsreel—Harry had his induction order in his pocket, was no longer wearing the uniform of an Air Force auxiliary, was making good-by calls, and going often, because there were seven more days to kill, to the movies—that the German Movietone News had something to say, quite marginally, about the dog Prinz.

The Führer's headquarters with demolished shack and living Führer was shown in the distance. And against the boots of the Führer, whose face under low-pulled cap seemed slightly swollen but otherwise unchanged, rubbed, black with erect ears, a male shepherd whom Harry identified without difficulty as the carpenter's dog's dog.

The bungling assassin, however, was taken to the gallows.

There was once a little girl,
whom forest Gypsies palmed off on a high school teacher who was sorting mica stones in an abandoned factory and was named Oswald Brunies. The girl was baptized with the name Jenny, grew up, and became fatter and fatter. Jenny looked unnaturally roly-poly and had to put up with a good deal. At an early age, the plump little girl took piano lessons from a piano teacher by the name of Felsner-Imbs. Imbs had billowing snow-white hair, which demanded to be brushed for a good hour every day. On his advice, Jenny, by way of keeping her weight in check, was sent to a ballet school to learn ballet dancing.

But Jenny went on swelling and promised to become as fat as Eddi Amsel, Dr. Brunies' favorite pupil. Amsel often came with his friend to look as the teacher's collection of mica stones and was also present when Jenny tinkled out scales. Eddi Amsel had many freckles, weighted 203 pounds, had ready wit, knew how to draw good likenesses quick as a flash, and in addition could sing clear as a bell—even in church.

One winter afternoon when snow lay all about and new snow kept falling on top of it, Jenny was transformed behind the Erbsberg, near the gloomy Gutenberg monument, into a snow man by playing children.

At the same hour, as chance would have it, fat funny Amsel, on the opposite side of the Erbsberg, was likewise transformed into a snow man; but those who transformed him were not playing children.

But suddenly and from all sides a thaw set in. Both snow men melted away and discharged: near the Gutenberg monument a dancing line; on the other side of the mountain a slender young man, who looked for his teeth in the snow and found them. Whereupon he made them rain down on the bushes.

The dancing line went home, represented herself when she got there as Jenny Brunies, fell slightly ill, soon recovered, and embarked on the arduous career of a successful ballet dancer.

The slender youth, however, packed Eddi Amsel's suitcase and in the guise of a Herr Haseloff took the train from Danzig via Schneidemühl to Berlin. There he had his mouth filled with new teeth and tried to cure a violent cold he had caught in the snow man; but his chronic hoarseness was there to stay.

The dancing line had to keep on going to school and working hard at ballet exercises. When the Stadttheater's children's ballet took part in the Christmas play, *The Snow Queen*, Jenny danced the role of the Snow Queen and was praised by the critics.

Then came the war. But nothing changed, or at most the ballet audience: Jenny danced in the Red Room of the Zoppot casino before high-ranking officers, Party leaders, artists, and scientists. The chronically hoarse Herr Haseloff, who had escaped from the Amselian snow man, had meanwhile become a ballet master in Berlin. As a prominent member of the ballet world, he had been invited to the Red Room, and now he said to himself over the long-lasting final applause: "What amazing sparkle! What heavenly arm movements! That line in the adagio! Somewhat lacking in warmth but classical to the finger tips. Clean technique, still rather self-conscious. Instep not high enough. Definitely talented. It would be a good thing to work with the child, work and bring out everything she's got."

Only after Dr. Brunies had been questioned by the police in connection with an embarrassing affair—he had diverted vitamin tablets intended for his pupils to his own mouth—arrested by the Gestapo, and sent to Stutthof concentration camp, did ballet master Haseloff find an opportunity to carry Jenny off to Berlin.

It was hard for her to part from the suburb of Langfuhr. She wore mourning and had fallen in love with a high school student by the name of Harry Liebenau. She wrote him many letters. Her tidy script told of a mysterious Madame Neroda, who headed the ballet, of the pianist Felsner-Imbs, who had followed her to Berlin, of little Fenchel, her partner in the *pas de deux*, and of ballet master Haseloff, who, chronically hoarse and always rather weird, directed exercises and rehearsals.

Jenny wrote of progress and minor setbacks. All in all she was getting ahead; there was only one trouble and there was no help for it. For all the praise Jenny earned with her *entrechats*, her instep was still flat and feeble, a source of dismay to the ballet master and to the dancer, because every true ballerina—ever since the days of Louis XIV—has had to have a fine high instep.

Several ballets, including some early German country dances and the usual bravura pieces from the venerable Petipa's repertory, were rehearsed and performed for the soldiers who had occupied half Europe. Long trips took Jenny all over. And from all over Jenny wrote her friend Harry, who answered now and then. Between rehearsals and during performances Jenny didn't sit there like a bonehead leafing through illustrated magazines; diligently she knitted baby clothes for a school friend who was expecting a baby.

When the ballet group returned from France in the summer of '44—taken unawares by the invasion, it had lost several sets and a number of costumes—ballet master Haseloff decided to work up a ballet in three acts, with which he had been fiddling ever since his childhood. Now, after the washout in France, he was in a hurry to put his childhood dream on its feet. He decided to call it *The Scarecrows* or *The Revolt of the Scarecrows* or *The Gardener's Daughter and the Scarecrows,* and expected it to open in August.

Since there were no suitable composers available, he had Felsner-Imbs arrange a blend of Scarlatti and Handel. The costumes that had been wrecked or badly damaged in France fitted nicely into the new ballet. The survivors of a group of midgets, who had belonged to Haseloff's propaganda unit and had also suffered losses at the beginning of the invasion, were taken on as acrobatic extras. This ballet was intended to tell a story with the help of masks, twittering machines, mobile automata, and a large illusionist stage.

Jenny wrote to Harry: "The curtain rises on the wicked old gardener's colorful garden, which is being looted by dancing birds. Half in league with the birds, the gardener's daughter—that's me—is teasing the wicked old gardener. As the birds whirl about him, he does a frantically funny solo dance and fastens a sign to the garden fence: 'Scarecrow wanted!' Instantly, jumping over the fence with a *grand jeté,* a young man in picturesque rags appears and offers his services as a scarecrow. After a choreographic discussion—*pas battus, entrechats,* and *brisés dessus-dessous*—the wicked old gardener agrees, exits left, and the young man scares away—*pas chassé,* and *glissades* in all directions—all the birds, the last being a particularly impudent blackbird—*tours en l'air.* Of course the pretty young gardener's daughter—that's me—falls in love with the bouncing scarecrow—*pas de deux* in among the wicked old gardener's rhubarb stalks—sweet adagio: *attitude en promenade*. With a show of timidity, the gardener's daughter shrinks back, then surrenders and is led away over the fence, another *grand jeté*. The two of us— little Fenchel plays the young man—exit right.

"In the second act—as you'll soon see—the young man's true nature comes out. He is the prefect of all scarecrows and rules over their underground realm, where scarecrows of every variety have to spin around ceaselessly. Here they engage in leaping processions, there they assemble for a scarecrow mass and sacrifice to an old hat. Our midgets, with old Bebra in the lead, combine to form a midget scarecrow, sometimes short, sometimes long, but always closely knotted. They weave picturesquely through history: shaggy Germani, baggy-panted lansquenets, imperial couriers, moth-eaten mendicant friars, mechanical headless knights, bloated nuns possessed of epilepsy, General Zieten emerging from the woods, and Lützow's intrepid band. Many-armed clothes trees are on the march. Cupboards vomit forth whole dynasties with court dwarfs. Then they all turn into windmills: the monks, the knights, nuns, couriers and lansquenets, the Prussian grenadiers and Natzmer uhlans, the Merovingians and Carolingians, and in between, popping like weasels, our midgets. Air is moved with wild wings but no grain is milled. Yet the big mill hopper is filled with rag entrails, lace clouds, flag salad. Hat pyramids and pants porridge mix into a cake, which all the scarecrows noisily devour. Growling rattling howling. A whistling of keys. A stifled moaning. Ten abbots belch. Farting of the nuns. Goats and midgets bleat. Rattling, scraping, guzzling, neighing. Silk sings. Velvet buzzes. On one leg. Two in one skirt. Wedded in pants. Sailing in a hat. They fall out of pockets, they multiply in potato sacks. Arias tangled in curtains. Yellow light bursts through seams. Trunkless heads. A jumping luminous button. Mobile baptism. And gods too: Potrimpos, Pikollos, Perkunos—among them a black dog. And right in the middle of this exercising, acrobatic, complexly ordered confusion—unclassical vibrati alternate with richly varied *pas de bourrée*—the prefect of all scarecrows, little Fenchel in other words, deposits the kidnaped gardener's daughter. And I, the gardener's daughter, am scared on frantic slippers. For all my love for the young man and prefect—only on the stage, mind you—I'm awfully frightened. After the nasty scarecrows have hung a moth-clouded bridal dress on me and crowned me with a rattling nutshell crown, I dance a terrified regal solo—the midgets carry my train—to solemnly tinkling court music; and with my dancing I, that is to say, the crowned gardener's daughter, succeed in dancing to sleep all the scarecrows, some standing singly, others in groups, one after the other: last of all, little Fenchel, that is, the prefect. Only the shaggy black dog, who is a member of the prefect's retinue, tosses restlessly about among sprinkled midgets, but is unable to stand on his twelve diabolical legs. Then, out of a perfect arabesque, I as the gardener's daughter bend down over the sleeping prefect, blow a sorrowful ballerina's kiss—without ever touching little Fenchel—and run away. Too late the black dog howls. Too late the midgets squeal. Too late the scarecrow mechanisms start up. And much too late the prefect wakes up. The second act ends with a furious finale: leaps and acrobatics. Music warlike enough to chase away Turkish armies. The hectically excited scarecrows scatter, boding trouble in the third act.

"The scene is the wicked old gardener's garden again. Sad and defenseless against the birds, he twists and turns in vain. Then shamefacedly—I have to play it half repentant, half defiant—the wicked old gardener's young daughter comes back in raggedy bridal dress and sinks down at her gardener father's feet. She clasps his knees and wants to be lifted up: *pas de deux,* father and daughter. A choreographic conflict, with lifts and promenades. In the end the old man's evil nature comes out: he rejects me, his daughter. I'm sick of living and I can't die. A roaring from behind: scarecrows and birds in strange alliance. A fluttering, chirping, whirring, squeaking, hissing monster rolls across the stage, holding up an enormous empty bird cage supported by the claws of innumerable scarecrows, bulldozes the garden, and catches the gardener's daughter with nimble midgets. The prefect shouts for joy when he sees me in the cage. Black, the shaggy dog describes swift circles. Triumph in every joint, the thousand-voiced monster rattles and squeaks away, taking me with it. Leaving the ruined garden behind. Leaving behind a limping figure in rags: the wicked old gardener. The teasing birds come back again—*pas de chat, pas de basque* —and encircle the old man. Wearily and as though to defend himself, he lifts his arms wrapped in tatters: and lo and behold, the very first movement frightens the birds, scares them away. He has turned into a scarecrow, forever after he will be gardener and scarecrow in one. On his macabre scarecrow solo—Herr Haseloff is toying with the idea of dancing this role—the final curtain falls."

This ballet, so sympathetically described by Jenny to her friend Harry, this ballet in three acts, so meticulously rehearsed, this sumptuously staged ballet—Haseloff in person had designed noise-making mechanisms and button-spitting automata—this scarecrow ballet was never to open. Two gentlemen from the Reich Propaganda Ministry, who attended the dress rehearsal, found the first act charming and promising, cleared their throats for the first time in the second act, and stood up right after the final curtain. In general, they thought the latter part of the story too sinister and allusive. The life-affirming element was absent, and the two gentlemen declared in unison: "Soldiers at the front want something gay, not some gloomy rumbling underworld."

Negotiations were carried on. Madame Neroda brought her connections to bear. The top authorities were showing signs of approving a new version when, before Haseloff had time to tack on a happy ending consonant with the situation at the front, a bomb hit demolished the costumes and sets. And the ensemble also suffered losses.

Though the rehearsal ought to have been interrupted during an air-raid alert, they kept right on: the gardener's daughter is dancing the scarecrows, the hellhound, all the midgets, and the prefect to sleep—Jenny was doing admirably, except that her instep still wasn't high enough and left the impression of a slight but disturbing blemish—Haseloff was just about to arrange the new and positive plot—Jenny was supposed to handcuff all the scarecrows and the prefect, after which she would put them to work for the benefit of the upper world, in other words, the formerly wicked gardener, who was now so good butter wouldn't melt in his mouth—just as Jenny, laden with cumbersome handcuffs, was standing alone on the stage, uncertain because of the changes that had been made, the bomb, meant for the radio tower next door, fell on the exhibition hall, which had been rigged up as a theater workshop.

The storeroom containing the sensitive mechanisms, flimsy costumes, and movable sets sank to its knees, never to rise again; Felsner-Imbs the pianist, who had accompanied all the rehearsals with ten fingers, was flattened aganst the keyboard for all time. Four little holes, two stoppers, the midget Kitty, and three stage hands were injured, only slightly thank heavens. But ballet master Haseloff came off with a sound skin and, as soon as the smoke and dust had settled, went looking for Jenny with hoarse cries.

He found her recumbent and had to extricate her feet from under a beam. At first they feared the worst, a ballerina's death. Actually the beam had only crushed her right as well as her left foot. Her ballet slippers had grown too tight for her swelling feet, and at long last Jenny Angustri appeared to have the perfect high instep that every ballerina ought to have.—Float hither, ye airy *sylphides*. Approach like brides, Giselle and Coppélia, or weep from enamel eyes. Grisi and Taglioni, Lucile Grahn and Fanny Cerito, come and weave your *Pas de Quatre* and strew roses on pitiful feet. Palais Garnier, burst into all your lights that the stones of the pyramid may join in the *grand défilé*: the first and second quadrille, the hopeful *coryphées,* the *petits sujets* and the *grands sujets,* the *premiers danseurs,* and, as embittered as they are unattainable, the Stars: Leap, Gaetano Vestris! Far-famed Camargo, still in command of the *entrechats huit*. Vaslav Nijinsky, slowly leaping god and specter of the rose, have done with butterflies and black spiders. Restless Noverre, break off your journey and make a halt here. Turn off the suspension machine, that moonbeams light as *sylphides* may cast their coolness. Wicked Diaghilev, lay your magical hand upon her. Anna Pavlova, for the time of this sorrow forget your millions. Chopin, once again, by candlelight, spit your blood upon the keys. Turn away, Bellastriga and Archisposa. Once again let the dying swan swoon away. And now, Petrushka, lie down beside her. The last position. *Grand plié*.

And yet Jenny went on living: a dismal life, never again on toes. The toes—how hard a thing to write!—of both feet had to be amputated. Shoes, ungainly things, were made for the stumps. And Harry Liebenau, whom Jenny had loved until then, received a matter-of-factly typewritten letter, the last. He too, Jenny asked, should write no more. All that was over. He should try to forget everything, almost everything. "I too will try hard not to think of us."

Some days later—Harry Liebenau was packing his bags, he was off to the wars—a package came with melancholy contents. In packets tied with silk ribbon: Harry's half-true letters; knitted jackets and rompers, finished, pink and blue. He found a necklace made of bottle washers. Harry had given it to Jenny when they were children playing by Aktien Pond, on whose surface floated bottle washers and no lotus blossoms.

There was once a streetcar—

it ran from Heeresanger in Langfuhr to Weidengasse in the Lower City and belonged to Line Number 5. Like all cars that ran between Langfuhr and Danzig, the Number 5 also stopped at the Main Station. The motorman of this particular car, concerning which it has been said: there was once a streetcar, was name Lemke; the conductor in the lead car was named Erich Wentzeck; and the conductorette in the trailer of this particular car was named Tulla Pokriefke. No longer was she working on the Number 2 Line to Oliva. Every day for nine hours she rode back and forth on the Number 5: quick, as though born to the trade, somewhat foolhardy; for in the evening rush hour when the car was overcrowded and it was impossible to get through inside, she jumped, with the car running at moderate speed, off the front platform and onto the rear platform. When Tulla Pokriefke collected fares, all those who rode with her coughed up their money: even her cousin Harry had to pay.

Two minutes after Tulla Pokriefke had rung the bell as a sign that this particular car, concerning which it has been said: there was once a streetcar, namely, the 10:05 P.M. car, due at the Main Station at 10:17, could and should push off from the Heeresanger terminus, a boy of seventeen got on at Max-Halbe-Platz, pushed a cardboard suitcase reinforced with leather corners onto the rear platform of the trailer, and lit a cigarette.

The car was empty and remained relatively empty. At "Reichskolonie" stop an elderly couple got on, and they got out at the Sporthalle. At "Halbe-Allee" four Red Cross nurses got into the trailer and asked for transfers to Heubude. The lead car was busier.

While on the rear platform of the trailer conductorette Tulla Pokriefke made entries in her trip book, the seventeen-year-old smoked awkwardly beside his lurching cardboard suitcase. It is only because the two of them, she with her trip book, he with the unaccustomed cigarette, knew each other—as a matter of fact they were related, cousins—

only because the two of them were about to part for life, that this car on Line Number 5 was a special car; in other respects it was running normally on schedule.

When Tulla had rung the bell at "Women's Clinic," she closed her trip book and said: "Leaving town?" Harry Liebenau, with his induction order in the breast pocket of his jacket, replied quite in the spirit of the indispensable leave-taking scene: "The farther the better."

Tulla's trip book, a prosaic prop, was encased in worn wooden covers: "Don'tcha like our town any more?"

Because Harry knew Tulla was no longer working on the Number 2 Line, he had decided in favor of a last trip on the Number 5: "I'm off to the Prussians. They're stymied without me."

Tulla jiggled the wooden covers: "I thought you were joining the Navy."

Harry offered Tulla a cigarette: "Nothing doing out there any more."

Tulla put the Juno away in the pigeonhole where the trip book was kept: "Watch out or they'll putcha in the infantry. It's no skin off their ass."

This dialogue drunk with parting was beheaded by Harry: "Maybe so. It's all one to me. So long as I get out of this lousy burg."

The particular car with trailer lurched down the avenue. Cars whished by in the opposite direction. Neither of them could look out, because all the windows in the trailer were blinded with blackout paint. So they had to keep looking at each other; but no one will ever find out how Tulla saw her cousin Harry when he stared at her as if to store up a supply: Tulla Tulla Tulla! The pimples on her forehead had dried out. But she had a fresh permanent, paid for with her own earnings. If you're not pretty, you've got to fix yourself up. But still and for the last time the smell of bone glue, carpenter's glue, rode back and forth with her between Heeresanger und Weidesgasse. The four Red Cross nurses inside the car were all talking at once in an undertone. Harry had his mouth full of artistically turned phrases. But no delicate phrase wanted to start out. After "Four Seasons," he put himself to the torture: "How's your father?" But Tulla replied with a shrug of the shoulders and the usual counter-question: "How's yours?"

At this Harry too had only a shrug of the shoulders to spare, although his father wasn't very well. Swollen feet had deterred the carpenter from taking his son to the station; and Harry's mother never went out without Harry's father.

Even so, a member of the family witnessed Harry's departure: the streetcar uniform was becoming to his cousin. The uniform skiff clung tilting to permanent waves. Shortly before "Oliva Gate," she removed two empty ticket pads from her ticket box: "D'you wanna ticket pad?"

The parting gift! Harry received two cardboard covers to which metal clasps fastened a finger-thick wad of ticket stubs. Instantly his fingers became childlike and made the thin paper purr. Tulla gave a bleating and almost good-natured laugh. But then she remembered something that had been forgotten amid protracted leavetaking: Her cousin hadn't paid his fare. Harry was playing with the empty ticket pads and hadn't provided himself with a valid ticket. Tulla pointed at the pads and at Harry's smugly playing fingers: "You can keep 'em, but you gotta pay your fare all the same. One to the station with baggage."

After Harry had let his purse slip back into his back pocket, he found a colorless slit in the blackout paint on the platform window; somebody had scratched with his fingernail in order that Harry might stop staring at his cousin and capture in one eye the panorama of the approaching city. Moonlight for his express benefit. He counted the towers. Not a one was missing. All grew toward him. What a silhouette! Brick Gothic strained his eye till it moistened: tears? Only one. For already Tulla was calling out his stop: "Main Station!"—and Harry let two empty ticket pads slip into his pocket.

When he clutched his cardboard suitcase by the handle, Tulla held out a little hand; a red rubber finger was supposed to protect the thumb and make it reliable at counting change. Tulla's other hand waited by the bellpull: "Take care of yourself, don't let 'em shoot off your nose, hear."

Tulla's cousin nodded obediently again and again, even after Tulla had rung for the car to push off and he for her and she for him—he on the sidewalk outside the station, she on the departing Number 5—were growing smaller and smaller.

No wonder that when Harry Liebenau was sitting on his

suitcase in the express, playing with empty ticket pads from
Danzig to Berlin, he had a Koshnavian ditty in his ears, which
ran to the rhythm of the joints in the tracks: "Duller Duller,
Tulla. Dul Dul Dul, Tulla. Tulla, Tulla, Dul."

There was once a ditty;
   it was about love, it was short, easy to remember, and so
strikingly rhythmical that armored infantryman Harry Liebenau, who had gone off with two purring ticket pads to learn
what fear was, had it between his teeth, kneeling standing lying, in his sleep, over his pea soup, while cleaning his
rifle, crawling hopping snoozing, under his gas mask, while
tossing real hand grenades, when falling in for guard duty,
weeping sweating miserable, on foot blisters, under his steel
helmet, on his ass in the latrine, while taking the oath to the
flag in Fallingbostel, kneeling without support, looking for the
bead in the notch, in other words, shooting swearing shitting,
and similarly while shining his shoes and lining up for coffee:
so persistent and universally appropriate was the ditty. For
when he hammered a nail in his locker to hang up a framed
photograph—Führer with black shepherd—hammerhead and
nailhead spoke up: Dul Dul, Tulla. When for the first time
bayonets were fixed in three steps, his three steps were
called: Tulla Tulla Dul! When he had to mount guard at night
behind Meat Depot 2, and drowsiness hit him behind the
knees with the flat of its hand, he awakened himself rhythmically: Duller Duller, Tulla! He worked the universally appropriate Tulla text into every marching song, regardless of
whether it featured Erika, Rosemarie, or Anushka, or dark-
brown hazelnuts. When he picked his lice and night after
night—until the company was deloused in Münster—
searched the seams of his drawers and undershirts with lice-
cracking fingernails, he didn't crush two and thirty lice,
but subjugated Tulla two and thirty times. Even when he had
a chance to stay out until reveille, to insert his member for
the first time and very briefly into an honest-to-goodness girl,
he didn't pick an Air Force auxiliary or a nurse, but screwed,
in Lüneburg's autumnal park, a Lüneburg streetcar conductress; her name was Ortrud but he, meanwhile and during,
called her Tulla Tulla Tulla! Which appealed to her only
moderately.

   And all this—Tulla song, oath to the flag, lice and Lüne-

burg—was recorded in love letters, three a week, to Tulla.
History was made in January February March; but he
searches for timeless words for Tulla. Between Lake Bala-
ton and the Danube the Fourth Cavalry Brigade is fighting off
counterattacks; but he describes the bucolic beauty of
Lüneburg Heath to his cousin. The relief offensive never
reached Budapest but comes to a standstill near Pressburg; he,
indefatigably, compares Lüneburg Heath with Tuchler
Heath. Slight gains in the Bastogne sector; and he sends Tulla
a little bag of juniper berries done up with violet greetings.
South of Bologna the 362nd Infantry Division parries armored
attacks by pulling back the main line of battle; but he writes
a poem—for whom, I wonder?—in which heather, at the beginning of January, is still in bloom: purple, purple! From
dawn to dusk a thousand American bombers attack targets
in the Paderborn, Bielefeld, Koblenz, Mannheim area; he, unmoved, reads Löns, who molds his epistolary style and
lends a purple coloration to the Tulla poem he has begun.
Full-scale offensive near Baranov; he, without looking up,
paints the one word, not blue, not red, with his fountain
pen. The Tarnow bridgehead is evacuated—breakthrough to
the Inster; but armored infantryman Harry Liebenau, who
has completed his training, is looking for a rhyme to conjure
up Tulla. Thrusts toward Leslau by way of Kutno—breakthrough at Hohensalza; but the armored infantryman of
Münster-North Company has still found no suitable rhyme
for his cousin. Enemy armored spearheads in Gumbinnen
and across the Rominte. At this point armored infantryman
Harry Liebenau, with marching orders and marching rations but without the vital word, is set in motion in the direction of Kattowitz, where he is supposed to make contact with
the 18th Armored Division, which is being transferred just
then from the northern Danube front to upper Silesia. Glei-
witz and Oppeln fall—he never gets to Kattowitz, for new
marching orders, accompanied by extra rations project armored infantryman Harry Liebenau to Vienna, where he has
a chance of finding the 11th Air Force Divison that has retreated from the southeast, and perhaps also the cover that
fits the pot named Tulla. The main line of battle is now
twelve miles east of Königsberg; in Vienna armored infantryman Harry Liebenau climbs to the top of St. Stephen's and
searches under the half-clouded sky. For what? Enemy ar-

mored spearheads reach the Oder and establish a bridgehead
near Steinau; Harry sends rhymeless picture postcards and
fails to find the headquarters of the Air Force division that
had been promised him. The battle of the Ardennes is
over. Budapest is still holding out. In Italy not much fighting. Colonel-General Schörner takes over Center Sector.
The barrier at Lötzen is forced. Near Glogau successful
defensive action. Enemy spearheads in Prussian Holland. Geography! Bielitz—Pless—Ratibor. Who knows where Zielenzig is located? For it is to Zielenzig, northwest of Küstrin,
that new marching orders are supposed to propel armored infantryman Harry Liebenau, who has just been issued fresh
rations; but he only gets as far as Pirna; there he is rounded
up and attached to a nameless replacement battalion, which
is expected to wait in an evacuated school building until the
21st Armored Division has been transferred from Küstrin to
the area north of Breslau. Combat reserves. Harry finds a
dictionary in the basement of the school, but refuses to
rhyme such names as Sulla and Abdullah, which yield no
meaning, with Tulla. The promised armored division fails to
materialize. But Budapest falls. Glogau is cut off. The combat reserve, including armored infantryman Harry Liebenau,
is set in motion in no particular direction. And every day,
punctually, there is a smidgin of four-fruit jam, a third of a
loaf of army bread, the sixteenth part of a two-pound can
of fat pork, and three cigarettes. Orders from Schörner's
Hq.: new combat unit set up. Spring breaks through. Buds
burst between Troppau and Leobschütz. Near Schwarz-
wasser four spring poems sprout. In Sagan, shortly before
crossing the Bober north of the city, Harry Liebenau makes
the acquaintance of a Silesian girl; her name is Ulla and she
darns two pairs of his socks. In Lauban he is swallowed up
by the 25th Armored Infantry Division, which has been pulled
back from the Western front and sent to Silesia.

Now at last he knows where he belongs. No more marching
orders sending him to units that cannot be found. Pondering
and looking for rhymes, he sits huddled with five other armored infantrymen on a self-propelled gun that is being
moved back and forth between Lauban and Sagan, but always
behind the lines. He receives no mail. But that doesn't prevent him from writing to his cousin Tulla, who, when she is
not cut off in Danzig-Langfuhr with elements of the Vistula

Army Group, goes on working as a streetcar conductress; for the streetcar runs till the bitter end.

There was once a self-propelled gun,

Panzer IV, old model, which was supposed to move up behind the main line of battle in mountainous Silesia. It weighed over forty tons, and to avoid being spotted from the air it backed up on two caterpillar treads into a woodshed secured only by a padlock.

But because this shed belonged to a Silesian glassblower, it contained, on shelves and bedded in straw, more than five hundred products of the glassblower's art.

The encounter between the self-propelled gun, backing on caterpillar treads, and the Silesian glass had two consequences. In the first place, the armored vehicle damaged quite a lot of glass; in the second place, the effect of the glass, breaking in several different keys, on Harry Liebenau, who, as a member of the infantry team assigned to the self-propelled gun, was standing outside the screaming glass shed, was a change of idiom. From this moment on, no more purple melancholy. Never again will he search for a rhyme to the name of Tulla. No more poems written with adolescent sperm and heart's blood. Once the screaming of that shed has splattered his ears like birdshot, his diary is restricted to simple sentences: The gun backs in to the glass shed. War is more boring than school. Everybody's waiting for miracle weapons. After the war I'm going to see lots of movies. Yesterday I saw my first dead man. I've filled my gas mask container with strawberry jam. We are due for transfer. I haven't seen a Russian yet. Sometimes I stop thinking of Tulla. Our field kitchen is gone. I always read one and the same thing. The roads are clogged with fugitives, who have lost all faith. Löns and Heidegger are wrong about lots of things. In Bunzlau there were five soldiers and two officers hanging on seven trees. This morning we fired on a wooded area. Couldn't write for two days because of contact with the enemy. Many are dead. After the war I'm going to write a book. We are to be moved to Berlin. There the Führer is fighting. I've been assigned to the Wenck combat team. They want us to save the capital. Tomorrow is the Führer's birthday. I wonder if he's got the dog with him.

Once there was a Führer and Chancellor,

who on April 20, 1945, celebrated his fifty-sixth birthday. Since the center of the capital, including the government quarter and the Chancellery, was under intermittent artillery fire that day, the modest celebration was held in the Führer's air-raid shelter.

Celebrities, several of whom were normally on hand for staff conferences—evening situation, noon situation—had come to offer their congratulations: Field Marshal General Keitel, Colonel General von John, Naval Commander Lüdde-Neurath, Admirals Voss and Wagner, Generals Krebs and Burgdorf, Colonel von Below, Reichsleiter Bormann, Ambassador Hewel of the Foreign Office, Fräulein Braun, Dr. Herrgesell, the Field Headquarters stenographer, SS Hauptsturmführer Günsche, Dr. Morell, SS Obergruppenführer Fegelein, and Herr and Frau Goebbels with all their six children.

After the congratulants had presented their best wishes, the Führer and Chancellor cast a searching look around him, as though missing a last and indispensable congratulant: "Where is the dog?"

The birthday company began at once to look for the Führer's favorite dog. Cries of "Prinz!" "Here Prinz!" SS Hauptsturmführer Günsche, the Führer's personal adjutant, combed the garden of the Chancellery, although the area was not infrequently marked by artillery hits. Inside the shelter a number of absurd hypotheses were formulated. Everybody had some suggestion to make. Only SS Obergruppenführer Fegelein had a clear grasp of the situation. Seconded by Colonel von Below, he rushed to the telephones connecting the Führer's bomb shelter with all the staff offices and with the MP battalion guarding the Chancellery: "Attention everybody! Attention everybody! Führer's dog missing. Answers to the name of Prinz. Stud dog. Black German shepherd Prinz. Connect me with Zossen. Attention everybody: the Führer's dog is missing."

In the course of the ensuing staff conference—report confirmed: enemy armored spearheads have advanced south of Cottbus and entered Calau—"Operation Wolftrap" is set up and all plans for the defense of the capital are co-ordinated with it. The Fourth Armored Corps postpones counterattack south of Spremberg indefinitely and secures Spremberg-Senftenburg highway against deserting Führerdog. Similarly the Steiner Group transforms the deployment zone for the relief offensive scheduled to move southward from the Eberswalde sector, into a deeply echeloned dogcapture zone. The operation proceeds according to plan. All available planes of the Sixth Air Fleet fly ground reconnaissance missions for the purpose of determining Führerdogescaperoute. Pursuant to "Wolftrap," the main battle line is pulled back behind the Havel. Führerdogsearchgroups are set up from combat reserves. They receive orders to maintain walkie-talkie contact with Führerdogcapturegroups consisting of motorcycle and bicycle companies. The Holste Corps digs in. But the Twelfth Army under General Wenck launches a relief escaperoute, for presumably Führerdog is planning to desert to Westenemy. To make Operation Wolftrap viable, the Seventh Army has to disengage itself from the Ninth and First American Armies and seal off the Western front between Elbe and Mulde. On the Jüterbog-Torgau line, projected antitank trenches are replaced by Führerdogtraptrenches. The Twelfth Army, the Blumentritt Army Group, the Thirty-eighth Armored Corps are placed under the direct orders of the Army High Command, which as of now is transferred from Zossen to Wannsee, where under General Burgdorf it sets up a "Wolftrap Command Staff"—WCS.

But despite all this vigorous regrouping the only dispatches to come in are the usual situation reports—Soviet spearheads reach Treuenbrietzen Königswusterhausen line—and no information about Führerdogescaperoute. At one nine four 0 hours, during the evening situation report, Field Marshal Keitel has a telephone conversation with Chief of Staff Steiner: "As per Führerorder, 25th Armored Infantry Division will close frontline gap at Cottbus and secure area against Führerdogbreakthrough."

Reply of Hq. Steiner Group: "As per instructions date one seven four, 25th Armored Infantry Division withdrawn Bautzen area and attached Twelfth Army. Available remaining units alerted against Führerdogbreakthrough."

Finally, in the early morning hours of April 20, not far from the bitterly contested Fürstenwalde-Strausberg-Bernau line, shots are fired at a black shepherd, who, however, when brought to the Führer's Headquarters and carefully examined by Dr. Morell, proves to be an impostor.

Thereupon, as per WCS instructions, all units in the Greater Berlin area are briefed on Führerdogdimensions.

The concentration between Lübben and Baruth receives support from Soviet armored spearheads pursuing identical aim. Forest fires spread despite drizzle and constitute natural dogbarrier.

On Arpil 22 enemy armor pushes across the Lichtenberg-Niederschönhausen-Frohnau line and enters outer defenses of the capital. Two reports of dogcapture in the Königswusterhausen area prove inaccurate, since neither captured object can be identified as a male.

Dessau and Bitterfeld are lost. American armored force attempts Elbe crossing near Wittenberge.

On April 23, Dr. Goebbels, gauleiter and Reich Defense Commissioner, issues the following statement: "The Führer is at his post in the capital and has assumed supreme command of all forces engaged in finishfight. As of now, Führerdogsearchgroups will obey only Führerinstructions."

WCS communiqué: "Köpenick railroad station retaken in counterattack. Enemy infiltration blocked by Tenth Führerdogcapturegroup, guarding area bordering Prenzlauer Alee. Two Soviet dogcapture appliances captured, proving that Eastenemy has intelligence of Operation Wolftrap." Due to sensation-mongering misrepresentation of Führerdogloss by enemy radio and press, WCS, as of April 25, transmits Führerinstructions in new, pre-established code—minuted by Dr. Herrgesell: "To what is the manifestness of the studdog Prinz attuned?"

"The original manifestness of the Führerdog is attuned to distantiality."

"What is the Führerdog attuned to distantiality acknowledged as?"

"The Führerdog attuned to distantiality is acknowledged as the Nothing."

Thereupon exlocution to all: "What is the Nothing attuned to distantiality acknowledged as?"

To which Hq. Steiner Group replies from combat position in Liebenwerda: "The Nothing attuned to distantiality is acknowledged as the Nothing in Steiner Group sector."

Whereupon Führerexlocution to all: "Is the Nothing attuned to distantiality an object or more generally an essent?"

Immediate reply from Command Staff Wenck Group: "The Nothing attuned to distantiality is a hole. The Nothing is a hole in the Twelfth Army. The Nothing is a black hole that just ran by. The Nothing is a black running hole in the Twelfth Army."

Whereupon Führerexlocution to all: "The Nothing attuned to distantiality runs. The Nothing is a hole attuned to distantiality. It is acknowledged and can be investigated. A black running hole attuned to distantiality manifests the Nothing in its original manifestness."

Whereupon supplementary WCS exlocutions: "First and foremost, modes of encounter between Nothing attuned to distantiality and Twelfth Army will be investigated for their encounter-structure. Primarily and a priori, penetration areas in Königswusterhausen sector will be investigated for their what-content. Manipulation-utilization of relation-inducing Wolftrap I equipment and supplementary Wolfpoint equipment will unconceal Nothing attuned to distantiality. The digressiveness of the not-at-hand will provisionally be passed over with a view to establishing authentic at-handness of bitches in heat, since the Nothing attuned to distantiality is fundamentally and at all times coexistence-oriented."

An urgent dispatch from contested Neubabelsberg-Zehlendorf-Neukölln line—"The Nothing is coming-to-be between enemy armor and our own spearheads. The Nothing is running on four legs"—is immediately followed by Führerexlocution: "The Nothing will be after-accomplished on the double. Each and every activity of the Nothing attuned to distantiality will be substantivized in view of final victory so that later, sculptured in marble or shell-lime, it may be at-hand in a state of to-be-viewedness."

Not until April 25 did General Wenck, Twelfth Army, reply from the Nauen-Ketzin sector: "Nothing being after-accomplished on double and substantivized. The Nothing attuned to distantiality discloses dread in every sector of the front. Dread is-there. We are speechless with dread. Out."

After the accomplishment reports of the Holster and Steiner combat teams have disclosed similar dread, a WCS exlocution of April 26 goes out, as per Fürerinstructions, to all: "Dread impedes apprehension of the Nothing. As of now, dread will be surmounted by speeches or singing. Negation of Nothing attuned to distantiality prohibited. Never must the Reichcapital in its locus-wholeness be infirmed by dread."

When accomplishment reports of all combat teams continue to show openness-to-dread, a supplement to Führer-instructions of April 26 goes out to all: "Twelfth Army will manifest counter-tonality to fusty atonality of Reichcapital. Unburdenings of Being in Steglitz and southern edge of Tempelhof Airfield will project advanced selfpoint. The final struggle of the German people will be conducted with regard to the Nothing attuned to distantiality."

In response to additional instructions from Burgdorf WCS staff to Air Fleet 6—"Between Tegel and Siemensstadt elucidate running Nothing in advance of enemy armored spearheads"—Air Fleet 6 reports after the all-clear: "Running Nothing sighted between Silesian and Görlitz stations. The Nothing is neither an object nor any essent, hence also no dog."

Thereupon, in accordance with Führerinstructions with new key, a direct exlocution signed Colonel von Below goes out to Air Fleet 6: "Jutting out into the Nothing, the dog has surpassed the essent and will as of now be referred to as Transcendence."

On the twenty-seventh Brandenburg falls. The Twelfth Army reaches Beelitz. After numerous dispatches from all sectors have reported increasing negation of the fugitive Führerdog Prinz and his code names "Nothing" and "Transcendence," a Führerorder to all goes out at one four one two hours: "Negative attitude toward running Transcendence will as of now be considered a court-martial offense."

When no accomplishment reports come in and openness-to-dread is registered even in the government quarter, drastic measures are taken, followed by an exlocution: "The prevailing negative attitude toward Transcendence attuned to distantiality is manifested primarily and decisively by the having-beenness of the following officers." (Names and ranks follow.) Only now, after repeated Führerinquiry—"Where are Wenck's spearheads? Where are Wenck's spearheads? Where is Wenck?"—command staff Wenck, Twelfth Army, replies on April 28: "Bogged down south Lake Schwielow. Joint missions with Air Fleet 6 reveal weather conditions bar visibility Transcendence. Out."

Nihilating reports come in from Halle Gate, from the Silesian Station, and from the Tempelhof Airfield. Space is split up into loci. Alexanderplatz dogcapturepost claims to have investigated twelve-legged Transcendence in advance of enemy armored spearheads. A conflicting dispatch reports three-headed Transcendence sighted in Prenzlau area. At the same time a message Twelfth Army is received at Führer-headquarters: "Slightly wounded armored infantryman claims to have seen and fed dog untranscendent in garden of villa on Lake Schwielow, and to have addressed him by the name of Prinz."

Whereupon inquiry direct from Führer: "Name of the armored infantryman?"

Twelfth Army: "Armored infantryman Harry Liebenau, slightly wounded on chowline."

Führer direct: "Armored infantryman Liebenau's present whereabouts?"

Twelfth Army: "Armored infantryman Liebenau in need of hospitalization removed westward."

Führer direct: "Terminate removal. Fly armored infantryman to garden area Reichchancellery per Air Fleet 6."

Whereupon General Wenck, Twelfth Army, to Führer direct: "Escape-permitting relegation to sinking locus-wholeness Greater Berlin to the point of finite transcending utilization lays bare end structure."

The following Führerexlocution—"The question of the dog is a metaphysical question, calling the entire German nation into question"—is followed by the famous Führerdeclaration: "Berlin is still German. Vienna will be German. And never will the dog be negated."

Whereupon an urgent report comes in: "Enemy armor entering Malchin." Followed by radio message, uncoded, to Reichchancellery: "Enemy radio reports dog sighted east bank Elbe."

Whereupon Soviet leaflets, secured in the contested Kreuzberg and Schöneberg sectors, announce that fugitive Führerdog has been captured by Eastenemy.

Situation report on April 29: "In the course of bitter house-to-house battle on Potsdamer Strasse and Belle-Alliance-Platz, Führerdogsearchgroups disbanding without orders. Morale increasingly impaired by Soviet loudspeakeraction with genuine amplified dogbarking. Beelitz retaken by enemy. No news of Ninth Army. Twelfth Army still trying to exert pressure on Potsdam, consequent to rumors of dogdeath on historical site. Reports of English dogcapture positions near

Elbe bridgehead in Lauenburg and of American dogcapture in Fichtel Mountains unconfirmed." In the light of which, final Führerinstructions to all, with new code: "The dog itself— as such—was-there, is-there, and will remain-there."

Whereupon General Krebs to Colonel General Jodl: "Request prospective orientation on Führersuccession eventuality death."

Whereupon, in accordance with the situation report of April 30, command staff Operation Wolftrap is disbanded. Dogcapture operations in Transcendence and on historical site having met with no success, the Army High Command withdraws the Twelfth Army from the Potsdam-Beelitz area.

Whereupon radio message signed Bormann to Grand Admiral Dönitz: "The Führer appoints you successor former Reichmarshal Göring. Written appointment and pedigree Führerdog on way."

Whereupon Führerdesign presentifies overclimb. Whereupon unofficial Swedish report to effect that Führerdog has been sent to Argentine by submarine is not denied. The Soviet announcement—"Tattered fur of twelve-legged black dog found in destroyed ballet storeroom"—is contradicted by accomplishment report of the Bavarian Liberation Committee on the Erding radio: "Black dogcorpse secured outside Feldherrnhalle, Munich." Simultaneously, reports come in to the effect that Führerdog corpses have been washed ashore: first, in the Gulf of Bothnia; second, on the east coast of Ireland; third, on the Atlantic coast of Spain. Ultimate Führerintimations, recorded by General Burgdorf and in Führertestament: "Dog Prinz will try to reach Vatican City. If Pacelli raises claims, protest immediately and invoke codicil to will."

Thereupon world twilight. Over the ruins of the artifactworld climbs world-time. Situation report May 1: "In the center of the Reichcapital the brave garrison is fighting in narrowed space, reinforced by disbanded Führerdogsearchgroups."

Thereupon at-handness takes its leave in the not-noticeableness of the inutilizable, giving rise to top secret message, Reichsleiter Bormann to Grand Admiral Dönitz: "Führer passed away yesterday one five three 0 hours. Testament in force and on way. As per instructions April 29, Führer's favorite dog Prinz, black, short-haired shepherd, is Führer's gift to the German people. Acknowledge receipt."

Whereupon the last radio stations play *Götterdämmerung*. Grounded on him. Whereupon there is no time for a minute of silence grounded on him. Whereupon the remnants of the Vistula Army Group, the remnants of the Twelfth and Ninth Armies, the remnants of the Holste and Steiner combat teams, try to reach English-and American-held territory west of the Dömitz-Wismar line.

Whereupon radio silence settles over the government quarter of the Reichcapital. Locus-wholeness, nihilation, open-to-dread, and togetherpieceable. Greatness. Entirety. The madeness of Berlin. Made finite. The end.

But the heavens did not darken over the structure of the end.

There was once a dog;

he belonged to the Führer and Chancellor and was his favorite dog. One day this dog ran away from the Führer. Why would he run away?

Ordinarily this dog cannot speak, but here, questioned as to the great why, he speaks and says why: "Sick of moving all over the place. No fixed dog-here, dog-there, dog-now. Bones buried everywhere and never found again. No allowed-to-run-loose. Always being-in-restricted-zone. Moving around for dog years, from operation to operation, and for every operation code names: Operation White goes on for eighteen days. While Weser maneuvers are in progress in the north, they have to start up Operation Hartmut to protect Weser maneuvers. Operation Yellow against neutral countries develops into Operation Red all the way to the Spanish border. And then Autumn Journey is arranged with a view to organizing Operation Sea Lion that will force perfidious Albion to its knees. It's called off. Instead, Marita rolls up the Balkans. Oh, what poet has he in his pay? Who writes his poetry for him? Christmastree against the Swiss; nothing comes of it. Barbarossa and Silverfox against subhumans; plenty comes of them. Operation Siegfried leads from Kharkov to Stalingrad. Thunderbolt and Blizzard don't help the Sixth Army one bit. A last try is made: Fridericus I and Fridericus II. Autumn Crocus soon fades. Landbridge to Demnyansk collapses. Typhoon has to straighten out the fronts. Operation Buffalo degenerates into stampede back to the stable. Home sweet home! In such a situation even a dog is fed up, but waits, faithful as a dog, to see if the newly planned bastion near Kursk will hold out, and to see what comes of Knight's-move against convoys headed for Murmansk. But alas! Gone are the happy days when Sunflower was transplanted to North Africa, when Mercury did business on Crete, when Mouse burrowed deep into the Caucasus. Nothing doing now but Spring Storm, Ball Lightning, and Poundcake against Tito's partisans. Oaktree is supposed to put Il Duce back in the saddle. But Westenemies Gustav, Ludwig, and Marten II land and provoke Sunrise at Nettuno. Enemy flowers blossom in Normandy. Griffin, Autumn Mist, and Sentinel try in vain to pluck them in the Ardennes. Before that the bomb goes off in rabbitless Wolf's Redoubt. It doesn't hurt the dog, but it blunts his enthusiasm: Fed up! Always being dragged this way and that way. Special trains. Special food, but no freedom, with juicy nature for miles around.

"Oh dog of many travels! From Berghof to Felsennest. From the Zoppot Winter Garden to the Tannenburg. From the Black Forest to Wolf's Lair I. Never did get to see anything of France and in Berghof nothing but clouds. Northwest of Vinnitsa, in a little forest allegedly full of foxes, lies Werewolf Camp. Shuttling back and forth between Ukraine and East Prussia. From Wolf's Redoubt propelled to Wolf's Lair II. One day's stay in the Eyrie, then down into the hole for good. Down into the Führer's airraid shelter. Day after day: nothing but air-raid shelters. After Eagle, Wolf, and again Wolf, air-raid shelters day in day out. After Cloudview and Crowsnest, after Tannenburg and the air of the Black Forest, nothing but a stuffy old air-raid shelter.

When things come to such a pass, a dog has his belly full. After the failure of Dentist and the fumbling of Baseplate, he decides to migrate with the Visigoths. To escape. To be-in-space. To give up being-faithful-as-a-dog. When things come to such a pass, a dog, who ordinarily and as a rule cannot talk, says: "I disengage myself."

While the birthday preparations in the Führer's shelter were going on, he slipped innocently across the inner courtyard of the Chancellery. Just as the Reichmarshal was driving in, he passed the sentry post and, having gathered from the situation reports that there was a gap in the front near Cottbus, started off in a southwesterly direction; but wide and attractive as the gap seemed to be, the dog, sighting Soviet armored spearheads, reversed his direction east of Jüterbog, abandoned the route of the Ostrogoths, and hurried toward the Westenemy: over the ruins of the inner city, around the government quarter, close call on the Alexanderplatz, guided through the Tiergarten by two bitches in heat, and damn near captured near the Zoological Gardens airraid shelter, where gigantic mousetraps were waiting for him, but he seven times circumambulated the Victory Column, shot down the Siegesallee, counseled by dog instinct, that wise old saw, joined a gang of civilian moving men, who were moving theater accessories from the exhibition pavilion by the radio tower to Nikolassee. But German loudspeakers as well as the far-carrying loudspeakers of the Eastenemy—alluring voices promising him rabbits—aroused his suspicion of residential suburbs like Wannsee and Nikolassee: not far enough west!—and he set himself a goal for the first leg of his journey: the Elbe bridge at Magdeburg-Burg.

South of Lake Schwielow he passed without incident the advance elements of the Twelfth Army that were supposed to relieve the pressure on the capital. After he had taken a short rest in the overgrown garden of a villa, an armored infantryman fed him still-warm pea soup and, without taking an official tone, called him by his name. Immediately thereafter enemy artillery subjected the villa area to harassing fire, slightly wounded the armored infantryman, but missed the dog; for what you see there, running with steady, reliable haunches, following the pre-established Visigothic migration route, is still one and the same self-grounded black German shepherd.

Panting between rippled lakes on a windy day in May. The ether teeming with weighty happening. Snapping at his goal, westward over the Prussian sand into which pine trees claw. A horizontal tail, fangs far in advance, waving tongue cut down the distance on sixteen times four legs: dog's leap in successive part movements. Everything in sixteenths: landscape, spring, air, freedom, tufty trees, beautiful clouds, first butterflies, singing of birds, buzzing of insects, kitchen gardens bursting into green, musical lath fences. Furrows spit out rabbits, partridges flush, nature without scale, no more sandbox but horizons, smells you could spread on bread, slowly drying sunsets, boneless dawns, now and then a wrecked tank, romantic against the five-o'clock-in-the-morning sky, moon and dog, dog eats moon, dog close-up, evaporating dog, dog project, dog deserter, get-out-of-here dog, count-me-out dog, dog-thrownness, genealogicals: And Perkun sired Senta; and Senta whelped Harras; and Harras sired Prinz . . . Dog greatness, ontic and scientific, dog deserter with the wind in his sails; for the wind too, like everybody else, is headed west: The Twelfth Army, the remains of the Ninth Army, what is left of the Steiner and Holste combat teams, the weary Löhr, Schörner, and Rendulic army groups, unsuccessfully the East Prussia and Kurland army groups from the ports of Libau and Windau, the garrison of Rügen Island, whoever is able to get away from Hela and the Vistula delta, in short, the remains of the Second Army; everybody who has a nose to smell with runs, swims, drags himself away: away from the Eastenemy toward the Westenemy; civilians on foot, on horseback, packed into former cruise steamers, hobble in stocking feet, drown wrapped in paper money, crawl with too little gas and too much baggage; behold the miller with his twenty-pound sack of flour, the carpenter, laden with doorframes and bone glue, relatives and in-laws, Party members, active and passive, children with dolls and grandmothers with photograph albums, the imaginary and the real, all all all see the sun rising in the west and take their bearings from the dog.

Left behind: mounds of bones, mass graves, card files, flagpoles, party books, love letters, homes, church pews, and pianos difficult to transport.

Unpaid: taxes, mortage payments, back rent, bills, debts, and guilt.

All are eager to start out fresh with living, saving, letter writing, in church pews, at pianos, in card files and homes of their own.

All are eager to forget the mounds of bones and the mass graves, the flagpoles and party books, the debts and the guilt.

There was once a dog,

who left his master and traveled a long way. Only rabbits pucker up their noses; but let no one who can read suppose that the dog didn't get there.

On May 8, 1945, at 4:45 A.M., he swam across the Elbe above Magdeburg almost unseen and went looking for a new master on the west side of the river.

BOOK THREE | **Materniads**

The dog stands central. Between him and the dog runs barbed wire, old and new, from corner to corner of the camp. While the dog stands, Matern scratches tin out of an empty tin can. He has a spoon but no memory. Everybody and everything are trying to give him one: the central dog; the tin can filled with air; the English questionnaire; and now Brauxel is sending advances and setting deadlines determined by the entrances and exits of certain planets: he wants Matern to shoot the shit about those days.

To begin is to select. What about this double row of barbed wire between dog and tin can: deprivation of freedom, prison camp jitters, all very graphic though the current has been turned off. Or stick to the dog, then you'll be central. Pour soup, noodled with names, into the tin can for him, expelling the air. Because you can always find scraps —dog food: the twenty-nine potato years. Memory soup. Remembrance dumplings. All those unseasoned lies. Theatrical roles and life. Matern's dehydrated vegetables. Gritty guilt: that's the salt.

To cook is to select. Which takes longer to cook, barley grits or barbed wire? Grits are spooned up, and yet underdone barbed wire between him and the dog induces grinding of the teeth. Matern could never abide wire and fences. Even his ancestor, who still called himself Materna, carried subversive grinding of the teeth with him to the Stockturm, the windowless tower.

To remember is to select. This, that, or the other dog? Every dog is central. What will drive a dog away? There aren't that many stones in the world; and Camp Munster— who doesn't remember it from the old days?—was built on sand and has scarcely changed. Barracks burned down, Nissen huts went up. The camp movie house, a few stray pines, the inevitable mess hall, and the whole enclosed in old wire, enriched by new wire: Matern, whom an English antifascist camp had spewed out, is spooning up barley grits behind the new barbed wire surrounding a discharge camp.

Twice a day he laps soup from a clattering tin can and follows his footprints in the sand along the double row of wire. Don't look around, the Grinder's around. Twice a day the selfsame dog refuses to eat stones: "Beat it! Clear out! Go back where you came from!"

For tomorrow or the day after the papers will be ready for somebody who wants to be alone, without a dog.

"Where will you go when you get your discharge?"

"Let's see, Mr. Brooks, let's say Cologne or Neuss."

"Date and place of birth?"

"April 1917, just a minute: the nineteenth, to be exact, in Nickelswalde, Danzig Lowlands District."

"Education and special training?"

"Well, first the usual: public school in the village, then high school. After graduating I was supposed to study economics, but I took up acting instead, under good old Gustav Nord, played Shakespeare marvelously, but he did Shaw, too, *Saint Joan* . . ."

"Then you're an actor by profession?"

"That's right, Mr. Broox. Played everything that came along. Karl and Franz Moor: Slavish wisdom, slavish fears! And once, in our good old Coffee Mill, when I was still a beginner, I even took the part of a talking reindeer. Those were the days, Mr. . . ."

"Ever a member of the C.P.? During what period?"

"Well, I graduated in '35. I must have started in with the Red Falcons at the beginning of second. Pretty soon I joined the Communist Party and stayed in until it was suppressed in Danzig, that was in '34. I worked illegally for a while after that, handing out leaflets and putting up posters, it was no use."

"Have you ever been a member of the National Socialist Party or any of its organizations?"

"A few months in the SA, for the hell of it. Sort of snooping around to see what was going on, and partly because a friend of mine . . ."

"During what period?"

"I just told you, Mr. Braux, a couple of months. From late summer '37 to spring '38. Then they threw me out. My sturm had me for trial for insubordination."

"What sturm?"

"If I could only remember! You see, I wasn't in very long. The whole thing was on account of this good friend of mine, who was a half-Jew. I was trying to protect him from the pack . . . All right, it was SA Sturm 84, Langfuhr-North. Belonged to Standarte 128, SA Brigade 6, Danzig."

"What was your friend's name?"

"Amsel. Eduard Amsel. He was an artist. We grew up together, so to speak. He could be awfully funny. Made stage sets, mechanical things. For instance, he wouldn't put on a suit or a pair of shoes until they'd been worn by somebody else. He was terribly fat but he had a good singing voice. A wonderful guy, really."

"What became of Amsel?"

"No idea. Had to leave town, because they'd kicked me out of the SA. I asked all over, for instance, I went to see Brunies, our former German teacher . . ."

"Where's the teacher now?"

"Brunies. He must be dead. Sent to a concentration camp in '34."

"Which one?"

"Stutthof. Near Danzig."

"Your last and next-to-last military unit?"

"Up to November, '43, 22nd AA Regiment, Kaiserhafen battery. Then I was court-martialed for insulting the Führer and undermining Army morale. They broke me from tech sergeant to private and sent me to the Fourth Punitive Battalion to clear mines. On January 23, '45, I deserted to the 28th American Infantry Division in the Vosges."

"Any other trouble with the authorities?"

"Plenty, Mr. Brooks. Well, first the business with my SA sturm. Then, just a year later—I'd gone to Schwerin to work in the theater—I was dismissed without notice for insulting the Führer and so on. Then I went to Düsseldorf. I did odd jobs on children's radio programs and played faustball on the side with the Unterrath Sports Club. A couple of the club members turned me in: I was held for questioning at the Kavalleriestrasse police headquarters, if that means anything to you. When they got through with me, I was ready for the hospital, and if the war hadn't broken out in the nick of time . . . Oh yes, I almost forgot the business with the dog. That was in midsummer 1939 . . ."

"In Düsseldorf?"

"No, Mr. Broox, that was back in Danzig. I'd had to volunteer or they'd have cooked me. So I was stationed in the former police barracks in Hochstriess, and during that time, maybe because I was mad or maybe just because I was against, I poisoned a dog, a shepherd."

"What was this shepherd's name?"

"Harras, and he belonged to a carpenter."

"Anything special about the dog?"

"He was a stud dog, as they say. And in '35 or '36 this Harras had sired a dog by the name of Prinz, honest to God, as true as I'm standing here, that was given to Hitler for his birthday and was supposed—there must be witnesses—to have been his favorite dog. In addition—and here, Mr. Braux, the story gets personal—Senta, our Senta, had been Harras' mother. In Nickelswalde—that's in the Vistula estuary— she whelped Harras and a couple of other pups under the jack of our windmill when I was just ten. Then it burned down. This windmill of ours was a very special mill . . ."

"In what way?"

"Well, it was known as the historical mill of Nickelswalde, because on her flight from Napoleon Queen Louise of Prussia spent the night in our mill. It was a fine German postmill. My great-grandfather built it, that was August Matern. He was a lineal descendant of Simon Materna, the famous hero of Polish independence, who in 1516 was arrested by Hans Nimptsch, the city captain, and beheaded in the Danzig Stockturm; but by 1524 his cousin, the journeyman barber Gregor Materna, was sounding the call for another uprising, and on August 14, while the St. Dominic's Day market was going on, he in turn, because that's the way we Materns are, we can't button up, we're always shooting our traps off, even my father, Anton Matern, the miller, who could predict the future, because the mealworms . . ."

"Thank you, Mr. Matern. You've given us sufficient information. Your discharge papers will be issued tomorrow morning. Here's your pass. You may go."

Through this door on two hinges, to give the sun outside a chance to show what it can do: on the camp grounds POW Matern, barracks, Nissen huts, the remaining pines, the crowded bulletin board, the double row of the barbed wire, and the patient dog outside the fence cast shadows, all in the same direction. Remember! How many rivers empty into the Vistula? How many teeth has a man? What were the names of the ancient Prussian gods? How many dogs? Were there eight or nine muffled figures? How many names are still alive? How many women have you . . . ? How long did your grandmother sit riveted to her chair? What did your father's mealworms whisper when the miller's son asked him how somebody was getting along and what he was doing? He whispered, remember, that this somebody was hoarse as a grater and nevertheless chain-smoked all day long. And when did we do Billinger's *The Giant* at the Stadttheater? Who played the part of Donata Opferkuch, and who did her son? What did Strohmenger the critic write in the *Vorposten?* Here's what it said, remember: "The gifted young Matern distinguished himself as the son of Donata Opferkuch, who, it should be added, was played sloppily but powerfully by Maria Bargheer; son and mother, two interesting, ambivalent figures . . ." *Chien . . . cane . . . dog . . . kyon!* I've been discharged. In my windbreaker I've got papers, six hundred reichsmarks and traveler's food tickets! My barracks bag contains two pairs of drawers, three undershirts, four pairs of socks, a pair of American combat boots with rubber soles, two almost new Ami shirts, dyed black, a German officer's overcoat, undyed, a real civilian hat from Cornwall, gentlemanlike, two packages of K-rations, a pound can of English pipe tobacco, fourteen packs of Camels, about twenty paperbacks—mostly Shakespeare Grabbe Schiller—a complete edition of *Being and Time*—still containing the dedication to Husserl—five cakes of first-class soap and three cans of corned beef . . . *Chien,* I'm rich! *Cane,* where is thy victory? Beat it, dog! Get thee behind me, *kyon!*

On foot, with his barracks bag over his shoulder, Matern takes steps on sand which outside the camp isn't trampled as hard as inside the camp. No more social life, that was the main thing! Accordingly, shank's mare and no trains for the present. The dog shrinks back and refuses to understand. A real or simulated throwing of stones drives him into plowed fields or up the path. Empty throwing motions make him tense; real stones he retrieves: *zellacken.*

With ineluctable dog Matern covers three sandy miles in the direction of Fallingbostel. Since the good dirt road is not like himself headed southwest, he drives the critter across the fields. Anyone who has noticed that Matern is striding normally on the right side will have to admit that on the left side he has a barely perceptible limp. All this was once a military terrain and will remain so for all eternity: damage to crops. A brown heath starts up and merges into young

woods. A felling makes him a present of a club: "Beat it, dog.
Faithfulasadog. You no-good bastard, beat it!"

I can't take him with me, can I? To live for once without
admirers. Haven't I been hounded enough? What can I do
with this flea bag? Rat poison, cuckoo clocks, doves of peace,
sharks, Christian dogs, Jewish swine, domestic animals,
domestic animals . . . "Beat it, dog."

This from morning to night till he was almost hoarse.
From Ostenholz to Essel his mouth full of self-defense and
names aimed not only at the dog but at the whole environing
world. In his cold homeland *zellacken* and not stones were
picked up from the fields whenever there was somebody to
be stoned. These, and clods of earth and the club as well,
are meant to hit the critter and just about everything else.
Never has a dog, unwilling to leave his self-chosen master,
had an opportunity to learn so much about the dog's function in mythology: is there any underworld he doesn't have
to guard; any river of the dead whose waters some dog
doesn't lap up? Lethe Lethe, how do we get rid of memories?
No hell but has its hellhound!

Never has a dog unwilling to leave his self-chosen master
been sent to so many countries and cities at once: Go
where the pepper grows. To Buxtehude, Jericho, Todtnau.
What multitudes of people this dog is told to nuzzle up to!
Names names—but he doesn't go to hell, doesn't go to Pepper
City, doesn't kiss the ass of strangers, but follows, faithfulasadog, his self-chosen master.

Don't look around, here comes the hound.

Then Matern gives a peasant a piece of advice in Mandelsloh—that makes him a Lower Saxon peasant, they had been
following the River Leine together. In exchange for four
Camels the peasant has let him sleep in a real bed, white
in and out. Over steaming fried potatoes Matern suggests:
"Couldn't you use a dog? He's a stray, he's been after me all
day. I can't get rid of him. Not a bad mutt, only kind of
run down."

But the following day from Mandelsloh to Rothenuffeln isn't
dogless for a single step, though in the peasant's opinion
the dog wasn't bad, only neglected, he'd sleep on it and
tell him in the morning. At breakfast the peasant was willing, but not the dog, his mind was made up.

The Steinhuder Sea sees them coupled; a load off Matern's
feet between Rothenuffeln and Brackwede when a three-

wheeled cart picks him up whereas the dog has to shake a leg; and in Westphalia, when their day's destination goes by the name of Rinkerode, the couple is still undivided: not a dog more, not a dog less. And as they are hiking from Rinkerode past Othmarsbocholt to Ermen, he begins to share with him: rye bread and corned beef. But while the dog bolts scraps, a club that has come along from Lower Saxony thuds dully on matted fur.

On which account he scrubs him next day—after the two of them have maintained a moderate distance from Ermen via Olfen to Eversum—in the River Stever, until he glistens black: coat and undercoat. A pipeful of tobacco is traded for an old dog comb. Matern receives an attestation: "He's a purebred." He can see that for himself, he knows a thing or two about dogs. "You're not telling me anything new, man. I grew up with a dog. Take a look at the legs. He's not cow-hocked or bowlegged. And the line from croup to withers: no sign of lumpiness, just that he isn't as young as he used to be. Take a look at the lips, they don't close tight. And those two gray spots over the stop. But his teeth will be good for years."

Appraisal and shoptalk with English tobacco in their pipes:

"How old would he be? Ten is my guess."

Matern is more exact: "More likely eleven. But that breed keeps lively up to seventeen. With proper care, mind you."

After lunch a few words about the world situation and the atom bomb. Then Westphalian dog stories: "In Bechtrup there was a male shepherd one time, long before the war, that quietly passed away at the age of twenty, which, I always say, makes a hundred and forty human years. And my grandfather used to tell about a dog from Rechede, raised in the Dülmen kennels, that lived to be twenty-two, even if he was half blind, which makes a hundred and fifty-four. Next to him your dog, with his eleven dog years, which makes seventy-seven human years, is still a youngster."

His dog, whom he doesn't send away with stones and hoarseness, but keeps close to him as a nameless possession. "What's he called anyway?"

"He isn't called anything yet."

"Are you looking for a name for the dog?"

"Don't look for names or you'll find names."

"Well, why don't you call him Fido or Towser, or Falko

or Hasso, or Castor or Wotan . . . I once knew a male shepherd, believe it or not, his name was Jasomir."

Oh lousy shit! Who has squatted here in the open fields, expelled a hard sausage, and is now contemplating his excrement? Someone who doesn't want to eat it, yet recognizes himself in it: Matern, Walter Matern, who is good at grinding his teeth: gravel in the dung; who is always looking for God and finding at best excrement; who kicks his dog: shit! But across the same field, cutting across the furrows, he whimpers back, and still has no name. Shit shit! Should Matern call his dog Shit?

Nameless, they make their way across the Lippe-Seiten Canal into the Haard, a moderately hilly forest. He really means to cut across the mixed forest to Marl with the nameless dog—should his name be Kuno or Thor?—but then they turn off on a path to the left—Audifax?—and, emerging from the woods, come across the railroad: Dülmen-Haltern-Recklinghausen. And here there are coal mines with names that would do perfectly well for dogs: Hannibal, Regent, Prosper? —In Speckhorn master and nameless dog find a bed.

Consult the books, draw up lists. Chiseled in granite and marble. Names names. History is made of them. Can should may a dog bear the name of Totila, Attila, or Kaspar Hauser? What was the first of the long line called? Maybe the other gods could supply a name: Potrimpos or Pikollos?

Who tosses and turns, unable to sleep, because names, now private ones unfit for any dog, are gouging his spine? In the early morning, through ground fog, the two of them stick to the railroad embankment, walk on ballast, step aside to let overcrowded morning trains pass by. Silhouetted ruins: that's Recklinghausen or, later on, Herne, to the right Wanne, to the left Eickel, Emergency bridges cross the Emscher Canal and the Rhine-Herne Canal. Nameless figures pick up coal in the mist. On headframes windlays turn or are silent over nameless mines. No noise. Everything bedded in cotton. At most the ballast speaks, or crows in their usual way: namelessly. Until something branches off to the right and has a name. Rails, single-tracked, come from Eickel and don't want to go to Hüllen. Over an open entrance, on a weatherbeaten sign, big letters: PLUTO BRANCH LINE.

That does it: "Here Pluto. Sit Pluto. Heel Pluto. Fetch it Pluto. Nice Pluto. Down, fetch it, eat, Pluto. Quick Pluto. Seek Pluto. My pipe Pluto." Godfather is Pluton, bestower of grain and shekels, who, like Hades—or old Pikollos—attends to the business of the underworld, shady business, templeless business, invisible business, underground business, the big pension, the elevator to the fill level, where they let you in but not out, he can't be bribed, you're there to stay, each and all go to Pluto, whom nobody worships. Only Matern and the Elians pile the altar: with heart, spleen, and kidneys for Pluto!

They follow the branch line. Weeds between the tracks mean there hasn't been a train here in a long time, and the rails are dull with rust. Matern tries the new name, loudly and softly. Now that he's taken possession of the dog, his hoarseness has been letting up. The name works. Surprise at first, then zealous obedience. That dog has had training sometime. He's no bum. When whistled, Pluto stands and lies down in the middle of the coal fields. Halfway between Dortmund and Oberhausen Pluto shows what he has learned and not forgotten, but only repressed a little because of the troubled, masterless times. Tricks. The mist has begun to curdle and swallow itself up. Around half past four, there's even a sun in these parts.

This mania for taking your bearings once a day: Where are we anyway? A memorable spot! To the left Schalke-North with Wilhelmine-Victoria Mine, to the right Wanne without Eickel, past the Emscher marshes Gelsenkirchen stops, and here, which is where the branch line with its rusty rails and weeds was headed, there lies, silenced and half destroyed by bombs beneath an old-fashioned knock-kneed headframe, that Pluto Mine which has given Pluto, the black shepherd male, his name.

What a war can do: everything closed down. Nettles and buttercups grow faster than the world can imagine. Crumpled walls that were expected to stand forever. T-girders and radiators twisted into iron bellyaches. Wreckage shouldn't be described but turned into cash; and so junk dealers will come and bend the scrap-iron question marks straight. Just as bluebells ring in the summer, so junk dealers will strike peaceful notes from scrap iron and announce the great smelting process. O ye unshaven angels of peace, spread your wings, bestir your battered mudguards and settle in places like this: Pluto Mine, between Schalke and Wanne.

The environment appeals to both of them: Matern and his four-legged buddy. Why not a little training right away?

A nice piece of wall, about four feet three inches high, is still standing. Go to it, Pluto. It won't be hard, not with those long withers and perfectly angulated forelegs, not with that comparatively short but powerful back, not with those efficient hindquarters. Jump, Pluto. Black bow-wow, without spots or markings on straight back: speed, staying power, willingness to jump. Go to it, doggy, I'll put a little something on top. Those two hocks will bring home the bacon. Away from the earthly. A little trip through the Rhenish-Westphalian air. Land softly, it's easier on the joints. Good-dog modeldog: shipshape Pluto!

Pants here, sniffs there. Nose to the ground, he collects scent marks: antiques. In a burned-out headframe he barks at dangling chain hoists and hooks, though second sight is needed to glimpse what's left of the rags of the last morning shift. Echo. It's fun to make a racket in abandoned ruins; but the master whistles his dog into the sun, out into the playground. In a wrecked shunting engine a fireman's cap is found. You can throw it up in the air or put it on. Fireman Matern: "All this belongs to us. We've got the head-frame. Now let's occupy the offices. The proletariat seizes the means of production."

But there wasn't a single rubber stamp in the thoroughly ventilated offices. And if not for the—"Say, there's a hole in the floor!"—they would have had every reason to go back to the sunlit playground. "Say, there's a way down!" an almost complete staircase. "But watch your step!" there might be a mine lying around from the day before yesterday. But there are no mines in the furnace room. "Let's take a look in here." Step by little step: "Where is my candle and what about my good old lighter? Picked it up in Dunkirk, it's seen Piraeus, Odessa, and Novgorod, and lighted my way home; it's always done its stuff, why not here?"

Every dark place knows why. All secrets are ticklish. Every treasure seeker has expected more. There they stand on six feet in the full-to-bursting cellar. No crates to break open; no little bottles to glug out of; neither displaced Persian carpets nor silver spoons; no church treasure nor castle valuables: nothing but paper. Not naked white paper, that might still have been good business. Or a correspondence between great men on handmade ragpaper. This paper was printed, in four colors: forty thousand posters still smelled fresh. One as smooth as the next. On each one He with low-pulled visor cap: solemn rigid Führergaze: As of four forty-five today. Providence has saved. When long ago I decided. Innumerable. Ignominious. Pitiful. If need be. To the very last. In the end. Remains, will again, never. Contemptible traitors. In this hour the whole world. The turning point. I call upon you. We will join ranks. I have. I will. I am well aware. I . . .

And every poster that Matern brushes from the pile with two fingers hovers for a time in midair and then settles in front of Pluto's forepaws. Only a few fall on the face. For the most part He stares at the furnace pipes on the ceiling: solemn rigid Führergaze. Matern's two fingers are indefatigable, as though he had reason to expect a different gaze from the next or next-to-next poster. Where there's life . . .

Then a siren swells in the pin-drop cellar. The Führergaze has set off this aria in the dog's heart. The dog croons and Matern can't turn him off. "Quiet Pluto. Lie down Pluto."

But the whimpering dog tips his erect ears, all four legs go limp, and his tail sags. Rising to the concrete ceiling, the sound threads its way into burst pipes, and Matern has nothing to oppose it with but a dry grinding of the teeth. Ineffectual, the grinding breaks off, and he spits: phlegm on a picture portrait taken before the attempt on his life; oysters into the solemn rigid Führergaze; lung butter loops the loop and strikes: him him him. But it doesn't lie for long, for the dog has a tongue, which licks, long and colorful, the Führer's flatlying face: snot from his cheek. No longer does spittle cloud the gaze. Laps saliva from the little square mustache: faithfulasadog.

Thereupon counteraction. Matern has ten fingers which crumple radically what smoothly records a four-tone face, what lies on the floor, what lies in piles, what looks up at the ceiling: He He He. No! says the dog. Growling in crescendo. Pluto's iron jaws: No! A dog says no: Stop that, stop it this minute! The fist over Matern's head relaxes: "O.K. Pluto. Sit Pluto. Come come. I didn't mean it that way, Pluto. Why don't we take a little nap and save the candle? Sleep and be nice to each other again? Nice Pluto, nice Pluto."

Matern blows out the candle. On piled-up Führergaze lie master and dog. Panting heavily in the darkness. Each breathes by himself. God in His heaven looks on.

SECOND MATERNIAD

They are no longer walking on six feet, one of which seems to be defective and has to be dragged; they are riding in a packjammed train from Essen via Duisburg to Neuss, for a man must have some goal or other: a doctor's degree or a sharpshooter's medal, the kingdom of heaven or a home of his own, on his way to Robinson Crusoe's island, world-record, Cologne on the Rhine.

The trip is hard and long. Lots of people, if not the whole population, are on the move with sacks of potatoes or sugarbeets. Accordingly—if sugarbeets are to be trusted—they are not riding into the spring but toward St. Martin's Day. And so, for Novemberly reasons, life, for all the crush of smelly overcoats, is more tolerable inside the packjammed car than on the rounded roof, on the jangling bumpers, or on running boards that have to be reconquered at every station. For not all the travelers have the same destination.

Even before the train pulls out of Essen, Matern gets Pluto settled. Inside the car an acrid smell mingles with the effluvia of late potatoes, earth-damp sugarbeets, and sweating humanity.

Out in the wind Matern smells only the locomotive. In league with his barracks bag, he holds the running board against enemy onslaughts at the Grossenbaum and Kalkum stations. It would be pointless to grind his teeth against the wind. In the old days, when he challenged the buzz saw with his jaws—the story was that he could grind his teeth even under water—in the old days his teeth would have spoken up even in the train wind. Silently, then, but his head full of dramatic parts, he speeds through the unmoving landscape. In Derendorf Matern makes room on the running board for a bilious watchmaker, who might also be a professor, by upending his barracks bag. The watchmaker is trying to convey eight briquettes to Küppersteg. At Düsseldorf Central Station Matern manages to save him, but in Benrath he is swallowed up by the mob along with his briquettes. Simply to be fair, Matern forces the character who in the watchmaker's place is determined to transport his kitchen scales to Cologne, to change in Leverkusen. Glances over his shoulder reassure him: Inside the car a dog is still standing on four paws and keeping an eye, faithfulasadog, on the window: "Good dog, good dog, just a little longer. That pile of bricks for instance promises to be Mülheim. We don't stop in Kalk. But from Deutz we can see the double prongs, the Devil's Gothic horns, the cathedral. And where the cathedral is, its secular counterpart, the Central Station, can't be far off. They go together like Scylla and Charybdis, throne and altar, Being and Time, master and dog."

So that's what they call the Rhine! Matern grew up by the Vistula. In recollection, every Vistula is wider than every Rhine. And it's only because the Materns must always live by rivers—the everlasting parade of water gives them a sense of being alive—that we've undertaken this crusade to Cologne. But also because Matern has been here before. And because his forebears, the brothers Simon and Gregor Materna, always came back mostly to wreak vengeance with fire and sword: that was how Drehergasse and Petersiliengasse went up in flames, how Langgarten and St. Barbara's burned down in the east wind; well, in this place others have had ample opportunity to try out their lighters. There's not much kindling left. "I come to judge with a black dog and a list of names incised in my heart, spleen, and kidneys. THAT DEMAND TO BE CROSSED OFF.

O acrid unglassed drafty holy Catholic Central Station of Cologne! Nations with suitcases and knapsacks come to see and smell you, disperse throughout the world, and can never again forget you: you and the double stone monstrosity across the way. Anyone who wants to understand humanity must kneel down in your waiting rooms; for here all are pious and confess to one another over watery beer. Whatever they do, whether they sleep with open jaws, embrace their pathetic baggage, quote earthly prices for heavenly lighter flints and cigarettes, whatever they may omit and pass over in silence, whatever they may add and repeat, they are working on the great confession. At the ticket windows, in the paper-blown station hall—two overcoats a plot, three overcoats in cahoots a riot!—and similarly down below in the tiled toilets, where the beer flows off again, warmed. Men unbutton, stand silently as though deep in thought in white-enameled bays, whisper with prematurely

worn-out cocks, seldom in a straight line, usually with a
slight but calculated elevation. Urine comes-to-be. Pissing
stallions stand for eternities with arched back on two legs in
pants, forming a roof over their excrescences with right hands,
mostly married, prop their hips with their left hands, look
ahead with mournful eyes, and decipher inscriptions, dedications, confessions, prayers, outcries, rhymes, and names,
scribbled in blue pencil scratched with nail scissors, leather
punch, or nail.

So too Matern. Except that he doesn't prop his hip with
his left hand, but holds behind him a leather leash, which
cost two Camels in Essen and in Cologne joins him with
Pluto. All men stand for eternities, but Matern's eternity is
longer, even after his water has stopped leaning on enamel.
Already he is fingering button after button, with pauses the
length of a paternoster in between, into the corresponding
buttonhole, his back no longer arched, but rather humped
like that of a reader. Nearsighted people hold their eyes that
close to printed matter or script. Thirst for knowledge.
Reading room atmosphere. The student of Scripture. Don't
disturb the reader. Knowledge is power. An angel passes
through the enormous tiled warm sweetandpungentsmelling
holy Catholic men's toilet of Cologne Central Station.

There it is written: "Deadhead, watch out." Recorded for
all time: "Dobshe dobshe trallala—Schnapps is good for
cholera." A Lutheran nail has scratched: "And though the
world were full of devils . . ." Hard to decipher: "Germany
awaken!" Perpetuated in capitals: "ALL WOMEN ARE SLUTS."
A poet has written: "In ice and flame—we're still the same."
And someone has stated tersely: "The Führer is alive."
But another handwriting knew more and added: "Right, in
Argentina." Brief ejaculations such as: "No! Count me out!
Chin up!" are frequent. So are drawings, which over and over
again have as their subject the indestructible Vienna roll
with its hairy halo, as well as recumbent women viewed as
Mantegna viewed the recumbent Christ, that is, by an eye
situated between the soles of their feet. Finally, wedged in
between the cry of rejoicing: "Happy New Year '46!" and
the obsolete warning: "Caution! Enemy ears are listening!,"
Matern, buttoned below, open on top, reads a name and address without rhymed or prose commentary: "Jochen Sawatzki—Fliesteden—Bergheimer Strasse 32."

Instantly Matern—with heart, spleen, and kidneys already

on his way to Fliesteden—has a nail in his pocket that wants to write. Significantly cutting across dedications, confessions, and prayers, across the strangely hairy Vienna rolls and the recumbent Mantegna ladies, the nail scratches the child's jingle: "DON'T TURN AROUND, THE GRINDER'S AROUND."

It's a village lined up along the highway between Cologne and Erft. The bus from the main post office to Grevenbroich by way of Müngersdorf, Lövenich, Brauweiler, stops there before Büsdorf, where it turns off to Stommeln. Matern finds his way without having to ask. Sawatzki in rubber boots opens: "Man, Walter, you still alive? Ain't that a surprise? Come on in, or wasn't it us you was coming to see?"

Inside it smells of boiling sugarbeets. Up from the cellar, head in kerchief, comes a doll who smells no better. "See, we're cooking syrup. Then we peddle it. It's rough work, but it pays. This here's my little wife. Her name's Inge, she's a native of Frechen. Inge, this here's a friend of mine, a buddy, kind of. We were in the same sturm for a while. My, oh my, haven't we been screwed: Shoilem boil 'em! remember, the two of us in the Kleinhammerpark, lights out—knives out! Get in there and fight. Christ, what a brawl! You remember Gustav Dau and Lothar Budczinski? Fränzchen Wollschläger and the Dulleck brothers? And Willy Eggers, man! And Otto Warnke, hell, and little Bublitz? Rough customers one and all, but good as gold, except they drank too much and you can say that again.—So there you are again. Man, I'm kind of scared of that mutt. Couldn't you lock him up in the other room?—All right, let him stay here. So give: where did you run off to at exactly the right time? Because once you left the sturm, we were through. Oh, it's easy to say when it's all over that we were damn fools to throw you out for nothing. It didn't amount to a hill of beans. But that's how they wanted it, especially the Dulleck brothers and Wollschläger too: Court of honor! An SA man don't steal! Robbing his comrades!—I really cried—honest to God, Inge —when he had to go. Well, here you are. You can take it easy in here or come into the laundry where the beets are cooking. You can flop in the deck chair and watch. Man, you old rascal. You can't lose a bad penny is what I always say to Inge, eh, Inge? I'm mighty glad."

In the cozy laundry room the sugarbeets cook away, spreading sweetness. Matern sprawls in the deck chair and has something between his teeth that can't come out because the two of them are so pleased and besides they're cooking syrup with four hands. She stirs the washtub with a shovel handle: pretty strong, though she's only a handful; he keeps the fire burning evenly: they have piles of briquettes, black gold. She's a regular Rhenish type: doll face with googoo eyes and can't stop googooing; he has hardly changed, maybe a little stouter. She just makes eyes and doesn't say boo; he bullshits about old times: "The storm troops march with firm and tranquil tread . . . Remember? Shoilem, boil 'em!" Why can't she stop making eyes? The bone I have to pick is with him, not with Ingewife. Cooking. What a racket! Out in the fields at night, stealing beets, peeling them, cutting them up, and so on. You won't see the last of Walter Matern so soon, because Walter has come to judge you with a black dog and a list of names incised in his heart, spleen, and kidneys, one of them exhibited for all to read in the Cologne Central Station, in the piss-warm part with the tiled floor and the cozy enameled bays: Sturmführer Jochen Sawatzki led the popular and notorious 84th SA Sturm, Langfuhr-North, through hell and high water. His terse but spirited speeches. His boyish charm when he spoke of the Führer and Germany's future. His favorite songs and favorite liquor: The Argonne Forest at midnight and for steady drinking gin with or without a plum. A good worker all the same. Energetic and trustworthy. Thoroughly disillusioned with the Commies, which is what made him so staunch a believer in the new idea. His operations against the Sozis Brill and Wichmann; the brawl at the Café Woike, the Polish student hangout; the eight-man action on Steffensweg . . .

"Say," says Matern across the dog reclining at his feet and through the sugarbeet mist. "What ever became of Amsel? You know whom I mean. The guy that made the funny figures. The one you beat up on Steffensweg, remember, that's where he lived."

This gets no rise out of the dog, but provokes a brief lull in the beet corner. "Man, whatcha asking me for? That little visit was your idea. I never could get it straight, seeing he was a friend of yours, wasn't he."

The deck chair answers through the steam: "There were certain reasons, private reasons that I won't go into. But this is what I want to know: What did you do with him afterwards, I mean after the eight of you on Steffensweg . . ."

Ingewife makes googoo eyes and stirs. Sawatzki doesn't

forget to put briquettes on the fire: "Whassat? We din't do nothing else. And whatcha asking questions for anyway, when there wasn't eight of us but nine, including you. And you were the one that really pasted him so there wasn't much left. Anyway, he wasn't the worst. Too bad we never caught Dr. Citron. He cleared out for Sweden. What am I saying, too bad? To hell with the final solution and final victory routine. It's finished and good riddance. Forget it. Forget all that crap, and don't try to put the finger on me or I'll get mad. Because, sonny boy, you and I were tarred with the same brush, and neither of us is any cleaner than the other, right?"

The deck chair grumbles. The dog Pluto looks up, faithfulasadog. Chunks of sugarbeet boil unthinking: Don't cook beets, or you'll smell of beets. Too late, by this time all smell in unison: Fireman Sawatzki, Ingewife with eyes in her head, the inactive Matern—even the dog has ceased to smell of dog alone. The washtub has begun to glug heavily: Syrup syrup thick and sweet is—flies are dying of diabetes. Ingewife's stirring shovel handle meets with resistance: Never when syrup is being stirred, stir up the past with a single word. Sawatzki puts on the last briquettes: Sugarbeets need husbandry—God has sugar in his pee!

Then Sawatzki decides it's done and sets up a double row of pot-bellied two-quart bottles. Matern wants to help but they won't let him: "No, my boy. When the bottles are full, we'll go upstairs and pour a little something under our belts. An occasion like this needs to be celebrated, whatcha say, Ingemouse?"

They do it with potato schnapps. Eggnog liqueur is on hand for Ingemouse. Considering their circumstances, the Sawatzkis have set themselves up pretty nicely. A large oil painting, "Goats," two grandfather clocks, three club chairs, a Persian carpet under their feet, the "people's radio" turned down low, and a glassed-in heavy-oak bookcase, containing an encyclopedia in thirty-two volumes: *A* as in "Afterbirth."—Aw, don't cry, maybe you'll get another sometime. *B* as in "Beerhouse brawl."—I've been through maybe fifty of them, ten for the Commies and at least twenty for the Nazis, but do you think I can even keep the places straight, Ohra Riding Academy, Café Derra, Bürgerwiese, Kleinhammerpark. *C* as in "Cuckold."—Hell no, nobody's jealous around here. *D* as in "Danzig."—In the East it was nicer,

but in the West it's better. *E* as in "Eau de Cologne."—
Believe you me. The Russians used to lap it up like water.
F as in "Father."—They sent mine down with the *Gustlow*.
What about yours?—*G* as in "Gunsight."—I took a bead on
him, ping ping. Out like a light. *H* as in "Hard feelings."—
Aw, stop stirring up the old shit. *I* as in "Inge."—Go on,
give us a little dance, something oriental. *J* as in "Jacket."—
Take your coat off, man. *K* as in *"Kabale und Liebe."*—You
used to be an actor, whyn't you do something for us?
L as in "Laughing gas."—Cut the giggling, Inge. He's doing
Franz Moor. *M* as in "Merriment."—If you ask me, we
should crack another bottle. *N* as in "Neutral."—Matern's
steam has subsided. *O* as in "Oasis."—Here let us settle
down. *P* as in "Palestine."—That's where they should of
sent them, or Madagascar. *Q* as in "Question mark."—What's
on your mind, man? *R* as in "Rabbi."—And he wrote on the
paper that I'd treated him decently. His name was Dr. Weiss
and he lived at Mattenbuden 25. *S* as in "Square."—Take
it from me, three is more fun than four. *T* as in "Tobacco."
—For twelve Lucky Streeks we got the whole dinner set with
the cups thrown in. *U* as in "U-boat."—A hell of a lot of
good they did us. *V* as in "Victory."—Well, that's for the
birds. *W* as in "Walter."—So go sit on his lap instead of
wearing your eyes out. *X* as in "Xanthippe."—That was a
dame for you, but I'll settle for Ingemouse. *Y* as in
"Yankee."—No Ami ever got his mitts on her, or any Tommy
either. *Z* as in "Zero hour."—And now let's all go beddy-
by together. Bottoms up! The night is young. Me on the right,
you on the left, and Ingemouse snug as a bug in a rug in
the middle. But not the dog. He can stay in the kitchen.
We'll give him something to eat to make it nice for him
too. If you feel like washing, Walter boy, here's the soap."

And after drinking potato schnapps and eggnog liqueur
out of coffee cups, after Ingemouse has done a solo dance
and Matern some solo acting and Sawatzki has told them both
stories from times past and present, after making up a bed
for the dog in the kitchen and washing themselves sketchily
but with soap, three lie in the broad seaworthy marriage
bed, which the Sawatzkis call their marriage fortress, purchase price: seven two-quart bottles of syrup brewed from
sugarbeets. NEVER SLEEP THREE IN A BED—OR YOU'LL WAKE
UP THREE IN A BED.

Matern prefers to lie on the left. As host Sawatzki contents himself with the right. To Inge belongs the middle. Oh, ancient friendship, grown cold after two and thirty beerhouse brawls, now rewarmed in lurching marriage fortress. Matern, who came with black dog to judge, explores Ingepussy with affectionate finger: there be meets his friend's goodnatured husbandfinger; and both, friendly affectionate goodnatured, as long ago on the Bürgerwiese, at the Ohra Riding Academy or the Kleinhammerpark bar, join forces, find a cozy nook, and take turns. She's having a fine time: so much choice and variety; and emulation spurs the friends on—for potato schnapps makes a body sleepy. A race is run in friendly competition: neck and neck. O night of open doors, when Ingemouse lies on her side, so the friend in front, with the husband politely following up from the rear: so spacious, though slight and Rhenish-maidenly, Ingepussy offers shelter and comfort. If only there weren't this restlessness. O friendship, so complex! Each the other's phenotype. Intentions, leitmotives, murder motives, the difference in education, the yearning for intricate harmony: so many arms and legs! Who's kissing whom around here? Did you —did I? Who in such a case can stand on possession? Who pinches himself to make his counterpart yell? Who has come here to judge with names incised in his heart, spleen, and kidneys? Let us be fair! Each wants to crawl across to the sunny side. Each wants a chance at the buttered side. Three in a bed always need a referee: Ah, life is so rich: nine and sixty positions has heaven designed, has hell granted us: the knot, the loop, the parallelogram, the seesaw, the anvil, the preposterous rondo, the scales, the hop-skip-jump, the hermitage; and names kindled by Ingepussy: Ingeknee—Suckinge—Ingescream—Snapinge Ingefish Yesinge Spreadumslegsinge, Blowinge Biteinge Ingetired Ingeclosed Ingeintermission—Wakeupinge Openupinge Visitorsinge Bringingcodliveringe Twofriendsinge Yourlegmyarminge Don'tfallasleepinge Turnaroundinge Itwassolovelyinge It'slateinge She'sworkedhardtodayinge: Sugarbeetsinge—Syrupinge—Dogtiredinge — Goodnightinge — Godinhisheaven'swatchinginge!

Now they are lying in the black, formerly square room, breathing unevenly. No one has lost. All have won: Three victors in one bed. Inge holds her pillow in her arms. The men sleep with open mouths. It sounds roughly as if they were sawing tree trunks. They are felling the whole Jäschkental Forest, round about the Gutenberg monument: beech

after beech. Already the Erbsberg is bare. Soon Steffensweg can be seen: villa after villa. And in one of these Steffensweg villas lives Eddi Amsel in oak-paneled rooms, building life-sized scarecrows: one represents a sleeping SA man;
the second represents a sleeping SA Sturmführer; the third
signifies a girl, splattered from top to toe with sugarbeet
syrup which attracts ants. While the plain SA man grinds
his teeth in his sleep, the SA Sturmführer snores normally.
Only the syrup girl emits no sound, but thrashes her arms
and legs, because everywhere ants. While outside the beautiful smooth beeches of Jäschkental Forest continue to be
felled one by one—to make matters worse, it would have been
a good beechnut year—Eddi Amsel in his villa on Steffensweg builds the fourth life-size scarecrow: a black mobile
twelve-legged dog. To enable the dog to bark, Eddi Amsel
builds in a barking mechanism. And then he barks and wakes
up the snorer, the grinder, the ant-maddened syrupfigure.

It's Pluto in the kitchen. He demands to be heard. The
three of them roll out of bed without saying good morning.
"Never sleep three in a bed—or you'll wake up three in a
bed."

For breakfast there's coffee with milk and bread spread
with syrup. Each chews by himself. All syrup is too sweet.
Every cloud has shed rain. Every room is too square. Every
forehead is against. Every child has two fathers. Every head
is somewhere else. Every witch burns better. And that
for three weeks, breakfast for breakfast: Each chewing by
himself. The triangle play is still on the program. Secret and
semi-overt designs to turn the farce into a one-man
play: Jochen Sawatzki soliloquizes as he cooks sugarbeets.
Into a whispering twosome: Walterkins and Ingemouse sell a
dog, grow rich and happy; but Matern doesn't want to sell
and turn into a whispering twosome, he'd rather be alone
with the dog. Sick of rubbing shoulders.

Meanwhile, outside the square bedroom-livingroom, that is
to say, between Fliesteden and Büsdorf, between Ingen-
dorf and Glessen, and similarly between Rommerskirchen,
Pulheim, and Quadrath-Ichendorf, a hard postwar winter has
set in. Snow is falling for reasons of de-Nazification: everybody is putting objects and facts out into the severe
wintry countryside to be snowed under.

Matern and Sawatzki have made a little birdhouse for the
innocent birds, who aren't to blame. They are planning to

set it up in the garden so they can watch it from the kitchen window. Sawatzki reminisces: "I've never seen so much snow piled up except once. That was in '37-'38, the time we paid Fatso a visit on Steffensweg. It was snowing like today, it just went on snowing and snowing."

Later on, he's down in the laundry room, corking two-quart bottles. Meanwhile the stay-at-home couple have counted all the outdoor sparrows. By that time their love needs an airing. They and the dog make tracks in the famous triangle: Fliesteden-Büsdorf-Stommeln, but see none of those villages, because of the snow drifting and steaming round about. Along the Büsdorf-Stommeln highway, only the telegraph poles coming from Bergheim-Erft and running toward Worringen on the Rhine, remind Walterkins and Ingemouse that this winter is numbered, that the snow is earthly, and that under the snow sugarbeets once grew, on whose coveted substance they are still living; all four of them, for, says he, the dog needs proper care; whereas she says we ought to sell it, it's a revolting mutt, she doesn't love anybody but him him him: "If it weren't so cold, I'd do it with you right here in the open, day and night, under the open sky, in the bosom of nature—but the dog has to go, see? He gets on my nerves."

Pluto is still black. The snow becomes him. Ingemouse wants to cry, but it's too cold. Matern is patient and speaks, between one-sidedly snow-laden telegraph poles, about parting, which must always be anticipated. He also pours forth his favorite poet. Self-immortelle, says the leavetaker, and: Last rose's dying. However, he doesn't lose himself in the causal-genetic, but transfers in the nick of time to the ontic. Ingemouse loves it when, snapping snowflakes, he roars, grinds, hisses, and squeezes out strange words: "I exist self-grounded! World never is, but worldeth. Freedom is freedom to the I. I essent. The projecting I as projecting midst. I, localized and encompassed. I, world-project! I, source of grounding! I, possibility—soil—identification! I, GROUND, GROUNDING IN THE GROUNDLESS!"

Ingemouse learns the meaning of these obscure words shortly before Christmas. Though she has got together any number of attractive and useful little presents, he leaves. He shoves off—"Take me with you!"—He wants to celebrate Christmas, I I I, alone with the dog—"Take me with you!"— Consequently, lamentations in the snow shortly before Stommeln: "Me with you!" But thinly as she threads her little voice into his hairy masculine ear: Every train pulls in. Every train pulls out. Ingemouse stays behind.

He who had come to judge, with a black dog and with names incised in his heart, spleen, and kidneys, leaves the sugarbeet environment and takes the train, after crossing off the names of Jochen Sawatzki and wife, to Cologne on the Rhine. In the holy Central Station, in view of the avenging double finger, master and dog stand once again centrally on six feet.

THIRD TO EIGHTY-FOURTH MATERNIAD

This was Matern's idea: We, Pluto and I, will celebrate Christmas all alone with sausage and beer in the big silent drafty holy Catholic waiting room in Cologne. We will think, alone, in the midst of humanity, about Ingemouse and Ingepussy, about ourselves and the Glad Tidings. But things turn out differently, they always do: There in Cologne's tiled men's toilet a message has been scratched on the wall in the sixth enameled bay from the right. Amid the usual meaningless outcries and proverbs Matern reads, after buttoning up, the significant entry: Captain Erich Hufnagel, Altena, Lenneweg 4.

And so they celebrate Christmas Eve not in Cologne's Central Station, but with a family in the Sauerland. A hilly wooded Christmas countryside, where for the rest of the year it mostly rains. A wretched climate that induces specifically regional ailments: isolated forest Westphalians succumb to melancholy and work and drink too-much too-quickly too-cheap.

127

To avoid too much sitting, master and dog leave the train in Hohenlimburg and start uphill early in the Holy Night. An arduous climb, for here too snow has fallen abundantly and gratis. Across Hohbräcker Rücken and on toward Wibblingswerde, Matern recites himself and Pluto through a forest made for robbers: by turns Franz and Karl Moor invoke fate, Amalie, and the gods: "Another complainant against God!—Continue." Step by step. Snow grinds, stars grind, Franz Moor grinds, virgin branches grind, nature grinds: "Do I hear you hissing, adders of the abyss?"—but from the sparkling valley of the Lenne Altena's unsmelted bells ring in the second postwar Christmas.

Lenneweg leads from homeofmyown to homeofmyown. Every homeofmyown has already lighted its Christmas tree candles. All Christmas angels lisp. All doors can be opened: Captain Hufnagel, wearing bedroom slippers, opens in person.

This time it doesn't smell of sugarbeets but instantly and overpoweringly of gingerbread. The slippers are new. The Hufnagels have already distributed their Christmas gifts. Master and dog are requested to wipe their six feet on the doormat. Without effort it becomes manifest that Frau Dorothea Hufnagel has been made happy with an immersion heater. The thirteen-year-old Hans-Ulrich in turn is immersed in a book on submarine warfare, and Elke, the gorgeous daughter, is trying out, on Christmas wrapping paper which in her mother's opinion really ought to be smoothed out and put away for next Christmas, a genuine Pelikan fountain pen. In capitals she writes: ELKE ELKE ELKE.

Without moving his shoulders, Matern looks round and round. Familiar environment. So here we are. Don't bother. Won't be staying long. No time for visitors, especially the visitor who has come on Christmas Eve to judge: "Well, Captain Hufnagel? Memory need refreshing? You look bewildered. Glad to help you: 22nd AA Regiment, Kaiserhafen battery. Magnificent country: lumber piles, water rats, Air Force auxiliaries, volunteers, crow shooting, pile of bones across the way, stank whichever way the wind was blowing, I initiated operation raspberry drop, I was your first sergeant: Matern, Tech Sergeant Matern reporting. The fact is that once, in the area of your excellent battery, I shouted something about Reich, nation, Führer, mound of bones. Unfortunately my poem didn't appeal to you. But that didn't prevent you from writing it down with a fountain pen. It was a Pelikan too, just like the young lady's. And then you sent in a report: court-martial, demotion, punitive battalion, mine removal, suicide team. All that because you with your Pelikan fountain pen . . ."

However, it's not the indicted wartime fountain pen, but a blameless postwar fountain pen that Matern grabs out of warm Elkefingers and crushes, smearing his fingers with ink. Phooey!

Captain Hufnagel grasps the situation in a flash. Frau Hufnagel doesn't grasp anything at all, but does the right thing: presuming the intruder in her fragile Christmas room to be a slave laborer from the East, now masterless, she holds out, with bravely trembling hands, the brand-new immersion heater, expecting the brute to blow off steam by demolishing this household utensil. But Matern, misjudged on account of his outspread inky fingers, declines to be fed the first thing that comes to mind. In a pinch he might find the Christmas tree to his taste, or maybe the chairs, or the whole kit and boodle: How much cozy comfort can you stand?

Fortunately Captain Hufnagel, who has a position in the civilian administration of the Canadian occupation authorities and is able to treat himself and his family to a genuine peacetime Christmas—he's even managed to scare up some nut butter!—takes a different and more civilized view: "On the one hand—and on the other hand. After all, there are two sides to every question. But meanwhile, Matern, won't you be seated. Very well, stand if you prefer. Well then, on the one hand, of course, you're perfectly; but on the other hand—whatever injustice you've—it was I who saved you from. Perhaps you are unaware that in your case the death penalty, and if my testimony hadn't led the court-martial to remove your case from the jurisdiction of the special court . . . Very well, you won't believe me, you've been through too much. I don't expect you to. However—and I'm saying this tonight, on Christmas Eve, in full consciousness—if not for me you wouldn't be standing here playing the raving Beckmann. Excellent play, incidentally. Took the whole family to see it in Hagen, pathetic little theater. Goes straight to the heart. Weren't you a professional actor? What a part that would be for you. That Borchert hits the nail on the head. Haven't we all of us been through it, myself too? Didn't we all become strangers to ourselves and our loved ones while we were out there at the front? I came back four months ago. French prison camp. Take it from me! Bad Kreuznach, if that rings a bell. But even that's better than. That's what we had coming to us if we hadn't cleared out of the Vistula sector before. Anyway, there I stood empty-handed with nothingness literally staring me in the face. My business gone, my little house occupied by Canadians, wife and children evacuated to Espel in the mountains, no coal, nothing but trouble with the authorities, in short, a Beckmann situation straight out of *Outside the Door*! And so, my dear Matern—won't you please be seated—I am doubly, triply, aware how you. After all I knew you in the 22nd AA Regiment as a serious young man, who liked to get to the bottom of things. I trust and hope you haven't changed. And so let us be Christians and treat this holy night as it deserves. My dear Herr Matern, from the bottom of my heart and in the name of my cherished family, I wish you a merry and a blessed Christmas."

And in this spirit the evening passes: Matern cleans up his fingers in the kitchen with pumice stone, sits down freshly combed at the family board, allows Hans-Ulrich to pet Pluto, cracks, in the absence of a proper nutcracker, walnuts with his hands for the whole Hufnagel family, receives a present of some socks, washed only once, from Frau Dorothea, promises the gorgeous Elkedaughter a new Pelikan fountain pen, tells stories about his medieval forebears, robbers and heroes of independence, until weariness sets in, sleeps with the dog in the attic, has dinner with the family on the first day of Christmas: sauerbraten with mashed potatoes; on the second day of Christmas barters two packs of Camels on Altena's black market for an almost new Mont-Blanc fountain pen, in the evening tells the assembled family the rest of his stories about the Vistula estuary and the heroes of independence Simon and Gregor Materna, plans, at a late hour when every weary head lies elsewhere, to deposit stocking-footed the Mont-Blanc fountain pen outside Elke's bedroom door; but instead of co-operating, the boards creak, whereupon a soft "Come in" threads its way through the keyhole. Not every room is barred. And so in his stocking feet he enters Elke's bedchamber to bestow. But he's welcome there and able to take vengeance on the father by: Elkeblood flows demonstrably: 128

"You're the first that ever. On Christmas Eve the moment you, and wouldn't even take your hat off. And now do you think I'm a bad girl? It's not the way I usually, and my girl friend always says. Are you as happy as I am now, without any other desire, except only. Do you know what? When I'm through with school, I'm going to travel, travel the whole time! Say, what's that? Is it a scar, and this one here too. Oh, that awful war! It didn't spare anybody. And now what? Are you going to stay here? It can be awfully nice around here when it's not raining: the woods, the animals, the mountains, the Lenne, the High Sondern, and all the dams, and Lüdenschied is an awfully pretty place, and wherever you look, woods and mountains and lakes and rivers and deer and dams and woods and mountains, oh, please stay!"

Nevertheless Matern, stocking-footed with black dog, goes his way. He even carries the almost new Mont-Blanc fountain pen away to Cologne on the Rhine; for he hadn't gone to the Sauerland to make presents, but to judge the father by dishonoring: Only God in His heaven looked on, this time framed and glassed above the bookshelf.

And so justice pursues its course. Cologne's station toilet, that warm Catholic place, speaks of a Sergeant Leblich, resident in Bielefeld, where underwear blooms and a children's choir sings. Accordingly, a long trip on rails with return ticket in pocket, up three flights, second door on the right, straight into the environment without knocking: but Erwin Leblich, through no fault of his own, has had an accident at work and is lying in bed with a high-hoisted plaster leg and an angular plaster arm, but with powers of speech unimpaired. "All right, do anything you please with me, let your dog eat plaster. All right. I chewed you out and made you doubletime with your gas mask on; but two years before that somebody chewed me out and made me doubletime with my gas mask on; and the same thing happened to him: running and singing with his gas mask on. So what the hell do you want?"

Questioned about his wishes, Matern looks around and wants Leblich's wife; but Veronika Leblich had died in '44 in the air-raid shelter. Whereupon Matern asks for Leblich's daughter; but the six-year-old child has recently started school and gone to live with her grandmother in Lemgo. But Matern is determined to build a monument to his vengeance at any price; he kills the Leblichs' canary, who has managed to come through the war in good shape, despite strafing and saturation bombing.

When Erwin Leblich asks him to bring him a glass of water from the kitchen, he leaves the sickroom, picks up a glass in the kitchen with his left hand, fills it under the faucet, and on the way back, quickly in passing, reaches into the bird cage with his right hand: except for the dripping faucet, only God in His heaven looks upon Matern's fingers.

The same onlooker sees Matern in Göttingen. There, without the help of the dog, he wrings the neck of some chickens —five of them—belonging to Paul Wesseling, an unmarried postman: because Wesseling, when still an MP, had picked him up in a brawl in Le Havre. The consequence had been three days in solitary; in addition Matern, who was to be rewarded with a transfer to Officers Training School for his resolute conduct during the French campaign, was prevented by this blot on his record from becoming a lieutenant.

The following day, between Cologne's cathedral and Cologne's Central Station, he sells the neck-wrung chickens unplucked for two hundred and eighty reichsmarks. His treasury is in need of replenishment; for the trip from Cologne to Stade near Hamburg, first class with dog and return, costs a tidy sum.

There behind the Elbe dike lives Wilhelm Dimke with dim wife and deaf father. Dimke, the assistant magistrate who had served as associate judge on the special court in Danzig-Neugarten while a case of undermining military discipline and insulting the Führer was being tried, had threatened Matern with the death penalty until, on the advice of Matern's former battery commander, the case was transferred to the competent court-martial. From Stargard, where he had last participated in the deliberations of a special court, Associate Judge Dimke had succeeded in rescuing a large stamp collection, possibly of considerable value. On the table, between half-emptied coffee cups, lie the albums: the Dimkes are engaged in cataloguing their possessions. Environmental studies? Matern has no time. Since Dimke remembers lots of cases on which he has deliberated, but not Matern's, Matern, by way of refreshing Dimke's memory, tosses album after album into the blazing pot-bellied stove, concluding with the colorful and exotic colonial issues: the stove is delighted, warmth spreads through the overcrowded fugitives' room; in the end, he even tosses in the stock of adhesive corners and the tweezers; but Wilhelm Dimke still can't remember. His dim wife is in tears. Dimke's deaf father utters the word: "Vandalism." On top of the cupboard lie shriveled winter apples. No one offers Matern any. Matern, who had come to judge, feels unappreciated and leaves the Dimke family with a dog who has shown little interest, but without saying good-by.

O eternal tiled men's toilet of Cologne Central Station. It has a memory. It doesn't lose a name: for as previously in the ninth and twelfth bays the name of the MP and the associate judge were inscribed, so now the name and address of

Alfred Lüxenich, sometime special judge, are etched legibly and precisely in the enamel of the second bay from the left: Aachen, Karolingerstrasse 112.

There Matern finds himself in musical surroundings. District Magistrate Lüxenich is of the opinion that music, the great consoler, can help us to live through hard and troubled times. He advises Matern, who has come to judge the former special judge, to listen first to the second movement of a Schubert trio: Lüxenich is a violin virtuoso; a Herr Petersen is no mean hand at the piano; Fräulein Oelling plies the cello; and Matern, with restless dog, listens resignedly, though his heart, his spleen, his kidneys are good and sick of it and are beginning in their introverted way to cough. Then Matern's dog and Matern's three sensitive organs are treated to the third movement of the same trio. Whereupon District Magistrate Lüxenich is not quite satisfied with himself or with Fräulein Oelling's cello playing: "My goodness! Let's have the third movement again; and then our Herr Petersen, who, it may interest you to know, teaches mathematics at the local high school, will play you the Kreutzer Sonata; I for my part should like to conclude the evening, before we enjoy a glass of Moselle together, with a Bach violin sonata. Now there's a piece for connoisseurs!"

All music begins. Unmusical from the waist up, Matern falls under the sway of classical rhythm. All music feeds comparisons. He and the cello between Fräulein Oelling's knees. All music opens up abysses. It tugs and pulls and supplies the background for silent films. The Great Masters. Imperishable heritage. Leitmotives and murder motives. God's pious Minstrel. If in doubt, Beethoven. A prey to harmony. It's lucky nobody's singing; for he sang silvery bubbling: *Dona nobis*. Voice always in the upper story. A *Kyrie* that could pull your teeth. An *Agnus Dei* that melted like butter. Like a cutting torch: a boy soprano. For in every fat man a thin man is hidden, who wants to come out and sing higher than buzz saw and band saw. The Jews do not sing; he sang. Tears roll down over the letter scales, heavy tears. Only the truly unmusical can cry over serious classical German music. Hitler cried when his mother died and in 1918 when Germany collapsed; and Matern, who has come to judge with black dog, sheds tears while Dr. Petersen, the school-teacher, plays the genius's piano sonata note for note. While District Magistrate Lüxenich bows the Bach violin sonata note for note on an instrument that has come through the war safe and sound, he is unable to dam the rising torrent.

Who is ashamed of manly tears? Who still has hatred in his heart as St. Cecilia glides through the music room? Who is not thankful to Fräulein Oelling when, all-understanding, she seeks Matern out, lets her woman's gaze strike roots, lays her well-manicured but clawlike cellist's fingers on his hand, and with whispered words plows Matern's soul? "Open your heart, dear friend. Please. You must have a great sorrow. May we share it? Ah, what can be going on inside you? When you came in with that dog, I felt as if a world were crashing down on me, a world torn by grief, lashed by storms, filled with despair. But now that I see you are a man, a human being, who has come among us—a stranger, yet somehow close to us—now that we have been privileged to help him with the modest means at our disposal, I find faith again, and courage. Courage to lift you from despair. For you too, my friend, ought to. What was it that moved you so deeply? Memories? Dark days rising up before your mind's eye? Is it some loved one, long dead, who holds your soul in thrall?"

Then Matern speaks bit by bit. He sets building blocks one on another. But the building he has in mind isn't the Danzig-Neugarten Courthouse with the Special Court on the fourth floor; rather, it is the thickset Church of St. Mary, which he erects Gothically, brick by brick. And in that acoustically superb vaulted church—cornerstone laid on March 28, 1343—a fat boy, supported by the main organ and the echo organ, sings a slender Credo. "Yes, I loved him. And they took him away from me. As a boy, I defended him with my fists, for we Materns, all my ancestors, Simon Materna, Gregor Materna, have always protected the weak. But the others were stronger, and I could only look on helplessly as terror broke that voice. Eddi, my Eddi! Since then a lot of things have broken inside me incurably: dissonance, ostracism, shards, fragments of myself, that can never be put together again."

At this point Fräulein Oelling disagrees and Herren Lüxenich and Petersen, sympathizing over sparkling Moselle, side with her: "Dear friend, it's never too late. Time heals wounds. Music heals wounds. Faith heals wounds. Art heals wounds. Especially love heals wounds!" Omnistickum. Gum arabic. The glue with the iron grip. Spittle.

Still incredulous, Matern is willing to make a try. At a

late hour, when both gentlemen are beginning to doze over their Moselle, he offers Fräulein Oelling his strong arm and the powerful jaws of his dog Pluto as an escort home through the nocturnal Aachen. Since their path takes them into no park and past no riverside meadows, Matern sits Fräulein Oelling—she's heavier than she sounded—down on a garbage can. She expresses no objection to offal and stench. Yes says she to the fermenting refuse, demanding only that love be stronger than the ugliness of this world: "Throw me, roll shove carry me wherever you please, into the gutter, into the foulest of places, down into cellars unspeakable; as long as it's you who do the throwing, rolling, shoving, and carrying."

Of this there can be no doubt: she rides the garbage can but doesn't make an inch of headway, because Matern, who had come to judge, is leaning against it three-legged; an uncomfortable position which only the desperate can profitably maintain for any length of time.

This time—it isn't raining snowing moonshining—someone besides God in His heaven is looking on: Pluto on four legs. He is guarding the garbage-can horse, the garbage-can equestrienne, the horse trainer, and a cello full of all-healing music.

Matern spends six weeks in Fräulein Oelling's care. He learns that her first name is Christine and that she doesn't like to be called Christel. They live in her attic room, where it smells of environment, rosin, and gum arabic. This is rough on Herren Lüxenich and Petersen. The district magistrate and his friend have to do without their trios. Matern punishes a former special court judge by forcing him to practice duets from February to early April; and when Matern leaves Aachen with dog and three freshly ironed shirts— Cologne has called him and he responds—a district magistrate and a schoolteacher have to find many comforting, pieces-mending, and faith-restoring words, before Fräulein Oelling is in any condition to round out the trio with her wellnigh flawless cello playing.

All music stops sooner or later, but the tiled men's toilet in Cologne Central Station will never for all eternity stop whispering names that are incised in the inner organs of railway traveler Walter Matern: now he has to pay a visit to former Kreisleiter Sellke in Oldenburg. Suddenly he realizes how big Germany still is; for from Oldenburg, where there are still honest-to-goodness court barbers and court pastry cooks, he must hurry via Cologne to Munich. There, according to the station toilet, lives his good old friend Otto Warnke, with whom he has to wind up certain discussions begun long ago at the bar of the Kleinhammerpark. The city on the Isar proves a disappointment—two days are more than enough; but he becomes very familiar with the hills of the upper Weser, for in Witzenhausen, as Matern can't help finding out in Cologne, Bruno Dulleck and Egon Dulleck, the so-called Dulleck brothers, have holed up. For a good two weeks, for all three soon run out of topics of conversation, he plays skat with them, after which he turns to further visitations. Next comes the city of Saarbrücken, where he enters the sphere of Willy Eggers, whom he tells about Jochen Sawatzki, Otto Warnke, Bruno and Egon Dulleck, all old friends: thanks to Matern, they are able to write each other postcards with greetings from buddies.

But even Matern doesn't travel for nothing. As souvenirs or spoils of the chase—for Matern is traveling with dog, to judge—he brings back to Cologne: a tightly knitted winter muffler, donated by former Kreisleiter Sellke's secretary; a Bavarian loden coat, for Otto Warnke's cleaningwoman possessed a supply of warm outer garments; and from Saarbrücken, where Willy Eggers briefs him on the frontier traffic between Gross-Rosseln and Klein-Rosseln, he brings, because the Dulleck brothers in the hills of the upper Weser had nothing to offer him but country air and three-handed skat, a good case of urban and French-occupied gonorrhea.

DON'T TURN AROUND—THE CLAP'S GOING AROUND. With pistol thus loaded, with barbed scourge of love, with serum-maddened hypodermic, Matern with dog visits the cities of Bückeburg and Celle, the lonely Hunsrück, the smiling Bergstrasse, Upper Franconia including the Fichtel Mountains, even Weimar in the Russian occupation zone—where he stops at the Hotel Elephant—and the Bavarian Forest, an underdeveloped region.

Wherever the two of them, master and dog, set their six feet, whether on the rugged Alb, on East Frisian marshland, or in the destitute villages of the Westerwald, everywhere the clap has a different name: here they say dripping Johnny, there they warn against lovesnot; here they count candledrops, there they tell of snipe honey; goldenrod and his lordship's cold, widow's tears and pistachio oil are pithy regional terms, as are cavalryman and runner; Matern calls it "the milk of vengeance."

Equipped with this product, he visits all four occupation zones and the quartered remains of the former national capital. Here Pluto is taken with nervous jitters, which subside only when they are west of the Elbe again, still delivering the milk of vengeance, which is nothing other than sweat gathered from the dripping forehead of blind Justitia.

Don't turn around, the clap's going around. And faster and faster, because Matern's avenging apparatus gives the avenger no rest and, leaping ahead of vengeance just inflicted, is off to a new start: on to Freudenstadt; around the corner, as it were, to Rendsburg; from Passau to Kleve; Matern doesn't shrink back from changing trains four times and even makes his way straddle-legged on foot.

Anyone who takes a look at the statistics on venereal disease in Germany during the first postwar years will be struck by a sudden increase in this benign but troublesome venereal ailment beginning in May '47. The curve attains its apogee at the end of October in the same year, then falls rapidly, and finally flattens off at its springtime level. The determining factors in the minor fluctuations that occur from then on appear to be demographic shifts and changes in the stations of the occupation troops, and no longer Matern who, privately and without a license, journeyed through the land to cross off names with a gonococcus-loaded syringe and to de-Nazify a large circle of acquaintances. Accordingly Matern, when postwar adventures are being retailed among friends, refers to his six-months case of gonorrhea as antifascist gonorrhea; and indeed, Matern was able to subject the female relations of former Party mediumshots to an influence which can be described, by extension, as salutary.

But who will cure him? Who will draw the pain from the root of him who has put the plague into circulation? Physician, heal thyself.

Now after forays through Teutoburg Forest and a brief stay in Detmold, he is in a little village near Camp Munster, where the rolling stone started rolling. Figures back and compares with his memo book: all around him heather in bloom and goldenrod as well, for in among the heath sheep and the heath peasants Matern finds any number of old friends; among others, Hauptbannführer Uli Göpfert who, in co-operation with Jungbannführer Wendt, had year after year directed the popular tent camps in Poggenkrug Forest near Oliva. He is living here in Elmke without Otto Wendt, but attached to a knot of long hair that formerly had been leading German girls, in two rooms which actually have electric light.

Pluto has plenty of freedom. Göpfert on the other hand sits fettered near the stove, putting on peat that he cut in the spring, grumbling at himself and the world, cussing out swine whom he never calls by name, and pondering: What now? Should he emigrate? Should he join the Christian Democrats, the Social Democrats, or the lost squadron of olden days? Later, after ups and downs, he will join the Liberals and carve out a career for himself in North Rhenish Westphalia as a so-called Free Democrat; but for the present—and here in Elmke—he is obliged to doctor himself without results for a case of gonorrhea brought into the house by a sick friend with a healthy dog.

Sometimes, when Frau Vera Göpfert is teaching school and her bun isn't there to tempt dripping Johnny, Göpfert and Matern sit peaceably by the warm stove, making each other soothing peat poultices, doctoring the selfsame misery in the manner of the heath peasants, and cussing out swine, some of them nameless and others who have made quite a name for themselves.

"How those bastards screwed us!" laments the former Hauptbannführer. "And we believed and hoped and trusted implicitly, we went along blindly, and now, what now?"

Matern reels off names from Sawatzki to Göpfert. So far he has been able to cross off some eighty entries in his heart, spleen, and kidneys. No end of common acquaintances. Göpfert remembers, for instance, the band leader of SA Brigade 6, Erwin Bukolt was his name: "That, my boy, wasn't in '36, but exactly on April 20th, '38, because believe it or not, you were there on monitor duty. At ten A.M. in Jäschkental Forest. Führerweather. Stage set up in the woods. Young people's Eastland celebration with a cantata by Baumann: 'Call from the East.' A chorus of a hundred and twenty boys and a hundred and eighty girls. All first-rate voices. Parade on three terraces. Out of the woods in measured tread over beechnuts from the year before. The girls were all doing their year of farm duty. I can still see them: full blouses, red and blue aprons and kerchiefs. That rhythmic marching flow. The merging of the choruses. On the main terrace stands the small boys' chorus, and after I have made a brief introductory speech, they ask the fateful questions. Two large boys' choruses and two large girls' choruses give the answers slowly and word for word. In between—do you remember?—a cuckoo called from the Gutenberg clearing. Regularly in the pauses between fateful questions and fateful answers: Cuckoo! But it doesn't upset those four boys, the solo speakers on the second terrace, raised above the choruses. On the third terrace stands the brass band. You fellows from the Langfuhr-North SA Sturm are standing at the lower left held in reserve behind Bukolt's band, because when it's over you'll have to organize the homeward march. Man, that was good! Jäschkental Forest has amazing echoes: they come back from the Gutenberg clearing, where the cuckoo goes on and on, from the Erbsberg, and from Friedrichshöhe. The cantata is about the destiny of the East. A horseman rides through German lands, proclaiming: 'The Reich is bigger than its borders.' The choruses and the four main questioners ask questions which the horseman answers as though hammering on metal: 'Yours to hold the fort and the gate to the East.' Slowly the questions and answers culminate in a single ardent profession of faith. Finally the cantata rises to a mighty close with a hymn to the Greater Germany. Echo effects. It was a beech forest. First-rate voices. The cuckoo didn't bother anybody. Führerweather. You were there too, my boy. Don't kid yourself. In 1938. On April 20th. Lousy shit. We wanted to set out for the Eastland with Hölderlin and Heidegger in our knapsacks. Now we're sitting here in the West with the clap."

Thereupon Matern grinds his teeth, rubbing East against West. He's fed up on avenging nettle juice, on the milk of vengeance, on love pearls and candledrops. Low and peat-warm is the peasants' room where he stands straddle-legged after four and eighty Materniads. Enough enough! cries his pain-inhabited root.

Enough is never enough! admonish other names incised in heart, spleen, and kidneys.

"Two shots of cement and every hour a fresh peat poultice," laments former Hauptbannführer Göpfert, "and still no improvement. Penicillin's out of sight and even belladonna's very scarce."

Thereupon Matern with pants wide open strides toward a white-washed wall that bounds the room on the east. This festive hour will have to get along without cuckoo and brass bands. Nevertheless he raises his honey-sweating penis to eastward. "The Reich is bigger than its borders!" Nine million refugees' identity cards pile up westward of Matern: "Yours to hold the fort and the gate to the East!" A horseman rides through German lands, but in the east he looks not for a door but for a simple wall socket. And between the socket and his penis contact is established. Matern, to put it plainly, pisses into the socket and obtains—thanks to an unbroken stream of water—a powerful, electric, skyhigh-sending, and salutary shock; for as soon as he can stand up again, pale and trembling under hair aghast, all the honey drains. The milk of vengeance curdles. The love pearls roll into cracks in the floor. The goldenrod withers. Dripping Johnny breathes again. Runner marks time. The widow's tears dry up. His lordship's cold has been cured by an electric shock. The physician has healed himself. Pluto has looked on. Former Hauptbannführer Göpfert has also looked on. And naturally God in His heaven has looked on too. Only Frau Vera Göpfert has seen nothing; for when she comes home from the village school with ample bun, all she finds of Matern is rumors and undarned woolen socks: Cured but unredeemed, master and dog leave the withered Lüneberg Heath. From this moment on, the clap is on the decline in Germany. Every pestilence purifies. Every plague has its day. Every joy is the last.

THE PHILOSOPHICAL EIGHTY-FIFTH AND THE CONFESSED EIGHTY-SIXTH MATERNIAD

What does Brauxel want? He's pestering the life out of Matern. As if it weren't bad enough vomiting up his guts for pages on end for a measly advance, now he has to send in a report every week: "How many pages today? How many tomorrow? Will the episode with Sawatzki and wife have consequences? Was snow falling when he began to shuttle back and forth between Freiburg im Breisgau and the ski slopes of Todtnau? In which bay of the men's toilet in Cologne Central Station did he find his travel order to the Black Forest? Written or scratched?"

O.K., Brauxel, here it is. Matern's excretion amounts to: Seven pages today. Seven pages tomorrow. Seven pages yesterday. Every day seven pages. Every episode has consequences. Snow wasn't falling between Todtnau and Freiburg. It is falling. In the twelfth bay from the left it wasn't written, it is written. Matern writes in the present: All Holzwege, all woodcutter's tracks, lead astray.

Crowds at every bay. The damp cold fills the men's toilet, for the cathedral is unheated. Matern doesn't shove, but when at long last he has occupied his bay, the twelfth from the left, he's in no hurry to leave it: Man is entitled to a resting place on earth. But already they're jostling behind him. All right, so he isn't entitled. "Hurry up, buddy. We gotta go too, buddy. He ain't pissing no more, he's just looking. What's so interesting to look at, buddy? Tell us about it."

Fortunately Pluto assures the reading Matern of privacy and leisure. Seven times he is able to lap up the delicate inscription that seems to have been breathed on the wall with silver point. After so much lust and pestilence he is comforted by spiritual fare. The passed water of all men in this world steams. But Matern stands alone and copies the subtle trace of the silver point in heart, spleen, and kidneys. The steaming Catholic men's toilet is a steaming Catholic kitchen. Behind Matern push cooks bent on cooking: "Hurry up, buddy. You're not the only pebble on the beach, buddy! Love your neighbor, buddy!"

But Matern stands central. The large ruminant ruminates every word in the twelfth bay from the left: "The Alemannic Stockingcap is capping between Todtnau and Freidburg."

Thus edified, Matern turns away. "At last!" He holds Pluto to heel. "Think it over, dog, but not with reason! He was with me when I flew gliders and played chess. With him—soul in soul, arm in arm—I roamed the streets and the waterfront. Eddi passed him on to me as a joke. Words that read like soft butter. He was good for headache and warded off thought when Eddi ratiocinated about sparrows. Think back, dog, but without reason. I read him aloud to Langfuhr SA Sturm 84. They were doubled up at the bar, I had them whinnying out of *Being and Time*. He wears a stockingcap that's longer than any march forward or backward. I took him with me in my musette bag from Warsaw to Dunkirk, from Salonika to Odessa, from the Mius front to Kaiserhafen battery, from police headquarters to Kurland, and from there—those are long distances—to the Ardennes; with him I deserted all the way to southern England, I dragged him to Camp Munster, Eddi bought him secondhand in Tagnetergasse: a copy of the first edition, published in 1927, dedicated to little Husserl, whom he later with his stockingcap . . . Get this straight, dog: he was born in Messkirch. That's near Braunau on the Inn. He and the Other had their umbilical cords cut in the same stockingcap year. He and the Other Guy invented each other. One day He and the Other will stand on the same pedestal. He is calling me, he is always calling me. Think it over, dog, but without reason! Where will the train take us this very day?"

They get out in Freiburg im Breisgau and drop in at the university. The environment is still ringing with the turgid speech he delivered in '33—"Our own selves: that is our goal!"—but there's no stockingcap hanging in any of the lecture halls. "He isn't allowed to any more, because he . . ."

Master and dog ask their way and find a villa with wrought-iron garden gate in front of it. They bellow and bark in the quiet residential quarter: "Open up, Stockingcap! Matern is here, manifesting himself as the call of care. Open up!"

The villa remains wintry still. No window is yellowed by electric light. But a note stuck to the mailbox beside the iron gate yields information: "The cap is capping on the ski slopes."

And so master and dog have to climb on six feet in the shadow of the Feldberg. Above Todtnau the snowstorm buffets them. Philosopher's weather—insight weather! Swirls in swirls, grounding. And no Black Forest fir to give information. If not for the dog without reason, they would be lost in errancy. Nose to the ground, he finds the ski hut, shelter from the wind. And instantly big words and dog's barking are clipped by the storm: "Open up, Stockingcap! Matern is here, manifesting revenge! We who have come here to enact our Being in Materniads and make visible Simon Materna, the hero of independence. He forced the cities of Danzig, Dirschau, and Elbing to their knees, sent Drehergasse and Petersiliengasse up in flames; that's what's going to happen to your cap, you skiing Nothing—open up."

Though the hut remains barred, doweled, chinkless, and inhospitable, there is a note, snow-powdered and barely legible, stuck on barkless Black Forest wood: "Stockingcap has to read Plato in the valley."

Downhill. This is no Erbsberg, it's the Feldberg. Without map through Todtnau and Cry-of-Anguish—such are the names of the places around here—to Care, Overclimb, Nihilation. For that very reason Plato fouled up. Why shouldn't *he*? What Syracuse was to the one philosopher, a rectoral address was to the other. Therefore settle down in the sticks. Why do we stay in the sticks? Because Stockingcap sticks to them. When he's not skiing up top, he's reading Plato down below. That is the subtle provincial distinction. A little game among philosophers: Peekaboo, here I am. Peekaboo, I fooled you: up down—down up. Applesauce! O Matern, seven times down the Feldberg without ever overtaking himself! Cap, capping, uncapped, cappedness: always ahead of oneself, never being-with, never being-already-in, no present-at-hand togetherness, always away-from-oneself-toward, neither curable nor incurable, hopelessly surrounded by fir environment, exceptionless. Once again Matern plummets from lofty attunedness to rockbottom contingency without at-handness; for in the valley, on the little square note beside the garden door, an already familiar script whispers: "Stockingcap, like all greatness, is out in the storm." And up above, storm-ventilated, he reads: "Stockingcap has to rake the field path below."

What hard work is the execution of vengeance! Rage snaps at snowflakes. Hatred sabers icicles. But the firs nihilate and guard the riddle of the enduring: if he isn't erring below, he's enacting his Being up above; if he isn't coming-to-be up top, he's grounding on a slip of paper beside the iron gate: "The amplitude of all the Black Forest firs that dwell around Stockingcap confers world and powder snow." Skiingweather skiingweather! O Matern, what will you do when after seven times up and down the Feldberg you haven't overtaken yourself, when seven times you have had to read down below: "Stockingcap up top" and seven times up top the words have flickered before your eyes: "Down below Stockingcap manifests Nothing."

Then in the quiet residential quarter master and dog stand panting outside a particular villa: exhausted duped fir-crazed, hatred and rage try to piss into a mailbox. Shouting climbs iron fences, larded with pauses: "Say, where can I catch you, Cap? What book is bookmarked with your cap?—In what cap have you hidden the lime-sprinkled forgetful of Being? —How long was the stockingcap you strangled little Husserl with? How many of your teeth do I have to pull to turn thrownness into essent stockingcapped Being?"

That's a lot of questions, but don't let it worry you. Matern answers them all by himself. He's in the habit. The questions of one who always stands central—phenotype, self-point-possessed—are never at a loss for answers. Matern doesn't formulate, he acts with two paws. First the iron gate outside the garden of a certain villa is shaken and cursed. But no more Alemannic stockingcap language; Matern's vituperation is down-to-earth and autonomously idiomatic: "C'mon out, ya louse! I'll show ya, ya clunk! Ya slimy gazoop! Ya big beezack! Ya—hatrack. I'm gonna kick ya in the slats and cut yer bleeding heart out. I'm gonna unravel you like an old sock. I'm gonna make hamburger out of ya and feed ya to the dog in little pieces. We're fed up on thrownness and existence-into-nuttin. Matern's gonna getcha. Matern's gonna getcha. C'mon out, philospher! Matern's a philosopher too: Shoilem boil 'em."

These words and Matern's claws do the trick: not that the philosopher follows the friendly invitation and steps out of the villa with Alemannic stolidness, in stockingcap and buckled shoes; instead, Matern lifts the wrought-iron garden gate off its hinges. He brandishes it, and Pluto falls speechless, for several times Matern succeeds in shaking it at the sky. And when the sky, black and smelling of snow, won't relieve him of the gate, he hurls it into the garden: an amazing distance.

The wrecker brushes off his hands: "That's that!" The hero looks around for witnesses: "Did you see? That's the way Matern does it. Phenomenal!" The avenger savors the after-taste of accomplished revenge: "He's got his. Now we're quits." But aside from the dog, no one can testify that it happened thus and not otherwise; unless God, despite the snow in the air, was eavesdropping from upstairs: nihilating essentiating catching-cold.

And the police have no objections when Matern with dog wants to leave the city of Freiburg im Breisgau. He has to travel third class because the ups and downs have exhausted his treasury: he has had to spend one night in Todtnau, two in Cry-of-Anguish, and once each in Nihilation and Over-climb; that's the price of associating with philosophers—and were it nor for charitable women and tender-hearted young girls, master and dog would hunger thirst perish.

But they journey after him, eager to cool a brow over-heated by philosophical disputation, eager to win a man who has narrowly escaped being shanghaied by Transcend-ence back to earth and its double beds: cello-playing Fräulein Oelling, Captain Hufnagel's gorgeous daughter, the brown-haired secretary from Oldenburg, Warnke's curly black-haired cleaningwoman, as well as Gerda, who gave him the dripping Johnny between Völklingen and Saarbrücken, all whom he enriched with and without goldenrod now want him and only him: Ebeling's daughter-in-law from Celle; Grete Diering from Bückeburg; Budzinski's sister leaves lonely Huns-rück; Irma Jaeger the flowering Bergstrasse; Klingenberg's Upper Franconian daughters Christa and Gisela; from the Soviet zone comes Hildchen Wollschläger without Franz Wollschläger; Johanna Tietz is sick of living with her Tietz in the Bavarian Forest; in search of him go: a Princess von Lippe with her girl friend, daughter of an East Frisian hotel-keeper, women from Berlin and maidens from the Rhine. German women grope for Matern with the help of newspaper ads and detective agencies. They bait their hooks with re-wards. An iron will lurks in wait with a dissyllabic goal. They chase find corner him, try to strangle him with Vera Göpfert's copious hair. They snap at him with Irmapussies, Gretetraps, cleaningwomen's chasms, garbage-can covers, Elkecracks, housewives' shopping bags, Berlin rolls, princess-quiffs, fishcakes, and Silesian meat pudding. In compensation they bring with them: tobacco, socks, silver spoons, wedding rings, Wollschläger's pocket watch, Budzinski's gold cuff links, Otto Warnke's shaving soap, their brother-in-law's microscope, their husband's savings, the special judge's violin, the captain's Canadian currency, and hearts souls love.

Matern isn't always able to evade these riches. They wait, touching to look upon, between Cologne's Central Station and Cologne's immovable cathedral. Treasures demand to be admired in air-raid-shelter hotels and one-night hotels, on Rhine meadows and pine needles. They've also brought sausage skins for the dog, lest counterpart payments be dis-turbed by demanding dog muzzle: "Don't do the same thing twice, or you'll be doing the same thing twice."

And whenever he sets out to visit the quiet men's toilet alone with dog, to meditate and practice detachment, de-manding girlfingers housewifefingers princessfingers touch him in the bustling station hall: "Come. I know where. I know a janitor who rents. A girl friend of mine has gone away for a few days. I know a gravel pit they're not using any more. I've taken a place for us in. Only a little while. Time enough to unburden our hearts. Wollschläger sent me. I had no choice. Afterwards I'll go away, I promise. Come!"

As a result of all this solicitude, Matern goes to the dogs and Pluto gets fat. O recoiling vengeance! Rage bites cotton. Hate excretes love. The boomerang strikes when he thinks he has struck five and eighty times: DON'T DO THE SAME THING TWICE—IT'S NEVER THE SAME. For with the best of fare he loses weight: Göpfert's shirts have begun to fit him; cool and soothing as Otto Warnke's birch tonic is to his scalp, Matern's hair is falling. Bankrupt! And who should turn up as the receiver but his old friend dripping Johnny; for what he thought he had got rid of in the Bavarian Forest or in the District of Arich, reinfects him in Upper Franconia, the Soviet zone, the backwoods. Leitmotives and murder motives: six times, on dripping Johnny's account, he has to piss into wall sockets. It knocks him cold. It flattens him. Horse medicine cures him. Gonococci infect him. Electricity sends Matern for the count. Double beds transform a traveling avenger into a leaky Don Juan. Already he presents the saturated look. Already he talks glibly and seductively about love and death. He can turn on the tenderness without even looking. He's begun to fondle his clap like the favorite child of genius. Minor madness has dropped its visiting card. Soon he'll be wanting to emasculate himself after shaving, to throw his lopped-off phenotype to Leporello, to the dog.

Who will save Matern? For what is all presumptuous philosophy compared to a single bounceback man without reason! What is the sevenfold stockingcap-maddened ascent of the Feldberg compared to six contact-crazed light sockets! And to make matters worse, the blubbering: "Make me a baby. Spill me one. Knock me up. Be careful, don't waste any. Pump me full. Curette me. Clean me out. Ovaries!" Who saves Matern, combs away the dead hair, and buttons up his pants till the next time? Who is kind to him, selfless? Who puts himself between Matern and the hairy soggy Vienna rolls?

At most the dog. Pluto manages to avert the worst: He chases Otto Warnke's cleaningwoman and Göpfert's Vera, the one in April, the other in May, across the Rhine meadows out of a gravel pit where they've been trying to suck

Matern's spinal fluid and bite off his testicles. And Pluto manages to sniff about and make it known when one of them turns up with dripping Johnny's love pearls in her purse. He barks, growls, gets between, and with butting nose indicates the treacherous focus of pestilence. By unmasking Hildchen Wollschläger and the princess's girl friend, the servant spares his master two additional electric shocks; but even he cannot save Matern.

Cologne's double prongs see him thus: broken, cavern-eyed, bald at the temples, with Pluto, faithfulasadog, frolicking around him. And this picture of misery, so close to the footlights, starts out again, makes his way through the bustle of Central Station, resolved to descend to quiet regions, tiled, Catholic, and whispering; for Matern still senses the presence of names, painfully incised in internal organs and demanding to be crossed off—be it with trembling hand.

And step by step with knotted stick he almost makes it. Thus she sees him: man and stick with dog. The picture moves her. Without hesitation she, the sugarbeet woman with whom all his vengeance began, comes toward him: compassionate charitable motherly. Inge Sawatzki pushes a baby carriage, in which dwells a Novemberly sugarbeet bunny, who came into the world syrupsweet a year ago next July and since then has been called Walli, for Walburga; for such is Inge Sawatzki's certainty that little Walli's father answers to a name beginning with *W*, such as Walter—although Willibald and Wunibald, the saintly brothers of the great witch-banishing saint, makers to this day of Walburga Oil, a product still in demand, are closer to her from a Catholic point of view.

Matern stares darkly into the occupied baby carriage. Inge Sawatzki curtails the usual period of silent admiration. "Pretty baby, isn't she? You're not looking at all well. She'll be walking any day now. Don't worry. I don't want anything of you. But Jochen would be pleased. You look all worn out. Really, we're both so fond of you. Besides, it's sweet the way he takes care of the baby. An easy confinement. We were lucky. Was supposed to be in Cancer, but she turned out to be a Leo girl, with Libra in the ascendant. They have an easy time of it later on: usually pretty, domestic, adaptable, versatile, affectionate, and with all that, strong-willed. We're living over in Mülheim now. We can take the ferry if you like, sailing, sailing over the bounding main. You really need rest and care. Jochen's working in Leverkusen. I advised against it, because wherever he goes he gets mixed up in politics, and he swears by Reimann. My goodness, you look tired. We could take the train too, but I like the ferry. Oh, well, Jochen must know what he's doing. He says a man has to show his colors. After all you were in there too. Is that where you met or was it in the SA sturm? You're not saying a word. I really don't want anything of you. If you feel like it, we'll baby you for a couple of weeks. You need a rest. A homey place. We've got two and a half rooms. You'll have the attic room all to yourself. I'll leave you alone, honest. I love you. But in a perfectly peaceful way. Walli just smiled at you. Did you see? She's doing it again. Does the dog like babies? They say shepherds love children. I love you and the dog. And I wanted to sell him, remember, I was dumb in those days. You've got to do something to save your hair."

They go on board: mother and child—master and dog. The well-fed sun cooks Mülheim's ruins and Mülheim's meagerly fed consumers in the same pot. Never has Germany been so beautiful. Never has Germany been so healthy. Never have there been more expressive faces in Germany than in the days of the thousand and thirty-two calories. But Inge Sawatzki declares while the Mülheim ferry is docking: "We'll be getting new money pretty soon. Goldmouth even knows when. What, you don't know him? Everybody that knows which way is up around here knows him. Take my word for it, he's got a finger in everything. The whole black market, from Trankgasse to the Amis in Bremerhaven, takes its cue from Goldmouth. But he says it's on the way out. He says we should reconvert. The new money won't be worthless paper; it'll be rare and precious, you'll have to work for it. He came to the christening. Hardly anybody knows his real name. Jochen says he's not a pure Aryan. I couldn't care less. Anyway he didn't come into the church, but gave us two sets of baby clothes and piles of gin. He himself doesn't touch it, he only smokes. My goodness, he doesn't smoke them, he eats them. Right now he's out of town. They say he has his headquarters near Düren. Other people say it's somewhere near Hanover. But with Goldmouth you never know. This is where we live. You get used to the view."

Staying with good old friends, Matern witnesses X-Day, the currency reform. This is the time to take stock of the situation. Sawatzki walks straight out of the C.P. For his money it stinks anyway. Everybody gets his quota. They don't drink it up. Certainly not: "This here is our investment capital. We'll live on our reserves. The syrup'll do us for twelve months at least. By the time we've worn out all the shirts and underwear, Walli will be going to school. 'Cause we haven't been sitting on our stocks, we saw what was coming, we unloaded. That was Goldmouth's advice. A tip like that is worth its weight in gold. He let Inge in on a way of getting CARE packages, just to be obliging, because he likes us. He's always asking about you, because we told him about you. Where you been keeping yourself all this time?"

With leaden pauses in between, Matern, who is slowly regaining his strength, lists German countrysides: East Frisia, the rugged Alb, Upper Franconia, charming Bergstrasse, Sauerland, the Hunsrück, the Eifel, the Saar, Lüneburg Heath, Thuringia or the green heart of Germany. He describes the Black Forest where it is highest and blackest. And his vivid geography lesson is enriched with the names of cities: "On my way from Celle to Bückeburg. Aachen, the ancient city founded by the Romans, where the Holy Roman emperors were crowned. Passau, where the Inn and the Ilz flow into the Danube. Of course I went to see the Goethe house in Weimar. Munich was a disappointment but Stade, the country behind the Elbe dikes, is a highly developed fruit-growing region."

Sawatzki's question "AND NOW WHAT?" ought to be embroidered, given a border, and hung up over the couch. Matern wants to sleep, eat, read the paper, sleep, look out the window, commune with himself, and look at Matern in the shaving mirror: Gone the bleary eyes. The hollows under the cheekbones excellently filled in. But there's no holding the hair, it's emigrating. His forehead grows, lengthening his character-actor's phiz, molded by thirty-one dog years. "And what now?" Eat humble pie? Go dogless into business now that things are starting up? Go back to acting, leave the dog in the checkroom? Grind teeth no longer on the open hunting ground, but only on the stage? Franz Moor? Danton? Faust in Oberhausen? Sergeant Beckmann in Trier? Hamlet in the experimental theater? No. Never! Not yet. His accounts aren't settled yet. Matern's X-Day hasn't dawned yet. Matern wants to pay his debts in the old currency, that's why he raises hell in Sawatzki's two-and-a-half-room apartment. With heavy hand he crushes a celluloid rattle and expresses doubts that Walli stems from the stem of Walter. Matern also wipes all the sure-fire tips grown in Goldmouth's garden off the breakfast table with the sugar bowl. He takes his cue from himself, from his heart, spleen, and kidneys. He and Sawatzki aren't calling each other by their first names any more, but denounce each other, according to mood and time of day, as "Trotzkyite, Nazi, you traitor, you crumby little fellow traveler!" But only when Matern boxes Inge's ears in the middle of the living room—let the reason lie buried in Matern's attic room—does Jochen Sawatzki throw his guest with dog out of the two-and-a-half-room apartment. Instantly Inge wants to be thrown out too with child. But Sawatzki brings a flat hand down on the oilclothed tabletop: "The kid stays here with me. She ain't going to be mixed up in this. Go where you please, go to the dogs. But not with the kid, I'll take care of her."

So without child but with dog and little of the new currency. Matern still has Wollschläger's pocket watch, Budczinski's gold cuff links, and two Canadian dollars. Between Cologne's cathedral and Cologne's Central Station they make merry on the proceeds of the watch. There's just enough left over for a week in a hotel in Benrath, offering a view of the castle with round pond and square garden.

"And what now?" she says.

He massages his scalp at the wardrobe mirror.

She points her thumb in the direction of the curtains: "It seems to me if you want work the Henkel works are over there, and over there on the right Demag is starting up again. We could look for a place to live in Wersten or right in Düsseldorf."

But at the mirror and later, out in the wet cold, Matern doesn't feel like working; he wants to wander. After all, he comes of a miller's family, and millers, says the poet, delight in wandering. Besides, the dog needs exercise. And before he raises a finger for those capitalist swine, he'll . . . "Henkel, Demag, Mannesmann! Don't make me laugh!"

Two with dog along the Trippelsberg, across the Rhine meadows to Himmelgeist. There they find an inn that has a room available and doesn't bother about marriage certificates and manandwife. A restless night, for from Mülheim Inge Sawatzki has brought not hiking shoes but an ornamental coverlet with the embroidered question "And what now?"

Won't let him sleep. Always in the same groove. Pillow-whispering: "Do something. Anything. Goldmouth says: invest, invest, and invest some more, it'll pay off in three years at the latest. Sawatzki, for instance, is going to quit his job in Leverkusen and go into business for himself in some small town. Goldmouth suggested men's coats and suits. Wouldn't you like to try something, anything? You're educated, after all, as you're always saying. A consultant's bureau, for instance, or a horoscope magazine, something serious-looking. Goldmouth says there's a future in that kind of thing. People have simply stopped believing in the old baloney. They want something different, really reliable information about what's written in the stars . . . You're Capricorn, for instance, and I'm Cancer. You can do whatever you please with me."

Obligingly Matern does for her next day. They have barely enough money left for the Rhine ferry from Himmelgeist to Üdesheim. The rain is free of charge. O wet cold bondage! In sopping shoes they hike in single file, the dog in the lead, to Grimlinghausen. There hunger is waiting but nothing to eat. They can't even change sides and ferry to Volmerswerth on the right bank. He does for her on the left bank of the Rhine, under the eyes of St. Quirinus, who was burned in Moscow under the name of Kuhlmann and nevertheless was powerless to protect the city of Neuss from bombs.

Where do you sleep without a penny to your name, but with a pious sinful heart? You get yourself locked up in a church, more precisely in an only true, unheated, namely, Catholic church. Familiar environment. Restless night. For a long time they lie, each in his own pew, until only she is lying and he with dog and dragging leg is roaming about the nave: everywhere scaffoldings and pails of whitewash. A cockeyed kind of place. A little of everything. Typical Transition style. Romanesquely begun when it was already too late, later pasted over with baroque, the dome for example. Damp plaster steams. With floating plaster dust is mingled the smell of elaborate pontifical offices from the dog years of the thirties. Still hovering indecisively and refusing to settle. Matern has been here before, in the days when he carried on conversations with the Virgin Mary. Today Inge-wife does the talking: "And what now?" is her ever-ready question. "It's cold," she says. And: "Can't you sit down?" And: "Should we get a rug?" And: "If it weren't a church, I'd say come on, would you like to too?" And then in the somnolent three-quarters darkness: "Say, look. There's a confessional. You think it's closed?"

It isn't closed but ready at all times. In a confessional he does for her. Something new for a change. In there it's a safe bet that nobody ever. So the dog has to go in where ordinarily the priest has his ear. For Pluto joins in the game. Matern with her enters the adjacent cubicle. And as she kneels, he bucks her uncomfortably from behind, while she has to blabber through the grating behind which Pluto is playing the father confessor. And he presses her fuckedout doll's face against the sinfully ornate wooden grille: baroque, masterly, Rhenish woodcarving outlives the centuries, doesn't break, but squashes the doll face's nose. Every sin counts. Works of penance are imposed. A prayer for intercession is offered up. Not, St. Quirinus, help! But: "Sawatzki, come and help me. Oh oh oh!"

Well, when it's all over, the confessional is undamaged. But she lies for a long while on cold flags and lets her nose bleed in the dusk. He goes roaming again, dog at heel, wordless. And back again at the indestructible confessional after two lonely echoing rounds, he snaps open his good old lighter with a view to lighting a comforting pipe; the lighter accomplishes more than he expected: first, it helps the pipe, second it proves that Inge's nose blood is red, and third it lights up a little card pinned to the confessional, and on the card something is written: a name in black and white: Joseph Knopf. Without further address, for at the moment the name is residing right here and has no need, like other names, to indicate street and number in Cologne's holy men's toilet; daily, for half an hour, from nine forty-five to ten fifteen this Knopf inhabits the indestructible confessional, making his certified ear available to each and all. O leit- and murder motives! O revenge, syrup-sweet! O justice plying the rails in all directions! O names crossed off and still to be crossed off: Joseph Knopf—or the Eighty-sixth Materniad!

Matern crosses him off on the dot of ten, solo and in person. Meanwhile he has tied Pluto—parting is sweet sorrow —to a bicycle stand still intact amid the ruins of Neuss. Still weeping, Inge slips away without a word shortly before early Mass and with squashed nose tramps back in the direction of Cologne. Some truck will pick her up—but he stays; on Batteriestrasse, almost exactly halfway between

Münsterplatz and the industrial port, he doesn't seek but finds ten pfennigs in one piece. Wealth! St. Quirinus has put it there especially for him; with it you can buy a butt; or the *Rheinische Post,* fresh off the press; it's the price of a box of matches or a stick of chewing gum; you could put it in a slot and, if you stood on the scales, out into the world would come a little card: your weight! But Matern smokes a pipe and when necessary snaps open his lighter. Matern reads newspapers in showcases. Matern has plenty to chew on. Matern doesn't need to be weighed. For ten found pfennigs Matern buys a beautiful long smooth chaste knitting needle —for what?

Don't turn around, knitting needle's going round.

This knitting needle is for the priest's ear and is intended to enter the ear of Joseph Knopf. With malice aforethought Matern, at nine forty-five, walks into the asymmetrical church of St. Quirinus to judge with a long knitting needle alienated from its function.

Ahead of him two old women confess briefly and meagerly. Now in the somnolent church night he kneels down in the very place where Inge, having been put into position, was going to confess to the dog. Anyone looking for evidence could probably find Ingeblood on the wooden grille and bear witness to a case of martyrdom. He takes aim and whispers. Joseph Knopf's ear is large and fleshy and doesn't quiver. There's room for the whole confession, sins checked off on fingers, and bang in the midst of it an old old story that happened in the dog years of the late thirties, involving a former SA man, then a Neo-Catholic, and a professional Old-Catholic who, on the strength of the so-called resolutions of Maria Laach, advised the Neo-Catholic to get back into a regular SA sturm in spite of everything and with the help of the Blessed Virgin to reinforce the Catholic wing of the inherently godless SA. A complicated story that turns cartwheels on thin ice. But the priest's ear doesn't quiver. Matern whispers names, dates, and quotations. He breathes: his name was Soandso, the other one's name was Soandso. No fly molests the priest's ear. Matern is still as busy as a bee: And the one whose name was Soandso said to the other one after devotions, that was in May of the year . . . The priest's ear is still hewn of marble. And from time to time substantial words issue from the other side: "My son, do you repent with all your heart? You know that Jesus Christ, who

died for us on the cross, knows of every sin, even the most
venial, and is watching us, whatever we do. Be contrite. Keep
nothing back, my son."

Such precisely were Matern's intentions. Once again he
reels off the whole story. From an ingenious music box
emerge the carved figures: Kaas, the prelate, Pacelli, the
nunzio, the former SA man, the repentant Neo-Catholic, the
crafty Old-Catholic, and the representative of the Catholic
wing of the SA. All, lastly the merciful Virgin Mary, do
their little dance and exit; but Matern still hasn't unreeled
the whole of his whispered spool: "And it was you, you and
no one else, who said that, get back into the SA. A lot of rubbish about the concordat and anecdotes from Maria Laach.
They even secretly blessed a banner and whined out prayers
for the Führer. You Dominican! You black shitbag. And to
me, Matern, you said: My son, resume the brown garment of
honor. Jesus Christ, who died on the cross and watches us in
all our works, has sent us the Führer to stamp out the seed
of the godless with your help and mine. That's right. Stamp
out!" But the priest's ear, mentioned several times by name,
is still the ingenious product of a Gothic stonecutter. When
the knitting needle, retail price ten pfennigs, is put in motion, when the instrument of vengeance rests on the ornate
grille of the confessional and is aimed knittingneedle-
sharp at the priest's ear, nothing quivers in alarm for the
eardrum; only the old man's voice, thinking the penitent has
finished, drones out wearily and with routine mildness the
everlasting words: *"Ego te absolvo a peccatis tuis in nomine
Patris et Filii et Spiritus Sancti. Amen."* The penance imposed consists of nine Paternosters and thirty-two Ave Ma-
rias.

Then Matern, who has come to judge with a ten-pfennig
knitting needle, lets his instrument recoil: this priest is lending his ear only symbolically. He is invulnerable. You can
tell him your whole story twice a day, all he hears is the
wind in the trees or not even. Joseph Knopf. Deaf-as-a-
button Knopf. Deaf-as-a-button priest absolves me in the
name of this one and that one, and in the name of the dove.
Behind the grille stonedeaf Joseph makes monkeysigns for me
to leave. Clear out, Matern! Other people have things to con-
fide in my deaf ear. Get thee behind me. All your sins are
remitted. O.K., get a move on, cleaner can't be did. Mingle
with the penitents: Maria Laach is near Neviges. Find your-

self some nice little Canossa. Take the knitting needle back to the store. Maybe they'll take it back and return your ten pfennigs. For that you can get matches or chewing gum. That's the price of the *Rheinische Post*. For ten pfennigs you can see how much you weigh after alleviating confession. Or buy your dog some sausage skins. Pluto has to be kept in form.

THE EIGHTY-SEVENTH WORM-EATEN MATERNIAD

Everybody has at least two fathers. They aren't necessarily acquainted with each other. Some fathers don't even know. Sometimes fathers get lost. Speaking of uncertain fathers, Matern possesses one who is particularly deserving of a monument, but doesn't know where he; or suspect what he; in whom he hopes. But he doesn't look for him.

Instead, and even in his dreams, whose work consists in felling a murmuring beech forest trunk by trunk, he gropes for Goldmouth, concerning whom mysterious things are being said on all sides. Yet, painstakingly as he searches every bay in the men's toilet of Cologne Central Station for hints about Goldmouth, no pointing arrow starts him on a dogtrot; but he reads—and this lesson puts him on the track of his father Anton Matern—a maxim freshly engraved in defective enamel:

"Don't listen to the worm. There's a worm in the worm."

Without striking his search for Goldmouth and his dream job of felling beeches from his program, Matern sets out in a fatherly direction.

The miller with the flat ear. Standing beside the historical postmill in Nickelswalde, situated to the east of the Vistula estuary and surrounded by Siberian frost-resistant Urtoba wheat, he shouldered a hundredweight sack until the mill, with turning sails, burned down from the jack via the flour loft to the sack loft. Thereupon the miller evaded the clutches of war, which was approaching from Tiegenhof by way of Scharpau. Laden with a twenty-pound sack of wheat flour —milled from the Epp variety—he, along with his wife and sister, found room on a ferry barge which had operated for years between the Vistula villages of Nickelswalde and

Schiewenhorst. The convoy included the ferryboat *Rothe-bude*, the railroad ferry *Einlage*, the tugboat *Future*, and a bevy of fishing launches. Northeast of Rügen the ferry barge *Schiewenhorst* had to be unloaded because of engine trouble and taken in tow by the Rothebude-Käsemark ferry. The miller, the twenty-pound sack of white flour, and the miller's family were allowed to board a torpedo boat. This vessel, overloaded with seasickness and children's screams, struck a mine west of Bornholm, and sank instantly, taking with it screams and collywobbles, not to mention the miller's wife and sister; he, however, managed to find standing room for himself and his sack of flour on the excursion steamer *Swan*, which had put out from Danzig-Neufahrwasser, destination Lübeck. Without further change of ship, miller Anton Matern, with flat ear and still-dry twenty-pound sack, reached the port of Travemünde, *terra firma*, the continent.

In the course of the following months—history goes right on: peace breaks out!—the miller is obliged to defend his shouldered refugee property often and craftily, for around him there are many who would like to eat cake but have no flour. He himself is often tempted to diminish the twenty pounds by a handful and cook himself a creamy wheat soup; but whenever his stomach prods him, his left hand gives his right-hand fingers, toying with the sack strings, a sharp smack. And it is thus that creeping misery, now engaged in environmental studies, finds him: lopsided, silent, and abstemious in waiting rooms, lodged in refugee barracks, squeezed into Nissen huts. The one ear protrudes enormously, while the flat ear is pressed by the undiminished twenty-pound sack. There the sack lies safe and—to an outside observer—as still as a mouse.

When, between the Hanover railroad station and the perforated but still long-tailed equestrian monument, miller Matern is caught in a police raid, taken to headquarters, and —because of the flour-filled sack—threatened with prosecution for black marketing, King Ernest Augustus, the Hanoverian, does not dismount from his charger to save him; a German official employed by the Allied military government takes his part, defends him and the twenty pounds with a fluent speech, and little by little in the course of his half-hour plea allows two and thirty gold teeth to glitter: Goldmouth vouches for miller Matern and takes the lopsided man and his sack of flour under his protection, nay more: in consideration of the miller's professional aptitudes, he buys him a slightly damaged postmill on the plains between Düren and Krefeld, and has the roof fixed, though he has no intention of having the tattered sails mended and turned into the wind.

For at Goldmouth's behest, the miller is to live a contemplative life on two stories: upstairs, under the main shaft and the dust-matted gears, in the so-called sack loft, he sleeps. Though cluttered with the big bedstone, the hopper, and the counterwheel which projects between the rafters, this loft, where formerly grist was piled, provides ample space for a bed, which, what with the proximity of the border, is an almost Dutch bed. The stone serves as a table. The damsel over the hopper contains shirts, underwear, and other belongings. Bats evacuate the counterwheel and lantern, arbor and windlay drive, to make room for Goldmouth's little presents: the radio, the lamp—he had electricity put in—the illustrated magazines, and the few utensils required by an old man who knows how to conjure up the smell of fried potatoes from a camp stove. The steps leading down are equipped with a new banister. For the spacious flour loft, marked in the center by the mill post, yields the miller's parlor and soon his consultation room. Under the iron plank and the overhung rail, under the inextricable clutter of machinery which formerly served to adjust the burrs, Goldmouth, who translates the miller's every whim into suggestions, places an imposing newly upholstered wing chair. Because one of its wings gets in the way of the shouldered twenty-pound bag, it ultimately has to be exchanged for a wingless easy chair. The mill creaks even on windless days. When the wind blows outside, dust still clouds up from the meal bin through the chute into the tattered bolter that hangs crooked in its frame. Easterly winds make the pot-bellied stove smoke. But usually the clouds, coming from the canal, scud low over the Rhenish Lowlands. Once, right after he has moved in, the miller oils the cotter that holds the oak lever in place and retightens the keys in the tenons to do justice to the occasion: a miller has moved into a mill. After that he lives in felt slippers and dark denims, sleeps until nine, eats breakfast alone or with Goldmouth when he happens to be visiting, and leafs through wartime or postwartime numbers of *Life*. He signs his contract right away, immediately after the momentous tightening of the keys in the tenons. Goldmouth doesn't demand much: with the exception of Thursday, the miller with his flat ear has to give consultations from ten to twelve every morning. In the afternoon, except for Thursday, which sees him hard at work from three to five, he is free. Then he sits with protruding ear by the radio, or goes to the movies in Viersen, or plays skat with two officers of the Refugee Party, to which he also gives his vote, because he holds that the cemeteries to the left and right of the Vistula estuary, especially the one in Steegen, are richer in ivy than any of the cemeteries between Krefeld and Erkelenz.

But who comes to consult the lopsided miller with the flat ear in the morning and Thursday afternoon office hours? At first the nearby peasants come to see him and pay in produce such as butter and asparagus; later on, small manufacturers from Düren and Gladbach come, bringing finished products with barter value; early in '46, he is discovered by the press.

What attracts these visitors, at first few and far between, then swelling to a stream that can hardly be regulated? For the benefit of anyone who is still in the dark: miller Anton Matern listens to the future with his flat ear. The lopsided miller knows important dates in advance. His recumbent ear, which seems to be deaf to everyday sounds, hears pointers with the help of which the future can be manipulated. No table tipping, laying out of cards, stirring of coffee grounds. Nor does he, from the sack loft, point a telescope at the stars. Nor unravel meaningful lines in hands. No poking around in hedgehog hearts and fox spleens or in the kidneys of a red-spotted calf. For the benefit of anyone who is still in the dark: it's the twenty-pound sack that knows so much. More specifically, mealworms, which in the flour milled from wheat of the Epp variety have survived the trip on the ferry barge, the swift sinking of the torpedo boat, in short, the turmoil of the war and the postwar period, at first with God's, later with Goldmouth's help, whisper predictions; the miller's flat ear—ten thousand and more hundredweight sacks of Urtoba wheat, of Epp wheat, of wheat flour milled from Schliephacke No. 5, have made it so flat, deaf and clairaudient—hears what the future has to offer and the miller's voice passes the mealworms' pointers on to those in quest of advice. For a reasonable fee, miller Anton Matern, abetted by East German worms, helps in no small degree to guide the destinies of West Germany; for when, after peasants and small manufacturers, Hamburg's future press moguls sit down facing his easy chair and write their questions on a small slate, he begins to wield influence: showing the way, molding opinion, influencing world politics, speaking the universal language of pictures, of reversed mirror images.

After handing out advice for many years in his native Nickelswalde, after guiding wheat production between Neuteich and Bohnsack with mealworm pointers and making it profitable, after predicting, with flat ear against mealworm-inhabited sack, plagues of mice, hailstorms, the devaluation of the Free City gulden, the collapse of the grain exchange, the date of the Reichspresident's death, and the ill-omened visit of the fleet to Danzig harbor, he now succeeds, with Goldmouth's support, in leaping from provincial obscurity to world fame throughout West Germany: three gentlemen drive up in a jeep belonging to the occupation authorities. Young and hence blameless, they take the stairs to the flour loft in two and a half steps, bringing with them noise, talent, and ignorance, pound on the mill post, potter with the windlay drive, and are determined to climb up to the sack loft and dirty their fingers in the mill machinery. But the "Private" sign on the banister of the sack-loft stairs enables them to show good breeding; they quiet down like schoolboys as they face miller Matern, who points to the slate and slate pencil, in order that wishes may be formulated and opened to fulfillment.

What the mealworms have to say to the three gentlemen may sound prosaic: the handsomest of the three is advised to insist, in his negotiations with the British authorities, on newspaper license No. 67, in order that, under the name of *Hör zu* (Tune In), it may run up a circulation and—just in passing—provide miller Matern with a free subscription; for the miller is wild about illustrated magazines and gone on the radio. License No. 6, titled *Die Zeit* (Time) at the worms' suggestion, is the advice given to the most agile of the three gentlemen. But to the smallest and most distinguished of the young gentlemen, who is bashfully chewing his fingernails and doesn't even dare to step forward, the mealworms whisper by way of the miller that he should have a try with license No. 123 and drop his unsuccessful experiment, known as *Die Woche* (The Week).

The smooth Springer taps the unworldly Rudi on the shoulder: "Ask Grampa what name to give your baby."

Instantly the blind mealworms send their message through the lopsided miller: *Der Spiegel* (The Mirror), which finds the pimple on the smoothest forehead, has its place in every modern household, but the mirror has to be concave; what's easily read can easily be forgotten and yet quoted; the truth isn't always essential, but the house number has to be right; in short, a good card index, ten thousand or more well-filled file drawers, take the place of thought; "people," so say the mealworms, "don't want to be made to think, they want to be accurately informed."

By right the consultation is over, but Springer sulks and sticks at the mealworm prognoses, because in his heart he doesn't want to start a radio magazine for the great masses, but is more inclined toward a radically pacifist weekly. "I want to stir people up, stir them up." At this the mealworms via miller Matern comfort him and forecast, for June 1952, the birth of an institution conducive to the general welfare: "Every morning three million reading illiterates will breakfast over an illustrated daily."

Quickly, before the miller can spring open his pocket watch a second time, the gentleman who only a moment before was as cheerful as a senator and whose manners Axel Springer and little Augstein are trying to copy, owns to perplexity bordering on despair, and pleads for help. At night, so he confesses on the slate, he has Social-democratic dreams, by day he dines with Christian heavy industry, but his heart is with avant-garde literature, in short, he can't make up his mind. Whereupon the mealworm informs him that this mixture—left by night, right by day, and avant-garde at heart—is characteristic and timely: wholesome, honorable, liberal, prudently courageous, pedagogic, and lucrative.

Question after question comes bubbling out. "Advertising rates? Who's going to be the vetoing minority in the house of Ullstein?"—but the mealworms, represented by miller Matern, decline to reply. Before they politely take their leave, all three gentlemen are permitted to carve their names in the mill post—which the miller exhibits to this day: the handsome Springer, the weltschmerz-tormented Rudi, and Herr Bucerius, whose family tree has its roots in the medieval enlightenment.

After a quiet week—a carpet is laid under miller Matern's feet; the lever, which formerly started or stopped the shaking movement of the hopper, serves as a temporary support for the glassed photograph of the aged President Hindenburg—; after a week of trifling domestic changes and of organizational initiative—Goldmouth has the path leading to the idle windmill widened and a sign put up on the highway between Viersen and Dülken—after a week, then, of quiet preparation, a number of big businessmen or their agents with decartelization troubles drive in over the freshly graveled driveway; and in a twinkling the mealworms, rested and communicative, cure the headaches of the tangled Flick group. On a hard stool sits Otto-Ernst Flick in person, representing his father and needful of advice. Not that the miller knows who is sitting there, crossing leg and leg, each time in a different way; with benign indifference he leafs through his worn illustrated magazines, while the slate fills up with urgent questions. The Allied decartelization law demands that Flick Senior should drop either iron or coal. The mealworm proclaims: "Unload your coal mines." So it happens that the holding company whose merger with Mannesmann has been dissolved takes over the majority of Essen Anthracite AG and later, as the mealworm advises, rejoins Mannesmann. Nine years later, or five years after his anticipated and mealworm-dated release from a term at hard labor, Flick Senior manages to get back into Harpener Coal, this time as a majority stockholder.

In the same year, incidentally, Dr. Ernst Schneider, who calls at the windmill shortly after Flick Junior, joins the Trinkhaus Bank; and with him the whole Michel group comes aboard: soft coal, soft coal!—and the carbon dioxide industry, whose chairman he is, thanks to the mealworm; for with a tongue as broad as the Vistula the miller hands out positions which shortly before were filled by the mealworms. Thus, for example, a retired cavalry captain, soon to be the key figure of the burgeoning German economy, is promised twenty-two board memberships including six chairmanships, because if Herr von Bülow-Schwante is to remain in the saddle, he will have to lead the entire Stumm Corporation over high and crowded hurdles that the Allies have put in his path.

Coming and going. Gentlemen exchange greetings on the stairs leading to the flour loft and to miller Matern. Resounding names begin to fill up the mill post, for nearly everyone wants to immortalize himself, Hoesch, or the Bochum Association in this famous place. Krupp sends Beitz, and Beitz learns how, with the fickle times working in Krupp's favor, decartelization is to be sidestepped. At an early date the mealworms also pave the way for the crucial interview between Messrs. Beitz and R. Murphy, U.S. Undersecretary of State. The mealworms speak, as Beitz and Murphy will do later on, of long-term credits to underdeveloped countries; but it is not the government that should open its moneybags, let Krupp pour out riches privately and with careful aim: iron foundries in India are projected by mealworms who, if they had been permitted to live in Nickelswalde to the right of the Vistula estuary, would have devised projects for the People's Republic of Poland; but the Poles refused to be helped by the East German mealworm.

Accordingly Siemens & Halske; Klöckner and Humboldt; Petroleum and Potash, wherever rocksalt flourishes. This honor is accorded miller Matern on a rainy Wednesday morning. Dr. Quandt comes in person and finds out how Wintershall AG is going to obtain a majority interest in the Burbach Potash Works. A deal is being arranged, in which Goldmouth, who has an interest in a shut-down potash mine between Sarstedt and Hildesheim, blandly participates.

But when on the ensuing free Thursday morning—it is still raining—which miller Matern spends driving nails into props and hanging the great President's picture now here, now there, Goldmouth, who to tell the truth had dropped in only to leave a pile of illustrated magazines for the miller, is gone again. Next day, however—the persistent downpour hasn't been able to discourage them—the IG-successors call in a body. Although decartelized, Baden Aniline, Bayer, and Hoechst come together and let the mealworm vote their policy for the ensuing years: "Don't pay dividends, increase your capital." But this mealworm slogan isn't restricted to the chemical industry; whoever calls, Feldmühle AG or Esso, the Haniels or North German Lloyd, all the big banks and insurance companies—the chorus of mealworms repeats emphatically: "No dividends. Increase your capital!" And concurrently the usual chickenfeed: How can the old-established Hertie Corporation, associated with the still-older-established firm of Tietz, transform itself into the Karg Family Foundation? Should Brenninkmeyer introduce customers' credit? What will the men's suit of the future look like—this refers to the doublebreasted number responding to revived consumer demand—which Peek & Cloppenburg will soon be putting on the market?

The mealworm answers all questions after advance payment at fixed rates. He refurbishes the Mercedes star, forecasts the rise and fall of Borgward, disposes of Marshall Plan funds, is present when the Ruhr Authority meets, dismisses the Constitution before it is approved by the Parliamentary Council, fixes the date of the currency reform, counts votes before the first Bundestag elections are held, builds the imminent Korean crisis into the shipbuilding program of the Howaldt Works of Kiel and Hamburg, arranges the Petersberg Agreement, picks a certain Dr. Nordhoff as the future pacemaker in the setting of prices, and, when it suits him and his ilk, exerts terrifying pressure on the stock market.

But by and large the trend is favorable, though the Thyssen ladies do not shun the path to the converted windmill. Is the mill a mill of youth? Are wrinkles smoothed, calves upholstered? Is the mealworm a matchmaker? An elderly Stahlhelm veteran who comes to attention at the sight of President von Hindenburg—who has meanwhile moved from the sack loft to the flour loft—and gives him an ingratiating salute, this gentleman, still hale and hearty, is advised to establish cordial family relations with the key figure Bülow-Schwante, as an encouragement to the construction industry: *"Tu felix* Portland Cement, *nube!"*—for family enterprises are favored by the mealworm.

Of course anyone who is on his way to the mealworm has to carry humility and childlike faith in his baggage. This is something the indestructible Hjalmar Schacht, the imp with the stand-up collar, can't get through his head, although he often shares the opinion of the mealworms. Both the worms and Schacht warn against overexpansion of the export trade, overaccumulation of dollars, overincrease of currency volume, and rising prices. But only the mealworms reveal the solution to future problems. Consulted separately by Schäffer, the future Minister of Finance, and Vocke, the future President of the Reichsbank—future pillars of the state, they will go down in history!—the mealworms advise them to loosen up: let the minister stop hoarding enormous reserves; let the bank president lend wings to his piles of gold. Once again, as in the mealworm-arranged Krupp-Beitz-Murphy conversations, the watchword is: "Dollar credits to under-developed countries."

A first boom. Wool markets strengthened by orders from Latin America. Bremen jute picks up. Warning against weakening Canadian dollar. A breathing spell, wisely ordered by the mealworms with a view to consolidation, prevents the market from running wild. The trend remains favorable. Goldmouth has the driveways surfaced with asphalt. The miller's crazy notion of getting married—a widow from Viersen seems to have been under consideration—comes to nothing, because it would have meant giving up a pension. Still alone but not lonely, the miller leafs through the illustrated magazines: *Quick* and *Kristall, Stern* and *Revue,* all supplied in gratitude and gratis: the *Frankfurter* and the *Münchner Illustrierte, Tune In,* now in its third year. And all who have been loyal to him from the very first, and those who have only belatedly found their way to the right faith, call regularly or bashfully for the first time, carve or reinforce their names in and on the imposing mill post, attentively bring little gifts, and cough when the stove smokes in the east wind: the gentlemen who have risen from the ranks: Münnemann and Schlieker, Neckermann and Grundig; the old foxes Reemtsma and Brinkmann; potential leaders such as Abs, Forberg, and Pferdmenges; the erstwhile future, then present Erhard comes regularly and is allowed to swallow a surplus mealworm: which lives to this day, miraculously miracle-working, in the exemplary paunch—expansion expansion! The free-market economy is run by the mealworm. From the very first the worm's been inside the father of the economic miracle, miraculously miracle-working. "Don't listen to the worm, there's a worm in the worm!"

So cackles the opposition, which doesn't come calling, doesn't pay, doesn't cough in the east wind, and doesn't consult miller Matern. In line with a decision of the Socialist Party in the Bundestag, it refuses to have any truck with medieval hocus-pocus. Certain trade union leaders secretly take the path to the mill notwithstanding. But although their mealworm-formulated directives have had a good deal to do with the present powerful position of the German Trade Union League, they are sooner or later exposed. For all Social Democrats brand the miller and his mealworm-counseled clientele as heretics. The lawyer Arndt harvests nothing but laughter when in the course of a question period in the Bundestag he tries to prove that association with, and taking counsel of, mealworms constitute an offense against Article 2 of the Constitution, because the rising mealworm cult represents a threat to the free development of the individual personality. Cynical worm jokes are hatched in the Bonn Socialist Party headquarters and when publicized as election slogans deprive the party of critically needed votes. Herr Schumacher and—as of August 1952—Herr Ollenhauer have not made a single election speech without heaping scorn and contempt on the consultations in the converted windmill. Party officials speak of the "capitalistic worm cure" and are still sitting—small wonder!—on the opposition benches.

But the clergy comes. Not, to be sure, in vestments, not with Cardinals Frings and Faulhaber at the head of field processions; those who come to the windmill that gives directives are for the most part anonymous Dominicans, seldom motorized, usually on foot, occasionally on bicycles.

More tolerated than favored, they sit outside the mill with open breviary and wait humbly until a Dr. Oetker of Bielefeld has received his personal order of the day: "Bake fleet of ships with Oetker's baking powder. Stir Oetker's pudding mix, bring it to a boil, let it cool, spill it carefully into all seven seas—and behold: Dr. Oetker's tankers are afloat." Later, after Oetker has immortalized himself on the mill post and left, Father Rochus is obliged to breathe on his spectacles in wild surprise, for as soon as he has quoted the catechism with shrill slate pencil: "Lord, send us Thy spirit and everything will be created anew . . ." the mealworms speak up as vicars: working through the Christian government party, the true Church must strive little by little to restore the ways of life of the Gothic and late Romanesque periods; Charlemagne's empire must be renewed, if necessary with Latin help; better lay off the torture and witch burning as a starter, because heretics like Gerstenmaier and Dibelius will eat out of the blessed Virgin's hand unasked: "Mary, virgin with the child, give us all thy blessing mild."

Overwhelmed with gifts, pious fathers return home on foot and on bicycles. Once the wind even blows six Franciscan nuns from the Convent of Our Lady in Aachen directly and decoratively to the mill. Though Sister Alfons-Maria, the mistress of novices, spends half an hour asking the miller for information, what the mealworms have to say to the nuns is a secret that no one must ever spill; only this much is certain: Catholic mealworms—miller Anton Müller is a Catholic—drafted pastoral letters for every conceivable situation; they whisper the name of a rising minister; *nomen est omen*—he will be Würmeling and, with the help of Catholic families, will create a state within the state; mealworms submit bills; mealworms demand measures in favor of denominational schools; for religious reasons Catholic mealworms oppose reunification; mealworms govern West Germany—for the East German government sends its planning expert too late.

Before the miller with his twenty-pound sack of wheat flour, which, it should be mentioned in passing, has had to be replenished with a few pounds of the Epp variety, obtained with difficulty from the now Polish Vistula delta—before miller Matern with his well-fed mealworms has a chance to participate in the planning of the Stalinstadt steel combine in the Oder marshes, in the building of the Black Pump power combine, in the uranium- and wolfram-mining operations of the notorious Wismuth AG, before he can help to organize socialist brigades, plain-clothes men are sent in to guard the area surrounding the speaking mealworms; for if Herren Leuschner and Mewis—and Ulbricht went so far as to send Nuschke—had been able in those days to slip two, three, or several times through the cordon set up by a general and his men, the German Democratic Republic would have a different look today, would have potatoes galore and paperclips to burn—while as things stand, it hasn't even enough barbed wire.

Equally slow in getting started, certain critics of the economic miracle, whose oratorical potshots at the symbolic Erhard are consistently wide of the mark, have also missed the bus to Düren. Herr Kuby and all the cabaret wits would have poisoned arrows, arguments, and biting satirical songs fit to shake an empire if they had only dropped in on miller Matern. For it is a mistake to suppose that partisan worms were always behind the one and only Konrad. Not at all! Early visitors to the mealworms, the gentlemen of the press and those with decartelization troubles, will testify that the dominant sentiment in the twenty-pound bag was strongly anti-Adenauer from the very start; it was not the mealworms who put forward the incompetent mayor as the first chancellor; why, he only visited the windmill four times, and then with nothing but questions of foreign policy on his mind. No, their vote was not for him, actually they cried out unanimously: "The man for us is Hans Globke, the modest resistance fighter who worked in the background."

It was not to be. But if mealworm-trained supporters, mindful of the mealworm's words, had not made a shadow chancellor of Dr. Hans Globke, so obtaining a hearing for the mealworm party in the Bundestag and for certain undersecretaries in the most important ministries, a great deal, everything perhaps, would have gone wrong.

And miller Matern? What honors was he accorded? Was a free subscription to this and that illustrated weekly, were the New Year's presents—calendars of corporations from Auto Union to Hanover-Hannibal Mines—his only profit? Did appointments, decorations, or blocks of shares come his way? Did the miller grow rich?

His son, who drops in with black shepherd in March 1949, doesn't get to see a red cent at first. Outside, the west wind is tugging at the idle sails. Neckarsulm Motors and United Boiler Works have just roared down the driveway. Visiting hours are over. The twenty-pound sack is resting in the safe. This article of furniture—donated by Krauss-Maffei, which has belonged to the Flick syndicate since Buderus acquired a majority interest—was installed by Goldmouth, who thought it unsafe just to leave the sack lying in the hopper. Other noteworthy acquisitions are nonutilitarian: in a spacious bird cage—the gift of Wintershall AG—bill and coo two parakeets —a gift of the Gerling Corporation. But father and son sit facing one another in silence, unless importance is attached to such exclamations as "Hmm" or "Well, well." The son politely opens the conversation: "Well, Pa, what's the mealworm been saying?"

The father waves the question aside. "What's he been saying? Just spinning yarns."

Then the son, as is fitting and proper, has to inquire after his mother and his aunt: "And Ma? And Auntie Lorrchen? Ain't they with you?"

The miller points his thumb up toward the flour loft: "They was all drownded on the way."

It occurs to the son to ask about old acquaintances: "And Kriwe? Lührmann? Karweise? What became of the Kabruns? Old Folchert and Lau's Hedwig from the Schiewenhorst side?"

Again the miller's thumb points at the ceiling timbers: "Drownded. They was all drownded on the way."

Even if mother, aunt, and all the neighbors have been swallowed up by the Baltic, there's no harm in asking about his father's mill. And again the miller has to announce a loss: "She burned down in broad daylight."

The son has to shout when he wants information of his father. At first cautiously, then directly, he comes out with his business. But the miller understands neither with his flat nor with his protruding ear. Accordingly, the son writes wishes on the slate. He asks for money. "Dough, dough!" —for he's as flat as the Vistula delta: "Hard luck, broke!" The millerfather nods understandingly and advises his son to go to work either in the coalfields or for him. "Make yourself useful around here. You can always find something to do. And we'll need to be doing some building pretty soon."

But before Matern, the son with black dog, makes up his mind to give his father a hand, he wants to know, just in passing, whether the miller knows a man, a heavy smoker, called Goldmouth, and whether it mightn't be possible to locate this Goldmouth with the help of the mealworms: "Whyn't you ask them?"

At this the miller turns to stone. The mealworms are silent in their safe: Krauss-Maffei. Only the parakeets—Gerling Corp.—go on chatting in their cage—Wintershall AG. Nevertheless, Matern Jr. stays on and hammers together a kennel for Pluto under the jack of the idle windmill. If there were a Vistula here and Vistula dikes from horizon to horizon, the village over yonder would be Schiewenhorst and here, where every morning except Thursday the coke barons and trustees drive up, would be Nickelswalde. Consequently the place will soon be called New Nickelswalde.

Matern Jr. makes himself at home. Father and son sign a contract in due form. From this day on, it will be the duty of the dog Pluto to guard the mill with contents and announce business visitors by barking. One of the son's duties will be to regulate the outward flow of the worm-guided economic process. As a superintendent receiving more than regulation wages, he arranges for a parking lot at the foot of the mill hummock, but refuses to have an Esso service station installed. While the gasoline pumps are relegated to the intersection of the driveway and the Düren highway, he allows the Federal Post Office department and Blatzheim Enterprises to build right here on the parking lot, flanking it on three sides, but only with one-story buildings, for he holds that the windmill—which has meanwhile become a national symbol, popularized in the form of lapel pins—must tower appropriately over the flourishing bustle down below. The telephone exchange and offices communicate and formulate worm instructions and worm logic. The main building harbors a relatively low-priced restaurant and provides twelve single and six double rooms for wormthinkers in need of sleep. The basement is the natural place for the bar, where in the late afternoon worm technocrats—nowadays they are called potential leaders—fasten themselves to bar stools. Over cold drinks, nibbling salted almonds, they develop the worm-promoted trend toward monopoly, discuss the worm-eaten competitive system, sell, pay dividends, support for the time being, mark time, fluctuate, depress, quote, record, rise sharply, and smile at a poster which Matern, the super, has hung up, white on red background, in the cellar bar:

THE WHEELS WON'T GO—WHEN THE MEALWORM SAYS NO.

For Matern Jr. joins in the conversation. Many of his sentences begin with the unvarying formula: "Marxism-Leninism has proved . . ." or: "On the wings of socialism the . . ."

The worm technocrats—for they never became leaders—wince on their bar stools when super Matern points with Lenin's famous gesture at the red-and-white poster and speaks of the mealworm collectivity, of the wormstructure of victorious socialism, and of history as a dialectical worm-process. While upstairs in the converted windmill the lop-sided miller, with the twenty-pound sack to his ear, helps the German postwar economy to gain world prestige—it is to his collaboration and tolerance that we owe the pioneering work by the economist W. Eucken: "The Tasks of Public-spirited Mealworms in a Constitutional State"—down below his son, the super, is lambasting monopolistic mealworm exploiters. Quotations crawl with worms. There are class-conscious and classless worms. Some practice collective self-education, others keep a brigade diary. Pioneering worms build the house of socialism. Under modified social conditions the capitalistic worm is converted to. They purge themselves, cast out, triumph. In the course of interminable conversations in the bar—upstairs Matern Sr. has long been asleep, dreaming of ivy-clogged cemeteries to the left and right of the Vistula estuary—Matern Jr., over gin and whisky, disseminates Marx-fed worm myths, which are made to sustain the theory of necessary development: "For there are worm planners and worm brigades, which on the wings of socialism have embarked on the path from the I to the We."

Matern, the super, isn't a bad talker. In the smoke-filled bar, his head on the way to baldness directly under the ceiling light, he clutches his whisky glass, brandishes his tinkling drink, points with oft-painted Lenin finger at the future, and performs didactic plays for a theater-loving public. For those who huddle on stools, the worm technocrats Abs and Pferdmenges, the Thyssen ladies and Axel Springer, Blessing, the business leader, and Stein, the trustee, the associates with unlimited liability, and the chairmen of seven boards of directors—all play along, because each one of them—"That's basic"—has a different opinion, which demands to be aired. Moreover, every one of them once upon a time in his youth—"cross my heart and hope to die!"—was somewhere on the left. After all, we're among friends: "Krauss-Maffei and Röchling-Buderus!" You old ruffians: "Lübbert and Bülow-Schwante, Alfred's witnesses and Hugo's heirs!" All in all, decides Matern the super, these people are open-minded—after midnight. They aren't all rolling in clover. Every one of them, even the widow Siemens, has his cross to bear. Every one of them, even the Gutehoffnung Foundry, had to start at the bottom of the ladder. Not a one of them, not even Phoenix-Rheinrohr, was built in a day. "But let's get one thing straight, you reinsurance and hail-insurance companies, you coal-tar wizards and steel manufacturers, you widely ramified and well-connected moguls, you Krupps, Flicks, Stumms, and Stinneses: Socialism will triumph! Bottoms up! Let the mealworm provide! Prost, Vicco! Outlook favorable. You're a good guy even if you were an SS leader. That's water under the bridge. Weren't we all? Each in his own way. Call me Walter!"

But only at midnight are all men brothers beneath the converted windmill; in the daytime, while the parking lot is overcrowded, the telephone exchange overloaded, and consultations at their peak, ideological guerrilla warfare prevails. No mysterious wirepullers finance the super; out of his own pocket he has leaflets printed, which serve a purpose thanks to their novel style.

On the left side quotations from Marx alternate with data from the family history of the Materns; on the right, quickly reacting pencils note the predicted annual capacity of the projected Rourkela Plant in Orissa, India.

On the left, class-struggle fighters Luxemburg and Liebknecht shower exclamation marks; on the right, a colon followed by the announcement that in a few years Opel will pay a superdividend of 66%.

On the left, the bandits Simon and Gregor Materna found —in the sixteenth century, mind you!—brigades consecrated to collective endeavor; on the right, the Mining Union is formulated.

On the left, anyone who is so inclined can read how the super's great-grandfather, who believed in Napoleon but sold scaling ladders to the Russians, acquired, thanks precisely to this ambivalence, money that had previously belonged to militarists and capitalists; on the right are listed the investments and write-offs of the Baden Aniline and Soda works for the still remote year 1955.

In short: while on the left side of his all-red leaflets super Matern makes himself known as someone who wishes to hasten the end of the decadent Western social order, the unprinted part of the same leaflets is filled with: graphs of costs, stock-market quotations, antitrust regulations—what a visual anticipation of present-day coexistence!

What gratuitous pleasure it would be, while this chronicle pauses for breath on its way to conclusion, to toss in an intermezzo or two; for who, in this day and age, hasn't got anecdotes up his sleeve? What happened to the movie industry, for instance, which sent its agents to New Nickelswalde too late? Who hasn't a lament to offer? About agriculture, for instance. Ah, what sins of omission, despite the fact that the mealworms, inspired by their environment, never cease to herald the impending agricultural crises. And who couldn't compile an almanac of social gossip? The Hamburg alliances, for instance: Rosenthal-China-Rowohlt-Publishers. Springer's grounds for divorce; tedious social criticism. We prefer to skip all this and to state succinctly: from March 1949 to summer 1953 Walter Matern, who had come to judge with black dog, serves as superintendent and insubordinate son to his father Anton Matern, who came to give advice with a whispering twenty-pound sack. This period has become generally known as the springtime of the economic miracle, whose germ-cell was New Nickelswalde. A good deal of what went on—rumors of wirepulling and international involvements—must and will remain in the dark. Matern, the super, for instance, never lays eyes on Goldmouth, though everybody knows who he and nobody knows where he—not even the mealworms. But they do leak the news of Stalin's death before it is officially announced. A few weeks later Pluto, the watchdog, who is allowed to run loose at night, announces: Fire under the mill! The fire is quickly checked. Only four small struts in the jack frame have to be changed. The damage to the saddle and to the corner beams of the flour loft is insignificant. The Düsseldorf police president drives up. Definitely a case of arson. But all attempts to establish a connection between this incident and the undoubtedly successful assault on the mill which occurred shortly thereafter amount to pure imagination; for to this day proofs are still lacking. Similarly, all those who suspect a link on the one hand between Stalin's death and the unsuccessful attempt at arson, or on the other hand between the successful assault and the workers' revolts in the Soviet-occupied zone, are indulging in unadulterated speculation. Nevertheless, Communists are still generally regarded as incendiaries and kidnapers.

And so miller Matern's son must submit to questioning over a period of weeks. But he knows the tune from the old days. He has always enjoyed games of question-and-answer. Every answer, he supposes, will bring him applause.

"Trained for what trade?"

"Acting."

"Present occupation?"

"Up to the time of the assault on my father's property, I was serving as superintendent."

"Where were you on the night in question?"

"In the basement bar."

"Who can testify to that effect?"

"Herr Vicco von Bülow-Schwante, chairman of the board of the Stumm Corporation; Herr Dr. Lübbert, partner in the firm of Dyckerhoff & Widmann; and Herr Gustav Stein, chief executive of the German Manufacturers' Association."

"What were you discussing with the witnesses?"

"First the tradition of the Uhlan regiment in which Herr

von Bülow-Schwante served; then the part played by the firms of Lenz-Bau AG and Wayss & Freytag in the reconstruction of West Germany; finally, Herr von Stein explained to me the many characteristics that cultural leaders and business leaders have in common."

But obstinately as the guilty parties avoid the public eye, the fact remains: in spite of the Gehlen Organization and the triple cordon, persons unknown succeed, in the night of June 15, 1953, in abducting miller Anton Matern from his residence in a shut-down mill at New Nickelswalde. In addition to the miller, the following objects are found missing from the windmill on the morning of June 16: in the sack loft: a framed and glassed picture of former President von Hindenburg and a Grundig radio. In the flour loft: issues, covering a period of five years, of the radio magazine *Tune In*, two parakeets with cage, and a twenty-pound bag of wheat flour, which had been locked in a safe that the criminals—it is assumed that there was more than one—succeeded in opening without resorting to force.

But since the abducted twenty-pound sack is a sack in which are living mealworms of East German origin and since by their central guidance these mealworms have ushered in a flowering of the West German economy, which, even now that its end is in sight, is still stimulating the market with its late bloom, the loss of the sack and of the miller who goes with it provokes extreme alarm. In the basement bar and on the parking lot, gentlemen who are not permitted to leave New Nickelswalde for the duration of the preliminary investigations, cast about for comparable disasters in the history of Germany and the Western world. The words Cannae, Waterloo, and Stalingrad are heard. With dark foreboding observers recall the dismissal of Bismarck as recorded in an English caricature of the time: "The pilot leaves the ship." Those who feel that this caption doesn't do justice to the situation intercalate an ominous adjective borrowed from a well-known adage about rats: "The pilot leaves the sinking ship!"

But the public is not permitted to share the anguish of the business leadership. Although no one orders a news blackout on the occurrence in New Nickelswalde, not a single newspaper, not even the *Bild-Zeitung*, runs alarmist headlines: "Mealworms leave Federal Republic." "Soviet Blow Against

West German Economic Center!" "Germany's Star on the Wane."

Not a word in *Die Welt*. Whatever calls itself a newspaper between Hamburg and Munich devotes its columns to the spreading revolt of the Berlin construction workers; but Ulbricht, supported by the sound of tanks, stays—while miller Matern vanishes without musical accompaniment.

Whereupon all those who have been living by his dialect-tinged mealworm utterances, the Krupps, Flicks, Stumms, and Stinneses; all those who continue to sail a mealworm-plotted course, the Deutsche Länder-Bank and Bahlsen's Cookies; whereupon all who stood in line outside a converted windmill, holding companies and chambers of commerce, savings banks and government associations; whereupon all those who have listened respectfully to the worm, dismiss the consultations in miller Matern's mill from their minds. Henceforth, at inaugurations cornerstonelayings shiplaunchings, the word is no longer: "This prosperity was inspired by mealworm whispers. What we possess we owe to the miller and his public-spirited twenty-pound sack. Long live miller Matern!" Instead, former worm technocrats, now vainglorious public speakers, who in calm or windy weather sound off about German Ability. About the industrious German People. About the Phoenix risen from the ashes. About Germany's miraculous rebirth. Or at best about the Grace of God, without which all effort is vain.

One man alone has been thrown off by the miller's departure. Matern, the former superintendent, grinds his way unemployed with black dog through the countryside. Every wave of prosperity ebbs in time. Every miracle can be explained. Every crisis has had its warning: "Don't listen to the worm—there's a worm in the worm."

THE EIGHTY-EIGHTH STERILE MATERNIAD

Trend dull: meanwhile bald up top, sullenly grimly on the move, but strict with the dog. Pluto obeys and isn't as young as he used to be. How strenuous to grow older; for every railroad station has bad things to say of the next. On every meadow others are already grazing. In every church the same

God: *Ecce Homo!* Behold me: bald-headed inside and out. An empty closet full of uniforms of every color. I was red, put on brown, wore black, dyed myself red. Spit on me: clothing for every kind of weather, adjustable suspenders; bounceback man walks on leaden soles, bald on top, hollow within, outside bedecked with remnants: red brown black— spit on me! But Brauxel doesn't spit, he sends advances, gives advice, speaks at random of export-import and the impending end of the world, while I grind: a bald-head demands justice. This is a question of teeth, thirty-two of them. So far no dentist has made a nickel on mine. Every tooth counts.

Trend dull. Even the Cologne Central Station isn't what it used to be. Christ, who can multiply loaves and turn off drafts, has had it glassed in. Christ, who has forgiven us all, has also had the bays of the men's toilet freshly enameled. No more names charged with guilt, no more treacherous addresses. Everybody wants to be left alone and eat new potatoes every day; only Matern still feels drafts and painful names incised in heart, spleen, and kidneys, demanding to be crossed off, every last one of them. A beer in the waiting room. Once with dog around the cathedral, so he can piss on all thirty-two of its corners. Then another beer across the street. Conversations with bums who take Matern for a bum. Then a last try at the men's toilet. The smell is still the same, although the beer used to be poorer and thinner. How absurd to buy condoms. With arched back and stallion-long: drainage and absolution in thirty-two bays, all nameless. Matern buys rubbers, ten packs. He decides to visit friends in Mülheim. "The Sawatzkis? They moved out long ago. Started a little business in Bedburg. Men's suits and coats. Then they bought into the garment industry. I hear they've just opened a big fancy place in Düsseldorf. Two stories."

So far he had always managed to steer clear of this pesthole. Gone through on the train, never got out. Cologne? Sure. And Neuss with knitting needle. A week in Benrath. The coalfields, from Dortmund to Duisburg. Two days in Kaiserswerth one time. Aachen, a pleasant memory. A few nights in Büderich, but never at Hans' Flophouse. Christmas in the Sauerland, but not at the Acrobats' Hostel. Never in Düsseldorf. Krefeld, Düren, Gladbach, the country between Viersen and Dülken, where Papa worked wonders with mealworms, all that was bad enough, but nothing compared to this abscess taped over with bull's-eye panes, this insult to a nonexistent God, this half-dried blob of mustard between Düssel and Rhine, this stories-high tub of stale, bitter beer, this monster that had come into the world after Jan Wellem straddled the Lorelei. City of art, they call it, city of expositions, city of gardens. Petit-bourgeois Babel. Fogbowl of the Lower Rhine and provincial capital. Godfather to the city of Danzig. Here Grabbe suffered and struggled. "He put up with the place. That makes us even. But in the end he cleared out." For even Christian Dietrich Grabbe refused to conk out in this hole, and preferred Detmold. Grabbe laughter: "I could laugh Rome to death, why not Düsseldorf!" Grabbe tears. Hannibal's ancient eye complaint: "It will do you good to cry, ye *aficionados*! At the most convenient time, when you've won all there is to win!" But without laugh-itch or bugs in his eyes, sober with black dog at heel, Matern comes to haunt the fair city of Düsseldorf, which at carnival time is governed by the blue-and-white Prince's guard, where money burgeons, beer blooms, art foams, a city good to live in from cradle to grave: merry merry!

But even at the Sawatzkis' the trend is dull. Inge says: "Boy, are you bald!" They live on Schadowstrasse over the store, in five rooms at once, furnished in style. Standing beside the medium-sized built-in aquarium, Jochen speaks correct German now, isn't it amazing? From the good old days in Mülheim—"Do you remember, Walter?"—they still have the encyclopedia in thirty-two volumes, which way back in Fliesteden the three of them never wearied of leafing through: *A* as in "Army."—They don't want you guys. *B* as in "Business."—We started small in Bedburg, but then. *C* as in "Currency."—Nowadays the mark isn't worth fifty pfennigs. *D* as in "Dinner."—Why don't you have a bite with us? No trouble. We'll just open a few cans. *E* as in "Easter." —Just think of it. Walli will be going to school after Easter. It's been a long time. *F* as in "Fanatic."—Like you. They never get anywhere in life. *G* as in "Goods."—Just feel it. No, it's not Scotch. We make it ourselves. That's why we can sell cheaper than. *H* as in "Harpsichord."—This one's Italian-made. We picked it up in Amsterdam. Pretty good buy. *I* as in "Igloo."—We're as snug as a bug in a rug. *J* as in "Journey."—Last year we went to Austria. Burgenland. You need a change now and then. It's dirt cheap and still so unspoiled. *K* as in "Kennel."—When are you going to get rid of that dog? *L* as in "Life."—This is the only one we've got.

M as in "Maid."—The one before last got fresh before the first week was out. *N* as in "Nature."—The grounds include two acres of woods and a duck pond. *O* as in "Oskar."—He's from Danzig, too, he was putting on a show in the Onion Cellar for a while. *P* as in "Pearls."—Jochen gave me these for our anniversary. *Q* as in "Qualm."—At first the Chamber of Commerce had qualms about us, but when Jochen showed them our credentials. *R* as in "Raspberries."—Raspberry jelly and yoghurt, that's what we eat for breakfast now. *T* as in "Textiles."—Goldmouth tipped us off. *U* as in "Underground." —No, no idea where he is. *V* as in "Vanished."—Oh well, maybe he'll turn up one of these days. *W* as in "Walli."—She's our child, Walter. Don't go making any claims. *X* as in "Xylophone."—Or cymbal, that's what they play at the Czikos. Should we drop in for a little while? *Y* as in "Yucatán."—That's another place we could go. Just been opened. *Z* as in "Zombie."—No, that's no good any more. Let's go to the Morgue. You've really got to see it. It'll shake you. Absolutely wild. The limit. Downright crazy. You'll love it. Well, anyway it's fun. You'lllaughyourselfsick. Medicalsotospeak. Nakednoofcoursenot. Everythingontop. Andsohighclass. Cutthroughthemiddle. Makesyouwanttothrowup. Sadistic bestial weird. Theyoughttocloseitdown. Buttheydon't. We've been there millionsoftimes. Theygiveyouyamstoeat. It's-Jochen'streat.

Inge's idea is that Pluto should stay with the maid in the five-room apartment to guard the sleeping Walli, but Matern insists that Pluto come along to the Morgue. Sawatzki suggests: "Hadn't we better go to the Czikos?" But Inge is dead set on the Morgue. The three of them with dog push off. Up Flingerstrasse, down Bolkertstrasse. Naturally the Morgue, like all authentic Düsseldorf nightclubs, is in the Old City. Who owns the place is uncertain. Some speak of F. Schmuh, owner of the Onion Cellar. Otto Schuster of the Czikos is also mentioned. Right now Film-Mattner, owner of the Choo-Choo and the Dacha, which they had first wanted to call the "Troika," is the coming man; just recently he opened a new joint, the Fleamarket. But at the time when Matern went out on the town with dog and Sawatzkis, he was only starting out. Along Mertenstrasse, before they venture into the Morgue, Inge Sawatzki racks her brains behind her doll's face that has grown five years older: "I really wonder who hit on the idea. Somebody had to think of it, didn't they? Goldmouth used to say such funny things sometimes. Of course we never believed the line he spills. In business matters you can trust him, but in other things? For instance, he tried to make us believe that he'd owned a whole ballet. And all that tripe about the Front Line Theater during the war and so on. And he's certainly not a pure Aryan. They'd have noticed that in those days. I asked him a couple of times: Tell me, Gold-mouth, where do you actually come from? Once he said Riga, another time: They call it Swibno today. What it was called before he didn't say. But there must be some truth in the ballet business. Maybe they really didn't notice. They say Schmuh's one too. He's the one with the Onion Cellar. They say he was some kind of an air-raid warden the whole time. But they're the only ones I. And they're both typical. That's why I say that an idea like the Morgue could only have been thought up by somebody like Goldmouth who. You'll see. I'm not exaggerating. Am I, Jochen? It's right after Andreasgasse, across from the Magistrate's Court."

There it is—in white letters on a black tombstone: THE MORGUE. And yet, if you don't look too closely, it could be a plain funeral parlor. In the window there's even an ivory-colored child's coffin—empty. And the usual: wax lilies and unusually attractive coffin mountings. Pedestals fitted with white velvet support photographs of first-class funerals. Wreaths as round as life preservers lean against them. In the foreground stands an impressive stone urn of the bronze age, found, as a small plaque informs one, in Coesfeld near Münster.

Inside, the guests find equally gentle reminders of human transcience. Although they have made no reservations, the Sawatzkis, with Matern and dog, are shown to a table not far from the Swedish movie actress killed in an automobile accident and now lying in state. She is under glass and naturally made of wax. A white quilt, showing no contours, the welted edges attenuated by clouds of lace, covers the actress to the navel; but from the softly wavy black hair to the waist, the left half of her, the cheek, the chin, the gently sloping neck, the barely delineated collarbone, the steeply rising bosom are of waxen, yet pink-and-yellow-skinned flesh; to the right, however, as seen by Matern and the Sawatzkis, the illusion is created that a surgeon's scalpel has laid her bare; also modeled in wax, but true to life: heart, spleen, and the left kidney. The prize package is the heart, which beats exactly as it should, and a few of the Morgue's customers are always standing around the glass case, trying to see how it works.

Hesitantly, Inge Sawatzki last, they sit down. In indirectly lighted wall niches the roving eye distinguishes various parts of the human skeleton, the arm with radius and ulna, the inevitable death's-head, but also clearly displayed in large labeled flasks, as though for purposes of instruction, the lobe of a lung, a cerebrum, a cerebellum, and a placenta. There is even a library offering book after book, not glassed in but ready at hand: volumes on general physiology, richly illustrated, and more exacting works for the specialist—an account, for example, of experiments in the grafting of organs and a two-volume study of the pituitary gland. And between the niches, all of the same format and framed in good taste, photographs and engravings of celebrated physicians: Paracelsus, Virchow, Sauerbruch, and the Greek god of medicine leaning on a snake-entwined staff watch the guests at dinner.

The menu is nothing unusual: wiener schnitzel, beef brisket with horseradish, calves' brains on toast, beef tongue in Madeira, lamb kidneys flambé, even common pig's knuckles, and the usual roast chicken with French-fried potatoes. At most the cutlery and china are deserving of mention: Matern and the Sawatzkis eat calves' knuckles with sterile dissecting instruments; around the plates runs the inscription: "Academy of Medicine—Autopsy"; the beer, common Düsseldorf brew, foams in Erlenmeyer flasks; but otherwise there is no exaggeration. The average restaurant owner or proponent of the Düsseldorf modern style, the now-prominent Film-Mattner and his interior decorators, for instance, would have made too much of a good thing. They might, for example, have run off tape recordings of operating-room sounds: the slow, chewinggum-sluggish counting before the anesthetic takes effect, whispered or sharp instructions, metal touches metal, a saw functions, something buzzes on one note, something else pumps more and more slowly, then faster, staccato instructions, heart sounds, heart sounds . . . Nothing of the kind. Not even muffled dinner music fills the Morgue with irrelevant sound. Softly the dissecting instruments tinkle over the main course. Evenly sprinkled conversation at every table; but the tables again, apart from the damask tablecloths, are authentic: operating-room tables, elongated, on rollers, adjustable, are not mercilessly illuminated by powerful operating-room lamps, but watched over and bathed in a warm, personal light by charmingly old-fashioned, definitely Biedermeier lampshades. Nor are the guests doctors in civilian clothes, but, like the Sawatzkis and Matern, business people with friends, an occasional member of the provincial diet, a sprinkling of foreigners whose hosts want to show them something special, rarely young couples, and in every case consumers who wish to spend money on their evening out; for the Morgue—originally it was to be called the "Mortuary"—isn't exactly cheap, and besides, it's full of temptations. At the bar sit none of the usual hostesses, encouraging liquor consumption, no such sexy tactics as at the Rififi or the Taboo; instead, conservatively dressed young men, in a word, graduate physicians, are prepared, over a glass of champagne, well, perhaps not to provide final diagnoses, but to tell instructive and yet generally intelligible tales out of school. Here, far from his overkindly family doctor, many a guest has been made aware for the first time that his ailment bears this or that name, arteriosclerosis, for instance. Deposits of a fatty substance, cholesterol for example, have caused a hardening of the blood vessels. Amiably, but without the familiarity characteristic of most barroom conversation, the learned employee of the Morgue calls attention to possible consequences, coronary thrombosis, apoplexy, or what have you, then beckons a colleague, sitting nearby over a drink, to come over: The colleague, a biochemist and authority on the metabolism of fats, enlightens the guest—they stick to champagne—about animal fats and vegetable fats: "You needn't worry, the only fats used in our establishment are those containing acids that reduce cholesterol: our calves' brains on toast are prepared with pure corn oil. We also use sunflower oil and, you may be surprised to learn, even whale oil, but never lard or butter."

The Sawatzkis, especially Inge Sawatzki, try to persuade Matern, who has been troubled by kidney stones of late, to join one of the "B-doctors," as Inge calls them, at the bar. But Matern dislikes the idea of crossing the room, and so Sawatzki with a gesture summons one of the young men, who introduces himself as a urologist. No sooner has the word "kidney stones" been dropped than the young man insists on ordering the juice of two lemons: "You see, we used to be glad if we could eliminate small stones with a long and troublesome treatment; our lemon cure brings better results and all in all it's less expensive. We simply dissolve the stones, but only the so-called urate stones, I have to admit. Generally speaking, our guests' urine is normal at the end of two months. On one condition, I'm sorry to say: absolutely no liquor."

Matern puts down the beer he has just picked up. Not wishing to outstay his welcome, the urologist—it has come out that he studied under big men in Berlin and Vienna— takes his leave: "Against oxalate stones—you can see them over there, in the second case from the left—we are still powerless. But our lemon cure—perhaps you'd like me to leave you a prospectus—is the simplest thing in the world. Herodotus tells us that the Babylonians were curing kidney stones with lemon juice more than two thousand years ago; of course when he speaks of stones the size of an infant's head, we have to bear in mind that Herodotus was sometimes given to exaggeration."

Matern has a rough time with his double lemon juice. Good-natured cracks from the Sawatzkis. Leafing through the Morgue's prospectus. Why, they've got everything: specialists for the diseases of the thorax and the thyroid. A neurologist. A special prostate man. Pluto is well behaved under the operating table. Sawatzki says hello to a radio dealer acquaintance and companion at another table. Business is going strong at the bar. The B-doctors aren't being stingy with their knowledge. The calves' knuckles were excellent. Now what? Cheese or something sweet? The waiters come unbidden.

Ah yes, the waiters! They, too, are true to life. White linen tunics, buttoned up to the neck and showing only discreet reminders of the operating room, white surgeon's caps, and a white mask over nose and mouth, making them anonymous sterile soundless. Naturally they don't carry the platters of beef brisket or pork tenderloin *en croûte* in their bare hands, but wear rubber gloves in accordance with professional standards. That's going too far. It is not Inge Sawatzki but Matern who finds the gloves exaggerated: "You've got to draw the line somewhere. But that's typical again: from one extreme to the other, always wanting to drive out the Devil with. Honest shopkeepers if you will, but so stupid and so infernally smug. And they never learn from their history, they always think everyone else is to. Determined to let well enough alone and never to tilt against. Wherever they can make themselves heard, they want to cure the world of what ails it. Salomé of nothingness. Over corpses to Neverneverland. Always missed their calling. Always wanting to be brothers with everybody, to embrace the millions. Always coming around in the dead of night with their categorical thingamajig. Any thought of change scares them. Luck was never on their side. Freedom always dwells in mountains that are too high—geographically speaking, of course. Wedged into a narrow, overcrowded. Revolutions only in music, but never want to foul their own. The best infantrymen all the same, though when it comes to artillery the French. Lots of great composers and inventors have been. Copernicus for instance wasn't a Pole but. Even Marx felt himself to be. But they always have to carry things to. Like those rubber gloves. Of course they're supposed to mean something. I wonder what the owner. Assuming him to be one. Because nowadays Italian and Greek, Spanish and Hungarian joints are springing up like mushrooms. And in every dive somebody has thought up some idea. Cutting onions in the Onion Cellar, laughing gas in the Grabbe Room—and here it's this waiter's rubber gloves. Say, I know that guy! Why, it's. If he'd just take that white rag off his face. Then! Then! His name was. What was it anyway? Got to leaf back, names names, in heart, spleen, and . . ." Matern came to judge with black dog.

But the waiter-surgeon doesn't remove the cloth from nose and mouth. Nameless, with discreetly downcast eyes, he clears the dissected remains of calves' knuckles from the damask-clothed operating table. He will come again and serve the dessert with the same rubber gloves. Meanwhile we can reach into kidney-shaped bowls and chew yams. They're supposed to be good for the memory. Matern has a respite, which he spends chewing on gnarled roots: Why, that was. It must be that bastard who. You've got him and the others to thank if you. I've got a little bone to. He was—I'm not seeing things—Number 4 when the nine of us came out of the woods and climbed the. I'll give his memory a jolt. Sawatzki doesn't notice? Or he knows and he isn't saying. But I'll settle his hash all by. Coming around here with rubber gloves and a white rag on his mug. If it were black at least like at Zorro's or like the time when we. It was a curtain. We cut it up with scissors into nine triangles: one for Willy Eggers, one for Otto Warnke, one and then another for the

Dulleck brothers, one for Paule Hoppe, one for somebody
else, one for Wollschläger, one for Sawatzki, there he sits
like a hypocrite, or maybe he really hasn't noticed, and the
ninth for that guy, just wait. So we climbed the fence into
the grounds of the villa on Steffensweg. The same fence
day in day out for dog years. Behind nine black cloths over
the fence. But not tied the same way as this character. Completely covering the eyes, with slits to look out of. While this
guy: you know those eyes all right. Snow lay heavy as lead. He
was a waiter even then, in Zoppot and later at the Eden.
Here he comes with the pudding. Bublitz. Of course. I'll
tear that rag off his. Alfons Bublitz. O.K., friend, just wait.

But Matern, who has come to judge and to tear a rag
from a face, doesn't tear and doesn't judge, but stares at
the pudding, served in plexiglass bowls such as those used
by dentists. With art and precision a pastry cook—there's
no limit to what those fellows can do—has reproduced the
human dentition in two colors: curved pink gums holding
shimmering pearly evenly spaced teeth together: the human
dentition numbers thirty-two teeth, to wit, above, below, and
on either side, two incisors, one canine, five molars—coated
with enamel. At first Grabbe laughter, which, as everyone
knows, had the power to laugh Rome to pieces, tries to
surge up in Matern and wreck the joint; but as Inge and
Jochen Sawatzki, his hosts to left and right of him, apply
spatula-shaped dental instruments to their pudding teeth, the
Grabbe laughter that has been building up languishes deep
within, Rome and the Morgue are not laid waste, but inside
him as he stores up breath for a grandiose and seldom enacted
scene, dissected calf's knuckle says no to more food, especially sweets. Slowly he slips off his round stool. With
difficulty he casts off from the white-covered operating table.
He has to prop himself against the glass case where the heart
of the Swedish movie actress beats imperturbably. Pilotless,
he drifts between occupied tables, at which dinner jackets
and muchtoomuchjewelry are eating liver *en brochette* and
breaded sweetbreads. Voices in the fog. Chatting B-doctors.
Position lights over the bar. Followed by Pluto, he lurches
past the blurred pictures of the benefactors Asclepius, Sauerbruch, Paracelsus, and Virchow. And reaches port: which,
except for the reproduction of Rembrandt's famous *Anatomy
Lesson*, is a perfectly normal toilet. He vomits thoroughly
and for years. No one looks on but God in His heaven,

for Pluto has to stay outside with the attendant. Reunited with his dog, he washes his hands and face.

When he's through, Matern has no change on him and gives the attendant a two-mark piece. "It's not so bad," she says. "A lot of people get that way the first time." She gives him advice for the homeward voyage: "Take some strong coffee and a slug of schnapps and you'll be all right."

Matern complies: from a clinical porcelain cup he sips black coffee; from cylindrical test tubes he pours down a first—drink one more schnapps, or you'll be short one schnapps—then—why not?—a second drink of framboise.

Inge Sawatzki is concerned: "What's the matter with you? Can't you hold it any more? Should we call back the urologist or maybe another one that specializes in this sort of thing?"

It's the same waiter who, after calves' knuckles, yams, and pudding teeth, serves the coffee and schnapps; but Matern has lost all desire to cross off a first or last name that keeps itself sterile behind a white surgeon's mask.

During a chance lull, Sawatzki says: "Check please, waiter, or should I say doctor, or professor, hahaha!" On a printed "death certificate" form, the disguised waiter serves up the check with rubber stamp, date, and illegible signature—doctor's scrawl—for the tax people: "It's deductible. Business expenses. Where'd we be if we couldn't regularly. If the tax collectors had their way, they'd. Don't worry, the government won't go hungry."

The costumed waiter pantomimes thanks and sees the Sawatzkis and their guest with black shepherd to the door. From there Inge Sawatzki, but not Matern, casts a last backward glance. She waves "so-long" to one of the B-doctors, probably the biochemist, quite inappropriately, especially as it's an authentic hospital double door. First leather, then white enamel, runs on rails. But you don't have to push, it responds to electrical pressure. The sterile waiter presses the button.

Helping each other into their coats in a normal cloakroom, they look behind them; over the double door a red light is shining: "PLEASE DO NOT DISTURB. OPERATION IN PROGRESS!"

"Christ!" Jochen Sawatzki draws a deep breath of fresh air. "I wouldn't want to eat there every night. Every two weeks at the most, what do you say?"

Matern breathes deeply, as though to suck in piece by piece the whole Old City with its leaded panes and pewter dishes, with its crooked St. Lambert's steeple and its antiquated wrought iron. Every breath can be the last.

The Sawatzkis are worried about their friend: "You ought to take up athletics, Walter, or you'll go to pieces one of these days."

THE EIGHTY-NINTH ATHLETIC
AND THE NINETIETH STALE BEER MATERNIAD

Been am sick. Got had the grippe. But I didn't put my fever to bed, I took it to the Choo-Choo, and propped it against the bar. What a joint. Latest Lower-Rhenish railroad style, all mahogany and brass like a club car. Sitting between this one and that one until four forty-five, the whole time clutching the same brand of whisky, watching the ice getting smaller and smaller in the glass, holding forth for the benefit of all seven bartenders. Chit-chat with phonies and floozies about the first Cologne football club, about the speed limit in towns and villages, about the end of the world on the fourth of next month, about poppycock and the negotiations over Berlin. Then all of a sudden Mattner gives me hell, because I've been scratching the fancy varnish off the wall with a pipe cleaner: the whole thing is phony! I got to see what's behind it, don't I? And all these people jammed into a club car. Squeezed into dinner jackets, with celluloid cunts in tow: crispy, crunchy, cute. But no place for a first-class act. The most I can do is to work off my manly play instinct: wind it up slowly and let it unroll fast. Out comes *Eine Kleine Nachtmusik*. In the end it was rich and schmaltzy. It seems that Mattner treated to a round of drinks, whereupon Franz Moor hollered, Act Five, Scene 1: "Slavish wisdom, slavish fears!—It's still a moot question whether the past is dead or whether there's an eye above.—Hum, hum! What whispered voice? Is there an avenger up there?—No, no!—Yes, yes! That awful whispering around me: Someone above. This very night I'll go to meet the avenger above. No! I say. Miserable subterfuge behind which. It's empty, lonely, deaf up there above.—And yet if there isn't! I command it: there isn't."

They applauded with hands as big as office folders and

snapped at Matern with powder boxes, encore: "Command it: there isn't."

What does an avenger do when his victims pat him familiarly on the back: "It's all right, boy. We get you: When you command, it isn't. Let bygones be bygones. Put on a new record. Weren't you a glider flier one time?—Sure, sure, you're perfectly right. You're an A-1 antifascist and we're lousy little Nazis, the whole lot of us. O.K.? But weren't you once, and didn't you once, and somebody told me you used to play faustball, a lineman, the captain . . ."

Bronze, silver, and gold. Every athlete refurbishes his past. Every athlete was better once upon a time. Every day both Sawatzkis, before and after dinner: "You've got to get some exercise, Walter. Go hiking in the woods, or goswimming-intheRhine. Think of your kidney stones. Do something about them. Take our bicycle out of the cellar or buy a punching bag and charge it to me."

Nothing can tickle Matern out of his chair. He sits, hands planted on both knees, as fused with the furniture as if he were planning to sit it out for nine years like his grandmother, old grandma Matern, who sat riveted to her chair for nine years, only rolling her eyeballs. And yet, what riches Düsseldorf and the world have to offer: thirty-two movie houses, Gründgens' Theater, up and down the Königsstrasse, tart Düsseldorf beer, the Rhine famed in song, the reconstructed Old City, the swan-mirroring castle gardens, Bach Society, Art Society, Schumann Hall, men's fashion shows, the carnival bells that ring in the carnival, athletic fields; the Sawatzkis list them all: "Why don't you go out to Flingern and have a look at the Fortuna Stadium? There's all sorts of things going on there, not just football." But none of these sports—and Sawatzki lists more than he has fingers—can lift Matern off his chair. And then by chance—his friends have already given up—the word "faustball" is dropped. It makes no difference who whispered it, Inge or Jochen, or maybe little Walli, mighty cute. In any event, no sooner has the word fallen than he is on his feet. Just as Düsseldorf and the world are about to write him off, Matern takes short steps on the pocketbook-thick carpet. Little limbering-up movements. Startled cracking of joints. Sudden loquacity: "Boy, it's been a long time. Faustball. '35 and '36 on Heinrich Ehlers Field. The Engineering School on the right, the crematory on the left. We won every tournament, crushed them all: the Athletic and Fencing Club, the Danzig Touring Club, Schellmühl 98, even the police. Played lineman for the Young Prussians. We had a marvelous center. He teased every ball up in the air for me and served with dauntless calm. His calm was Olympian, I'm telling you; with machinelike underhand shots he hit one ball after another down to the line, and I just pounced: sharp forehand shots and long shots that the opposing team couldn't. Just before the war, I played here for a while with the Unterrath Atheletic Club, until they. Well, better not talk about that."

It's not far, you take the Number 12 from Schadowplatz to Ratingen, up Grafenberger Allee to the Haniel and Lueg plant, then turn off to the left through vegetable gardens, through Mörsenbroich and the Municipal Forest, to the Rath Stadium, a medium-sized setup at the foot of Aap Forest. A fine flourishing piece of woods, with a view through the nearby gardens down to the city immersed in the usual mist: churches and factories alternate significantly. Empty lots, fenced-in building sites, and, massive on the other side, the Mannesheim Corporation. Here and there: activity on every field. They're always laying out fresh cinders somewhere. Junior handball teams, sloppy playing, three-thousand-meter runners trying to better their time; and on a small field off to one side and surrounded by Lower-Rhenish poplars, the Unterrath Seniors are playing the Derendorf Seniors. Seems to be an unscheduled game. The field is sheltered from the wind, but Unterrath is losing. Matern with dog can see that at a glance. He can also see why: the lineman is no good and doesn't co-ordinate with the center, who under different circumstances wouldn't be bad.

Overhead return shots are all right for the backs, but not for the man on the line. The left forward is pretty good, but they're not using him enough. Actually the team hasn't got a playmaker, the center—he looks mighty familiar to Matern, but that could be because of the gym suit, and as a rule a lot too many look familiar to him—well, all the center does is to bounce the ball high, so anybody at all can come running up: both backs, the lineman; naturally the Derendorfers, who aren't really so hot, get in close and pile up points by smashing. Only the left forward—he too looks as if Matern had seen him somewhere sometime—stays put and manages, mostly with backhand shots, to save the

honor of the Unterrath Seniors. The return game also ends
with a defeat for the home team. They've switched the lineman and the right back; but up to the final whistle the new
lineman exhibits no prowess capable of saving the day.

Matern with dog stands at the entrance to the field: anyone heading for the locker rooms has to pass by him and his
inquiring gaze; the moment they come in sight with their
gym suits over their shoulders, he's sure. His heart hops.
Something presses against his spleen. Painful kidneys. It's
them. Once Unterrath Juniors like himself: Fritz Ankenrieb
and Heini Tolksdorf. Even then, so and so many dog years
ago, Fritz played center and Heini played left forward, while
Matern was lineman: what forwards! What a team altogether, the backs—what were their names anyway—were
class too. They even beat the stuffings out of a Cologne
University team and the boys from the Düsseldorf SS, but
then the team suddenly went to pot, because . . . I'll ask
the boys if they remember why, and who it was that
turned, if it wasn't a certain Ankenrieb that, and even Heini
Tolksdorf agreed that I . . .

But before Matern has a chance to confront them: I've
come with a black dog . . . Ankenrieb starts jawing at him
from one side: "Christ, is it possible? Is it you or . . . Take
a look, Heini, who's been watching our lousy playing. I said
to myself before, when we were changing sides: You know
that guy. Look at that posture, the same old. Hasn't changed
a bit, except on top. Well, none of us can claim that his looks
are improving. Once we were the hope of Unterrath, today
we get one drubbing after another. Christ, those were the
days, remember the police meet in Wuppertal. And you on the
line. The whole time right under the nose of that cop
from Herne. You've got to come to our bar, we still have
all the pictures and scrolls. As long as we had you for a
lineman, nobody could, after that, am I right, Heini, we
went downhill fast. We never did recover. Lousy politics!"

A group of three, with a black dog frolicking around them.
They've put him in the middle, they talk about victories and
defeats, they blurt it out quite frankly, yes, they were the
ones who went to the club manager, so he'd. "You just
couldn't keep your trap shut, though of course you were
right about a good many things." A few whispered remarks
in the locker room had done it. "If you'd said that to me at
home or somewhere else, I'd have listened, maybe even

agreed with you, but that's how it is. Politics and sports have never mixed. They still don't."

Matern quotes: "This is what you said, Ankenrieb: We can do without a lineman who spreads Jewish-Bolshevist propaganda. Is that right?"

Heini Tolksdorf comes to the rescue: "We were brainwashed, the whole lot of us. You yourself didn't always say the same things. They threw dust in our eyes for years. We had to foot the bill. Our backs, do you remember, little Rielinger and Wölfchen Schmelter, never came back from Russia. Christ! And what for?"

The club's hangout is where it always was, on Dorotheenplatz in Flingern. With four five old friends, Matern is affably constrained to remember the game in Gladbach, the quarter finals in Wattenscheid, and the unforgettable end game in Dortmund. The corner reserved for the Unterrath Club isn't lacking in decoration. He has a chance to admire himself, the lineman, in twelve photographs of the team, all framed and glassed. From late fall '38 to early summer '39 Matern played, here he has it in black and white, on the Unterrath team. Barely seven months, and what relics of victory! What thick rebellious hair he had! Always serious. Always the center of attraction, even when he was standing on the right wing. And the scrolls. Brown calligraphy under the eagle emblem of those days. "You really should have stuck something over that. I just can't stand the sight of the animal. Memories well and good, but not under that bankrupt gallows bird."

That's a suggestion worth discussing. At a late hour— the drinks are beer and gin—they patch up an exemplary compromise: Heini Tolksdorf borrows a tube of paste from the owner and, encouraged by cheers, sticks common beer mats, Schwaben-Bräu, over the offensive emblem on all the honor scrolls. In return, Matern makes a solemn promise—all the club members rise to their feet—never again to waste a word on the stupid old incident and to play lineman again—shake hands on it—for the Unterrath Seniors.

"Good will is the main thing. We'll make out. What comes between us shall be forgotten, what unites us shall be held in honor. If everybody makes a concession or two, strife and dissension will be things of the past. For true democracy is unthinkable without readiness to compromise. We're all sinners, we've all. Who will cast the first? Who can say, I am without? Who can claim to be infallible? Therefore let us. We of Unterrath have always. And so let us first, in honor of our comrades who in Russian soil. And then to the health of our good old, who is with us today, and lastly to the old and the new comradeship among athletes. I raise my glass!" —Every toast is the toast before last. Every round has no end. Every man is merriest among men.—Under the table Pluto licks spilled beer.

So things seem to be on the mend. Inge and Jochen Sawatzki are delighted when Walter Matern parades his brand-new gym suit: "Boy, has he got a figure!" But the figure is deceptive. Of course you have to get back into the feel of the game. It would be dumb to put him on the line right off. But for the present he's too slow for a back—a back has to get away fast—and he proves a failure at center because he wants to cover the whole field and can't manage to maneuver the ball effectively from the backfield to the line. He plays neither to the left forward nor to the lineman. He takes everything that comes up from the backs as intended for him personally, cuts the ball off from his own men, and then half the time proceeds to lose it. A solo artist, who hands the opposing team set-up shots on a platter, just asking to be smashed. Where can they put him if it's too soon to put him on the line?

"He's got to be on the line."

"And I'm telling you he has to get back into shape first."

"His type can only be used on the line."

"His reactions aren't quick enough."

"Anyway, he's big enough for a lineman."

"He's got to taste blood, then he'll perk up."

"Too ambitious for a center."

"All right, put him up front, we'll see."

But playing right forward, all he can manage is an occasional trick serve that drops square in front of the opposition's feet. Only seldom does he surprise the Oberkassel or Derendorf Seniors with tricky backspins; but then, when the ball takes a sharp, flat, and unpredictable bounce in enemy territory, one gets an inkling of the lineman that Matern once was. Ankenrieb and Tolksdorf exchange wistful nods: "Man, what a champ he used to be! Too bad." And keep their patience. They give him good passes, they keep the ball up high for him, and he shoots it down the drain. He's hopeless. "But we've got to be sporting about this. How can you expect him to be in form after all these years? And besides, there's his leg injury. It's hardly noticeable, but just the same. Why don't you make him a reasonable proposition, Heini? Something like this: 'See here, Walter, it seems to me you've lost some of the old zip. I can understand that. God knows there are more important things than being a lineman for the Unterrath Athletic Club, but couldn't you referee the next game or two, just until you get the feel of the thing?' "

Team members try to make things easy for Matern. "Sure! Why not? There's nothing I'd like better. I'm only glad you're still willing to. Whatever you like: line watcher, scorekeeper, referee. Like me to make you a cup of coffee or bring you a coke? Can I have a real referee's whistle?" That's something Matern has always longed for. His true calling: to make decisions. "Foul ball. The score is now nineteen to twelve in favor of Wersten. You're wrong. I know all the rules. When I was knee-high to a grasshopper, at home on Heinrich Ehlers Field. Man, what a center we had. A fat kid with freckles, but light on his feet like lots of tubbies, and, boy, was he calm! Nothing could rattle him. And always cheerful. Like me, he knew all the rules: The player who puts the ball into play must have both feet behind the line of play. At the moment of hitting the ball and putting it into play, he must have at least one foot on the ground. The open hand or a fist with disengaged thumb may not be used in putting the ball into play. Any one player may only once, and in general three times is the limit. The ball may strike the ground only once between strokes, neither the goalpost nor the line must be, only arm and fist may be—Ah, if only I could play again with Eddi, he in midfield, I on the line!—any infringement turns the ball into a foul ball, the whistle is blown twice, which means: The ball is dead!" Who would have thought it: Matern, who had come with black dog to judge, makes out fine as a referee and trains his mutt to be a line judge: Pluto barks at every foul; Matern, who had always been hot on the heels of an enemy, knows no opponent, but only teams which are all, without exception, subject to the same rules and regulations.

His old faustball friends, Fritz Ankenrieb and Heini Tolksdorf, admire him. They talk Matern up at meetings of the club's officers, and especially to the Juniors. "You can take an example from him. When he saw that his form wasn't what it used to be, he gave up his position on the line without a single bitter word and unselfishly offered his services as referee. He'd be a swell coach for you, what a guy! Went through the whole war. Wounded three times. Always ready for a suicide mission. When he begins to tell stories, your eyes pop out of your head."

Who would have thought it: Matern, who had come to judge the Seniors Ankenrieb and Tolksdorf, turns into an unbiased referee, declines when someone, in a well-meant attempt at subordination, offers him a half-time job at Mannesmann's, which would keep master and dog in style, and strands incorruptible, with dog at heel, among the Juniors of the Unterrath Athletic Club. The boys in the blue gym suits form a loose semicircle, and he in crimson gym suit explains his raised striking fist, showing the surfaces employed in the backhand shot and the inside shot. While he demonstrates his lowered fist, showing the surfaces used in the forehand shot and the snap shot, the Sunday morning sun does a headstand on his hairless dome: how it glitters. The boys can hardly wait to apply what Matern has drummed into them: his horizontal fist shows the surface employed in the backhand shot and the risky roundhouse shot. And then, after a lively practice game and the starting exercises for the backs—his own idea—he tells the boys stories from wartime and peacetime. Seated, the dark-blue gym suits around him, the crimson-clad coach, form a loose but tense semicircle. At last somebody who knows how to get at the youngsters. No question falls unanswered on the turf of the faustball field. He knows about everything. Matern knows how it happened; how things came to such a pass; what an undivided Germany was and could be; who is to blame for all this; what jobs the old-time murderers are holding down again; and how to make sure it will never happen again. He has the right tone for the youngsters. He makes what was jellyfish-soft woodcut-clear. His leitmotives unmask murder motives. He simplifies labyrinths into straight broad highways. When coach Matern says: "And that is our still unconquered past!," every Unterrath youngster looks upon him as the one and only true conqueror of the past. After all, he has set an example, not once but many times: "For instance, when I stepped up to that member of the special court and a little later to the judge himself, those bastards crawled, crawled I'm telling you, and Local Group Leader Sellke in Oldenburg, who used to talk so big, began to snivel when I and the dog . . ." In general, allusions to Pluto, who is never absent when past and present are being clarified in the loose semicircle, are the refrain of Matern's long didactic poem: "And when I went to the Upper Weser country with the dog. The dog was there when in Altena-Sauerland. The dog is a witness that in Passau I." The boys applaud whenever Matern tumbles one of the old-time big-shots. They are carried away. Model and coach in one. But throughout these pleasurable Nazi funerals Matern unfortunately can't refrain—and not just in subordinate clauses—from making socialism triumph.

"What business has Marx on an athletic field?" asks the executive committee unanimously.

"Can we allow Eastern propaganda to be encouraged on our athletic fields?" runs the question which the field manager submits in writing to the Unterrath Athletic Club.

"Our young athletes will not tolerate this state of affairs," maintains the honorary chairman at the bar in Dorotheen-platz. He knows Matern from before the war. "He made the same kind of trouble even then. Can't adapt himself. Poisons the atmosphere." In his opinion, which is seconded by nods and murmurs of "exactly," a true Unterrath athlete must not only give himself wholly and cheerfully to his elected sport, but must also be clean inside.

After soandso many dog years, for the soandsomanieth time in Matern's medium-length life, a court of honor takes up his case. Exactly like the Young Prussians on Heinrich Ehlers Field and the men of Langfuhr SA Sturm 84, the members of the Unterrath Athletic Club decide to expel Matern a second time. As in '39, the vote to exclude him from club and athletic field meets with no opposition. Only members Ankenrieb and Tolksdorf abstain, an attitude which meets with silent approval on all sides. In conclusion the honorary chairman remarks: "He can be glad that these proceedings will remain among ourselves. The last time the affair had further repercussions, police headquarters on Kavalleriestrasse, if that rings a bell." DON'T GO IN FOR SPORTS. YOU'LL BE MADE SPORT OF.

O Matern, how many defeats must you check off as victories? What environment spat you out after you had subjected it? Will they someday print maps of both Germanies and unroll them in schoolrooms as a visual record of your battles, marked in the usual way—two crossed sabers? Will they say: Matern's victory at Witzenhausen became evident on the morning of the? The battle of Bielefeld saw the victor Mater in Cologne on the Rhine the following morning? When Matern triumphed in Düsseldorf-Rath, the calendar read June 3, 1954? Or if your victories, marked with crosses and counted, do not find their way into history, will at least grandmothers surrounded by grandchildren remember half-truthfully: "Then, in the dog year '47, a poor dog, who had a black dog with him, came to see us and tried to make trouble for Grampa. But I took the fellow, not a bad sort really, quietly aside until he calmed down and began to purr like a kitten, all cuddly."

Inge Sawatzki, for example, has often revived the tired victor Matern and nursed him back to health, which is just what she does now that the wounds inflicted on the Unter-rath athletic field are in need of being dressed. It was bound to happen. Inge can wait. Every warrior comes home now and then. Every woman welcomes with open arms. Every victory demands to be celebrated.

Even Jochen Sawatzki can see that. Accordingly he says to his wife Inge: "Go ahead if you can't help it." And they—the classical great lovers—do what they still can't help. The apartment is big enough after all. And now that he's kind of worn out, it's actually more fun than in the days when you only had to look at his knob for the machine to spring into action and finish the job much quicker than necessary. Always that craving for records: "I'll show you. I can do it any time, at high speed. I could show you seven times and climb the Feldberg when I'm through. That's the way I am. All the Materns have been like that. Simon Materna, for instance, always had a big chunk of meat up front, even on horseback when he was on his way to wreak vengeance between Dirschau, Danzig, and Elbing. That was a man. And as for his brother Gregor Materna, you can still read in the Danzig city archives that 'after al manner of mysdeedes, murther, and the sheddyng of Christian blode, lorde Materna cam that autumn to Danczk for to wreak al manner of fiercenesse, and eke to hank Claus Bartusch by the neck, at which tyme he set vp his passyng styffe peter for a gallows, whereat wondyrment was of alle the robboures and mar-chants.' That's the kind he was. And in the old days, in the

Army, for instance, you could have hung, well, maybe not a sack of pepper, but anyway a twenty-pound weight on my handle without preventing it from giving you the works quickly and very effectively."

Nevermore would he hammer nails into the wall with turgid tool. Now she takes him in hand—slowly and gently. "Mustn't panic right away, we have time. These are the best years of life, when potency levels off and we watch it like a savings account. After all there are other things in life. For instance, we could go to the theater sometime, you used to be an actor yourself. You don't feel like it? Never mind, we'll go to the movies, or we can go watch the Martinmas procession with Walli: lantern lantern, sun, moon, and stars. Or it's nice having coffee in Kaiserswerth and looking out over the Rhine. We could go to Dortmund for the six-day bicycle race, and this time we'll take Sawatzki with us. I've never been to the Moselle for the wine harvest. Ah, a beautiful beautiful year with you. It'll be something I can feed on for the rest of my life. You seem so much more settled than you used to be. You even leave the dog home once in a while. Of course there are always exceptions, like at the last Men's Garment Fair when we bumped into that tubby little Semrau man, and you went off your rocker and started arguing with him and Jochen behind our booth. But then you had a few beers together, and Jochen even closed a deal with Semrau: for several dozen duffel coats. Or in Cologne at the Mardi Gras parade: they've been marching by for over an hour, and then comes a float with a regular windmill on it, and a lot of nuns and knights in real armor are dancing around it. But headless the whole lot of them. They're carrying their heads under their arms. Or playing catch with them. I'm just on the point of asking you what they're suppose to symbolize when off you go, trying to break through the barrier and get at the nuns. Lucky they didn't let you through. Heaven knows what you would have done to them, and they to you, because they don't pull any punches on Mardi Gras. But then you calmed down, and at the station it was gay again. You went as some kind of medieval soldier; Sawatzki was a one-eyed admiral; and you made a regular robber's moll out of me. Too bad the picture turned out so fuzzy. Because if it were clear, you could see what a bay window you've put on, my sugarbun. That's because we take such good care of you. You've got nice and plump since you gave up athletics. It doesn't agree with you—clubs and meetings and all that stuff. You'll always be a lone wolf. The only reason you make out with Jochen is that he always does what you say. He's even against the atom bomb because you're against it and signed that petition. And I'm against it too, I wouldn't want to get bumped off now that we're so cozy together. Because I love you. Don't listen. I could eat you up, because I, do you hear? Everything about you. The way you look through walls and the way you clutch a glass. When you cut bacon against your thumb. When you talk like an actor, trying to grab hold of heaven knows what. Your voice, your shaving soap, or when you cut your, or the way you walk, you walk as if you had an appointment with God knows who. Because sometimes I can't make you out. But that doesn't matter. Just don't listen when I. But I would like to know how you spent the time with Jochen in the old days when. You don't have to start up with your teeth right away. Didn't I tell you not to listen? Say, there's a shooting match on the Rhine Meadows, hear? Should we go? Tomorrow? Without Jochen? I've got to be over there in the branch store until six. How about seven at the Rhine Bridge? On the Oberkassel side."

Matern is on his way to his date, without dog. Good old Pluto, he isn't allowed out in the street so often any more, for fear of his being run over. Matern walks quickly straight ahead, because he has an appointment at a definite time. He has bought cherries, a whole pound. Now he's spitting cherry pits in the direction of his appointment. People walking toward him have to dodge. The cherries and minutes grow fewer. When you cross the bridge on foot, you notice how wide the Rhine is: from the Planetarium on the Düsseldorf side to Oberkassel: a good pound of cherries wide. He spits in the head wind, which pushes the cherry pits in the direction of Cologne; but the Rhine carries them down to Duisburg or farther still. Every cherry cries out for the next. Eating cherries puts you in a rage. Rage mounts from cherry to cherry. When Jesus chased the money-changers out of the Temple, He ate a pound of cherries before He. Othello also ate a whole pound before he. The Moor brothers, both of them, day in day out, even in winter. And if Matern had to play Jesus, Othello, or Franz Moor, he'd be obliged to eat a whole pound before each performance. How much hatred ripens with them or is preserved along with them in jars? They only seem to be so round; in reality cherries are pointed triangles. Especially sour cherries set the teeth on edge. As if he had any need of that. He thinks shorter than he spits. Ahead of him homeafteroffice-goers hold their hats tight and are afraid to look behind them. Those who look back have someone behind them. Only Inge Sawatzki, who also has an appointment, mirrors the ever more menacingly approaching Matern fearlessly and punctually in googoo eyes. How can she be expected to know that he has almost a pound of cherries under his belt? Fresh-white blows her flimsy dress. Tight above, wide below. Waist still twenty-one, though it takes a girdle. She can afford sleeveless expectation. Wind in Ingedress brushes jumpy knees, towardly knees: smiling toward, running toward, four-and-a-half Italian sandal steps: and then plunk between her towardly breasts; but nothing can get Inge Sawatzki down; under the impact she stands staunch and vertical: "Aren't I punctual? The spot looks good on my dress. It needed some red. Were they sweet or sour cherries?"

For the bag has vented all his rage. The cherry-pit spitter can drop it. "Should I buy you some more, there's a stand over there."

But Inge Sawatzki would like "to ride the high-flier, for ever and ever." So off across the Rhine Meadows. In amid the surge of others and instantly included in the count. But no description of the environment, for she doesn't want ice cream, she doesn't know how to shoot, the scenic railway appeals to her only when it's dark, sideshows are always a disappointment, all she wants is the high-flier, for ever and ever.

First he wins two roses and a tulip for her at the shooting gallery. Then she simply has to let herself be bumped around with him in a dodgem car. During which, hermetically sealed off against the outside world, he meditates on mass man, materialism, and transcendence. Then with three shots he wins her a little yellow bear for Walli, but it can't growl. Then he has to drink two consecutive beers standing up. Then he buys her burnt almonds whether she wants them or not. A try at a target—it'll only take a minute: two eights, a ten. At last she gets to ride the high-flier with him, but not for ever and ever. The high-flier is two-thirds empty, it's gradually going out of style. But Inge is wild about old-fashioned things. She collects music boxes, dancing bears, cutouts, magic lanterns, whistling tops, decalcomanias, she's just the type for the high-flier. Her dress and undies made specially to order for this circular journey. Hair loose, towardly knees anything but pressed together; for anyone who is as hot as Inge Sawatzki, obliged to carry a feverquiff around with her hour after hour, keeps wanting to hang it and herself out in the wind. But he doesn't enjoy subjection to the laws of gravitation. Round and round for two and a half minutes, regardless of whether or not you roll up and let the change of direction unwind you: round and round until the music stops. But Inge wants to hang herself in the wind: "One more time. One more time!" Not to be a spoilsport for once in his life. There's no cheaper way of making her dizzy. Take a look at the environment while it goes round and round. Still one and the same leaning St. Lambert's Tower means Düsseldorf over there. Still the same ugly mugs crowded in a circle, with or without ice cream, with objects bought or won by shooting or dicing, and waiting for Matern's return. Mass man believes in him and trembles at his approach. Slavish wisdom, slavish fears! all, without distinction, cooked according to the same recipe. Bankbooks in their hearts, jungle without claws, hygienic pipedreams, neither good nor evil, but *phenomenal*, all in one gravy. Scattered peas. Or if you prefer, raisins in a cake. Forgetful of Being, in search of an *ersatz* for transcendence. Taxpayers, all cut from the same cloth, excepting one. All identical; one stands out. Just an irregularity in the weave, but even so he stands out. From round to round, impossible to ignore. Got himself a sharpshooter's hat like all the other members of the rifle club, and is nonetheless here again, gone, back again, gone: a very special sharpshooter. O names! why, that's, of course, wait a minute! Gone— here again: that's all I needed. The jig is up, sharpshooter police major. The revels will soon be ended, Police Major Osterhues. Shall we ride the high-flier? Chase murder motives with leitmotives? What do you say, Heinrich, shall we?

Some of the sharpshooters want to, but this particular one doesn't. He wanted to before, but now that someone jumps off the starting high-flier and shouts his name plus his superannuated rank to the ends of the world, the meanwhile alderman and sharpshooter Heinrich Osterhues has lost all inclination and wants only to make himself scarce. "Police major"; those are words he doesn't like to hear. Even old friends aren't allowed to. That was once upon a time and has no business here.

Happened before and often filmed: nothing is easier than running away at a shooting match. For everywhere friendly fellow sharpshooters with their hats—half forester's hats, half sou'westers—stand in readiness and take him under cover. They even run a few steps to lead the wolf up a false trail. Fool him by scattering, which just about halves or quarters the wolf. Split into sixteenths—that's what Matern would have to do. Nab him, nab him! Leitmotive chases murder motive! Ah, if only he had Pluto with him, he'd know the way to Heinrich Osterhues. Ah, if only he had marked him, the police major of rib-smashing years, with cherry pit and cherry spot and not Ingedress. "Osterhues Osterhues!" Don't turn around—cherry pit's going around.

Only after an hour of Osterhues-screeching and Osterhues-searching—he must have seized a whole regiment of sharpshooters by the buttons of their uniforms and released them in disgust—does he find the trail again: he picks up a photograph, badly trampled, from the trampled grass. It doesn't show this one or that one or Osterhues the sharpshooter: no, it shows the onetime police major Osterhues, who in the year 1939 personally questioned Walter Matern, prisoner held for investigation, in the cellar of the Kavalleriestrasse police headquarters.

With this photograph—it must have slipped out of the fleeing sharpshooter's sharpshooter's jacket—Matern makes the rounds of the beer tents. No sign of him. Or he threw it away—evidence! Armed with this warrant, he races through sideshow booths, pokes around under the trailers. Night is falling over the Rhine Meadows—white Ingedress follows him pleading respectfully and wants to ride on the scenic railway, for ever and ever—when Osterhues-hungry, he enters a last beer tent. Whereas all the other tents, inflated like beer bellies, could scarcely hold the noise of the singing, under this tent silence prevails. "Psst!" warns the monitor at the entrance. "We're taking a picture." With catlike tread Matern treads on beer-sour sawdust. Neither folding chairs nor rows of tables. Osterhues-seeking eyes take in the scene: What a picture, what a photograph, the rifle club photographer is planning! Amidst hushed emptiness a platform raises one hundred thirty-two sharpshooters toward the tent roof. Arranged into tiers—kneeling, sitting, standing, and in the very back row towering-over. One hundred thirty-two sharpshooters wear their sharpshooter hats—half forester's hat, half sou'wester—slightly tilted to the right. Sharpshooter braid and rosettes are equitably distributed.

None silvers more strikingly, no chest is less bemedaled. Not one hundred thirty-one sharpshooters and one sharpshooter king, but one hundred thirty-two brother sharpshooters of equal rank smile slyly goodnaturedly eagerly in the direction of Matern, who, armed with the police major's photograph, is trying to distinguish and select. All resemblance is purely fortuitous. All resemblance is denied. All resemblance is admitted one hundred thirty-two times; for between raised platform and tent roof Sharpshooter Heinrich Osterhues smiles in tiers, kneels sits stands towers-over, wears his sharpshooter's hat tilted slightly to the right, and is photographed one hundred thirty-two times with one flash bulb. A family portrait. One hundred thirty-twolets. "That's all, gentlemen!" cries the photographer. One hundred thirty-two Heinrichs rise chatting lumbering beer-sodden, rise from the festival-photograph platform, all bent upon shaking hands immediately and one hundred thirty-twofold with an old friend from one-hundred-thirty-twofold police-major days: "How's it going? Back on the old stamping ground? Ribs mended O.K.? Those were rugged times all right. All hundred thirty-two of us will lay to that. It was hew to the line, boy, or else. But at least the guys sang when we took 'em in hand. They weren't pampered like nowadays . . ."

Whereupon Matern turns and runs, across beer-sour sawdust. "What's the hurry, man? A meeting like this wants to be celebrated!" The shooting match spews him out. O starry sky, with vanishing points! The tireless Inge and God in His heaven are waiting for him. In His hands and keeping, the Rhine Meadows are streaked with dawn by the time she has calmed him down—her teeth-chattering lover.

THE NINETY-FIRST, HALFWAY SENSIBLE MATERNIAD

What good is his cast-iron head if the walls to dash it against are made pervious on purpose? Is this an occupation: pushing revolving doors? Converting whores? Making holes in Swiss cheese? Who wants to tear open old wounds if the opening of wounds gives pleasure? Or dig a pit for the other guy so he can help you out of it afterward? Shadowboxing? Bending safety pins? Driving nails into solid-rubber enemies? Going through telephone directories or address books, name by name?—Call off the vengeance, Matern! Let Pluto rest by the fireside. Enough de-Nazification! Make your peace with this world; or combine your obligation to heed your heart, spleen, and kidneys with the security of a monthly income. Because you're not lazy. You've always worked full time: making the rounds, crossing-off, making the rounds. You've often strained yourself to the limit and beyond: women to take with you, women to drop. What else can you do, Matern? What have you learned at the mirror and against the wind? To speak loudly and distinctly on the stage. Well then, slip into roles, brush your teeth, knock three times, and get yourself hired: as a character actor, phenotype, Franz or Karl Moor depending on your mood—and announce to all the loges and to the orchestra as well: "But soon I will come among you and hold terrible muster!"

Too bad! Matern isn't prepared yet to make a halfway profitable business of revenge. In Sawatzki's easy chair he hatches out gaping nothings. He drags himself and his kidney stones from room to room. Friends support him. His mistress takes him to the movies. When he goes walking, with dog and on business, no one dares to turn around. What hammer blow will have to stun him before he learns to steer clear of people who hear him, the Grinder, behind them.

And then in 1955, when all the children born in '45, the year peace set in, turn ten years old, a cheap, mass-produced article floods the market. Secretly, though not illicitly, a well-oiled and hence soundless sales organization functions. No newspaper ads herald this hit of the season; in no shop window does it bait the eye; in no toyshops or department stores does this article sell like hotcakes; no mail-order house sends it out postage paid. Instead, peddlers peddle it on fairgrounds, on playgrounds, outside school buildings; wherever children condense; but also outside vocational schools, apprentice-homes and universities, a toy intended for the generation between seven and twenty-one is obtainable.

Not to make an additional mystery out of an already mysterious commodity, the object in question is a pair of glasses.

No, not the kind of glasses through which you can study indecent goings-on in different colors and positions. No disreputable manufacturer is out to corrupt the West German postwar youth. No competent authorities or injunctions are called for or necessary. No pastor finds occasion to fling hairraising parables from the pulpit. And yet the glasses that are offered for sale at strikingly low prices do not serve to correct the usual defects of vision. Glasses of a very different kind, which neither corrupt nor cure, approximately—we have only estimates to go by—one million four hundred thousand pairs of them, make their appearance on the market: price fifty pfennigs. Subsequently, after investigating commissions have had to concern themselves with this article in the provinces of Hesse and Lower Saxony, the official estimates are corroborated: a certain firm of Brauxel & Co., located in Grossgiessen near Hildesheim, has manufactured one million seven hundred forty thousand pairs of the wrongfully incriminated item and succeeded in selling exactly one million four hundred fifty-six thousand three hundred twelve of these mass-produced articles. Not a bad venture in view of the low production costs: crudely stamped plastic. Still, though the glasses are like windowpanes, without any special grind, they must have required long and painstaking research: Brauxel & Co. would seem to have employed the specialized skill of Jena-trained opticians, fugitives from the Democratic Republic. But Brauxel & Co.—a highly reputable firm I might add—is able to prove to both investigating commissions that no optician was working in the laboratory, but that a special mixture, patent applied for, had been brought to the melting point in the small glassworks connected with the enterprise: to the well-known mixture of quartz sand, sodium carbonate, sodium sulphate, and limestone is added a quantity, measured to the gram and therefore secret, of mica, such as may be gained from mica gneiss, mica slate, and mica granite. Thus no Devil's broth, nothing of a forbidden nature, is brewed; scientific data are confirmed by the affidavits of well-known chemists. The proceedings initiated by the provinces of Lower Saxony and Hesse are quashed. And yet there must be something special about the things—caused no doubt by the little mica mirrors. But only the younger generation from seven to twenty-one respond to the gimmick, for there is, in those glasses, a gimmick to which grownups and younger children are impervious.

What are the glasses called? Various names, not all of them developed by Brauxel & Co., are current. Originally the manufacturers present their article as a nameless toy, but once its appeal is obvious, they put out a name or two as slogans for vendors.

Matern, who has gone for a stroll hand in hand with the now eight-year-old Walli, hears of the "miracle glasses" for the first time at the Düsseldorf Christmas fair on Bolkerstrasse. Between the potato pancake booth and a stand selling Christmas stollen, an unobtrusive little man, who might just as well be selling Christmas cookies or cut-rate fountain pens or razor blades, is holding out a half-filled cardboard box.

But neither on the left where fat-saturated odors are meant to lure, nor on the right where powdered sugar is not being spared, are so many customers jostling as around the soon empty cardboard box. The vendor, doubtless a seasonal worker, doesn't shout but whispers: "Miracle glasses. Try them. Look through 'em." But for all its fairytale quality, the name is intended more for the grown-up pocketbook holders; for the nature of the miracle has got around among the younger generation: thirteen-year-old boys and sixteen-year-old girls mostly call the glasses "recognition glasses"; students in their last year of high school, newly licensed automobile mechanics, and students in their first year at the university speak of "knowledge glasses." Less current and probably not of juvenile origin are the terms: "father-recognition glasses" and "mother-recognition glasses" or "family unmaskers."

As the last names suggest, the glasses, which Brauxel & Co. has thrown on the market by the millions, enable the young to see through their families. The glasses uncover, recognize, worse, unmask father and mother, in fact, every adult who has reached the age of thirty. Only those who are not yet thirty or who are over twenty-one in the year '55 remain indifferent and can neither unmask nor be unmasked by their younger brothers and sisters. Is this crude arithmetical hocus-pocus supposed to solve the problem of the generations? Are the indifferent—nine complete age groups —written off as incapable of essential knowledge? Has the firm of Brauxel & Co. ambitions; or is it not, quite simply, that modern market research has succeeded in spotting and satisfying the needs of the rising postwar generation?

On this controversial point as well, the counsel of the firm Brauxel & Co. has been able to produce affidavits whose acuteness and sociological insight dissipate the misgivings of two investigating commissions. "The coincidence between product and consumer," says one of these affidavits, "can be calculated only up to the moment of delivery, at which time the consumer begins to produce independently and to transform the acquired product into his means of production, in other words, into an inalienable possession."

Let skeptics hold their peace; for whatever motives may have been at work when it was decided to produce and distribute miracle glasses, the success of this passing fad is unquestionable and modified the social structure of West Germany considerably, regardless of whether the structural change, or consumer modification as Schelsky calls it, was intended or not.

The young people acquire knowledge. Even if over half of all the glasses sold are destroyed shortly after purchase, because the parents suspect that there's something fishy about these glasses, this leaves some seven hundred thousand eyeglass wearers, who are able at their leisure to form a complete picture of their parents. Favorable moments arise, for instance, after supper, on family excursions, or while Papa is running around in circles with the lawn mower. The presence of miracle glasses is registered throughout the Federal Republic; but alarming concentrations occur only in the provinces of North Rhine-Westphalia, Hesse, and Lower Saxony, whereas in the southwest and in Bavaria sales amount to no more than a steady but slow trickle. Only in the province of Schleswig-Holstein are there whole districts (Kiel and Lübeck are exceptions) which show no evidence of glasses, for there, in the districts of Eutin, Rendsburg, and Neumünster, the authorities have gone so far as to confiscate the glasses by the carton, straight from the wholesaler. An injunction was issued *post factum*. The firm of Brauxel & Co. was able to collect damages; but only in the cities and the vicinity of Itzehoe have the glasses found a clientele able and willing to form a picture, a picture of their parents.

But what exactly is seen through the miracle glasses? Inquiries have thrown little light on the question. Most of the youngsters who have formed, or are still engaged in rounding out, a picture of their parents, are reluctant to talk. At the most they admit that the miracle glasses have opened their eyes. Interviews on athletic fields or outside movie houses tend to go roughly as follows: "Would you kindly tell us, young man, how our glasses have affected you?"

"That's quite a question. Well, after wearing the glasses a few times, I knew my old man pretty well."

"It's the details we're interested in. Please speak freely and without reservation. We are from the firm of Brauxel & Co. In the interest of our customers we should be glad to perfect our glasses . . ."

"They don't need any perfecting. They're just fine. I looked through them a few times and now I know what's what. Nothing could be any clearer."

All those questioned answer evasively, but this much is certain: a young person sees his father differently with the naked eye and with an eye that takes aim through miracle glasses: the miracle glasses show youthful wearers varied images of their parents' past, often, though it takes a little patience, in chronological sequence. Episodes which are kept from the younger generation for one reason or another are made palpably clear. Here again questioning by the agents of Brauxel & Co., or by the school authorities, has not proved very fruitful. Nevertheless all indications are that, surprisingly enough, no staggering quantities of erotic secrets are aired—little beyond the customary escapades. The scenes that recur over and over again in the twin spheres of the father-recognition glasses are acts of violence performed tolerated instigated eleven twelve thirteen years ago: murders, often by the hundreds. Aiding and abetting. Smoking cigarettes and looking on while. Certified decorated applauded murderers. Murder motives become leitmotives. With murderers at one table, in the same boat, bed, and officers' club. Toasts, emergency directives. Record entries. Blowing on rubber stamps. Sometimes mere signatures and wastebaskets. Many roads lead to. Silence as well as words can. Every father has at least one to hide. Many lie buried curtained siloed, as if they had never happened until in the eleventh postwar year miracle glasses appear on the market.

No isolated cases. Here and there a young person consented to the statistical use of his "knowledge" but sons and daughters alike kept the concrete details secret, just as fathers and mothers had been discreet even in their dreams. Feelings of shame may have inhibited the youngsters. A boy who resembles his father physically may fear that people will infer other similarities. Furthermore, students are disinclined to jeopardize their educational careers, financed by their parents often at a great sacrifice, by calling their parents to account. Surely not the firm of Brauxel & Co., but someone who developed the miracle glasses, who obtained mica mirrors from gneiss and added them to the usual glass mixture, may have expected and even hoped that the eyeglass campaign would bring radical results. But a revolt of the children against their parents did not materialize. Family feeling, instinct of self-preservation, cold self-interest, and for that matter blind love of those who had been exposed prevented a revolution which might have netted our century a few headlines: "New edition of children's crusade!—Cologne Airfield seized by teen-ager organization!—Martial Law Decreed.—Bloody clashes in Bonn and Bad Godesberg.—Not until early morning did police detachments and Bundeswehr teams succeed in.—The Hessian Radio is still in the hands of.—To date, 47,000 young persons, including eight-year-old children, have been.—Suicide wave among youngsters cornered in the area of Lauenburg, Elbe.—France honors extradition treaty.—The fourteen- to sixteen-year-old ringleaders have already signed a confession. —Cleanup operations concluded. Tomorrow all stations will broadcast an address by.—The search for the Communist agents who instigated and led the uprising is being continued. —After an initial slump the stock market seems.—German securities again in demand in Zürich and London.—December 6 proclaimed a day of national mourning."

Nothing of the kind. Cases of illness are reported. The parental image is too much for a certain number of girls and boys: They leave home: emigration, Foreign Legion, the usual. Some return. In Hamburg four suicides are registered in rapid succession, in Hanover two, in Cassel six, causing Brauxel & Co. to suspend delivery of the so-called miracle glasses shortly before Easter.

The past flares up for a few months and then blacks out— forever, it is to be hoped. Only Matern, who is here being spoken of in Materniads, sees the daylight in spite of inner resistance; for when at the Düsseldorf Christmas fair he buys his daughter Walli a pair of these miracle glasses, the child puts them right on: Walli had just been laughing and nibbling Christmas cookies, now she sees Matern through the glasses, drops cookies and gold-beribboned package, starts to scream, and screaming runs away.

Matern with the dog after her. But both of them—for Walli sees the dog too accurately and terribly—become more and more terrifying in the eyes of the child, whom they overtake shortly before the Rating Gate. Passers-by feel sorry for the screaming little girl and demand that Matern identify himself as her father. Complications! Words begin to fall: "He was trying to rape the child, that's a sure thing. Just look at him. It's written over his face! Swine!" Then, at last, a policeman breaks up the crowd. Identities are established. Witnesses claim to have seen or not seen this and that. Walli is screaming and still has the glasses on. A patrol car deposits Matern, Pluto, and the horrified child at the Sawatzki residence. But even in the familiar apartment, surrounded by all her expensive toys, Walli doesn't feel at home, for she still has the glasses on: Walli sees not only Matern and the dog, but also Jochen and Inge Sawatzki with new eyes, accurately and terribly. Her screaming drives Pluto under the table, turns the grownups to stone, and fills the nursery. Intermittent words, garbled by screams yet charged with meaning. Walli stammers something about piles of snow and blood dripping in the snow, about teeth, about the poor nice fat man, whom Papa and Uncle Walter and other men, who all look awful, are hitting, hitting the whole time with their fists, most of all Uncle Walter. The nice fat man; he's not standing up any more, he's lying in the snow, because Uncle Walter . . . "Don't! It's not right. Hitting and being cruel to people flowers animals. It's forbidden. People who do that don't go to heaven. God sees it all. Stop stop . . ."

Only when Inge removes the glasses from the face of the delirious child does she calm down a little; but hours later, in her little bed and surrounded by all her dolls, she is still sobbing. Temperature is taken, she has a fever. A doctor is called. He speaks neither of incipient flu nor of the usual children's ailments, but thinks the crisis must have been brought on by a shock, something impossible to put your finger on, she needs rest, the adults should keep away from her. If she doesn't get better, she'll have to be taken to a hospital.

Which is just what happens. For two days the fever refuses to come down and indefatigably, without fear of repetitiousness, spawns the wintry scene: snow lies, blood drips, fists talk, fat man falls, tumbles time and again, into what? into the snow, because Uncle Walter and Papa too, into the snow and so many teeth are spat out, one two five thirteen thirty-two!—No one can bear to count them any more. And so Walli with her two favorite dolls is taken to St. Mary's Hospital. The men, Sawatzki and Matern, don't sit beside the intolerably empty child's bed; they sit in the kitchen, drinking out of water glasses until they slide off their chairs. Jochen has retained his preference for the kitchen-livingroom environment: in the daytime he is a businessman, correctly clad in well-nigh wrinkleless material; in the evening he shuffles in bedroom slippers from icebox to stove and plucks at suspenders. In the daytime he speaks his brisk business German, to which vestiges of military jargon lend pithiness and time-saving succinctness: "Let's cut the goldbricking, let's wade in!" So, in his time, spoke Guderian, the military genius, and today Sawatzki takes a leaf from his book when he decides to flood the market with a certain single-breasted number; but toward evening, in kitchen and slippers, he eats crisp potato pancakes and speaks at great length and in broad dialect of the good old days and what it was like back home in the north. Matern too learns to appreciate the cozy warmth of the kitchen-livingroom. Tearfully two old buddies clap each other on the back. Emotion and unadulterated schnapps bring tears to their eyes. They push halfhearted feelings of guilt back and forth on the kitchen table, and quarrel only about dates. Matern says something or other happened in June '37. Sawatzki disagrees: "That was exackly in September. Who'da suspected the end was gonna be so rotten." But both are convinced that even then they were against it: "When you come right down to it, our sturm was kind of a hideout for the inner emikrashun. Don'tcha remember the way we slung the philosophy at the bar? Willy Eggers was there, the Dulleck brothers, naturally Fränzchen Wollschläger, Bublitz, Hoppe, and Otto Warnke. And you went on gassing about Being, until we wuz all nuts. Shoilem boil 'em! And now? Now what? Now a guy's own kid comes home saying: murderer murderer!"

After one of these laments, the kitchen-livingroom environment is as still as a mouse for a minute or two, except perhaps for the coffee water singing its peace-on-earthly song, until Sawatzki starts up again: "And all in all, what do you think, Walter, did we deserve that? Did we? No, we didn't. We don't."

When Walli was discharged from the hospital exactly four

weeks later, the so-called miracle glasses had vanished from the apartment. Neither did Inge Sawatzki throw them in the garbage pail nor did Jochen and Walter demolish them in the kitchen-livingroom; maybe the dog chewed up, swallowed, digested them. But Walli asks no questions about her missing toy. Quietly the little girl sits at her desk and has to catch up, because she has missed a lot of school. Grown solemn and a little peaked, she can already multiply and add. All hope that the child has forgotten why she has grown so solemn and peaked, why she isn't plump and bumptious any more. Because that's what Walli was in the hospital for: good care to make Walli forget. Little by little this becomes the first principle of all concerned: Forget! Maxims are embroidered on handkerchiefs, pillow slips, and hat linings: Learn to forget. Forgetfulness is natural. The mind should be occupied by pleasant memories and not by nasty tormenting thoughts. It's hard to remember constructively. Ergo, people need something they can believe in: God, for instance; or if you can't manage that, there's beauty, progress, the good in man, etcetera. "We, here in the West, believe implicitly in freedom, always have."

In any event, activity! And what activity is more productive than forgetting? Matern buys a large eraser, stations himself on a kitchen chair, and begins to erase the names, crossed off and not crossed off, from his heart, spleen, and kidneys. As for Pluto, that four-legged hunk of past, feeble with age though still running around, he'd be glad to sell him, send him to a rest home for dogs, erase him; but who'd buy an elderly hound? Moreover, mother and child are opposed: not for any price would Inge Sawatzki. She's got used to the dog in the meantime. Walli cries and promises to get sick again if the dog. So, black and ineluctable, he stays. And the names, too, offer stubborn resistance to Matern's big eraser. For instance: while he effaces one and blows eraser crumbs from his spleen, he stumbles, in the course of his newspaper reading, across another, who writes articles about the theater. That's what comes of doing something else while erasing. Every article has an author. This one is a man of the theater, who has pondered his way to wisdom. He says and writes: "Just as man needs the theater, so, and in equal measure, the theater needs man." But a few lines later he deplores: "Today man finds himself in a state of increasing alienation." Yet this he knows for certain: "The history of mankind has its most exemplary parallel in the history of the theater." But if, as he anticipates: "The three-dimensional theater should once again flatten into a picture-frame stage," this man, who signs himself R.Z., can only second the great Lessing in crying out: "To what end have we toiled so bitterly to achieve dramatic form?" His article embodies at once a warning and an exhortation: "The theater does not stop when man ceases to be man; it is the other way around: Close the theaters and man will cease to be man!" In general Herr Rudolf Zander—Matern remembers him from his theatrical days—is hipped on the word "man." For example: "The man of coming decades." Or: "All this calls for a stormy reckoning with the problem of man." Or in a polemical vein: "Dehumanized theater? Never!" Be that as it may, R.Z., or Dr. Rolf Zander —onetime director of the Stadttheater in Schwerin—has forsaken the "theatrical mission"; of late he has been with the West German radio in an advisory function, an activity which does not deter him from writing articles for the Saturday supplements of several important newspapers: "It is not enough to show man the catastrophe; violent emotion remains an end in itself unless it culminates in exegesis, unless the purifying effect of catharsis tears the wreath from nihilism and lends meaning to chaos."

Salvation twinkles humanely between the lines. There's a man for Matern to turn to, all the more so as he knows him well from former days and carries the name of Rolf Zander around with him, incised somewhere: either in the heart or in the spleen or in kidney script; no eraser, not even the newly purchased one, can efface it.

Everybody has an address. R. Zander is no exception. He works in the beautiful new Radio Building in Cologne; and he resides—so whispers the phone book—in Cologne-Mariendorf.

With or without dog? To judge—or to ask advice in a situation of human-chaotic distress? With revenge in my baggage or with a little human question? Both. Matern cannot desist from. He is looking simultaneously for work and revenge. Carnage and entreaty slumber in the same fist. With identically black dog he calls on friend and enemy. Not that he makes a beeline to the door, saying: "Here I am, Zander, for better or for worse!"; several times he creeps—Don't turn around—through the old park, determined to strike, if not the former theater director, then at least the trees in his park.

One stormy evening in August—all this is perfectly true:
it was August, it was hot, and a storm came up—he vaults
the wall with dog and lands on the soft ground of Zander's
park. He bears neither ax nor saw but a white powder. Oh,
Matern has a hand with poison! He is experienced: exactly
three hours later Harras was dead. No sprinkling of nux
vomica; plain rat poison. This time it's plant poison. From
tree to tree he scurries with dog shadow. A dance of nature
worship. Minuet and gavotte determine the sequence of steps
in the dusky, goblin-inhabited, ninefold green, nymphean
lovers' maze of Zander's park. A figure bows low, a hand is
held out: on dragon-thick roots he strews his powder without
muttering spells. However, Matern grinds as usual:

> Don't turn around:
> the Grinder's around.

But how can the trees be expected to! They don't even feel
like rustling, for not a breeze is stirring under the sultry sky.
No magpie warns. No jay denounces. Moss-covered baroque
putti are in no mood for giggling. Even Diana, with hunting
dog at hastening heel, is disinclined to turn around and bend
her unfailing bow; out of a dusky thinking-grotto Herr Zander
in person addresses the winged powder strewer: "Gracious!
Do my eyes deceive me? Matern, is it you? Goodness, and
what amiable occupation are you engaged in? Putting chemical fertilizer on the roots of my giants? Aren't they big
enough for you? But you've always been drawn to the colos-
sal! Chemical fertilizer! How absurd and yet delightful.
But you haven't taken the weather into account. Any minute
a storm is going to pour down on us mortals and the park.
The very first shower will wash away the traces of your
horticultural enthusiasm. But let us not tarry! The first gusts
of wind herald the storm. Undoubtedly the first drops have
been released on high, they are coming, coming . . . May I
invite you, as well as that magnificent specimen of a dog, to
my modest home!"

A light tug at a reluctant arm, guidance in the direction of
shelter. The last few steps, now over gravel paths, are rapid:
only on the veranda is the conversation resumed: "Gracious,
what a small world it is! How often I've wondered: what
can Matern be doing? That child of nature, that—begging
your pardon—ecstatic drinker?—And here you are, standing

in my library, feeling my furniture, looking around, and your
dog as well, both casting shadows in the lamplight, a warm
human presence. Welcome!"

Herr Zander's housekeeper hastens to brew strong manly
tea. Brandy is in readiness. Environment, undescribed, gains
the upper hand again. While outside, as Herr Zander would
put it, the storm hits the stage, a useful conversation about
the theater runs its course in dry and comfortable armchairs.
"My dear friend—you've done well to come right out with
your grievances—but you're mistaken and you do me a
grave injustice. Admitted: it was I, I couldn't help myself,
who canceled your contract with the Schwerin Stadttheater.
However, the reason why all this was done to you—and had
to be—was not, as you now suppose, political, but—how shall
I put it?—purely and simply alcoholic. It just wouldn't do.
Yes, yes, we all of us enjoyed a glass or two. But you went
to extremes. Quite frankly: even today in our more or less
democratic Federal Republic, any responsible director or stage
manager would have to do the same: you came to rehearsals
drunk, you came to performances drunk and without your
lines. Yes, of course I remember your ringing speeches. No
objection, not the slightest even then, to their content or ex-
pressiveness, but plenty, then and today as well, to the place
and time of your resounding declamations. Nevertheless, my
hat off to you: You pronounced, a hundred times, what the
rest of us may have thought but didn't dare to state in
public. I admired your magnificent courage, I still do; the
freedom with which you spoke of certain very delicate
matters would have been highly effective if not for your advanced alcoholic state. As it was, denunciations, mostly from
stagehands, piled up on my desk. I stalled, smoothed things
over, but in the end I had to take action, not least in order
to protect you, yes, protect you; for if I hadn't, by a simple
disciplinary measure, given you an opportunity to leave
Schwerin, which had gradually got to be a very hot place for
you, Lord, I don't like to think what would have happened
to you. You know, Matern, when those people struck, it
wasn't with kid gloves. The individual counted for nothing."
Outside, the stage thunder doesn't miss a cue. Inside, Matern
ponders what might have become of him but for the philan-
thropic Dr. Zander. Outside, wholesome rain washes away
the plant-killing poison from the roots of age-old all-knowing
trees. Inside, Pluto sighs out of dog dreams. Outside, Shake-

spearean rain functions like clockwork. Naturally a clock is ticking in the dryness too, no, three costly timepieces are ticking at once, variously pitched, into the silence between former theater director and former *jeune premier*. Peals of thunder do not traverse the footlights. Moistening of lips. Massaging of scalps. Inside, illuminated by outside lightning: Rolf Zander, an experienced host, gets back into the conversation: "Good Lord, Matern! Do you remember how you introduced yourself to us? Franz Moor, Act Five, Scene 1: Slavish wisdom, slavish fears! You were magnificent. No no, I mean it, shattering! An Iffland couldn't have wrung such horror from his entrails. A discovery, fresh from Danzig, which has given us full many an outstanding mime—think of Söhnker, or even, if you wish, of Dieter Borsche. Fresh and promising, you came to us. If I'm not mistaken, the excellent Gustav Nord, so lovable both as a man and as a colleague, who was to perish so wretchedly at the end of the war, was your teacher. Wait: You attracted my attention in a beastly play by Billinger. Didn't you play the son of Donata Opferkuch? Right, and La Bargheer saved the show with her Donata. I could still die laughing when I think of Fritzchen Blumhoff playing the Prince of Arcadia, in '36-'37 I think it was, with his excruciating Saxon accent. Then there was Carl Kliever, the indestructible Dora Ottenburg. Heinz Brede, whom I remember in a very decent performance of *Nathan the Wise*, and of course your teacher: what a versatile Polonius! A fine Shakespearean actor and magnificent at Shaw too. Mighty courageous of your Stadttheater to put on *Saint Joan* as late as '38. I can only repeat: if it weren't for the provinces! What was it you people called the building? That's it. The Coffee Mill! I hear it was totally destroyed. Hasn't been rebuilt. But I'm told they're planning to on the same site and in the same neoclassical style. The Poles are amazing, always were. The heart of the Old City, too. I hear that Langgasse, Frauengasse, and Jopengasse have already been laid out. Why, I'm from the same neck of the woods: Memel. Am I thinking of? No, my friend, never marry the same. The spirit that presides over our West German theaters really doesn't. Theatrical mission? Theater as a medium of mass communication? The stage as a mere generic concept? And man as the measure of all things? Where everything becomes a purpose in itself and nothing culminates in exegesis? What of purification? Catharsis?—Gone, my dear Matern—or perhaps not, for my work on the radio satisfies me completely and leaves me time for short essays that have wanted to be written for years. And what about you? Enthusiasm gone? Act Five, Scene 1: Slavish wisdom, slavish fears!"

Matern sulks and drinks tea. Knotted in his entrails, twined round heart, spleen, and tortured kidneys, the rosary chatters: Opportunist! Potential Nazi! Phony! Opportunist! Potential Nazi! But over the teacup a sheepish voice: "Theater? Never again. Self-confidence gone? Possibly. There's also the leg injury. Hardly noticeable, yes I know, but on the stage? The rest is in good shape, organ of speech, energy, enthusiasm. Ah yes, everything but the opportunity."

Then, after three Empire clocks have been permitted to tick for a minute or two undisturbed, the redeeming words fall from Rolf Zander's mouth. The rather delicate little man paces the floor of the suitable room, speaking softly, sagely, sympathetically. Outside, in the park, trees drip a reminder of the short-lived August storm. As Dr. Zander talks, his hand caresses book spines on broad shelves, or he takes out a book, opens it, hesitates, imparts a quotation which fits easily into his monologue, puts the book away booklovingly. Outside, the dusk brings the trees closer together. Inside, Zander comes to rest among the fruits of a lifelong collector's passion—Balinese dance masks, demonic Chinese marionettes, colored morris dancers—without damming his flow of speech. Twice the housekeeper comes in with fresh tea and pastry; she too a rare piece like the Empire clocks, first editions, and musical instruments from Hindustan. Matern sprawls in the armchair. The standing lamp communicates with his polished skull. Pluto makes rattling sounds in his sleep: a dog as old as the trees outside. Inside, Zander speaks of his work on the radio. He takes care of the early morning hours and bedtime: children's program and late night program. No contradiction for Zander, on the contrary. He speaks of tensions, of building bridges between. We must find our way back if we are to. At one time Matern too was allowed to sound off on a children's radio program. He was Little Red Riding Hood's Wolf; he devoured the seven kids. "Splendid!" Zander joins the threads: "We need voices, voices like yours, Matern. Voices that stand up in space. Voices that resemble the elements. Voices that carry, voices that bend the bow. Voices that give resonance to our past.

For instance, we've been working up a new program, thinking of calling it 'Discussion with the Past,' or better still, 'DISCUSSION WITH OUR PAST.' A young colleague of mine, a countryman of yours, incidentally—talented, dangerously so, I'm almost inclined to think—is trying to develop new forms of radio entertainment. I can easily imagine that in our station you, my dear Matern, you in particular, might work your way into a vocation commensurate with your talents. Urgent search for truth. The eternal question of man. Whence come we—whither are we going? Silence has barred the way, but now speech will open the gate!— What do you say?"

Thereupon the age-old dog awakens hesitantly, and Matern says yes. Shake on it?—Shake on it. Day after tomorrow, 10 A.M. at the Radio Building?—Day after tomorrow at ten. But be punctual.— Punctual and sober. May I call you a cab?— Dr. Rolf Zander is entitled to charge the West German Radio. All expenses are deductible. All risks are tax-exempt. Every Matern finds his Zander.

THE HUNDREDTH PUBLICLY DISCUSSED MATERNIAD

He speaks rumbles roars. His voice enters every home. Matern, the popular radio speaker. The children dream of him and his voice, which awakens all their terrors. It will go rumbling on and little children grown into shriveling old folks will say: "In my childhood we had a radio uncle, whose voice gave me, took away from me, inspired me, forced me, so that sometimes even now, but that's how it is with any number of Maternoids, who in those days." But right now adults, upon whom other voices have set their stamp, make use of Matern's voice as an aid in child rearing; when the kids act up, their mother threatens: "Do you want me to turn the radio on again and let the wicked uncle speak?"

Over medium wave and short wave, a bogeyman can be brought into the room. His voice is in demand. And other stations want Matern to speak, rumble, and roar in their broadcasting rooms. His colleagues, it is true, remark in private that his pronunciation is bad, that he lacks training, but they have to admit that his voice has a certain something: "That atmospheric quality, that barbaric uncouthness, that voracious naïveté is worth its weight in gold—people are sick of perfection nowadays."

Matern buys a date book, for every day, sometimes here sometimes there and at specified hours, his voice is recorded. He speaks rumbles roars mostly over the West German Radio, sometimes over the Hessian Radio, never over the Bavarian, occasionally on the North German, with alacrity and in Low German on the Bremen Station, very recently on the South German Radio in Stuttgart, and, when time permits, on the Southwestern Radio. He steers clear of trips to West Berlin. Consequently, RIAS and the Free Berlin Radio have had to drop their plans for live broadcasts that would rely on the very special character of Matern's voice, but within the exchange program they relay Matern's children's broadcasts from the West German Radio Station in Cologne, where his precious voice is at home.

He has set up housekeeping, he has an address: new building, two rooms, incinerator, kitchenette, built-in cupboards, bar, wide couch; for over the weekend inalienable Ingewife turns up, alone or with Walli. Sawatzki, the gentlemen's outfitter, sends his best. The dog is in the way. It's high time they had a little privacy. The mutt is a nuisance—like a grandmother who can't contain her water. Though still alert and well trained. How can there be any domestic wellbeing with this animal on the scene? Bleary-eyed, gone to fat in places, and even so, the skin sags on his neck. Still, no one says: "He ought to be done away with." On the contrary, Matern, Ingewife, and Wallichild are agreed: "Let him enjoy his pittance. Our Pluto won't be with us very long anyway. While there's enough for us, there'll always be enough for him." And Matern remembers at his shaving mirror: "He was always a friend in need. Stuck by me in hard times, when I was restless and unstable, when I was chasing a phantom that had many names and yet refused to be captured. The dragon. Evil. Leviathan. The Nothing. Errancy."

Yet occasionally, for all his fine-checked vests, Matern sighs over his omelet. At such times his hunter's eye excepts Ingewife and searches the wall for wallpaper script. But the Bauhaus pattern is unequivocal, and despite their ambivalent modernism the framed prints disclose no secrets. Or there's a pounding in the radiators, Matern pricks up an ear, Pluto stirs, the signals stop, and once again sighs blow copious bubbles. Not until early spring, when the first flies begin to stir, does he find an avocation that makes him forget to sigh for hours on end. Even the doughty little tailor started out with a flyswatter and went on to capture the unicorn. No one will ever know the names he gives to what he catches on the panes, what names he cracks between fingers, the names of his transmigrated enemies, from whom he plucks flyleg after flyleg and lastly the wings, without regret. The sighing persists, wakes up with Matern, goes to bed with him, sits with him at tables in the Radio Building canteen, while he is rehearsing his scoundrelly lines for the last time. Because he'll be going on the air in a minute. Matern will have to speak rumble roar. He will have to abandon this half glass of beer. Around him the ladies of the forthcoming programs: the woman's touch. The farmer's voice. Music in the afternoon. The good word for Sunday. Band music. Fifteen minutes of meditation. Our sisters and brothers behind the Iron Curtain. Sports news and racetrack news. Poetry before midnight. Water-level report. Jazz. The Gürzenich Orchestra. The children's program. Colleagues and their colleagues: that one over there, or that one, or the one in the checked shirt without a tie. You know him. Or you might know him. Wasn't he the one who in '43 on the Mius front? Or the one in black and white with the milkshake? Didn't he once? Or wouldn't he have? The whole lot of them! Checked flies, black-and-white flies. Fat blue-bottles over skat chess crosswordpuzzles. Interchangeable. Keep cropping up. O Matern, slowly cicatrizing names are still itching you. There he sighs in serenely bored broadcasting room, and a colleague who hears Matern's heavily laden sigh rising from the center of the earth, pats him on the back: "Man, Matern. What have you got to sigh about? You have every reason to be pleased. You're working full time. Happened to turn on the agony box yesterday, and whom do I hear? This morning I look into the children's room. They've moved the box in there. The kids are sitting there with their tongues hanging out, and whose voice do I hear? You lucky bastard!"

Matern, the booming radio pedagogue, speaks rumbles roars as a permanent robber, wolf, rabble rouser, or Judas. Hoarse as a polar explorer in a snowstorm. Louder than wind velocity 12. As a coughing prisoner with rattling radio chains. As a grumbling miner just before the awful explosion. As the ragingly ambitious mountain climber on the inadequately organized Himalaya expedition. As the gold prospector, the refugee from the East zone, the martinet, the SS guard, the Foreign Legionary, the blasphemer, the slave overseer, and a reindeer in a Christmas play; this last role he has played once before, on the stage as a matter of fact, in his dramatic school days.

Harry Liebenau, his countryman, who directs the children's program under Dr. R. Zander's guidance, says to him: "I'm rather inclined to think that was my first meeting with you. Stadttheater. Children's show. The little Brunies girl, you remember, danced the part of the Snow Queen, and you did the talking reindeer. Made an enormous impression on me, a lasting impression. A fixed point in my development, so to speak. Decisive childhood experience. All sorts of things can be traced back to it."

That shithead with his file-card memory. Wherever he goes stands sits, always shuffling cards. Nothing he hasn't got the dope on: Proust and Henry Miller; Dylan Thomas and Karl Kraus; quotations from Adorno and sales figures; collector of details and tracker down of references; objective onlooker and layer-bare of cores; archive hound and connoisseur of environments; knows who thinks left and who has written right; writes asthmatic stuff about the difficulty of writing; flashbacker and time-juggler; caller-into-question and wise guy; but no writers' congress can dispense with his gift of formulation, his urge to recapitulate, his memory. And the way he looks at me: Interesting case! He thinks I'm grist for his mill. He pinpoints me, closely written, on file cards. Seems to think he knows all about me, because he saw me that time as a talking reindeer and maybe twice in uniform. He was much too young to. When Eddi and I. He couldn't have been more than. But his kind think they know. That capacity for patient listening, for playing the gumshoes with a knowing smile: "Never mind, Matern, I know. If I'd been born a couple of years sooner, I'd have fallen for it just like you. I'm certainly the last one to moralize. My generation, you know, has seen a thing or two. Besides, you adequately demonstrated that you could also. Someday we ought to go over the whole thing objectively and without the usual resentment. Maybe in the 'Discussion' series we've been planning. How does it appeal to you? These children's programs may be useful, but they can't satisfy us in the. Noises, to help people put their children to bed. When you come right down to it, they're nothing but ground-out hokum. The beep-beep between programs is more meaningful. Why not put some life on the air? What we need is facts. How about really spilling your guts? Unburdening your heart. Stuff that hits you in the kidneys!"

Only the spleen is missing. And what the asshole will wear! English custom-made shoes and ski sweater. Maybe a homo too. If I could only remember the guy. Goes on the whole time about his cousin and blinks at me: suggestively. Says his father was the carpenter with the dog—"Hm, you know!" —"And my cousin Tulla—her real name was Ursula—was crazy about you, back in the shore battery, remember, and later on in Kaiserhafen." He even claims that I was his gunnery instructor—"The Number 6 mans the fuze setter"—and that I introduced him to Heidegger's calendar mottoes—"Being withdraws, losing itself in the . . ." The guy has collected more facts on the subject of Matern than Matern himself could dream up. Yet smooth and affable on the surface. Just thirty, going fat around the chin, and always ready for a joke. He'd have done fine as a Gestapo dick. He dropped in on me recently—ostensibly to go over a part with me—and what does he do? He grabs Pluto by the muzzle and feels his teeth or what's left of them. Like a vet. And with an air of mystery: "Strange, very strange. The stop too, and the line between withers and croup. Old as the animal is—my guess is twenty or more dog years—it's obvious from the structure of the forequarters and the excellent carriage of the ears. Tell me, Matern, where did you dig up that dog? No, better still, we'll discuss the question publicly. In my opinion this is a situation—I've told you about my pet idea—that ought to be developed dynamically and in public. But not in a dull naturalistic vein. The subject calls for formal ingenuity. If you want to hold an audience, you've got to stand your intellect on its head but still let it declaim. A kind of classical drama. Boiled down to one act, but keeping the good old structure: exposition peripeteia castastrophe. Here's how I visualize the set: a clearing in the woods, beeches if you like, birds twittering. You remember Jäschkental Forest, don't you? Well then: the clearing around the Gutenberg monument. We'll throw out old Gutenberg. But we'll keep the temple. And where the father of the printed book used to be, we'll put you. That's right, you, for a starter we drop you, the phenotype Matern, into the temple. So you're standing there under the roof, looking toward the Erbsberg, two hundred and fifty feet above sea level. On the other side of the Erbsberg there's Steffensweg, villa after villa, but we won't show that, only one set, the clearing. Facing the former Gutenberg monument, we'll put up a grandstand for the public, big enough for, well, in round numbers, thirty-two persons. All children and young people between the ages of ten and twenty-one. To the left we might have a small platform for the discussion leader. And Pluto—amazing animal, troubling resemblance—the dog can sit beside his master."

And that's exactly how this character—with hardly any musical trimmings—sets up his show. Zander is wildly enthusiastic, all he can talk about is this "exciting new form of broadcast." From the start he detects—"over and above the radio"—possibilities for the theater: "Neither picture-frame nor three-dimensional stage. Orchestra and stage merge for all time. After a centuries-long monologue, man finds a way back to dialogue; nay, more—this great Western debate warrants a new hope of exegesis and catharsis, interpretation and purification."

Rolf Zander points, in no end of articles, to the future; but the wisenheimer is thinking entirely of today. He isn't out to save the theater from subsidized stagnation, but to crucify Matern and dog. He is knitting a pitfall, but questioned as to his intentions, he lays it on smoothly, confidentially: "Believe me, Matern, with your help we will work out a valid technique for getting at the truth. Not only for you, but for every one of our fellow men, this is a matter of vital necessity: we must break through between master and dog, design a window that will give us back our perspective; for even I— you can tell by my modest literary efforts—lack the vital grip, the quivering flesh of reality; the technique is there but not the substance: I've been unable to capture the this-is-how-it-was, the substantial reality that throws a shadow. Help me, Matern, or I'll lose myself in the subjunctive."

And this play is enacted under trees. The fellow has even succeeded in scaring up some beeches and a cast-iron temple, in which the phenotype Johannes Gutenberg waits for his relief. For six weeks, not counting rehearsals, Matern with dog is squeezed to the last drop in the presence of a changing audience. The final manuscript, with which this wisenheimer and his Dr. Rudolf Zander have tinkered a bit, but solely for artistic reasons, reads as follows. Matern— "You're an actor after all!"—is expected to memorize the main part, so as to be able to speak, rumble, roar it on the specified recording date.

AN OPEN FORUM

PRODUCER: West German Broadcasting Station, Cologne.
SCRIPTS: R. Zander and H. Liebenau.
DATE OF BROADCAST: (approximate) May 8, 1957.
PARTICIPANTS IN THE DISCUSSION:

    HARRY L.—Discussion leader.
    WALLI S.—Assistant with miracle glasses.
    WALTER MATERN.—The Topic under discussion.
    SUPPORTING ROLE: Pluto, the black shepherd.

Thirty-two children and young people of the postwar generation participate more or less actively in the open forum. None is under ten or over twenty-one.

TIME: Approximately one year ago, when the so-called miracle glasses, or knowledge glasses, were withdrawn from the market.

SCENE: An oval clearing in a beech forest. To the right rises a grandstand in four tiers, on which the children and young people, boys and girls, take their places without formality. A platform to the left bears a table, behind which sit the discussion leader and his assistant. To one side a blackboard. Between grandstand and platform, but somewhat farther to the rear, a small cast-iron temple with chain garlands and a mushroom roof. Three granite steps lead up to the temple.

Inside the temple a cast-iron statue—obviously of Johannes Gutenberg—is laid on its side by movingmen, wrapped in woolen blankets, and finally carried away. "Heave-ho," the workmen call to each other. A hubbub among the younger generation.

The discussion leader spurs on the workers with such cries as: "We've got to get started, gentlemen. The old man can't be any heavier than a Bechstein piano. You can have breakfast as soon as the temple is clear."

Over it all the twittering of birds.

As the movers exit, Matern enters the clearing with a black shepherd.

Walli S., the assistant, a little girl of ten, removes a pair of glasses from their case, but does not put them on.

Matern's entrance is greeted by enthusiastic stamping on the part of the younger generation. He does not know where to go.

The discussion leader points to the temple and the younger generation explains, speaking in chorus: "Matern will have to stay in the printer's house today. In Gutenberg's old place Matern will show his face! Matern just loves to answer questions. A topic will be discussed, where stood old Johann in his rust! With man and beast, we'll have a discussion feast! Matern has come. Welcome! Welcome!"

The verses of greeting are followed by applause and stamping. The assistant toys with her glasses. The discussion leader rises, makes a gesture that sweeps away all sound except for the twittering of the birds, and opens the discussion:

DISCUSSION LEADER: Fellow participants in this forum! Young friends! The word has become flesh again and has come to dwell among us. In other words: we have come here to discuss. Discussion is our generation's medium of expression par excellence. In former times discussions were carried on at the family board, in circles of friends, on playgrounds: they were secret, muffled, or aimlessly playful; but today we have succeeded in liberating the great, dynamic, never-ending discussion from the four walls that formerly confined it, and in putting it out into the open, under the sky, among the trees!

A BOY: The discussion leader has forgotten the birds!

CHORUS OF BOYS AND GIRLS: A discussion feast
            with man and beast.

DISCUSSION LEADER: Yes indeed! They, too, the sparrows, blackbirds, and wood pigeons, answer us. Rookedykroo, rookedykroo! All speak! All demand to be informed. Every stone gives us information.

CHORUS: What's the stone's name today?
        Stones are people too, I say.

TWO BOYS: If it's Fritz, let him go,
        if it's Emil, let him blow.
        Let Hans and Ludwig run away,
        if it's Walter, let him stay.

DISCUSSION LEADER: That's it! Walter Matern has come among us in order that we may discuss him through and through. And when I say "him," I mean the reality that casts a shadow and leaves footprints.

A BOY: Has he come of his own free will?

DISCUSSION LEADER: Because we are alive, we discuss. We do not act, we . . .

CHORUS: . . . discuss!

DISCUSSION LEADER: We do not die . . .

CHORUS: We discuss death.

A BOY: I ask again: Has Matern come of his own free will?

DISCUSSION LEADER: We do not love . . .

CHORUS: We discuss love!

DISCUSSION LEADER: Consequently there is no topic we cannot discuss dynamically. God and liability insurance; the atomic bomb and Paul Klee; to us the past and the provisional constitution are not problems but topics of discussion. Only those who welcome discussion are fit . . .

CHORUS: . . . to be members of human society.

DISCUSSION LEADER: Only those who enjoy discussion become, through discussion, human beings. Therefore, to be a man is . . .

CHORUS: . . . to be willing to discuss!

A BOY: But is Matern?

CHORUS: Is Matern willing to discuss
his kidneys with us?

TWO GIRLS: We girls are curious to see
Matern's heart spout poetry.

TWO BOYS: And Matern's spleen we fondly hope
to study through a microscope.

CHORUS: Nibble nibble, crunch crunch,
from secret pockets let us munch.

TWO GIRLS: Another thing we wouldn't miss:
to see how thoughts and feelings kiss.

CHORUS: If Matern says: I'm willing!
it will be just thrilling.

DISCUSSION LEADER: And so we ask you, Matern, are you willing to be open, uncoded, and dynamically aired? Are you willing to think what you say; are you willing to speak out what you have buried? In other words: Are you willing to be the topic of this dynamic open forum? If so, answer loudly and plainly: I, Walter Matern, welcome discussion.

A BOY: He's not willing. I told you so: he's not willing.

A BOY: Or he hasn't understood yet.

A BOY: He doesn't want to understand.

CHORUS: If Matern won't understand,
make him discuss by command.

DISCUSSION LEADER: I must request you to give your comments a choral form or to state them in writing. Mob emotions cannot be permitted to erupt in a public discussion.— I ask you for the second time: Walter Matern, do you feel the need of communicating yourself to us in order that the public . . .

(*Whispering among the younger generation. Matern is silent.*)

A BOY: Close the temple if he's not willing.

A BOY: I demand a compulsory discussion. The Matern case is of general interest and must be discussed.

DISCUSSION LEADER: (*to the assistant*): Members number fourteen to twenty-two are obstructing discussion and therefore barred from discussion. (*Walli S. takes down the numbers on the margin of the blackboard.*) In line with the dynamism we are aiming at, the chair has decided to take account of certain comments that have not been cast in the proper form. If the topic of discussion persists in his hostility to discussion, a state of compulsory discussion will be declared. In other words: our assistant will make use of a special device, the so-called knowledge glasses, and so provide us with the facts, for every discussion must be based on facts.

CHORUS: If he keeps his secrets in,
glasses will see through his skin.

DISCUSSION LEADER: And so for the third time I ask Walter

MATERN: Are you willing, in this cast-iron temple, which only a short time ago housed Johannes Gutenberg, inventor of the printing press, to make yourself available as a topic of discussion, that is, to answer our questions? In a word: Do you welcome discussion?

MATERN: Hm . . . (*pause*) Damn it! . . . I . . . (*pause*) In the name of Satan and the Blessed Virgin . . . welcome discussion!

(*Walli S. writes on the blackboard: He welcomes discussion.*)

CHORUS: He says: I'm game,
he'll play our game.

MATERN: As in the Last Judgment,
where everyone speaks,
I have, I was,

I touched a hair,
I shot at the mirror, twice, struck home.
I wakened the mirror from purblind sleep.

TWO BOYS: He flailed at butter with a spindle,
till water gushed and cried: A swindle.

MATERN: I dashed the pigeon from the tower steep,
I buried the worm in the earth down deep.

TWO BOYS: Once when he'd stabbed an oven dead,
he saw an oven, he saw red.

TWO BOYS: He choked his towel, he was fit to be tied.
His towel was always a thorn in his side.

MATERN: I smothered the stone, I sweetened the salt,
I cut a goat's bleat out of her throat.

CHORUS: He wrote with chalk on the kitty's house:
Death in disgrace to Mister Mouse.

MATERN: And now I'm a topic of discussion;
being dragged to a foregone conclusion.

(*The younger generation clap and stamp. The discussion leader rises and motions for silence.*)

DISCUSSION LEADER: With great pleasure and interest we have just heard that Walter Matern is willing to unburden himself. But before question and answer, beginning as a rivulet but soon swelling into a broad-beamed torrent, carry him and us away, let us pray: (*The younger generation and the assistant rise with clasped hands.*) O great Creator of dynamic and everlasting world discussion, Thou who hast created question and answer, who givest and takest away the floor, sustain us this day as we proceed to discuss the discussion-welcoming topic of discussion, Walter Matern. O Lord of all discussions . . .

CHORUS: . . . give us this day the maturity indispensable to all discussion.

DISCUSSION LEADER: O wise and omniscient Creator of language, Thou who commandest the stars to discuss in the universe . . .

CHORUS: . . . loosen our tongues.

DISCUSSION LEADER: O Thou Creator of great sublime topics of discussion, Thyself the most sublime of all topics of discussion, loosen the tongue of the discussion-welcoming Walter Matern . . .

CHORUS: . . . loosen his tongue.

DISCUSSION LEADER: And let us in Thy name embark upon this discussion which honoreth Thee and Thee alone . . .

CHORUS: Amen. (*All sit down. Repressed murmurs. Matern wishes to speak. The discussion leader shakes his head.*)

DISCUSSION LEADER: The first question is the prerogative of the discussion club and not of the topic under discussion. But before we proceed to the usual exploratory questions, I wish to introduce Walli S., assistant to the chair, and to thank the firm of Brauxel & Co., which has supplied us, for purposes of the present discussion, with a pair of knowledge glasses, an article that has become extremely rare since it was taken off the market. (*Applause from the younger generation.*) But we intend to make use of this device only in case of necessity and on a motion supported by a majority of those present. Perhaps this will prove unnecessary since the topic under discussion has professed his readiness for discussion and since control by means of the Brauxel knowledge glasses is in order only if a state of compulsory discussion is declared. Nevertheless, by way of highlighting the efficient and every-ready presence of the glasses, the chair requests Walli S. to explain, for the benefit of our topic and of the new members of our discussion club, what these knowledge glasses are and how Walli S. first found occasion to put them to dynamic use.

WALLI S.: Approximately from the autumn of last year until shortly before Easter of the current year, the firm of Brauxel & Co. manufactured roughly one million four hundred forty thousand pairs of glasses, which were put on the market during this period under the name of miracle glasses and chalked up sensational sales. These miracles glasses, which are now known as knowledge glasses, cost fifty pfennigs a pair and enabled the purchaser, provided he was not under seven or over twenty-one years of age, to know all adults over thirty.

DISCUSSION LEADER: Walli, would you mind telling us more specifically what became known when you, for example, put the glasses on?

WALLI S.: Last year, on the third Sunday of Advent, my uncle Walter, who is the topic under discussion today, and to whom, because I know so much about him, I owe the honor of serving as assistant to the chair in spite of my tender years—my uncle Walter took me to the Düsseldorf Christmas fair. There were lots of colored electric signs and booths where you could buy everything under the sun: Christmas cookies and marchpane, antitank guns and

Christmas buns, hand grenades, household articles, aerial bombs, cognac snifters, and suicide teams, leitmotives and murder motives, Christmas tree stands and close combat badges, dolls with washable hair, dollhouses, dolls' cradles, dolls' coffins, doll replacement parts, doll accessories, dolls' radar . . .

CHORUS: To the point! To the point!

WALLI S.: And the so-called miracle glasses were also on sale. My uncle Walter—there he is!—bought me a pair. I put the glasses on right away, because I always have to try things right away. I looked at him through the glasses and I saw him very plainly as he used to be: it was simply awful. Of course I began to scream and ran away. (*She lets out a short scream.*) But he—my uncle Walter—ran after me and caught me near Rating Gate. He had his dog with him. But since he didn't take the glasses off me, I kept seeing him and the dog too and their past. He looked like a terrible monster and I couldn't stop screaming. (*She screams again.*) After that my nerves were affected and I had to go to St. Mary's Hospital for four weeks. I had a nice time, though the food didn't amount to much. Because the nurses, one of them was called Sister Walburga like me, and another one was called Sister Dorothea, and the night nurse was called . . .

CHORUS: Please come to the point!

A BOY: No hospital stories!

A BOY: Such digressions are quite superfluous.

WALLIS S.: Well, that is my experience with the miracle glasses, now known as knowledge glasses, which I shall put on today if the topic under discussion makes statements such as would inhibit discussion. Brauxel's knowledge glasses should be present at every public discussion. If speech should fail . . .

CHORUS: Brauxel's knowledge glasses never fail!

WALLI S.: Anyone who like my uncle is a topic under discussion . . .

CHORUS: . . . should never forget that Brauxel's knowledge glasses are always ready.

WALLI S.: Many thought the past was dead and buried . . .

CHORUS: . . . but Brauxel's knowledge glasses can make the past present.

WALLI S.: If, for instance, I were to put the glasses on now to look at my uncle Walter, I'd have to start screaming something awful like last year, on the third Sunday of Advent.— Want me to? (*Matern and dog grow restless. Matern pats the dog's neck. The discussion leader motions Walli S. to be seated.*)

DISCUSSION LEADER (*amiably*): Forgive us, Herr Matern, the members of our discussion club relapse occasionally into their usual childlike to adolescent state. Then what should be treated as work threatens to become a game; but for your peace of mind and our own, the chair will find means to prevent gruesome jokes from getting out of hand.—The discussion ban on members fourteen to twenty-two is lifted. We shall now open our discussion with exploratory questions which should be kept simple and as direct as possible! Questions, please! (*Several members raise their hands. The discussion leader calls on them successively.*)

A BOY: First series of exploratory questions, addressed to the topic under discussion: How many stations?

MATERN: Thirty-two.

A BOY: And counting backwards?

MATERN: Thirty-two.

A BOY: And how many have you forgotten?

MATERN: Thirty-two.

A BOY: Then you remember exactly . . .

MATERN: . . . thirty-two in all.

A BOY: What is your favorite dish?

MATERN: Thirty-stew.

A BOY: Your lucky number?

MATERN: Thirty-two times thirty-two.

A BOY: And your unlucky number?

MATERN: Ditto!

A BOY: Do you know your multiplication tables?

MATERN: Eight—sixteen—twenty-four—thirty-two.

A BOY: Thank you. The first series of exploratory questions is concluded.

DISCUSSION LEADER: Second series, please.

A BOY: Can you form simple sentences beginning with the indefinite pronoun "every"?

MATERN (*quickly*): Every tooth counts. Every witch burns better. Every knee hurts. Every station says bad things about the next. Every Vistula flows in retrospect wider than every Rhine. Every livingroom is always too rectangular. Every train pulls out. Every music begins. Every event casts its shadow. Every angel lisps. Every freedom dwells in mountains that are too high. Every miracle can be explained. Every athlete refurbishes his past. Every cloud has rained several times. Every word may be the last. Every candy is too sweet. Every hat fits. Every dog stands central. Every secret is ticklish . . .

DISCUSSION LEADER: That will do, thank you. And now, if you please, the third and last series of exploratory questions. Go ahead.

A BOY: Do you believe in God?

MATERN: I object; the question of God cannot be called an exploratory question.

DISCUSSION LEADER: The question of God is perfectly admissible as an exploratory question provided it is formulated without such modifiers as "triune" and "only true."

A BOY: Very well. Do you believe?

MATERN: In God?

A BOY: That's right. Do you believe in God?

MATERN: You mean . . . in God?

A BOY: Exactly: in God.

MATERN: In God up there?

A BOY: Not just up there. Everywhere, in general.

MATERN: You mean in something up there and elsewhere . . .

A BOY: We don't mean something, we mean God, neither more nor less. Out with it! Do you or don't you . . . ?

CHORUS: Scissors or stone,
        yes or no!

MATERN: Every man, whether he likes it or not, every man, regardless of his upbringing and the color of his skin, regardless of the idea he lives by, every man who thinks, feels, eats, breathes, acts, in other words, lives . . .

DISCUSSION LEADER: Herr Matern, the question addressed by the members of the discussion group to the topic under discussion is: Do you believe in God?

MATERN: I believe in the Nothing. Because sometimes I have to ask myself in earnest: Why are there essents rather than nothing?

A BOY: That's a quotation from Heidegger. We're thoroughly familiar with it.

MATERN: So perhaps pure Being and pure Nothing are the same.

A BOY: Heidegger again!

MATERN: The Nothing never ceases to nihilate.

A BOY: Heidegger!

MATERN: The Nothing is the source of negation. The Nothing is more fundamental than the not and negation. The Nothing is acknowledged.

CHORUS: Heidegger hid, Heidegger hod!
The question is: Do you believe in God?

MATERN: But sometimes I can't even believe in the Nothing; then again I think I could believe in God if I . . .

A BOY: Our question has been stated. There's no need to repeat it. Yes or no?

MATERN: Well . . . (*pause*) . . . In the name of the Father, the Son, and the Holy Ghost: No.

DISCUSSION LEADER: The third and last exploratory question may be considered answered. We sum up: The lucky and unlucky number of the topic under discussion is: thirty-two. The topic under discussion can form any number of sentences beginning with the indefinite pronoun "every." He does not believe in God. This constellation—thirty-two, every, God—justifies an additional question. Let's have it. (*Walli S. notes the answers to the exploratory questions on the blackboard.*)

MATERN (*indignant*): Who sets up these rules? Who's running this discussion, who's pulling the strings? Who?

DISCUSSION LEADER: Our discussion, carried on by a discussion-loving group, has come to a point where it seems advisable to steer it in a direction that will lend it the necessary dynamic gradient, that will give promise of a catastrophe in the traditional classical sense. I therefore request a supplementary question, based on the conclusions drawn from our exploratory questions: Thirty-two, every, God.

A GIRL: Do you love animals?

MATERN: That's absurd! Can't you see I've got a dog?

A GIRL: That doesn't answer my supplementary question.

MATERN: The dog is well treated. Correctly and when the occasion arises firmly.

A GIRL: It seems hardly necessary to repeat, but I'll do it just the same: Do you love animals?

MATERN: Take a look, young lady. What do you see? An elderly, half-blind dog, hard to feed, because his scissors bite is, to say the least, incomplete, and yet . . .

A GIRL: Do you love animals?

MATERN: This dog . . .

DISCUSSION LEADER: Ruling from the chair. In view of the

topic's obvious and deliberate evasiveness, appropriate sub-questions will be permitted within the framework of the supplementary question. Questions, please!

A BOY: Did you ever kill an animal with your bare hands?

MATERN: Admitted: a canary with this hand, because the bird's owner—that was in Bielefeld—was an old-time Nazi and I as an antifascist . . .

A BOY: Did you ever shoot an animal?

MATERN: In the Army: rabbits and crows, but during the war everybody shot at animals, and those crows . . .

A BOY: Did you ever kill any animals with a knife?

MATERN: Like every boy who lays his hands on a pocket-knife: rats and moles. A friend gave me the knife and with that knife we both of us . . .

A BOY: Did you ever poison an animal?

MATERN (pause): Yes.

A BOY: What kind of animal?

MATERN: A dog.

CHORUS: Was he white, blue, or purple?
Red, green, yellow, or purple?

MATERN: It was a black dog.

CHORUS: Was it a spitz, dachshund, or pekinese?
A St. Bernard, boxer, or pekinese?

MATERN: It was a black-haired German shepherd answering to the name of Harras.

DISCUSSION LEADER: The supplementary question, supported by appropriate subquestions, has shown that Walter Matern, the topic under discussion, has killed a canary, several rabbits, a number of crows, moles, rats, and a dog; I therefore repeat the supplementary question based on thirty-two, every, and God: Do you love animals?

MATERN: Believe it or not: yes.

DISCUSSION LEADER (motions to Walli, the assistant. She writes "loves animals" on the blackboard): We note that on the one hand the topic under discussion has poisoned a black shepherd, and that on the other hand he takes ex-cellent care of a black shepherd. Since he professes to love animals, dogs—as such and in this case a black shepherd—seem to become the fixed point of discussion in reference to the topic under discussion. For safety's sake may I re-quest exploratory questions calculated to check the unques-tionably dynamic result of our exposition, namely, a black-haired German shepherd, possibly the fixed point of this whole discussion. (*Walli S. writes "black-haired German shepherd" on the blackboard.*)

A BOY: For example: Are you afraid of death?

MATERN: I'm a bounceback man.

A BOY: Then perhaps you'd like to live a thousand years?

MATERN: A hundred thousand, because I'm a bounceback man.

A BOY: In case you should die notwithstanding, would you prefer to die in your room, in the open, in the kitchen, in the bathroom, or in the cellar?

MATERN: A bounceback man couldn't care less.

A BOY: What would you prefer: illness or traffic accident? Or do you favor battle, the duel as a form of existence, war as casualty, revolution as potentiality, or a good honest free-for-all?

MATERN (*good-humoredly*): My good friend, for a bounceback man like me, all those are mere opportunities of showing what a bounceback man can do. You can discuss me to death with knives and firearms; you can hurl me from television towers; and even if you bury me fathoms deep and weigh me down with arguments as hard as granite—tomorrow I'll be standing on my lead soles again. Bounceback man, bounce!

CHORUS: Buried below and gladly we
    will take the bet: what's buried below
    comes out no more to the light, the sparkle,
    and stirs no more nor spoons;

MATERN: for the spoon too lay in the cellar
    melted down, but when outside
    Aurora with policeman's whistle
    blew back the darkness, Matern

CHORUS: stood on molded leaden soles
    with heart spleen kidneys, was hungry
    and spooned, ate, shat, and slept.

MATERN: The bolt struck low, I fell from the tower.
    The pigeons were troubled not at all.
    I was an epitaph, flat on the pavement,
    an inscription read by passers-by:

CHORUS: Here lies and lies and lies flat, lies he
    who fell from above and here he lies;
    no rain washes him, nor hail taps
    or types his letters, eyelashes,
    or open forums;

MATERN: but comes Aurora on two legs
and blasts the pavement where I lie,
first stands the pecker, then the man,
and squirts and fathers and laughs himself sick.

CHORUS: Shot he was, through and through;
a tunnel they had just been planning,
and through him, through him, freshly shot,
the railroad soon was running.

MATERN: The special trains, the kings,
had to pass straight through me when
they wished to visit other kings
out past me, and the Pope
spoke in nine languages through the hole.

CHORUS: He was funnel, tunnel, megaphone,
and green grew the customhouses on either end,

MATERN: but when Aurora with the heavy
far-famed hammer of resurrection
plugged me up at both ends,
Matern, once freshly shot,
stood up and breathed spoke lived and hollered!

(*Pause. Walli S. writes "bounceback man" on the blackboard.*)

DISCUSSION LEADER: And so I take it that you're not afraid of death?

MATERN: Even bounceback men have their weak moments.

DISCUSSION LEADER: Then perhaps you wouldn't like to live for a thousand years or more?

MATERN: Good God! You have no idea what a bother lead soles can be.

DISCUSSION LEADER: Well, should the occasion arise and supposing you had your choice between death in bed and death out of doors?

MATERN: Definitely in the open air.

DISCUSSION LEADER: Heart disease, accident, or war injury?

MATERN: I'd like to be murdered.

DISCUSSION LEADER: With knives or firearms? Would you like to be hanged or electrocuted? Suffocate or drown?

MATERN: I'd like to be poisoned and collapse in the presence of a first-night audience in an open-air theater. Suddenly. (*He sketches the motion of collapsing.*)

CHORUS: Listen to that. Poison!
Matern swears by poison!

A BOY: What kind of poison?

A BOY: Old-fashioned toad's eyes?

A BOY: Snake venom?

A BOY: Arsenic or poisonous mushrooms: death cup, sickener, jack-o'lantern, fly agaric, Satan's boletus?

MATERN: Plain ordinary rat poison.

DISCUSSION LEADER: The chair wishes to put a question: When you poisoned the black shepherd Harras, what poison did you select?

MATERN: Plain ordinary rat poison!

CHORUS: O strangest of men!
        Rat poison again!

DISCUSSION LEADER (to Walli S.): Under "bounceback man" you'd better note: death urge, colon, poison. And branching off to the right: Harras' dogdeath, colon, rat poison. (Walli S. writes in capitals.) But for the present, rather than follow up this first confirmation of "black shepherd" as a fixed point, I suggest a second exploratory question that will place the fixed point in a more general perspective.

A BOY: Under what constellation were you born?

MATERN: I haven't the faintest idea. The date is April 19th.

WALLI S.: It is my duty as assistant to point out to the topic under discussion that false statements will result in immediate compulsory discussion: my uncle, that is, the topic under discussion, was born on April 20, 1917.

MATERN: That kid! That's what it says in my passport, but my mother always insisted I was born on the nineteenth, at exactly ten minutes to twelve. The question is: Whom is the world going to believe, my mother or my passport?

A BOY: Nineteenth or twentieth of April, regardless, you were born in the sign of the Ram.

CHORUS: Passport date or mother's claim,
        in either case the Ram's the same.

A BOY: What famous men besides yourself were born when the sun was in the house of the Ram?

MATERN: How do I know? Professor Sauerbruch.

A BOY: Nonsense. Sauerbruch was Cancer.

MATERN: What about John Kennedy?

A BOY: A typical Gemini.

MATERN: His predecessor, then.

A BOY: I think it is generally known that General Eisenhower was born when the sun was in the sign of Libra?

DISCUSSION LEADER: Herr Walter Matern: Please concentrate. Who else was born in the sign of the Ram?

MATERN: You incompetents! You wisenheimers! This isn't a public discussion, it's degenerating into a witches' sabbath. In the same month and, as it says in my passport, on the twentieth of April, Adolf Hitler, the greatest criminal of all time, was whelped.

DISCUSSION LEADER: Exception! Cognizance is taken only of the name, not of the irrelevant apposition. We have come here not to sling mud but to discuss. The chair takes note of the fact that Walter Matern, the topic under discussion, was born in the same sign and on the same date as Adolf Hitler, builder of the Reichsautobahn, a topic recently discussed by our group. Very well then: in the sign of the Ram.

A BOY: Have you anything else in common with the Ram-born Adolf Hitler?

MATERN: All men have something in common with Hitler.

A BOY: We wish to make it clear that the topic under discussion is not "all men," and certainly not "mankind," but you and you alone.

WALLI S.: I know something. Something I can testify to without having to put on the knowledge glasses. Something he even does in his sleep and when shaving. He doesn't even have to suck a lemon to do it.

MATERN: Well, in school and later too, they called me "Grinder," because sometimes when I don't like the way things are going, I grind my teeth. Like this (*he grinds long and loud into the microphone*). And Hitler is also said to have ground his teeth now and then! (*Walli S. makes a note: "teeth grinding or the Grinder."*)

CHORUS: Don't turn around,
the Grinder's around.

A BOY: Anything else in common with the builder of the Reichsautobahn?

CHORUS: Don't go to the woods,
in the woods are woods.
He who goes through the woods,
looking for trees,
seek him not in the woods.

A BOY: We wish to know whether the topic under discussion, Walter Matern, alias the Grinder, has other points in common with Adolf Hitler, topic of a previous discussion.

CHORUS: Have no fear.
fear smells of fear,
He who smells of fear

> will be smelled
> by heroes who smell like heroes.

A BOY: The topic under discussion is moistening his lips.

CHORUS: Don't drink of the sea,
> it whets the appetite.
> If you drink of the sea
> you'll thirst eternally
> for ocean.

A BOY: Dynamic compulsory discussion stands starkly menacing, without smoke trailer, on the horizon.

CHORUS: Don't build a home
> or you'll be at home.
> If you're at home,
> you'll expect
> late visitors and open up.

A BOY: Walli S., our assistant, has already begun to remove documents from the document case: postcards, blood spots, certificates, specimens of feces, affidavits, neckties, letters . . .

CHORUS: Don't write letters,
> letters are filed away.
> When you sign a letter,
> you're signing
> what you were yesterday.

A BOY: He who always stood central, whose phenotypes are the bounceback man and the Grinder, whose posthumous papers we will examine in his lifetime, thinks he still stands central.

CHORUS: Don't stand in the light,
> the light can't see you.

TWO BOYS: Don't have courage,
> courage takes courage.

TWO GIRLS: Don't sing in the fire,
> nobody sings in the fire.

TWO BOYS: Don't lapse into silence,
> or you'll break silence.

CHORUS: Don't turn around,
> the Grinder's around.

MATERN: To further your search for clarity, I'll talk again. What is it you wish to know, hear, nibble on?

A BOY: Facts. Characteristics in common with that other Ram-born topic. We know you grind your teeth.

CHORUS: Don't turn around.

MATERN: Always glad to oblige: this dog. Like me, Hitler

was fond of black-haired German shepherds. And the black shepherd Harras, who belonged to a carpenter . . .

DISCUSSION LEADER: This definitely confirms the black-haired shepherd as our fixed point. Do any of our members, nevertheless and for safety's sake, wish to ask further questions? (*Walli S. notes and underlines the "fixed point."*)

A BOY: The fixed point, German shepherd, should at least be tested from the erotic standpoint.

A BOY: Member No. twenty-eight is surely referring to the sexual implications of the fixed point.

DISCUSSION LEADER: The supplementary exploratory question is approved. Go ahead.

A BOY: With what famous women have you, or would you like to have had, sexual intercourse?

MATERN: In the year 1806 with Queen Louise of Prussia, twice in quick succession. She was in flight from Napoleon at the time and spent the night with me in my father's windmill, which was guarded by a black shepherd by the name of Perkun.

A BOY: The queen in question is largely unknown to the members of this discussion club . . .

DISCUSSION LEADER: Nevertheless, Walli S., please make a note of the watchdog Perkun, but add the word "legendary" with a question mark.

MATERN: Furthermore, from late summer '38 to spring '39, I intercoursed fairly regularly with the Virgin Mary.

A BOY: Any good Catholic can re-enact fictitious intercourse with the Virgin Mary; moreover, the same re-enaction is open to every so-called unbeliever.

MATERN: Just the same, it was she who persuaded me to poison the black shepherd Harras with rat poison, because this Harras . . .

DISCUSSION LEADER: Very well, at the request of the topic under discussion please note in parentheses "Marianic influence" before the key phrase "Harras' dogdeath by rat poison."

A BOY: We still need something more definite, something that isn't grounded in the irrational.

MATERN: All right, here's your candy. I slept with Eva Braun at a time when she was already his mistress.

A BOY: Please describe the coitus in every detail.

MATERN: A gentleman doesn't talk about his adventures in bed.

A BOY: The objection is unwarranted. After all, this is an open forum.

A GIRL: The topic's obscene secretiveness is an insult to the female members of this discussion club.

CHORUS: The discussion soon will be
made compulsory.

DISCUSSION LEADER: Objection from the chair. The topic under discussion has adequately answered the question about coitus with celebrated women. After legendary intercourse with the here largely unknown Queen Louise of Prussia, after fictitious intercourse with the Virgin Mary, he has admitted to coitus with Fräulein Eva Braun. Consequently questions concerning the details of this coitus are superfluous; at most the topic under discussion might be asked whether the sexual act between the sexual subjects Matern and Braun was or was not performed in the presence of spectators.

A BOY: For instance: was the builder of the Reichsautobahn present?

MATERN: He and his black and favorite dog Prinz, as well as the Führerphotographer Hoffmann.

DISCUSSION LEADER: The exploratory question has been answered. The answer has confirmed the sexual implications of the "black-haired shepherd dog," already recognized as a fixed point of discussion. We can manage without the photographer, I should think. (*Walli S. makes a note.*) Before we proceed to discuss the ownership status of the dog here present, who not only functions as our topic's fixed point but is actually present at his feet, the topic under discussion is authorized to ask the members of our discussion club a question.

MATERN: What is all this? Why am I standing here in Johannes Gutenberg's place? How can you call this public third degree a public discussion? How can you say it's dynamic when I, talented and trained in dynamic striding, have to stand still between columns? For I, as actor and phenotype, as Karl Moor and Franz Moor: "Slavish wisdom, slavish fears!" hunger for pacings back and forth, for entrances sudden and unexpected, for phrases to hurl across footlights, exits that give promise of new and terrible entrances: "But soon I will come among you and hold terrible muster."—Instead of all this, statics and question games. By what right are these know-it-all snot-noses questioning me? Or, to put it more politely: What is the purpose of this discussion?

DISCUSSION LEADER: The last question is in order.

A BOY: Through discussion we inform ourselves.

A BOY: Public discussion plays a legitimate role in every democracy.

A BOY: Lest there be any misunderstanding, I wish to point out that public discussion, precisely because it is carried on in public, differs fundamentally from the Catholic institution of confession.

A BOY: Nor is there any justification for analogies between our efforts and the so-called public confessions of countries under Communist rule.

A BOY: Neither in the secular nor in the religious sense does democratic discussion culminate in absolution; it ends without commitment. Or it might be more accurate to say that true discussion doesn't end at all, for after every open forum we discuss our findings in small groups, and at the same time cast about for interesting topics to discuss in future open forums.

A BOY: When we have finished with topic Walter Matern, for example, we plan to discuss the denominational school, or we shall take up the question: Have savings encouraged by fiscal policy become of interest again?

A BOY: We recognize no taboos.

A BOY: Recently we discussed the philosopher Martin Heidegger, the man and his work. I feel justified in saying that this topic of discussion holds no further enigmas for us.

CHORUS: Stockingcap croaks
          metaphysical jokes.

A BOY: When you come right down to it, problems solve themselves. All you need is a little patience. Take the Jewish question. Such a thing could never happen in our generation. We'd have gone on discussing with the Jews until they emigrated of their own free will and conviction. We despise all violence. Even when we engage in compulsory discussion, the conclusion is in no way binding on the topic of compulsory discussion: when the discussion is over, he's perfectly free to hang himself or to drink beer if he prefers. We're living in a democracy after all.

A BOY: We live for discussion.

A BOY: In the beginning was discussion.

A BOY: We discuss in order not to have to soliloquize.

A BOY: For here and here alone are our social ties forged. Here no one is lonely.

A BOY: Neither class struggle ideology nor bourgeois political economy can replace the stratification mechanism of applied sociology, namely, free discussion.

A BOY: After all, the technical efficiency of our life apparatus depends on great social organizations such as the World League of Free and Discussion-welcoming Discussion Groups.

A BOY: To discuss is to master the problems of existence.

A BOY: Modern sociology has demonstrated that in a modern mass state free discussion alone offers the possibility of developing personalities mature enough for discussion.

CHORUS: We are one big happy public international independent dynamic discussion family.

TWO BOYS: If we didn't welcome discussion, there would be no democracy, no freedom, and consequently no life in a free democratic mass society.

A BOY: Let us sum up: (*All stand up.*) We have been asked by the topic under discussion why we discuss. Our answer is: We discuss in order to prove the existence of the topic under discussion; if we were silent, Walter Matern, the topic under discussion, would cease to exist!

CHORUS: Therefore we all agree:
without us Matern would not be! (*Willi S. writes on the blackboard.*)

DISCUSSION LEADER: The topic's question has been answered. And now we ask: Do you wish to ask a supplementary question?

MATERN: Don't mind me. I'm beginning to catch on, and I agree to play along—without reservation.

DISCUSSION LEADER: In that case let's get back to the fixed point, the black shepherd, who has proved himself three times, the last time in his erotic significance.

MATERN (*with pathos*): If you want me, friends, to spill my guts, hold out the basin!
I'll vomit up without restrain
peas spooned up dog years ago.

DISCUSSION LEADER: We shall now proceed to clarify and discuss the ownership status of a black shepherd.

MATERN: Potatoes gobbled many dog years past
will demonstrate to you today
that even then potatoes grew.

Yesterday's murder motives
are today's leitmotives.

DISCUSSION LEADER: In other words, we shall check into a black shepherd who, present here in person, represents the fixed point of this discussion, which, as we have seen, is "black shepherd."

MATERN: For now the bars are down.
What tickled my palate then
makes me retch today.
What took the road to the high Caucasus
and down to pale Ladoga Lake,
shall now roll back: methodical, half-digested,
gall-bitter,
and stink till it rises sour to your mouths.

DISCUSSION LEADER: And so I invite questions relating to the ownership status of the black shepherd here present.

MATERN: Murder: an old-fashioned word!

A BOY: What is the name of the black shepherd here present?

MATERN: Rear sight, front sight.
The whites of their eyes.
Holding enfolding squeezing.

A BOY: I repeat my question: The name of the dog here present?

MATERN: Corpses, who counts them any longer?
The bones have all been processed.
The blood flows on the stage.
And hearts beat *moderato*.
Death has been run out of town! (*Pause*)
And the dog's name, as if you didn't know, is Pluto.

A BOY: To whom does Pluto belong?

MATERN: To the man who feeds him.

A BOY: Did you purchase Pluto?

MATERN: He attached himself to me.

A BOY: Did you make inquiries as to the dog's former owner?

MATERN: He attached himself to me shortly after the end of the war. There were lots of masterless dogs running around in those days.

A BOY: Has the topic under discussion any intimation as to whom Pluto may have belonged to, probably under another name?

MATERN: I'm willing to tell you what I've eaten, touched,

done, experienced, but I refuse to let my intimations be discussed.

DISCUSSION LEADER: Since the topic under discussion, for reasons connoting hostility to discussion, wishes to remove his notions from the scope of our discussion, the members of our discussion club are authorized to question Pluto, the black shepherd, directly, since the dog, in fact and in his capacity as a fixed point, belongs to the topic under discussion. We shall submit three musical themes to the dog. Suggestions, please. (*Walli S. notes: "Musical interrogation of the dog Pluto."*)

A BOY: Why not begin the musical interrogation with *Eine Kleine Nachtmusik*? (*Walli S. puts on a record. Music plays briefly.*)

DISCUSSION LEADER: We observe that the dog Pluto does not react to Mozart. Second suggestion.

A BOY: How about Haydn? Or something of the sort, maybe *Deutschland, Deutschland über Alles.* (*Walli S. puts on the record. The dog wags his tail as soon as the music starts.*)

DISCUSSION LEADER: The dog reacts with pleasurable animation, so demonstrating that his former owner was a German national. This makes it clear that ownership cannot be imputed to members of the then occupying armies. Accordingly, we can dispense with Handel or with themes from the French opera *Carmen*. Neither *Nutcracker Suite* nor the Don Cossacks. Similarly there is no need to consider spirituals or ballads from American pioneering days. The third suggestion, please.

A BOY: Why beat about the bush? I suggest a direct approach: some typical Wagner, the Siegfried motif or the Helmsmen's Chorus . . .

A BOY: We might as well start right in with *Götterdämmerung.*

CHORUS: *Göt-ter-dämmerung!*
Göt-ter-dämmerung!

(*Walli S. puts on the record. The music from* Götterdämmerung *plays at length. The dog howls throughout.*)

DISCUSSION LEADER: Here we have conclusive proof that the dog Pluto must have belonged to an admirer of Wagner. On the strength of conclusions thus far arrived at in the course of our discussion—I call your attention to our notes—we shall make no mistake in presuming former Chancellor Adolf Hitler, whom we have recently discussed as the builder of the Reichsautobahn and whose predilection for Wagner is well known, to have been the rightful owner of the black shepherd here present, currently named Pluto. By way of avoiding unnecessary delay, we shall now proceed to a dynamic confrontation: black shepherd—Hitlerportrait, if you please.

MATERN: Preposterous. The dog is almost blind.

DISCUSSION LEADER: A dog's instinct never goes blind. My father, for example, an honorable carpenter, kept a shepherd as a watchdog; incidentally, he was black, his name was Harras, and he was poisoned with rat poison. Though he never studied cynology as a science, the chair, having grown up so to speak with this Harras, regards himself as a pretty fair judge of dogs, especially black shepherds. If you please, the confrontation! (*Willi S. stands up and unrolls a large color print of Hitler over the blackboard. Then she moves the blackboard forward until it faces the cast-iron temple. Long pause. The dog becomes restless, sniffs in the direction of the picture, suddenly breaks loose, stands whimpering in front of the picture, gets up on his hind legs, and begins to lick Hitler's colored face. At a sign from the discussion leader, Walli S. rolls up the picture. The dog continues to whimper and Walli S. has difficulty in leading him back to the temple. The blackboard is moved back to its former place. Clamor among the discussion club members.*)

A BOY: It's plain as day.

A BOY: Dynamic confrontation has again proved its value as a promoter of discussion.

CHORUS: Shrewdly confronted,
            his instinct was unblunted.
            He whimpered and licked the place
            where he discovered a face.

DISCUSSION LEADER: Quite apart from its relevance to our discussion, the confrontation has obviously taken on the character of a historic event. We therefore request our members to rise and join me in a brief moment of meditation: O great Creator of everlasting world discussion, O Thou maker of sublime topics of discussion . . . (*Protracted silence. The members of the discussion club are filled with awe.*) Amen! (*The members sit down again.*) Meanwhile the archives of our discussion club have disclosed the following data:

WALLI S. (*who has not joined in the prayer, is holding a sheaf of papers*): Among several shepherds in the kennels of former Chancellor Adolf Hitler, it was a black-haired shepherd by the name of Prinz who attracted the most attention. He was a present to the Chancellor from Adolf Forster, Gauleiter of Danzig. The first months of his life were spent in the police kennels at Danzig-Langfuhr. He was then transferred to the Führer's residence, the so-called Berghof, where, up to the outbreak of the war, he was free to romp and run untrammeled in God's great out-of-doors. Then, however, the vicissitudes of war led him from one Führer's Headquarters to another, and finally to the Führer's air-raid shelter in the Chancellery.

DISCUSSION LEADER: And there the following happened:

WALLI S.: On April 20, 1945 . . .

A BOY: On the day when the builder of the Reichsautobahn and our topic of discussion Walter Matern celebrate their birthdays . . .

WALLI S.: During the birthday celebration, attended by General Field Marshal Keitel, Lieutenant-Colonel von John . . .

A BOY: Naval Captain Lüdde-Neurath . . .

A BOY: Admirals Voss and Wagner . . .

A BOY: Generals Krebs and Burgdorf . . .

WALLI S.: Colonel von Below, Reichsleiter Bormann, Ambassador Hewel of the Foreign Office . . .

A BOY: Fräulein Braun!

WALLI S.: SS Hauptsturmführer Günsche and SS Obergruppenführer Fegelein . . .

A BOY: Dr. Morell . . .

WALLI S.: And Herr and Frau Dr. Goebbels with all their six children—while congratulations were still being tendered, the black-haired German shepherd Prinz ran away from his master.

A BOY: And then what? Was he halted, captured, shot?

A BOY: Did anyone see him running? Deserting?

A BOY: And to whom did he desert?

WALLI S.: After brief misgivings the dog decided to follow the movement of the hour and disengage in a westerly direction. Since at the time of his projected and executed flight violent finishfights were in progress all around the capital, it proved impossible to catch the dog Prinz despite the untiring efforts of the dogsearchtroops that were immediately set up. At 8:45 A.M. on May 8, 1945, the dog Prinz swam across the Elbe above Magdeburg and went looking for a new master on the west shore of the river.

CHORUS: Matern was the master he chose
   with his legs and eyes and nose.

WALLI S.: But since in his last will of April 29th, the then Führer and Chancellor bequeathed his black-haired shepherd Prinz to the German people . . .

DISCUSSION LEADER: . . . we are forced to conclude that Walter Matern, the topic under discussion, cannot be the rightful owner of the shepherd Prinz—presently known as Pluto. We can regard him at the very most as the administrator of the Führerlegacy, the aforesaid black shepherd Prinz.

MATERN: This is an outrage! I'm an antifascist.

DISCUSSION LEADER: Why shouldn't an antifascist be the administrator of the Führerlegacy? We shall be glad to hear the opinions of our members on the subject.

MATERN: I was with the Red Falcons. Later I was a card-carrying member of the C.P. . . .

A BOY: As administrator of the Führerlegacy, the topic under discussion can lay claim to qualities that predestine him to this historic task . . .

MATERN: I distributed leaflets as late as '36 . . .

A BOY: For instance, he was born in the sign of the Ram, like the dog's former owner.

MATERN: If I joined the SA later on, it was only for a year, a brief interlude.

A BOY: Like the dog's late owner, dogadministrator Matern can grind his teeth.

MATERN: And then the Nazis kicked me out. Court of honor.

A BOY: But must it not be taken as an argument to the contrary that the selfsame dogadministrator Matern once poisoned a black dog?

MATERN: Yes, and with rat poison, because that Nazi dog, who belonged to a carpenter, mated with a bitch in the police kennels who later . . .

A BOY: Yet the topic under discussion claims to love animals.

A BOY: Would it not be fruitful to discuss our fixed point, namely "black shepherd" and the ownership status of the black shepherd Prinz, now Pluto, in conjunction with the pedigree of the black shepherd Pluto and the dynamic past of the topic under discussion?

MATERN: As an antifascist, I protest forcefully against this association of unrelated and purely fortuitous factors.

DISCUSSION LEADER: Objection upheld. We amend our project as follows: The fixed point and the dog pedigree will be dynamically discussed in the light of our topic's antifascist past.

A BOY: But only the final outcome of our discussion can show whether the Führerlegacy Prinz—now Pluto—is in reliable hands with the present dogadministrator.

DISCUSSION LEADER: The member's motion is approved. Anticipating the probable existence of a second fixed point, the chair prefers for the present to invite questions without direct bearing on the fixed point or on the ownership status of the black shepherd. (*Walli S. notes: Fixed Point 2, colon.*)

A GIRL: Can the topic under discussion think of any important childhood experiences that left their mark on him?

MATERN: Actual happenings? Or are you more interested in atmosphere?

A GIRL: Every level of consciousness can provide us with discussion-promoting data.

MATERN (*with a sweeping gesture*): Here Nickelswalde—over there Schiewenhorst.

> Perkunos, Pikollos, Potrimpos!
> Twelve headless nuns and twelve headless knights.
> Gregor Materna and Simon Materna.
> The giant Miligedo and the robber Bobrowski.
> Kujave wheat and Urtoba wheat.
> Mennonites and breaches in the dikes . . .
> And the Vistula flows,
> and the mill mills,
> and the narrow-gauge railway runs,
> and the butter melts,
> and the milk thickens,
> a little sugar on top,
> and the spoon stands upright,
> and the ferry comes,
> and the sun gone,
> and the sun back again,
> and the sea sand goes,
> and the sea licks sand . . .
> Barefoot barefoot run the children,
> and find blueberries,
> and look for amber,

and step on thistles,
and dig up mice,
and climb barefoot into hollow willows ...
But he who looks for amber,
who steps on the thistle,
jumps into the willow,
and digs up the mouse,
will find a dead dried maiden in the dike:
that's Duke Swantopolk's daughter,
who was always shoveling about for mice in the sand,
who bit with two incisor teeth,
and never wore shoes or stockings ...
Barefoot barefoot run the children,
and the willows shake themselves,
and the Vistula flows for evermore,
and the sun now gone, now back again,
and the ferry comes or goes
or lies fast and groans

while the milk thickens till the spoon stands, and slowly
runs the narrow-gauge railway ringing fast on the bend. And
the mill creaks when the wind at a rate of twenty-five feet
a second. And the miller hears what the mealworm says.
And teeth grind when Walter Matern from left to right.
Same with his grandmother: all around the garden she chases
poor Lorchen. Black and big with young, Senta crashes
through a trellis of broad beans. For terrible she approaches,
raising an angular arm: and in the hand on the arm the
wooden cooking spoon casts its shadow on curly-headed Lorchen and grows bigger and bigger, fatter and fatter, more
and more . . . also Eddi Amsel . . .

A BOY: Was this Eddi Amsel a friend of the topic under
discussion?

MATERN: The only one I ever had.

A BOY: Did your friend die?

MATERN: I can't imagine Eddi Amsel being dead.

A BOY: Was the aforementioned Eddi Amsel an intimate
friend?

MATERN: We were blood brothers! With one and the same
pocketknife we scored each other's left . . .

A BOY: What became of the knife?

MATERN: No idea.

A BOY: The question is vital. We repeat: what happened to
the pocketknife?

MATERN: Actually I wanted to throw a *zellack* into the Vistula. In those parts we called stones *zellacken*.

A BOY: We are waiting for news of the pocketknife!

MATERN: Well, stone or *zellack*, I looked for one in both pockets, but didn't find anything but the . . .

A BOY: . . . pocketknife.

A BOY: The knife had . . .

MATERN: . . . three blades, a corkscrew, a saw, and a leather punch . . . Nevertheless, I threw it . . .

A BOY: . . . the knife!

MATERN: into the Vistula. What does a river like the Vistula carry away with it? Sunsets, friendships, pocketknives! What rises to memory, floating on its stomach, with the help of the Vistula? Sunsets, friendships, pocketknives! Not all friendships last. Rivers that set out for hell empty into the Vistula . . .

DISCUSSION LEADER: Therefore let us recapitulate: As children and with the help of a pocketknife, Walter Matern, the topic under discussion, and his friend Eddi Amsel swore blood brotherhood. Still a boy, Matern threw the same pocketknife into the Vistula. Why the pocketknife? Because no stone was available. But in a more general sense, why?

MATERN: Because the Vistula flowed straight ahead for evermore. Because the sunset behind the opposite dike, because after we had sworn blood brotherhood, my friend Eddi's blood flowed inside me, because—because . . .

A BOY: Was your friend a Negro, a Gypsy, or a Jew?

MATERN: (*eagerly*): Only a half-Jew. His father was. His mother wasn't. He had reddish-blond hair from his mother and next to nothing from his father. A wonderful guy. You'd have liked him, boys. Always in a good humor, and what ideas he had! But he was kind of fat and I often had to protect him. All the same I loved him, admired him, even today I'd . . .

A BOY: If, for instance, you were annoyed with your friend, which must have happened now and then, what bad names did you call him?

MATERN: Well, at the worst, because he really was so monstrously fat, I'd call him a fat pig. Or to kid him, I'd call him fly shit, because he had millions of freckles all over. I'd also, but more as a joke and not when I was sore, call him milliner, because he was always building weird figures out of old rags, and the peasants used them for scarecrows and stood them up in their wheat.

A BOY: Can't you think of any other bad names?

A BOY: Something more specific.

MATERN: That was all.

A BOY: For instance, when you really wanted to wound him, to hurt his feelings?

MATERN: I never had any such intentions.

DISCUSSION LEADER: We are obliged to point out that we are discussing not intentions, but actions. So out with that big bad last dramatic dynamic word?

CHORUS: Let him cough up that little word,
   or under pressure he'll be heard.

WALLI S.: Perhaps I shall have to put on the knowledge glasses after all and peer into long past situations, in the course of which the topic under discussion, my uncle Walter, lost his temper.

MATERN (shakes his head): Then—at times when I couldn't control myself, because he was starting up again, or because he wouldn't stop, or because Eddi—I called him sheeny.

DISCUSSION LEADER: The discussion will be suspended while the insulting word "sheeny" is being analyzed. (Muttering among the members. Walli S. stands up.) I request your attention for our assistant Walli S.

WALLI S.: "Sheeny" is a contemptuous term, meaning Jew, dating roughly from the middle of the nineteenth century. It is thought to derive from the Yiddish word shane, meaning "fine," "lovely," "very good," which is often overheard in conversation among Jews, though what reason they had for regarding anything as fine, lovely, or very good has not been established. Cf. the popular jingle which developed early in the twentieth century . . .

CHORUS: Jewish sheeny,
   his legs are skinny,
   Roman nose,
   shits in his close.

A BOY: But our topic's friend, whom he insulted by calling him a sheeny, was fat.

DISCUSSION LEADER: As we have seen in previous discussions, insulting epithets are not always used with the strictest logic. The Americans, for instance, call all Germans "krauts," although not all Germans love sauerkraut or eat it regularly. Consequently, the term "sheeny" can also be applied to a

Jew or—as in the present case—a half-Jew with a tendency to corpulence.

A BOY: In any event we cannot fail to note our topic's penchant for anti-Semitic utterances.

MATERN: As a man and as a pronounced philo-Semite, I protest. Yes, I lost my temper now and then and said things I shouldn't have said, but I always defended Eddi when other people called him a sheeny; when, for instance, you, Herr Liebenau, aided and abetted by your snotnose cousin, grossly insulted my friend in the yard of your father's carpenter shop—for no reason at all, he was only sketching your watchdog Harras—I came to my friend's defense and rebuffed your childish but slanderous remarks.

A BOY: The topic under discussion apparently wishes to broaden the discussion by bringing up episodes from the private life of our discussion leader.

A BOY: He has called our discussion leader's cousin a snotnose.

A BOY: He has dragged in the carpenter shop where, as we know, our discussion leader enjoyed a carefree childhood amid lumber sheds and gluepots.

A BOY: He has likewise mentioned the carpenter's watchdog Harras, who is identical with the black shepherd Harras, later poisoned by the topic under discussion.

DISCUSSION LEADER: The chair can only interpret the unfair personal attacks to which it has just been subjected as a further indication of our topic's uncontrolled reactions. We therefore ask a counterquestion: Was there any connection between the already-noted legendary dog Perkun, the likewise noted bitch Senta, who belonged to the father of the topic under discussion, namely, miller Matern, and the black shepherd Harras, who belonged to the discussion leader's father, namely carpenter Liebenau—was there, I ask, any connection between them apart from the fact that the miller's son Walter Matern on the one hand and on the other hand the carpenter's son Harry Liebenau and his cousin Tulla Pokriefke called the topic's friend a sheeny?

MATERN: O ye dog years, biting each other's tails! In the beginning there was a Lithuanian she-wolf. She was crossed with a male shepherd. The outcome of this unnatural act was a male whose name does not figure in any pedigree. And he, the nameless one, begat Perkun. And Perkun begat Senta . . .

CHORUS: And Senta whelped Harras . . .

MATERN: And Harras sired Prinz, who is living on my charity today. O ye dog years hoarse from howling! What guarded a miller's mill, what watched over a carpenter shop, what in guise of favorite dog rubbed against the boots of your Reichsautobahn builder, attached itself to me, an antifascist. Have you fathomed the parable? Do your accounts of accursed dog years balance to the last decimal? Are you satisfied? Have you anything more to say? May Matern take his dog away and have a beer?

DISCUSSION LEADER: Our public and dynamic discussion is hurrying to a close. But though we take justified pride in our partial findings, it is too soon to speak of full satisfaction. There are still a few threads left to tie. Let us recollect. (*He points to the blackboard.*) The topic under discussion has killed many animals . . .

A BOY: He poisoned a dog!

DISCUSSION LEADER: And yet claimed . . .

A BOY: . . . to love animals . . .

DISCUSSION LEADER: . . . to be an animal lover. So far we know that on the one hand the topic under discussion, who likes to speak of himself as an antifascist and philo-Semite, protected his friend, the half-Jew Eddi Amsel, from the persecutions of ignorant children, and on the other hand insulted him by calling him a sheeny. We therefore ask:

CHORUS: Matern loves animals;
      does Matern also love the Jews?

MATERN (*with pathos*): By God and the Nothing! The Jews have been gravely wronged.

A BOY: Answer in so many words: Do you love the Jews as you love animals, or don't you?

MATERN: We have all of us gravely wronged the Jews.

A BOY: That is generally known. The statistics speak for themselves. Reparation, a topic recently discussed by us, has been under way for years. But we are speaking of today. Do you love them today or haven't you come around to it?

MATERN: In an emergency I would defend every Jew with my life.

A BOY: What does the topic under discussion mean by an emergency?

MATERN: For instance, my friend Eddi Amsel was beaten up one cold day in January by nine SA men, and I was powerless to help him.

A BOY: What were the names of the nine assaulting SA men?

MATERN (*in an undertone*): As if names could stand for deeds! (*Aloud*) But never mind: Jochen Sawatzki. Paule Hoppe. Franz Wollschläger. Willy Eggers. Alfons Bublitz. Otto Warnke. Egon Dulleck and Bruno Dulleck.

CHORUS (*who have been counting on their fingers*):
We've counted only eight.
What was the name of the ninth?
Nine foes, nine crows,
nine symphonies,
and nine holy kings
adoring on their knees!

DISCUSSION LEADER: Though promised the names of nine thugs, our members have counted only eight names. May we, to obviate the need for dynamic compulsory discussion, assume that the topic under discussion was the ninth thug?

MATERN: No! No! You have no right . . .

WALLI S.: Aha, but we have the knowledge glasses! (*She puts on the glasses and moves halfway to the temple.*)
Nine climbed the garden fence,
my uncle was one.
Nine trampled the January snow,
my uncle in the snow was one.
A black rag on every face,
my uncle disguised was one.
Nine fists battered a tenth face,
my uncle's fist was one.
And when nine fists were tired,
my uncle wasn't done.
And when all the teeth had been spat,
my uncle stifled a cry.
And sheeny sheeny sheeny was
my uncle's litany.
Nine men escaped over the fence,
my uncle was one. (*Walli S. takes off the glasses, returns to the blackboard, and draws lines indicating nine little men.*)

DISCUSSION LEADER: We have only a few last questions:

A BOY: Which SA strum?

MATERN (*crisply*): Langfuhr-North, Eighty-four, SA Brigade Six.

A BOY: Did your friend defend himself?

MATERN: At first he wanted to make us coffee, but we didn't want any.

A BOY: What then was the purpose of your visit?

MATERN: We wanted to teach him a lesson.

A BOY: Why had you hidden your faces?

MATERN: Because it's the style: when you want to teach a lesson, you hide your face.

A BOY: What form did this lesson take?

MATERN: Hasn't that been made clear enough?—The sheeny got beaten up. Shoilem boil 'em! He got it square in the puss.

A BOY: Did your friend lose any teeth?

MATERN: All thirty-two of them!

CHORUS: To us the number isn't new.
　　　　　We keep on hearing thirty-two.

DISCUSSION LEADER: And so we find that the lucky and unlucky number obtained through our first series of exploratory questions is identical with the number of teeth that his friend Eddi Amsel had knocked out by nine disguised SA men. This makes it clear that in addition to "black shepherd," the personality of Walter Matern, the topic under discussion, has a second fixed point, which enables us to form a dynamic picture of him. This second fixed point is the number thirty-two. (*Walli S. writes on the blackboard with capital letters.*) The value of public discussion has again been fully confirmed.

A BOY: How, in conclusion, shall we characterize the topic under discussion?

DISCUSSION LEADER: How, if he were asked, would the topic under discussion characterize himself?

MATERN: Shoot the shit, crack wise, do what you like! I, Matern, was and am an out-and-out antifascist. I've proved it thirty-two times over, and . . .

DISCUSSION LEADER: Then we may characterize Walter Matern, the topic under discussion, as an antifascist who feeds Adolf Hitler's legacy, the black shepherd Pluto—formerly Prinz. Our discussion has brought results. Let us then give thanks and pray (*the boys and girls rise and clasp their hands*): O Thou great Guide and Creator of everlasting dynamic world discussion, Thou who hast given us a discussion-welcoming topic of discussion and shown us the way to a universally valid conclusion, let us offer up a hymn of thanksgiving, singing two and thirty times the praises of the black-haired German shepherd. As he was, and as he is:

CHORUS: Long-bodied, stiff-haired, with erect ears and a long tail.

TWO BOYS: A powerful muzzle with dry tight lips.

FIVE BOYS: Dark eyes slightly ovoid.

A BOY: Erect ears tilted slightly forward.

CHORUS: Neck firm, free from dewlap or throatiness.

TWO BOYS: Barrel length two inches in excess of shoulder height.

GIRLS: Seen from all angles, the legs are straight.

CHORUS: Toes well closed. His long, slightly sloping croup. Pads good and hard.

TWO BOYS: Shoulders hocks joints:

A GIRL: powerful, well muscled.

CHORUS: And every single hair: straight, smooth, harsh, and black.

FIVE BOYS: And black too the undercoat.

TWO GIRLS: No dark wolf markings on gray or yellow coat.

A BOY: No, all over him to the erect, slightly forward-tilting ears, on his deep curled chest, on the slightly fringed legs, his hair glistens black.

THREE BOYS: Umbrella-black, blackboard-black, priest-black, widow-black . . .

FIVE BOYS: SS-black, Falange-black, blackbird-black, Othello black, Ruhr-black . . .

CHORUS: violet-black, tomato-black, lemon-black, flour-black, milk-black, snow-black . . .

DISCUSSION LEADER: Amen! (*The discussion club disbands.*)

THE HUNDRED AND FIRST FUGITIVE MATERNIAD

Matern reads this final broadcasting script of an open forum in the canteen of the Radio Building. But twenty-five minutes later—the members of the discussion group haven't yet reeled off their final prayer and the loudspeaker is summoning Matern to broadcasting room four—he leaves the brand-new Radio Building with Pluto. He doesn't want to speak. His tongue doesn't feel like it. He holds that Matern isn't a topic to be publicly discussed. From eagerly contributed discussion material, gumshoes and wisenheimers have built him a watertight house, in which he absolutely refuses

to live, not even for the time of a single broadcast; but
he still has a fat fee, earned with his popular children's-
program voice, coming to him. The voucher, signature-
blessed, may be presented at the cashier's office: bills fresh
from the bank crackle shortly before he leaves the Cologne
Radio Building.

In the beginning, when Matern was traveling to pass judgment, Cologne Central Station and Cologne Cathedral had
been eloquent partners; now, with his final fee in his pocket
and again in a mood for travel, he abandons the tension-
charged triangle—Central Station, cathedral, Radio Building. Matern breaks away, withdraws, takes flight.

And finds reasons aplenty for flight: first, that revolting
dynamic discussion; in the second place, he's had enough of
the capitalistic, militaristic, revanchistic, and Nazi-logged West
German rump state—he hears the call of the future-building,
peaceloving, virtually classless, healthy, and East Elbian
German Democratic Republic; and in the third place, Inge
Sawatzki—the slut wants to divorce good old Jochen—has
been getting flight-provokingly on his nerves.

Farewell to the Gothic pigeon-nourishing double prongs.
Farewell to the still drafty railroad station. There's still time
for a farewell glass of beer in Cologne's holy waiting room
between the penitent and the hardened of heart. Just time
for a last leak in Cologne's warm, tiled, sweet-and-pungent-
smelling Catholic men's toilet. Oh no! No sentimentalities! The
Devil and his philosophical equivalents take all the names
which, scribbled in enamel bays, once made his heart thump,
his spleen swell, his kidneys ache! A phenotype demands to
be relieved. A bounceback man wants to make a fresh bed
for himself. A legacy administrator no longer feels responsible. Matern, who journeyed through the Western camp
with black dog to judge, makes his way to the Eastern,
peaceloving camp without dog: for he deposits Pluto, alias
Prinz, with the station mission. Which mission? Two are in
competition. But the Protestants are kinder to animals than
the Catholics. Oh, Matern has meanwhile learned a thing or
two about religions and ideologies. "Would you mind keeping this dog for me? Only for half an hour. I'm a war in-
valid. My certificate. I'm only passing through. I've got
a business errand, and I can't take the. God will reward
you. A cup of coffee? Gladly and gratefully when I get

back. Be a good boy, Pluto. I won't be more than half an hour."

Parting of the ways. Heaves a sigh of relief in the hurried draft. Burns his ships in thought, word, and deed. Shakes off dust on the run: track four. The interzonal train via Düsseldorf, Duisburg, Essen, Dortmund, Hamm, Bielefeld, Hanover, Helmstedt, Magdeburg, to Berlin-Zoological Gardens and Berlin-East Station is about to pull out. All aboard!

O pipe-smoking certainty. While Pluto is probably lapping up his milk in the Protestant mission, Matern rides away dog-less and second class. Nonstop to Düsseldorf. Adopts a candid foreign look; faustball players, sharpshooters, members of the Sawatzki family might come in and compel him by their mere presence to get out. But Matern is able to keep his seat and to go on carrying his well-known character actor's head unalienated on his shoulders. It's none too comfortable sharing a compartment with seven interzonal travelers. All peace lovers, as he soon finds out. None of whom wants to stay in the West, though it's ever so much cushier than.

Because they all have relatives over there. "There" is always where you aren't. "He was over there until last May, then he came over here. The people who stay over there have their reasons. And all the things you have to leave behind. Over here there's Italian tomato paste, over there you can get the Bulgarian stuff now and then." Conversations as far as Duisburg: palatal soft plaintive cautious. The one grandma from over there does all the complaining: "Over there at home they were out of brown thread for a while. So my son-in-law said: lay in a supply while you're over here, heaven only knows when you'll get another chance. At first I couldn't get used to it over here. Everything is so crowded. And the advertisements. But then when I saw the prices. They wanted to keep me over here: Grandma, why don't you stay? What's the use of going back over there, when over here with us. But I said no. I'm only a burden to you, I said, and over there at home maybe things will gradually get better. Young people are more adaptable. Last time I came over here, I said: My, how quickly you've settled into the life over here. And my second daughter's husband said: What do you think, Grandma. What kind of a life did we have over there? But neither of them thinks we'll ever be reunified. My second daughter's boss, who only came over four years ago, says when all's told, the Russians and the Amis are in cahoots. But everybody says something different. Not just over there at home, over here too. And every year come Christmas I think: Well, next Christmas. And every year when I put up fruit from the garden, I say to my sister Lisbeth, maybe we'll all be peacefully unified by the time we have the plums for Christmas. Well, this time I brought two jars of preserves over. They were mighty pleased. Tastes like home, that's what they said. Though over here they've got plenty of everything. Every Sunday pineapple!"

This music in Matern's ears while outside a film unrolls: an industrial landscape working to capacity under the sign of the free-market economy. No commentary. Chimneys speak for themselves. Anyone who feels like it can count them. Not a one made of cardboard. All jutting skyward. Industry's Song of Songs. Sustained dynamic solemn; blast furnaces are no joke. Legal wages, subject to revocation. Capital and labor, eye to eye. Coalandchemicals ironandsteel RhineandRuhr.—Don't look out the window or, spooks is what you've got in store. The show begins in the coal basin and rises to a climax on the plains. In the smoking compartment plaintive palatal music: "My son-in-law over there says, and my second daughter over here wants to," while outside—Don't look out the window!—first from kitchen gardens, then from fields of spring-green grain, the uprising spreads. Mobilization—spook dynamics—scarecrow movements. They race along while the interzonal train runs on schedule. But they don't overtake it. No spooks jumping aboard a moving train in defiance of regulations. Just continuous running. While in the smoking compartment the grandma says: "I didn't want to come over without my sister, though she's always saying: Go on over, who knows when they'll close the border," outside—Don't look out the window—scarecrows tear themselves away from their fixed stations. Functionally dressed hatracks leave salad beds and knee-high wheat. Beanpoles buttoned up for winter start and take hurdles. What a moment before was blessing gooseberries with wide-sleeved arms, says amen and trots off. But it's not a flight, more like a relay race. It's not as if they were all hightailing it eastward to the Peaceloving Camp; no, their purpose is to pass something on over here, some news or a watchword; for scarecrows uproot themselves from their vegetable gardens, hand on the baton with the terrible message rolled in it, to other scarecrows who have hitherto been guarding rye, and as the vegetable scarecrows are catching their breath in rye, the rye scarecrows sprint beside the interzonal train until, in a good stand of barley, they encounter scarecrows ready to start, who take over the spook post, relieve breathless rye scarecrows, and with bold checks and beanpole joints keep pace with the on-schedule train, until once again herringbone-patterned rye scarecrows take over. One two six scarecrows—for teams are battling for victory—carry six handily rolled letters, an original and five copies—or is the treacherous import of one and the same message conveyed in six different versions?—to what address? But no Zatopek takes the baton from a Nurmi. No athletic uniforms suggest that Wersten (blue-and-white) is leading but that the Unterrath Athletic Club is coming up, passing the Derendorf boys, fighting neck and neck with Lohhausen '07. Distances are being devoured in civilian clothes of every conceivable style: under velours hats, night-caps, and helmets of all sorts flutter coachmen's capes, Prussian Army coats, and carpets—chewed by whom?—long strides are taken by trouser legs ending in galoshes and buckled shoes, army boots, and friar's sandals. A duffel coat relays a Glasenapp Hussar. Loden passes on the baton to raglan. Rayon to muslin. Scarlet to synthetic fiber, poplin to herringbone, nankeen and piqué send brocade and chiffon on their way. Dutch bonnet and trenchcoat fall behind. A heavy ulster outdistances a wind-filled negligee and the Second Empire. Directoire and functional fashions are relayed by the twenties and by fusty furbelows. A genuine Gainsborough in collaboration with Prince Pückler-Muskau demonstrates the classical method of handing on the baton. Balzac catches up. Suffragettes hold their own. And then for quite some time a princess' skirt is in the lead. O bold and muted colors: shot silks, pastel shades, rainbow! O you prints: millefleurs and modest stripes. O you changing trends: the neoclassical note gives way to the functional, the military to the casual. The waist moves down again. The invention of the sewing machine contributes to the democratization of ladies' fashions. Crinolines have seen their day. But Makart opens the old chests, liberating velvet and plush, tassels and pompons: see how they run: Don't look out the window or, spooks is what you've got in store!, while in the smoking compartment!—O story without end!—the grandma

from over here and over there is still at it when the Westphalian landscape passes on the baton with scarecrow-ease
to the incoming Lower Saxon landscape, speeding it on its
way from over here to over there: for scarecrows know no
borders: parallel to Matern, the scarecrow message journeys
to the Peaceloving Camp, shakes off the dust, leaves capitalistic rye behind it, is taken up by class-conscious scarecrows in
socialized oats: from over here to over there without customs inspection or pass; for scarecrows don't, but Matern does
have to show his papers, and so does the grandma, who was
over there and is now coming back over here.

Matern sighs with relief: oh, how different the sausages
smell in the Socialist Peaceloving Camp. Gone forever that
capitalistic curry smell. Matern's heart bursts iron bands:
Marienborn! How beautiful the people are here, and even
the tenements, Vopos, windowboxes, and spittoons. And the
well-fed redness of the flags, and the billowing streamers
with their slogans. After all the bad years, with black dog
at heel, at last socialism triumphs. No sooner is the interzonal train in motion than Matern wants to communicate the
red jubilation of his heart. But as he starts to speak and to
praise the Peaceloving Socialist Camp, quietly and suit-
casedraggingly the smoking compartment empties. The
smoke is getting too thick, there must be room in a compartment for nonsmokers. No offense and a pleasant trip.

All the fellow travelers on their way to Oschersleben,
Halberstadt, and Magdeburg, and finally the grandma who
is changing in Magdeburg for Dessau leave him. In his lone-
liness Matern is haunted by the rhythm of the rails: posts
ghosts posts ghosts.

Message-bearing, they are on their way. Now clad like
Spartacus or the toiling masses. Strike pickets hand on the
baton. Sansculottes smell blood. Even in mixed forests Matern
thinks he sees rebellious proletarians. Woods spit out scarecrows in windbreakers. Brooks are no obstacles. Hedges
taken at a leap. Long-legged over knolls. Swallowed up, there
again. Stockingless in wooden shoes, in Phrygian caps.
Cross-country scarecrows. Field and stream scarecrows. Peasants' Revolt scarecrows: Bundschuh and Poor Konrad,
vagabonds and iron miners, mendicant friars and Ana-
baptists, the monk Pfeiffer, Hipler and Geyer, the Fury of
Allstedt, the peasants of Mansfeld and Eichsfeld, Balthasar
and Bartel, Krumpf and Velten, on to Frankenhausen, where

already the rainbow of rags and tatters, of leitmotives and murder motives . . . At this point Matern changes his view; but on the corridor side of the interzonal train he is horrified to find the same spooks behind sash windows, all moving in the same direction.

Out! At every station where the train doesn't stop, he wants to get out. Distrust germinates. Every train has a different destination. And will the Peaceloving Camp really take me to its bosom when this locomotive, hitched to first and second class, hitched to my dreams, says amen? Matern checks his ticket: all in order and paid for. What, seen through sash windows, is happening outside, is happening free of charge. Why should he have forebodings just because he sees a few plain ordinary scarecrows running? After all, it's the nationalized Magdeburg Bowl, famed for its sugarbeets, and not the capitalistic desert of Nevada that is being traversed by swift dynamic scarecrows. Besides, there have always been scarecrows. He wasn't the first and won't be the last to make dozens of them out of old rags and chicken-wire. But these here—a glance out of the window—might have been made by him. His style. His work. Eddi's deft fingers.

Thereupon Matern takes flight. Where can you run to on a speeding interzonal train, rendered transparent to left and right by sash windows, mostly stuck, if not to the john. He even manages to take a shit and so motivate his flight. Relax. Settle down. Put away all fear; for, generally speaking, the toilet windows of all trains, whether fast or slow, are made of frosted glass. Frosted glass windows negate spooks. O peaceful idyl. Almost holy and just as Catholic as the station toilet that Cologne held in readiness for him when he went to Cologne and was looking for a quiet place. Here too scribble-scrabble on damaged enamel. The usual: verses, confessions, suggestions for doing something this way or that way, names unknown to him; for neither heart, spleen, nor kidneys quiver as he tries to decipher individual words. But when the hand-sized and cross-hatched drawing catches his eye—the black-sketched dog Perkun Senta Harras Prinz Pluto jumping over a garden fence—his heart blackens, his purple spleen darkens, the urine curdles in his kidneys. Once again, this time from a skillfully sketched dog, Matern takes flight.

But where can you run to on a speeding interzonal train if you leave the one refuge which frosted glass windowpanes secure against the spook show? At first, quite logically, he wants to get out in Magdeburg, but then, like a hypnotized rabbit, remains faithful to the destination on his ticket, expecting salvation from the River Elbe. The Elbe forms a barrier. The Elbe is the natural frontier of the Peaceloving Camp. Bird-repellent spooks and anyone else who may be headed in that direction will halt at the Western shore of the Elbe and send their scarecrow screams or other spectral howlings heavenward, while the interzonal train hurries off across the not yet fully repaired Elbe bridge.

But as Matern and the meanwhile half-empty interzonal train—most of the travelers have got out in Magdeburg—leave behind that saving event, the Elbe bridge, multiplied evil bursts forth from the rushes of the East-Elbian shore: not only are the usual news-pregnant scarecrows racing along as from Marathon to Athens; in addition, his coat still Elbe-wet, a dog glistening deep black knows only one direction: after the interzonal train! A race begins, neck and neck, dog versus express train roaring through the Peaceloving Camp. For a time the animal takes the lead—the train is running slightly late because the roadbed is soggy in the Peaceloving Camp and, timetable or not, can't afford to be in too much of a hurry—but then drops back, enabling Matern to feast his eyes on blackness.

Oh, if you had only left Pluto at the Catholic mission instead of its animal-loving competitor! If you had given him reliable poison, or if a club, properly handled, had destroyed the half-blind mutt's drive and his passion for the chase. But as it is, a black shepherd grows dog years younger between Genthin and Brandenburg. Rises in the ground swallow him up. Hollows spit him out. Fences split him into sixteenths. Fine steady driving gait. Soft landings. Powerful hind quarters. No one but he can jump like that. The line from the withers to the slightly sloping croup. Eight—twenty-four—thirty-two-legged. Pluto draws up and leads the field of scarecrows. Evening sun edges silhouettes. The Twelfth Army surges toward Beelitz. Götterdämmerung. Structure of the end. If I only had a camera: cut cut. Spook close-up. Final victory close-up. Dog close-up. But you're not allowed to take pictures of the Peaceloving Camp from moving trains. Unfilmed, the Wenck combat team, disguised as an army of scarecrows, and a dog by the name of Perkun Senta Harras Prinz Pluto remain on a level with the teeth-grinding

Walter Matern behind a sash window. Beat it, dog. Scram, dog. Get thee behind me, *kyon*!

But only after Werder, near Potsdam, in among the vast expanse of lakes, do scarecrows and dog lose themselves in league with the land-engulfing darkness. Matern sticks to the plastic upholstery of his second-class seat and stares at the framed photograph across from him: in oblong the fissured landscape of the Elbsandstein Mountains advertises itself. Hikes through Saxon Switzerland. Something new for a change, especially as neither scarecrows nor Pluto are to be seen among the crags. Sturdy comfortable hiking shoes, if possible with double soles. Woolen stockings, undarned. Knapsack and map. Large deposits of granite, gneiss, and quartz. Brunies used to correspond with a geologist in Pirna and exchange specimens of mica gneiss and mica granite. Quantities of Elbe sandstone besides. That's the place for you. It's quieter. There nothing will sneak up on you from behind. With or without dog, you've never been there. In general people should only go to places where they've never: to Flurstein, for instance, and then up the trail and along the Ziegenrück road to Polenz View, a rock platform without a railing, offering a marvelous view of the Polenz Valley: then follow Amsel Valley to Amsel Falls and the Hockstein. Stop for the night at the Amsel Valley Hunting Lodge. I'm a stranger in these parts. Matern? Never heard of him. Why is Amsel Valley called Amsel Valley and Amsel Falls Amsel Falls? No connection with your friend by the same name. In addition we have here Amsel Gulch and Amsel Rock. We're not interested in your past. We have other, socialist worries. We're engaged in rebuilding the beautiful city of Dresden. The old Zwinger Palace with new Elbe sandstone. In people's quarries we're cutting house fronts for the Peaceloving Republic. Nobody grinds his teeth in these parts, and neither will you. So show your papers and turn in your pass. Steer clear of West Berlin, that bastion of capitalism. Go right on through to East Station, then come and see socialism being built in the Elbsandstein Mountains. Stay right in your seat when the train has to stop at the warmongers' and revanchists' station. Be patient until Friedrichstrasse Station bids you welcome. For God's sake don't get out at Zoological Gardens Station.

But shortly before the interzonal train stops at Zoological Gardens Station, Matern remembers that he still has a fat chunk of his radio fee in his pocket. He decides to stop for a minute, exchange his West marks for East marks at the profitable capitalistic rate, one to four, and take the "L" to the Peaceloving Camp. Besides, he has to buy a razor and blades, two pairs of socks, and a change of shirts; who knows whether these vital necessities are available over there at the moment?

With these modest desires he leaves the train. Along with him others, who doubtless have greater desires. Relatives welcome relatives, taking no notice of Matern, whom, as he reflects with a note of bitterness, no relatives are expecting. Nevertheless, a reception has been provided for Matern. Reception jumps up on him with forepaws. Reception licks him with long tongue. Glad barking, whimpering jubilation. Don't you remember me? Don't you love me any more? Did you want me to stay in that station mission forever, until dog-death? Haven't I a right to be faithful as a dog?

Of course of course! It's all right, Pluto. Now you've got your master back again. Let's have a look at you. It's him and it isn't him. An obviously black stud dog answers to the name of Pluto, but the scissors bite is gapless to the touch. Gone are the ice-gray islands over the stop, the eyes are no longer bleary. Why, at the most that dog can't be a day over eight. Rejuvenated and new. Only the dog tag is still the same. Dog lost, dog found again; and—as usual in railroad stations—here comes the honest finder: "Pardon me, is this your dog?"

He removes the Borsalino from his smoothly combed hair: a slim, affected stringbean, as hoarse as a grater, which doesn't prevent him from sucking a coffin nail: "The animal ran up to me and insisted on dragging me to Zoological Gardens Station; he pulled me right through the entrance hall and up these stairs to where the big expresses come in."

Is he after a reward or does he want to strike up an acquaintance? Still with hat in hand, he doesn't spare his vocal cords: "I don't wish to be obtrusive, but I am glad to have met you. Call me what you like. Here in Berlin most people call me Goldmouth. An allusion to my chronic hoarseness and the twenty-four-carat substitutes for teeth that I am obliged to wear in my mouth."

Thereupon Matern's internal cash drawer gets a checking over: coins of every kind jingle together. Inflamed with red only a moment before, his heart is now wrapped in gold leaf.

Spleen and kidneys are heavy as ducats: "My, what a surprise! And in a railroad station of all places. I can't say what is more amazing, finding my Pluto again—I lost the dog in Cologne—or this momentous, I can't think of any other word, meeting."

"The pleasure is all mine!"—"But haven't we friends in common?"—"You think so?"—"Why yes, the Sawatzkis. Wouldn't they be flabbergasted if they."—"Why then I must be—or can I be mistaken?—talking to Herr Matern?"—"As he lives and breathes. What a coincidence! We really have to drink on it."—"Suits me."—"Where do you suggest?"—"Wherever you like."—"I'm pretty much of a stranger around here."—"Then let's start our little round at the Barfuss place."—"Anything you say. But first I'd like—my trip was unexpected—to buy a change of shirts and a razor. Heel, Pluto! My, is he happy!"

THE HUNDRED AND SECOND FIREPROOF MATERNIAD

Here you see God's gigolo with his one and only prop! In between mincing pigeon steps, the guy is actually whirling an ebony cane with an ivory handle. In this station as in all others, familiar and welcomed: "Hi, Goldmouth. In town again? How's your love life?"

And smokes Navy Cut the whole time at high speed. While inside the station—the shops here are open until late—Matern buys his vital razor and the blades that go with it, the little fellow smokes without interruption and, when he runs out of matches, asks a policeman for a light: "Good evening, officer." And the officer salutes the idling smoker.

And everybody winks at Goldmouth and, so it seems to Matern, points to him and the rejuvenated dog: Among friends. Complicity. That's a hot one, Goldmouth. Some bird you've scared up.

Talk about birds! When Matern comes back with two pairs of woolen socks and a fresh shirt, five or six kids are surrounding his new friend. And what are they doing? Horsing around between the Heine Bookstore and the ticket windows of the "L," dancing around him while he offhandedly beats time with his cane, twittering like telegraph wires, cackling and chirping sound effects. They turn their jackets inside out; with the lining out they look like members of the scarecrow family that was staging a relay race on both sides of the just-arrived interzonal train, as though intending, even before the train pulled in at Berlin-Zoological Gardens, to make known, deliver, and loudly proclaim the tidings, message, watchword: "He's coming! He's coming! He'll be here in a minute and needs to buy a razor and socks and a change of shirts."

But all the boys evaporate as soon as Matern steps up to Goldmouth with parcels and rejuvenated dog: "O.K. Let's go."

It's not far. The place is no longer in existence, but at the time when the trio is crossing Hardenbergstrasse is situated across the way from the Newsreel Theater, which today is projecting the news somewhere else. Not into the Bilka department store, but across Joachimstaler on the green light, and a few steps up Kanstrasse. After the Ski Hut sporting goods store, an electric sign over the usual Berlin pub makes it clear that ANNA HELENE BARFUSS—who by now must be rinsing glasses behind the heavenly bar——still reigns behind an earthly cash register as our trio is approaching. The place used to be a coachmen's hangout. Today traffic cops gather there after hours. Also teachers of art from Steinplatz and couples who are ahead of time for their movie. And now and then the kind who are often between jobs. They stand at the bar shifting their weight from leg to leg between glasses. For good measure one might mention a flighty old biddy who, always under the same hat, is enjoying a free lunch, in return for which she has to tell Anna Helene about the repertory at the Volksbühne from the latest Adamov to the last time Elsa Wagner brought the house down; for Anna Helene's cash register rings so steadily that she can never get out to the theater.

Here too Goldmouth is a familiar figure. His order: "A hot lemonade, please!" surprises no one but Matern. "For your throat, I suppose. That's a bad cold you've got. No, it must be smoker's cough. You sure smoke like a chimney."

Goldmouth listens attentively to the voice. He connects himself with the hot lemonade by means of a straw. But listening to Matern and sucking lemonade are only two activities; in addition, he smokes cigarettes, lights the fresh smoke-stick with the last third of the old one, and throws the burning butt behind him, whereupon la Barfuss, deep in retrospective theatricals at the free-lunch counter, motions the waiter with her eyebrows to stamp out the butt. The gentlemen pay for two beers, a hot lemonade, and three meatballs. Dutch, except that Matern pays for the dog.

But Goldmouth and Matern with newly found Pluto haven't far to go: up Joachimstaler, across Kurfürstendamm on the zebra stripes, and at the corner of Augsburger into the White Moor. There Matern consumes two beers and two schnapps; Goldmouth drains a hot lemonade to the sweet dregs; the dog is served a portion of fresh blood sausage—homemade! The waiter has to stamp out four butts in all behind the smoker's back. This time they don't cling to the bar but stand at a small table. Each becomes the other's opposite. And Matern counts as the waiter reduces to silence what Goldmouth flips smoking behind him. "You ought to quit smoking so much. It doesn't make sense when you're as hoarse as a grater."

But the several times admonished smoker expresses, as though in passing, the opinion that his constant smoking is not the cause of his chronic hoarseness, but that, thinking much further back, to a time when he was still a nonsmoker submitting to athletic discipline, something, a certain someone, had roughed up his vocal cords: "Hm, you surely remember. It happened early in January."

But strenuously as Matern swirls the remnant of beer in his glass, he can't seem to remember: "What am I supposed to? Are you trying to pull? But joking aside, you really ought to cut out the chain smoking. You won't have any voice left. Waiter, the check. Where do we go now?"

This time Goldmouth pays for everything, including the blood sausage for the newly found dog. Obviously their legs need no more stretching. A stone's throw up Augsburger. Scenes of welcome in the springtime air that has a hard time preserving its balminess against the curry vapors of nearby snack bars. Unaccompanied ladies are glad to see him, but not obtrusive: "Goldmouth here, Goldmouth there!" And the same song and dance at Paul's Taproom, where they sit on bar stools, because the circular sofa around the big table is fully occupied: trucking men with ladies and interminable stories which even Goldmouth's feted arrival can interrupt only briefly, and that because they feel obliged to say something about the dog. "Mine—sit, Hasso—is a good ten years old." Dog talk and curiosity: "That's a purebred. Where'd you get him?" As if the dog belonged not to Matern but to this smoker who, rising above all the questions, gives the order: "Hey, Hannchen. A beer for the gentleman. For me the usual. And a schnapps too for the gentleman, if it's all right."

It's all right. So long as he doesn't mix his drinks. Better be careful, keep a clear head and a steady hand in case of trouble. You never can tell.

Matern's refreshments are served. Goldmouth sucks the usual with a straw. The newly found dog, described as a pure-bred by one of the trucking men, receives a hard-boiled egg, which Hannchen in person peels for him behind the counter. A free and easy atmosphere: questions, answers, and some-what ambiguous remarks are exchanged between tables. A three-lady table near the ventilator is curious to know whether Goldmouth is in town for business or pleasure. The round table—against a background adorned with photographs of wrestlers and boxers waiting, most of them at the vertical, for the next full nelson or left hook—inquires, without so much as a lull in its internal conversation, how Goldmouth's business is doing. Trouble with the Internal Revenue Service is mentioned. Goldmouth complains of slow deliveries. The circular sofa counters: "What would you expect, with your export orders?" Hannchen wants to know how his love life is prospering. A question which was already asked by the bustling Zoological Gardens Station and which in both cases Goldmouth answers with a suggestive smoke line in the air.

But here again, in this pub, where everybody is in the know except for the hick Matern, the smoker insists on flip-ping his cigarette butts behind him every time Matern pushes up the ash tray: "Some manners you have, I must say. Oh well, these people are used to your routine. Why don't you try a filter for a change? Or try to fight it off with chewing gum? It's sheer nervousness. And that throat of yours. It's none of my business. But if I were you, I'd cut it out com-pletely for two weeks. I'm really worried."

Goldmouth is pleased to hear Matern's concern expressed so prolixly. Though it keeps reminding him that his chronic hoarseness doesn't come from immoderate smoking, but can be dated with precision: "One January afternoon, years ago. You surely remember, my dear Matern. There was a lot of snow on the ground."

Matern counters that there's usually a lot of snow on the ground in January, that all this is a silly subterfuge to distract attention from his cigarette consumption, because the root of his throat trouble is coffin nails and not any perfectly normal winter cold he caught many years ago.

The next round is stood by the trucking men, whereupon Matern feels called upon to order seven slugs of gin—"because where it comes from is where I come from"—for the occupants of the round table. "From Nickelswalde, and Tiegenhof was our county seat." But despite rising spirits, Goldmouth, Matern, and newly found dog gather little moss at Paul's Taproom. Despite urgent pleas to hang around from the three-lady table—whose occupants change frequently—from the social stability of the trucking men's table, and from the universally popular Hannchen: "You're always dropping in for half a second; and you haven't told us a story in ages"—the gentlemen prefer to ask for the check, which doesn't mean that Goldmouth—he's already standing by the ventilator with Matern and dog—has no story up his sleeve.

"Tell us about the ballets you used to put on."

"Or when you were a so-called cultural-affairs officer in the occupation."

"The one about the worms is good too."

But this time Goldmouth's mood is running in a very different direction. Facing the round table, grazing the three-lady table, and taking in Hannchen, he hoarsely whispers words which the trucking men, nodding weightily weightily, load up.

"Just a very short story, because we're all so cozy here together. Once upon a time there were two little boys. One of them, out of friendship, gave the other a lovely pocketknife. With this gift the other boy did all sorts of things, and once, with that very same pocketknife, he scored his own arm and the arm of his friend whom friendship had made generous. And so the two little boys became blood brothers. But one day when the boy to whom the pocketknife had been given wanted to throw a stone in the river, but found no stone for throwingintheriver, he threw the pocketknife in the river. And it was gone forever."

The story makes Matern pensive. They're out in the street again: up Augsburger, across Nürnberger. The smoker is on the point of turning right to pay a visit to Rankestrasse and somebody he calls Prince Alexander, when he notices Matern's somber thoughtfulness and decides that he himself, Matern, and the newly found dog need a little exercise: up Fugger-strasse, across Nollendorfplatz, and then to the left down Bülowstrasse.

"See here." That's Matern. "That story about the pocket-knife sounds mighty familiar to me."

"That's perfectly natural, my friend," Goldmouth croaks. "It's a story out of a German schoolbook, so to speak. Every-body knows it. Even the men at the round table nodded in the right places, because they knew the story."

Matern suspects there's something behind all this and bores deep holes that are meant to get to the bottom of the enigma: "And what about the symbolism of it?"

"Nonsense! A common ordinary story. Just think, my good friend: two boys, a pocketknife, and a river. That's a story you can find in every German schoolbook. Edifying and easy to remember."

Even though the story oppresses him less since he has de-cided to call it symbolic, Matern can't help arguing some more: "You very much overestimate the quality of German schoolbooks. Still the same old rubbish as before. Nothing to enlighten the young people about the past and all that. Lies! Nothing but lies!"

Goldmouth smiles all around his cigarette: "My dear good friend, my story, too, though extremely edifying and easy to remember, is a lie. Just look. The end of my fable goes: The boy threw the pocketknife in the river. And it was gone forever— But what have I here? Examine it closely. It's lost its sparkle after all these years. Well, what do you say?"

In the flat of his hand lies, as though conjured out of the air, a rusty pocketknife. The street lamp, under which Matern, the dog, and Goldmouth are standing, bends over the object: used to have three blades, a corkscrew, a saw, and a leather punch.

"And you think it's the same one as in your story?"

Gaily and always glad to do tricks with his ebony cane, Goldmouth replies in the affirmative: "That's the pocket-knife out of my lying schoolbook story. You really oughtn't to make derogatory remarks about German schoolbooks. They're not so bad. If they mostly omit the point, as in the case of the knife that was found again, it's because the truth is too unbearable and might be harmful to a child's innocent mind. But German schoolbooks smell good, the stories are edifying and easy to remember."

Already the Hermitage is opening its arms to the trio, already Goldmouth is about to give the recovered pocketknife back to the air, his spacious prop room, already the hasty imagination sees the trio standing at the bar or sitting in the Green Room, already the Hermitage is snapping its jaws at them with no intention of disgorging them before dawn—for none of the bars around the Church of the Apostles has a stomach better able to hold its guests—when a magnanimous mood carries the smoker away.

As they cross the street and, turning off to the right, succumb to the compulsion of Potsdamer Strasse, Goldmouth's gift-endowment-bequest is formulated: "Listen, my dear friend: the night—almost cloudless and extravagantly supplied with moonlight—has put me in a generous mood: take it. Of course we're neither of us boys any more, and with rusty blades such as these it would be dangerous to score arms, to swear blood brotherhood, but take it just the same. It comes from the heart."

Late in the night—the month of May has populated all the drives and cemeteries, the Tiergarten and Kleist Park—Matern, who has already acquired a rejuvenated dog, receives a present of a heavy and, as he soon discovers, unopenable pocketknife. He thanks Goldmouth kindly but in return, as it were, can't refrain from expressing his sincere concern over Goldmouth's extreme hoarseness: "As a favor to me. I'm not a monster and I won't ask the impossible, but couldn't you skip every third cigarette? I've only known you a few hours, but even so. Maybe you think I should mind my own business. But I'm really worried."

What good can it do for the smoker to keep harping on the true source of his chronic hoarseness, that January frost which suddenly turned to a thaw; Matern continues to put the blame on cigarettes, which Goldmouth persists in terming harmless and a vital necessity: "Not tonight, my dear friend. Your company stimulates me. But tomorrow, yes tomorrow, we shall live abstinently. And so, let us stop in here. I have to admit that a hot lemonade would do me and my throat good. Here, this wooden shed, temporary premises to be sure, will be glad to receive us and the dog. You shall have your beer and your *petits verres;* to me the usual will be served; and our good Pluto will be fed meatballs or weenies, hard-boiled eggs or a cutlet in aspic—ah, the world is so rich!"

What a set! In the background menaces the Sports Palace, a barn whose wheat was threshed years before; the foreground is occupied, with gaps in between, by wooden booths employed for various trades. One promises bargains. The second, amid undying curry aroma, provides shashlik and fried sausages. In the third, ladies can have ladders in their stockings picked up at any hour of the day. The fourth booth awakens hope of tombola winnings. And the seventh shed, hammered together from remnants of other sheds and bearing the name of Chez Jenny, will provide the trio with their next environment.

But before they go in, a question jells within Matern, a question that doesn't want to emerge in the seventh shanty, but to unfold in the balmy spring air: "Tell me this: This knife—it's mine now—where'd you get it? Because I can't really believe it's the same one as the little boy—the one in the story, I mean—is supposed to have thrown in the river."

Already the smoker has hooked the ivory crook of his cane into the door handle—he has opened the doors of all the joints in this way: Anna Helene Barfuss' place, Lauffersberger's White Moor, Paul's Taproom, and the Bülow Hermitage almost—already Jenny, the proprietress of the place that is not called Chez Jenny for nothing, is anticipating the arrival of new customers—she suspects who is coming and is starting to squeeze lemons—when Goldmouth's sandpapered vocal cords bring forth words of explanation: "Try to follow me, my good friend. We have been talking about a pocketknife. In the beginning every pocketknife is new. Then every pocketknife is used for what it is and ought to be, or it is alienated from its proper function and utilized as a paperweight, a counterweight, or—for lack of stone missiles—as a missile. Every pocketknife gets lost someday. It is stolen, forgotten, confiscated, or thrown away. Now, half of all the existing pocketknives in this world are found knives. These in turn may be be subdivided into common and preferred pocketknives. It is undoubtedly to the preferred class that we must assign the one I found in order to return it to you, its original owner. Or would you, here on the corner of Pallasstrasse and Potsdamer, here in the presence of the historical and actual Sports Palace, here, before this shed engulfs us, claim you never owned one, secondly that you never lost one, forgot one, or threw one away, and finally, that you haven't just recovered one?—And believe me, I had my troubles arranging this little reunion. My schoolbook story says: The pocketknife fell into a river and was gone forever. Forever is a lie. For there are fish that eat pocketknives and end, made manifest, on a kitchen table; what's more, there are dredges which bring everything to light, including pocketknives that have been thrown away; in addition there is chance, but that doesn't enter into the present case. —For years, just to give you an idea of the pains I've taken, for years and shunning no expense, I sent in petition after petition, I went so far as to bribe high officials of various flood-control commissions. Finally, and thanks to the complaisance of Polish officialdom, I obtained the desired permit: in the Vistula estuary—for as you and I know, the knife was thrown into the Vistula—a dredge, put to work especially for me by a high-level bureau in Warsaw, brought the object to light approximately where it had taken leave of the light in March or April 1926: between the villages of Nickelswalde Schiewenhorst, but nearer the Nickelswalde dike. No doubt was possible. And to think that I'd been having the Gulf of Bothnia and the southern coast of Sweden dredged for years, that the alluvial deposits off Hela Peninsula had been dug over any number of times at my expense and under my supervision. And so, to wind up our discussion of lost and found objects, there seems to be every reason to conclude that it's absurd to throw pocketknives into rivers. Every river gives back pocketknives without asking anything in return. And not only pocketknives! It was equally silly to sink the so-called Hoard of the Nibelungs in the Rhine. For if someone should come along who is seriously interested in the treasures hoarded by that restless race—as I, for instance, was in the fate of the pocketknife—the Hoard of the Nibelungs would come to light and, unlike the pocketknife whose rightful owner is still in the land of the living, find its way to a provincial museum.—But enough of this chatting in doorways. Don't thank me! Just bear with me and accept a little piece of advice: take better care of your newly found property. Don't throw it in the Spree as you once threw it in the Vistula; although the Spree surrenders pocketknives with less resistance than the Vistula, where you grew up—your accent still shows it."

And once more Matern stands at a bar, with dog at heel,

anchored to a beer glass on the left and a double-decker schnapps on the right. While he ponders: How does he know all this, where did he . . . Goldmouth and the woman in charge of the otherwise empty bar play out a reunion scene, in which titles such as "Jennyofmyheart," "Jennymyconsolation," "dearest Jenny," show that the withered person behind the bar means more to Goldmouth than four plank walls can hold. While the faded spinster in the limp knitted jacket is squeezing the juice from lemon halves, Matern is told that this Jenny is among other things a silver Jenny and a Snow Queen to boot: "But we won't call her Angustri, though it's her real name, because that puts her in a melancholy frame of mind and reminds her of Bidandengero, in case you've heard of him."

Matern, who in his innermost soul is still arguing with the pocketknife, refuses to burden his memory with unpronounceable Gypsy names and to appraise a silver ring that has been worn thin. As far as he is concerned, this fulsomely praised Jenny—a single glance is enough—is some shopworn dancing girl; an acute observation that is confirmed by the décor of the shanty: while Paul's Taproom is graced with the photographs of flatnosed boxers and wrestlers, Jenny has decorated her joint with a *corps de ballet* of dance-worn ballet slippers: from the low ceiling they dangle pale-pink, once-silvery, and Swan Lake-white. Of course there are also pictures of various Giselles. With well-informed finger Goldmouth points to attitudes and arabesques: "That's la Deege at the lower left. Always lyrical, always lyrical. There's Svea Köller, la Skorik, Maria Fris in her first big part, as Dulcinea. And there, next to the ill-starred Leclerq, our Jenny Angustri with her partner Marcel, whose real name in those days, when Jenny was dancing the gardener's daughter, was just plain Fenchel."

A dancers' hangout. After the show you drop in for a moment Chez Jenny, and if you're in luck you'll meet little Bredow or Reinholm, the Vesco sisters, Kläuschen Geitel, or Rama the ballet photographer, who has retouched most of the photographs here displayed, for no neck must show strain and every instep wants to be the highest.

Ah, what ambition and ephemeral beauty these ballet slippers have danced away! And now the place, for all its tap beer, in spite of Mampe's Schnapps and Stobbe's Juniper, persists in smelling of chalk, sweat, and sour jersey. And that careworn goat face behind the bar, which, Goldmouth claims, is capable of making him the best and most soothing hot lemonade in the world. Even now, after the first greedy gulps, so the smoker assures us in his enthusiasm, relief is suffusing his throat, and his voice—as a boy, he informs me, he was able to sing steeple-high—is beginning to remember the most high-climbing of Mozart arias, and soon—only a few more glasses of Jennyhot Jennylemonade—he'll be able to awaken the angel within him and let him sing for joy.

Although Matern has ear enough to detect a few relatively smoothed-out notes in Goldmouth's voice, he can't help giving tongue once again to his concern: "It may be that the lemonade here is particularly good and, for my money, tasty as well. All the more reason why you should stick to soft drinks and give up that immoderate and, I might almost say, cynical smoking."

Back on the old subject: "Don't smoke too much or you'll smoke too much!" Whereupon the smoker with practiced fingernail tears open a fresh pack of Navy Cut, offers them neither to Matern nor to Jenny, helps himself, and dispenses with a match, brightening his fresh weed with the remnant of his veteran smoke-stick: flip! over his shoulder flies the butt, landing on boards, where it is permitted to burn on, to burn out, or to find nourishment—who knows?

For this time no waiter creeps up behind Goldmouth, no heel worn to a slant grinds out the honored guest's afterglowing excrement; for that is what Goldmouth calls the cast-off butts he flips behind him: "They, my dear friend, are my existential bowel movements, so to speak. Which is not to disparage the term or, for that matter, the indispensable function it connotes. Offal offal! Aren't we all? Or won't we be? Don't we live on it? Look, but without horror I beg of you, upon this glass of hot lemonade. I'm going—you won't mind, my dear Jenny?—to let you in on a secret. For what makes this glass, full of the usual, into something special is not selected lemons and choice water: a pinch of mica, got from mica gneiss and mica granite, is mixed—please observe the little silvery fishes!—into the lemonade; then—an old Gypsy recipe—three drops of precious and delicious essence, which my Jenny holds in readiness for me at all times, give this favorite drink of mine a magic, make it flow down my throat like balm. You've guessed. You've got the ugly yet grandiose word on the tip of your tongue and suspect the presence of a similar essence in your yellow beer, you're about to turn

away, disgust in both corners of your mouth, and to cry out
in horror: urine! urine! woman's urine!—but my Jenny and
I are used to being suspected of operating an abominable
witches' cauldron. No matter, you've already—right, Jenny?
—been forgiven; already and once again harmony reigns
between us under a sky of tired ballet slippers; already, and
not for the last time, glasses are being filled; beer and clear
grain spirits will suit my friend; meatballs will cheer the dog;
and as for me, who smoke in order that the world may understand: Behold, he still lives, for he is still smoking!—for me,
whose voice was sandpapered one January afternoon by a
sudden thaw; for me, whose genius for retrieving no pocketknife can resist; for me, who have at my fingertips any number of schoolbook stories, such as the story of the burning
christening goose or the one about the milk-drinking eels,
the story of the twelve headless knights and the twelve headless nuns, not to mention the highly edifying tale about the
scarecrows who were all created in man's image; for me, the
surviving chain smoker, who tosses behind him what a moment before hung burning from his lips: excrement excrement! for me, Goldmouth, who as a child longed to wear two
and thirty gold teeth in my mouth instead of my tiresome
natural teeth; for me, then, the smoker with the gold teeth—
a friend helped me to acquire them by redeeming me from
my natural-grown dentition—for me, the redeemed one, let
hot lemonade, to which biotite and muscovite have contributed a pinch of sparkling mica, let lemonade ennobled by
Jenny's essence fill this glass, that we may drink—to what?
To friendship, to the Vistula that flows for evermore, to all
windmills, whether turning or standing still, to a black
buckled patent-leather shoe that belonged to the little daughter of the village mayor, to the sparrows—sworraps!—over
far-billowing wheatfields, to the grenadiers of Frederick II
of Prussia, who was overly fond of pepper, to the button off
a French grenadier's uniform, which, deep down under the
Church of the Trinity, bore witness to history, to jumping
frogs and quivering salamander tails, to the German game of
schlagball, no, to Germany in general, to Germany's destiny
sauces and Germany's cloud dumplings, to primordial pudding and noodle inwardness, likewise to Adebar the stork,
who brings the babies, to the reaper who invented the hourglass, but also to Adler's Beer Hall and to the zeppelin high
over Heinrich Ehlers Field, to master carpenters and con-

cert pianists, to cough drops and the bone-glue imp, to oak
paneling and Singer sewing machines, to the Municipal Coffee Mill and a hundred slim paperbacks, pregnant with roles,
to Heidegger's Being and Heidegger's Time, similarly to
Weininger's standard work, in other words, to song and the
pure idea, to simplicity, modesty, and dignity, to awe of and
emotion over, to honor and the profound Eros, to mercy
love humor, to faith, to the oak tree and the Siegfried motif,
to the trumpet and SA Sturm Eighty-four; let us then drink
to that January day's snow man, who released me that smoking I might survive: I smoke, therefore I am! Let us drink to
me and to you, Walter! Yet, it's me, so let us drink. You
say something's burning; let us drink all the same. You say
we ought to call the fire department; let us drink without the
fire department! You say my excrement, which you call cigarette butts, has set fire to this haven of exhausted ballet
slippers, which you call a shack; I beg of you, let us finally
drink, because I'm thirsty: hot lemonade, delicious hot lemonade!"

The friends clink their glasses, while the fire on the floor
spreads and begins to lick the plank walls. Beer glass and
lemonade glass meet and tinkle obediently, while in the increasing heat the chorus of martyred ballet slippers under the
ceiling begins a little dance: *échappé croisé, échappé effacé,
assemblé assemblé, petits battements sur le cou-de-pied*. What
an inspiring ballet master fire can be! But the truly applause-
worthy miracle is wrought by the hot lemonade: Jenny's drops
and the pinch of sparkling mica produce a miraculous effect:
with a gentle voice, a trifle too high, rather too soft, so that
whole words are drowned out by the ballet-directing work
sounds of the fire, Goldmouth, who despite the flaming environment refuses to stop smoking, tells exciting schoolbook
tales, with and without points. Not to be outdone, Matern
tells stories of his own, which fill in certain gaps in Goldmouth's stories. And Jenny, too, knows stories. Around this
quartet, busy entertaining each other—for Pluto listens—the
fire tells a story which appeals to the hot-air ballet under the
ceiling: the *corps de ballet* reacts with precise *pas de chat*
and doesn't ever want to stop alternating feet: *pas de bourrée,
pas de bourrée*! And while the photographs full of attitudes
and arabesques turn brown at the lower edges; while at the
bar the Goldmouth story, supported by Materniads, flows
into a lemonade-hot Jenny story; while photographs curl,

then shrivel, while stories find no end and the ballet unleashed above the fire executes daring glissades, outside the
fire department begins to tell its hose-long story.

Presto! Goldmouth has to hurry through his scarecrow
stories; Matern really ought to unwind his dog stories more
quickly; Jenny would do well to hurry her mica-gneiss leg-
ends, in which forest hussars and Gypsies, tinkers and
Tsiganes hunt hedgehogs, toward the final feast, the hedgehog
banquet; for neither Goldmouth nor Jenny nor Matern, who
takes a symbolic view of the dog, can narrate as fast as the
blaze is devouring wood. Already attitudes and arabesques
have left rigid photographed poses to join in the play of the
fire. Already ingenious choreography mingles the *pas as-
semblés* of the slipper-dancers with the sweeping *pas jetés*
of male flames. In a word, the whole shack, except for a
small part of the story-obsessed bar, is going up in smoke.
Quickly then the story about the scarecrows who turned the
tables at the battle of Leuthen. And follow up with Matern's
tale about how he poisoned a black dog with the help of
the Virgin Mary. And Jenny—how the fire becomes the withered Giselle, what fine fresh bloom the heat lends her—in
swift words set with tiny mica mirrors, a newly kindled
beauty tells how a little seasoning transformed common hot
lemonade into Goldmouth's elixir. With every new cigarette,
Goldmouth lashes on the company, now huddled on top of
the bar with dozing dog. "More stories. More stories. Keep
going! As long as we're telling stories, we're alive. As long as
stories keep coming, with or without a point, dog stories, eel
stories, scarecrow stories, rat stories, flood stories, recipe
stories, stories full of lies and schoolbook stories, as long as
stories have power to entertain us, no hell can take us in.
Your turn, Walter. Tell stories as long as you love your life."

Gone the ballet, replaced by crackling applause. Nine-
tailed flames wag their tails and mate. Shanty wood goes to
meet its destiny. The fire department does its duty. The heat
would be oppressive if not for Matern's frost-crunching January stories: "Only in the East are winters that cold. And
when it snowed up there, it snowed in earnest, for days and
days. The snow covered everything over, everything. That's
why the snow men in the East were always bigger than the
snow men in the West, even way back. And when it began to
thaw, we had our hands full, believe me. It was in January,
when the sea was frozen over from Hela to Weichsel-

münde, that my ancestors, who still called themselves Materna, liked best to ..."

Oh, Matern knows how to evoke the remote past when the lighting is right. The fire serves up its second course, spits out bone gnawed soft and red-hot nails, gobbles loudly, laps up rivers of beer, makes rows of bottles burst: Stobbe's Juniper, jugs of Steinhäger, Double Juniper, rot-gut schnapps and fine spirits, framboise and mild Bisquit, blended brandy and genuine arrack, Mampe's Half and Half, White Horse, sherry, blackberry brandy, chartreuse and gin, slender kümmel, curaçao so sweet, Hussar's Coffee . . . spirits! what a lovely, transcendence-caressing word. Spirit kindles spirit while Matern, thinking back to the past, sets up a row of Materniads: "There were two of them, brothers. And the story begins with Gregor Materna in the year 1408. In that year he went from Danzig to London, where he was given short weight of salt, a mortal insult. Paid back in blood, by God! And he went back home and demanded justice, but didn't get it. And he raised hell outside the Artushof, where no one was allowed to bear arms, but he did, and used them. Whereupon they outlawed him, yes, outlawed him! But he didn't let the grass grow under his feet, he gathered henchmen: what was left of the dispersed band, once led by Hans Briger, the journeyman butcher, which had set fires such as this one and committed murders: Bobrowski joined him and Hildebrand Berwald, to mention only a few. To make a long story short: One thing happened near Subkau, something else was swung in Elbing; in January frost he raided the length and breadth of the Knights' country, cut the throat of the councillor Martin Rabenwald and filled him chock-full of lead. Then, because the cold refused to subside, he specialized in arson: Langgarten, along with the Church of St. Barbara and the howling Hospital of St. Barbara, went up in flames. He razed the beautiful, gaily painted Breitgasse. Finally Zantor, the voivod in Posen, caught him and hanged him. On September 14th, that's it, 1502. But if you think that was the end of it you're mistaken and doomed to burn. For now comes his brother, Simon Materna, avenges Gregor Materna, and regardless of the seasons sets fire to timber-frame houses and proud-gabled granaries. He maintains a storehouse for pitch, tar, and sulphur on Putzig Bay, and employs over three hundred maids, who all have to be maidens, winding tinder matches. He supplies the monasteries of Oliva and Karthaus with funds, and zealous monks make him pitch torches. Thus equipped, he sets Petersiliengasse and Drehergasse flaming to high heaven. In this fire, laid especially for the purpose, he roasts twelve thousand pork sausages, a hundred and three sheep, and seventeen oxen to a fine crisp—not to mention the poultry, Island geese and Kashubian ducks—and feeds, yes by God, feeds the city's poor, the beggars from the suburbs, the cripples from Holy Ghost Hospital, and all those who come hobbling from Mattenbuden and the New City. And the houses of the patricians sizzle and sputter in rooster-red fire. Pepper sacks season the blaze, while food is roasted for the sick and hungry. Oh, Simon Materna—if they hadn't caught him and hanged him, he'd have set the world on fire to provide all the downtrodden with juicy roasts from the spit. And from him, the first class-conscious pyrotechnist, I am descended, yes, by God. And socialism will triumph, yes, by God."

This uproar, soon followed by endless gales of laughter—Goldmouth has launched a merry schoolbook story or two—lends the shanty fire, seen from outside, a touch of fiendish terror; for not only are the usual onlookers, an easy prey for anything that smacks of ghosts, gripped with dread; but even the fire fighters of West Berlin, though good Protestants by birth and upbringing, have no thought but to cross themselves. The next wave of diabolical laughter sweeps away all four fire brigades. The helmeted men barely take time to roll up valuable hoses. Leaving the shanty fire to its own resources—strange to say, it shows no inclination to spread and consume the whole row of sheds—the fire fighters drive off with the well-known din. And not even a fire warden comes forward to hold vigil by the fire, for all ears are plugged with horror: in the heart of the furnace, diabolical guests are carousing; by turn they roar Communist slogans and burst into bestial laughter, after which the stage is taken over by a tenor, who sings higher than darting flames and fiery glow can sing: Latin, as sung in Catholic churches, desecrates Potsdamer Strasse from the Control Commission Building past Bülowstrasse.

The Sports Palace has never heard anything like it: a *Kyrie* that strikes sparks, a *Gloria in excelsis Deo* that teaches long-fingered flames to fold their hands. The arias are Goldmouth's offering. With mica-spiked, lemon-slim voice and childlike, forthright faith, he—the fire has finished the third course and is still nibbling hungrily at the dessert—believes: *in unum Deum*. The tenderly clinging *Sanctus* is followed by a *Hosanna* to which Goldmouth manages to lend an echo-like polyphony. But when, in the velvety andante, the *Benedictus* breaks all altitude records, Matern, whose eyes have withstood all the smoke, can no longer hold back the tears: "Spare us the *Agnus Dei!*" But it's the jubilant round that pours Matern's emotion, which is threatening to spread to Jenny and Pluto, into a silk handkerchief: Goldmouth goes on singing *Dona nobis* until the grateful listeners have regained their composure and the flames, tongues, and sparks have all gone to sleep. The volutes of a pianissimo *amen* are spread like a blanket over the charred beams, molten glass, and the hot-air ballet that has sunk dead-tired to ashes.

Themselves tired, they crawl over the unharmed bar and leave the slumbering scene of the fire. Cautiously, step by little step, the dog in the lead, they reach the deserted Potsdamer Strasse, guarded only by street lamps. Jenny says how tired she is, and wants to go right off to bed. The drinks still have to be paid for. Goldmouth appoints himself host. Jenny wants to go home alone: "Nobody is interested in me." But the gentlemen insist on lending their protection. In Mansteinstrasse, across from Leydicke's, they say good night. At the house door Jenny, poor creature who is always being left behind, says: "You'd better go beddy-by too. You old night owls. Tomorrow's another day."

But for the two others, who are more likely to leave than to be left behind, the night is still young. And nature's immortal creation also stands fresh and attentive on four legs: "Heel, Pluto."

For there is still a leftover that wants to be tasted. On the one hand a leftover of cigarettes, lighted one from another, wish to go their way up Yorckstrasse past the Memorial Library, on the other hand an insubstantial leftover demands to be spoken of; it lodges between teeth and sets them on edge, all thirty-two of them.

But Goldmouth dotes on music such as this: "How happy it makes me, dear Walter, to hear you grind your teeth as in the blessed days of Amsel."

Matern, however, doesn't like to hear himself. In his innermost being—for the Grinder has an innermost being—he is staging wrestling bouts. Across Zossen Bridge, along Urban Harbor, the wrestlers grunt and groan. Lord knows who's trying to throw whom. Probably the whole Materna tribe is in there fighting: all conquering heroes on the lookout for worthy opponents. Is Goldmouth, for instance, fit for the ring? There he goes again with cynical talk, cynically smoking cigarettes that call everything into question. What in the fiery furnace was a jubilant credo without ambiguity, degenerates, not far from Admiral Bridge, into hoarse and cacophonous ifs and buts. Nothing in him is pure. Always standing values on their heads, so the pants slip down to the knees. His favorite theme: "The Prussians in general and the Germans in particular." Words of insidious praise for this people, among which he was doomed to suffer before and after the snow man. That won't do, Goldmouth! Even if it's May and the buds are popping: how can a man be in love with his murderers!

But even his love of Germany, when you listen carefully, is a twining of cynical laurel, taken from wax funeral wreaths. For instance, Goldmouth strews professions of faith across the Landwehr Canal: "I have found out, and you can take it from me, that the best and most long-lasting stamp pads are manufactured and utilized in the area bounded— as the song puts it—by the Adige and the Belt, the Meuse and the Memel."

With voice gone hoarse, again, the smoker tosses sententious utterances into the claw-studded air along Maybach-Quay. His coffin nail participates in his remarks, shuttling from corner to corner of his mouth: "No, my dear Walter, you may still feel bitterness toward your great fatherland— but I love the Germans. Ah, how mysterious they are, how full of the forgetfulness which is pleasing to God! Not giving it a thought, they cook their pea soup on blue gas flames. And another thing: what other country in the world can boast such brown, velvety gravies?"

The scarcely flowing canal runs straight as a die. But then comes a fork: the left prong heads for the eastern port; up ahead lies the border of the Soviet sector; the right prong develops into the Neukölln Ship Canal. As the two of them with faithful dog stand on this memorable spot— across from them lies Treptow: everybody has heard of the war memorial—Goldmouth indulges in words which, though worthy of the fork in the canal, carry noxious flotsam in their flow: "Of course you may say that every man is a potential scarecrow; for after all, this should never be forgotten, the scarecrow was created in man's image. All nations are arsenals of scarecrows. But among them all it is the Germans, first and foremost, even more so than the Jews, who have it in them to give the world the archetypal scarecrow someday."

Not a word out of Matern. And the little birdies, who were already awake, pretend to be sleeping again. The usual grinding of teeth starts up. The aimless groping of a shoe on flat pavement: no stone. What will I? Nowhere a *zellack*. My change of socks and shirts? I left my razor in the smoke-filled shanty. It looks like I'll have to. Or I'll clear out, beat it to the Soviet sector. That's where I was going in the first place, and I'm still hanging around here. So I'll just . . .

He thrusts his closed hand behind him, a wind-up; what a fine powerful thrower's stance! Goldmouth delights in the harmony of the movement. Pluto tenses. And Matern throws —well, what do you think?—the newly recovered pocketknife far away. What the Vistula, not without resistance, gave up, he gives to the Berlin Landwehr Canal, at the point where it forks. But no sooner has the pocketknife vanished with the usual splash, and seemingly for good, than Goldmouth is on the spot with well-meaning advice: "Don't worry, my dear Walter. For me it's the merest trifle. That section of the canal will be drained. There isn't much current at this point. You'll have your good old pocketknife back in two weeks at the most.—It made us into blood brothers, you know."

O impotence brooding eggs from which rage will hatch: naked and without fuzz. Matern releases a word. O human rage, always looking for words and finding one in the end. Matern flings a single word, which aims and strikes home. Human rage, which never has enough and heaps up repetitions intended as intensives. Several times in succession the word. The dog stands still. The canal forks. Goldmouth neglects to take a light from an almost burned-down cigarette. Leitmotive slips into murder motive. Matern takes aim and says: "SHEENY!"

At last the sparrows wake up. O lovely balmy May dawn under a bipartite sky. O night gone and day not yet come. O long in-between moment when the word "sheeny" is spoken, and doesn't feel like falling to the ground, but wants to hang in midair awhile!

It's Matern who sinks to the ground. He's overreached himself. It's really been too much for him: "First the inter-

zonal trip with all the fuss and bother. Then the round from
bar to bar. The change of air. The joy of finding his friend
again. Most anybody would be floored. Every explanation
applies only to the circumstances. Every word is too much.
Do what you please with me."

And so Goldmouth's ebony cane summons a taxi: "Tempelhof Airport. Departure gate. This gentleman, the dog, and
I are in a hurry. We've got to catch the first plane for
Hanover. We have to visit a plant that's situated below
ground. The firm of Brauxel & Co. You've heard of it?"

THE HUNDRED AND THIRD
AND BOTTOMMOST MATERNIAD

Anyone wishing to travel below ground will do well to take
a start in the air: ergo, British-European Airways to Han-
over-Langenfeld. The remaining miles on the flat surface
are diminished by a company car: past cows and building
sites, guided by detours and feeders, through a spring-green
yet pallid countryside. A striking sight from the distance,
the destination is stuck to the horizon: the conical waste
pile, the brick-red buildings: lab, changehouse, boiler house,
administration building, storehouse—and over all the roofs,
towering above the waste pile and the dumping gear that
goes with it: the stilt-legged headframe.

Who would want to build cathedrals in a day when the
sky is held up by stagesets like this! This is Brauxel & Co., a
firm which, though registered with the Hanover Potash Association and responsible to the Hanover Bureau of Mines,
extracts not so much as a single ton of potash and yet lowers
men in three shifts: powdermen, licensed muckers and drillers, all told one hundred and eighty-two miners.

And as long as pulleys in the headframe continue to
drive cables over the whim, the man who alights first from
the company car will no longer be called Goldmouth, but
Herr Director or Herr Brauxel: so says the driver, so says
the porter.

And the figure who gets out of the company car behind
Brauxel is not yet Matern, but a black, full-grown shepherd,

whom both Brauxel and the finally alighting Matern call Pluto.

But when they pass through the wrought-iron gate, which was installed in potash-mining days, the porter takes his cap off to greet Herr Director Brauxel. Thereupon Matern, whom neither a night rich in wonders and not poor in startling conversations, nor a wonderfully serene flight along the Berlin-Hanover air corridor has deprived of his native capacity for amazement, cannot help asking a question: "How is it that the porter employed here looks so embarrassingly like my father, miller Anton Matern?"

To this Director Brauxel, who leads his guest straight to the changehouse, meanwhile whistling Pluto to heel as though the dog belonged to him, has the ultimate answer: "Porter Anton Matern does not look like miller Matern, he is the miller, he is your father."

Whereupon Matern, who likewise, but without results, whistles the dog to heel, draws the obscure but high-sounding conclusion: "In the end every father becomes a porter to every son."

The changehouse attendant submits to Matern a paper that has to be signed. Regulations prescribe that strangers to the mine, desirous of being lowered below ground with a view to visiting same, must confirm their intention with a signature. Matern signs and is led to a bathroom where, standing beside a dry tub, he is expected to remove his traveling clothes and put on light denims, woolen socks, high clodhoppers, a woolen scarf, and a new, yellow-varnished, and ill-fitting hard hat. He changes garment for garment and through the partition asks Director Brauxel in the adjoining bathroom: "What's become of Pluto?"

And Brauxel, who though director also has to exchange traveling clothes for a mine outfit, garment for garment, answers through the same partition: "Pluto's with me. Where else would he be?"

And thus attired, Brauxel and Matern, followed by Pluto, leave the changehouse. Each carries a carbide lamp in his left hand. The lamps as well as the denims and the twice-yellow hard hat efface the differences between director and visitor. But as they are passing the administration building, a hunchbacked little man, whom cuff protectors identify as the chief clerk, steps out of the door and obliges the gentlemen to pause. At the supposed chief clerk's request, Brauxel has to sign some papers that have accumulated during his absence. The chief clerk is glad to meet Herr Matern Junior. Then wishing them good luck, he lets them proceed to the headframe.

Followed by the dog, the two of them, Matern and Brauxel, cross a yard, where quantities of nailed-up crates are being hauled back and forth by forklift trucks; but there is no potash either in the crates or in warehouse bins.

And when they reach the foot of the headframe and Brauxel is about to step on the iron staircase leading to the shaft collar, Matern asks a question: "Is the dog going down too?" Brauxel isn't joking when he says: "Every dog comes from below and has to be lowered again in the end."

Matern has misgivings: "The dog has never been below ground."

Whereupon Brauxel with authority: "The dog is company property and will have to get used to it."

This loss—a few hours ago he was still a dog owner—is too much for Matern: "He's my dog. Heel, Pluto!" But Brauxel whistles up ahead and the black shepherd takes the stairs to the shaft collar, which straddles the headframe at mid height. It's drafty on the platform. From obliquely below them, the drive wheel moves the pulleys above their heads: upper and lower cable tense in anticipation of the mine run.

But when strokes of a bell—four strokes meaning "go slow"—announce the arrival of the cage from the bottom, Matern wants to make a suggestion before it is too late: "Why not leave Pluto on the platform? God knows what the rapid descent will do to him, and I hear it's hellishly hot down below."

Only when they are weighing down the cage—Pluto wedged in between Brauxel and Matern—is the director prepared to answer. The cage gate is closed. The trammer signals "ready" with three strokes, "go" with five strokes, and Brauxel says: "Every hell has its climate. The dog will have to get used to it."

And now the last daylight has been left upstairs. The descent from the platform (a hundred feet above the earth's surface) to the fill level on the pit bottom (twenty-eight hundred feet under the earth's surface) marks the beginning of the official tour of inspection, intended to give the stranger Walter Matern on-the-spot instruction.

He is advised to open his mouth and to breathe evenly. The pressure on his ears is explained by the speed of the lowering, the slight burnt smell by the friction between the falling cage and the guide rails of the shaft. The fingers of the updraft become more and more southerly; it finds its way through denim and up trouser legs. Matern claims to have noticed that Pluto is trembling; but Brauxel says everybody shivers who has to drop so far in barely one minute.

And before they reach the bottom, he enlightens Matern, for educational purposes, about the activities of potash-mining days and days within the memory of Brauxel & Co. The words "gangue rock" and "mine rock" drop fifty feet a second with them. At the same lowering speed there is talk of shutdowns and cable inspections: the cage cable consists of seven times thirty-two wire strands wound around a hemp-clad steel core. Loosening of the outer strands, overloaded steel cores, screw dislocations resulting in kinks, and cable jumping—these are the main causes of cable breaks, which, it should be added, are infrequent. Nor should rust erosion be forgotten, which digs its grooves even while the cable is running. For this reason grease, but it has to be nonacidic, must be applied to the cable, which has to be dry, and never must grease be applied to the whole length of the cable, but only in three-hundred-foot stretches, for fear that fresh grease will get on the drive wheel, for this cable that's lowering us is the soul of the whole plant, its alpha and omega, it raises us to the light of day and carries us down below, so God help us if it.

And so Matern has no leisure to pay attention to the stomach flutter which is sometimes felt even in ordinary elevators. Pressure on the temples and watering of the eyes go unnoticed, because Brauxel is giving him a mental diagram of the shaft from the pulley covers to the return guides for cable and the so-called shaft sump.

With four warning strokes and the single stroke that calls the engine to halt, the trammer puts an end to the lesson which Brauxel has been able to funnel into the visitor in barely a minute; so vastly does a drop by cable enhance man's gift of assimilating and remembering.

The fill level has light, electric light, in readiness. And as they set foot on the pit bottom with Pluto in the lead, they return the *"Glück auf"* of Wernicke, the head foreman, who, in response to instructions from the surface, has come from the waste stall, where he had been checking the trap doors, to give Matern, the stranger, an account of the mine.

But Brauxel, who is as familiar with all scooped-out stalls, drifts, adits, and blind shafts as with the labyrinthine Old City where he went to school, admonishes the foreman: "Don't wander. Begin, as customary in our country, with a description of the situation after 1945; then come to the main point, how we stopped mining potash and began to turn out finished products bearing the trade mark of Brauxel & Co."

Thus admonished and accompanied by the three-tracked activity of the fill level, the foreman launches into his account of the mine: "Well then, in 1945, as our director has said, we in West Germany were left with only 39 per cent of Germany's over-all prewar potash production. The rest and, there's no denying it, the largest and most modern potash works were at the disposal of Soviet-occupied Central Germany. But even if things looked dark for us at first, West Germany had overtaken the East zone by the middle of '53, though by then our plant had given up potash and gone into the manufacture of finished products. But to get back to potash: Our operation was based on a large deposit extending from the Salzdetfurth Works in the eastern part of the Hildesheim Forest through Gross-Giessen, where our mine was located, to Hasede, Himmelsthür, Emmerke, and Sarstedt. As a rule these salt veins are situated almost ten thousand feet below the surface, but here they are compressed into domes covered only by a layer of sandstone. Our mining rights covered roughly fourteen miles along the dome, some four miles of which had actually been tapped at the time when Brauxel & Co. gave up potash mining. Our company owns two shafts, two miles apart, going down to the twenty-eight-hundred-foot level. These two shafts, the one a mining, transportation, and fresh-air shaft, the other a vent shaft— are connected horizontally by four main galleries. On these galleries drifts lead to the stalls. Formerly the twenty-four-hundred-foot level was the pit bottom. There the rich Ronneberg deposit, containing for the most part 24 per cent of sylvinite and barely 14 per cent of carnallitite, was worked to a width of as much as sixty-five feet. In February 1952, when the drilling and blasting began on the Stassfurt reserve deposit, Wintershall AG took over the Burbach Potash

Works, and our mine, allegedly because the Stassfurt deposit wasn't rich enough to be profitable, was first leased and then sold to Brauxel & Co. But most of the men stayed on because, in addition to our base pay and the tax-free miner's bonus of two marks fifty per shift, we were promised an extra indemnity for work unrelated to mining. But it wasn't until June 1953, after we had struck the plant for two weeks, that our bonus was paid regularly. It might also be worth mentioning that our own power plant, equipped with steam generators and substation, provides us with power and heat. Of the sixty-eight stalls, only a fraction of which had been worked out in mining days, thirty-six have had to be filled in with waste for reasons of safety. After a long-drawn-out inspection by the Bureau of Mines, Brauxel & Co. obtained permission to use the remaining thirty-two. Though at first it was hard for us experienced miners to give up our usual business of working muck holes, of operating scoops and shaking-conveyors, though the new working conditions struck us at first as unbefitting a miner, we finally got used to them. Thanks to Herr Brauxel's firmness, we were allowed to keep our membership in the miners' union."

Here Brauxel, the director, puts in: "That will do, Wernicke. And I hope no one will dare to set potash, coal, and iron ore above our finished products. What we raise from below can bear inspection from all sides."

But when Walter Matern, the stranger below, asks why it stinks so here at the fill level, where the smell comes from and what it's composed of, the director and foreman have to admit that the place still smells predominantly of potash-mining days: "The smell of brine oozing from the still damp waste blends with the earthy smell of sandstone and with lingering powder smoke, which is full of saltpeter because they used blasting gelatin to open up the roof. In addition, sulphur compounds deriving from algae and diatoms, mixed with the ozone generated by the sparks of electric cars and tramways, impregnate the air throughout the galleries and stalls. Further ingredients of the smell are: the salt dust that fills the air and settles everywhere, billows of acetylene from the lamps, traces of carbon dioxide, and stale grease. When the ventilation isn't too good, you can even guess what brand of beer was consumed here and is still being consumed in the era of Brauxel's finished products, namely,

Herrenhäuser Pilsner, the bottled beer with the horse of Lower Saxony on the label."

And Matern, the stranger below, enlightened about the smell prevailing in all the well-ventilated galleries and in the poorly ventilated stalls, is of the opinion that in addition to the acrid smell there is also an oppressively warm draft blowing from the pit bottom to the fill level, although any amount of fresh spring air is available on the surface.

When they begin—and Pluto is not left behind—to move at first horizontally through the gallery on an electric trolley, and then vertically by cage to the waste stall—two thousand feet below the surface—they enter into a sultry August fug, the content of which is brine on top, sulphur compounds in the middle, and at the very bottom ancient blast smoke compounded with recent trolley ozone. The sweat dries faster than it breaks out.

"This is hell itself," says Matern.

But foreman Wernicke corrects him: "This is the place where our materials are made ready for the manufacturing process. This stall, which we call the first in accordance with the program of our visit, is where our new materials, requisitioned from above, are degraded, as we call it."

Dog in the lead, they enter the first stall through the narrow gangway. A room the size of a church nave opens up. Marked by neatly halved drill holes, layers of salt—overhanging cuts, face cuts, and underlying cuts—extend toward the far wall of the stall, which towers in such sacral remoteness as to suggest a chancel. But the room contains only two rows of enormous vats, sixteen on each side, extending at knee height from the narrow gangway to the far wall of the stall. In the narrow passage between the rows, Hinrich Schrötter, formerly a powderman, services the vats with a long spoon-billed pole.

And the man in charge of the brine baths in stall No. 1 informs the stranger Matern: "We chiefly process cotton, synthetic wool, popeline, twill, calico, quick-shrinking flannel, jersey, taffeta, and tulle, but also raw silk and rayon. Not so long ago we handled a sizable lot of corduroy and twelve bolts of shot silk; occasionally there is a demand for small to medium lots of cashmere, cambric, and chiffon. Today, since the beginning of the night shift eight bolts of Irish linen, forty-eight inches in width before treatment, are in the first stage of degradation. We also have furs on hand, mostly pony, Persian lamb, and South African goat, and in the last three vats, on the upper left, a few brocades, an assortment of Brussels lace, and small quantities of piqué, crepe de Chine, and suede are in process of degradation. The remaining vats are degrading lining materials, denim, onion sacks, English sailcloth, and rope of every thickness. We work for the most part with cold caustic solutions, consisting of the usual waste brine with an admixture of magnesium choride. Only when intensive degradation of new materials is required do we make use of a hot sylvinite solution to which magnesium bromide is added. Actually all our degradation baths, especially those containing bromide, call for above-average ventilation. But unfortunately, and Herr Wernicke, our foreman, will back me up, the ventilation on the two-thousand-foot level wasn't up to regulation even in the past, when they were still blasting open the stalls."

But Director Brauxel takes the reference to inadequate ventilation lightly. "Everything will be all right, boys, when the centrifugal ventilators come. They'll speed up the intake."

And they leave the first stall, over whose caustic solutions white vapors swirl, and find their way, foreman with raised lamp in the lead, to the second stall, where caustic-treated materials and new materials are subjected to dry degradation: a scoop driven by a sprocket wheel is moving a mountain of materials over loose muck, a leftover from potash-mining days.

But when with dog as chipper as ever they enter the third stall, no sprocket wheel is roaring, no magnesium chloride develops vapors; here, in lateral lockers, men's suits and overcoats and an assortment of uniforms are being devoured by moths. The articles here being degraded require attention only once a week. But Wernicke, the foreman, has the power of the keys and opens one of the lockers; moth silver sweeps up in a cloud. Quickly the door is closed.

In the fourth stall the visitors are introduced to an assortment of machines operated by former muckers and drillers, which on the one hand give caustic-scoop-moth-degraded materials an additional tearing, subject them to searing heat, and mark them with oil, ink, and wine spots, and on the other hand cut the now fully degraded materials to pattern, line them, and stitch them up. The director with dog, the overseer, and Matern the stranger are then received by the fifth stall, which rather resembles an engine room.

Scrap from the all-devouring surface, accumulated by auto graveyards, engendered by wars and wrecking operations, scrap sorted out after boiler explosions, an anthology of scrap lies here in mounds, travels on conveyor belts, is disentangled with blow torches, takes rust-removing baths, hides a little while, and then returns galvanized to the conveyor belt: parts are assembled, ball joints play, gears come through the sand test unclogged, index wheels with chain hooks form a conveyor system that runs empty. Piston rods, clutches, bushings, governors, and suchlike gadgets obey electric motors. On man-high frames hang mechanical monsters. In busy skeletons elevators dawdle adagio from floor to floor. In stiffly vaulted thoraxes hammer mills have undertaken the never-ending task of crushing loud steel balls. Noise, noise!

And still more educational training in the sixth stall. Their ears are subjected to an experience which first makes Pluto restless, then sets him to howling under the steep late-Gothic roof.

And Matern, the stranger, says: "This is hell, indeed! We ought to have left the dog up top. The poor fellow is suffering."

But Brauxel, the director, is of the opinion that the dog's howling, flung vertically at the roof, blends admirably with the pretested electronic systems of the skeletons in process of manufacture: "Yet what has unthinkingly been termed a hell gives bread and wages shift in shift out to thirty miners, trained by internationally known metal sculptors and sound experts. Our head foreman, the worthy Herr Wernicke, will bear me out when I say that muckers and drillers, who have been working in the mine for twenty years, are inclined to find hell anywhere on the surface, but no proof of hell below ground, not even when the ventilation is poor."

The mine-wise foreman nods several times and leads his director, the director's perseveringly howling dog, and the stranger out of the sixth stall, where the noise is unable to catch up with itself, through the muffling gangway, and out to the gallery, where the noise continues to recede.

They follow his buzzing carbide lamp to the mining shaft which at the beginning of the visit carried them from the pit bottom to the waste stall and the vent shaft.

Again descent is re-enacted, but only briefly, down to the level which the foreman traditionally calls the pit bottom but the director refers to as the "path of first-class disciplines."

In the seventh, eighth, and ninth stalls, the stranger below is exposed, in the interest of training, to the three cardinal emotions and their echo effects.

And once again Matern ventures to cry out: "This is hell, indeed!" although the weeping, every human variety of which is here represented, is tearless. Dry emotion turns the stall into a house of woe. Swathed in degraded mourning garments, frames, which only a little while before were scrap iron and then, resurrected as skeletons, were invested with noisy or soundless mechanisms and submitted to various mechanical and acoustical tests, now stand in weeping circles on the bare-scraped floor. Each circle has set itself a different tear-promoting yet desert-dry task. Here it begins. The next circle can't turn off the whimpering. This circle sobs deep within. Wailing, crescendo and decrescendo, dents and distends every circle. Muffled weeping, as into pillows. Blubbering as though the milk had been burned. Sniveling, handkerchief between teeth. Misery is contagious. Knotted into convulsions and threatened with hiccups. Plaintive to tearful: Bawling Suzy and Blubbering Lizzie. And above the shoulder-shaking, the breast-beating, the silent inward weeping, a voice on the verge of tears recites sob stories, snot-and-water stories, stories to soften a stone: "And then the cruel bailiff said to the frozen little flower girl. But when the poor child held out her hands in supplication to the rich peasant. And when the famine was at its height, the king commanded that every third child in the land. The blind old woman was so lonely she thought she would have to. And when the brave young warrior lay thus miserably in his blood. Then grief spread like a shroud over the land. The ravens croaked. The wind moaned. The horses went lame. The deathwatch ticked in the beams. Woe! Woe! That will be your fate. There shall not be left one stone upon another, nor shall any eye remain dry. Woe!"

But those who in the seventh stall are subjected to the discipline of weeping, have no glands to open the floodgates. Here not even onion juice would help. These automats weep, but the coins refuse to jingle. And how indeed could this lacrimal discipline, encompassed as it is by salt above, below, and on all sides, be expected to release fountains with a crystalline residue, capable of seducing a goat?

And after so much futility, the director with dog and the foreman followed by the stranger leave the seventh chamber of the first emotion, to follow the busy gallery in silence until the foreman's lamp leads them through a gangway into the eighth stall, which seems almost too small to contain so much glee.

And once again Matern cannot hold back his cry: "What hellish laughter!" But actually—as Director Brauxel immediately points out—in the eighth stall only the gamut of the second emotion, human laughter, is assembled. We know the scale from tittering to splitting a gut. "It should be pointed out," says Wernicke, the foreman, "that the eighth stall is the only one in our entire plant which, because of the continuous explosions, has to be secured against cave-in with three rows of the finest mine props."

This is understandable. Frames, which sackcloth-clad were practicing grief and lamentation only a short time ago, are now guffawing bleating laughing in bright-colored, though also degraded, Scotch plaids and cowboy shirts. They double up, they lie down, they roll on the ground. Their built-in mechanisms permit belly-holding, thigh-slapping, and stamping. And while limbs make themselves independent, it bursts from a fist-size opening: the roar of people laughing themselves sick and sound, old men's laughter, tapped from beer barrels and wine cellars, staircase and lobby laughter, insolent, groundless, Satanic, sardonic laughter, nay more, insane and desperate laughter. It resounds in the cathedral with its forest of columns, mingles mates multiplies, a chorus struggling for breath: here laugh the company, the regiment, the army, the loons, homerically the gods, the people of the Rhineland, all Germany laughs at, with, in spite of, without end: German scarecrow laughter.

It is Walter Matern, the stranger below, who first speaks the characterizing word. And since neither the director nor the foreman corrected him when he spoke of hellish laughter, he calls the jokes that run back and forth between the laughing automats, which may as well be termed scarecrows, scarecrow jokes: "You heard this one? Two blackbirds and a starling meet in the Cologne Central Station . . . Or this one? A lark takes the interzonal train to Berlin for Corpus Christi, and when it gets to Marienborn . . . Or this one, it's really good: Three thousand two hundred and thirty-two sparrows decide to go to a whorehouse together, and when they come out, one of them has the clap. Which one? Wrong! Once again now, listen carefully: Three thousand two hundred and thirty-two sparrows . . ."

Matern, the stranger below, pronounces this brand of humor too cynical for his taste. To his mind, humor should have a liberating, healing, often even a saving effect. He misses human warmth, or call it kindness, charity. Such qualities are promised him for the ninth stall. Whereupon all, including the never laughing Pluto, turn away from the scarecrow laughter and follow the gallery until a gangway branching off to the left announces the stall inhabited by the third cardinal emotion.

And Matern sighs, because the foretaste of dishes not yet served embitters his palate. At this Brauxel has to raise his curious lamp and ask what there is to sigh about. "I'm sorry for the dog, who hasn't a chance to romp about up above where the spring is green, who has to follow at heel down below and live through this meticulously organized inferno."

Brauxel, however, who is carrying not the usual plain walking stick but an ebony cane with an ivory crutch, which only a few hours before belonged to an immoderate smoker calling himself Goldmouth, never smokes below ground but says: "If this, our plant, absolutely has to be called an inferno by a stranger to the mine, it only goes to show that the company needs a hellhound of its own; just see how our light teaches the animal to cast a hellish shadow that devours the gallery: already the gangway is sucking him in. We must follow."

Here narrow-eyed hate, never oxidizing rage, cold and hot revenge keep school. In wind-inflated and consequently voluminous battle dress, which repeated caustic degradation has injected with the traces of seven boiler battles. Scarecrows which sackcloth-clad operated a tear pump that persistently said no, scarecrows which in bright checks and loud polka dots let their built-in humor-developer unwind, are standing in the empty stall, each scarecrow by himself. So this is the homework imposed on rage, hate, revenge: full-grown crowbars must be bent into question marks and suchlike gewgaws. Patched countless times, rage must burst and blow itself up again with its own lungs. Hate has to burn holes in its own knee with its narrow-set eyes. But cold and hot revenge must go round— Don't turn around, revenge is around—

and grind whole spoonfuls of quartz pebbles between their teeth.

So that's what the meal sounds like that Matern, the stranger, had a foretaste of. School fare. Scarecrow fare. For not satisfied with bursting and with burning holes, not finding expression enough in the bending of crowbars, rage, the great valve burster, and hate, the blowtorch, spoon themselves full from feed troughs into which two employees of Brauxel & Co. hourly shovel a supply of the pebbles—food for grinding teeth—which are plentiful on the green surface of the earth.

Thereupon, Matern, who from earliest childhood has ground his teeth whenever rage rode him, hate compelled him to stare at a fixed point, and revenge commanded him to make rounds, turns away from these scarecrows who have raised his particularity to the level of a universal discipline.

And to the foreman, who with upraised lamp is leading them from the ninth stall to the gallery, he says: "I should think that these immoderately expressive scarecrows would sell well. Man loves to see his mirror image in a blind rage."

But Wernicke, the foreman, counters: "It is true that formerly, in the early fifties, our odonto-acoustical models were in great demand both on the domestic and on the foreign market, but now that the decade has come of age, collections based on the third cardinal emotion find takers only in the young African states."

Whereupon Brauxel smiles subtly and pats Pluto on the neck: "Don't worry about the marketing problems of Brauxel & Co. Hate, rage, and roving revenge will be back in style one of these days. A cardinal emotion that promotes the grinding of teeth can't be a passing fad. To abolish revenge is to take revenge on revenge."

These words mount the electric trolley with them and demand to be mulled over during the long ride through two trap doors, past barred blind shafts and waste-filled stalls. Only at their destination, where the foreman promises a visit to the tenth to twenty-second stalls, is Brauxel's proposition about unabolishable revenge forgotten, though without loss to it succinctness.

For even in the tenth, eleventh, and twelfth stalls, where athletic, religious, and military exercises, in other words, relay races, skipping processions, and changes of the guard, are being performed, rage, hate, the revenge which, because it is always roving, cannot be rooted out, the futile tear pump, and the built-in humor-developer, in short, the cardinal emotions weeping, laughter, and the grinding of teeth provide the deep-seated foundation on which athletic scarecrows are able to break records at pole vaulting, penitent scarecrows at split-pea racing, and newly recruited scarecrows at close combat. How scarecrow outdoes scarecrow by a scarecrow head, how scarecrows keep bettering their time at elevating scarecrow crosses, how they overcome barbed-wire entanglements, not with old-fashioned wire cutters but by eating them up, barbs and all, then evacuate them barbless in scarecrow fashion, deserves to be recorded on charts, and recorded it is. Employees of Brauxel & Co. measure and enter: Scarecrow records and rosary lengths. Three stalls that were blasted in potash-mining days until they attained gymnasium length, church height, and the width of broad-shouldered antiaircraft dugouts, provide over four hundred team-spirited scarecrows, halleluia scarecrows, holdouttothelastgasp scarecrows per shift with room in which to develop their electronically guided energies. Remote-controlled for the present—the control room is where the windlass platform used to be—indoor sport festivals, pontifical offices, and autumn maneuvers, or the other way around, athletic events for recruits, divine services in the front lines, and the blessing of scrap-iron scarecrow weapons fill schedules in order that later on, when, as they say, an emergency arises, every record can be broken, every heretic unmasked, and every hero find his victory.

The director with his dog and the visitor with Wernicke, the mine-wise foreman, leave the caustic-degraded athletes, the moth-degraded monks' habits, and the scoop-degraded fatigue uniforms, which have to creep and crawl toward the enemy while the scarecrow enemy likewise creeps and crawls, for in the schedule it is written: Creeping and crawling. Creeping and crawling toward. Mutual creeping and crawling up to.

But when, as the visit continues, the thirteenth and fourteenth stalls are inspected, the scarecrow collections in training are no longer dressed in athletic costumes, altar-boy red, and camouflage fatigues; the goings-on in these two stalls are strictly civilian. For in a family stall and an administrative stall the democratic virtues of the scarecrow state, whose form of government is determined by the needs of its citizens, are inculcated, developed, and put into daily practice. Harmoniously scarecrows sit at the table, at the television screen, and in moth-degraded camp tents. Scarecrow families—for the family is the germ cell of the state—are instructed concerning every article of the provisional constitution. Loudspeakers proclaim what polyphonic families repeat, the scarecrow preamble: "Conscious of its responsibility before God and men, inspired by the will to preserve our national and political scarecrow unity . . ." Then Article 1, dealing with the dignity of scarecrows, which is inviolable. Then the right, guaranteed in Article 2, of the scarecrow personality to develop freely. Then one thing and another, and finally Article 8, which guarantees to all scarecrows the right to assemble peacefully and unarmed, without notice and permission. And nodding their heads, scarecrow families acquiesce in Article 27: "All German-blooded scarecrows are uniformly stamped with the trade mark of the firm of Brauxel & Co."; nor is there any opposition to Article 16, Paragraph 2: "Victims of persecution will enjoy the right of asylum below ground." And all this political science, from the "universal right to grouse" to "forced expatriation," is practiced in the fourteenth pit: scarecrow voters step into polling booths; discussion-welcoming scarecrows discuss the dangers of the welfare state; scarecrows whose journalistic talent condenses in a daily newspaper invoke the freedom of the press, Article 5; the parliament convenes; the Scarecrow Supreme Court rejects a last appeal; in questions of foreign policy, the opposition supports the government party; party discipline is exerted; the tax collector holds out his hand; freedom of coalition connects stalls that do not border on the same gallery; in accordance with Article 1 B, 3 a, scarecrow analysis with the help of the lie detector developed by Brauxel & Co. is declared unconstitutional; political life flourishes; nothing hampers communication; the self-government of scarecrows, guaranteed by Article 28 A 3, begins below ground and extends, on the flat and hilly surface, to the Canadian wheatfields, to the rice paddies of India, to the endless cornfields of the Ukraine, to every corner of the earth where the products of Brauxel & Co., namely, scarecrows of one variety or another, do their duty and put a stop to the depredations of birds.

But Walter Matern, the stranger below, says once again after the thirteenth and fourteenth stalls have shown themselves to be civilian and civic: "Heavens above, this is hell. It is hell itself!"

And so, in order to refute the stranger, Wernicke, the foreman, raising his lamp, leads Walter Matern and the director with compliant dog to the fifteenth, sixteenth, and seventeenth stalls, which house Eros unleashed, Eros inhibited, and phallic narcissism.

For here all uniformed discipline and civic dignity are defied, because hate, rage, and roving revenge, which only a short time before seemed to be checked by the administrative apparatus, bloom afresh, covered with degraded yet flesh-pink skin. Because all unleashed, inhibited, and narcissistic scarecrows nibble on the same cookie, the recipe for which makes dough of all lusts but satisfies no one regardless of how strenuously and in what positions the bare-assed mob fucks and squirts. Such results, to be sure, are registered only in the fifteenth stall, where the unleashed Eros permits none of the rutting scarecrows to ring the knell of an erection which has been at it for innumerable shifts. No stopper can withstand the flood. No intermission bell rings for this permanent orgasm. Unchecked flows the scarecrow snot, a sylvinite-containing product, as foreman Wernicke explains, which has been developed in the laboratories of Brauxel & Co. and injected with gonococcuslike agents, so that the unleashed, steady-flowing scarecrows enjoy the benefit of irritation and itching similar to those observed in cases of common gonorrhea. But this pestilence is allowed to spread only in the fifteenth and not in the sixteenth and seventeenth stalls. For in these two there is no ejaculation and in the inhibited stall not even the indispensable erection. In the narcissistically phallic stall the solo scarecrows struggle in vain, despite the sultry music with prurient words which tries to help them, despite the sexy movie excerpts that occupy the screens which have been hung on the far walls of the repressed and narcissistic stalls. No sap may rise. Every snake lies dormant. All satisfaction has remained above ground; for Matern, the stranger below, says: "That's unnatural. Those are the torments of hell. Life, real life, has more to offer. I know. I've lived it!"

Suspecting at this point that the stranger is troubled by a lack of cultural life here below, Wernicke, the foreman, leads him and the director, who is smiling subtly to himself and holding Pluto loosely by the collar, to the eighteenth, nineteenth, and twentieth stalls, which are all situated on the next lower, the twenty-five-hundred-foot level, and provide room respectively for philosophical, sociological, and ideological knowledge, achievements, and antinomies.

No sooner has he arrived on this level than Matern turns away: the stranger doesn't want to go on; hell fatigues him; he would like to breathe in the daylight again; but sternly tapping his ebony cane, which only a few hours before belonged to a certain Goldmouth, Brauxel refers to something that Matern is supposed to have done up above: "Has the stranger forgotten under what circumstances he, in the early morning of this very day, threw a pocketknife into the Landwehr Canal, which flows through Berlin, a city situated on the sunlit surface?"

And so Matern, the stranger, is not allowed to turn away; he is obliged to pass through the gangway and face up to the philosophical insights that dwell loquaciously in the eighteenth stall.

But not Aristotle, not Descartes or Spinoza, from Kant to Hegel not a soul. From Hegel to Nietzsche: a vacuum! Nor any sign of a neo-Kantian or neo-Hegelian, no Rickert of the lion's mane, no Max Scheler, nor does the phenomenology of any goateed Husserl fill the stall with eloquence, permitting the stranger to forget what hellish torments the vulgarian Eros had to offer; no below-ground Socrates contemplates the world above ground; but He, the pre-Socratic, he multiplied a hundredfold. He capped with a hundred caustic-degraded, once Alemannic stockingcaps, He in buckled shoes, in a linen smock: a hundred times He, coming and going. And thinks. And speaks. Has a thousand words for Being, for time, for essence, for world and ground, for the with and the now, for the Nothing, and for the scarecrow as existential frame. Accordingly: Scareness, being-scared, scare-structure, scare-view, primeval scare, scaring-away, counter-scare, scare-vulnerable, scare-principle, scare-situation, un-scared, final scare, scare-born time, scare-totality, foundation-scare, the law of scare. "For the essence of the scare-crow is the transcendental threefold dispersal of scare-crow suchness in the world project. Projecting itself into the Nothing, the scarecrow *physis,* or burgeoning, is at all times beyond the scarecrow such and the scarecrow at-hand . . ."

Transcendence drips from stockingcaps in the eighteenth stall. A hundred caustic-degraded philosophers are of one and the same opinion: "Scarecrow Being means: to be held-out-into Nothing." And the anxious question of Matern, the stranger below, who casts his voice into the stall: "But what of man, in whose image the scarecrow was created?" is answered by one and a hundred philosophers: "The scarecrow question calls ourselves—the askers—into question." At this Matern withdraws his voice. A hundred matching philosophers come and go on the salt floor, greeting each other essentially: "The scarecrow exists self-grounded."

With oldtime buckled shoes they have even trampled down paths. Now and then they fall silent, then Matern hears their mechanisms. The principle of sufficient scare is starting up again.

But before the hundred-times present, moth-scoop-and-caustic-degraded philosopher can run off his built-in sound tape again, Matern escapes to the gallery. He would gladly run for it, but can't, for he is still a stranger to the mine and would certainly go astray: "The scarecrow comes-to-be in errancy, where, erring in circles, it fosters error."

So thrown back upon Wernicke, the mine-wise foreman, and reminded of hell by Pluto's blackness, he is driven through stalls whose numbers make it clear that no stall is spared him.

Under the nineteenth roof sociological insights are gathered together. The forms of alienation, the theory of social stratification, the introspective method, the pragmatic nihilism that dispenses with values, pure behaviorism, factual statements, and analyses of concepts, the static and dynamic approach, not to mention sociological ambivalence and divers stratification structures, are embodied as mobiles. Degraded in a variety of ways, modern society listens to lectures on collective consciousness. Habit scarecrows develop into environment scarecrows. Secondary scarecrows correspond to the scarecrow norm. Determined scarecrows and undetermined scarecrows carry on a debate, the outcome of which neither Matern, the stranger below, nor Brauxel the mine-wise director, with dog and foreman, is inclined to wait for; for in the twentieth stall all ideological differences are argued out: a scarecrow controversy which Matern is able to follow, because a similar muddle prevails inside him. Here as in Matern's interior the question is: "Is there a hell? Or is hell already on earth? Do scarecrows go to heaven? Is the scarecrow descended from the angels, or were there

scarecrows before the angels were conceived of? Are scarecrows themselves angels? Did the angels or the scarecrows
invent the bird? Is there a God, or is God the first scarecrow? If man was created in God's image and the scarecrow in the image of man, is the scarecrow not the image
and likeness of God?"—Oh, Matern would like to say yes to
every question, he would like to hear a dozen more questions forthwith and to answer them all in the affirmative:
"Are all scarecrows equal? Or are there elite scarecrows?
Are scarecrows the property of the people? Or is every peasant entitled to claim scarecrow ownership? Of what race are
scarecrows members? Is a Germanic scarecrow superior to a
Slavic scarecrow? Is a German scarecrow allowed to buy
from a Jewish one? Don't Jews lack the gift? Is a Semitic
scarecrow even conceivable? Scarecrow sheeny, scarecrow
sheeny!" And once again Matern escapes to the gallery; it
asks no questions which he must answer blindly, all in the
affirmative.

Soothingly, as though director and foreman wished to
bandage the exhausted visitor's wounds, the twenty-first stall
opens up to him: a feast for the eyes, to be contemplated in
silence. Here the turning points in history are scarecrowified.
Degraded yet dynamic, scarecrow history unfolds in its proper order, reciting dates, defenestrations, and peace treaties.
After caustic bath and moth feast, old-time brooch and Wellington hat, Stuart collar and rakish sombrero, Dalmatic and
two-cornered seafarer's hat embody fateful hours and years
of destiny. They revolve and bow according to the fashion.
Winged words—here Guelf, here Ghibelline!—Under my rule
every man can save his soul according to his own lights
. . . Give me four years' time . . . ! occupy the air and are
replaced by others. And all the striking poses, still or in
pantomime: The bloodbath at Verden. The victory on the
Lechfeld. Canossa. Young Konradin rides and rides. Gothic
madonnas make no attempt to economize on drapery. Sable
predominates when the council of Electors is established.
Who is stepping on the fathoms-long train of that houppe-
lande? Hussites and Turks influence customs. Knights and
rust mate. Splendor-loving Burgundy contributes red, brocade, and silk tents lined with velvet. But when codpieces
swell and braguettes can scarcely contain their exuberant
contents, the monk nails his theses to the door. O Hapsburg
lip casting its shadow on a century! Bundschuh goes round,

scratching pictures from walls. But Maximilian tolerates slit doublets, jerkins, and low-crowned caps bigger than haloes. Above the Spanish black stand foam-born and thrice-starched ruffs. The rapier replaces the broadsword and ushers in the Thirty Years' War, which whimsically modifies the styles. Outlandish plumes, leather jerkins, and top boots move into winter quarters here and there. And no sooner have the Wars of Succession designed the full-bottomed periwig than the three-cornered hat, in the course of three Silesian wars, becomes more and more severe. But bag wig, *baigneuse,* and *trompeuse* are no safeguard against scissors-grinders and sansculottes: heads must fall. Represented in a striking mobile in the twenty-first stall. And yet, for all its discolored Bourbon white, the Directoire hatches the flowery Restoration. The Congress dances in split skirts and calf-pinching nankeen. The swallowtail survives the censor-ship and the riotous days of March. The men of the Pauls-kirche speak into their top hats. To the strains of the Yorck March, the Düppeln redoubts are scaled. The Ems Dispatch, teacher's pet of all history teachers. Bismarck resigns in a cape. In frock coats enter: Caprivi, Hohenlohe, and Bülow. The Kulturkampf, the Triple Alliance, and the Herero upris-ing yield three color-saturated images. And don't forget to mention the red dolman of the Zieten Hussars at Mars-la-Tour. And then in moth-degraded Balkan environment shots are fired. Victory bells are sounded. That little river is the Marne. Steel helmets replace spiked helmets. The gas mask has come to stay. In wartime crinoline and high boots, the Kaiser leaves for Holland, because of the dagger thrust from the rear. Whereupon cockadeless soldiers' councils. Kapp makes his putsch. Spartacus rises up. Paper money crackles. The Stresemann suit votes for the Enabling Act. Torchlight parades. Books burn. Brown predominates. A No-vember tableau: a kaftan stuffed with straw. Then fancy-dress balls. Then prison stripes. Then army boots, special communiqués, Winter Aid, earmuffs, snow hoods, camou-flage uniforms, special communiqués . . . And in the end the radio symphony orchestra in its brown work clothes plays something from *Götterdämmerung.* That is always appro-priate, a leit- and murder motive that flits like a spook through the entire history, imaged and resurrected in scare-crows, which fills the twenty-first stall.

Thereupon Matern, the stranger below, bares his head and

with company-owned scarf dries the beads from his scalp. Even in his schooldays, historical dates dropped from his book to the floor and vanished in cracks. Only his family history finds him in command of figures; but here scarecrows do not mime regional Materniads, here the war of investitures and Counterreformation are enacted; mechanically and by means of fist-size electric motors negotiations are carried on: the Peace of Westphalia; in scarecrow fashion assemble those who—when, where, with whom, against whom, without England—voice grievances, make proclamations, put under ban, in brief make history; appropriately costumed from turning point to turning point.

And when the corny round begins anew, flits across the Lechfeld to Canossa, and makes the young Hohenstaufen scarecrow ride again, the stranger is unable to behead his ever-ready comment: "A hell! This is indeed a hell!"

And he has similarly infernal words at his command when with dog they leave the twenty-second stall, which, made to look like the floor of a stock exchange, seems to be too small for the investing, market-conquering, and prosperity-creating potential leaders. The mere sight of scarecrow-nimble trust formation, the acoustic charm of slight market fluctuations, the board of directors meeting raised to monumental stature wring from Matern the unminerly cry: "This is hell. Hell AG."

He is no more loquacious when discharged by the twenty-third stall, which, fifty feet in height, houses, between overhanging salt and underlying salt, a highly acrobatic discipline that calls itself "internal emigration." One might suppose that only scarecrows could knot themselves so inextricably, that only scarecrows would have the power to crawl into their own viscera, that scarecrows alone could give the subjunctive body within and clothing without. But since—according to the statutes—the scarecrow mirrors the image of man, there must be similar walking subjunctives on the sunlit surface of the earth.

The stranger below has loaded his voice with scorn: "Your hell hasn't forgotten anybody. Not even the ichneumon."

And Brauxel, the director, replies with shadow-casting ebony cane: "What can we do? The demand is great. The catalogues we distribute internationally are remarkable for their completeness. We have no remainders. The twenty-third stall is especially vital to our export program. People still emigrate internally. It's warm inside, you know your way around, there's nobody to bother you."

But though equally double-jointed, the goings-on are less sedentary in the twenty-fourth stall, the stall of the degraded opportunists. Here reaction speed is tested. At regular intervals, lamps hanging from the roof, not unlike the traffic lights of the upper world, flash sharp colors and political symbols: and naked scarecrows, whose inborn mechanism hangs unconcealed within their skeletons, have to change their rags at high speed under the prodding of the second hand and make parts in their caustic-degraded hair: for a time the hairdo was divided on the left side; now the part is worn on the right; shortly thereafter a part in the middle becomes the fashion; and every shading: half-left, half-right, and hairdo without any part at all can also, or might, be in demand.

This act amuses Matern—"What diabolical fun!"—all the more so as his yellow-varnished hard hat protects a skull, the forehead of which has been considerably heightened by the raging succession of opinions characteristic of conditions above ground, until with the help of the fair sex, as Matern has to admit, the whole meadow refuses to grow. The stranger is deeply relieved at the thought that no one will ever again be able to make him change his hairdo, to shift his part in accordance with a trend. "If you have rehearsed still other farces, I shall gladly look upon hell as a playhouse."

Matern is beginning to feel at home below ground. But Wernicke, the foreman, raises his buzzing carbide lamp. On the twenty-five-hundred-foot level, he has only one horror play left—in the twenty-fifth stall. This virtually plotless one-acter, which under the title *Atomic Particularities* has been on the program since potash-mining days, stifles Matern's high spirits at once, although the words of a classical poet provide the background for the silent action. What above ground is called absurd has the taste of reality below; separate members act independently. Jumping heads, for whose particularity even a neck was too much, are unable to scratch themselves. In short: each of the items that make the body a composite structure lives on independently. Arm and leg, hand and torso pose to an accompaniment of high-sounding words which, ordinarily spoken in front of the footlights, are here recited behind the curtain: "O God,

O God! This marriage is terrible, but eternal." "Welcome, my worthy friends. What important business brings you all to me?" "But soon I will come among you and hold terrible muster."

In Schiller, to be sure, there is the parenthetical instruction: "They exit trembling." But these obstinate scarecrow fragments are long-playing mimes, which never exit. An inexhaustible repertory of quotations permits of solitary genuflections. Solo hands speak for themselves. Heads heaped up like chunks of rock salt lament in chorus: "No greater sorrow than to recall happy days in a time of misery."

During a brief descent—with a double stroke of the bell, the trammer announces the pit bottom, where lies the fill level and hence also the hope that hell may be exhausted and ascent decided upon—Matern, wedged into the cage between director and foreman with dog, is informed that the mobile scarecrow fragments he has just seen have recently been in great demand, especially in the Argentine and in Canada, where the wide expanse of the wheatfields necessitates echeloned scarecrows.

And as the three of them with dog stand on the twenty-eight-hundred-foot level, the director gives Wernicke the cue for the lines introducing the final phase of the tour of inspection, and the foreman complies: "We have followed the stages of production on the three upper levels and have witnessed the various kinds of degradation as well as the assembly process. We have tried to make it clear that all the disciplines, from the athletic to the atomic-particular, are based upon the three central motives. We still have to show how the scarecrows are familiarized with the tasks they will have to perform on the surface. In the twenty-sixth, twenty-seventh, and twenty-eighth stalls we shall witness object lessons, tests from which no scarecrow produced by Brauxel & Co. has ever been exempted."

"That is cruelty to animals," says Matern even before the twenty-sixth stall is opened. "Leave the animals in peace," he shouts up at the roof when he is compelled to hear that sparrows, which Brauxel calls "our dear, unassuming citizens of the world," cannot stop chirping even below ground.

And the director says: "Here our export scarecrows are made acquainted with sparrows and with the varieties of wheat that they will soon have to guard against the depredations of birds. Each scarecrow to be tested—here a collection of Zealand rye scarecrows, whose sphere of action will be southwestern South Africa—is expected to protect a limited radius of attraction, rendered alluring by rye seed, from the incursion of test sparrows. In the course of this shift, as I see, still other collections are being tested: twelve assortments of Odessa scarecrows, which will have to prove their mettle over South Russian Girka wheat and Ukrainian Sandomir wheat. In addition our La Plata scarecrows, very much in demand, which have helped the Argentines to achieve record wheat harvests. Further, éight assortments of Kansas scarecrows will be familiarized with the protection of the Kubanka variety, a summer wheat which, I might add, is also grown in South Dakota. Smaller lots of wheat scarecrows will have to keep sparrows at a distance from Polish Sandomirka and from the bearded and frost-resistant Banat wheat. Here as in the twenty-seventh and twenty-eighth stalls, we shall test collections that are in demand for two-rowed Poltava barley, for Northern French brewer's barley, Scandinavian panicled oats, Moldavian corn, Italian cinquantino corn, and the North American and Soviet varieties of corn, grown in southern Russia and the Mississippi lowlands. While in this stall only sparrows are to be excluded from the radius of attraction, in the next stall birds of the pigeon family, especially rock pigeons, which also prey on rape seed, flax seed, and peas, are applied to the export scarecrows to be tested. Occasionally crows, daws, and meadowlarks are admitted as test material, while in the twenty-eighth stall thrushes and blackbirds test our orchard scarecrows and starlings our vineyard scarecrows.—But we can set the stranger's mind at rest: all of our test birds, from the sparrows to the rock pigeons, finches, larks, and starlings, have been brought down from the surface with the approval of the authorities. The S.P.C.A. of Hanover and Hildesheim inspects our testing stalls every three months. We are not unfriendly to birds. We co-operate with them. Our scarecrows have the utmost contempt for air rifles, lime twigs, and bird netting. Indeed, I am proud to say that Brauxel & Co. has repeatedly and publicly protested against the barbarous catching of song birds by the Italians. Our success on all continents, our Ohio and Maryland scarecrows, our Siberian Urtoba scarecrows, our scarecrows in Canadian Manitoba wheat, our rice scarecrows, which protect Javanese rice and the Italian ostiglione variety grown near Mantua, our corn scarecrows, which have helped Soviet corn harvests to approach the records set in America, all our scarecrows, whether they protect native rye, Moravian Hanna barley, the Milton oats of Minnesota, the celebrated Bordeaux wheat, the rice paddies of India, the Cuzco corn of southern Peru, or Chinese millet and Scottish buckwheat from the depredations of birds, all the products of Brauxel & Co. without exception are in harmony with nature; they themselves *are* nature: crows and scarecrows form a harmony; indeed, were it not for the scarecrow, there would be no crows; and both, crow and scarecrow—created by the same God—contribute to solving the mounting problem of feeding the world. The bird pecks the larvae of the corn fly, the black corn borer, and the malignant wild mustard seed, while over the ripening corn the scarecrow turns off all bird song, the cooing of pigeons and the chattering of sparrows, and banishes the starlings from vineyards, the blackbirds and thrushes from cherry trees."

And yet, eloquently as Director Brauxel lauds the harmony prevailing between birds and scarecrows, the words "cruelty to animals" keep falling from the lips of Matern, the stranger below. When he is now doomed to hear that Brauxel & Co., in line with its rationalization program, has begun to let sparrows, rock pigeons, and blackbirds nest, brood, and hatch in the mine, when it dawns on him that whole generations of birds have never seen the light of day and look upon rock salt ceilings as the sky, he speaks of the infernal torments of infernal birds, though all three stalls sound as merry as the merry month of May: the song of the finches and larks, the cooing of pigeons, the music of the daws, unorganized sparrow hubbub, in short, the sound effects of a sap-fomenting day in May fill the three stalls; and only very seldom, when the ventilation of the twenty-eight-hundred-foot level weakens, are employees of Brauxel & Co. obliged to gather up feathered folk, whose *joie de vivre* has been impaired by the atmospheric conditions.

The stranger affects indignation. He speaks of a "hellish outrage." If the foreman hadn't promised him that in the twenty-ninth stall he would witness the end of all scarecrow training, the graduation exercises, the great scarecrow mass meeting, he would run blindly for the fill level, there—if he ever made it—to scream for light and air, the light of day and the month of May.

But under the circumstances he consents to watch the shindig from the sidelines. In this scarecrow show the graduates of all the preceding stalls are represented. Halleluia scarecrows and close-combat scarecrows, and whatever scarecrow society has to offer: many-headed scarecrow families, the scarecrow cock at the head. Unleashed, inhibited, narcissistic scarecrow sex fiends. In degraded glad rags they have come to the scarecrow get-together, the scarecrow ball: the stockingcap scarecrow and the standardized secondary scarecrows, elite angelic scarecrows and the scarecrows of history: Burgundian nose and Hapsburg lip, Stuart collar and Suvorov boot, Spanish black and Prussian blue; in among them the touts of the free-market economy; internal refugees, almost indiscernible, because they have crawled back into their own wombs; who is speaking resolute language over there? Who is keeping up scarecrow morale and fostering scarecrow development? It's the universally popular opportunists, who wear red under brown and will slip into ecclesiastical black any minute. And with this gathering of the people—for a republic is here represented by its average citizens—mingle the atomic and stage-struck particularities. A colorful gathering: scarecrow-colored. Beloved scarecrow German makes friends. Scarecrow music appeases hate, rage, and roving revenge, the cardinal emotions bred in stalls, which oil every scarecrow's mechanism and, serving as monitors, brandish the scarecrow whip: "God help you if. God help you if you!"

But the graduates are well mannered, though at all times ready for mischief. Pickaback scarecrows tease singing Salvation Army scarecrows. The scarecrow vulture can't stop thieving. The historical group, "Wallenstein's Death," has been joined by hospital-pale nurses. Who would have expected the pre-Socratic stockingcap scarecrow to be conversing with the stale theory of social stratification? Flirtations are in the making. Laughter, acquired in the seventh stall and unjustly called "infernal laughter," mingles with the weeping of the eighth stall and the teeth-grinding of the ninth; for where has there ever been a party at which jokes were not laughed at, the loss of a pocketbook wept over, and a sharp but soon settled quarrel ironed out amid a grinding of teeth?

But as now, accompanied by the mine director with dog and the stranger following the foreman, the graduates are led from the graduation celebrations into the nearby thirtieth stall, silence prevails for a moment.

A sense of shame commands Matern to avert his face, for the assembled guild of scarecrows, guided as he knows by remote control, "soulless automats," as he puts it, take the oath to the firm of Brauxel & Co. And the scarecrows have the audacity to babble: "So help me God." What begins with the customary "I solemnly swear . . ." ends, after scarecrows have taken the oath never to deny their origin, namely the pit below, never irresponsibly to desert the field assigned them, always to carry out their primary mission of firmly but fairly discouraging birds, ends with Him, whose eye also watches the pit below: "So help me God."

It remains to be mentioned only that in the thirty-first stall individual scarecrows and scarecrow collections are packed and bedded in crates for export; that in the thirty-second stall cases are labeled, bills of lading made out, and trucks dispatched.

"This," said Wernicke, the foreman, "brings us to the end of our long production process. We hope you have been able to form a rough idea. Certain features, such as all the laboratories situated on the surface, the automation, and our electrical workshops, are not included in the tour of inspection. Similarly our glassworks may be visited only by special permission. Perhaps you would like to ask Herr Brauxel."

But Walter Matern, the stranger below, has had enough. He craves to return to the light faster than the trolley can reach the shaft. Matern is supersaturated.

For that reason he has no heart to protest when Brauxel, the director, takes Pluto, the black shepherd, by the collar and chains him in the place where the tour of inspection began, where the view of the mine ends, where, as Brauxel has ordered, the mine-joyous inscription *"Glück auf"* has its place, but where, as Matern suggests, what ought to be written is: "Abandon hope all ye who enter here!"

Already the cage is opening for the ascent when the stranger drags up final words: "See here, that's my dog."

Whereupon Brauxel utters words of conclusion: "What object worthy of his guardianship has the bright surface of the earth to offer a dog such as this? This is his place. Here where the mining shaft says amen and the ventilators breathe forth spring air from above. He shall be guardian here, yet he will not bear the name of Cerberus. Orcus is up above."

O ascent two together—they have left the foreman below.
O ye fifty feet gained in every second.
O well-known feeling that every elevator imparts.

The roar in which they are silent stuffs cotton in every ear. And everyone smells the burnt smell. And every prayer beseeches the cable to remain united, in order that light, daylight, once again the sun-embroidered May . . .

But when they set foot on the platform of the shaft collar, it is raining outside and dusk is creeping over the land from the Harz Mountains.

And this man and that man—who now will call them Brauxel and Matern?—I and he, we stride with doused lamps to the changehouse, where the changehouse attendant takes our hard hats and carbide lamps. I and he are led to cabins where Matern's and Brauxel's clothes are in keeping. He and I strip off our mine outfits. For me and him bathtubs have been filled. I hear Eddi splashing next door. Now I too step into my bath. The water soaks me clean. Eddi whistles something indeterminate. I try to whistle something similar. But it's difficult. We're both naked. Each of us bathes by himself.

NOTES

13   *Adalbert,* Bishop of Prague, 955-997, known as apostle of the Prussians, came down the Vistula, according to legend, and baptized more than a thousand pagans. He was killed by a pagan priest.—*Dukes Swantopolk* and *Mestwin II,* Dukes of Pomerelia, around whose castle Danzig was built. Mestwin II died in 1294 without a male heir.—*Duke Kynstute* (r. 1345-77) ruled Western Lithuania at a time when it was constantly raided by the Teutonic Knights (see below).

55   *Uniformed scarecrows:* the references are to the wars of Frederick the Great of Prussia. In the battle of Leuthen, 1747, the Prussians defeated the armies of the Austrian Empire.—*The Poor Man of Toggenburg* is the sobriquet of a Swiss mercenary who participated in the Seven Years' War, and later published his autobiography under this title.—*General Seydlitz,* one of Frederick's generals, pursued and defeated the head of the Austrian army, *Hildburghausen.*

66   *The Teutonic Knights,* a military and religious Order dedicated to the extension of the borders of Christendom. In 1208, Duke Conrad of Masovia invited the Order to settle along the Vistula in order to help protect his territories against the savage Prussians. In 1308, in alliance with the Poles, the Knights ousted the Prussians from Danzig, but forced their Polish allies out also. The Order established a Germanic military outpost on the Baltic which thrived at the expense of the Slavs. Eventually, the Order degenerated and its power waned. In 1410, the Knights were defeated by the combined Lithuanian and Polish forces in the battle of Tannenberg.—Hitler and his SS revived the mystique of the Order's mission as instrument of Germanic expansion in the East and the enslavement of the Slavs, and used the fortress castles of the Order as

schools for the Nazi elite.—*Jagello*, Grand Duke of Lithuania, a pagan chieftain who brought about the union of Poland and Lithuania in 1386 and became Wladislaus II, Catholic King of Poland, founder of a dynasty which ruled Poland for two centuries, and devoted itself to keeping the Teutonic Order, the old enemy of their race, in check.—*Kasimir III, the Great*, 1333-70, King of Poland.—*Stanislaus Lesczynski*, King of Poland 1704-09 and again 1733-34, besieged by the Russians in Danzig, his last refuge; vanquished and exiled.—*Kniprode, Letzkau, and von Plauen*, Grand Masters of the Teutonic Knights.—*Albrecht Achilles*, 1414-86, Elector of Brandenburg, established his house as regnant over Pomerania.—*Zieten, Hans Joachim von*, 1699-1786, Prussian cavalry general under Frederick the Great.

72ff   The Teutonic Order was joined by the flower of European chivalry in its crusade against the heathen. *Henry Derby*, Duke of Lancaster, later King Henry IV of England, made two journeys to Prussia, 1390-91 and 1392.   Other foreign knights participating in raids against Lithuania were *Jacob Doutremer, Pege Peegott, Thomas Percy, Fitzwater*. At the time of Henry Derby's visits, *Konrad Wallenrod* was Grand Master of the Order (1391-93). *Engelhard Rabe*, Marshal of the Order (1387-92), led the Order's army into the trackless woods of Lithuania, starting his raids from one of the frontier castles, *Ragnit*. Traditionally, the *St. George's banner*, insignia of all Christian knights, was carried by a German knight, but Thomas Percy insisted on his own smaller banner. This led to bloody quarrels among German and English knights. Henry Derby also brought his own St. George's banner but was frustrated by Wallenrod, who conferred the privilege of carrying the banner on the German knight *Hattenstein*. *Simon Bache, Erik Cruse, Claus Schone, Richard Westrall, Spannerle, Tylman,* and *Robert Wendell* were artisans who supplied the Duke of Lancaster with various necessities on his Prussian campaigns.

111   *Sleeping lights:* candles made from the fat of stillborn children. Before breaking into a house, as many sleeping lights are lighted as there are sleepers in the house. If a light extinguishes, it is a sign that someone inside the house has woken up.

161   *Angela Raubal*, Hitler's widowed half-sister and housekeeper.—*Rudolf Hess*, Hitler's aide who helped him write *Mein Kampf*, and during the war undertook a sensational flight to Scotland.—*Ernst (Putzi) Hanfstaengl*, Harvard graduate, son of an American mother, befriended Hitler during his early Munich days and was later made chief of the

Foreign Press Department of the Party.—*Hermann Rausch-ning*, President of the Danzig Senate 1933-35, helped National Socialism to victory in Danzig but was soon disillusioned. He went into exile and wrote *Conversations with Hitler* and *The Revolution of Nihilism*.—*Albert Forster*, National Socialist Gauleiter of Danzig. Proclaimed the annexation of Danzig to the German Reich on September 1, 1939, and appointed himself administrator of Danzig City and District.—*Wilhelm Brückner*, SA Commander and Hitler's personal adjutant.—*Gregor Strasser*, one of the earliest adherents of National Socialism and chief organizer of the nascent Party. He quarreled with Hitler and was liquidated in 1934.—*General Kurt von Schleicher*, last Chancellor of the Weimar Republic, who played a devious role in Hitler's rise to power. He was liquidated during the purge of June 30, 1934.—*Ernst Röhm*, one of Hitler's earliest supporters, who helped create and organize the SA, whose commander he was until his assassination at Hitler's orders on June 30, 1934.—*Count Joseph Arthur Gobineau*, French man of letters, whose *Essay on the Inequality of Races* profoundly influenced Nazi racial theories.

176   *Franz and Karl Moor*, rebels against society in Schiller's early revolutionary drama *Die Räuber*.

184   *Arthur Greiser*, National Socialist, succeeded Hermann Rauschning as President of the Danzig Senate and signed a treaty with the Nationalist Socialists regarding relations between Poland and Danzig.

193   *Houston Stewart Chamberlain*, 1855-1927, son-in-law of Richard Wagner, propagated Count Gobineau's racial theories. His main work, *Foundations of the Nineteenth Century*, exalts the Teutonic race and laid the groundwork for ideological anti-Semitism in Germany.

204   *SA man Brand*, propaganda figure of National Socialism, touted as hero and martyr of the Movement.—*Herbert Norkus*, Hitler youth, killed in 1932 in one of the bloody battles between Nazis and Communists.—*Horst Wessel*, SA leader of dubious morals, killed in a fight with Communists. Author and composer of the "Horst Wessel Lied," which became the second National Anthem in the Third Reich.

206   *Wilhelm Löbsack*, Nazi publicist and speaker, who edited the speeches and writings of the Danzig Gauleiter Albert Forster.

244   *Richard Billinger*, Austrian dramatist, dealt with the conflict between progress and mechanized city life on the one hand and the demonic world of the peasant on the other. In *The Giant* (1937), a peasant girl succumbs to the temptations of the city and finally drowns herself. Her seducer is the son of Donata Opferkuch.—*The phenomenology of a stockingcap:* the reference is to Martin Heidegger, who studied under Edmund Husserl, the founder of a new philosophical method which he called phenomenology. In 1927, Heidegger published his principal work, *Being and Time*. Soon after Hitler's rise to power, Heidegger came out in favor of the Nazi regime. His predilection for the stockingcap of the Alemannic peasant betokened his attachment to the simple life and the soil of his native Baden. He lives in Todtnau, in the Black Forest.—*Abstrusely secular lyric poetry* is a reference to the Expressionist poet Gottfried Benn (1886-1956), who also supported National Socialism from 1932 to 1934, but was later disillusioned and attacked by the regime. The fragments cited in the text are from his poem "Das späte Ich" (The late I). One of his early works is entitled "Morgue."

388   *The raving Beckmann* is a reference to the protagonist of the postwar play *Outside the Door* by Wolfgang Borchert, which describes the plight of the returning and unwanted soldier.

407   *Max Reimann*, Communist Party leader in postwar Germany.

410   *Quirinus Kuhlmann*, 1651-89, great lyric poet of the baroque, burnt in Moscow as a heretic.

418   In article 12 of the Potsdam Pact, signed at the end of the war, the Allies outlawed "undue concentration of German economic power." A number of "decartelization laws" were issued, affecting all cartels, or trusts, and many other corporations and private businesses. Their purpose was to break the power of German heavy industry which had helped establish Hitler's rule. It was argued that excessive concentrations of economic power impeded the functioning of democratic institutions and that German economic life should be guided by the spirit of free competition prevailing in the United States, France, and England. But the worm was in the economic system from the start—the expansion following the currency reform led to the formation of new trusts and monopolies. The old and new men of power: *Axel Springer*, who soon after the war founded the radio magazine *Hör Zu* (Tune In), published under British license, which today has the largest circulation of any German periodical (four million). He now directs the largest and most influential news-

paper chain in Germany, which publishes the newspapers *Bild, Die Welt,* and the magazine *Kristall.* Springer also controls two publishing houses, Ullstein AG and Propyläen Verlag.—*Gerd Bucerius,* founder of Zeit-Verlag GmbH, which own an interest in the Henry Nannen Verlag. These houses publish the weekly *Die Zeit* and *Stern,* one of the big illustrated magazines. From 1949 to 1962 Bucerius was a Christian Democratic member of the Bundestag.—*Rudolf Augstein,* after a short-lived experiment with the weekly *Die Woche,* in 1946 founded the news magazine *Der Spiegel* on the model of *Time* magazine.—*Otto-Ernst Flick,* son of the industrialist Friedrich Flick, who was sentenced to a prison term by the Nuremberg War Crimes court. Friedrich Flick KG was obliged by the decartelization law to withdraw from mining. Today it again holds an interest in Harpener Bergbau AG and is influential in numerous corporations, such as Daimler Benz AG. Otto-Ernst Flick is a board member and executive in these firms.—*Ernst Schneider,* chairman of the board and a large shareholder in Kohlensäure-Industrie AG, in which the C. G. Trinkhaus private bank also holds an interest.—*The Michel group,* whose holdings in the Soviet zone were confiscated, built up a new soft-coal corporation on the basis of four mines it had retained in West Germany.—*Vicco von Bülow-Schwante,* landowner in Mecklenburg and retired ambassador, is chairman of the board of the Stumm family's mining company in the Saar—*Bertold Beitz* was director of the Polish oil fields during the war. In 1953 he became chairman of the board of Friedrich Krupp von Bohlen und Halbach and directed the rebuilding of the Krupp Corporation, which was largely dissolved in 1945.—*Carl F. W. Borgward,* owner of the Borgward Automobile Corporation, which has meanwhile gone into bankruptcy.—*Heinrich Nordhoff,* chairman of the board of Volkswagen AG, Europe's largest producer of automobiles.—*Herbert Quandt* directs in partnership with his brother Harald the concern inherited from their father, which has absorbed the Burbach Potash Works.—*I-G Successors:* In 1945 I-G Farben (the German Dye Trust) was the largest of German corporations. On the strength of Law No. 35 of the Allied High Commission it was split up into the following concerns: Badische Anilin- u. Soda-Fabrik AG, Farbenfabriken, Bayer AG, Farbwerke Höchst AG.—*Hjalmar Schacht,* economist, banker, former finance minister and president of the Reichsbank, in 1946 acquitted of war crimes charges by the Nuremberg court. Today he is part owner of the Schacht & Co. export-import bank, in Düsseldorf.—*Julius Münnemann* became, thanks to a new method of industrial financing, one of the most successful German financiers in the years after the war.—*Willy H. Schlieker* developed, in the same period, an important government enterprise in the Ruhr. After having built the world's most modern shipyard in Hamburg, his firm went into bankruptcy.—*Joseph Neckermann* in 1950 founded the Neckermann Versand KG, a mail-order house, which with ninety-one outlets is today the leading German enterprise of its kind.—*Max Grundig* developed after the war a small radio business into a large corporation which is now one of the world's foremost producers of radios, phonographs, and other electrical appliances.—*Hermann F. Reemtsma* vastly expanded the production of the Reemtsma cigarette factories after the war.—*Rudolf Brinckmann*, banker, part owner of the Brinckmann, Wirtz & Co. bank (formerly M. M. Warburg).—*Hermann J. Abs*, chairman of the Deutsche Bank AG, one of the three largest German banks. Member of the board of almost thirty leading corporations.—*Kurt Forberg*, banker, part owner of the C. G. Trinkhaus bank; member of the board in some twenty-five concerns.—*Robert Pferdmenges*, banker, part owner of Sal. Oppenheim Jr. & Cie. bank. Helped to found the Christian Democratic Party in the Rhineland. Long-time friend of Chancellor Konrad Adenauer.—*Rudolf August Oetker* expanded the flourishing baking powder factory inherited from his father and subsequently founded the largest German steamship company.—*Kurt Schumacher*, 1930-33 Social Democratic member of the Reichstag, spent the years 1933-45 in a concentration camp. He was the first postwar chairman of the German Socialist Party and up to the time of his death in 1952 the most prominent figure in the opposition.—*Erich Ollenhauer*, chairman of the German Socialist Party after Schumacher. During the war he was a member of the executive committee of the Socialist Party in exile.—*Dr. Eugen Gerstenmaier*, Protestant theologian and member of the German resistance movement during the war. Since 1949 a member of the Bundestag, of which he is now president.—*Dr. Otto Dibelius*, Protestant Bishop of Berlin since 1945. From 1954 to 1961 he was chairman of the World Council of Protestant Churches.—*Franz Joseph Würmeling* became Minister for Family Affairs in 1953. Known for his proposed legislation in favor of large families. —*Bruno Leuschner* became vice-chairman of the Council of Ministers of the German Democratic Republic in 1955, in 1960 a member of the state council, in charge of the co-ordination of economic plans. He died February 11, 1965.— *Otto Nuschke*, first chairman of the Communist Party in the German Democratic Republic, long vice-chairman of the Council of Ministers.—*Kurt Mewis*, appointed in 1960 to the Council of State of the German Democratic Republic. In 1961 became a minister and first chairman of the State Planning Commission.—*Petersberg Agreement:* an agreement concluded in May 1952 between the three Western occupation powers and the German Federal Republic.—*Erich Kuby*, left-wing journalist.—*Hans Globke*, one of the jurists who formulated the notorious Nuremberg laws by which the Nazis deprived the Jews of the rights of citizenship. In postwar Germany, he became chief assistant to Chancellor Adenauer.

434-435   *Jan Wellem*, popular name of John William, elector palatine, 1679-1716, whose equestrian statue stands on Düsseldorf market place.—*Christian Dietrich Grabbe*, 1801-36, German dramatist, who visited Düsseldorf and left it after a quarrel. Among his historical tragedies is the unfinished drama *Hannibal*.

518f   *Bundschuh and Poor Konrad, the monk Pfeiffer, Hipler and Geyer, the peasants of Mansfeld and Eichsfeld, etc.* are all references to the Peasants' War in South Germany in 1525. The Anabaptist Thomas Münzer (the Fury of Allstedt) was one of the leaders of the revolt. The insurgents were defeated at Frankenhausen and their leaders executed.